## The Better Wo

'What sort of job do you have in mind for me?' said C.J.

'I'm not sure yet,' said Reggie. 'But I promise you it'll be worthy of your talents. Come and give it a try. After all, the proof of the pudding is caviar to the general.'

'That's true,' said C.J. 'That's very true. I'm not sure if it's my line of country, though.'

'You'll have board and lodging and a salary of eight thousand pounds a year.'

'On the other hand, no doubt I could soon adjust to it,' said C.J.

They shook hands, and Reggie bought another round.

'When I've got my staff together,' he said, 'there'll be a period of training.'

'Training, Reggie?'

'We'll all have to learn how to be nice.'

'Oh.'

C.J. gazed morosely at his whisky.

'I didn't get where I am today by being nice,' he said.

'You'll get used to it,' said Reggie. 'Once you are nice, you'll find that it's really quite nice being nice.'

David Nobbs

# The Better World
# of Reginald Perrin

Mandarin

**A Mandarin Paperback**

THE BETTER WORLD OF REGINALD PERRIN

First published in Great Britain 1978
by Victor Gollancz Ltd
First paperback edition published 1979
by Penguin Books
This edition published 1990
by Mandarin Paperbacks
Michelin House, 81 Fulham Road, London SW3 6RB

Mandarin is an imprint of the Octopus Publishing Group

Copyright © David Nobbs 1978

A CIP catalogue record for this book
is available from the British Library
ISBN 0 7493 0468 5

Printed in Great Britain by
BPCC Hazell Books
Aylesbury, Bucks, England
Member of BPCC Ltd.

# Contents

*To my mother*

# 1  *The Plan*

He awoke suddenly, and for a few moments he didn't know who he was.

Then he remembered.

He was Reginald Iolanthe Perrin and he was fifty years of age.

Beside him his lovely wife Elizabeth was sleeping peacefully.

It took him a few moments longer to realize *where* he was.

He was in room number two at the George Hotel in Netherton St Ambrose in the county of Dorset. The pale light of a late October morning was filtering through the bright yellow patterned curtains on to the bright green patterned wallpaper and the bright red patterned carpet.

On a small round table by the window stood the wherewithal for making tea and coffee.

Soon hotels would expect you to print your own morning newspaper.

He closed his eyes, but the decor faded only slowly.

Suddenly he sat bolt upright. He wasn't Reginald Iolanthe Perrin at all. He was Arthur Isambard Gossamer, and it was the lovely Jennifer Gossamer who was sleeping so peacefully beside him.

It was still late in the month of October, and he was still fifty years of age.

Three days ago they had left their old clothes on the pebbles of Chesil Bank and set off in disguise towards a new life.

Wait a minute. He was Reginald Iolanthe Perrin, former

senior sales executive at Sunshine Desserts. He had caught the eight-sixteen every weekday morning for twenty-five years. He had given the best years of his life to puddings. How had he come to be wandering the world disguised as Arthur Isambard Gossamer?

Perhaps it was all a dream.

Perhaps he was a dream.

He stepped out of bed carefully, not wishing to wake his wife, whether she was called Elizabeth or Jennifer, whether she was part of a dream or not. He tiptoed across the room, and drew back the curtains gently. There was nothing there. Just a white wall of absolute blankness.

'Oh my God,' he said.

'What is it?' said his wife sleepily.

'There's nothing. There's nothing outside the window at all.'

'It's fog, you fool. They forecast it.'

A double-decker bus edged slowly past the hotel, its outline faintly visible in the thick autumn fog, the passengers wraiths. A wave of relief swept over Reggie.

'We really do exist,' he said.

'We can go where we like and be whoever we like,' said Reggie as they finished their breakfast alone in the autumnal dining room.

'The world is our oyster, as C.J. would say,' said Elizabeth.

'Yes, I'm afraid he probably would,' said Reggie.

He smiled at the memory of his former boss, who had also left his clothes on Chesil Bank and set off for a new life, dressed as a tramp. Reggie wondered how he was faring on this raw October morning.

There was silence save for the hissing of the gas fire and the crunching of toast by middle-aged teeth. There were hunting scenes on their table mats.

'We're free from the grinding wheels of commerce. We're

8

free to shake off the bonds of an acquisitive society,' said Reggie.

'Yes.'

Reggie's coffee spilt over the scarlet coat of the Master of Foxhounds. He rubbed it around the mat, spreading the thin grey liquid over man and hound alike.

He gave a curious half-smile. For a moment he looked like the Mona Lisa's brother.

'Let's go home,' he said. 'Let's become Mr and Mrs Perrin again. We'll sell the house. We'll sell Grot. We'll sell the shops, the prime sites, the juggernauts. Then, when we're rich, we'll really be free to shake off the bonds of an acquisitive society.'

The sun shone out of a cloudless early December sky. The Mediterranean was deep blue. Seven cats lurked, waiting for crumbs.

They were breakfasting on the terrace of their hotel in Crete. They had sold the house in Coleridge Close. They had sold Grot. They had sold the prime sites, the juggernauts. They had set off on a world tour. Even allowing for the depredations of Capital Gains Tax, they were rich.

Below them a ragged olive grove fell stonily towards a tiny private beach. Across the bay the stern masculine mountains wrapped their secrets firmly to their dark breasts.

The tea came in tea-bags which you made in the cup. The instant coffee came in individual sachets.

The cats waited.

Reggie sighed.

'Happy?' said Elizabeth.

'Wonderfully happy,' said Reggie, tugging at the lid of his individual jar of apricot jam.

'I'm glad,' said Elizabeth.

'I'm glad you're glad,' said Reggie, 'It makes me very happy, darling, to know that you're glad I'm happy.'

'I'm glad,' said Elizabeth.

An old woman dressed in black rode her donkey through the olive grove. Behind her trailed a mangy goat. She did not look at the gleaming white hotel. Nor did the mangy goat.

Reggie removed the tea-bag from his cup and placed the sodden lump in his saucer. It oozed a thick acrid liquid. When he lifted his cup, drops spilt on his fawn holiday trousers and his buff short-sleeved holiday shirt.

'Yes,' he said. 'This is sheer bliss.'

He sighed.

The cats waited.

'If you're so happy, why do you keep sighing?' said Elizabeth.

'Sheer bliss isn't enough,' he said.

'Did you mean what you said yesterday?' said Elizabeth.

Reggie sipped his beer slowly. They were sitting on the terrace of the tourist pavilion at Phaetos.

'That sheer bliss isn't enough?' he said. 'Oh, yes.'

Below them, the fertile Messara Plain stretched to the foot of Mount Dhikti and the Lasithi Range.

They were weary after exploring the remains of the Minoan palaces.

'Is it guilt?' said Elizabeth.

'I expect so,' said Reggie glumly. 'It usually is. Guilt, the curse of the middle classes.'

Far away, cow bells jingled.

A robin hopped on to a nearby table.

More than fifteen hundred years before Christ, the unique, intricate and artistically joyous civilization of the Minoans had flourished here. Now, far overhead, a plane laid a thin vapour trail across the clear blue sky, like planes the world over.

'Summer in England, winters in Crete and Gozo, it isn't for me,' said Reggie.

Eighteen French tourists with blue guide books and painful feet invaded the winter peace of the tourist pavilion.

'There must be something that it's absolutely right for me to do next,' said Reggie.

The French tourists sat noisily all about them. They had bought oranges and postcards.

Far above, two vultures waited.

For what?

The French tourists sucked their oranges.

The cow bells tinkled.

A scooter roared briefly, then spluttered into silence.

'It's simply this,' said Reggie. 'I'm just an ordinary bloke, old Goofy Perrin from Ruttingstagg College. I'm no different from anyone else who walked out on his job, faked suicide, started a new life, returned home in disguise and remarried his wife, opened a shop selling goods that were guaranteed useless, to his amazement succeeded, walked out again, faked another suicide and started another new life.'

'But no one else has done that,' said Elizabeth.

'Exactly,' said Reggie. 'So there must have been some purpose behind it.'

The bones of ten red mullet were eloquent evidence of their greed. In the wine bottle only a few drips of retsina remained. In the salad bowl, one piece of cucumber floated bravely in the succulent dark-green olive oil of Greece.

Elizabeth smiled at Reggie.

Reggie smiled at Elizabeth.

'This is the life,' said Elizabeth.

'That's just it,' said Reggie. 'It isn't the life at all.'

He clasped Elizabeth's right hand, firmly yet tenderly.

'I want a home again,' he said.

She smiled at him.

'Oh so do I,' she said.

'Then I can start on my plans,' said Reggie.

A spontaneous outbreak of singing began. They smiled and clapped.

When they had entered the restaurant, they had bought

11

twenty plates, to break when the spontaneous singing began. They broke them now. The plates were English. The Cretans found that they broke more easily than other plates, and imported them in bulk.

'There are still some things we British do best,' mouthed Reggie across the hubbub.

Elizabeth grinned.

The singing and dancing and breaking of plates ended as suddenly as they had begun.

'What plans?' said Elizabeth.

'I don't know,' said Reggie.

On their first day back in /London Reggie discovered what their plans were.

They were staying in a hotel, tourists in their own town. It was eleven days before Christmas and tawdry angels hung listlessly over the Oxford Street crowds. Elizabeth had gone to buy shoes. It was an afternoon of raw mist and intermittent drizzle, eminently suited to the purchase of footwear.

It was three minutes to two when Reggie entered the bank where the fateful revelation was to come to him.

There were queues of equal length at the windows of Mr F. R. Bostock and Miss J. A. Purves. Reggie didn't join the queue of Miss J. A. Purves, who was moderately attractive. Looking at the breasts of bank clerks was a thing of the past, and so he chose the queue of Mr F. R. Bostock, who was moderately unattractive.

Rarely can virtue have been so instantly rewarded. At that very moment Miss J. A. Purves closed her window and set off, did Reggie but know it, to have a late lunch with her friend from the Halifax Building Society, Mr E. D. Renfrew (withdrawals).

A large, florid man moved angrily over from Miss Purves's window and stood in front of Reggie.

The man behind Reggie, a small, leathery man with a

spectacularly broken nose, leant forward and prodded the florid man in the back.

The florid man turned and glared at Reggie.

'What's the big idea?' he said.

'It wasn't me,' said Reggie.

'This man was 'ere before you,' said the small, leathery man with the broken nose.

'I have been waiting twenty minutes,' said the florid man, with the careful enunciation that follows a large liquid lunch, 'and I'm in a tearing hurry.'

'Listen mush, that man was before you,' said the broken nose.

'Thank you, but it's quite all right,' said Reggie, turning towards him.

'What did you say?' said the large, florid man slowly.

'I said, "Thank you, but it's quite all right",' said Reggie, whirling round to face him.

'Not you. Him,' said the florid man, pointing dismissively at the leathery man.

'I said, "That man was before you",' said the leathery man.

'Nobody orders me around,' said the florid man.

'What did you say?' said the broken nose.

'It honestly is quite all right,' said Reggie, turning first to one, then the other, smiling desperately. 'I'm in no particular hurry.'

'I said, "Nobody orders me around",' said the florid man. 'So kindly mind your own business.'

The queue shuffled forward towards Mr F. R. Bostock's window, but the argument continued.

'Ah, but it is my business, innit?' said the broken nose. 'This gentleman 'ere 'as waited just as long as what you have, and then, lo and behold, you barge in in front of him, you great fat pig.'

'Please, it's all right,' said Reggie. 'It's raining outside, so why hurry?'

'What did you say?' said the florid man with icy anger.

Reggie swung round to face him.

'I said, "It's raining outside, so why hurry?" ' he said.

'Not you. You keep out of this,' said the florid man.

'Next,' said Mr F. R. Bostock, who now had an empty window.

'Thank you for standing up for me,' said Reggie to the broken nose. 'I'm very grateful, but let's forget it.'

'I won't bleeding well forget it,' said the broken nose. 'If you won't stand up for yourself, I will.'

'You called me a fat pig,' said the large, florid man.

'Come on, come on, who's next?' said Mr F. R. Bostock.

'I do not like being called a fat pig and I'll ask you to kindly keep your hideous broken nose out of my business,' said the large man, who was growing steadily more florid.

The small man, who had no comparable chance of growing steadily more leathery, grabbed hold of Reggie and used him as a screen against the florid man.

'Oh, it's aspersions on my wonky hooter now, is it?' he said, prodding the florid man with Reggie. 'It's down to personal abuse, is it? Well sod off, you fat drunken pig.'

'You started it. You called me a fat pig,' said the florid man, prodding Reggie to emphasize his point.

'You are a fat pig,' said the broken nose, thumping Reggie's back.

'Please,' said Reggie, shaking himself clear of the two men.

'Will somebody come and get served?' said Mr F. R. Bostock.

'If you're in a tearing hurry, do go ahead,' said Reggie, to the florid man.

'I'm not in such a hurry that I'll allow a pipsqueak short-house with a nose as bent as West End Lane to call me a fat drunken pig and then accuse me of using personal insults,' said the florid man.

'You did,' said the broken nose. 'A broken nose, that's a personal disability, allied to your squints and your 'are-lips. Being a fat drunken pig, that's your bleeding character, innit?

14

That's having too many double brandies down the bleeding golf club.'

'Please, gentlemen,' said Reggie.

'Sling your hook, you,' said the broken nose. 'My quarrel's with alcoholics anonymous here.'

'Come outside and repeat that,' said the florid man.

'With pleasure,' said the broken nose.

Reggie, who had been feeling more and more like a United Nations Peace Keeping Force, suddenly stopped whirling dizzily about. He smiled broadly.

'Thank you, gentlemen,' he said.

He shook them both warmly by the hand.

'Thank you once again,' he said.

They stared at him in astonishment, their quarrel momentarily forgotten.

'Please,' pleaded Mr F. R. Bostock. 'Will somebody come and get served.'

'Shut up,' said Reggie.

He walked briskly out of the bank. He knew now what he had to do.

He hummed gaily as he walked through the Oxford Street drizzle towards the shoe shop.

Then he remembered that he'd forgotten to draw out any money.

He returned to the bank and joined the back of Mr F. R. Bostock's queue.

Reggie and Elizabeth just had time for a corned beef sandwich and a drink before closing time. The big-eared landlord opined that the weather was bad for trade. It was the worst pre-Christmas trade since he'd moved from the Plough at Didcot.

They sat in the corner by the grimy window. Elizabeth showed Reggie her new shoes. In vain. He was far, far away, in the land of his plans. But how could he tell Elizabeth? How could he persuade her to spend the rest of her life in the way he wanted? Not here. Not in this inhospitable hostelry.

Tonight, in an intimate restaurant, over the last of an excellent burgundy.

'You aren't listening to a word I say,' said Elizabeth.

'Sorry,' he said. 'I was thinking. What were you saying?'

'It doesn't matter.'

'Darling, I'm not one of those male chauvinist pigs who think that the conversation of women consists largely of idle chitter-chatter. I'm sure it was well worth hearing and I'd like to hear it. Now, what did you say?'

'I said these corned beef sandwiches aren't too bad.'

'Oh. No they aren't, are they? Not too bad at all. Well, mine isn't anyway. I can't speak for yours. But if mine's nice, it's hardly likely that yours will be repulsive. Especially as you say it isn't.'

It was three o'clock. The landlord opened both doors wide. Raw, damp air poured in.

'What's wrong?' said Elizabeth.

'I've had an idea,' said Reggie. 'This isn't the time to tell you about it.'

It was one minute past three. The landlord switched the Xpelair fans on. Cold air blew down their necks.

'When is the time?' said Elizabeth.

'Tonight, after a good dinner,' said Reggie.

'That sounds ominous,' said Elizabeth. 'Am I going to be so hostile to it?'

'No, of course not.'

'Tell me now, then.'

Reggie swallowed nervously.

'In the bank just now there was an argument,' he said. 'I started to think about all the unnecessary hatred and anger and violence in the world.'

'Come on you lot, haven't you got homes to go to? What do you think it is? Christmas?' yelled the landlord.

'Thank you, landlord,' Reggie called out. 'An apt intervention!'

'Well, go on,' said Elizabeth. 'What was your idea?'

16

Reggie swallowed again.

'I intend to set up a community, where middle-aged, middle-class people like us can learn to live in love and faith and trust,' he said.

'I think that's a marvellous idea,' said Elizabeth.

'People will be able to come for any length of time they like,' said Reggie over the aforementioned burgundy, at the end of an excellent dinner in Soho. 'They'll be able to use it as a commune where they can live in peace and happiness, or as a therapy centre where our staff can help them to find the love and goodness that lurks inside them.'

Their brandies arrived.

'Where will it be?' said Elizabeth.

'Cheers,' said Reggie.

'Cheers. It could be anywhere, I suppose.'

'Absolutely.'

'An old country house. An island. The Welsh hills. Anywhere.'

Reggie stretched his hand out under the table and patted Elizabeth's knee affectionately. She had taken the idea of the community better than he had dared to hope, but this was going to be a bitter pill for her to swallow.

'I'm sorry, old girl,' he said. 'But I want to live in an ordinary suburban house in an ordinary suburban street.'

'Thank God for that,' said Elizabeth. 'So do I.'

# 2  The Recruitment

It didn't take Reggie and Elizabeth long to realize that Number Twenty-One, Oslo Avenue, Botchley, was the ideal setting in which to begin their immense task. It was, in the eloquent words of Messrs Blunstone, Forrest and Stringer, a spacious detached residence of unusual desirability even for this exceptionally select area of Botchley.

'Listen to this, darling,' said Reggie as they entered the hall. '"Accustomed as we are to inspecting three or four properties a day, we were, nevertheless, very greatly surprised on entering this residence to find such an astonishing sense of space, particularly within the Principal Reception Room, the Added Conservatory, the Master Bedroom and the Kitchen Area."'

'Do you have to read from that thing?' said Elizabeth. 'Can't we just look at it for ourselves?'

They walked briskly through the Genuine Hall, pausing only to observe the timbered wainscoting and double-doored integrated cloaks hanging cupboard, and entered the Principal Reception Room.

'My word,' said Reggie, 'this room affords an unrivalled view over the terraced gardens, fringed by a verdant screen of trees that endows the said gardens with a sense of peacefulness which bestows the final accolade on this exceptionally characterful property.'

'Reggie!' said Elizabeth.

They admired the integrated double-glazed windows, noted the modern power circuitry with four conveniently sited power access points, and were impressed by the handsome integrated brick fireplace.

Then they entered the Dining Room.

'Stap me!' said Reggie. 'More modern power circuitry, and if this isn't an intimate yet surprisingly spacious setting for formal and informal dining, I'm the Queen of Sheba's surprisingly spacious left tit.'

'Reggie! Please!' said Elizabeth. 'I thought you were excited about buying the house.'

'I am,' said Reggie. 'Almost as excited as Messrs Blunstone, Forrest and Stringer.'

They paused briefly to admire the low-level Royal Venton suite and integrated wash-basin in the spacious Separate Downstairs WC, the amply proportioned Study, the splendid Added Conservatory, and the exceptionally commodious kitchen with its Scandinavian-style traditional English fully integrated natural pine and chrome storage units and work surfaces.

Then they went upstairs to the Master Bedroom.

'Here we find the same impression of spacious living as is afforded throughout the ground floor,' said Reggie. 'This handsome room enjoys integrated double-glazing with sliding units, and it is patently obvious that the unusually tasteful decorations are in absolutely pristine order, affording an elegant background to Scandinavian or traditional English sex activities both anal and oral with fully integrated manking about and doing exceptionally spacious naughty things.'

'It doesn't say that,' said Elizabeth.

'Of course it doesn't.'

They laughed. Their lips met. A feeling of happiness and tenderness ran through them. For all they cared, the double-floored fully integrated floor-to-ceiling wardrobe units might not have existed.

It was approaching the end of January, and the weather was unseasonably mild. Fruit farmers felt the balmy winds

19

morosely and worried about spring frosts. The going at Market Rasen and Plumpton was 'good to firm'.

Reggie and Elizabeth took up residence in a relatively cheap hotel in one of the less fashionable parts of Hendon while they waited to move to Botchley.

'We must husband our resources. I want to pay my staff good salaries,' Reggie explained over their tagliatelle bolognese in one of the best Italian restaurants in Hendon.

'What sort of staff are you looking for?' asked Elizabeth.

'People who are intelligent, mature, kind and trustworthy,' said Reggie.

'How will you find them?' said Elizabeth.

'Personal contacts,' said Reggie. 'Leave all that to me.'

'And me?' said Elizabeth. 'Where do I come in?'

Reggie poured a little more of the rough carafe wine into Elizabeth's glass. It was a placatory gesture.

'I want you to be secretary,' he said. 'It's a very important job. Taking bookings, allocating rooms, handling correspondence. A highly responsible post.'

Their escalopes and chips arrived. On top of each escalope there were three capers and half an inch of anchovy fillet. They each had fifteen chips.

'I've always thought of secretaries of institutions as cool, hard, efficient, grey-haired, sexless,' said Elizabeth.

'You'll be the exception that proves the rule,' said Reggie.

'You mean I'm not efficient?' said Elizabeth.

'No!' said Reggie hastily.

She laughed. Both the other customers turned to look. The proprietor beamed.

'I'm teasing you, darling,' said Elizabeth.

'Teasing?' said Reggie.

'I'd love to be secretary,' she said.

Reggie's recruitment of his first intelligent, mature, kind and trustworthy member of staff had been concluded.

He popped a caper into his mouth.

\*

The recruitment of the second intelligent, mature, kind and trustworthy member of staff took longer.

It was C.J.

Reggie's former boss at Sunshine Desserts lived at Blancmange Cottage, Godalming. Reggie phoned him from the only unvandalized phone box in Hendon. It was outside the cemetery. Mrs C.J. answered.

'I haven't seen him since October,' she said. 'I understood he was last seen dressed as a tramp.'

'Yes. You mean he . . . he hasn't been . . . he's still . . . good God!'

'Yes. I had a letter from him at Christmas. Shall I read it to you?'

'Please.'

'Hang on.'

Light rain fell. A pale, harassed woman came out of the cemetery and stood anxiously outside the phone box. She looked at her wrist although she had no watch. Reggie shrugged. The pips went. He inserted 10p. The woman opened the door.

'I won't be long,' he said.

'But you aren't talking,' she said.

'The person on the other end has gone to fetch something,' said Reggie.

'Only I'm ringing my friend, and she goes out.'

'I won't be long,' said Reggie.

'Only she's not well.'

'I'm very sorry.'

'No, but it's her leg, you see.'

'I'm sorry about her leg, but what can I do?'

'She's not well, you see,' said the woman.

The woman closed the door and waited impatiently. The pips went. Reggie inserted 10p. The woman made an angry gesture and set off down the road.

'Hello,' said Mrs C.J. 'Are you still there?'

'Yes,' said Reggie.

'Sorry to keep you. He says "Dear Mrs C.J. This is to wish

you a happy Christmas. I wish I could send you something, but times are hard. I make a bit working the cinema queues. I haven't much to say. Least said, soonest forgotten. With love, C.J."'

'I see. Good . . . er . . . Good God!'

'Yes.'

'Have you tried to find him?'

'No.'

'Did you have a happy Christmas?'

'Wonderful. I spent it with my friends in Luxembourg.'

When Reggie rang off, the harassed woman started to walk back towards the phone box.

A smooth young man got out of a taxi and stepped into the phone box just before she could reach it.

For four days Reggie trudged round the West End cinema queues. The buskers were most varied, but all had one thing in common. They weren't C.J.

On the fifth day, his travels took him to a fringe cinema in North London. A few earnest young people were waiting to see a double bill of *avant-garde* West German films. One of them was called *L* and the other one was called *The Amazing Social, Sexual and Political Awakening of the Elderly Widow Blumenthal*. The *avant-garde* youngsters appeared to be mean, impecunious, and sound judges of music. None of them put any money in the cloth cap of the middle-aged man who was strumming his banjo so insensitively, and singing, stiffly and very flat, the following unusual words:

> 'Love and marriage,
> Love and marriage,
> They go together like a horse and carriage.
> Dad was told by mother:
> I didn't get where I am today without knowing that you
> can't have one without the other.'

'It's good to see you, Reggie,' said C.J., when they were settled in the Lord Palmerston round the corner.

'Really?' said Reggie.

'Of course,' said C.J., downing his whisky rapidly. 'You know what they say. Absence is better than a cure.'

'Prevention makes the heart grow fonder,' said Reggie.

'In a nutshell, Reggie,' said C.J. 'Same again?'

'I'll get them.'

'Please!' said C.J. 'It's my round. A few people have been kind enough to reward my efforts with some pennies, enough to buy a whisky and a half of Guinness, anyway.'

Reggie smiled as he watched C.J. at the bar, trying to look dignified in his beggar's rags. A woman with large holes in her tights thought he was smiling at her, and he stopped smiling rapidly.

'Cheers', said Reggie on C.J.'s return.

'Bottoms up,' said C.J.

Reggie's lips felt carefully through the froth to the cool, dark, smooth beer below.

'So, you've stuck at being a tramp, then?' he said.

'When I do a thing, I do it thoroughly,' said C.J. 'I see it through.'

'You certainly do, C.J.'

C.J. glanced round the drab, run-down pub as if he feared that the three Irish labourers standing at the bar might be CIA agents.

'I've had enough, Reggie,' he said quietly. 'Busking isn't really my bag.'

'I imagine not, C.J.'

Reggie took a long sip of his Guinness. He laid the glass down and looked C.J. straight in the eye.

'I want to offer you a job,' he said.

'What is it this time? Another mad idea like Grot? More humiliations for your old boss? More farting chairs?'

'Grot was a success, C.J., and you had a good job. But even that will be as nothing compared to your future work.'

A young man won the jackpot on the fruit machine.

Reggie described the community that he was going to form.

'Where will it be? Some sunny off-shore island?' asked C.J. hopefully.

'Twenty-one, Oslo Avenue, Botchley.'

'Oh.'

The barman came over to their table. He seemed angry.

'You gave me the wrong money,' he told C.J. scornfully. 'You gave me thirty-five pee, three pesetas, two pfennigs and a shirt button.'

C.J. managed to find the correct money, and handed it to the barman.

'You want to be careful of these types,' the barman warned Reggie.

'Thank you, I will,' said Reggie.

C.J. pocketed the pesetas, the pfennigs and the shirt button.

'Mean bloody unwashed long-haired louts,' he grumbled.

'That's not the way you should talk about them, if you're joining my community,' said Reggie.

'Oh. How should I talk about them if I'm joining your community?'

'Fascinating, somewhat misguided, rather immature, socially confused, excessively serious but potentially highly creative and absolutely delightful mean bloody unwashed long-haired louts,' said Reggie.

He bought another round, the better to further his persuasion of C.J.

'What sort of job do you have in mind for me?' said C.J.

'I'm not sure yet,' said Reggie. 'But I promise you it'll be worthy of your talents. Come and give it a try. After all, the proof of the pudding is caviar to the general.'

'That's true,' said C.J. 'That's very true. I'm not sure if it's my line of country, though.'

'You'll have board and lodging and a salary of eight thousand pounds a year.'

'On the other hand, no doubt I could soon adjust to it,' said C.J.

They shook hands, and Reggie bought another round.

'When I've got my staff together,' he said, 'there'll be a period of training.'

'Training, Reggie?'

'We'll all have to learn how to be nice.'

'Oh.'

C.J. gazed morosely at his whisky.

'I didn't get where I am today by being nice,' he said.

'You'll get used to it,' said Reggie. 'Once you are nice, you'll find that it's really quite nice being nice.'

'This free board and lodging, Reggie, where will that be?'

'Erm . . . with us.'

'With you? Ah!'

'There won't be room for everyone actually in the house,' said Reggie. 'Some of you'll have to live under . . . er . . . canvas.'

C.J.'s hand shook slightly as he lifted the whisky to his lips.

'Under canvas? You mean . . . in a tent?'

'Yes.'

'Good God.'

'Yes.'

'Eight thousand pounds?'

'Yes.'

'Not that I'd mind, Reggie. It's Mrs C.J. She's a different kettle of fish.'

'She certainly is,' said Reggie. 'And you feel that she might be a different kettle of fish out of water?'

'Exactly. By no stretch of the imagination can Mrs C.J. be described as a frontierswoman.'

'No.'

'She's wedded to her creature comforts, Reggie.'

The eyes of the two men met.

'I seem to recall that she has friends in Luxembourg,' said Reggie.

'Yes. Delightful people.'

'Luxembourg *is* delightful.'

'Absolutely delightful.'

'All the charms of European civilization in microcosm.'

'Well put, Reggie.'

Reggie smiled faintly.

'Perhaps it would be a rather nice gesture if you were to sacrifice your marital pleasures and let her stay in Luxembourg for a while,' he said.

'What an excellent idea, Reggie. Just for a few months till we get things straight. You're on. Consider me recruited.'

'You're the first person I've come to,' said Reggie.

'Ah!'

'Start at the top.'

'Quite! Thank you, Reggie.'

'After Everest, the Mendips.'

'Absolutely. What? Not quite with you, Reggie.'

'Perfectly simple,' said Reggie. 'If I can make you nice, I can make anybody nice.'

The next intelligent, mature, kind and trustworthy recruit to be signed up by Reggie was Doc Morrissey.

It wasn't difficult to trace the ageing ex-medico of Sunshine Desserts. Reggie soon discovered that he had installed himself in a bed-sitter in Southall.

The bed-sitter turned out to be above a shop that sold Indian spices, next door to a launderette. Asian women of indeterminable age and inaccessible beauty were setting off with Tesco carrier bags from houses that had been built for Brentford supporters and old women who liked a bottle of stout before the pubs filled up on a Saturday morning.

Over the road the Gaumont, designed for films with Richard Todd in them, had gaudy posters for a double bill of romances from the sub-continent.

Beside Doc Morrissey's door there were three bells. Above each bell, untidily secured with Sellotape, there was a name. The names were Patel, Mankad and Morrissey. Reggie rang Doc Morrissey's bell.

The air was full of the scents of cumin, garam masala and Persil.

There was no reply. He tried the bell marked Patel. Mr Patel had a chubby face and told Reggie that he would probably find the Professor in the park.

The park was small and bleak. The grass was thin and patchy. The backs of the surrounding houses were shabby and blackened. Grot's erstwhile Head of Forward Planning was sitting on a bench, feeding crumbs of poppadum to sceptical starlings.

'Reggie!' he said, a smile of heart-warming delight spreading across his weatherbeaten face.

'Morning, Professor,' said Reggie.

Doc Morrissey gave an abashed grin.

'It goes down well in these parts,' he said. 'I've set myself up as an English teacher.'

'How's it going?' said Reggie, sitting beside him on the bench.

'Extremely well.'

'How many pupils have you got?'

'These are early days, Reggie.'

'How many pupils?'

'One. I'm not unhappy here, Reggie. I suppose that since I'm one of nature's exiles, I'm better off where it's natural for a white man to feel an exile.'

It was the middle of February. The weather was still quite mild, but a keen wind was sending occasional reminders about loneliness gusting across the park.

'Old age must be rather depressing for a doctor,' said Reggie. 'Knowing exactly what's happening to your body.'

'Yes it must,' said Doc Morrissey.

He flexed the fingers of both hands.

'Why are you doing that?' said Reggie.

'Preventing the onset of arthritis in the joints.'

The starlings, their glorious plumage dulled by the city

grime, had deserted Doc Morrissey and were exploring the lifeless ground around a derelict swing.

Two crows and a blackbird joined them.

'Even the birds are black here,' said Doc Morrissey.

'Are you depressed?' said Reggie.

'No. No. Southall's a million laughs. And I find a certain consolation, Reggie, in the knowledge that by being the worst doctor in England I have saved somebody else from that ignominy. No man's life is entirely pointless.'

'Oh good,' said Reggie. 'I'm glad you're not depressed.'

He trailed his arm over the back of the bench and turned to face Doc Morrissey.

'This is no chance meeting,' he said. 'I've come to offer you a job.'

Doc Morrissey gawped.

'Again?' he said.

Reggie explained about the community and its aims.

'It sounds marvellous,' said Doc Morrissey excitedly. 'What sort of role do you have in mind for me?'

'A medical role,' said Reggie.

'Oh. Isn't there anything else I could do?'

'A different branch of medicine, though. You'll be our psychologist.'

'Oh!'

'It's your undiscovered metier, Doc.'

'It is?'

'Psychology is your nettle and I'm confident that you'll grasp it.'

'You are?'

'You will have a salary of . . . five thousand pounds, plus board and lodging.'

They went to the pub to celebrate. They drank pints of bitter and ate gala pie with brinjal pickle.

'I'm no expert, you know,' said Doc Morrissey.

'The experts have had their chances,' said Reggie. 'They

have failed. It's precisely your lack of expertise that excites me.'

'Oh.'

On the nineteenth of February, Reggie and Elizabeth moved into Number Twenty-one, Oslo Avenue, Botchley.

Vans brought the furniture that Elizabeth had chosen from the great furniture emporia of London Town.

Men came to connect up the gas and electricity.

The neighbours offered them cups of tea. These olive branches were not spurned.

The houses of the neighbours were smaller than Number Twenty-one. They only had three bedrooms.

The neighbours at Number Twenty-three were Mr and Mrs Penfold.

The neighbours at Number Nineteen were Mr and Mrs Hollies.

Mrs Penfold talked little and seemed neurotically shy. Her tea was too weak.

Mrs Hollies talked a great deal and seemed obsessively extrovert. Her tea was too strong.

The exceptionally mild weather continued. The snowdrops were on the rampage in front gardens. The crocuses were swelling expectantly and sticky buds were forming on the trees.

Mrs Hollies had never known anything like it. But then we didn't get the seasons like we used to. Everything had gone absolutely haywire. Mrs Hollies blamed the aeroplanes. People could scoff, but it stood to reason that all those great big things up there disturbing the atmosphere must make everything go haywire.

The views of Mrs Penfold on the subject were a closed book.

That evening Reggie and Elizabeth explored their neighbourhood. They walked down Oslo Avenue, past pleasant detached residences, several of which had mock-Tudor beams and bay windows. They turned right into Bonn Close. The timing devices of the street lamps were on the blink, and the lights were pale pink and feeble. Bonn Close brought them to the High Street.

They visited the Botchley Arms, where Reggie had two bottles of diabetic lager while his partner opted for two medium sherries.

They walked down Botchley High Street, past supermarkets, shoe shops, betting shops and dress shops, past the George and Dragon, until they came to a parade set back from the High Street. Here there were three restaurants – the New Bengal, the Golden Jasmine House, and the Oven D'Or. They dined at the Oven D'Or. They were the only diners.

Before returning home they sampled the delights of the George and Dragon. It was run by a small man with a large wife and an even larger mother. The locals called it the George and Two Dragons.

Their route home took them along Nairobi Drive, and round Lisbon Crescent to the other end of Oslo Avenue. A right turn brought them back to their new home. They stood by the garden gate and looked at the placid, commonplace frontage of their surprisingly spacious dwelling. Soon it would be bursting with life and love and hope.

A light rain began to fall. Reggie lifted Elizabeth up and staggered in over the threshold.

The work of recruitment continued. The targets were Reggie's old colleagues at Sunshine Desserts and Grot. He felt about them as he felt about his ageing pyjamas. They might not fit, they might be somewhat torn in vital places and permanently stained in other vital places, but a man felt comfortable with them.

He called next at the flat occupied by Tony Webster and his wife Joan. It was in the Lower Mortlake Road. It was ten fifteen on a Saturday morning. Reggie was disappointed to find that his former secretary was out. It fact he only just caught Tony. He was sporting a brown suit and matching suitcase, and carried a lightweight topcoat over his arm.

'Sorry. Were you just going out?' said Reggie.

'Business trip. Frankfurt. Off to hit the fatherland, score a few exports. I'll get a later flight. No sweat,' said Tony. 'Come in. Great to see you.'

The flat bore evidence of both opulence and poverty. There was a threadbare carpet and a heavy, stained three-piece suite. There was also a colour television set, a cocktail trolley and expensive stereo equipment.

'Joan at work?' Reggie asked, installing himself in one of the heavy armchairs.

'Yeah. She does one Saturday morning in three. I don't want her to work, but you know what women are.'

'Things are going well, are they?' said Reggie.

'Fantastic. Great. Knock-out.'

'I came here with a proposition,' said Reggie. 'But there doesn't seem much point in putting it as you're doing so well.'

'Well, pretty well. This is Success City, Arizona. But I've always been interested in your ideas, Reggie.'

Reggie described the community and offered Tony and Joan jobs.

'Knock-out,' said Tony. 'Absolute knock-out. We'll let you know.'

When Reggie left, Tony set off with him. The suitcase came open on the stairs and his central-heating brochures cascaded into the hall.

'OK,' said Tony. 'Frankfurt doesn't exist. But this central heating job's a knock-out. No basic, but fantastic commission.'

That afternoon Reggie invited himself to tea with David and Prue Harris-Jones.

They had a flat in a new block in Reading. Already the paint on the outside was peeling and the walls on the inside were cracking. Their fourteen-month-old boy was Reggie's godson. His name was Reggie. David and Prue greeted Reggie with something approaching adoration. Young Reggie greeted him with something approaching an attack of wind.

David said that he was very happy with the building society, and Reading was much maligned. When Reggie offered them jobs, their response was unequivocal.

'Super,' they said.

Later, over his second slice of sponge cake, David Harris-Jones did venture a cautious criticism.

'You know what I think of you, Reggie,' he said. 'I look up to you.'

'Oh dear, oh dear,' said Reggie.

'Well exactly,' said David Harris-Jones. 'I look up to you as the sort of person who doesn't expect or want people to look up to him.'

'I agree,' said Prue.

'Well, thank you,' said Reggie.

'I mean the community idea is super,' said David Harris-Jones. 'But I don't think Prue or I would be happy if you were . . . how can I put it? . . . well, not exactly a cult figure, but . . . er . . . not exactly sort of too big for your . . . but sort of . . . er . . .'

'Thank you for speaking so frankly,' said Reggie. 'If you mean that I'm in danger of becoming self-important, please don't worry. The community's the thing. I'll just be the shadowy catalyst that enables it to function.'

'Super,' said David and Prue Harris-Jones.

'What are you going to call it?' said Prue, crossing her attractive but sensible legs.

'Perrins,' said Reggie.

'Super,' said David and Prue Harris-Jones.

Steady rain was falling as Reggie drove home from Reading. The lights in Lisbon Crescent were out, and the February night was very dark. As he turned into Oslo Avenue, he found himself following the single-decker bus, the W288, which ran through these quiet streets to places with deliciously dull names, gloriously ordinary Coxwell, exquisitely prosaic Spraundon.

This was his world.

When he entered the living-room, he felt as if he had been there for a thousand years. The phone was ringing. It was Tony.

'We'll take the job,' he said. 'No sweat.'

'Reggie?' said Elizabeth next afternoon, as they were about to wash up the Sunday dinner things in the deceptively commodious kitchen.

'Yes?'

'What's happening about the staff? You haven't told me a thing.'

'We agreed that the recruiting would be my responsibility and the furniture would be yours,' he said.

'Well I haven't kept the furniture secret,' said Elizabeth.

'That is rather different,' he said. 'I mean, we couldn't sit on it if you did.'

He donned the real ale apron and began to stack the dishes in the integrated sink with double drainers. He arranged the dishes in a pyramid so that the water would pour over them like a fountain.

'Is there some reason why you don't want to tell me about the staff?' said Elizabeth, wrapping the remains of the meal in the *Botchley and Spraundon Press* (*Incorporating the Coxwell Gazette*).

'Of course not, darling.'

He turned on the hot water. It gushed on to a dessert spoon and sprayed out all over the floor. He moved the spoon hurriedly, and added a few squirts of extra-strength washing-up liquid.

'I've engaged six excellent people,' he said.

'Who?' she asked. 'I know their names won't mean much, but I'd like to know.'

'Er . . . one or two of the names may mean something. C.J., for instance.'

'C.J.?'

'Yes.'

'You've appointed C.J.?'

'Yes. He won't be on top of us all the time, darling. He'll probably spend quite a lot of his time in his . . . er . . . in his tent.'

There was a pause. Reggie lost his dishmop.

'In his what?' said Elizabeth.

'He's going to live under canvas,' said Reggie. 'Mrs C.J. won't be with him. She's no frontierswoman.'

'Reggie, where is this tent of C.J.'s going to be?' said Elizabeth.

'Damn, I've broken a cup,' said Reggie.

He hunted for the remains of the cup in the sud-filled bowl, for, like many a good man before him, he had sadly under-estimated the power of the extra-strength washing-up liquid.

During his hunt he found the dishmop. Life is often like that. In hunting for one thing, we find another.

'Where is this tent going to be?' repeated Elizabeth. 'Near here?'

'Er . . . quite near.'

'How near?'

'Er . . . not in the front garden.'

'Are you trying to tell me that C.J. is going to live in a tent in the back garden?' said Elizabeth.

'Right at the back of the back garden,' said Reggie. 'Miles from the house, really.'

'What will he do about food? Open tins of pemmican down by the compost heap?'

'I thought he'd . . . er . . . have some of his meals with us.'

'Which meals?'

'Er . . . breakfast, lunch and dinner.'

'So we live together, the three of us. That sounds dangerous,' she said.

'Good heavens no. *Ménages à-trois*, Bermuda triangles, that
would be dangerous. No, they'll all live here.'

'All?'

'All the staff.'

'So I'm expected to share my house with total strangers?'

'They . . . er . . . they won't be strangers.'

'What will they be?'

'Well . . . people like Doc Morrissey, Tony and Joan, David
and Prue.'

'All the old mob?'

'They've proved their worth, darling. Look what they did
for Grot.'

'And what about our daughter? Hasn't she proved her
worth?'

'Linda and Tom too. I was going to ask them next. And
Jimmy.'

'It's going to get a bit crowded, isn't it?'

'That's the whole point of a comminity,' said Reggie.
'There's not much point in having a community if nobody's
there.'

'Am I expected to cook for them?'

'We'll employ a cook, darling.'

Reggie advanced towards her. Suds dripped from his green
washing-up gloves.

'I'm sorry,' he said. 'I should have told you everything. I
just didn't know how you'd take it.'

'I think it's all very exciting,' said Elizabeth.


After they had finished the washing-up, they had their coffee
in the living-room. The chairs and settee that Elizabeth had
chosen had comfort as their main objective, while not neglect-
ing the aesthetic element. Three pictures of bygone Botchley
adorned the walls. The smokeless fuel burned placidly. They

sat on the settee, and Elizabeth nestled her head against Reggie's chest.

'Did you really mean that?' said Reggie. 'Do you really think it's all very exciting?'

'After Grot, I'll never doubt your judgement again,' said Elizabeth.

It was cosy in the living-room in the fading half-light. Reggie put his arm round Elizabeth.

'We're going to have to learn different values,' he said. 'We're going to have to forget that an Englishman's home is his castle. From now on, our home is everyone else's castle.'

The front doorbell rang.

'Damn, damn damn,' he said. 'Who the hell is that?'

He smiled ruefully.

It was his son-in-law Tom.

'Oh, it's you. Come in,' said Reggie.

'I haven't come at an unfortunate time, have I, Reggie?' said Tom.

'Every time you visit us, Tom, it's . . . absolutely delightful. Wot, no prune wine?'

Tom had brought some of his usual appurtenances – his beard, his briar pipe – but none of his home-made wine.

'I haven't had the heart to make any lately,' he admitted. 'You'll have to forgo it.'

'Oh, what a shame.'

They went into the living-room.

'This room is surprisingly spacious,' said Tom, after he had kissed his mother-in-law.

'Once an estate agent, always an estate agent,' said Reggie.

Elizabeth went to make some coffee for Tom, who plonked himself down on the settee. His legs stretched out in front of him till they seemed to fill the room.

'How are things with you, Reggie?' he asked.

'Not bad, Tom. I smiled ruefully just before you came. First time I can recall actually smiling ruefully. I've read about it, of course. Always wanted to do it.'

'I'm not smiling ruefully,' said Tom.

'No.'

'I'm looking lugubrious.'

'Yes.'

'Even when I'm wildly excited I look lugubrious, so it's difficult for people to tell when I actually am lugubrious.'

'You've got no lugubriosity in reserve.'

'Exactly.'

Tom relit his pipe.

'Do you remember what a success I was with my adverts for Grot?' he said.

'I certainly do.'

'I was known as the McGonegall of Admass. Well, you may find this difficult to believe, but I've been unable to get another job in advertising.'

'You amaze me. So, it's back to the estate agent's boards, is it?'

Tom relit his pipe before replying.

'I couldn't go back to that,' he said. 'I've burnt my boats.'

'Burnt your boats, Tom?'

Tom stood up, as if he felt that it would relieve the burden of his folly.

'When I left, Norris asked me if I'd continue to write my witty house ads. I said . . .' Tom shuddered at the memory. 'I said: "You can stick your house ads up your fully integrated exceptionally spacious arse unit."'

Reggie laughed.

'Yes.'

'Very good,' he said. 'I'm surpri . . . no, I'm not. Why should I be?'

'He's told every estate agent from Bristol to Burnham-on-Crouch.'

'They'll have forgotten.'

'Estate agents never forget. They're the elephants of the professional world.'

37

Tom sat down again, and managed to achieve the impossible by looking even more lugubrious than he had before.

'I popped in at a party last night, at the show house on that new estate at High Wycombe,' he said. 'I was snubbed. Even Harrison, of Harrison, Harrison and Harrison, cold-shouldered me. I wouldn't have been surprised if it had been Harrison or Harrison. They're bastards. But Harrison! He was my friend.'

He relit his pipe.

'I've got bitten by the crafts bug,' he said. 'Thatching, basket-weaving, coopering. I can't seem to get a foot in, though. I can't get any work, Reggie. We're in trouble.'

'I'm sorry, Tom.'

Tom shifted nervously in his seat.

'I've never asked for charity, Reggie,' he began.

'I'm glad to to hear it,' said Reggie.

'I'm not a charity person.'

'Oh good. That is a relief.'

'I don't like having something for nothing.'

"Oh good. For one awful moment there I thought you were going to ask me for help. I misjudged you, Tom. Can you forgive me?'

Tom looked at Reggie in hurt puzzlement.

'I should have known better,' said Reggie. 'I always thought that our daughter had married a real man.'

'Oh. Thank you, Reggie.'

'A man with pride.'

'Oh. Thank you, Reggie.'

They sat in silence for a few moments. Tom looked acutely miserable.

'I'm also glad you didn't ask for charity, because you don't need it,' said Reggie.

He explained his project, offered Tom and Linda jobs, agreed salaries, and suggested that they sell their house, but not through Harrison, Harrison and Harrison.

Elizabeth brought the coffee, switched on the light, and drew the curtains on the gathering mists of night.

The front doorbell rang again. Early indications were that it was coping splendidly with its role in the smooth running of the household. It was Linda, and she was angry. She swept past her father's affectionate embrace and confronted Tom.

'You bastard!' she said.

Tom stood up slowly.

'Hello, darling,' he said. 'How did you get here?'

'I borrowed the Perrymans' car. You did it, didn't you? You bastard!'

'Linda!' said Elizabeth.

'To what do I owe the reception of this unmerited description?' said Tom.

'Oh shut up,' said Linda. 'You did it, didn't you?'

'I can't answer you and shut up,' said Tom.

'Oh, shut up,' said Linda. 'Well, did you or didn't you?'

Reggie put a fatherly arm on Linda's shoulder.

'What is it?' he said.

'He came to you and begged,' she said. 'I asked him not to. He promised. I can't stand people abasing themselves and begging. I went down on one knee and cried: "Tom, please if you love me, don't abase yourself. Don't beg." He promised.'

'You've got it all wrong, Linda,' said Reggie. 'Come on. Sit down and discuss this sensibly. There's all this splendid new furniture just waiting to be sat on. Pity to waste it.'

They all sat down except Linda.

'What have I got wrong?' she demanded.

'Tom didn't beg,' said Reggie. 'He obviously took your words to heart, because he rushed all the way over here to tell me . . . now, what was his exact phrase? . . . Yes . . . "I'm not a charity person".'

'That's right,' said Tom.

'And I offered him a job,' said Reggie.

He squeezed up towards Tom, making room for Linda to sit on the other end of the settee.

He put his arm round her shoulder and explained about the project and the jobs he had offered them and how he

39

wanted them to come and live at Perrins. When he had finished Linda burst into tears.

'It's not as bad an idea as all that, is it?' said Reggie.

Everyone played their part in cheering Linda up. She blew her nose, Elizabeth poured her a brandy, Reggie squeezed her affectionately, and Tom remained silent.

Reggie's squeeze meant: 'We love you so much. You're all we've got now that our son is lost to us.'

They had last heard from Mark almost three years ago, after he had been kidnapped by guerillas while presenting *The Reluctant Debutante* to an audience of Angolan mercenaries. They had drifted into silence about him. His absence was a constant presence which they never acknowledged. Reggie hoped that Linda would understand his squeeze.

'Well,' he said. 'What do you think of my idea?'

'I learnt my lesson over Grot,' said Linda. 'I'm never going to criticize your ideas again.'

A car horn began to blare outside.

'What's that rudely disturbing the calm of our suburban Sunday?' said Reggie.

Linda leapt up.

'Oh, my God,' she said. 'I left Adam and Jocasta in the car.' She rushed outside.

Tom relit his pipe.

'Oh, my God,' said Reggie. 'Adam and Jocasta will be living with us as well.'

Reggie felt a lurking sadness that his friends, relatives and colleagues weren't meeting with more success in their various lives.

Surely somebody would stand out against him and his purse? It didn't seem likely. Only Major James Gordonstoun Anderson remained.

Since Elizabeth's elder brother had been made redundant by the Queen's Own Berkshire Light Infantry on the grounds of age in his forty-sixth year, success had not courted him assiduously. He had been divorced from his first wife, Sheila. His marriage to his second wife Lettuce had failed to survive his non-arrival at the church. His secret right-wing army had collapsed when his colleague, Clive 'Lofty' Anstruther, had vamoosed with all the funds and weapons. His brief career as Head of Creative Thinking at Grot had ended when the organization had been disbanded.

An inquiry at his old bed-sitter revealed that he had moved to a house near Woburn Sands. It was called Rorke's Drift.

What could Jimmy be doing in the Woburn area? Army recruiting officer for Milton Keynes? Chief Giraffe Buyer for the Duke of Bedford?

There were pools of water at the roadside, after the overnight rain. Heavy yellow clouds hung over Dunstable Downs, and it was still very mild for March.

Rorke's Drift turned out to be a small, unprepossessing modern bungalow that stood like a tiny corner of some seaside suburb in a clearing surrounded by fine woods. It was deserted. No smoke rose from its rustic chimney. A brief ray of sunshine lit up the clearing, then died away.

A large woman marched fiercely along a track that led out of the woods past the bungalow. She was towing a reluctant and severely over-stretched chihuahua.

'Looking for the colonel?' she barked, perhaps because she knew that the little dog was too exhausted to do so.

'The . . . er . . . yes.'

'He's out. At work.'

'Ah! Do you . . . er . . . do you happen to know where he works?'

'Sorry. Can't oblige. Come on, Rastus. Chop chop.'

She led the exhausted chihuahua remorselessly towards fresh pastures. Trees against which it would have loved to cock its little legs were glimpsed like pretty villages from an express train.

At equal speed from the opposite direction came a mild and tiny woman being pulled by a huge Alsatian.

'Looking for the colonel?' she managed to gasp.

'Yes.'

'Narkworth Narrow Boats. Outskirts of Wolverton.'

And then she was gone.

Reggie was happy to leave this strange place. There was more than an air of *Grimm's Fairy Tales* about the silent woods, the nasty bungalow in the little clearing, and the women with their wildly unsuitable pets. What grotesque pair would arrive next? A dwarf pulled along by a lion? A giant, exercising his field mouse?

The clouds were breaking up rapidly. The sun gleamed on the puddles.

Reggie found Narkworth Narrow Boats without difficulty. It was situated on a long straight stretch of the Grand Union Canal. He parked in a heavily rutted car-park and picked his way gingerly between the puddles into a small yard surrounded by workshops and store-rooms. A smart sign-board carried the simple legend 'Reception'. It pointed to a newly painted single-storey building.

Jimmy sat at the desk, almost hidden behind a huge pot of flowers. His face broke into a delighted smile.

'Reggie!'

They shook hands. Jimmy's handshake was a barometer of his circumstances and now it had the unrestrained vigour of his palmiest days.

'Nice to see you, Colonel,' said Reggie.

'Nice to see . . . ah! Yes. You've . . . er . . . you've met some of my neighbours. A harmless deception, Reggie. Practically a colonel. Should have been, by rights.'

Reggie sat down, and faced Jimmy round the edge of the flowers.

'Running this show,' said Jimmy. 'Excellent set-up. Landed on my feet.'

'I half thought you might be running another secret army,' said Reggie.

'No fear. Once bitten, twice shy. Bastard took the lot.'

'Clive "Lofty" Anstruther?'

'Lofty by name and Lofty by nature,' said Jimmy mysteriously. 'If I ever run into him . . .'

What he would do was evidently beyond expression in mere words.

He led Reggie on a tour of inspection, while Reggie described his community persuasively.

'It's a kind of army,' he said. 'An army of peace. Fighting together, living together, messing together. Living under canvas. Think of the camaraderie, Jimmy.'

Jimmy stood in the yard, thinking of the camaraderie.

Then he shook his head.

'Two months ago, jumped at the chance,' he said. 'Good set-up here, though. Leisure explosion. Canals booming.'

'Good. Good. Is there a Narkworth, incidentally?'

'Cock-up on the marital front. Kraut wife.'

Jimmy had never forgiven the Germans for losing the war before he was old enough to fight.

'Sold out, dirt cheap, fresh start, sad story,' said Jimmy.

The sun was beaming now from a cloudless sky.

'Care for a spin?' said Jimmy.

All along the canal there were bollards, and fifteen narrow boats of various lengths were tied up. They were all painted green and yellow. In some of them, renovation was in progress beneath waterproof sheeting.

Jimmy chose a full-length seventy-foot converted butty boat, and they chugged slowly up the cut. Little blue notices abounded by the towpath. They carried messages such as 'Shops, 700 yards', 'Next Water Point, 950 yards', thus ensuring that those who came to get back to nature were reassured that it had been thoroughly tamed in their absence.

Cows stopped chewing the cud to watch their slow progress. They disturbed a heron, which flapped with lazy indignation ahead of them.

'How do you turn round?' said Reggie.

'Winding hole two pounds up the cut,' said Jimmy.

43

'Pardon?'

'There's a widened bit after we've been through two locks.'

'Ah!'

'Good life,' said Jimmy. 'Only one bugbear.'

'What?'

'Johnny woman.'

'You've got woman trouble?'

'Yes.'

'What's the trouble?'

'No women.'

'Ah!'

'Renewed vigour. Indian summer. Bugbear, no Indians.'

'What about the doggy ladies near your cottage?'

"Odd chat,' said Jimmy. 'Time of day. Haven't clicked.'

He negotiated a sharp bend with skill. Ahead was a pretty canal bridge.

'Should have married Lettuce,' he continued. 'Poor cow.'

A black and white Friesian lowed morosely.

'Not you,' said Jimmy. 'Nice woman, Lettuce. Fly in ointment, bloody ugly.'

'She isn't that ugly,' said Reggie.

'Yes, she is. Got her photo, pride of place, bedroom. Felt I owed it to her.'

They ducked as the boat chugged peacefully under the mellow brick bridge. On the other side there was an old farmhouse. Lawns swept down to splendid willows at the water's edge. Muscovy ducks paddled listlessly in a reedy backwater. Reggie stood up again, but Jimmy remained in his bent position.

'Reggie?' he said, in a low voice.

Reggie bent down to hear.

'Yes?'

'Something I want to confess.'

'Fire away.'

'Started to do something. Something I've never done before.'

44

'For goodness' sake, Jimmy, what?'

Jimmy lowered his voice still further, as if he feared that a passing sedge-warbler might hear. Little did he know that the sedge-warblers were far away, wintering in warmer climes.

'Self-abuse,' he whispered hoarsely.

'Well for goodness' sake,' said Reggie. 'At your age that's a cause for congratulations, not remorse.'

'Never done it before,' said Jimmy. 'Not in regimental tradition.'

'I should hope not, overtly,' said Reggie. 'I don't know, though. It's quite a thought. The new recruit up the North West Frontier. "One thing you should know, Hargreaves. Friday night is wanking night. And Hargreaves, you can't sit there. That's Portnoy's chair. Oh, and a word of advice. Don't have the liver."'

'Not with you,' said Jimmy.

'Literary allusion,' said Reggie.

'Ah! Literature. Closed book to me, I'm afraid.'

'I really can't see why masturbation should be frowned upon by a nation that's so keen on do-it-yourself,' said Reggie.

'Thing is . . .' began Jimmy.

But Reggie was never to learn what the thing was, because at that moment, with both men bent below the level of the engine casing and unable to see ahead, the narrow monster ploughed straight into the bank.

They walked forward over the long roof, and stepped off on to the towpath. The boat was firmly wedged in the bank, and there was damage to the bows.

'Damn!' said Jimmy. 'Cock-up on the bows front.'

They pulled and heaved. They heaved and pulled. All to no avail.

A Jensen pulled up by the bridge and two men in gumboots and cavalry twill walked along the towpath.

'Having trouble, brigadier?' said one.

'Er . . . yes.'

With three men shoving and Jimmy throwing the engine into full reverse, they managed to shift the boat.

'Thanks,' said Jimmy.

'No trouble,' said the first man.

'Regards to Beamish,' said the other.

Jimmy picked Reggie up at the next bridge, and they chugged on towards the winding hole.

'Brigadier?' said Reggie.

'Might have been eventually, if I hadn't been flung out.'

'Beamish?'

'My partner. Tim "Curly" Beamish. Wish you could meet him. Sound fellow. Salt of earth. Top drawer.'

Reggie's next quest was for a chef. He placed adverts in the catering papers.

He received replies from George Crutchwell of Staines, Mario Lombardi of Perugia, and Kenny McBlane from Partick.

He invited all three to Perrins for interviews.

George Crutchwell spoke with great confidence in an irritatingly flat voice. He was unemployed – 'resting', he called it – but had wide experience. He was reluctant to give a reference but eventually named the Ritz.

Mario Lombardi was good-looking and smiled a lot. He assured Reggie that Botchley was more beautiful than Perugia, and told him that they didn't have houses like Twenty-one, Oslo Avenue in Umbria. He gave a reference willingly.

Kenny McBlane might have been good-looking if it hadn't been for his spots, and didn't smile at all. Reggie had no idea what he said because his Scottish accent was so broad. He gave a reference willingly, writing it down to ensure that there was no misunderstanding.

Reggie soon received the three references.

The Ritz had never head of George Crutchwell and Reggie crossed his name off the list.

Mario Lombardi's reference was excellent. If praise for his culinary skills was fulsome, the lauding of his character was scarcely less so. He sounded like a cross between Escoffier and St Francis of Assisi.

Kenny McBlane's reference was a minor masterpiece of the oblique. It didn't actually state that he was a bad cook, and it didn't actually say anything specifically adverse about his character. It just left you to deduce the worst.

Reggie showed Elizabeth the two references.

'Which do you think?' he asked.

'It's obvious,' said Elizabeth. 'Lombardi.'

'I'd say it was obviously McBlane,' said Reggie. 'Lombardi's employers want to get rid of him. McBlane's want to keep him.'

He appointed the thirty-three-year-old Scot.

The remainder of March was a time of preparation.

Tom and Linda sold their house, and made arrangements for Adam and Jocasta to go to school in Botchley. Adam was seven now, and Jocasta six. They had decided not to have any more children, as they weren't ecological irresponsibility people.

David and Prue Harris-Jones sold their flat in Reading.

Tony and Joan sold their flat and had a ceremonial burning of three thousand central heating brochures.

Doc Morrissey borrowed every book on psychology that Southall library possessed. He read them both avidly, long into the cumin-scented night.

C.J. returned to Blancmange Cottage, Godalming. He told Mrs C.J. of his new job, and suggested that it might be better, for the time being, if she were to visit her friends in Luxembourg. He was surprised by the speed with which she acceded to this proposition.

Elizabeth bought three tents.

March gave way to April, and the mild winter proved to have a sharp sting in its tail.

The great day approached.

\*

McBlane arrived three days before the others. Reggie had booked him into the Botchley Arms. He was dark, tense and slim, with a hint of suppressed power. His spots had got worse and there were three boil plasters on his neck.

He spent much of the first day examining his equipment. He also examined the kitchen and the range of utensils that Elizabeth had provided.

Reggie and Elizabeth dined at the Oven D'or. They were the only diners. They felt too nervous to do justice to their meal.

They were worried about McBlane. If the eating arrangements were a fiasco, morale would slump.

On the second day, McBlane stocked up his commodious deep-freeze, his spacious fridge, his ample herb and spice racks.

When he had gone back to the Botchley Arms for an evening of hard drinking, Elizabeth examined his purchases. They were varied, sensible and interesting.

Reggie and Elizabeth dined at the New Bengal Restaurant. They were the only diners. They felt too nervous to do justice to their food.

On the third day their doubts about McBlane were swept away on a wave of glorious cooking smells.

Reggie went into the kitchen towards the end of the morning.

'Is everything all right, McBlane?' he asked.

McBlane's reply sounded to Reggie like 'Ee goon awfa' muckle frae gang doon ee puir wee scrogglers ye thwink.'

'Sorry,' said Reggie. 'Not . . . er . . . not quite with you.'

'Ee goon awfa' muckle frae gang doon ee puir wee scrogglers ye thwink.'

'Ah. Jolly good. Carry on, McBlane.'

That evening, Reggie and Elizabeth dined at the Golden Jasmine House. They were the only diners. They felt too nervous to do justice to their food.

*

The day of the staff's arrival dawned. The sun was warm between the scudding clouds. In his letter of instructions Reggie had asked them to be there by noon. C.J. arrived at ten fifty-eight.

'You're the first to arrive,' said Reggie, ushering him into the living-room.

'I didn't get where I am today without being the first to arrive,' said C.J.

'We'll erect the tents this afternoon.'

'Ah. Yes. The tents. Splendid.'

Elizabeth entered with a tray of coffee. C.J. leapt up.

'My dear Elizabeth. Splendid,' he said.

He kissed her on the hand.

'You grow more beautiful as you grow . . . er . . . as you grow more beautiful,' he said.

Elizabeth's eyes were cool as she met C.J.'s gaze.

'Coffee, C.J.?' she asked.

'Thank you.'

'I'm community secretary,' she said. 'Anything you need, indent for it with me please.'

'Ah . . . er . . . quite,' said C.J.

He sat on the settee. Elizabeth chose the furthest armchair and pulled her skirt down over her knees.

There was an awkward pause.

'Well!' said C.J. 'Well well well!'

'Quite,' said Reggie.

'Exactly. I'm looking forward to getting to know the other staff,' said C.J.

'You'll know some of them already,' said Reggie.

'Really? Good Lord.'

Doc Morrissey arrived next. He looked astonished to see C.J.

'Well well well!' he said.

'Precisely,' said C.J. 'How are you, are you well?'

'Pretty well,' said Doc Morrissey. 'I seem to have picked up

49

a touch of arthritis in the joints of my hands. My doctor puts it down to over-exercise.'

'You mustn't believe all the doctors say, Doc,' said Reggie.

Elizabeth smiled radiantly at Doc Morrissey as she handed him his coffee. He sat beside C.J. on the settee.

At eleven twenty-seven David and Prue Harris-Jones arrived. Young Reggie was sleeping peacefully in his carry-cot. They seemed astonished to see C.J. and Doc Morrissey.

'Well well well!' they said.

'Exactly,' said C.J. and Doc Morrissey.

'I hope you aren't alarmed to see your old friends,' said Reggie.

'No. Super,' said David and Prue Harris-Jones.

At eleven forty-nine Tom and Linda arrived. Tom carried a bottle wrapped in tissue paper.

'Well well well,' he said, when he saw the others.

Everybody laughed.

'Why are you laughing?' said Tom.

'That's what everyone said,' said Reggie.

'I see. I'm unoriginal. Good,' said Tom.

'Oh, Tom,' said Linda.

'Well, I'm sorry, but I just can't see anything riotously funny in the fact that I said "Well well well",' said Tom.

Tom sat in the remaining armchair, leaving Linda to squat on the pouffe. Elizabeth poured coffee busily.

'We're putting up our tents this afternoon,' C.J. told Doc Morrissey.

'Tents. Ah. Jolly good,' said Doc Morrissey.

'A heavy shower splattered fiercely against the french windows.

'I forgot this,' said Tom, handing Reggie a bottle. 'It's the last bottle of my prune wine.'

'Thank you, Tom,' said Reggie. 'We must keep it for a really suitable occasion. I know. My funeral.'

Everybody except Tom laughed.

'Sorry, Tom,' said Reggie. 'It was just a little joke.'

'I've said it before and I'll say it again,' said Tom. 'I'm not a joke person.'

'No,' said Linda.

The doorbell rang again. It was Tony and Joan.

Tom turned towards them expectantly, hoping that Tony would say 'Well well well!'

'The whole gang!' said Tony. 'You crafty sod, Reggie. Knock-out.'

Lunch was a triumph. It consisted of vichyssoise, boeuf bourguignon and zabaglione.

After lunch, Elizabeth thanked McBlane profusely.

'I thanked him profusely,' she told Reggie.

'Was he pleased?'

'I don't know. There was a sentence in the middle that I thought I understood, but I must have got it wrong.'

'What was it?' said Reggie.

'It sounded like "Bloody foreign muck".'

They spent the afternoon settling into their living quarters.

'I hope you don't mind Adam and Jocasta sharing a room,' said Reggie.

'We insist on it,' said Linda. 'We don't want to give them a thing about sex.'

'Premature sexual segregation promotes incalculable emotional introversion,' said Tom.

The rain held off, and it wasn't too difficult to erect the tents on the back lawn.

The tents were erected by C.J., Doc Morrissey and Tony.

Joan walked across the lawn. She looked displeased.

'Tony?' she said.

'Yeah?' said Tony, who was bent over a recalcitrant rod.

'Who are these tents for?'

'C.J., Doc Morrissey and us.'

'Us?'

'Yes.'

'Stand up, Tony. I can't talk to you like that.'

'I can't stand up or the tent'll collapse,' said Tony.

'Let it collapse.'

'What?'

'You never told me we were going to live in a tent.'

'Didn't I? I thought I did.'

At last Tony was free to stand up.

'Easy,' he said. 'No sweat.'

'Tony?'

'Yeah?'

'Why didn't you tell me we were going to live in a tent?'

'You didn't ask.'

'Tony?'

'Yeah?'

'I'm not living in a tent.'

'Oh, come on, Joany. It'll be fun. A summer under canvas. Knock-out.'

Reggie approached them across the lawn.

'What's the trouble?' he said.

'Joan refuses to sleep in a tent,' said Tony.

'I'll get double pneumonia,' said Joan.

'Rubbish,' said Tony. 'It'll be Health City, Arizona. Anyway, you're as tough as old boots.'

'Lovely,' said Joan. 'What a delicate, feminine compliment.'

Behind them, C.J. stood back and surveyed his completed tent with ill-concealed pride.

'It'll be lovely in a tent, Joan,' said Reggie. 'I wish I could sleep in one.'

'Why don't you, then?' said Joan.

'I'd like to,' said Reggie. 'But I'm head of this community. It wouldn't look right. It's only till the clients arrive, Joan. I'll buy other houses then, and as soon as I do, you'll be the first to move. I promise.'

Joan gave in reluctantly.

Behind them, Doc Morrissey stood back and surveyed his completed tent with ill-concealed pride.

It collapsed.

Later that afternoon, Reggie held a staff meeting.

His purpose was to allocate duties and responsibilities.

They assembled in a wide circle around the living-room, which no longer looked quite so surprisingly spacious.

Outside through the french windows, the three white tents gleamed in the April sun.

Reggie stood with his back to the fireplace.

'A lot of work here will be communal,' he said. 'We'll have group sessions, the first of which will be tomorrow morning at nine. But you'll also have individual roles to play and during your training you will familiarize yourselves with these, with other members of staff taking the place of clients. I will hold a watching brief, and Elizabeth, as you know, is secretary.'

Elizabeth smiled in acknowledgement.

'Doc Morrissey will naturally be our psychologist.'

Doc Morrissey smiled in acknowledgement.

'Tom, equally naturally, will be responsible for sport.'

'Sport?'

'Sport.'

'I know nothing about sport, Reggie.'

'That's all right. Doc Morrissey knows nothing about psychology.'

Everyone laughed.

'Just a minute,' said Doc Morrissey. 'I'll have you know I've been swatting it up like billyo.'

'Have you really?' said Reggie. 'That is bad news. No, Tom, it's sport for you.'

'But I'm just not a sports person,' said Tom.

'It's true,' said Linda. 'He doesn't know one end of a cricket racket from the other.'

'They're bats. I know that much,' said Tom.

'It was a joke,' said Linda.

'Ah, well, there you are,' said Tom. 'I've said it before and I'll say it again. I'm not a joke person. Seriously though, Reggie, I was hoping to do something with old English crafts. I've been rather bitten by the crafts' bug. Thatching, basket-weaving, that sort of thing. I'd prefer it if the popular Saturday evening TV programme was called "Craft of the Day", and its Sunday equivalent was . . .' Tom paused roguishly '. . . "The Big Thatch".'

One or two people smiled.

'You see,' said Tom. 'When I do make a joke you don't take any notice.'

C.J. laughed abruptly.

'Just got it,' he said. '"The Big Thatch". Well done, Tom. I didn't get where I am today without recognizing a rib-tickling play on words when I hear it.'

'No, Tom,' said Reggie. 'Sport it is. We have to be unconventional, if we're to free our sport from competition and aggression, so your pathetic ignorance is just what I want.'

'Oh. Well, thanks, Reggie.'

Reggie smiled at Joan, who was sitting on the pouffe.

'You'll be responsible for music,' he said.

Tony snorted.

'Why do you snort?' said Joan, whipping round to glare at him.

'You're tone deaf,' said Tony.

'Thank you,' said Joan. 'You really know how to make a woman feel good.'

'Tony, you'll be responsible for culture,' said Reggie.

It was Joan's turn to snort.

'Culture?'

'Culture.'

'Culture. Fine. With you. No sweat,' said Tony. 'I'll really hit culture.'

'Prue,' said Reggie, turning towards the hard chair where Prue sat, slightly out of the circle. 'You'll be responsible for crafts. Thatching, basket-weaving, that sort of thing. Excellent therapy.'

'Super,' said Prue.

'I must say, Reggie, I think that's a bit thick,' said Tom.

'Need you for sport. Sorry,' said Reggie. 'C.J., your work will be work.'

'I don't follow you, Reggie,' said C.J.

'Nobody understands the problems of man's relationship with his work better than you.'

'Thank you, Reggie.'

'You've caused so many of them.'

'Thank you, Reggie.'

'A lot of the people who come to Perrins will be unhappy in their work. You'll simulate work situations and help them overcome their problems. Linda, you'll deal with art. Painting, drawing, etcetera.'

'Must I?' said Linda.

'And finally David,' said Reggie.

David Harris-Jones smiled nervously.

'You'll deal with sex,' said Reggie.

David Harris-Jones fainted.

'Art's dreary,' said Linda. 'Can't I have sex?'

'Not while you're married to me,' said Tom.

Dinner consisted of pâté, grilled trout, and trifle. It was excellent.

Dark uncompromising night descended upon Number Twenty-one, Oslo Avenue, Botchley.

Dark uncompromising night descended upon the back garden of Number Twenty-one, Oslo Avenue, Botchley.

Dark uncompromising night descended upon the three tents lined up at the bottom of the lawn in the back garden of Number Twenty-one, Oslo Avenue.

A Tilley lamp shone on C.J. as he lay in his sleeping-bag, looking up at the narrowing angle at the top of his tent.

He was thinking.

He had decided to write a book about Reggie Perrin's community.

He had never written a book before, but there was a first time for everything.

He began to write.

'A Tilley lamp shone on me,' he wrote, 'as I lay in my sleeping bag, looking up at the narrowing angle at the top of my tent.'

I was thinking.

I had decided to write a book about Reggie Perrin's community.

I had never written a book before, but there was a first time for everything.

I began to write.

What an unimaginative way of starting a book.

'What an unimaginative way of starting a book,' wrote C.J. 'I ripped up the paper and hurled it to the far corner of the tent.'

In the other two tents, the lamps were already out. Doc Morrissey was trying to sleep, and Tony was trying to persuade Joan to make love.

The aims were different, the failures equal.

Tom was sitting on the bed, in his underpants. The wallpaper was floral.

'Come to bed,' said Linda.

Tom began to put on his pyjamas.

'Don't put your pyjamas on,' said Linda.

'They said it might be pretty cold later on,' said Tom. 'Minus two by dawn in sheltered inland areas.'

He clambered into bed and kissed Linda on the cheek.

'Night, Squelchypoos,' he said.

'Tom! Please don't call me Squelchypoos, Tom.'

'Well, come on, tell me what you want me to call you.'

'A proper term of endearment, Tom.'

'Such as?'

'Well, Cuddlypuddles.'

'Cuddlypuddles is as bad as Squelchypoos.'

'To you it is. To me it isn't.'

Tom propped himself up on his left elbow, the better to assume mastery of the conversation.

'I'm sorry, Linda,' he said. 'But for the life of me I can't distinguish any great difference between Squelchypoos and Cuddlypuddles.'

'Oh stop being pompous, Tom.'

Tom abandoned mastery and plumped for being hurt. This involved lying on his back and staring fixedly at the ceiling.

'I can't help being pompous, Linda,' he said. 'I drew the ticker marked pomposity in the lottery of life. I'm a pomposity person.'

'That's another thing, Tom.'

'What?'

'Do try and stop saying "I'm a whatsit person" all the time.'

'I never say "I'm a whatsit person".'

'You just said "I'm a pomposity person".'

'I've never said "I'm a whatsit person".'

Linda turned angrily on her side, facing away from Tom.

'You know what I mean,' she said. 'Whatever it is we're talking about, you say, "I'm not a whatever it is person".'

'It's just a phrase I'm going through, Linda. I can't help it. It's like C.J. can't help saying "I didn't get where I am today". I just don't happen to be an "I didn't get where I am today" person. I'm an "I'm a whatever it is person" person.'

'Oh, Tom, for God's sake. We're supposed to be setting up an ideal society here.'

'Perhaps I'm just not an ideal society person, Cuddlypuddles.'

'It's been an excellent first day,' whispered Reggie.

Oslo Avenue lay draped in the thick velvet of suburban sleep, eerie, timeless, endless.

57

Reggie began to stroke Elizabeth's stomach.

'No,' she said, stiffening.

'Stop stiffening,' he said. 'Leave that to me.'

'People will hear,' she whispered.

He put his ear to the wall.

'Reggie, don't,' she whispered. 'That's disgraceful. It's intruding on people's privacy. Can you hear anything?'

'David Harris-Jones just whispered "No. People will hear",' he whispered.

And he laughed silently, joyously.

# 3  The Training

In the morning the temperature was close to freezing point. Joan curled up in her sleeping bag and pretended to be asleep.

'Come on,' said Tony. 'Lovely fresh morning. Knock-out. Let's go and hit some breakfast.'

Joan groaned.

'Oh come on, darling,' said Tony. 'Let's get this show on the road and score some fried eggs.'

He crawled inelegantly out of the tent. A heavy dew lay on the lawn and rose bushes. The sky was a diffident blue.

C.J. was returning from the house after performing his ablutions. He was wearing a purple dressing gown over his trousers and vest and carried a large pudding basin. Neatly folded over the edge of the basin was a matching purple face flannel. Among the toilet requisites in the basin were a luxuriant badger-hair shaving brush, a cut-throat razor and a strop.

'Only just up?' said C.J. 'You've missed the best part of the morning. The early bird gets first use of the lavatory.'

Reggie came over the patio towards the lawn, rubbing his hands.

'Morning,' he said. 'Everybody up? That's the ticket. Lovely fresh morning.'

'I.e. perishing,' said Tony.

At that moment three things happened simultaneously. Mr Penfold looked over the hedge from Number Twenty-three, a tiny double-decker bus, hurled from the children's bedroom, struck Reggie's shins, and Doc Morrissey's tent collapsed.

Mr Penfold closed his eyes, as if he hoped that when he opened them again it would all be gone. Doctor Daines had warned him that there might be side-effects from giving up smoking. Perhaps this whole scene was simply a side-effect.

He opened his eyes. The scene was still there. A child was bawling in an upstairs room, and Doc Morrissey was moaning inside the collapsed tent. Mr Penfold met Reggie's eyes.

'It's a sharp one, isn't it?' he said, and fled.

Reggie joined C.J. and Tony outside Doc Morrissey's tent.

'Are you all right, Doc?' he called out.

'I can't move,' groaned Doc Morrissey. 'I've broken my back.'

It was nine o'clock. Time for the group meeting to begin.

Reggie sat in his study, looking out on to the pebble-dash wall of Number Twenty-three.

In his lap sat Snodgrass, the newly acquired community cat. She wriggled uneasily.

'It's time for my great project to begin, Snodgrass,' said Reggie, tickling her throat gently. 'But I shall enter slightly late, in order to impress.'

Snodgrass averted her eyes haughtily, in order to impress.

'Is it too ridiculous for words, Snodgrass?' said Reggie. 'Should I go in there and say "Sorry. It's all been a mistake. Go home"?'

Snodgrass made no reply.

'I can't, can I?' said Reggie. 'They've sold their homes. They've given up their jobs. I'm committed.'

Snodgrass miaowed.

'You're wrong, Snodgrass,' said Reggie. 'It isn't ridiculous. It will work. We aren't going to be sod worshippers in Dorset or mushroom sniffers in the Welsh hills. We aren't going to pray to goats or sacrifice betel nuts. We aren't going to live in teepees and become the lost tribe of Llandrindod Wells. I'm not going to shave my hair off and chant mantras in Droitwich High Street. I'm not going to become the Maharishi of Forfar or the Guru of Ilfracombe. It's going to be an ordinary place, where ordinary, unheroic, middle-class, middle-aged people can come. It's going to be a success. I'm going to make another fortune.'

He lowered Snodgrass gently to the floor.

He smoothed his hair and straightened his tie. He might have been setting off for the office, not starting an experiment in community living.

He entered the living-room.

There was nobody there.


It was almost ten o'clock before the chaos of that first morning was sorted out and the staff were assembled in the pleasant surburban room.

The only absentee was C.J. It was still the school holidays, and, as luck would have it, he had drawn first blood at looking after the children.

Reggie stood in front of the fireplace and looked grimly at his watch.

'It's nine fifty-eight,' he said. 'Not an auspicious start. Now, who'll set the ball rolling?'

He sat between Prue and Tom on the settee, and looked round expectantly.

'Come on,' he said. 'We've wasted enough time already. You're supposed to discuss your problems openly, criticize each other frankly, and so learn to express yourselves and realize your potential more fully. So come on, let's be having you.'

He looked round the room imploringly.

'All right,' he said. 'Let's try a different approach. Why are you all late? Doc?'

He glanced hopefully at his psychologist.

'My tent fell down,' said Doc Morrissey.

'How is the tent now?'

'I find myself suffering from a feeling of deep insecurity in my tent,' said Doc Morrissey, who seemed to have made a remarkable recovery from his broken back. 'I just toss that into the maelstrom of speculation.'

'Ah!' said Reggie. 'Now that is just the kind of thing these meetings are for. Well done, Doc. We're off. We're on our way. The project is launched.'

He looked round the room, embracing them all in his smile of encouragement.

'Has anyone got any ideas why Doc Morrissey should feel insecure in his tent?' he asked.

'Yes,' said Tony. 'The bloody thing keeps falling down.'

Reggie looked pained.

'Isn't that a bit facile?' he said.

'I spoke of a deeper insecurity than that,' said Doc Morrissey. 'As I lie on my back, in my tent, in a tactile me-to-ground situation, I feel a strong sense of the natural world, the earth, beneath me, and the fragile structure of civilization, the tent, above me, and I realize, I sense, the fragility of our domination over the world of nature around us. And it gives me a real sense of pain.'

'Cobblers,' said Tony.

'Yes, I do have a bit of pain in the cobblers as well. It's the dew, I think. Incipient arthritis of the testicles.'

'Well, that was splended, Doc,' said Reggie. 'You see, you've taken to psychology like a duck to water. Excellent. So that's why you were late. Anyone else got any interesting reasons why they were late?'

'Because I didn't get up,' said Joan.

'Ah!' said Reggie. 'But why didn't you get up?'

'Because I was in a tent.'

'Yes, I think maybe we could move on from the subject of tents now,' said Reggie.

'Tony'll soon be wanting to,' said Joan. 'He isn't going to get his end away while we're under canvas.'

'Joan!' said Tony, giving her leg a sharp kick.

'Tony!' said Reggie. 'Don't kick Joan.'

'Well what a thing to say. Honestly. Crudesville, Arizona,' said Tony.

'I won't miss it much. Your not all that fantastic at it, anyway,' said Joan.

'Joan, please!' said Tony.

'I think this is going a bit far, Joan,' said Reggie.

'I thought we were supposed to criticize each other frankly,' said Joan, bending down and examining her leg.

'We *are* supposed to criticize each other frankly,' said Reggie, 'but frankly I think you're criticizing Tony too frankly. Not that he should have kicked you.'

'Excuse me a moment,' put in Elizabeth, leaning forward in her armchair. 'Aren't we going to be teaching very largely by example?'

'That's right,' said Reggie. 'Example from above.'

'Well, then, should you give aggressive orders like "Don't kick Joan"?'

'Well, I mean to say . . .'

'Surely it's wrong to counter aggression with aggression, if aggression is wrong?'

'We're quibbling now,' said Reggie.

'Mother-in-law's right,' said Tom. 'It should be a democratically arrived at decision whether Tony should have kicked Joan.'

'I suppose I should have said . . . er . . . er . . . has anyone any idea what I should have said?'

'"Tony, do you think it's in your best interests to kick Joan?"' said Prue. '"Might it not lead to her kicking you in retaliation?"'

'Good,' said Reggie, patting the top of her sensible head affectionately. 'Very good.'

'"Tony, don't you think that if you kick Joan you might bruise her legs and render those exquisite long slender limbs a little less pleasant to plant little hot kisses on?"' suggested Doc Morrissey.

Joan gave him a cool look.

'Just a suggestion,' he said. 'What we psychologists call the appeal to self-interest.'

'Right,' said Reggie. 'Well, if we can now leave the question of Joan's legs and move on . . .'

C.J. burst in. There were lumps of plasticine on his face. He shook his trousers angrily. A green frog dropped to the floor.

'I've had enough,' he thundered. 'I didn't get where I am today by having green frogs dropped down my crutch.'

'Had enough already?' said Reggie. 'You're going to need a bit more perseverance than that if you're to succeed in the great work for which I have enrolled you. You're getting the perfect training with those kids. There isn't a person in this room who wouldn't willingly exchange places with you, but there you are, you picked the plum. Linda, where are you going?'

Linda, who was sidling towards the door, stopped.

'I was going to see if the children were OK,' she said.

'Please. Please. Faith and trust. I'm sure that if C.J. has the backing of our trust and faith, he will go in there and start earning his salary.'

C.J. scowled.

'But what'll I do?' he said.

'What about trying simple argument?' said Reggie. 'What about saying, "I say, Adam, old fruit, do you really think Kermit wants to have a trip down my crutch. It's frightfully dark inside trousers, you know".'

'Yes,' said C.J. 'But what'll I do after that?'

'Why not tell them a story?' said Reggie.

C.J. looked as near to panic as Reggie had ever seen him.

'Oh, all right,' he said. 'But I don't intend to make a habit of looking after the children.'

'Their behaviour will get much better once we adults set them a consistent example,' said Reggie.

'Hm!'

C.J. left the room with a wistful glance at the comparative safety of the group meeting.

'I see,' said Tom. 'So we haven't been bringing the children up properly. Is that the insinuation?'

'There was no insinuation whatsoever,' said Reggie. 'But the fact that you insinuate that there was suggests that you feel guilty. Maybe we can examine this feeling without interruption.'

C.J. burst in once more.

'Reggie's wet himself,' he announced.

'Then change him,' said Reggie irritably.

Prue fetched a nappy and safety pins, and handed them to C.J. He received them as if they were a grenade and its pin.

'I fold them by the kite method,' said Prue.

'The . . . er . . . ah!' said C.J. 'I . . . er . . . I've never actually changed a nappy before.'

'There's a first time for everything,' said Reggie.

'That's true,' said C.J., grudgingly admitting the force of Reggie's remark.

'In changing the nappy you'll help yourself,' said Doc Morrissey. 'Try and look on it as a wonderful journey of self-discovery.'

C.J. smiled faintly at Doc Morrissey.

'Your turn for the wonderful journey of self-discovery will come,' he said, and he closed the door behind him.

'Right,' said Reggie. 'It is now ten twenty-six and we've still hardly got started. This emphasizes the importance of starting punctually at nine. It's not good enough and it won't happen again.'

He glared fiercely at them.

'Excuse me,' said David Harris-Jones. 'I may be quite wrong, but . . . er . . . if you're the example that we're to follow, isn't it wrong that you should give orders and . . . er . . . virtually . . . as it were . . . threaten us. I mean maybe I'm wrong and it isn't wrong. But I think I'm right and it is wrong.'

He looked anxiously at Prue. She smiled reassuringly.

'Super,' she said.

'David has a good point,' said Reggie. 'I'd like to rephrase what I said. We should have started at nine, but we didn't and that is . . . er . . . absolutely splendid because obviously you didn't want to start at nine, but I would suggest that it would be even more absolutely splendid in future if you did want to start at nine.'

'Too early,' said Joan.

They decided to decide democratically what time their group sessions would start and end. They decided to have a vote on it. Then they debated democratically what form the vote should take. Then they voted on what form the vote should take. Then they voted.

The consensus of opinion was that they should begin at nine thirty and break for lunch at twelve thirty. By that time it was twelve thirty. They broke for lunch.

'It's been an excellent first morning,' said Reggie.

Life at Number Twenty-One, Oslo Avenue, Botchley, began to settle into a pattern.

Twice a week they held a meeting to discuss their group meetings.

The rest of the time they discussed their problems with Doc Morrissey and their sex lives with David Harris-Jones, wove baskets with Prue, painted with Linda, sang with Joan, sported with Tom, were cultural with Tony, and entered into simulated work situations with C.J.

At first some of these activities were not very successful, while others were worse.

At the third group meeting they decided to set up a rota system for doing the various household activities like dusting, hoovering, helping McBlane and answering the door.

At the fourth group meeting Doc Morrissey suggested that each day they should select a different word, and try to live in accordance with it. He explained that this would be an excellent form of self-discipline and would help to weld them into corporate entity.

They each chose ten words. The hundred words were put into a hat. Each evening the hat was shuffled, and the next day's word was drawn by a member of the staff.

The member of the staff who would choose the word was chosen out of another hat.

The scheme began on May the second. The word was Courtesy, and it was Tom's turn to answer the door.

'Good morning, Jimmy,' he said. 'Wonderful to see you. What an unexpected pleasure. What a bonus.'

Jimmy stared at him in amazement.

'Courtesy's our word for the day,' said Tom.

'Oh, I see. That explains it,' said Jimmy. 'Jolly good. Like to see Reggie privately. Personal. My car. Case nothing comes of it.'

Reggie went outside and sat in Jimmy's rusty old Ford. There were two dents in the off-side.

All the street lights were on due to a failure in the timing devices.

'This army of yours going well?' said Jimmy, when they were settled inside the car.

'Very well indeed,' said Reggie, nodding to the milkman, who was returning to the depot on his float.

'Offer of a job still open?'

'Well, yes,' said Reggie, surprised.

'On beam ends.'

'But, Jimmy. The narrow boats.'

'Sold out, Reggie. Cut losses. Kaput.'

Jimmy was tapping the steering wheel nervously.

'Let down,' he mumbled.

'Tim "Curly" Beamish?'

Jimmy nodded miserably.

'His share of money. Stolen,' he said. 'Ran up debts. Casanova Club, Wolverton. Copacabana Club, Bletchley. Paradise Lost, Milton Keynes. Women. Gambling. Paid for equipment with dud cheques. Our names mud from Daventry to

67

Hemel Hempstead. Clive "Lofty" Anstruther all over again. Bastard!'

Jimmy sank his head in misery and the horn shattered the stillness of the domestic morning.

'What the hell is that noise?' he said.

'You're leaning on the horn,' said Reggie.

Jimmy sat up hastily.

'Funny thing. Wasn't working earlier,' he said.

He switched the ignition off. He seemed marginally cheered by the revival of his horn.

'Don't expect you'll have me now,' he said.

'Of course I'll have you,' said Reggie. 'You did sterling work for Grot. I have no doubt you'll do sterling work here.'

'What as?' said Jimmy.

'Leader of expeditionary forces,' said Reggie. 'Helping old ladies across road, clearing litter, whatever you like. A sort of commando unit for good works.'

'Thanks Reggie,' said Jimmy. 'Kiss you if we were French.'

'Thank God we aren't, then,' said Reggie.

'Yes. Postman might think we were bum-boys.'

They got out of the car, and Jimmy locked up carefully.

'Cock-up on the judgement of men front,' he said. 'Always choose the wrong chap. My Freudian heel.'

'Achilles heel.'

'You see. Wrong chap again. Useless. No wonder army made me personnel officer.'

Next day, a fourth tent appeared on the lawn.

On the following day, the word of the day was Quietude. The peace was shattered at seven o'clock when Jimmy emerged from his tent and blew 'Come to the cookhouse door, boys' on his bugle. Reggie took him quietly to one side before breakfast. They sat in the study, looking out over the pebble-dashed side wall of Number Twenty-three.

'Jimmy, today's word is quietude,' whispered Reggie.

'Damn,' whispered Jimmy. 'Slipped my mind. Get the picture. No bugle till tomorrow.'

'When I said I was running a sort of army,' whispered Reggie, 'I didn't mean it literally.'

'Very literal cove,' whispered Jimmy. 'Leave imagination to you brain boxes.'

'I was using a figure of speech,' whispered Reggie.

'Ah! Figures of speech not my line. Not many metaphors in Queen's Own Berkshire Light Infantry. Hyperbole exception rather than rule in BFPO thirty-three.'

'No doubt you see what I'm driving at,' whispered Reggie.

'Never see what people are driving at, Reggie.'

'Ah! What I'm driving at is this, Jimmy. I don't think that blowing "Come to the cookhouse door, boys" on your bugle is quite our style.'

'I see.'

'Besides, what will the neighbours say?'

'Ah! Admit it. Forgot the neighbours. Great boon of army life, no neighbours. "Guns one to eight, fire!" "Excuse me, sir?" "Yes, Smudger, what is it?" "Won't we wake the neighbours, sir?" "Good God, so we will. Cancel the firing. We'll have some cocoa instead. Good thinking, Smudger." Doesn't happen. World might be different if it did. Thought?'

'It certainly is, Jimmy.'


But neighbours there assuredly were in Oslo Avenue, Botchley, and shortly after breakfast on the Saturday morning they made their presence felt. The weather was showery.

Mr Penfold, from Number Twenty-three, was the first to arrive. Prue, whose turn it was for answering the door, ushered him into the living-room. He had a small head and stick-out ears.

'I'd like to have a word with you if I may, Mr Perrin,' he said.

'Certainly,' said Reggie. 'Would you like coffee? My wife makes excellent coffee.'

Doc Morrissey served coffee and biscuits. When he had gone Mr Penfold said, 'Er . . . excuse me, but this place is a little unusual, and unusual things are really quite usual these days. So . . . er . . . well . . .'

He swallowed hard.

'That wasn't your wife, was it?' he said.

Reggie laughed heartily.

'No,' he said. 'That was my Doc Morrissey. We share all duties in our community.'

'Community?'

'Yes.'

'Ah. I really must . . . er . . . lovely coffee . . . I really must put my foot down. Well, it isn't really me. It's Mrs Penfold.'

'You really must put Mrs Penfold's foot down.'

Mr Penfold sat perched on the edge of his chair, taking his coffee in tiny sips.

'After all, Oslo Avenue isn't the King's Road, Chelsea,' he averred.

'It isn't the Reeperbahn in Hamburg,' agreed Reggie.

'I'm glad you see it my way,' said Mr Penfold.

'It isn't the red light district of Amsterdam either.'

'Precisely.'

'It's a pity, isn't it?'

Careful, Reggie. You need these people on your side.

Mr Penfold leant forward so far that he almost toppled off the chair.

'Not to me, it isn't,' he said. 'Mrs Penfold is not a well woman, Mr Perrin. I'm afraid that all this . . .'

'All this, Mr Penfold?'

Mr Penfold waved his arms, including the french windows, the three pictures of bygone Botchley and the standard lamp in the environmental outrage that was being perpetrated on him.

The doorbell rang again, and Prue ushered in Mrs Hollies, from Number Nineteen.

Doc Morrissey produced an extra cup, and Mrs Hollies's verdict on the coffee reinforced that of Mr Penfold.

'Don't worry. That's not his wife,' said Mr Penfold, when Doc Morrissey had gone.

'What?' said Mrs Hollies.

'That man who served coffee. He's not Mr Perrin's wife.'

Mrs Hollies looked at Mr Penfold in astonishment.

'Do we owe the pleasure of your visit to any particular purpose?' Reggie inquired pleasantly.

'It's Mr Hollies,' said Mrs Hollies. 'Mr Hollies has to take things very easily. The slightest disturbance to his routine, and Mr Hollies goes completely haywire. It's his work. These are perilous times in the world of sawdust.'

'Sawdust?' said Reggie.

'Mr Hollies is in the sawdust supply industry,' said Mrs Hollies.

'What exactly does that mean?' asked Reggie.

'He supplies sawdust.'

'I see.'

'To butchers, bars, zoos, furriers, circuses.'

'Where sawdust is needed,' said Reggie, 'there is Mr Hollies.'

'Exactly.'

'Do I deduce that thing's aren't good in the world of sawdust?' said Mr Penfold.

'Not what they were, but then, what is?' said Mrs Hollies.

'You can say that again,' said Mr Penfold.

Mrs Hollies spurned the invitation. Instead, she said: 'In and out like the tide. Up and down like Tower Bridge. These biscuits are delicious. Where do you get them?'

'Finefare,' said C.J., passing through with the hoover.

There were pretty blue flowers round the edge of C.J.'s pinny.

'They share everything here,' explained Mr Penfold.

'Some share more than others,' said C.J. darkly, and with that ominous thrust he departed.

71

'I must admit that I came round to . . . er . . . inquire what exactly is going on here,' said Mrs Hollies. 'I don't mind myself, an Englishman's home is his castle, but it's Mr Hollies's nerves.'

'What exactly are you complaining about?' said Reggie politely.

'Tents in the garden,' said Mrs Hollies. 'It isn't natural.'

'Babies crying at all hours. Comings and goings,' said Mr Penfold.

'Goings and comings,' said Mrs Hollies.

'That's the same complaint twice,' said Reggie. 'One man's coming is another man's going.'

'No, it isn't,' said Mr Penfold.

'Just testing,' said Reggie.

Careful, Reggie.

'Anything else?' said Reggie.

'Cars parked outside the house,' said Mr Penfold. 'You probably think that's petty, but it's Mrs Penfold.'

'Mr Hollies is the same,' said Mrs Hollies. 'Me, you could park juggernauts outside.'

'As far as I'm concerned,' said Mr Penfold, 'you could have a line of pantechnicons stretching from Beirut Crescent to Buenos Aires Rise.'

'But it's Mr Hollies,' said Mrs Hollies. 'Mr Hollies is very jealous of his front view. Cars parked in front of our house, they prey on his mind.'

'Mrs Penfold's exactly the same,' said Mr Penfold. 'Cars parked in front of our verge, they're a red rag to a bull.'

'It's the number of people you have here,' said Mrs Hollies. 'It's the uncertainty.'

'I mean, this is a residential street, let's face it,' said Mr Penfold.

'It's wondering what you're up to, with the tents and the bugle and that,' said Mr Hollies.

Reggie stood up.

'I'm in a position to set your minds at rest,' he said. 'First, the bugle. I can give you a unilateral assurance that there will be no more bugling.'

'Oh well. You can't say fairer than that,' said Mr Penfold.

'So far as it goes,' said Mrs Hollies. 'But what about everything else?'

'Secondly, everything else. You are privileged to live next to an amazing and historic development. In this road, hitherto barely known in Botchley, let alone in the great wen beyond, you are going to see the formation of an ideal society.'

'A utopia, you mean?' said Penfold.

'I suppose you could call it that,' said Reggie.

'If you wanted a utopia, you'd have done better to take one of those big houses in Rio De Janeiro Lane,' said Mr Penfold. 'They've got forecourt parking, you see.'

'The people here at present are my staff,' explained Reggie. 'They're in the middle of their training, learning how . . .'

Tom burst in from the direction of the kitchen. He had a bucket of water and a chamois leather.

'C.J. has accused me of not pulling my weight,' he said. 'Either he goes or I do. Oh, I'm sorry. I didn't know you had visitors.'

'Tom, these are our neighbours, Mr Penfold and Mrs Hollies. This is Tom, our sports wizard,' said Reggie.

Tom fixed Mrs Hollies with an intense gaze.

'Anyone who knows anything about me knows that I'm just not a pulling my weight person,' he told her.

'Where was I?' said Reggie, sitting down again after Tom's departure. 'Oh yes. These people are in the middle of training, learning how to be happy, generous, perfect people.'

Mrs Hollies produced a thinly veiled sneer.

'I know what you're thinking,' said Reggie. 'Well, yes. We all have a long way to go. That's what makes it fascinating. Who'd bother to climb Everest if it was flat?'

'Mrs Penfold and I,' said Mr Penfold. 'It'd be just about our mark.'

'People will flock to this place, as soon as it's open to the public,' said Reggie. 'Casualties of our over-complicated society will seek help in their hundreds.'

Mr Penfold and Mrs Hollies turned pale.

'I hope I've set your minds at rest,' said Reggie.

The next day was Sunday. It rained on and off. There was only play in one John Player League cricket match. The word of the day was Knowledge.

Reggie sat in his study, reading an encyclopedia. The door handle slowly turned. It was Jocasta, bringing him a cup of coffee. Not all of it had spilled in the saucer.

He thanked her gravely.

'Adam's got a willy and I've got a hole,' she said.

'What a satisfactory arrangement,' said Reggie.

'I wouldn't want a willy.'

'Quite right.'

'Has C.J. got a willy?'

'Yes.'

'Have you seen it?'

'No.'

Reggie tipped the spilt coffee back into his cup.

'How d'you know he's got a willy if you haven't seen it?'

'The balance of probabilities.'

'Has he got a hole?'

'No.'

'Liar. He's got one in his bum.'

Reggie sipped the coffee. It was lukewarm.

'Mankind, Jocasta, is distinguished from the lower orders by his capacity to conceptualize about abstract matters of ethical, moral, aesthetic, scientific and mathematical concern,' he said. 'I know you're only six, but I think you ought to be turning your mind to slightly higher questions than you are at present.'

'Does C.J. sit down when he does his wee-wees?'

That evening Reggie told Tom and Linda about Jocasta's thirst for knowledge. Tom looked glum.

'Her failure is a mirror of our failure,' he said.

'Your failure is a mirror of my failure,' said Reggie.

On Monday it rained all day. There was no play in the Schweppes County Championship or the Rothmans Tennis. The word of the day was Innovation.

Tom called on Reggie in his study. He was wearing a blue tracksuit and carried an orange football.

'I've got an innovation,' he said.

'Fire away,' said Reggie.

Tom sprawled in an upright chair that might have been designed specifically to prevent sprawling.

'Football,' he said.

'It's been done before,' said Reggie.

'With a difference,' persisted Tom. 'Football with no aggro, no fouls, no tension, no violence.'

'What's the secret?' said Reggie.

'No opposition,' said Tom.

'Pardon?'

'You asked me to be unconventional. This is unconventional. We have eleven members of staff. The perfect team. Only nobody plays against us. We use skill, passing, teamwork, and tactics. It's pure football, Reggie.'

'Interesting,' said Reggie.

'I've been in touch with Botchley Albion,' said Tom. 'They play in the Isthmian League. They can rent us some costumes for a consideration. We don't want to look ridiculous.'

Tuesday dawned cloudy but dry. The word of the day was Connect.

It was C.J.'s turn to be analysed by Doc Morrissey. The chaise-longue, purchased at the Botchley Antique Boutique, seemed out of place in Doc Morrissey's tent.

'Lie down on the couch,' he told C.J.

C.J. clambered on to the chaise-longue with bad grace.

Doc Morrissey lay back on his sleeping bag.

'A little word association,' he said. 'Both of us making random connections. Sex.'

'Table tennis,' said C.J.

'Why?'

'Random.'

'When I say random, I mean that you're to let subconscious logical associations replace your conscious logical associations. Let's start again. Sex.'

'Table tennis.'

'Oh for goodness sake, C.J.'

'In my palmier days,' said C.J., 'I had relations with a table tennis player in Hong Kong. She had a very unusual grip.'

'What happened?'

'She beat me twenty-one-seventeen, twenty-one-twelve, twenty-one-nine. Then she took me home and I beat her. She seemed to enjoy that sort of thing. Very disturbing. So did I. Even more disturbing.'

'Why did you say it was a random association, then?'

'I was lying.'

Doc Morrissey sighed.

'You're on this project, C.J.,' he said. 'You might as well take it seriously.'

'Oh very well.'

C.J. stared at the cool white roof of Doc Morrissey's tent. He could feel his mind going blank.

'Table tennis,' said Doc Morrissey.

'Sex.'

'Girl.'

'Dance.'

'Gooseberry.'

'Raspberry.'

'Fool.'

'Jimmy.'

'Army.'

'Resistance.'

'Underground.'

'Rush-hour.'

'Red buses.'

'Moscow.'

'St Petersburg.'

'Dostoyevsky.'

'Idiot.'

'Jimmy.'

'Very interesting,' said Doc Morrissey when they had finished. 'Why do you associate Jimmy with fool and idiot?'

'He is a fool and an idiot.'

'People can't help what they are,' said Doc Morrissey. 'Their behaviour is conditioned by many things. You should say, "The many environmental and hereditary influences to which I have been subjected lead me to believe Jimmy is an idiot".'

'He is an idiot.'

'All right. The many environmental and hereditary influences to which I have been subjected lead me to believe that the many environmental and hereditary influences to which Jimmy has been subjected have made him an idiot.'

C.J. clambered stiffly off the couch.

'Is that all?' he said.

'No,' said Doc Morrissey. 'Many factors influence our behaviour. The state of the planets. Our biorhythmic cycle. The weather.'

'The many environmental and hereditary influences to which I have been subjected, allied to my low biorhythmic cycle, the relationship of Pluto to Uranus, the fact that it's pissing down in Rangoon and that my auntie was jilted by a tobacconist from Wrexham lead me to believe that you're talking a load of balls,' said C.J.

Wednesday dawned dry but cloudy. The word of the day was Bananas. For the best part of an hour, they struggled to think bananas, talk bananas and be bananas.

Then they gave it up.

Thursday began brightly but fell off fast. The word of the day was Bananas.

They examined the slips that remained in the hat, and found that eight more carried the legend 'Bananas'. They never found out who had chosen bananas for all their ten words.

They abandoned having a word of the day after that. Doc Morrissey explained that it was stifling individual responses and preventing a steady emotional development.

Friday was extremely cold for May. Severiano Ballasteros shot a five under par sixty-six to win the Tampax Invitation Classic by three strokes.

In the evening Reggie put a little plan into action.

McBlane's excellent dinner was already but a memory. Little Reggie was asleep. Adam and Jocasta were watching Kojak. Reggie and Elizabeth waited for their guests in the living-room. Four guests were invited. But only Mr Penfold and Mrs Hollies arrived. Their loved ones were indisposed.

They accepted small medium sherries.

'I have great news for you,' said Reggie. 'I've decided that you were right. This is not a suitable environment for our project. We're selling up.'

Mrs Hollies and Mr Penfold tried not to show their relief. They accepted more sherry with pleasure and praised the decor with sudden enthusiasm.

'The would-be purchaser is calling round shortly,' said Reggie. 'You'll be able to meet him.'

Quite soon the doorbell rang.

'This may be him now,' said Reggie.

Elizabeth answered the door. Mr Penfold and Mrs Hollies stood up expectantly. Elizabeth returned with Tony, who was heavily blacked up.

'Ah, there you are, Winston,' said Reggie.

'Here ah is, man,' said Tony.

'This is Mr Winston Baldwin Gladstone Vincent Fredericks,' said Reggie.

Tony flashed his carefully whitened teeth, and extended a blackened hand. He was worried lest the boot-polish came off – unnecessarily. Neither Mr Penfold nor Mrs Hollies seemed over-anxious to shake his hand.

'I don't think my new neighbours dig me man,' said Tony. 'Because I'm a black man, man. Sure is a sad thing. I was really looking forward to scoring some curried goat barbecues with them this summer.'

On Tuesday afternoon Tom led his team out for their football match versus nobody. A 'For Sale' board was being stuck in the soft earth outside Number Nineteen.

The eleven members of staff turned left, past the 'For Sale' board in the garden of Number Twenty-three. They looked self-conscious and sheepish in the Botchley Albion strip. Varicose veins and white legs abounded.

They turned right into Washington Road, Doc Morrissey behind Joan, gazing at her legs.

'Yellow and purple suits you,' whispered Jimmy to Linda. 'Legs as top-hole as ever.'

They turned left into Addis Ababa Avenue.

'I'm playing a four-three-three line-up,' Tom confided to Reggie.

The line-up was C.J.; David Harris-Jones, Elizabeth, Tom and Prue; Tony, Reggie and Linda; Doc Morrissey, Jimmy and Joan.

As they were not all in the full bloom of youth and fitness, they only played twenty minutes each way. It began to rain at half time.

It proved rather boring playing with no opponents and they had the rain and wind against them in the second half. Even so, the result was something of a disappointment.

'We should have won by far more than four-one,' said Tom

as they walked wearily back down Addis Ababa Avenue, hair flattened by the rain, legs reddened by exertion. 'We frittered away our early advantage.'

Next day, a West Indian who bore a striking resemblance to Tom was shown round Number Twenty-three.

The following day another dusky-hued gentleman examined the bijou charms of Number Nineteen. He sounded more like a Southern gentleman than a West Indian.

'You sure has a mighty fine residence here, Ma'am,' he told Mrs Hollies. 'Ah didn't get where ah is today without recognizing a mighty fine residence when ah sees it, no sirree ma'am ah didn't.'

Two days later, 'For Sale' boards went up outside Numbers Twenty-five and Seventeen.

By the end of June the community had bought Numbers Seventeen, Nineteen, Twenty-three and Twenty-five.

The tents had gone.

Alterations were in progress in all the houses. Kitchens, dining-rooms and living-rooms were converted into bedrooms.

C.J., Doc Morrissey, David Harris-Jones and Jimmy became house wardens. McBlane moved reluctantly into Number Twenty-one.

The weather was changeable and temperate. It was a year without seasons.

The evenings began to draw in. The training intensified. Jimmy tried to persuade Linda to let him paint her in the nude. She refused.

'Come to my room,' he said.

'I can't, Jimmy. We're supposed to be nice, perfect human beings.'

Jimmy buried his head in her lap.

'Come and do nice perfect things in my room,' he said.

Linda stroked his greying, receding hair gently.

'That's all over, Uncle Jimmy,' she said.

'Absolutely. Should never have started,' said Jimmy. 'Just for ten minutes.'

'No!'

'Quite right. Glad you said "no". Best thing. Some time next week, perhaps.'

'No, Jimmy. Never again.'

'Absolutely right. Bang on. Like to paint you in nude, though.'

The opening day was fixed for August the fifteenth. Soon there was only a fortnight to go. Reggie placed an advert in several newspapers and journals. It read:

> Does your personality depress you?
> Has life failed you?
> Do you hate when you'd like to love?
> Are you aggressive?
> Are you over-anxious?
> Are you over-competitive?
> Are you over eighteen?
> Then come to PERRINS for PEACE, GOOD LIVING and CARE.
> STAY as LONG as you LIKE.
> PAY ONLY what YOU think it was WORTH.
> Apply 21, Oslo Avenue, Botchley.

Behaviour improved all round. Reggie Harris-Jones hadn't cried for fifteen days and sometimes Adam and Jocasta went for several hours without doing anything beastly.

Only one week remained before the opening day.

Excitement was at fever pitch, dampened only by the fact that there wasn't one single booking.

Reggie began his final assessment interviews with his staff.

First he saw his psychologist.

Doc Morrissey leant forward and banged Reggie's desk so hard that the knob fell off one of the drawers.

'I have an awareness explosion, Reggie,' he said. 'A sensory tornado. An auto-catalystical understanding of my complete orgasm.'

'Don't you mean organism?'

'Possibly, Reggie. Rather a lot of terms, you know. Can't remember them all. Anyway, the point is, my visual, tactile and acoustic lives are amazingly enhanced. You know what that's called, don't you?'

'No.'

'Extrasensory perception, Reggie.'

He banged the desk, and the knob came off again.

'We seem to have a bit of desk castration here,' said Reggie, replacing the knob.

'You know what's done all this for me, Reggie? Confidence.'

Doc Morrissey raised his hand to bang it down again. Reggie removed the knob.


The Websters also expressed themselves delighted with their progress. Joan was enjoying the musical training, even though the staff weren't a musical lot, and Tony was really into culture. Shakespeare was the kiddie, and old Ibsen was a knock-out, for a Norwegian. Tony reckoned they could have been really commercial if they weren't so famous.

'We haven't had a row for three days,' said Joan.

'That's not very long,' said Reggie.

'Well, we like a good argument,' said Tony.

'I don't,' said Joan.

'You don't want to be like those bloody Harris-Joneses, do you?'

'What's wrong with the Harris-Joneses?' said Reggie.

'They always agree about everything,' said Tony.

'I think that's rather nice,' said Joan.

'Well, I don't,' said Tony. 'I'd hate to be married to somebody who always agreed with me.'

'I disagree,' said Joan.

Tony kissed her affectionately on the cheek.

\*

On the Tuesday, a day marred by thunder and the non-arrival of any bookings, it was the turn of the Harris-Joneses to have their assessment interviews.

David Harris-Jones was wearing sandals, fawn trousers and a yellow sweater.

Prue was wearing sandals, fawn trousers and a yellow sweater.

They sat very close together and held hands.

'How are you getting along?' said Reggie.

'Super,' they said.

'It has been suggested that you spend so much time thinking alike that you hardly exist as separate entities any more,' said Reggie.

'I don't think that's fair,' they said.

'Oh, sorry. After you,' they added.

They laughed. Reggie smiled.

A peal of thunder rumbled around Botchley.

'You answer, David,' said Reggie. 'Why don't you think it's fair?'

'Well, I think our marriage is happy because we agree about so much,' he said.

'I agree,' said Prue. 'I think it would be pointless to have to find things to disagree about in order to prove that you could agree to disagree.'

'I agree,' said David. 'Anyway, we sometimes disagree.'

A flash of forked lightning illuminated the room.

'I mean, when we first discussed which side of the bed we like to sleep on, we both said the right side,' said David.

'That was agreeing,' said Prue.

'I disagree,' said David. 'I think it was disagreeing. Because we couldn't both sleep on the right side. To agree would have been to disagree about our favourite side, so that we'd have slept on different sides. As we in fact do, by agreement.'

'Well, it does seem as if, so far as you are concerned, everything's going amazingly satisfactorily,' said Reggie.

'I agree,' they said.

*

On Wednesday there was great excitement. A Mr C. R. Babbacombe wished to visit the community.

His travel instructions were sent, and he was advised to arrive between three and six on Sunday. The floodgates were open.

It was Elizabeth's turn to have her assessment interview.

'I can't assess you,' said Reggie. 'Give us a kiss.'

'Sexy beast,' said Elizabeth.

Reggie went over to her chair, sat on her lap and kissed her. He kissed her again, harder. The chair tipped over backwards and they fell to the floor.

'I love you,' he said.

'I love you too,' she said.

Reggie kissed her. Neither of them heard the tentative knock on the study door.

Nor did they see Jimmy come in.

'Sorry,' he said. 'Haven't seen anything. Best thing, slope straight out, say nothing.'

Reggie and Elizabeth disentangled themselves, and stood up, dishevelled and embarrassed.

'What did you say?' said Reggie.

'I said, "Haven't seen anything. Best thing, slope straight out, say nothing".'

'Ah!'

'Sorry. Didn't mean it to come out loud.'

'That's all right,' said Reggie. 'Elizabeth was just having her assessment interview.'

'Ah!'

'Sorry to barge in,' said Jimmy awkwardly, when Elizabeth had gone. 'Didn't mean to catch you . . .'

'*In flagrante delicto.*'

'Is it? Ah! Never mind. Want to ask a favour, Reggie. Go AWOL, Friday lunch,' said Jimmy, pacing nervously up and down.

'Stop marching, Jimmy.'

'Oh. Sorry. Nerves.'

Jimmy sat down stiffly.

'Remember a girl called Lettuce?' he said.

'Of course. We talked about her on the canal.'

'Built like a Sherman tank.'

'I wouldn't say that exactly,' said Reggie. 'More a Centurion.'

'Not turning up at church like that,' said Jimmy. 'Being here, niceness everywhere. Realized pretty rotten thing to do to a girl. Want to do the decent thing.'

'The decent thing, Jimmy?'

'Marry her.'

Reggie began to pace around the room, then remembered that he had told Jimmy not to, and sat down again.

'Remember the cove I told you about on the canal?' said Jimmy.

'Tim "Curly" Beamish?'

'No. Self-abuse. Images spring to mind. Erotic. ATS parades, Kim Novak, that sort of caper. Yesterday morning, Reggie, I . . .'

'Self-abuse?'

'Yes. Dear old Lettuce sprang to mind, Reggie.'

'And this image proved er . . . not unconducive to . . . er . . .?'

'Enemy position stormed and taken, Reggie, no casualties. With me?'

'Yes.'

'Anyway, long story short, rang her people, posed as insurance agent, white lie, wheedled address, gave her tinkle, public phone, George and Two Dragons, back bar: "Lettuce? Jimmy here. Remember our wedding? Rotten show. Sorry and all that. Suppose dinner's out of the question?" Surprise, surprise, by no means. Now. Here's the rub. Friday night, Lettuce, Greek Islands, month, on tod. Only time free, short notice, Friday lunch.'

'And you want to get your claim in before she goes?'

'In nutshell, Reggie. Strike while iron's hot.'

'Faint heart never won Sherman tank. Of course you can go, Jimmy.'

On Thursday, there were no more applications to join the community.

The floodgates had not opened.

Reggie held his final assessment with Tom and Linda.

They seemed happier than he could ever remember seeing them.

'Tom did a wonderfully nice thing last night,' said Linda.

'Congratulations,' said Reggie.

'I found a bottle of my sprout wine that we overlooked,' said Tom.

'Oh, I see.'

'I drank the whole lot myself, Reggie.'

'Well done.'

Reggie also held his final assessment interview with C.J.

C.J. seemed happier than he could ever remember seeing him.

It was one of the few warm days of that dreadful summer, so they walked through the quiet streets of Botchley.

C.J. clasped his hands behind his back and took long strides.

'This beats orgies into a cocked hat,' he said.

'You're settling in now, are you?' said Reggie.

'In the early days,' said C.J., 'I felt like leaving.'

'You did terrible things, C.J. That helping old women across roads expedition of Jimmy's. Terrible.'

'I helped her across the arterial road.'

'You helped her half-way across, C.J.'

Their walk had taken them into Rio De Janeiro Lane, known in Botchley as Millionaire's Row. Here there were many-gabled Mock Tudor fantasies. Here the nobs hung out.

'Then I realized that you have me by the short and goolies,' said C.J.

'Curlies.'

'What?'

'The expression is "curlies".'

'All right then. I thought, "He has me by the curlies and goolies. I'll make the best of it."'

'Well . . . good.'

'I've done two unselfish things, Reggie,' said C.J. 'I laughed at one of Tom's jokes, and I've told Mrs C.J. to stay six more months in Luxenbourg.'

'Well done,' said Reggie.

On Friday there were again no applicants, and Reggie felt a twinge of fear.

Jimmy felt more than a twinge as he walked towards his rendezvous in Notting Hill Gate.

The weather was fine and sunny.

Good stick, Lettuce, he thought. Looks aren't everything. Looks fade.

But does ugliness?

No miracle. Still ugly. Not horrendous, though. No means as bad as feared. On credit side, not horrendous.

'Hello, Lettuce,' in odd-sounding voice.

'Hello, Jimmy.'

Presence of traffic overwhelming, strangely far away yet absurdly near.

'Right. Wop nosh party fall in.'

No! Control nerves. No military jargon.

They walked to the La Sorrentina in silence, handed in their coats as in a dream, found themselves sitting with drinks in their hands and a large menu at which they stared without seeing.

The tables were too close together but as yet the restaurant was empty.

'Well!' said Jimmy.

'Yes.'

'Well, well!'

'Yes.'

More silence.

'About wedding,' said Jimmy. 'Sorry. Cock-up.'

'Please!'

'Sorry. Greek islands, then?'

'Absolutely.'

'Blue sea. Dazzling white houses. Olive groves. Music. Wine. Informal. Joyous. Spot-on.'

'You've been there?'

'No.'

The waiter loomed.

'Bit rusty on my Itie nosh,' said Jimmy, smiling at him. 'Ravioli. Those are the envelope wallahs, aren't they? Lasagne? Aren't they those long flat green Johnnies?'

'Lasagne verde, sir. Excellent.'

'Ah! Well then! There we are.'

Soon they had ordered. The wine arrived, and Jimmy talked about Reggie's project until the arrival of the lasagne verde.

'M'm,' he said. 'Excellent. Theory. Bad soldier, good cook. Your average Frenchie, magnificent coq au vin, come the hostilities, buggers off to Vichy. Ities, tanks with four gears, all reverse. Pasta magnifico. English, spotted dick and watery greens. Fights till he drops. Reason. Nothing to live for. Waffling. Evading issue. Nerves.'

Lettuce smiled.

'Please don't be nervous,' she said. 'The wedding's forgotten.'

She shovelled a forkful of pasta into her mouth.

'Marry me,' said Jimmy.

Lettuce stared at him in open-mouthed astonishment. Then she remembered that her mouth was full of lasagne and she hastily stared at him in closed-mouth astonishment.

'Meant it,' said Jimmy, clasping her hand under the table. 'Thoroughly good stick.'

Two middle-aged women entered. They were on a shopping spree. They had the reckless air of women who have already spent too much and now see no obstacle to spending far too much.

Although there was plenty of room, the waiter put them at the next table to Lettuce and Jimmy.

It is rare for the English to live with such intensity that they are unaware of the table next to them, but Jimmy and Lettuce were unaware of it now. The result was a great treat for the two shoppers.

'Thank you for calling me a thoroughly good stick,' said Lettuce. 'That's one of the nicest things anyone's ever said of me. But you don't want to stare at my ugly mug every morning.'

'I do,' said Jimmy. 'I do.'

The implications of this remark flashed transparently across his honest face.

'Not that your mug's ugly,' he added hastily.

Lettuce smiled, and took another mouthful of lasagne. Immediately she wanted to talk. She ploughed through the mouthful as hastily as she could, but it resisted, as mouthfuls are wont to do at such moments.

'Shall I tell you the story of my life?' she said, and the two shoppers nodded involuntarily. 'As a girl I was big and gawky. I felt extremely visible. I became shy. Later I learnt, painfully, to seem less shy, although I was just as shy really. I was emotionally frustrated. I 'ate too much, in compensation. I became larger still. Now I drink too much in compensation as well. Soon I'll look haggard as well as large. You don't want to marry me.'

'Nonsense,' said Jimmy stoutly. 'Won't pretend you're a raging beauty. No Kim Novak. Got something that's worth all the Kim Novaks in the world, though. Character. A beauty? All right, maybe not. A damned handsome woman? Yes, every time.'

Suddenly, oblivious of the watching shoppers, he began to cry.

'Lonely,' he said. 'So bloody lonely.'

Lettuce stared at him in horror.

'Jimmy, don't cry. Don't cry, my darling.'

She lent him a hankie and he blew a trumpet voluntary.

She held his hand under the table.

'I hate to see men cry,' she said.

It seemed that in this respect her views differed from those of the lady shoppers.

'Marry me,' he said.

'I'm middle-aged and ugly,' said Lettuce. 'And my name is Lettuce. If I was a character in a novel, I'd be a figure of fun.'

'Horsewhip the author personally if you were,' said Jimmy. 'Bastards. Read some. E. M. Forster? Wouldn't give him house room. Virginia Woolf? Some drivel about a lighthouse. Wouldn't have lasted long in my regiment, I can tell you. No, Lettuce, nobody's a figure of fun, in my book. You least of all.'

'I couldn't bear it if . . . if . . .'

'If I didn't turn up at church again? No fear of that. Jilted at altar twice? Not me. Marry me. Lettuce.'

'Oh yes,' said Lettuce. 'Yes, please.'

'Duck, sir?' said the waiter.

Jimmy stared at his duck with uncomprehending astonishment. He felt as if he had ordered it a thousand years ago.

Jimmy and Lettuce lingered. They had brandies after the meal.

The two shoppers left the restaurant before them. When they got out into the bright sunshine, one of the women sighed deeply.

'I know just what you mean,' said the other. 'When I get home tonight, Ted won't believe a word of it.'

'Ronald won't even listen.'

On Saturday there was one letter in the mail. It informed them that a new restaurant was to open in War Memorial Parade. It was called the Thermopylae Kebab House. They could have twenty-five per cent off a bill for two on presenting the enclosed voucher. No voucher was enclosed.

The study of Number Twenty-one had been transformed into the secretary's office. On the walls, Elizabeth had pinned several sheets of paper. They revealed the full nature of the accommodation that was available.

There were eight bedrooms, four kitchens, four dining-rooms and two living-rooms as bedrooms for guests. Seven of these had been fitted out as double rooms, so there was accommodation for twenty-five guests.

Reggie had worried that it wouldn't be sufficient.

At the moment it was sufficient.

There was only one name on the charts: Mr C. R. Babbacombe.

'Oh my God,' said Reggie. 'What have we done?'

'You felt like this at the beginning of Grot,' said Elizabeth. 'And look where that ended up.'

'Yes, but what's Mr C. R. Babbacombe going to think when he finds he's got to face the lot of us on his own?'

It began to rain. The two-day summer was over.

Reggie's expression brightened.

'Perhaps he won't turn up,' he said.

# 4   *The Early Days*

But Mr C. R. Babbacombe did turn up. He arrived, small, neat, shy, shiny and eager at twenty-five past three on Sunday afternoon.

'Hello. I hope I'm not the first,' he said in a thin, metallic voice.

'You're certainly in good time,' said Reggie.

He led Mr Babbacombe to Number Twenty-three, where he would have the room next to the Harris-Joneses.

David Harris-Jones opened the door.

'Oh. Ah. You must be Mr . . . er . . .'

'Babbacombe,' said Mr Babbacombe. 'Must be difficult for you to remember all our names.'

'Er . . . yes,' said Reggie.

'Yes, well . . . er . . . come in and I'll show you to your . . . er . . .' said David Harris-Jones.

He led the way up the narrow stairs.

'. . . room,' he said, when everyone had forgotten that he still had a sentence to finish.

'Pardon?' said Reggie.

'I said I'd . . . er . . . show Mr Babbacombe to his . . . er . . .'

'Oh I see,' said Reggie.

'. . . room,' said David Harris-Jones. 'I was just finishing my . . . er . . .'

'Sentence,' said Reggie.

'. . . that I'd started earlier,' said David Harris-Jones.

Mr Babbacombe looked from one to the other with some alarm.

On the door of his room a card announced 'Mr C. R. Babbacombe'.

David opened the door, and they entered. There was a single bed, an armchair, a hard chair, a small desk, a gas fire and a print of Botchley War Memorial.

'I can't wait to meet all the others,' said Mr Babbacombe.

'Ah. Yes. The others,' said Reggie.

Mr Babbacombe went over to the window, which afforded a fine view over the spacious garden. It was chock-a-block with flowers, of wildly clashing colours, all about one foot six high. It had been Mr Penfold's pride and joy.

The sky was leaden.

'I'm an undertaker,' said Mr Babbacombe.

'Ah!' said Reggie.

'How . . . er . . . interesting,' said David Harris-Jones.

'But then you know that. It sticks out a mile, doesn't it?' said Mr Babbacombe.

'Good lord, no,' said Reggie. 'Does it, David?'

'Certainly not,' said David Harris-Jones.

'My face bears the stigmata of my profession,' said Mr Babbacombe, sitting on the pink coverlet and testing the bedsprings gingerly. 'My clothes are permeated with the stench of decay.'

'No, they're very nice,' said Reggie.

'I'm an outcast, a pariah. That's why I'm looking forward to this . . . er . . . course.'

'To meet the others?'

'Yes.'

Reggie looked at David Harris-Jones helplessly.

'Among the other . . . er . . . what do you call us? Patients?' said Mr Babbacombe.

'Good heavens no,' said Reggie. 'Guests.'

'Among the other guests I hope to be accepted as an equal,' said Mr Babbacombe.

David Harris-Jones looked helplessly at Reggie.

Mr Babbacombe released the clasp of his suitcase decisively. His packing was orderly and spare. He had two-tone pyjamas.

'I'm afraid I have a disappointment for you,' said Reggie.

'Oh?'

'Yes. You ... er ... you won't be meeting the others ... yet. We'd like to give you some solitude to ... er ...'

'Get in the right frame of ... er ...' said David Harris-Jones.

'... mind,' said Reggie.

'I see,' said Mr Babbacombe. 'I don't meet the others until dinner, is that it?'

'You'll ... er ... dine alone in your room tonight,' said Reggie.

'Oh.'

'This will enable you to prepare yourself mentally and physically for tomorrow when you ... er ...'

'Meet the others.'

'Broadly speaking, yes. You'll have a group meeting at nine thirty.'

Reggie called an emergency meeting of the staff and explained the situation. It was decided that the only solution was for five members of the staff to pretend to be guests. The names of the staff were put into the hat, except for Reggie's.

'As head of the project I cannot take part, however much I might want to,' he explained.

The five names drawn were David Harris-Jones, Elizabeth Perrin, C.J., Joan Webster and Doc Morrissey.

They spent the evening preparing their roles for the next day's deception.

Mr Babbacombe spent the evening lingering over an excellent but lonely dinner and getting himself into the right mental and physical state for meeting them.

In the morning Mr Babbacombe's breakfast was brought to his room. Then, in a trance-like state of expectation, he drifted along Oslo Avenue, under the grey August sky, to Number Twenty-five.

Jimmy opened the door and led him into the living-room.

It was even more surprisingly spacious than the living-room of Number Twenty-one. There were no french windows. Three pictures of bygone Botchley adorned the walls. Twelve assorted chairs stood in two semi-circles of six, facing each other.

Mr Babbacombe didn't know in which semi-circle to sit, so he remained standing, looking out over the banal garden with unseeing eyes.

C.J. arrived next.

'Lucas is the name,' he said, in a thin metallic voice.

'Babbacombe,' said Mr Babbacombe, and C.J. realized with horror that his assumed voice was identical to Mr Babbacombe's real one.

'I feared I might be alone,' said C.J.

'I have the impression there are quite a few of us,' said Mr Babbacombe.

'Oh good,' said C.J. 'One swallow doesn't make a summer.'

'That's true,' said Mr Babbacombe.

'I wonder which chairs we sit in,' said C.J. 'Let's plump for these.'

'Righty ho,' said Mr Babbacombe.

No sooner had they sat, in the chair facing the handsome brick fireplace, than they had to stand to greet Joan and Elizabeth. Doc Morrissey arrived next, then the staff entered *en masse* and finally David Harris-Jones sidled into the end seat. He had suddenly realized that Mr Babbacombe knew him, and he'd made frantic efforts to disguise himself as the road manager of a pop group. These efforts were not an unqualified success.

Reggie stood up. Beside him were Linda, Tom, Tony, Jimmy and Prue.

'Good morning,' he said. 'Now the idea of these group sessions is that we all get to help each other. We, the staff, help you, and you, the guests, help each other, bringing up your problems, and discussing them among yourselves.'

95

He smiled at Mr Babbacombe, Doc Morrissey, C.J., Elizabeth, Joan and David.

'And you, the guests, can help us,' said Reggie. 'By the end, if the meeting's going well, it'll be hard to tell who are the staff and who are the guests. Huh huh. Now, I'll call upon the Doc to say a few words. Doc?'

Doc Morrissey stood up.

'Thank you,' he said.

Oh my God, thought Reggie, I forgot Doc was one of the guests. He glared desperately at Doc Morrissey.

'Oh, I'm sorry,' said Doc Morrissey. 'I've just remembered. I'm not the Doc.'

He sat down.

Reggie fixed his glare at Tom.

'Doc?' he said.

Tom seemed to be miles away, but Jimmy stood up.

'Sorry miles away, brown study,' he said. 'I'm the Doc. Word of advice. If you fancy the local bints, keep well away. Go for a long hike instead. Cold shower every morning, and Bob's your uncle. Carry on.'

He sat down.

'Good advice there from the Doc,' said Reggie. 'Now if any of you have any problems, any neuroses, any phobias, anything, however little, however large, do please tell us about it. Now, who'll get the ball rolling?'

He sat down.

Doc Morrissey stood up.

'I think I'd better explain why I stood up just then,' he said. 'I'm prey to the delusion that I'm a member of the medical profession. It's embarrassing. People say, "Is there a doctor in the house?" "I'm a doctor," I cry. I leap up. "I'm a doctor. Make way. Make way," I cry. I get to the scene of the disaster, they all say, "Thank God you've come, Doc," and I say. "I've just remembered I'm not a doctor. Sorry".'

Doc Morrissey sat down.

'Fascinating,' said Reggie. 'Any comments, Doc?'

Doc Morrissey stood up.

'Not really,' he said.

Reggie glared at him.

'Sorry,' said Doc Morrissey. 'You see. There I go again.'

He sat down and wiped his brow.

Jimmy stood up.

'Just remembered. I'm the Doc,' he said. 'Sorry. Memory's a bit dicey lately. Touch of . . . er . . .'

'Amnesia?' suggested Reggie.

'Yes. Bit tired this morning. Cock-up on the kipping front. Fascinating tale of yours, Doc.'

'Why do you call him Doc if he isn't the Doc?' said Mr Babbacombe.

'Ah!' said Reggie. 'Yes. Er . . . why do you call him Doc, if he isn't the Doc, and of course he isn't the Doc, Doc?'

'Er . . . er . . .' suggested Jimmy.

'I don't want to put words into your mouth,' said Reggie.

'Please do,' said Jimmy.

'You're thinking that if you tell our deluded friend here that he isn't the Doc, he feels rebuffed, but if you pretend he is the Doc, he has the opportunity to deny it himself, he is a part of his own cure, he feels rewarded. Well done, Doc.'

'Took the words out of my mouth,' said Jimmy.

He sat down.

C.J. stood up.

'I can't make friends,' he said, in his assumed voice. 'I'm just waiting for the day when I need the services of the undertakers, that fine body of men.'

'You know, don't you?' said Mr Babbacombe.

'No, I don't,' said C.J. 'Know what?'

'It sticks out a mile.'

'No, it doesn't,' said C.J.

'Since you all know already, I may as well tell you. I'm an undertaker. Surprise, surprise.'

'Good heavens, are you really?' said C.J. 'Well, well, bless my soul.'

'Come off it. Anyone can tell an undertaker from everyone else,' said Mr Babbacombe in his thin, metallic voice.

'Nonsense,' said C.J. in his thin, metallic voice. 'I didn't get where I am today by telling undertakers from everyone else.'

'When I first saw you yesterday, Mr Babbacombe,' said Reggie, 'I thought, "That man's a research chemist, or I'm a Dutchman".'

'I'd got you down for a civil engineer,' put in Linda.

'Any other problems anyone would like to raise?' said Reggie, wiping his brow. 'Mrs Naylor, how about you?'

Joan and Elizabeth hesitated. Both thought the other one wasn't going to speak. Both said, 'Not at the moment, thank you.'

'Ah! you're both called Naylor. Are you related?' said Reggie.

'No,' said Joan.

'Yes,' said Elizabeth.

'This is interesting,' said Reggie. 'There seems to be some doubt about the matter. I'll ask you again. Are you related?'

'No,' said Elizabeth.

'Yes,' said Joan.

'I think I understand,' said Reggie desperately. 'Mrs Naylor denied being related to Mrs Naylor because she's ashamed of her. Mrs Naylor, realizing this, tried to protect Mrs Naylor by pretending not to be a relative, but Mrs Naylor had by this time decided to acknowledge her. Am I right, Mrs Naylor?'

'Brilliant,' said Joan and Elizabeth.

'It's what I'm here for,' said Reggie. 'Why are you ashamed of Mrs Naylor, Mrs Naylor?'

'She . . . er . . .' said Joan.

'I drink,' said Elizabeth.

'She drinks,' said Joan.

David Harris-Jones decided that it was time for him to come to the rescue.

Now Reggie remembered that Mr Babbacombe had met David.

'I'm a roadie for a super pop group,' continued David Harris-Jones, standing with his face averted from Mr Babbacombe. 'I'm sorry to turn away from you like this. I guess I just can't face you face to face. I guess I can't face myself, know what I mean? I have to make trips, all over the country, one night stands, and on these trips I . . . er . . . I make trips, know what I mean? I mean am I into acid? Am I? Well, I'll tell you. I am. Like you finish a gig, back to some chick's pad, a real super laid-back scene, man. Know what I mean? But what are you, identity crisis wise? Nobody. A bum. I'm fed up with being into music, man. I'm fed up with being into acid. I guess I've wised up. I'm just not into being into things any more. I want out. I mean, like it's . . .' He glanced apologetically at Tony. '. . . it's Coldsoupsville, Arizona. I wanna kick the habit, keep off the grass, know what I mean, man? Like I just don't know who I am.'

'I do,' said Mr Babbacombe. 'You're the warden.'

'I mean like I . . . what?'

'You're the warden of Number Twenty-three,' said Mr Babbacombe.

David Harris-Jones looked round wildly. Prue smiled encouragingly.

'Oh, that creep,' said David. 'I saw him. Like I'm a dead ringer for him, know what I mean?'

'The only good ringer is a dead ringer,' said C.J.

'Where's the warden now?' said Mr Babbacombe.

'He's . . . er . . . he's ill,' said Reggie. 'He's got food poi . . . no, not food poi . . . er . . .'flu. That's it. 'Flu. He's got 'flu. He's definitely got 'flu.'

'He's the warden,' said Mr Babbacombe. He pointed at Doc Morrissey. 'He's the doctor. Neither of them are called Mrs Naylor. You're all staff.'

'Some of what you say is true,' said Reggie. 'To the extent that . . . er . . . he's the doctor . . . er . . . and he is the warden . . . and . . . er . . . neither of them are called Mrs Naylor . . .

and we are all staff. Well done, you've come through the test with flying colours.'

'Test?'

'Spotting who are staff and who aren't. It's a little psychological test to ... er ... test your ... er ... ability to understand psychological tests.'

'Where are your guests?'

'You are.'

'What?'

'It's our first day, Mr Babbacombe, and you are our only guest.'

Reggie pleaded with Mr Babbacombe to give them another chance, and the little mortician was reluctantly persuaded.

They moved the chair around. There were now eleven chairs with their backs to the fireplace, and one chair facing it.

Mr Babbacombe sat facing the full complement of staff.

Reggie stood up.

'Good morning again,' he said. 'Now we hold these little group meetings, Mr Babbacombe, so that we, the staff, can meet you, the ... Mr Babbacombe, and so that you, Mr Babbacombe, can meet us, the staff. We can help you and you can help ... er ... yourself, bringing up your problems, discussing them among ... er ... yourself and ... er ... so let's get on with things, shall we? Now, who's going to start the ball rolling? Mr Babbacombe?'

Mr Babbacombe stood up.

'We can stay as long as we like and at the end we pay according to what we feel we've got out of it, is that right?' he said.

'Exactly,' said Reggie. 'It seems the fairest way to me.'

'I think so too,' said Mr Babbacombe.

'Oh good. I am glad,' said Reggie.

'Good-bye,' said Mr Babbacombe.

When Mr Babbacombe had gone, Reggie turned to his staff. 'I'll be honest,' he said. 'This start has not been as auspicious as I hoped. But, we must not panic. I have just one thing to say to you. Aaaaaaaaaaaaaaaaagh!'

Even McBlane's excellent lunch and dinner couldn't raise morale.

And that evening the great chef himself came under the lash of disapproval. His ears would have burned, had they not been burning already, due to an attack of Pratt's Ear Itch.

The incident involving McBlane began when Linda entered the children's bedroom, to hear Tom saying, 'They're a famous Italian film director and an Irish air-line. Now go to sleep.'

'What are?' said Linda.

'Nothing,' said Tom.

It was eleven fifteen. The children had just sat exhausted and bored through a documentary on the life-cycle of the parasitic worm on BBC 2. In the interests of personal freedom, Tom and Linda had not told them to go to bed. In the interests of personal pride, they had kept their red little eyelids open.

'Well, come on, Tom,' said Linda, when they had closed the children's door behind them. 'What are a famous Italian film director and an Irish air-line?'

'Jocasta said that she finds Uncle McBlane's stories boring,' said Tom, 'and Adam asked what fellatio and cunnilingus are.'

'Don't worry,' said Reggie, who happened to be passing on his way to bed. 'I'll deal with McBlane in the morning.'

Next morning Reggie tackled the unkempt Hibernian genius in his lair. Vegetables covered the kitchen table. Pots and pans lay ready on the Scandinavian-style traditional English fully integrated natural pine and chrome work surfaces.

McBlane was crying. Reggie hoped it might be remorse, but it was only onions. McBlane swept the chopped onions imperiously into a large pan in which butter had melted. One of his boil plasters was hanging loose.

'Morning, McBlane,' began Reggie.

McBlane grunted.

'McBlane, I must have a word with you,' said Reggie.

McBlane grunted again.

'I must speak to you frankly,' said Reggie. 'Er . . . the salmon mousse yesterday was superb.'

McBlane proved a master at varying his grunts.

'But,' said Reggie. 'Life doesn't consist of salmon mousse alone. And . . . er . . . the navarin of lamb was also superb.'

McBlane barked an incomprehensible reply.

'On the other hand,' said Reggie, 'the duchesse potatoes were also superb. Incidentally, I understand you're telling stories to Adam and Jocasta. Thanks. It's much appreciated.'

'Flecking ma boots wi' hae flaggis,' said McBlane.

'Quite,' said Reggie. 'Point taken. But . . .'

McBlane swivelled round slowly from the stove, and looked Reggie straight in the face. He had a stye above his left eye.

'But,' said Reggie, 'I wouldn't like you to think that my praise of the potatoes implied any criticism of the choucroute à la hongroise.'

This time there was no mistaking McBlane's reply.

'Bloody foreign muck,' he said.

'Absolutely,' said Reggie.

McBlane glowered.

'I protest,' said Reggie. 'The choucroute à la hongroise was delicious.'

McBlane re-glowered.

'Well, fairly delicious,' said Reggie. 'Talking about the stories you're telling Adam and Jocasta . . . er . . . I hope you'll remember their age, as it were, and keep them . . . er . . . er if you see what I mean. Point taken?'

McBlane grunted.

'Jolly good,' said Reggie.

He walked briskly to the door. Then he turned and faced the dark chef fearlessly.

'Wonderful rhubarb crumble,' he said.

Later that day Reggie told Tom, 'I saw McBlane this morning. I gave him a piece of my mind.'

Reggie accepted much of the blame for the initial failure of his venture. He admitted that he had seriously under-estimated the amount of advertising that would be needed. He had been reluctant to cash in on the name that he had made through Perrin Products and Grot. He was reluctant no longer. Soon adverts for Perrins began to appear in national and local newspapers, on underground stations, buses, and hoardings.

Some of the advertisements said simply: 'Perrins'.

Others were more elaborate.

One read:

> Whatever happened to Reginald Perrin?
> Remember Grot and its useless products?
> Now Perrin rides again.
> This time his product is USEFUL.
> It's called HAPPINESS.
> Visit PERRINS.
> Stay as long as you like.
> Pay as little as you like.

Another simply read: 'Perrins – the only community for the middle-aged and middle class.'

Others stated: 'Perrins – the In-place for Out-people', 'Perrins – where misfits fit', 'Are you a backward reader? Then come and be cured at Snirrep', 'Lost all faith in experts? Then come to Perrins. Guaranteed no experts in anything' and 'Want to drop-out but don't like drop-outs? At Perrins the drop-outs are just like you. They're more like drop-ins. Next time you feel like dropping-out, why not drop-in?'

The saturation coverage began on September the first.

The W288 carried the legend 'Perrins' past the front door.

McBlane wrapped the remnants of dinner in newspapers that all carried advertisements for Perrins, even though they were as divergent as the *Financial Times*, the *Daily Express*, and the *Botchley and Spraundon Press* (*Incorporating the Coxwell Gazette* and the remains of twelve lamp chops).

The saturation coverage took effect immediately.

On Monday, September the twelfth the staff swung into action once more.

And this time there wasn't just one client.

There were two.

Reggie decided to give all the clients an introductory interview before subjecting them to the rigours of a group meeting.

His new study was in Number Twenty-three, to the right of the front door. It had a brown carpet and buff walls. There were two upright chairs and a heavy oak desk. Two pictures of bygone Botchley adorned the walls.

It was a quiet September morning. Autumn was coming in modestly, as if bribed to conceal the ending of the summer that had never begun.

Reggie's first interviewee was Thruxton Appleby, the textiles tycoon. Thruxton Appleby was a large paunchy man with a domed shiny bald head. His nose was bulbous. His lips were thick and flecked with white foam. His enormous buttocks crashed down politely on to the fragile chair provided. 'Call this furniture?' they seemed to cry. 'We eat chairs like this in Yorkshire.' Reggie quaked. His whole organization seamed weak and fragile.

'I read your advert in *Mucklethwaite Morning Telegraph*,' said Thruxton Appleby. 'I liked its bare-faced cheek. I admire bare-faced cheek. Are you a Yorkshireman?'

'No,' said Reggie. 'A Londoner.'

'That's odd. You don't often find bare-faced cheek among namby-pamby Southerners.'

His paunch quivered over his private parts like junket in a gale.

'I'm a textiles tycoon,' he said. 'Everything I'm wearing is

104

from my own mills. I don't usually bother with quacks, crack-pots and cranks, but I've tried everything. Head-shrinkers, health farms, religion. You're my last resort.'

'How flattering,' said Reggie. 'What is your problem?'

'I'm not likeable, Mr Perrin.'

Reggie drew a sheet of paper towards him and wrote, 'Thinks he isn't likeable. He's right.'

Thruxton Appleby leant forward, trying to read what Reggie had written.

'Professional secret,' said Reggie, shielding the paper with his hand.

'I'm not liked for myself, do you see?' continued Thruxton Appleby. 'I've made Mucklethwaite. I've fought a one-man battle against the depredations of Far East imports. You can go in the Thruxton Appleby Memorial Gardens, past the Thruxton Appleby Memorial Band-stand, and look out over the whole of Mucklethwaite to Scrag End Fell, and what are you sat on? The Thruxton Appleby Memorial Seat.'

'Shouldn't memorials be for after you're dead?' said Reggie.

'What use is that?' said Thruxton Appleby. 'You're gone then.'

A blue tit was hanging under a branch on the bush outside the window. Thruxton Appleby's eyebrows rose scornfully. 'Call that a tit?' they seemed to say. 'In Yorkshire we call yon a speck of fluff.'

The blue tit flew away.

'I expect money to carry all before it,' said Thruxton Appleby. 'Cure me of that, and you can name your price.'

Reggie felt that he could do nothing for this man.

'My first impressions are unfavourable,' said Thruxton Appleby. 'Thruxton, I say to myself, tha's landed up in a tin-pot organization, staffed by namby-pamby Southerners. I'll give it a go while Tuesday. So get on with it, Mr Perrin, and do it quickly. Time is money.'

Thruxton Appleby glanced at his watch, as if to see how

rich he was. Reggie wondered what it said. Ten past six hundred thousand pounds?

Stop having silly thoughts, Reggie. Concentrate. Having silly thoughts and not concentrating are symptoms of lack of confidence.

How right you are.

Be confident. Be bold.

Look at him. He's all wind and piss. Already he's uneasy because you aren't speaking and it isn't what he expects. He's used to bullying. Bully him in return.

I think you're right.

Reggie smiled at Thruxton Appleby.

'Smoke?' he said.

'Please.'

'Filthy habit.'

He wrote 'smokes' on the piece of paper.

'I don't offer cigarettes,' he said. 'Do you like coffee?'

'Please.'

'Milk and sugar?'

'Please.'

'Takes coffee with milk and sugar,' Reggie muttered as he made another note. 'Caught you twice. Thick as well as nasty.'

Thruxton Appleby gasped.

'What did you say?' he said.

'Thick as well as nasty.'

'I'm not used to being spoken to like that.'

'Excellent. Why do you think you're so loathed?' said Reggie.

'Not loathed, Mr Perrin. Not even disliked. Just "not liked". I'm rich, you see.'

'I can easily cure you of that.'

Reggie shielded the piece of paper with his hand, wrote 'Nosey Bastard' on it, and left the room.

He talked briefly with C.J., asking him to interrupt in thirty seconds on a matter of no importance and be dismissive towards Thruxton Appleby.

He returned to the study. Thruxton Appleby didn't appear to have moved.

'I don't think I'm a nosey bastard,' he said.

Reggie laughed.

'Come in,' he said.

'Nobody knocked.'

'Give them time. Don't be so impatient. Come in.'

'Why do you keep saying "Come in"?'

'Third time lucky,' said Reggie. 'Come in.'

C.J. entered.

'Is this important?' said Reggie.

'No,' said C.J.

'Good. Take your time.'

'I just wondered if you'd heard the weather forecast.'

'I'll ring for it,' said Reggie, lifting the phone and dialling. 'Excuse me, Mr Dangleby, but this *is* a waste of time.'

He listened, then put the phone down.

'Yes, C.J., I have now heard the weather forecast,' he said.

'Oh good. I'll be on my way then,' said C.J.

'Oh, this is the chemicals tycoon, Throxton Dangleby,' said Reggie.

'Textiles,' said Thruxton Appleby.

'Nice to meet you, Mr Textiles,' said C.J.

'Appleby,' said Thruxton Appleby.

'You've probably heard of the Throxton Ingleby Memorial Hat-Stand,' said Reggie.

'Band-stand,' said Thruxton Appleby.

'Nice to meet you, Mr Dimbleby,' said C.J., and he closed the door gently behind him.

'Not very subtle tactics,' said the unlovely industrialist.

'For a not very subtle man,' said Reggie. 'Now. I can cure you, but it'll take time. Within a fortnight, you'll no longer be obnoxious. Irritating and mind-bogglingly boring, but not obnoxious. Within three weeks, you'll be tolerable in mixed

107

company in medium-sized doses. Within a month, give or take a day or two either way, this is not an exact science, you'll be likeable.'

'Thank you,' said Thruxton Appleby hoarsely.

The bloated capitalist removed his unacceptable face from the study.

The second guest was known to Reggie already. He was Mr Pelham, owner of Pelham's Piggery, where Reggie had swilled out in the dark days before he had even thought of his Grot shop.

'You've done well for yourself, old son,' said Mr Pelham.

'Not bad,' acknowledged Reggie.

Mr Pelham's honest, God-fearing, pig-loving face had a grey, uninhabited look. The chair, so puny under attack from Thruxton Appleby's buttocks, seemed ample now.

'I always liked you,' said Mr Pelham. 'You were different from the other hands. Chalk and cheese, Reg. Chalk and cheese, old son.'

'Thank you,' said Reggie.

'I shouldn't be talking to you like this,' said Mr Pelham. 'You're the guv'nor now.'

'Please,' said Reggie, waving a deprecatory hand.

'I read your advert for this place, I thought, "That's the self-same Perrin that swilled out my porkers".'

Reggie's heart sank. Why did anyone he knew have to come, and especially so soon? He could do nothing for Mr Pelham. Probably he could do nothing for anybody. He smiled, trying to look encouraging.

'Well, I am the self-same Perrin,' he said.

'You certainly are, old son,' said Mr Pelham. 'You certainly are. He's the man to go to with my problems, I thought.'

'Tell me about your problems,' said Reggie.

Mr Pelham told Reggie about his problems. He had diversified since the old days. He had bought the premises of his neighbours, the Climthorpe School of Riding and the old chicken farm that Reggie had called Stalag Hen 59. Pelham's Piggery had become Associated Meat Products Ltd. He sold pigs, chickens and calves. An abbatoir in Bicester gave him group rates. His daughter never came near him. His son worked in a bank and had espoused vegetarianism. It was more than ten years since his wife had been knocked down by a bus outside Macfisheries. The shop wasn't even there any more. The nearest branch was at Staines.

'I'm alone in the world, Reg,' he said. 'And there's blood on my hands.'

'Aren't you exaggerating?' said Reggie.

'All those chickens in rows, Reg, living in the dark with their beaks cut back. All those calves, deliberately made anaemic so that people can eat white meat. How can people sleep in their beds with all that going on? How can I sleep in my bed?'

Reggie didn't know what to say, so he said nothing.

The blue tit returned to the bush outside the window. It clearly didn't see Mr Pelhan as a threat to its security.

'I get dreams, Reg,' said Mr Pelham.

'Dreams?' repeated Reggie, writing 'Dreams' on his sheet of paper. 'What sort of dreams?'

'Dreams of Hell, old son,' said Mr Pelham. 'I dream about what'll happen to me when I get to Hell. And I will, don't you worry.'

'I will worry,' protested Reggie.

'I won't get a gander at those pearly gates, not if I live to be a thousand I won't.'

He dreamt of a Hell in which there were rows and rows of Mr Pelhams, kept side by side in the dark, their innumerable cages soiled with the stains of centuries of Pelham faeces, their noses cut off, their diet unbalanced, the better to produce anaemia and white meat, while opposite them, lit by thousands of bare bulbs, hundreds of chefs turned thousands of Mr Pelhams on spits, and beyond, in a gigantic cavern, beneath vast crystal chandeliers that stretched to infinity, Satan and his thousands of sultry mistresses sat at long tables with velvet cloths, drinking dark wine out of pewter goblets and moistening their scarlet lips with spittle in anticipation of their finger-licking portions of Hades-fried Pelham.

'I'm in a cage among all the rows of me,' said Mr Pelham. 'And I get brought a portion of me, on a silver tray, with barbecue sauce. And I try to eat me. I'm not bad. I taste like pork. But I stick in my throat.'

'Has it ever occurred to you that maybe you're in the wrong line of business?' said Reggie.

'It's all I know,' said Mr Pelham.

Reggie wrote 'God knows what to do' on the sheet of paper. Mr Pelham tried to see what he had written, but he shielded the paper behind a pile of books.

'Professional secrets,' he said.

'Can you help me, Reg?' said Mr Pelham.

Reggie opened his mouth, convinced that no sound whatsoever would emerge, that it would open and shut like the mouth of a stranded grayling. Imagine his astonishment, then, when he heard confident and coherent sentences emerging.

'We can help you to make your personality whole,' he said. 'We can send you from here a kindly, nice, peaceful man, content with his personality, yet not complacent. This we *can* do. What we can't do is solve the problems posed by your work. We can't increase society's awareness of the methods by which its food is produced or its willingness to pay the increased costs that more humane methods would entail. We can't tell you what you should do about your conscience. We can only send you off in the best possible frame of mind to deal with these problems. The rest is up to you.'

Mr Pelham smiled happily. It was as if a great burden had been taken from his shoulders. His trust was absolute.

'Thank you,' he said. 'I knew you could do it, old son.'

When Mr Pelham had gone, Reggie found that he was trembling.

He hadn't known that he could do it.

Three days after the arrival of the two clients, neither of them had left. It wasn't a triumph, but it was something. And one or two forward bookings were beginning to deflower the virgin sheets on the walls of the secretary's office.

The weather was discreetly unsettled.

It was not a busy time. When Jimmy applied to have Thursday lunchtime off, Reggie granted it without hesitation.

The purpose of his brief furlough was to visit Restaurant Italian Sorrentina La, Hill Notting, 12.30 hours, Horncastle Lettuce Isobel, engagement for the breaking off of.

It had all been a dreadful mistake.

This time there would be no cowardly desertion in the face of a church. This time he would face Lettuce bravely, across a restaurant table, and say, 'Sorry, old girl. Just not on. Still be friends, eh? Meet, time to time, meals, odd opera, that sort of crack? Be chums?'

Mustn't be frightened of a woman, he told himself, as the train sped with perverse punctuality towards Waterloo. Imagine her as Rommel. Come to think of it, she didn't look altogether unlike Rommel. A touch more masculine, perhaps. His face softened with affection. Poor, dear Lettuce!

No! He hardened his heart. Eventually, warmed by four double whiskies, he made his way to La Sorrentina.

They sat at the same table. They were served by the same waiter. They ordered the same food. Only the two lady shoppers were missing.

Lettuce was fiercely bronzed by the Hellenic sun. She showed him her snapshots of Greece. He gazed at blue skies and azure seas, at dazzling white hotels and cafés, at huge Horncastle thighs that began the holiday gleaming like freshly painted lighthouses and ended up like charred trunks of oaks blackened in some forest fire.

'Who's the tall man with the beard?' he asked.

'Odd.'

'Odd?'

'That's his name. Odd.'

'Odd name, isn't it?'

'It's common in Sweden.'

'And was he?'

'What?'

'Odd.'

'Not that I know of.'

She showed him the next picture.

'Who's the blond giant?'

'Bent.'

'Bent?'

'It's a common name in Denmark.'

'And was he?'

'What?'

'Bent.'

'No.'

'How do you know?'

'He didn't appear to be.'

She produced the next picture.

'This is Mikonos,' she said. 'Very touristy.'

'Odd and Bent all present and correct.'

'Are you jealous?'

'Course not.'

'Naxos,' she said, of the next snap. 'This was the hottest day. Thirty-four degrees Celsius.'

'Odd and Bent aren't absent on parade, I see.'

Lettuce put her photos away. They had done their job.

Jimmy was jealous.

They decided to get married on Wednesday, December the twenty-first, and spend Christmas in Malta.

The money continued to drift out of the once-fat bank account of Reginald Iolanthe Perrin. The evenings drew in. The equinoctial gales began to blow.

On Sunday, September the eighteenth, a third client arrived. He was an insurance salesman who had lost his motivation.

'It's a dreadful thing to say,' he told Reggie at his first interview, 'but I couldn't care less if there are hundreds of people walking the streets of Mitcham seriously under-insured.'

To Reggie's incredulous relief, both Thruxton Appleby and Mr Pelham were showing definite signs of progress.

Under Linda's expert tutelage, Mr Pelham produced several paintings. Porkers were his favourite subjects, but sometimes, for a change, he would paint other kinds of pig.

Thruxton Appleby was making even more spectacular progress. On one of Jimmy's tactical exercises without troops, he helped a blind writer of Christmas card verses across Botchley High Street, and enjoyed the experience so much that he waited seven minutes to help him back again.

Joan reported few triumphs with her singing classes, but Prue was making steady progress, between the rain storms, with the thatching of the garden shed at Number Twenty-one.

One or two areas gave Reggie cause for concern.

Sporting activity was conspicuous by its absence, and culture was another area where progress was tardy.

Reggie found it necessary to speak to Tom and Tony about the slow progress of their departments.

On the afternoon of Thursday, September the twenty-second, he entered the garden of Number Seventeen. The beds around the surprisingly spacious lawn were given over predominantly to roses, and he noted with pleasure that C.J. had proved diligent in removing dead heads.

Reggie knocked on the door of the garden shed, alias the Sports Centre. Tom let him in reluctantly. On the shelves all round the shed there were bottles. On the floor there were more bottles. Some of the bottles contained spirits, others contained liquids of strange exotic hue. Still others were empty. In one corner a work table had been erected. On it

113

were huge glass bottles connected together with drips and pipes. Under the table there were many trays of fruit. Reggie's heart sank.

'Do you remember that I used to make home-made wine?' said Tom.

'I seem to recall something of the kind,' said Reggie. 'You've started making them again, have you?'

'Oh no,' said Tom.

'Oh good,' said Reggie.

'I'm making spirits now.'

'Oh my God.'

'Sloe gin, prune brandy, raspberry whisky.'

'Oh my God! May I sit down?'

Reggie sat in the one chair provided. Tom looked at him earnestly.

'I'm afraid I've got a disappointment for you, Reggie,' said Tom.

'Oh dear. Well, tell me the worst. Let's get it over with.'

'None of them is ready to drink yet.'

'Oh dear, that is disappointing. Tom, I am prepared to accept against all the odds that these things will be delicious, but I have to ask you, are they sport?'

'I don't follow you, Reggie,' said Tom, taking his unlit pipe out of his mouth as if he thought that might help his concentration.

'You were put in charge of sport.'

'Oh that. I'm just not a sport person, Reggie.'

Reggie stood up, the better to assert his authority.

'I thought you accepted it as a challenge, Tom,' he said. 'And it got off to such a good start with that football.'

Tom gazed at Reggie like a walrus that has heard bad news.

'I've let you down,' he said. 'I've allowed myself to be discouraged by our early failures.'

Reggie patted him on the shoulder.

'There's still time, Tom,' he said. 'The community is young. Instigate some lively sports activities, and I'll let you carry on with the booze production. No promises, but I may even drink some myself.'

'Thanks,' said Tom. 'I won't let you down again, father-in-law.'

Reggie went straight round to the Culture Room which was situated in the garden shed of Number Twenty-five. This garden had been largely dug up and devoted to the production of greens. The door of the shed was painted yellow. On it hung a notice which read, 'Culture Room. Prop: T. Webster, QCI.'

He knocked and entered.

The hut had been converted into a living-room with two armchairs and a Calor Gas fire. All round the uneven wooden walls were pin-ups of girls with naked breasts, taken from the tabloid newspapers.

Reggie gawped.

'Knock-out, eh?' said Tony, looking a little uneasy.

'What are they supposed to be?' said Reggie.

'Culture.'

'They aren't culture. They're boobs.'

'They're actresses,' said Tony. 'What are actresses if they aren't culture?'

'Actresses!'

'Read any one of the captions.'

Reggie approached the endless rows of breasts nervously, and read one of the captions that nestled timorously under the vast swellings.

'Vivacious Virginia's a radiologist's daughter,' he read. 'Her dad made some pretty startling developments in X-ray techniques, but you don't need an X-ray to see vibrant Virginia's startling developments. Volatile Virginia has plans to be a classical actress. Well, she might reveal some talents, but unfortunately she'd have to hide her biggest assets!'

'Culture,' said Tony.

Reggie peered at the equally well-developed female on Virginia's right.

'Curvaceous Caroline's a colonel's daughter,' he read. 'Dad might think she's improperly dressed for parade, but then she's fighting a different battle of the bulge from the one he got a DSO for. Come to think of it we wouldn't mind giving Cock-A-Hoop Caroline a medal. We might even pin it on ourselves. Cultivated Caroline plans to become a Shakespearian actress. It's a case of "from the bared to the Bard!".'

'What did I tell you?' said Tony.

Reggie turned away from the multi-nippled walls of the garden shed and looked disgustedly at Tony.

'There are hundreds of boobs in here,' said Tony. 'A ton of tits.'

'What does QCI stand for?'

'What?'

Reggie swung the door open. Daylight streamed into the little hut.

'Prop: T. Webster, QCI,' said Reggie.

'Oh, that,' said Tony. 'Qualified Culture Instructor.'

'I can't talk in there,' said Reggie. 'Come into the garden.'

They stood on the tiny lawn, surrounded by vast beds of autumn cabbages.

'Tony,' said Reggie. 'If a prospective client gets in touch with me, and says, "Do you have any cultural activities?" and I say. "Yes. We have a qualified culture instructor and he has a garden shed with a ton of tits", what do you think will happen?'

'He'll sign on.'

'Yes, well, very possibly. Forget that, then. But remove those boobs. And get some culture going. I'm not one for issuing threats, Tony. This community runs on love and trust. But if you let me down, I'm warning you, I will issue threats. And you know what they'll be threats of, don't you? Chucked out without a pennysville, Arizona.'

*

116

On Sunday, September twenty-fifth, two more clients arrived. The month expired quietly. There were no mourners.

October began gloomily. The weather was unremittingly wet. There was a race riot in Wednesbury. Four headless torsos were found in left-luggage cubicles at Temple Meads Station, Bristol. A survey showed that Britain came fifth in the venereal disease tables of the advanced nations. A Ugandan under-secretary was taken to a West London hospital with suspected smallpox and claimed that it was impossible as he had diplomatic immunity. Third-form girls in a school in South London terrorized teachers after a drinks orgy.

But there was one bright spark amidst all this gloom. The fortunes of Perrins were looking up. Seven new clients arrived on Sunday, October the second, making the total twelve. And there were several forward bookings dotted around the wall charts in the secretary's office, including one from a fortune teller who was going to have a nervous breakdown in April.

The twelve clients were Thruxton Appleby; Mr Pelham; the insurance salesman who had lost his motivation; an arc-welder from Ipswich named Arthur Noblet; Bernard Trilling, Head of Comedy at Anaemia Television; Hilary Meadows, a housewife from Tenterden; Diana Pilkington, an account executive from Manchester; a VAT inspector from Tring, who hated the fact that he liked his work; a probation officer from Peebles, who hated the fact that he hated his work; a director of a finance company that specialized in pyramid selling; an unemployed careers officer, and a middle manager in a multi-national plastics concern. The work of Perrins began in earnest.

The five suburban houses in Oslo Avenue, Botchley, were alive with activity.

Reggie wandered proudly around, watching the guests at their various activities.

In the Art Room he admired the work of Diana Pilkington, who painted as Monet would have painted if he'd been totally

117

devoid of talent. The work of the VAT inspector from Tring was very different, however. He painted as Lowry would have painted if *he'd* been totally devoid of talent.

He listened with pleasure to the distortions of Gilbert and Sullivan that came from the Music Room.

'Keep it up,' he told the probation officer from Peebles. 'Any genius can sing like Tito Gobbi. It takes a real talent to persist when he sings like you.'

He attended group meetings, watched the progress of the thatching and went on expeditions with Jimmy. All the time he fought against a desire to take a more active part in things.

When he burst in unannounced upon Doc Morrissey, he fully intended to take a back seat.

Lying on the couch in the study of Number Nineteen was Bernard Trilling, Head of Comedy at Anaemia Television. Only the haunted expression in his eyes revealed the inner torment of the man.

Outside, the moisture hung from the trimmed privet hedge in the front garden, but the rain had stopped at last.

'Carry on,' said Reggie. 'My job is just to watch.'

'Let's try some simple word associations,' said Doc Morrissey. 'Mother.'

'Comedy,' said Bernard Trilling.

'Ah!' said Reggie.

'Please don't interrupt,' said Doc Morrissey. 'I want to go on and on, associating freely till we reach a totally uninhibited level of association. If we stop after each association, our future associations are affected by what we associate with the past associations.'

'I'm sorry,' said Reggie. 'I didn't mean to interrupt. It was just the way he came out with the mother/comedy association.'

'Yes, yes,' said Doc Morrissey impatiently. 'He resents his job and he resents his mother. Child's play.'

'I love my mother,' said Bernard Trilling.

118

'All right,' said Doc Morrissey. 'We may as well explore this area now. The thread's been broken.'

He glared at Reggie.

'Sorry,' said Reggie, moving his chair right back into a dark corner. 'Carry on. Behave as if I'm not here.'

'Why do you think you associated mother with comedy?' said Doc Morrissey.

Bernard Trilling was lying with his hands under his head. He glared at the ceiling.

'We're planning a situation comedy about a happy-go-lucky divorced mother who tries to bring up her three happy-go-lucky children by writing books,' he said gloomily. 'It's called "Mum's the Word".'

He turned his face to the wall and uttered a low groan.

'I started in documentaries,' he said. 'What went wrong?'

'Right. Let's start again,' said Doc Morrissey.

Reggie looked out of the window. A Harrods van drove past. He tried to let his mind go blank, in the hope that he would find some interesting associations with the Harrods van.

It reminded him of Harrods.

Perhaps I'm imaginatively under-nourished, he thought.

He forced himself to concentrate on the events that were going on in the little room. He didn't want to miss anything.

Gradually he became aware that there was nothing to miss.

Nothing was going on in the little room.

Bernard Trilling lay hunched up on the couch.

Doc Morrissey was staring intently into space.

'Sorry,' said Doc Morrissey. 'My mind's going a blank. It's you, Reggie. You're unsettling me.'

'Please,' said Reggie. 'Take no notice of me. I'm not here.'

'But you are,' said Doc Morrissey.

'Make yourself believe I'm not,' said Reggie. 'Mind over matter. It's all psychological.'

'I know,' said Doc Morrissey glumly. 'Right. Here we go.'

There was silence for fully a minute.

'It's the enormity of the choice that's inhibiting me,' said Doc Morrissey.

'I don't want to interfere,' said Reggie. 'But shall I suggest one or two things, just to get you over your blockage?'

'All right,' said Doc Morrissey. 'But once you've started, don't stop.'

'Right,' said Reggie. 'Here we go. Farmhouse.'

'Comedy,' said Bernard Trilling.

'Egg-cup,' said Reggie.

'Comedy,' said Bernard Trilling.

'It's pointless if you're just going to say "comedy" all the time,' said Reggie.

Bernard Trilling sat up.

'It's all I ever think of,' he said. 'Every news item, every chance remark in the pub, I think, "Could we make a comedy series about that?" I'm on a treadmill. The nation must be kept laughing. I need just one successful series, and I'd be laughing. Well no, I wouldn't. I've no sense of humour.'

'You must try and think of other things or Doc Morrissey can't help you,' said Reggie.

'I'll try,' promised Bernard Trilling.

'Right,' said Reggie. 'Here we go again. Or would you rather do it, Doc?'

Doc Morrissey shrugged resignedly.

'Right,' said Reggie. 'Taxidermy.'

'Comedy,' said Bernard Trilling.

'Oh Bernard!' said Reggie.

'We're planning a new comedy series about a happy-go-lucky taxidermist,' said Bernard Trilling. 'It's called "Get Stuffed".'

The W288, grinding along Oslo Avenue on its slow progress towards Spraundon, sounded very loud in the ensuing silence.

'It . . . er . . . it sounds an unlikely subject,' said Reggie.

'It's what we in the trade call the underwater rabbi syndrome,' said Bernard Trilling.

'Ah!' said Doc Morrissey, with a flash of his former spirit. 'You dislike Jews?'

'It just means that in our desperation we're hunting for ever more unlikely subjects,' said Bernard Trilling. 'The unlikeliest we can think of is an underwater rabbi.'

'It needn't have been a rabbi, though,' said Doc Morrissey. 'It could have been an underwater Methodist minister. The fact that it's a rabbi suggests prejudice, albeit unconscious. It's what we call a psycho-semitic illness.'

Doc Morrissey smiled triumphantly, then frowned, as if vaguely aware that he had got it wrong.

'I've got nothing against Jews,' said Bernard Trilling. 'Some of my best friends are Jews. My parents are Jews.'

He blushed furiously.

An extremely noisy lorry drove by, carrying a heavily laden skip.

'I was born Trillingstein,' admitted Bernard Trilling. 'I'm not ashamed of being Jewish. Very much the reverse. I just felt that if I was a big success people would ascribe it to my Jewishness. "Of course he's clever. He's a Jew." And I wanted them to say "Of course he's clever. He's Bernard Trilling." Some hope I should have that anyone should say I was clever.'

He smiled.

'I feel better already,' he said. 'I've kept that secret for fourteen years. And you've unlocked it. You're a wizard, Doc.'

'Me?' said Doc Morrissey. 'I did nothing.'

'Well it wasn't me,' said Reggie. 'I wasn't there.'

It was the same when he looked in on David Harris-Jones at the Sex Clinic, which was yet another garden shed, at Number Nineteen. Outside, it appeared to be an ordinary, rather tumbledown wooden shed. Inside, there was a carpet, a desk and hard chair, and three armchairs. The walls and ceiling had been painted in restful pastel shades as recommended in Weissburger and Dulux's *Colour and Emotional Response*.

Reggie moved his armchair back, out of the limelight.

David sat behind his desk.

Hilary Meadows, the housewife from Tenterden, sat in the armchair. She was in her mid-forties, her face crinkled but attractive, her sturdy legs crossed.

'Now, Hilary,' said David, 'as I was saying before Reggie . . . er . . .'

'Don't mind me,' said Reggie. 'I'm not here.'

'As I was saying there's no need to feel . . . er . . . er . . .'

'Nervous,' said Reggie.

'Yes,' said David Harris-Jones. 'That's what I was going to . . . er . . . but I'm a little . . . er . . .'

'Nervous,' said Reggie.

'Yes. Maybe if you didn't . . . er . . .'

'Interrupt.'

'Yes.'

'Sorry. I won't interrupt any more. It's just that you go so . . . how can I put it . . . er . . .'

'Infuriatingly slowly.'

'Yes.'

'I know. I just seem to sort of go to pieces when you're here, Reggie.'

'You'll have to get over that, David,' said Reggie, 'because I won't always be here to pick up the pieces.'

Hilary Meadows uncrossed her legs, and watched the two men with amusement.

'Carry on, David. I'll leave it all to you,' said Reggie.

David Harris-Jones fiddled with the papers on his desk.

'As I was saying, Hilary,' he said, 'there's no need to be nervous.'

'I'm not,' she said.

'I want you to feel completely . . . er . . . oh good, you're not. Super.'

He moved to the third armchair.

'No need to be formal,' he said. 'Now the subject I deal with, Hilary, is . . . er . . .'

'Sex,' said Hilary Meadows.

'Yes. As it were.'

As he talked, David Harris-Jones's eyes moved restlessly round his restful den.

'Lots of people . . . er . . .' he began. 'At times, anyway. After all, life's full of . . . well not problems exactly. Difficulties. And . . . er . . . there's nothing to be . . . er . . . I mean . . .'

'Oh for God's sake David,' said Reggie. 'What David is trying to say, Hilary, and we must remember that he had an unusually sheltered upbringing in Haverfordwest and its environs, what David is trying to say, in his nervous, roundabout way, and he's probably going about it in a roundabout way because he's nervous, after all you are only the second woman that he's ever . . . er . . . talked to in this way, what as I say he's trying to say is . . . well, I mean everybody at some time or other . . . in some degree or other . . . and there's no disgrace in that.'

'I have no sexual problems at all,' said Hilary Meadows.

'So if you . . . er . . . no se . . . se . . . oh good. Good.'

'Super.'

'My husband and I have it very happily at what I understand is roughly the national average.'

'Oh you do. Good. Good.'

'Super.'

Hilary Meadows crossed her legs.

'Well, that's got that off our chests,' said Reggie. 'That's got that out in the open.'

'Yes, but when we talk about . . . er . . . sex,' said David Harris-Jones, 'we don't just mean . . . er . . .'

'Sex,' said Hilary Meadows.

'Exactly. Modern . . . er . . . psychology, as you know . . . I mean the gist of it is that . . . er . . . sex, and our attitude towards it, rears its ug . . . let me put it another way. Much of our life is influenced by sex,' said David Harris-Jones.

'And much more of it isn't,' said Hilary Meadows. 'You poor unimaginative creatures. You can't imagine any problems except sexual ones. Let me tell you why I'm here. Because I'm bored out of my not so tiny mind. I'm bored with having my cooking taken for granted, not being listened to by my husband, not being helped and thanked by my children. Bored with not going out to work. Bored with cleaning the house so that the cleaning woman won't leave. Bored with slow check-out girls at unimaginative supermarkets and time-killing conversations at coffee mornings and playing golf with other women with thick calves and thin white elderly legs and garish ankle socks. Bored, bored, bored.'

'Splendid,' said Reggie. 'Well, I think we can help you there.'

'I don't need help,' said Hilary Meadows. 'I've only come here for a change. I couldn't go to the Bahamas or my family wouldn't feel guilty. You poor men. You look so disappointed. No nice cure to do. No little toys to play with.'

'Well, I'll leave you two to it,' said Reggie. 'You're doing absolutely splendidly, David.'

Next day there was watery sunshine at last. Very slowly, the sodden gardens began to dry out.

At the long, crowded breakfast table, Reggie told C.J. that he'd like to see how his work on people's attitude to their work was progressing.

'Excellent,' said C.J. through a mouthful of McBlane's rich, creamy scrambled egg. 'We've got a pretty little role-playing session lined up for this morning. Arthur Noblet is applying to Thruxton Appleby for increased fringe benefits at the Hardcastle Handbag Company.'

'Excellent,' said Reggie. 'I'll just sit and watch.'

'You have to play a role too,' said C.J. 'According to Doc Morrissey, everyone has to play a role.'

'It's against my policy,' said Reggie. 'I don't like to trespass on my staff's preserves.'

'Talking about trespassing on the staff's preserves, could I have the marmalade?' said the insurance salesman who had lost his motivation.

Reggie passed him the marmalade.

'You can be holding a watching brief for the industrial relations research council, Reggie,' said C.J.

'Wonderful,' said Reggie. 'What role will you be playing?'

'I'll be Thruxton Appleby's secretary,' said C.J.

Tony Webster choked in mid-toast.

'What'll I be called?' said Reggie.

'Perrin,' said C.J. 'I stick to the facts as far as possible.'

'What'll you be called then?' said Reggie.

C.J. glanced at Tony.

'Cynthia Jones,' he said.

Tony spluttered again.

'There's nothing ludicrous about it,' said C.J. 'It's a valuable exercise. But I couldn't expect you to see that. You know what they say. Small minds make idle chatter. How people change. It's hard to believe that you were once my golden boy at Sunshine Desserts.'

After breakfast they walked along Oslo Avenue in the pale sunshine.

At the gate of Number Seventeen, Reggie stopped.

'I don't want to interfere,' he said. 'But wouldn't this be a more valuable exercise if Arthur Noblet played the boss and Thruxton Appleby played the worker.'

'How come?' said C.J.

'Well,' said Reggie. 'They might learn something about the them and us situation which bedevils British industrial relations so tragically.'

'I didn't get where I am today by learning about the them and us situation which bedevils British industrial relations so tragically.'

'You certainly didn't, C.J. Maybe it's about time you did. But, as I say, it's entirely up to you.'

'Yes.'

'It might be more fun my way, though.'

'You have a point, Reggie.'

They entered Number Seventeen and went into the sun room extension which now formed C.J.'s office.

The room, built for suburban relaxation, was filled with office furniture. There were three desks, two typewriters, six chairs, green filing cabinets, two waste-paper baskets, and a hat-stand.

The watery sun streamed in.

Thruxton Appleby and Arthur Noblet were waiting. C.J. explained the revised scenario.

C.J. settled himself behind his typewriter and the other three went into the back garden.

Reggie knocked.

'Come in,' said C.J. in a mincing, psuedo-female voice.

Reggie entered.

'Can I help you?' minced C.J.

Reggie laughed.

'Reggie!' said C.J. 'This is an important social experiment, and all you can do is laugh. Immerse yourself in your role as I do. I become Cynthia Jones. C.J. is dead, long live Cynthia Jones. Now get out and come in.'

'Sorry, C.J.'

Reggie went back into the garden.

He re-entered the sun room.

'I meant, "Sorry, Cynthia",' he said. 'Sorry, C.J.'

'Get out.'

Reggie went out and knocked on the door.

'Come in,' said C.J.

Reggie came in.

'Mr Noblet's office,' minced C.J. 'Can I help you?'

'The name's Perrin,' said Reggie. 'Industrial relations research council.'

'Ah, yes. Welcome to Hardcastle Handbags, Mr Perrin. Mr Noblet'll be in in a jiffy.'

There was a knock.

'Come in,' said C.J.

Arthur Noblet entered.

'No, no,' said Reggie. 'It's your office. No need to knock.'

'Sorry,' said Arthur Noblet.

'Sorry, I didn't mean to butt in,' said Reggie. 'But now that I have, may I make a point?'

'Go ahead,' said C.J.

'Come in with a bit of authority,' said Reggie. 'Make some remark about your journey. "Twelve minutes late. Traffic lights out of order at Hanger Lane." That sort of thing.'

'Excellent,' said C.J. 'First-class remark. Take an umbrella.'

Arthur Noblet took an umbrella.

'Go out and come in,' said C.J.

Arthur Noblet went into the garden, where Thruxton Appleby was examining the veins on a rose leaf.

He re-entered the sun room.

'Twelve minutes late,' he said, hanging his umbrella on the hat-stand. 'Traffic lights out of action at Hanger Lane.'

'This is Mr Perrin, Mr Noblet,' minced C.J. 'He's from the industrial relations research council.'

'I'm holding a watching brief,' said Reggie.

'Ready for dictation,' minced C.J., hitching up his trousers and crossing his legs.

There was a knock. Nobody answered.

'Oh, that'll be for me. It's my bleeding office,' said Arthur Noblet. 'Come in.'

Thruxton Appleby entered with massive authority.

'We want more fringe benefits, Noblet,' he thundered.

'OK. You deserve them,' said Arthur Noblet.

'No, no, no!' said Reggie. 'Pathetic! Abysmal! Appleby, you wouldn't enter your office with massive authority if you were about to be interviewed by you. And Noblet, you mustn't give in like that. You must get inside each other's roles. Take your example from C.J., the Deborah Kerr of Botchley.'

C.J. waved the compliment aside modestly.

'Right,' said Reggie. 'We'll take it from Noblet's entrance.'

Arthur Noblet and Thruxton Appleby went out into the sun-filled garden, where they could be seen arguing about their roles.

'Nice morning, Miss Jones,' said Reggie.

'Very nice,' said C.J., crossing his legs.

'Have you planned your holiday yet, Miss Jones?' said Reggie.

'Well no, I haven't had time to draw breath yet, truth to tell, what with moving flats and my boy friend's promotion and that. I'm in a right tiswas,' said C.J.

Arthur Noblet burst into the sun room.

'Morning, Miss Jones,' he said, hanging his umbrella on the hat-stand. 'Sixteen minutes late. Jack-knifed juggernaut at Neasden. Have you typed the letter to Amalgamated Wallets?'

'I'm just doing it, Mr Noblet,' said C.J. 'This is Mr Perrin, of the industrial relations research council.'

'I'm extremely grateful to you, Mr Noblet,' said Reggie, 'both on behalf of myself and everyone at Research House, for letting me witness your arbitration procedures at ground roots level.'

'Don't mention it,' said Arthur Noblet.

There was a knock.

'Come!' roared C.J.

'No, no, no,' said Reggie.

Thruxton Appleby entered.

'Sorry,' said C.J. 'My fault that time. A case of the pot calling the kettle a silver lining, I'm afraid. Let's take it from Appleby's entrance. Appleby, go out and come in again.'

The massive textiles tycoon left the room meekly.

Almost immediately he knocked.

'Enter,' said Arthur Noblet, with a shy smile at his powers of verbal invention.

Thruxton Appleby entered. His demeanour was cowed, yet implicitly insolent.

128

'Sit down, Appleby,' said Arthur Noblet. 'This is Mr Perrin, of . . . er . . .'

'IRRC,' said Reggie. 'I'm holding a watching brief.'

'Now, what's this little spot of bovver, Appleby?' said Arthur Noblet.

'The chaps on the floor want more fringe benefits,' said Thruxton Appleby. 'Silly of them, the lazy good-for-nothings, but there it is.'

'What do you mean, silly of them?' said Arthur Noblet. 'How you blokes are expected to make ends meet when berks like me cop for twenty thousand a year defeats me.'

'No, no, no,' said Regie. 'Useless. Oh, sorry, C.J. I didn't mean to get involved. Oh well, I've started now. Appleby, you really believe you deserve the fringe benefits. Noblet, you seriously believe you can't afford them. But you say the rest, C.J. This is your show.'

'Thank you, Reggie,' said C.J. through clenched teeth. 'Right, we'll take it from Appleby's entrance. We'll take your knock as read, Appleby.'

'I'd rather knock, if you don't mind,' said the burly West Riding chrome-dome.

'OK, bloody well knock, then, but just get on with it,' snapped C.J.

Thruxton Appleby knocked, Arthur Noblet yelled 'Come!', Thruxton Appleby came, C.J. simpered flirtatiously at the typewriter, Reggie was introduced, and the negotiations began.

'The lads are a bit cheesed off,' said Thruxton Appleby. 'I know times have been hard, with the fluctuating of the yen, and we've had to announce a reduced dividend of seven and a half per cent, but the lads would like improved fringe benefits.'

'What kind of improved fringe benefits?' said Arthur Noblet.

Thruxton Appleby thought hard. He'd never taken much interest in workers' fringe benefits.

'Five weeks' holiday, automatic membership of the golf club, free investment advice, company cars, and increased share holding, and an improved dividend,' he said.

'Piss off,' said Arthur Noblet.

'No, no, no,' said Reggie. 'No, no, no, no, no. Mind you, that was better. I won't say another word, C.J. This is your show.'

'Well . . .' said C.J.

'Just an idea,' said Reggie. 'Supposing you and I demonstrate our idea of negotiation techniques?'

'Would that really have much value?' said C.J.

'With you as the powerful boss and me as the downtrodden worker,' said Reggie.

'It might be worth a try, I suppose,' said C.J. 'Hang it on the clothes line, see if the cat licks it up.'

And so Arthur Noblet became Cynthia Jones, Thruxton Appleby became the man from the Research House, Reggie became the workman, and C.J. became C.J.

Arthur Noblet installed himself behind the typewriter, while the others went into the garden.

Arthur mimed a last glance at the mirror, Thruxton Appleby entered and was introduced, C.J. entered, hurled his umbrella at the hat-stand, missed, said, 'Twenty-two minutes late. Failure of de-icing equipment at Coulsdon,' and sat down, and Reggie knocked, was invited to enter, and did so.

'Now then, Perrin, what's the trouble?' said C.J.

'It's like this, guvnor,' said Reggie sitting down facing C.J. 'We're falling be'ind as regards differentials and that.'

'Who's falling behind as regards differentials?'

'Everybody.'

C.J. looked pained.

'Everyone can't fall behind as regards differentials,' he said.

'No, what I mean is,' said Reggie, 'we're falling behind vis-à-vis workers in strictly comparable industries, i.e. purses, brief-cases, and real and simulated leather goods generally, like.'

'You had a rise eight months ago, in accordance with phase three of stage eight,' said C.J. 'Or was it phase eight of stage three? Anyway, there's a world-wide handbag slump. Do you expect me to run at a loss?'

'Course not, guv,' said Reggie. 'Stone the crows, no. You're in it for the lolly, same as what we all are. You're forced to be. Forced to be. Course you are. You're forced to be forced to be. Course you are. We aren't arguing about the basic wage. Basically the basic wage is basically fair. It's the fringe benefits, innit?'

'What sort of fringe benefits?' said C.J.

'Areas where I could suggest amelioration of traditional benefits would include five weeks' 'oliday a year, rationalized shift bonuses, increased production incentives, longer tea breaks, coffee breaks brought up to the tea break level, a concessionary handbag for every year of service, and fifteen minutes unpenalized latitude for lateness due to previously notified genuine unforeseen circumstances.'

'I see,' said C.J. 'Well, Perrin, I might see my way to recommending the board to give a day's extra holiday and a seasonal shift bonus adjustment, and we might be able to work something out on incentives, and then report back to you.'

'Well,' said Reggie, 'I can put that to my members, and see if we can draft a resolution that the negotiations committee might be prepared to put to the steering committee, but I have a feeling my members will want something on the table now.'

'I'm afraid that may not be possible,' said C.J.

'We just want a fair share of the cake,' said Reggie.

'Ah, but can you have your fair share of the cake and eat it?' said C.J.

'We want deeds, not words,' said Reggie. 'Otherwise we're coming out.'

'I will not yield to threats motivated by political scum,' said C.J.

'I don't think my members will appreciate that nomenclature,' said Reggie.

'It's what they are, isn't it?' shouted C.J. 'Marxist scum. Reds under the handbags. I will flush them out.'

'Right. It's all out then,' said Reggie quietly.

'You're all sacked,' said C.J.

'You bastard!' said Reggie.

There was a moment's silence.

'Yes, well, you get the general idea,' said Reggie. 'Seeing the other person's point of view, that's what it's all about.'

That evening Reggie and Elizabeth went to the George and Two Dragons after dinner. Several other members of the community were in evidence, both staff and guests. C.J. was drinking with Thruxton Appleby. Reggie was delighted when Arthur Noblet joined them. Tony Webster was chatting up Hilary Meadows, and getting nowhere expensively. The middle manager was talking to Mr Pelham. Subjects discussed included porkers and other kinds of pigs. McBlane popped in for a few minutes. He was on dry gingers as he'd found that alcohol played havoc with his psoriasis.

'I've just realized what's missing,' Reggie told Elizabeth. 'All these people shouldn't be down the pub every night. A community should have social evenings.'

Two days later, at the group meeting, Reggie made an announcement.

'Every evening, after dinner,' he said, 'there will be a social gathering. These gatherings will be totally voluntary. Obviously I hope everyone will attend, but there's no obligation.'

That evening, Reggie and Elizabeth sat in the living-room of Number Twenty-one, waiting.

Nobody came.

At the next group meeting, Reggie spoke to them all again.

'I can't see how any guest who intends to get full value

from the community wouldn't come to some at least of these gatherings, and I'd be very disappointed if members of staff didn't set an example by frequent attendance,' he said. 'Though of course I will emphasize once again that it is entirely voluntary.'

'You, you and you,' said Jimmy.

Reggie gave him a cool look.

'Sorry,' said Jimmy. 'Slipped out. Army volunteering. You, you and you. Wasn't suggesting that here. No need. Stampede.'

'You didn't exactly stampede last time,' said Reggie.

'Prior engagement,' said Jimmy. 'Wedding plans. All invited. Refusal *de rigueur*.'

'*De rigueur* means essential,' said Reggie.

'Exactly,' said Jimmy. 'Essential, all present, church parade, twenty-first December. Hope all be on parade tonight too. As I will, living-room, twenty-thirty hours, delights social various for the enjoyment of.'

Jimmy was as good as his word. In fact he was the first to arrive that evening.

Others swiftly followed. Soon the living-room was packed. Every available seat was occupied, and latecomers had to find a place on the floor.

The smokeless fuel glowed in the grate. The curtains were drawn on the cold October night.

Present were Reggie, Elizabeth, C.J., Doc Morrissey, Jimmy, Tom, Linda, Joan, David, Prue, Thruxton Appleby, Mr Pelham, the insurance agent who had lost his motivation, Diana Pilkington, Hilary Meadows, the VAT inspector from Tring, the probation officer from Peebles, the unemployed careers officer, the director of the finance company, and the middle manager.

Absent were Tony (down the George and Two Dragons), Arthur Noblet (down the Botchley Arms), and Bernard Trilling (watching TV).

The evening began stickily, but slowly began to develop its

style. They shared cigarettes, passing them round after each puff.

'This is just as much fun as smoking pot,' said Reggie.

'I didn't get where I am today by smoking pot,' said C.J., who was sitting on the rug in front of the fire.

When the conversation flagged, Reggie asked if anybody had seen anything beautiful during the day.

'The sunset was beautiful,' volunteered Hilary Meadows.

'Yes, it was. I really noticed it,' said the unemployed careers officer. 'Too often I close my eyes to beautiful things like the sunsets.'

'We all do,' said Diana Pilkington from the settee. Her legs were crossed, revealing an expanse of slender, rather glacial thigh.

'I saw an old tramp in the High Street, and he picked up this sodden fag end and smoked it,' said Linda.

'I can't see anything beautiful in a sodden fag end,' said the insurance salesman who had lost his motivation.

'It was beautiful for the tramp,' said Tom. 'That's Linda's point.'

His eyes met Linda's and he smiled.

'It was a very beautiful thing, Linda darling,' he said, 'because it shows your understanding of people. I've said it before and I'll say it again. We're people people.'

Elizabeth, seated on the settee, put her hand on Reggie's shoulder. He stroked her leg. It made them happy to see Tom and Linda so happy.

'I'm still on the side of the sunset,' said Diana Pilkington.

'I'd like to talk to you about your social drives tomorrow, Di,' said Doc Morrissey, who was sitting between Elizabeth and Diana Pilkington on the settee.

'Any more beautiful experiences?' said Reggie.

'I saw a really beautiful missel thrush,' said the VAT inspector from Tring.

'Super,' chorused David and Prue Harris-Jones.

'It was eating a worm,' added the VAT inspector from Tring.

134

'Oh,' said David and Prue Harris-Jones.

'You wouldn't think it was beautiful if you were a worm,' said the middle manager in the multi-national plastics concern.

'I'm not a worm,' said the VAT inspector from Tring.

'Matter of opinion,' said Jimmy. 'Just joking,' he added hastily.

He looked round to see if Linda approved of his sally. She smiled at him, and mouthed the single word 'Lettuce'. He nodded, his nod saying 'Oh, quite. Engaged. Eyes for one woman only. Looked at you out of affection. Favourite niece, that sort of crack. Other thing, past history, water under bridge. Self-abuse, ditto. New man. New leaf.'

'I saw a beautiful thing,' said David Harris-Jones. 'Well, perhaps it wasn't all that beautiful.'

'Tell us,' said Reggie. 'Let us decide.'

'I saw the driver of the W288 pull up between two stops to let an elderly woman on,' said David Harris-Jones.

'Yes, that is beautiful,' said the probation officer from Peebles.

'It's a miracle,' said Reggie.

'I wish you'd told me about the bus driver,' said Prue.

'Why?' said David.

'It's interesting,' said Prue.

'It isn't that interesting,' said David.

'It's interesting because you saw it, darling,' said Prue.

Elizabeth waited for Reggie to explode. He beamed.

'Any other beautiful sights?' he said.

'Yes. I saw Tony's private parts,' said Joan.

'Come, come,' said C.J. 'Really!'

'They're beautiful,' said Joan.

'Yes, they are,' said Reggie. 'I mean I assume they are. I haven't seen them myself. But I mean surely if Joan thinks they're beautiful she should be able to say so. And surely the human body is beautiful?'

'I don't think so,' said Diana Pilkington.

'I think we might touch on that tomorrow, too, Di,' said Doc Morrissey.

C.J. shifted uncomfortably on the floor.

'Sorry,' he said. 'Not used to squatting on floors. Neither Mrs. C.J. nor I has ever been used to squatting on floors.'

'Give C.J. your seat, Tom,' said Linda.

'I'm not a sitting on floors person either,' said Tom.

'Now's the time to start, then,' said Reggie.

'You're right,' said Tom. 'I've got to become less rigid in my attitudes.'

Tom snuggled up against Linda on the floor, and C.J. took the armchair he had vacated.

More beautiful experiences were related. More cigarettes were shared. The probation officer shyly produced a guitar. Joan sang a protest song. Mr Pelham sang a pig song. Thruxton Appleby sang a textiles song. The insurance salesman sang an insurance song. The middle manager tore up a fiver and threw it on the fire. They examined his motives. Linda kissed Tom. Not to be outdone, Prue kissed David.

'Touch,' said Doc Morrissey suddenly.

Everyone looked at him in astonishment.

'We should touch each other,' he said. 'We should make physical contact. It's the outward expression of inward togetherness.'

He put his hand on Diana Pilkington's knee.

'Touching is good,' he said.

He slid his hand along her leg.

'Feeling is beautiful,' he said.

He pushed his hand right up inside her skirt, between her thighs.

She gave his arm a karate chop that numbed it completely.

'Smacking is good,' she said.

Doc Morrissey held his injured arm tenderly.

'Twelve karate lessons in Chorlton-cum-Hardy are beautiful,' said Diana Pilkington.

'I was only giving the outward expression of inward togetherness,' said Doc Morrissey. 'I only touched you because I was sitting next to you. I'd have done the same thing if I'd been sitting next to Reggie.'

'Thank God you weren't,' said Reggie.

'No, but touching each other is beautiful,' said David and Prue Harris-Jones, entwining their fingers with intense tenderness.

Reggie walked up to the VAT inspector from Tring, and put his hand in his.

'Foreign countries do it all the time,' he said. 'It's natural. You don't mind, do you, Mr VAT inspector from Tring?'

'Not at all,' said the VAT inspector from Tring. 'I rather like it.'

'Oh,' said Reggie.

He removed his hand.

'Not in that way,' said the VAT inspector from Tring. 'Just as friendliness.'

'Ah!' said Reggie.

He clasped the hand of the VAT inspector from Tring once more.

'Come on. Everybody touch everybody,' he said.

'I didn't get where I am today by touching everybody,' said C.J.

'I'm game,' proffered the probation officer from Peebles.

'Me too,' put in the unemployed careers officer.

'So am I,' agreed Tom. 'It's about time I broke the barriers of habit that have enslaved me.'

Everyone began to wander round the room, touching each other. At first there were a few giggles. Somebody said, 'We're groping towards success,' and there was laughter.

Soon, however, the giggles and laughter died down, and there was only the quiet, rather solemn ritual of touching.

The middle manager kissed the director of the finance company. Tom kissed Reggie. His beard tickled. All over the room people held hands, kissed, touched, regardless of age, sex and occupation.

'It's the new Jerusalem,' said Doc Morrissey.

Arthur Noblet entered, slightly unsteady after his evening at the Botchley Arms, took one look at the New Jerusalem, said 'Bloody Hell,' and lurched out.

'It went off very well,' said Elizabeth that night in bed.

'Too well,' said Reggie.

Elizabeth kissed the lobe of his hear. Her face wore a charming admixture of affection, amusement and exasperation.

'Will you never be content?' she said.

'Seriously, darling,' said Reggie. 'We're getting a bit of a problem. Nobody's leaving. That means nobody's giving us any money.'

The following day an incident occurred which delayed the likely departure of Thruxton Appleby, the wealthiest of Reggie's guests.

Reggie was accompanying Jimmy on one of his expeditions. A small group stood on the front porch of Number Twenty-one, in the pale golden sunlight, and Jimmy briefed them.

'Object of exercise,' he said, 'Litter clearance. Done some major work already. Cleared Threadwell's Pond, flushed out old bedsteads in Mappin Woods. Today, mopping-up operations, isolated pockets of litter throughout borough. Place your litter in the king bin liners provided.'

They moved off down Oslo Avenue, their king bin liners in their hands, and turned left into Bonn Close, where Mr Pelham dealt summarily with a 'Seven-up' tin.

When they turned left into Addis Ababa Avenue, Reggie saw the unmistakable domed head of Thruxton Appleby in the phone box at the junction with Canberra Rise.

'Walk back the other way,' he said. And Jimmy led his

team back down Bonn Close with the instinctive obedience of a military man.

Reggie tackled Thruxton Appleby, who admitted that he had been phoning his office and tearing them off a strip.

'You're the sort of person who pays a fortune to a health farm and then sneaks out to gorge himself on cream cakes,' said Reggie.

'You don't understand. Bilton's cocked up the forward orders,' said Thruxton Appleby.

'How many phone calls have you made?' said Reggie.

'Three,' said Thruxton Appleby. 'I just can't trust them a minute.'

A vein was throbbing ominously around his temple. Reggie thought of all Thruxton Appleby's money and sighed.

'One more phone call and you leave,' he said.

'If I promise not to make any more calls . . .?'

'You can stay.'

'I promise,' said Thruxton Appleby.

He glanced at his watch.

'They're open,' he said. 'Do you fancy a drink?'

They walked down Nairobi Drive to the High Street, and entered the saloon bar of the George and Two Dragons. Thruxton Appleby stood back politely to let Reggie get to the bar and his wallet first. They were the first customers. Hoovering was in progress, and there was a strong smell of furniture polish. The old dragon served them.

'What are you having?' said Reggie.

'Whisky and soda,' said Thruxton Appleby.

Reggie ordered a whisky and soda and a pint of bitter.

'No, by God, I'll have a beer too,' said Thruxton Appleby. 'And I'm paying.'

They sat in a window alcove.

'I'm getting almost likeable, aren't I?' said Thruxton Appleby.

'You're on the verge, Thruxton.'

'I might have done it by now if it hadn't been for those phone calls.'

'They've set you back, I'll not deny it.'

'We've got a word for people like me, where I come from,' said Thruxton Appleby. 'Am I to tell you what it is?'

'Please.'

'Thrifty. Canny. Cautious. In a word, mean as arseholes. But when I leave, Mr Perrin, I'm not going to be mean. I'll give you a goodly whack.'

'Well, thank you,' said Reggie. 'Cheers.'

'I'll be staying quite a while yet, though.'

'Oh. Well . . . good . . . splendid.'

'You'll have to take my generosity on trust.'

'Yes . . . well . . . splendid.'

'I might stay for ever, you never know.'

'Huh huh. Huh huh huh. Splendid.'

That Friday afternoon, however, the departures began at last. The first to call in at Reggie's study in Number Twenty-three was Mr Pelham. He entered shyly.

'Afternoon, Reg,' he said. 'May I sit down?'

'Of course,' said Reggie.

Mr Pelham's inquiry had not been an academic one. Informed that he might sit, he did so.

'I've come to the end of the road, old son,' he said.

Reggie's heart began to beat faster than he would have wished.

'Is this an admission of success or defeat?' he asked.

If he'd hoped for a simple answer, he didn't get it.

'Who knows?' said Mr Pelham. 'I came here, with blood on my hands, hoping for a miracle. What have I learnt? I'm a bloody awful painter, I can't thatch for toffee, and I sing like a pregnant yak.'

'Oh dear.'

'Sex clinic? Damp squib. My sex life finished years ago, old son. Analysis? My subconscious is as dull as my conscious.'

140

'Oh dear, oh dear.'

Mr Pelham looked out at the passing W288 to Spraundon much as a docker might watch the luxury liner whose hawsers he had handled slipping away to glamorous foreign parts.

'This is dreadful,' said Reggie.

'Don't get me wrong, Reg,' said Mr Pelham. 'I've enjoyed myself. Good food, new people. I haven't said much, but I've soaked it all up. I expected I don't know what. I know now that there isn't any don't know what. There's only what there is, old son. And I know now who I am.'

'Er . . . who are you?'

'I'm the meat man. When I go in the pub, the landlord says "Morning, meat man". When I meet the assistant bank manager in the street, he says, "And what sort of a weekend did the meat man have?" That's who I am, Reg. Not Leonardo da Vinci. Not Kim Novak. Not a tramp. Not the Headmistress of Roedean. The manager of the Abbey National Building Society doesn't say, "Hello, Mr P, can I enter our Sandra for your school?" The milkman doesn't say, "Saw the old Mona Lisa last week. Nice one, Leonardo. Stick at it." And so, I build up a dossier of my identity. I'm the meat man.'

'I don't know what to say,' said Reggie.

Mr Pelham got out his cheque book.

'I've been thinking while I've been here, Reg,' he said. 'And that's good. I'm returning to my chosen career which I do well. If the world wants my meat, they can have it. I'm not happy and I'm not miserable. You haven't succeeded and you haven't failed. I'm giving you a cheque for five hundred pounds.'

'Well, I . . . er . . .' began Reggie.

'You aren't going to turn it down, are you?' said Mr Pelham.

'No, actually I'm not,' said Reggie.

They shook hands.

'Good-bye, old son,' said Mr Pelham.

'Good-bye, Mr P,' said Reggie. 'And Mr P?'

Mr Pelham turned to face Reggie.

'Yeah?'

'Give my love to the pigs.'

The next person to call in at the drab, dark study was the insurance salesman who had lost his motivation.

'I'm very grateful. I'd give you more if I was richer,' he said, handing Reggie two hundred pounds in cash.

Reggie unlocked a drawer in his desk, put the bundles of notes in, and locked the drawer.

'You've done wonders for me,' said the insurance salesman who had lost his motivation.

'You realize that it doesn't matter that you've lost your motivation,' said Reggie. 'Splendid.'

'No, no. Much better than that. I've found my motivation again.'

'Oh. Well that really wasn't what I . . .'

'Large amounts of cash lying in drawers all weekend. Have you thought of increasing your protection against burglary?' said the insurance salesman who had found his motivation again.

The mellow weather continued. Arrivals outpaced departures, and the advance booking charts were dotted with names.

McBlane discovered that dry ginger inflamed his dermatitis and reverted to Newcastle Brown. The food remained as delicious as ever.

The social evenings became a permanent and valued feature of life.

One day, Tom announced that he had developed a new concept in sporting non-competition.

'Solo ball games,' he explained. 'You play squash and tennis on your own.'

Squash on one's own proved tolerable, though tiring. Solo

tennis was much less enthusiastically received. Frequent changes of end were necessary to retrieve the balls.

When this complaint was voiced, Tom solved it almost immediately.

'A load of balls,' he told the group meeting excitedly.

But even with an adequate supply of balls, the drawbacks of solo tennis proved too great. Each rally consisted of only one stroke. It was a service-dominated sport, and when the weather broke it was abandoned without regret.

Hilary Meadows returned home to the bosom of a family who would no longer take her for granted.

'My husband'll send you a cheque,' she told Reggie. 'I'll tell him to send whatever he thinks my happiness and sanity are worth. You'll get more that way. I hope.'

Reggie came across Bernard Trilling, Head of Comedy at Anaemia Television, putting the finishing touches to a splendid basket that he had woven.

'So, I've woven a basket already,' he said, no longer hiding his Jewishness under a bushel. 'If I could weave a television series, I'd be all right maybe.'

And he laughed.

'My wife's often said that she could knit funnier series than some you put on,' said Reggie.

'I know,' said Bernard Trilling. 'Some of our comedy series are a joke.'

He laughed again.

'Is this hysteria, I ask myself,' he said. 'I'd better leave before I answer.'

He gave Reggie a cheque for five hundred pounds, and two tickets for the pilot show of 'Mum's the Word'.

On the last day of October, Thruxton Appleby discharged himself reluctantly. He still appeared far too large for the little

143

chair in Reggie's office, but this time his vast buttocks seemed gentle, apologetic giants.

Two blue tits flitted without fear from branch to branch on the bush outside the window.

The rain poured down. The brief summer was over.

'This is the moment of truth,' said Thruxton Appleby, getting his cheque book out slowly. 'Now, how much?'

'It's up to you,' said Reggie.

'Well,' said Thruxton Appleby, 'you've certainly succeeded. I'm likeable, aren't I?'

'Thoroughly likeable.'

'Lovable?'

'Perhaps not lovable yet. On the way, though. And the more you can get over your natural meanness and learn the pleasures of generosity, the quicker you'll be lovable.'

'So I ought to give you a fat sum?'

'For your own sake,' said Reggie, 'I think you should.'

Thruxton Appleby roared with laughter.

'I like your bare-faced cheek,' he said. 'I admire bare-faced cheek.'

And he made out a cheque for a thousand pounds.

'It's worth every penny,' he said. 'I'm a new man. All I've thought about for years is money and business. Money and business.'

Reggie slipped the cheque into the safe that had been installed the previous day.

'Please don't start worrying that it's too much,' said Thruxton Appleby. 'It's tax deductible.'

That night, the wind rattled the double-glazed windows of the surprisingly spacious master bedroom in Number Twenty-one. Reggie sighed. Once more Elizabeth put her book down and gave her husband a searching look over the top of her glasses.

'Still not fully content, darling?' she asked.

'Oh yes,' said Reggie. 'The money's pouring in. Cures are

144

being made. New people are arriving. I really am fully content at last.'

He sighed.

'Then why are you sighing?' said Elizabeth.

'Contentment worries me,' said Reggie.

November took a dismal grip on Great Britain. Fierce winds destroyed three seaside piers, twelve scout huts, and the thatched roof of the garden shed at Number Twenty-one, Oslo Avenue, Botchley. For four days pantechnicons were unable to cross the Severn Bridge. Fieldfares and redwings reached Norfolk from Scandinavia in record numbers, to collapse exhausted on cold, sodden meadows and wonder why they had bothered. A survey showed that Britain had sunk to fifteenth place in the world nutmeg consumption league, behind Bali and Portugal. There were strikes by petrol tanker drivers, draymen at four breweries, and dustmen from eight counties. Twelve-year-old girls were found to be offering themselves to old men for money behind a comprehensive school in Nottinghamshire. Seven hundred and twenty-nine hamsters arrrived dead at Stansted Airport from Cyprus, and a Rumanian tourist died after being caught between rival gangs of Chelsea and Leeds fans in West London.

But at Numbers Seventeen to Twenty-five, Oslo Avenue, Botchley, things were far from gloomy. Guests were arriving in steadily increasing numbers. The majority of guests who departed were in expansive mood and gave generously. The engagement between Jimmy and Lettuce was proceeding placidly. The marriages of Reggie and Elizabeth, David and Prue, and Tom and Linda were going smoothly. Young Reggie Harris-Jones was proving a model child, and the behaviour of Adam and Jocasta had improved beyond the expectations of the most sanguine idealist.

Not everything was perfect, of course. The first of Tom's sloe gin and raspberry whisky was ready for drinking, and the behaviour of Tony Webster still gave cause for concern.

One day, Reggie called unexpectedly at the Culture Room, in the garden shed of Number Twenty-five. The dreary, functional garden was dank and lifeless in the raw November mist. The notice 'Culture Room: Prop T. Webster, QCI' still adorned the yellow door.

There was a delay before Tony opened the door.

His hair was tousled.

He led Reggie into the Culture Room. The naked breasts had been removed, and the walls were bare.

Diana Pilkington sat on one of the armchairs.

Her face was flushed.'We've been rehearsing *Romeo and Juliet*, Act Two, Scene Two,' said Tony.

And indeed, two copies of French's Acting Edition lay open on the floor.

'Excellent,' said Reggie.

'I know what you're thinking,' said Tony.

'I wasn't thinking anything of the kind,' said Reggie.

'I haven't told you what I know you're thinking,' said Tony.

'I know what you think I'm thinking,' said Reggie.

'Touché Town, Arizona,' said Tony.

Reggie flinched, and Diana Pilkington smiled, revealing small white teeth.

'I know,' she said. 'Doesn't he use *the* most dreadful phrases? You'd have thought a bit of Shakespeare would have rubbed off on him by now. No such luck.'

'Come on, Di,' said Tony. 'Let's really hit Capulet's Garden.'

And indeed they did give a spirited rendition.

'Well done, Di,' said Tony when they had finished. 'You're beginning to let it all hang out.'

That evening Reggie went to the George and Two Dragons in search of Tony. He found him chatting up the buxom barmaid, under the jealous glare of the young dragon. It was George's night off.

Tony brought Reggie a drink.

'I know what you're thinking,' he said, when they were settled in the corner beyond the food counter. 'And you're right. Di's a frigid lady, Reggie. She's got this computer programmer from Alderley Edge sniffing around her, and I'm just warming her up. It's a hell of a bore, but you've got to take your responsibilities to the community seriously, haven't you?'

'It's Joan I'm thinking of, Tony,' said Reggie.

'It's Joany's idea,' said Tony.

'What?'

'I'm a changed man, Reggie. I have a wonderful wife. Extramarital activity is Outsville, Arizona, with a capital O. Joany trusts me. So, I'm the obvious man to warm up our cold career lady. No sweat.'

The young dragon cleared their table noisily and wiped it with a smelly rag.

'You never come to our communal evenings,' said Reggie. 'You're never with Joan.'

'Each in his own way, Reggie. Faith and trust. I'd have left Di to Tom or David, but they couldn't warm up a plate of custard. And I tell you what, Reggie. It'll be dynamite when it's warmed up. Its computer programmer won't know what's hit him.'

Four under-age drinkers from the fifth-form debating society of Botchley Hill Comprehensive entered the bar. The young dragon listened to their order. Then, because it wasn't expensive enough to be worth the risk, she refused to serve them.

'May I venture a brief word of criticism of your linguistic habits, Tony?' said Reggie.

'Sure,' said Tony. 'Feel free. Shoot.'

'Doc Morrissey would no doubt suggest that you're compensating for the ageing process which you refuse to admit by larding your language increasingly with what you take to be the argot of the young,' said Reggie.

'I know what you mean,' said Tony. 'And I think you'll see a dramatic improvement pretty soon.'

'Oh good. That is encouraging. Any particular reason?'

'Yeah. OK, I made out I was into culture, but I wasn't. I'm really into it now, Reggie. Know what changed my attitude?'

'No,' confessed Reggie.

'Shakespeare. He's a real laid-back bard.'

Soon there were only forty-four basket-weaving days to Christmas.

Tom told a group meeting, 'I've got an idea for a whole new concept of non-aggressive football. Playing with no opposition hasn't been the answer. We've had the occasional good result, like last week's 32-0 win, but basically it's boring. So we'll play in two teams, but we're only allowed to score for the other side. That should get rid of the worst affects of aggresssion and partisanship.'

'Super,' said David and Prue Harris-Jones.

Soon there were only thirty-nine rethatching days to Christmas.

For the first time there wasn't a single empty bed. Extra accommodation would have to be found. Reggie and Elizabeth faced the problem fair and square.

'We can get one extra room by teaming up C.J. and Doc Morrissey,' said Reggie in bed that night. 'It'll mean rejigging the wardenships, but it's worth it. Every little helps.'

'They'll never agree,' said Elizabeth.

'I'll use psychology,' said Reggie. 'And you'll be with me, so that they can't get too angry.'

The next morning Reggie asked C.J. and Doc Morrissey to come to the secretary's office. Elizabeth sat behind her desk, and Reggie sat in front of it, with the wall charts behind him.

C.J. came first.

'These wall charts reveal the expanding state of our business,' said Reggie.

'I always knew it would succeed,' said C.J. 'Out of the mouths of babes and little children.'

148

'We're going to need more accommodation,' said Reggie. 'Everyone is going to have to make sacrifices.'

'I'm glad to hear it,' said C.J.

'You'll have to share a room with McBlane.'

C.J.'s mouth opened and shut several times, but no sound emerged. At last, he managed a hoarse, piteous croak.

'I think I know what you're trying to say,' said Reggie. 'You didn't get where you are today by sleeping with pox-ridden Caledonian chefs.'

C.J. nodded.

'I didn't realize you'd feel so strongly,' said Reggie. 'All right. You can share a room with Doc Morrissey instead.'

'Thanks,' said C.J. 'Thanks very much, Reggie.'

When C.J. had gone, Reggie smiled triumphantly at Elizabeth.

'If you'd asked him to share with Doc Morrissey straight off, he'd have gone berserk,' she said.

'Exactly. But now he agrees eagerly, in gratitude at being spared the odiferous Scot. Thrill to my shrewdness now, as I try the same trick on Doc Morrissey.'

Doc Morrissey was soon installed in the chair that C.J. had so recently warmed.

'Psychological side of things still going well?' said Reggie.

'Damned well,' said Doc Morrissey, courteously including Elizabeth in his beaming smile. 'It's having a good effect on me, too.'

'Physician heal thyself.'

'Quite. Think I could take anything on the chin now.'

'Oh good. I want you to share a bedroom with McBlane.'

'What?'

'We're getting very crowded, due to our success. I want you to share your bedroom with McBlane.'

Doc Morrissey laughed. Then he smiled at Elizabeth.

'He had me going for a moment there,' he said.

Elizabeth smiled nervously.

'It isn't a joke,' she said. 'We really are awfully crowded.'

'Well, I know, but . . . McBlane!'

'He's a superb cook,' said Reggie.

'Red Rum's a fine horse, but I have no intention of sharing a bedroom with him,' said Doc Morrissey.

Reggie could hardly conceal his smugness as he made his master stroke.

'All right, then,' he said. 'I'll tell you what I'll do. You can share a bedroom with C.J. instead.'

Doc Morrissey fainted.

Two days later, Reggie called a staff meeting in the living-room of Number Seventeen, to outline his plans for increasing the accommodation. Making C.J. and Doc Morrissey share a bedroom no longer featured in those plans. Assorted chairs, from large sagging armchairs to scruffy kitchen chairs, hugged the walls. A row of mugs hung on hooks at either side of the fireplace. Each mug bore the name of a member of the staff.

Reggie outlined their plans. Folding beds would be installed in the staff bedrooms, so that the various activities could be staged in them during the day. Reggie's office would move to the sun-room of Number Twenty-one and C.J.'s office would be in London, enabling work activities to take place within the context of commuting.

Eight bedrooms, four dining rooms, two studies, two sun-rooms, four kitchens and four garden sheds would be available as double bedrooms for guests. The unusual nature of the accommodation and the sharing of rooms would become an integral part of the exciting social journey on which the guests had embarked.

David Harris-Jones's hand shot up. Then he realized that he didn't really want to say what he had been going to say. He lowered his arm as unobtrusively as he could.

Not unobtrusively enough.

'You wanted to say something,' said Reggie.

'No,' said David Harris-Jones. 'Just . . . er . . . just a touch of lumbago. Exercise does it good.'

He raised and lowered his hand twice more.

'That's better,' he said.

'You were going to say something,' said Reggie. 'Don't be afraid!'

'David was going to say that you and Elizabeth still have your bedroom, and both your offices,' said Prue.

'Well, I was sort of going to say something along those . . . er . . .' said David Harris-Jones.

'Fair enough,' said Reggie. 'I'm glad you mentioned it.'

'. . . lines,' said David Harris-Jones.

'We'd like to give up our use of three rooms,' said Reggie. Sacrificing one's comforts in the interests of the community is a real pleasure, but it's one that we'll have to sacrifice. I have to command authority and respect. I have to inspire confidence. It's regrettable, but there it is.'

He told them that he would be opening other branches. There would be great chains of Perrins, from Land's End to John O'Groats. The great work had only just begun. These other communities would need managers. The jobs would command high salaries and great prestige, and Reggie would be looking for people experienced in this kind of work.

'It would be invidious to mention names,' he said. 'But I think it would be super and a knock-out if I could find some of these people among my own staff, because I'm a loyalty person. I didn't get where I am today without knowing that you have a cock-up on the staffing front if you aren't a loyalty person.'

There were no more complaints.

Work began on the alterations. Elizabeth was a frequent visitor to the Botchley Slumber Centre, and barely a day passed without the arrival of new beds at one or other of the five houses. The bank accounts, briefly swollen by generous donations, began to dip alarmingly. Soon it would all pay off.

Perrins was a success.

All the time, they were growing more experienced and more confident.

All the time, life in the community was improving.

Reggie witnessed an eloquent example of this improvement when he entered Adam and Jocasta's bedroom on the very last day of that November.

The ecological wallpaper contained thirty-eight of the most threatened species in the world. Adam had some sheets of paper in his hand. Jocasta was sitting peacefully on the floor. Snodgrass was purring on Jocasta's bed. The room was tidy.

'I'm reading Jocasta a story, Uncle Reggie,' said Adam. 'I read better than her, but only because I'm older.'

'What's the story?' said Reggie.

'Uncle C.J. wrote it for us,' said Adam. 'It's all about ants. It's frightfully good.'

I like Uncle C.J.,' said Jocasta.


December was a quiet month. Fewer people came to Perrins, although forward bookings remained good.

The alterations proceeded steadily.

The weather remained wet and windy.

The great days of Perrins lay ahead.

# 5  *Christmas*

Christmas really began on the morning of Saturday, December the seventeenth.

That was when the snow came.

And the letter.

The letter was curiously brief.

'Dear Mother and Father,' it read. 'This will come as a complete surprise, I'm in Paris on my way back to England. I got your address from one of your adverts. My news can wait until I see you. I'll arrive on Friday, 23 December. I'm looking forward to seeing you all. Your loving son, Mark.'

The snow began at half past ten. It wasn't heavy, but it caused the cancellation of eleven football matches.

Their festive plans received a further boost that morning. C.J. announced that he was going to spend Christmas with Mrs. C.J. in Luxembourg.

Doc Morrissey would also be absent. He had committed himself to an Indian Christmas in Southall. He would miss the festivities at Perrins, but he couldn't let his old friends down.

The majority of the guests would be going home.

'It's going to be more a family Christmas than a community Christmas,' said Elizabeth in bed that night, snuggling against Reggie's chest.

'The community is a family,' said Reggie.

'I enjoy being secretary,' said Elizabeth. 'But I want to be a wife over Christmas.'

'So you will be, darling.'

'There's a fly in the ointment.'

'Fly? What fly?'

'McBlane.'

'I realize he needs a lot of ointment. I didn't know he was a fly in it.'

'Reggie!'

A carload of revellers squished homeward through the soft snow that carpeted Oslo Avenue.

'I want to cook the Christmas dinner myself,' said Elizabeth.

'No problem,' said Reggie. 'I imagine McBlane will be going home to his family.'

'Has he got a family?'

'Yes. He told me all about them the other day. I think. It was either that or the history of Partick Thistle.'

'He frightens me sometimes.'

'Nonsense, darling. I'll go and see McBlane tomorrow, and tell him that he's having Christmas off. No problem.'

Next day Reggie's predictions proved partly true and partly false.

He did go and see McBlane. There was a problem.

It was four o'clock on a Saturday afternoon, and the slim, dark culinary wizard was slumped on a wooden chair at the kitchen table. There was a pint bottle of Newcastle Brown in his hand, and his vest was stained with fat, oil and sweat. He had a rash on both arms.

'Good afternoon, McBlane,' said Reggie. 'I just called in to say that we ... er ... the ... er ... carbonnades of beef were wonderful today.'

'Bloody foreign muck,' said McBlane.

'Well, everyone is entitled to his opinion. At the risk of upsetting you, McBlane, I have to admit that we found them delicious. Now, the thing is, McBlane, the thing is that we ... er ... my wife and I ... would like it if ... if we could have the carbonnades again some time.'

McBlane grunted.

154

'Oh. Good. That's settled then.'

McBlane took a long swig of beer.

'Oh yes. There is one other thing,' said Reggie. 'Not long till Christmas now.'

'Ee flecking wae teemee hasn't oot frae grippet ma drae wee blagnolds,' said McBlane.

'Well of course it is a bit over-commercialized,' said Reggie. 'But I expect you're looking forward to seeing your family.'

'Och nee I nivver flecking wanna same baskards ee flecking baskards ee immeee lafe wathee dunter mice stirring baskard done baskard firm baskard ling wasna flecking low dove haggan brasknards.'

'Well, no family's perfect, of course, McBlane. You'll go and stay with friends in Scotland, will you?'

'Willy fleck in ell? Wazz cottle andun firm ee? Eh? Fock loo her. Fock loo her. Banly sniffle baskards. Albie Stainer.'

'You'll spend Christmas with Albie Stainer! Absolutely splendid. Where does he live?'

'Albie Stainer. Albie Stainer.'

'You'll be staying here! Ah! Oh, what a relief. Oh, good, you'll be able to . . . er . . . cook the Christmas dinner then. That is splendid news.'

Reggie hastened from the kitchen, and McBlane tossed off the remains of his Newcastle Brown. A smile hovered around his sensitive, powerful lips. He had a cold sore coming.

The wedding between James Gordonstoun Anderson and Lettuce Isobel Horncastle was scheduled for two thirty on Wednesday, December the twenty-first. The venue was St Peter's church in Bagwell Heath, the very church at which, more than twenty months ago, Jimmy had failed to arrive. Once again the weather was wintry. Overnight there had been four inches of snow, and more snow fell intermittently throughout the morning. The same organist gave the same spirited rendition of the same old favourites. The same heating system accompanied him with a slightly increased cacophony of squeaks and gurgles.

It was an unevenly balanced congregation that had gathered in the spacious fifteenth-century church, with its famous Gothic font cover.

On the left of the aisle there sat just one person. Lettuce's mother was a formidable lady in her late sixties, with a large square face. She wore her moustache defiantly, as if relishing the displeasure that the world felt in looking at it.

On the right were the friends and relatives of the groom. There were Tom and Linda, with Adam and Jocasta, C.J., Doc Morrissey, the Websters, and the Harris-Joneses. There were the same old army colleagues, their noses even redder from liquid indulgence, and the same assorted cousins with their even more assorted wives, and thirty-six past and present guests of Perrins had made the wintry journey to Bagwell Heath to pay homage to the leader of their expeditionary forces.

Altogether there were seventy-one people on the right-hand side of the church, yet it was Lettuce's mother who looked proud, and the seventy-one who looked sheepish.

Lettuce's mother's isolation seemed to say, 'We could have filled our pews twice over for a suitable groom.'

The massed ranks of Jimmy's friends and relations seemed to say, 'We felt we had to come, in case he doesn't.'

Outside, the snow fell steadily, carpeting Bagwell Heath in silence.

Elizabeth stood by the handsome lych-gate, sheltering from the snow under a smart, red umbrella.

The bride and her father sat in an upstairs room at the Coach and Horses, from which a fine view of the church could be obtained. They had large brandies in their hands. The beribboned car was parked in the pub car-park, whence it would not stir until the groom had put in his appearance.

The vicar turned to his wife, said, 'Oh, well, may as well be hung for a sheep as a lamb', and set off through the snow in his Wellington boots. He carried his shoes in a Waitrose carrier bag.

Reggie's beribboned car slowly approached the churchyard, with the groom sitting petrified in the passenger seat beside his best man.

It was twenty-seven minutes past two.

The car skidded on a patch of ice concealed beneath the fresh snow, and struck a lamp-post. Jimmy, who had forgotten to do up his safety belt, was jerked forward and cut his nose against the windscreen.

Blood gushed out.

'Oh my God,' said Reggie.

'Bit of blood, no harm,' said Jimmy, attempting to staunch the flow with his demob handkerchief. All to no avail.

'Lie down,' said Reggie.

'No time,' said Jimmy. 'Think I'm not turning up again.'

'I can't drive on till you're bandaged,' said Reggie, 'or you'll be having your reception at the blood transfusion centre.'

He ripped the ribbons off the bonnet, and managed to produce a make-shift bandage.

It was two thirty-four.

The vicar changed his shoes. Lettuce and her father sipped their brandies and watched. Elizabeth stood at the lych-gate and waited. The organist returned to the beginning of his meagre repertoire, but he played it more slowly this time.

Uneasiness grew, inside the church and out.

'It's flooded,' said Reggie. 'And there's no juice left in the battery.'

'Done for,' said Jimmy, slumping in his seat.

They set off to walk to the church, trudging frantically through the snow.

A car came towards them. They thumbed it. Reggie pointed at Jimmy, whose face was criss-crossed with yards of ribbon, and tried frantically to mime a wedding. He mimed church bells, standing at the altar, putting on the ring, eating and drinking at the reception. When he got to the honeymoon night, the driver accelerated, lost control of his vehicle and crashed into a lamp-post on the other side of the road.

'We've got to see if he's all right,' said Reggie.

'Absolutely. First things first,' said Jimmy stoutly, public-spirited even in his greatest crisis.

They approached the motorist.

'Are you all right?' said Reggie.

'Go away, you bloody lunatics,' said the motorist. 'Get back to your bloody asylum.'

'He seems all right,' said Reggie.

They struggled on desperately through the snow. An AA break-down truck approached. They hailed it and it stopped.

'Wedding. Two-thirty. Bagwell Heath. Cock-up on car front,' said Jimmy.

'That your car back there?' said the driver.

'Yes,' said Reggie. 'Never mind the car.'

'Are you AA members?' said the driver.

Jimmy produced his membership card.

'Fair enough,' said the driver.

It was two forty-six.

Inside the church, Lettuce's mother rose majestically to her feet, turned scornfully towards Jimmy's seventy-one friends and relations, and strode off up the aisle, like a footballer who has been sent off for a foul that he hasn't committed. She strode out of the church just as the AA van pulled up at the lych-gate. She watched Jimmy step gingerly out, the ribbons heavily stained with red.

'You're bleeding,' she said accusingly.

'A mere bagatelle,' he countered bravely.

He marched proudly up the aisle. Lettuce's mother slunk in behind him.

The vicar entered, and smiled with grim astonishment at Jimmy.

Reggie took his place beside the wounded groom, and Elizabeth slid unobtrusively into her seat from the side-aisle.

It was two fifty-one.

At last they had a groom, but they still had no bride. Lettuce was arguing with her father in the car-park of the Coach and Horses.

'I want to arrive by car,' she said.

'There's no time,' expostulated her parent. 'We'd have to go right round the new experimental one-way system.'

'Whose life is this the greatest day of, yours or mine?' said Lettuce. 'I've waited twenty-one months. Jimmy can wait five minutes.'

Lettuce's father's mistake was to try and knock a minute off that estimated time. At the furthest point from the church, the car slid across the snow into the hedge.

The desperate organist began his repertoire for the third time.

Jimmy whispered, 'Serves me right. Biter bit. Shove off?' to Reggie.

'Give her five minutes,' whispered Reggie.

Lettuce's mother didn't know whether to smirk or have a nervous breakdown.

It was two minutes past three.

Lettuce and her father limped exhaustedly through the drifts.

Behind them, two tearful little bridesmaids tried unavailingly to hold the train out of the snow.

The procession hobbled into the church at seven minutes past three.

The organist, in his incredulous relief, made a horrible mess of the first bars of the wedding march.

It was twenty-four minutes past three before Jimmy mouthed the first sentence of the day that even he was unable to shorten.

'I do,' he said.

'I really feel festive now,' said Elizabeth, as they lay in bed on the morning of Friday, December the twenty-third. 'Mark's arriving, C.J.'s leaving, and we're going to have a white Christmas.'

Mark did arrive, C.J. did leave, but they didn't have a white Christmas. All day it thawed, slowly at first, then faster, mistily, steamily, nastily. The snow was already losing its sparkle by the time the postman arrived. One of the cards which he delivered contained the heart-warming message 'Dynamite. Thanks. The computer programmer from Alderley Edge.' The W288 was churning up waves of brown slush by the time C.J. set off for Luxembourg. By the time Mark arrived there were great pools of water lying on the snow.

Mark looked well. Africa hadn't heightened him. He was still five foot seven, but he had filled out and looked even more disconcertingly like a smaller and younger version of Reggie. He kissed Linda affectionately, and was even polite to Tom. That was the trouble. He was too polite. As the evening went gently on its way, it was as if he wasn't really there at all. Reggie tried hard to venture no criticism of his way of life, and to avoid those awkward phrases like 'old prune' which he had always found himself using to his son. They told him about the Perrins set-up. He seemed interested, but not unduly impressed.

Reggie discovered that he desperately wanted him to be impressed.

They told him about 'Grot', and the departure in disguise of Reggie and Elizabeth. He seemed interested, but not unduly surprised.

Reggie discovered that he desperately wanted him to be surprised.

McBlane laid on a good dinner. Reggie felt proud of it.

Mark ate well, but made no comment.

Afterwards, the family held a private gathering in Tom and Linda's bedroom. The new double bed had been folded away, and comfortable armchairs had been moved in for the evening. Tom provided the drinks. There was apple gin, raspberry whisky and fig vodka. Mark praised the drinks politely. Linda took the bull by the horns, and said, 'Now then, shorthouse, what was all that theatre business in Africa?'

But Mark was not to be drawn on the subject of the group of freelance theatrical mercenaries, dedicated to the incitement of revolutionary fervour through the plays of J. M. Barrie, freely adapted by Idi 'Post-Imperialist Impression' Okombe.

Nor did he call Linda 'fatso', as in days of yore.

'Let's just say it was a phase I went through,' he said. 'Everyone's got to go through their wanting-to-overthrow-the-established-order phase. Anyway, it's over and done with. I don't really want to talk about it.'

'Supposing we do want to talk about it, old prune?' said Reggie.

Damn! Damn! Damn!

Mark shrugged.

'Well, this is nice. All together again,' said Elizabeth too hastily.

'Another drink, anyone?' said Reggie. 'More fig vodka, Mark, or would you prefer to enjoy yourself?'

Mark held out his glass, and Reggie poured a goodly measure of fig vodka. It was extremely pale green.

'It doesn't matter if we get a bit olivered tonight,' he said.

'Olivered?' said Mark.

'Oliver Twist. Pissed,' said Reggie. 'You were always coming out with rhyming slang in the old days.'

'Was I?' said Mark. 'I think I must have been going through a solidarity-with-the-working-classes phase. Everybody has to go through their solidarity-with-the-working-classes phase.'

'Unless they're working class,' said Linda.

'I never did,' said Tom, pouring himself some of his raspberry whisky as if it was gold dust. 'I know the working classes are the salt of the earth, but the fact remains, I don't like them. I'm just not a working class person.'

'You still haven't told us what you were doing in Paris,' said Elizabeth.

'No,' said Mark.

'Oh come on, shorthouse, don't be infuriating,' said Linda.

'I met this film director in Africa,' said Mark, 'and he wanted me to make a couple of films in Paris.'

'How exciting,' said Elizabeth. 'When will we see them?'

'Never, I hope,' said Mark. 'They're blue films. I think I'm going through a reaction-against-my-political-period phase.'

When it was time to go to bed, Elizabeth said that she hoped Mark could stay a long time.

'Fraid not,' he said. 'I've got to go to Stockholm on the twenty-seventh, I'm making a film there.'

'Are you still in your blue period?' said Reggie.

'Fraid so,' said Mark. 'It's about a randy financier. It's called "Swedish loss adjustor on the job".'

In the morning, all traces of snow had gone.

Christmas day was grey, still and silent, as if the weather had gone to spend the holidays with its family.

Elizabeth had to agree that McBlane's dinner was a good one. As he himself put it, if she understood him aright, 'There's none of that foreign muck today'. The turkey was moist and tasty, the home-made cranberry sauce was a poem, and even the humble bread sauce was raised to the level of art by the scabrous Caledonian maestro. If there was any criticism, it was perhaps of a certain native meanness with regard to the monetary contents of the Christmas pudding.

The wine flowed smoothly, the smokeless fuel glowed smokelessly, Mark passed cruets and sauce bowls with unaccustomed assiduousness, David Harris-Jones got hiccups, Linda found a pfennig in her pudding, Prue Harris-Jones got hiccups, Joan told Prue that her togetherness was slipping because her hiccups were out of phase with David's, Tom informed them that some people were hiccup people and other people were burp people and he was a burp person,

162

Jocasta didn't cry when she found a shirt button in her pudding, Reggie asked McBlane to join them for the port and stilton, and received an incomprehensible reply, the four guests joined in as best they could, Tony proposed a toast to Absentfriendsville, Arizona, there was speculation about the honeymooning activities of Jimmy and Lettuce, some of it ribald and the rest of it obscene, everyone agreed that the jokes in the crackers were the worst ever, the candles flickered, the grey light of afternoon faded, and the very last, somewhat drunken toast was to the future of Perrins.

And what of those absent friends?

Doc Morrissey was sitting beside a gas fire in a much smaller room in Southall. He was surrounded by his friends. He had consumed a large meal of turkey musalla, with chipolata dhansk, korma bread sauce, sprout gosht and Bombay potatoes, followed by Christmas pudding fritters. His Indian friends were hanging on his every word, and he basked in the glory of their respect and adulation as he told them of his magnificent work at Botchley. He realized that they had journeyed to a far land in order to learn the mystical secrets of life. On that grey afternoon, Southall was Shangri-La, the mysterious occident, and Doc Morrissey was the guru who would reveal to them the transcendental secrets of metaphysics.

It was some minutes since he'd spoken, and they began their eager questioning again.

The guru was asleep.

C.J. and Mrs C.J. walked peacefully among the Luxembourgeoisie in the grey, still afternoon.

Clearly the weather hadn't gone to Luxembourg for yuletide.

C.J. held his hands behind his back. Mrs C.J. tried to link arms and failed.

'Don't you love me any more, C.J.?' she said.

'Of course I do, darling,' he said.

They walked slowly over the bridge which spans the ravine in Luxembourg City.

C.J. allowed Mrs C.J. to link arms.

'You're happy in Luxembourg, aren't you?' he said.

'Of course I am,' said Mrs C.J.

'Your friends are nice.'

'Delightful. But I miss you, C.J.'

'You seemed happy enough to come here.'

'Maybe I was, but I've grown to miss you.'

They stood, looking out over the ravine.

'Nice ravine, eh?' said C.J. 'I didn't get where I am today without knowing a nice ravine when I see one.'

'Don't change the subject,' said Mrs C.J.

'There isn't any subject,' said C.J. 'So how can I change it? We're walking in Luxembourg City. We come from a large country, and this is a small country, but I don't think we should be patronizing on that account. I don't think we should just barge through, willy-nilly, wrapped up in our problems, ignoring nice ravines. Nice ravines don't grow on trees, you know. I mean, if we get back to England, and I say, "Nice ravine, that ravine in Luxembourg" and you say, "Which ravine?" and I say "You know. That nice ravine" and you say, "I don't remember any ravine", I'm going to look pretty silly. Women don't always understand the rightness of time and place, my dear, and the time and place to talk about a nice ravine is when you're looking at it. That's what marriage is all about. Sharing things. And that includes ravines.'

C.J. gazed at the ravine. The light was fading slowly.

'That's the whole point,' said Mrs C.J. 'When *am* I going to get back to England? When *am* I going to share you? You don't want me there, do you? There's somebody else.'

'There isn't anybody else.'

'Why don't you want me there then?'

'Darling, it's Christmas. Hardly the time to be arguing.'

'Perhaps it's the time to be loving, C.J.'

C.J. drew his eyes away from the ravine and smiled earnestly at Mrs C.J.

'I want to come to Botchley and share your work,' she said.

'Botchley's dull. Suburban.'

'No ravines?'

'You're laughing at me.'

'I'm trying to get through to you. I'm lonely.'

C.J. put his arm round his wife, and hugged her. Slowly they began to retrace their steps.

'We lead a monastic life at Perrins,' said C.J. 'Celibacy is the order of the day.'

Mrs C.J. looked at him in amazement.

'But Reggie,' she said. 'Tom. David. Tony. I thought they all had their wives with them.'

'Their wives are there,' said C.J., 'but they lead segregated lives. We sleep in dormitories. It's a strict community. They can stand it. I just couldn't stand being near you and yet not fully with you. Frustration is the thief of time, and that's all there is to it.'

Mrs C.J. kissed him.

'Oh, C.J.,' she said.

'Oh, Mrs C.J.,' he said.


Jimmy and Lettuce had wakened to the growl of thunder and the drumming of heavy rain. Then had come gusty warm winds from the south, driving away the clouds. The wind had fallen away, and there had been hot sun. Now a cool breeze was setting in from the north.

Clearly, all the weather had gone to Malta for its holidays.

Jimmy and Lettuce looked out over the ruffled, dark blue surface of the Mediterranean from the terrace of their hotel restaurant.

'Happy?' said Jimmy.

'Happy.'

'Stout girl. Bus ride tomorrow?'

'We had a bus ride yesterday.'

'Aren't rationed. Different bus, different ride.'

'I don't know if I'll feel like a bus ride tomorrow.'

'Fair enough. Nice bus ride yesterday?'

'Yes.'

'Interesting ticket system they have.'

'It seemed much like ticket systems everywhere.'

'To the uninitiated. Top hole hotel?'

'Lovely.'

'A1 grub?'

'Yes.'

'Everything up to expectation in marital rights department?'

'Lovely. Don't worry, Jimmy!'

'Bus ride Tuesday?'

'Must we make plans, Jimmy?'

'No. Course not. Honeymoon. Liberty Hall. You're right. Good scout. Bus ride not out of the question, then?'

'This interest in buses has come as a bit of a surprise, Jimmy.'

'Always been a bit of a bus wallah on the QT. If not Tuesday, maybe Wednesday.'

'Maybe.'

'You don't like bus rides, do you?'

'I just don't want to make plans.'

'Wonder if there'll be normal schedules tomorrow. Don't know if Maltese have Boxing Day as we know it. Ask at desk.'

'Does it matter?'

'Interesting. Little titbits, foreign ways. Nervous, Lettuce. Know why?'

'No.'

'Happy. Admit it, cold feet. Probably guessed it, not turning up at church. One failed marriage. Don't want another. So happy now. Insecure. Don't want to lose it.'

'Oh, Jimmy.'

166

'See that kraut, table in corner, big conk. At bus station Friday morning.'

'I didn't know you went to the bus station on Friday morning.'

'Just popped in. Asked the cove there if they have any equivalent of a Red Rover. Didn't understand what I was on about.'

Mark left on Boxing Day as he had things to do before he went to Stockholm.

In bed that night, Reggie and Elizabeth were in pensive vein.

'I wonder how Jimmy and Lettuce have got on,' said Elizabeth.

'Very well,' said Reggie. 'Jimmy's so much more relaxed since we started the community.'

'I wonder how C.J. and Mrs C.J. have got on.'

'Very well. C.J.'s so much kinder since we started the community.'

Elizabeth pressed the soles of her feet against the top of Reggie's feet.

'Poor Mark,' she said.

'Yes.'

'We seem to have lost him in a way.'

'I know.'

'He's gone away from us.'

'Maybe it's we who've gone away from him. The community's our whole life now, my darling. Christmas has just been an interlude, that's all. Our life has been suspended.'

'Is that bad?'

'No. But it's just as well the community's such a success.'

'Is it really such a success, Reggie?'

'Of course it is, darling. A tremendous success. What's happened so far is just a start. The best days lie ahead.'

# 6 *The Best Days*

January began quietly. Winter flirted with Botchley. There was snow that didn't settle, rain that didn't last, sun that didn't warm. The number of guests at Perrins increased steadily. There was an article about the community in a national newspaper. It was inevitable, since journalists read each other's papers, that the article would be followed by others. It was inevitable, since the bulk of television's magazine programmes are made up of ideas taken from the newspapers, that Reggie should appear on television. It was inevitable, given the nature of Reggie Perrin's life, that the interviewer should be Colin Pillock.

Reggie was nervous.

When he had been interviewed by Colin Pillock about Grot, he had not been nervous, because he had been bent on self-destruction.

The researchers made wary, desultory conversation with him over drinks and sandwiches in the spartan, green hospitality room. The researchers wolfed all the sandwiches. Colin Pillock entered, surveyed the large plates covered only in wrecked cress, and told the researchers, who already knew, 'You've wolfed all the sandwiches, you bastards.'

'They always wolf all the sandwiches, the bastards,' he told Reggie.

Reggie sympathized.

Colin Pillock gave Reggie a run-down of the questions he would ask.

When they got on the air, he asked totally different questions.

They went down to the ground floor in the goods lift and walked across the studio floor, past the huge hanging sign that said, simply, 'Pillock Talk'.

They were made up so that they'd look unmade-up under the lights.

Reggie felt increasingly nervous.

They sat in elegant armchairs, with a small circular table between them.

It was all very cool.

Reggie was not cool. If he made a fool of himself now, all would be destroyed.

When he'd been bent on self-destruction, he had failed dismally.

Would he fail equally dismally now, when he was bent on success?

They tested him for level.

The opening music began. His heart thumped. The four cameras stared at him impassively. The cameramen were calm and moderately bored.

'Good evening,' said Colin Pillock. 'My first guest this evening is a man whom I've had on the programme before, when he was head of the amazing "Grot" chain, Reginald Perrin.'

Reggie tried to smile, but his mouth felt as if it was set in concrete.

'Good evening,' he said.

'I didn't do too well with Reginald Perrin on that occasion,' said Colin Pillock. 'But I must be either a brave man or a fool.'

'Or both,' said Reggie.

No, no, no.

'I still can't get over your name,' said Reggie. 'Pillock.'

No, no, no.

No, no, no, no, no.

169

Take a grip on yourself.

Confine yourself to minimal answers till you're settled in.

'You're now running a community called Perrins, Mr Perrin?'

'Yes.'

'People come to your community for as little or as long as they like, and at the end they pay as little or as much as they like.'

'Yes.'

'Perrins has been described as part community, part therapy centre, part mental health farm. Would you say that was a fair description?'

'Yes.'

'It's been described as a community for the middle-class and the middle-aged, set in what used to be Middlesex.'

'Yes.'

Colin Pillock twitched.

Many people had had cause to regret the onset of Colin Pillock's twitch. Would Reggie be one of them?

'Do you intend to confine yourself entirely to this monosyllabic agreement?' said Colin Pillock.

'No.'

'Oh, good, because our viewers might feel it was rather a waste of time for you to come here and say nothing but "yes".'

'Yes.'

No! No, no, no, no, no!

'Mr Perrin, are you genuinely doing all this for the good of humanity, or is it basically a money-making venture, or is it a giant con, or is it simply a joke? What's your honest answer?'

'Yes.'

'Mr Perrin!'

'I'm serious. It's all of them. That's the beauty of it.'

That stopped him in his tracks. That made him think.

'Well?' said Colin Pillock.

Reggie realized that he had been asked a question, and he had no idea what it was.

'Sorry,' he said. 'I was just thinking very carefully about my answer.'

'Which is?' said Colin Pillock, smiling encouragingly.

'My answer is . . . would you mind repeating the question?'

Panic flitted across Colin Pillock's eyes. He smiled desperately.

'What kind of people come to your community?'

'Well, perhaps it would be helpful if I told you who we have at this moment?'

'Fine.'

'We've got a stockbroker, a pub landlord, a time and motion man, the owner of a small firm that makes supermarket trolleys, a systems analyst, a businessman who answers to the name of Edwards, and a housewife who wishes that she didn't answer to the name of Ethel Merman.'

'I see. And . . .'

'An overworked doctor, a disillusioned imports manager, an even more disillusioned exports manager, an extremely shy vet, a sacked football manager, an overstressed car salesman and a pre-stressed concrete salesman.'

'Splendid. And . . .'

'A housewife who longs to be a career woman, a career woman who longs to be a housewife, a schoolteacher who's desperate because he can't get a job and another schoolteacher who's even more desperate because he has got a job.'

Colin Pillock smiled uneasily.

'So work is a major problem that causes people to come to you, would you say?' he asked.

'They have a wide variety of problems. Some have sexual problems, some have social problems, some have professional problems, some have identity problems. Some have sexual, social, professional and identity problems. There are women who are exhausted by the strain of trying to be equal with men, and men who are exhausted by the strain of trying to remain more equal with women. There are people who live above their garages and their incomes, in little boxes they can't afford on prestige estates they don't understand, where families are two-car, two-tone and two-faced, money has replaced sex as a driving force, death has replaced sex as a taboo, sex has replaced bridge as a social event for mixed foursomes, and large deep-freezes are empty save for twelve packets of sausages. They come to Perrins in the hope that here at last they'll find a place where they won't be ridiculed as petty snobs, scorned as easy targets, and derided by sophisticated playwrights, but treated as human beings who are bewildered by the complexity of social development, castrated by the conformities of the century of mass production, and dwarfed by the speed and immensity of technological progress that has advanced more in fifty years than in millions of years of human existence before it, so that when they take their first steps into an adult society shaped by humans but not for humans, their personalities shrivel up like private parts in an April sea.'

'I . . . er . . . I see,' said Colin Pillock.

'Not *too* monosyllabic for you, I hope,' said Reggie.

On Thursday, January the nineteenth, Reggie had a visit from Mr Dent, a planning officer from Botchley Borough Council. The weather was cold. Ominous clouds were moving in from the east. Oslo Avenue was lined with cars, and Mr Dent had to park in Washington Road. On his way towards Number Twenty-one, he passed Tom and a group of footballers dressed in the Botchley Albion strip.

They were about to instigate a new system of playing football. Scoring goals for the opponents hadn't worked. As each team played entirely for the opponents, they became the opponents, who became them. The result was two teams playing against each other in an absolutely conventional way. So now they were going to play as two normal teams, but with goals not permitted. If you scored, the opponents got a penalty. If they scored from it, you got a penalty. Etcetera etcetera.

Mr Dent knew none of this, as he walked resolutely up the front path towards Number Twenty-one. He was a short man with thinning dark hair, a small mouth, a receding chin and large ears. He would have passed unnoticed in a crowd and might even have passed unnoticed on his own.

Reggie led him into the sun-room and established him in an uninteresting chair.

'I'll come straight to the point,' said Mr Dent.

'Good,' said Reggie. 'I welcome that.'

'We've had complaints about the parking of cars in Oslo Avenue, Mr Perrin,' he said.

'They never block entrances,' said Reggie, 'and there's no noise or unseemly behaviour.'

'The cars themselves aren't my pigeon,' said Mr Dent. 'They come under the Highways Department. My worry is that you're conducting a business in private premises. We'd have been on to you long ago, but there's been a work to rule and an epidemic. Then, when we saw you on the other BBC . . .'

'The other BBC?'

'We call Botchley Borough Council the BBC.'

'Ah!'

'Because of its initials being BBC.'

'Quite.'

'We call the people over in the new extension in Crown Rise BBC 2. Not a hilarious crack, but it causes mild amusement in the town hall canteen.'

'I can believe it.'

'Anyway, we felt that matters were getting out of hand. Now . . .'

'I'm not conducting a business,' said Reggie.

'You place adverts in the newspapers. Clients arrive. They receive treatment. They pay. Is that or is it not a commercial venture?'

'No,' said Reggie.

173

Mr Dent sighed.

'I'm a busy man, Mr Perrin,' he said. 'I don't particularly enjoy my job. My life is spent examining trivia, and I have a boss who invariably leaves me to do the dirty jobs.'

'I see,' said Reggie. 'I'm one of the dirty jobs, am I?'

The little council official looked round the immaculate sunroom, at the large gleaming picture windows, the tidy desk, the new filing cabinets.

'Not dirty,' he said. 'Awkward. Unusual. My boss shrinks from the unknown.'

'I invite people to come here, as my guests,' said Reggie. 'If at the end they want to give me something, fine. It would be heartless to refuse it.'

'But you advertise?'

'Suppose I advertised, "Party every night. All welcome. Presents not refused". Would that be a commercial undertaking?'

'We're splitting hairs now.'

'In my houses . . .'

'Houses?'

'I own Numbers Seventeen to Twenty-five.'

'I thought Numbers Nineteen and Twenty-three were purchased by non-white gentlemen?'

'Good friends of mine,' said Reggie. 'If they believe in me so much that they buy houses for me, who am I to say them nay?'

He spread his hands in a gesture of helplessness.

'I'm a remarkable man,' he said.

Mr Dent's eyes met his, and he had the impression that the Planning Officer would have smiled, if he had dared.

'What exactly are you aiming to provide in these houses of yours, Mr Perrin?' he asked.

'The universal panacea for all mankind,' said Reggie. 'Would you like some coffee?'

'No, thank you,' said Mr Dent. 'This business of the change of use becomes rather more important if we're dealing with five adjoining houses. I shudder to think what Mr Winstanley will say.'

'Mr Winstanley?'

'My boss.'

'You think he'd ruin an attempt to save mankind from suicide simply because of an infringement of council planning regulations regarding five detached houses in Oslo Avenue, Botchley?'

'Definitely,' said Mr Dent.

'A petty streak in his character, is there?'

'Most definitely,'

'But you're a man of a different kidney?'

'I'd like to think so, Mr Perrin.'

'So would I, Mr Dent. So would I. Are you sure you won't have some coffee?'

'Well, perhaps a small cup.'

Reggie left the sun-room, soon returning with a tray, decorated with a picture of Ullswater. On the tray were two cups of coffee and a plate of ginger nuts. Mr Dent was looking out over the garden.

'Looks like snow,' he said, regaining his seat.

Reggie handed him the coffee.

'Don't get me wrong,' said Mr Dent, 'I'm in favour of your universal panacea for all mankind. It might do a bit of good.'

'Thank you.'

'M'm. Delicious ginger nut.'

'Thank you.'

'But my job is to make sure that there are no unauthorized changes of use,' said Mr Dent, through a mouthful of crumbs.

'I've made no structural changes,' said Reggie. 'Another ginger nut?'

'May I? They're tasty. Structural changes aren't the be all and end all, Mr Perrin.'

'I realize that,' said Reggie.

'M'm. Nice ginger nut,' said Mr Dent. 'Quite as nice as the first.'

'Thank you,' said Reggie.

'You're welcome,' said Mr Dent.

'You're a shrewd judge of a biscuit,' said Reggie.

'Are you trying to soft soap me?' said Mr Dent.

'It wouldn't work,' said Reggie. 'You're a man of too much moral fibre.'

'Thank you,' said Mr Dent. 'So you've made no structural changes?'

'None,' said Reggie. 'It's true that I'm using kitchens and garden sheds as bedrooms, but they could return to their former use at the drop of a hat. Where does it end? If the Jack Russell does big jobs in the dining room, is it on that account a downstairs toilet?'

Mr Dent stood up, and dumped his empty cup in the middle of Ullswater. He put his hands on Reggie's desk and leant forward till his face was close to Reggie's.

'I could get you,' he said, with greater mildness than the gesture had led Reggie to expect. 'I could get you on inadequate air vents. I can get anybody on inadequate air vents. Though I say it myself, as shouldn't, I'm mustard on inadequate air vents.'

Mr Dent sat down, and gave a shuddering sigh.

'What a pathetic boast,' he said. 'I'm mustard on inadequate air vents. What an abysmal claim. What a dismal piece of human flotsam I am.'

'Nonsense,' said Reggie stoutly, walking over to put his arm on Mr Dent's chair. 'I like you. Look, don't go straight on to your next dreary task. Watch us at work. Sit in on one of Doc Morrissey's group sessions.'

Doc Morrissey's group session was held in the spacious living-room of Number Twenty-five. Thick yellow cloud, pregnant with snow, hung over the pocked lawns and heavy vegetable beds. A calor gas fire stood in front of the empty fireplace. It was turned to maximum and provided a steady heat. In front of it slumbered Snodgrass.

176

Reggie introduced Mr Dent to Doc Morrissey, and Doc Morrissey introduced him to the six guests who were present. They were the systems analyst, the stockbroker, the businessman who answered to the name of Edwards, the owner of the small firm that made supermarket trolleys, the extremely shy vet, and Ethel Merman.

'Who's going to set the ball rolling by talking about their problems?' said Doc Morrissey, who was seated in an old wooden chair with curved arms, at the centre of the group.

He beamed at them encouragingly.

Nobody spoke.

'Splendid,' said Doc Morrissey. 'Has anyone got anything to add?'

Again, nobody spoke.

'Does anybody feel they're over-aggressive?' said Doc Morrissey. 'Does anyone feel a need to dominate any group they're in?'

Nobody spoke.

'Obviously not,' said Doc Morrissey.

'I don't feel that I'm a dominating person at all,' said the systems analyst, flicking ash gently off the end of his cigarette into the shell-shaped ashtray on the table beside his chair. 'I'm cool, controlled, systematic, analytical, as befits a systems analyst.'

He looked round the group and gave a cool, controlled, systematic smile.

Reggie nodded encouragingly at Mr Dent, as if to say, 'We've started at last.'

'But underneath I'm a bubbling cauldron,' continued the systems analyst. 'I get aggressive in two areas really. Driving and . . . er . . .'

'Ah!' said the stockbroker. 'That's probably your sex drive. The car represents a woman.'

'Auto-suggestion!!' said Doc Morrissey.

Again there flitted across his face a look of professional

satisfaction, almost immediately followed by the dawning of self-doubt.

'Maybe,' said the systems analyst. 'Because the second area is . . . er . . .'

The yellow gloom outside grew thicker. There was the distant roar of a pneumatic drill in Lisbon Crescent.

'The second area?' prompted Doc Morrissey gently.

The systems analyst looked shiftily at Ethel Merman.

'Lately I've developed an almost irresistible desire to . . . to . . .'

'To?'

'To punch pregnant women in the stomach.'

Ethel Merman drew in her breath sharply.

'You must have given this some thought,' said Doc Morrissey. 'Have you any idea why you want to . . . er . . .?'

He swung his arms in imitation of a vaguely aggressive gesture, but couldn't bring himself to say the words.

'I think I must hate women,' said the systems analyst. 'I see that complacent swelling, that maternal arrogance, that sheen of self-absorbed pregnancy, and I want to go . . . whoomf! whoomf!'

He punched an imaginary mother-to-be. His face was transformed by hatred.

Ethel Merman flinched.

'Oh, I've never done it,' said the systems analyst. 'I very much doubt if I ever will. I've too much to lose. Friends, acquaintances, work, insurance policies, credit rating. I'll never do it, but . . . wanting to's just as bad.'

The extremely shy vet looked at him sadly. Ethel Merman edged to the far side of her chair.

Reggie nodded towards Mr Dent, as if to say, 'You don't get that sort of stuff in the town hall canteen, do you?'

'You find that shocking, naturally?' said the systems analyst to Ethel Merman.

'I wouldn't be a woman if I didn't, would I?' she said.

She glanced round the wide circle of chairs nervously. The extremely shy vet smiled extremely shyly at her.

'I'm Ethel Merman,' she said, defiantly.

'Not the legendary Ethel Merman?' said the stockbroker.

'No, the unlegendary Ethel Merman,' she replied.

Reggie produced another of his meaningful smiles for Mr Dent. 'Life is such a rich tapestry,' this one seemed to say.

Ethel Merman fixed him with a baleful stare.

'It's no laughing matter,' she said. 'It's bugged my life. It's brought home to me just how dreary Erith is. It's the same with my friend.'

She paused. She was still looking at Reggie, and he felt drawn into a reply.

'Your friend?'

'Mrs Clark. I said to her the other day, "Pet," I said, "Who'd have thought it? The two of us in the one street, with the names of famous international artistes, and nobody has ever heard of either of us. It's not fair." I said the same thing to her at the corner shop. "It's not fair, Shirley," I said.'

Reggie felt as if he was taking part in a double act of which only his partner knew the script.

'Shirley Bassey?' he heard himself saying.

'No. Shirley McNab. Shirley Bassey's the singer,' said Ethel Merman.

Reggie nodded resignedly. He *had* been taking part in a double act of which only his partner knew the script.

'Still,' said Ethel Merman. 'We all have our cross to bear.'

'I certainly do,' said the owner of the small firm that made supermarket trolleys. 'I'm a homosexual.'

The little gathering was stunned, less by the revelation itself than by the fact that it was this particular man who was making it. He spoke with an accent inappropriate for such admissions. Under the western edge of the Pennines the voices are flatter than anywhere else in Britain. In the Eastern Potteries there are still traces of the Midland drawl, mingling with the purity that finds its peak of flatness in the cotton

179

towns of East Lancashire. In his case this complex Staffordshire accent had been diluted but not destroyed by his transition into the managerial classes. It had geography and social history in it, failure and success. It seemed strange that it should be used, bluntly, flatly, to say, 'I'm a raving pouf.'

'It's no disgrace these days,' said the businessman who answered to the name of Edwards.

It began, gently at first, to snow.

'Not in certain circles, I'll grant you. It's practically a badge of office in some quarters, I've heard tell. But it's not expected in a self-made secondary school lad who started out in a bicycle shop in Leek, saw the way the wind was blowing, got out before the virtual demise of that mode of transport, shrewdly anticipated the growth of the supermarket and ended up with his own firm making trolleys and wire baskets.'

'It's nothing to be ashamed of,' said the systems analyst. 'Not nearly as bad as wanting to punch pregnant women.'

'I agree. Why should I be ashamed, just because I have an unusual distribution of my comatose? But it's bad for trade if you're widely known as a jessie. It's tantamount to extinction. "You don't get your trolleys from that bloody Jessie, do you?", as if the very trolleys themselves were contaminated. And so I lead a double life. By day, the solid businessman. By night, a shadowy figure in the gay clubs of the Five Towns. And it's bad for your morale and self-respect, is leading a double life.'

The snow began to fall in earnest, settling on lawns, flower beds, paths and roofs alike, turning the drab garden into a wonderland. They all watched in silence for a while, hypnotized by the big, gentle, creamy flakes. Reggie was aware of the aggression inside himself. He wanted the snow to go on and on, plunging the mundane world into chaos, cutting off towns and villages, blocking main roads, teasing the Southern Region of British Rail to despair.

'I lead a double life as well,' said the stockbroker. 'I'm an ant on the floor of the stock exchange and a king in armour.'

'I don't understand,' said Doc Morrissey.

'I go to a place in Marylebone once a fortnight. There's all kinds of equipment there, for sexual pleasure. I wear armour, and a crown, and I'm suspended in irons.'

There was a pause.

'How long can you keep it up?' said Doc Morrissey.

'All the time I'm hanging there.'

'No, I meant, how long do you hang there?'

'Oh. Two hours. It's ten pounds an hour. Rather steep, but beggars can't be choosers.'

'Splendid,' said Reggie. 'Excellent. Oh, I don't mean it's excellent that you . . . er . . . have to be . . . er . . . in order to . . . er . . . what I mean is, it's splendid that, as you do have to be . . . er . . . in order to . . . er . . . you've had the courage to tell us about your . . . er . . .'

'Kink.'

'Kink. No, I wouldn't say kink. Preference.'

It was eerily yellow now as the fierce snow storm swirled around Botchley. The blue-white flame of the gas fire glowed brightly, and Snodgrass stirred to the rhythm of a distant dream.

'I'm trying to give it up, as a matter of principle,' said the stockbroker.

'Well done,' said Doc Morrissey.

'The mistake you're making,' said the stockbroker, 'is in thinking that I'm giving it up for moral reasons. I have no feelings of guilt about it. It is totally absurd, and rather inconvenient, that I should find sexual gratification in this way, but I don't see it as wrong. Nobody else is involved. I don't mess about with small children.'

'Or men,' said the owner of the small firm that made supermarket trolleys. 'It's all right for you, the city smoothie, with your sophisticated bloody perversion. I'm the yokel, the simple straightforward jessie. Talk about the unjust society. Not even equality of perversions.'

'I honestly am sorry that you should take it so personally,' said the stockbroker. 'I'm not a happy figure that you should envy. I'm miserable. The mistake you make is in thinking that I'm miserable because of the two hours in Marylebone. I'm happy there. I make jokes. "You have heavy overheads," I comment as the mechanism is lowered to receive me. "This is the stockbroker belt," I say as I strap myself in. I'm miserable because the other three hundred-odd hours in every fortnight are so empty and sterile. I'm a hollow man, envying you your bicycle shop in Leek and your wire basket factory.'

There was almost an inch of level snow in the garden already. The pneumatic drill had stopped. The workmen had knocked off.

'Why do you intend to give it up on principle, then?' said Reggie.

'They're going to charge VAT,' said the stockbroker. 'And I'm convinced that a business like that wouldn't be VAT registered.'

He smiled. There was no warmth or coldness in his smile. He smiled because he had learnt from experience that a smile was the appropriate facial arrangement for such an occasion.

'I may like being strapped up,' he said, 'but I don't intend to be taken for a ride.'

Doc Morrissey looked towards the extremely shy vet, who shook his head and sank deeper into the threadbare old recliner in which he was sitting.

'Oh well. I suppose I'd better have a go,' said the businessman who answered to the name of Edwards.

He had dark hair and a thin sallow face, and he was wearing fawn trousers and a blue blazer with gold buttons.

'As you know, I answer to the name of Edwards,' he said.

'Yes,' agreed Reggie.

'What you don't know is that I also answer to the name of Jennings. And Levingham. And Brakespeare. Not to mention Phipps-Partington.'

Everyone looked at him in astonishment.

'I'm a con man,' he explained. 'Sometimes it's convenient to cover one's tracks, you see. Each of us has a different personality. Phipps-Partington is a gentleman down on his luck. Levingham's an out-and-out bastard who separates old ladies from their savings. Brakespeare's a likeable rogue who sets up rather wild, florid schemes, like collecting for a fund to build a replica of the Menai Bridge in Wisconsin, and have a corner of the USA that is for ever Welsh. You'd be surprised how many hard-bitten rugby players give to that with tears in their eyes on a Saturday night.'

'What made you decide to come here?' said Reggie.

The con man looked round the dark, warm living-room, at the respectably dressed people in their assorted armchairs.

'I want to find out who I am,' he said. 'But there are thirteen people in this room, and five of them are me.'

'Thank you for telling us, all of you,' said Doc Morrissey.

He looked at the shy vet hopefully. The vet shook his head.

'I can only talk to animals,' he mumbled.

To Reggie's surprise, Mr Dent began to speak.

'I know perfectly well who I am,' he said. 'I'm a friendly, genial, delightful man, not physically brave, but lit up from within by a generosity of spirit, an eagerness to love the human race. It's just that it never seems to come out that way. I do a rather dull, tiring, nit-picking sort of job, I don't have enough money to live with any style, I have a lot of administrative problems, all getting steadily worse with the financial cut-backs, and somehow, what with one thing and another, well, the real me doesn't stand a chance. Maybe here it will. Oh yes, I'll stay, Mr Perrin. Sod the council.'

He stood up and grinned down at the little gathering in the darkened room.

'Sod the air vents,' he said.

The meeting dispersed. The snow had almost stopped. The sky was lightening.

Reggie walked back along the white pavement to Number Twenty-one, for lunch. At his side was Mr Dent.

'Thank you,' said Reggie.

'Thank *you*,' said Mr Dent.

183

They stood in the hall, taking off their coats and stamping the snow off their shoes, bringing life back to numbed feet.

'I look at life, going on around me,' said Reggie. 'Ordinary, mundane. I look at the crowds in the streets or on the floor of the stock exchange, or streaming over London Bridge. The crowds on trains and buses. The crowds at football and cricket matches. Ordinary people, mundane. Then I read the papers. Court reports, sex offences, spying cases, fantasies, illusions, deceits, mistakes. Chaos. Rich, incredible chaos. Human absurdity. And I just can't reconcile the two. The ordinary crowds. The amazing secrets. This morning, in that room, they were reconciled.'

His face was alight with triumph. He banged his right fist into his left palm.

Tom, passing through the hall on his way to lunch, stood stockstill and stared at him.

'Eureka,' he said.

The whiteness of sun on snow flooded in through the frosted glass window in the front door, illuminating the stained glass of its central pane. As they went in to lunch, the sun shone brilliantly on the virgin snow. Within three hours, all traces of snow had gone. Botchley was grey and dark once more.

The explanation of Tom's excited cry of 'Eureka' didn't come until lunchtime the following day. Tom sat at Reggie's left hand, Tony Webster on Reggie's right. The guests all congregated towards the middle of the table, as if for protection.

'You remember when I said "Eureka" yesterday,' said Tom.

'I do indeed,' said Reggie.

'I had a brainwave, but decided to sleep on it. It's a new idea to take the aggression out of sport.'

He took a large mouthful of succulent roast pork and chewed it thirty-two times. At last he'd finished.

'Boxing,' he said.

'Once again, events have moved too fast for you,' said Reggie. 'The thing's been invented, I fear.'

'Non-aggressive boxing,' said Tom, taking a mouthful of McBlane's exquisite red cabbage.

'Boxing's the most aggressive sport there is,' said Tony Webster.

Tom chewed his red cabbage impassively. At last he had finished.

'It was your gesture that suggested it, Reggie,' he said. 'When you hit your palm with your fist.'

'Suggested what?' groaned Reggie.

'Each person hits himself instead of his opponent,' said Tom.

Reggie and Tony stared at him.

'That's a very interesting idea, Tom,' said Reggie.

'Knock-out,' said Tony.

'That's exactly what it won't be,' said Reggie. 'Well done, Tom.'

The following Wednesday afternoon, Reggie had another visitor from Botchley Borough Council. He was Mr Winstanley, Mr Dent's boss.

The weather was bright and breezy. Reggie was relaxed after his lamb cutlets with rosemary. Mr Winstanley was resentful after his cottage pie and chips. Reggie escorted him into the sun-room.

Mr Winstanley was a shambling, untidy, shiny man, with a paunch like a vast tumour. He could have looked like a gentleman who had fallen on hard times, if he hadn't let himself go.

'Did our Mr Dent come to see you last week?' he asked in a hoarsely resonant voice.

'He did indeed,' said Reggie. 'He sat in that very chair, and spoke kindly of my ginger nuts. Would you like some coffee and biscuits?'

Mr Winstanley shook his head and stifled a burp.

'You're getting too much starch and grease,' Reggie informed him.

'Mr Dent has disappeared,' said Mr Winstanley.

'That's odd,' said Reggie. 'I saw him at lunch.'

'At lunch? Where?'

'Here, of course.'

'Here?'

'Mr Dent has joined our community. Didn't he tell you?'

Mr Winstanley's eyes bulged.

'He most certainly did not,' he said. 'He has a secretive streak.'

'I didn't realize that,' said Reggie.

'He plays it very close to the chest.'

'It probably comes of having to keep things private at public inquiries,' said Reggie.

'Possibly,' said Mr Winstanley. 'But if you ask me he's a bit of a loner. Take my advice, Mr Perrin. Beware of loners.'

'Thank you, Mr Winstanley. I'll remember that.'

'Mr Dent is a bit too fond of stealing plums from under my nose. Anything with a touch of novelty. A hint of the unusual. Off he trots. Doesn't put it in the diary. A good man, mind, if he wasn't so secretive.'

Snodgrass appeared at the window of the sun-room, miaowing to be let in.

'Cats exacerbate my asthmatic condition, I'm afraid,' said Mr Winstanley. 'Yes, Mr Dent telephoned us to say that he had the 'flu, which didn't surprise me, as he's not as robust as some of us. No resistance at all. Anyway, I didn't think twice about it.'

'You wouldn't. It's so boring.'

'Well, exactly. Then yesterday it came to light that he'd phoned Mrs Dent to say that he'd been sent off to a town planning conference in Harrogate. Of all the flimsy excuses! We've tried to trace him through his diary, which was inadequately entered up.'

'The secretive streak.'

186

'Precisely. Eventually our Mr Pennell remembered that he'd said something about checking up on you.'

'Which you would have loved to do yourself as I've made totally unauthorized changes of use and am running a business from five adjoining residential houses with overloaded drains and inadequate air vents, and which I purchased in a most irregular way involving the impersonation of non-whites.'

Mr Winstanley's air was one of mystification, rather than gratification.

'It rather spoils the fun, doesn't it, when I admit it all like this?' said Reggie. 'It offends the hunter and the sportsman in you. Because unless I'm very much mistaken, Mr Winstanley, you are a sportsman.'

'You wouldn't be trying to flatter me, would you, Mr Perrin?' said Mr Winstanley.

'Of course not. You're far too shrewd,' said Reggie.

'Thank you,' said Mr Winstanley. 'We can go into the matter of the houses later. What are we going to do about Mr Dent, that's the pressing question.'

Snodgrass miaowed pitifully at the window.

'It's our sports afternoon. He'll be taking part in a boxing match. He's immensely game,' said Reggie.

Mr Winstanley's eyes bulged again.

'Mr Dent's taking part in a boxing match?'

'Yes.'

'Mr Dent of Botchley Borough Council?'

'Yes.'

'Little shorthouse with big ears?'

'Yes.'

Suddenly, Mr Winstanley smiled. His face was miraculously transformed.

'This I must see,' he said.

A small ring, hurriedly ordered from the Botchley Sports Centre, had been erected in the centre of the living-room of

Number Twenty-five. There was barely room for the single row of hard chairs which had been placed round the walls for the spectators. Reggie entrusted Mr Winstanley to Doc Morrissey's care. They took their seats. There were some twenty spectators, staff and guests.

'This is a very exciting experiment,' Doc Morrissey told Mr Winstanley. 'Turning aggression upon oneself in order to come to terms with it.'

'I don't understand,' said Mr Winstanley.

There was a red sash on the ropes behind one of the boxers' chairs, and a blue behind the other. The two seconds entered with their towels and bowls, and took up their stations behind the chairs. The second in the red corner was the disillusioned imports manager. The second in the blue corner was the even more disillusioned export manager.

Mr Dent and the pub landlord stepped into the ring, discarded their dressing gowns and limbered up.

Mr Dent, in the red corner, was five foot four and thin, his matchstick legs gleaming white beneath the shorts that Elizabeth had bought for him at Lionel of Botchley.

The landlord was six foot three and broad-shouldered.

'It's not fair,' said Mr Winstanley, his resentment of his deputy's secretive ways temporarily forgotten. 'He should fight someone his own size.'

'He is,' said Doc Morrissey.

Mr Dent caught sight of Mr Winstanley and waved. Reggie stepped into the ring and called the ill-assorted fighters together. He inspected their gloves.

'And now, ladies and gentlemen,' he boomed. 'We come to the first bout of the afternoon. This is a three-round, heavy-weight and fly-weight contest between, in the red corner, Mr George Dent, of Botchley, and himself, and in the blue corner, Mr Cedrick Wilkins, of Epsom, versus himself. May neither man win.'

Mr Winstanley looked at Doc Morrissey in bewilderment.

The grand old man of the couch beamed. The bell rang. Both pugilists leapt from their chairs and the first round began.

The styles of the two men were as contrasting as their physiques.

Mr Dent put up a determined if somewhat over-cautious defence which his determined if somewhat over-cautious attack was totally unable to penetrate.

Mr Wilkins's defence was somewhat wild and uncoordinated, so that, although his blows were somewhat wild and uncoordinated, he was able to get in some pretty effective punches, pinning himself against the ropes for long stretches.

At the end of the round both seconds were enthusiastic about their man's chances.

'You're seeing yourself off,' Mr Dent's second told him, fanning the little council official's face with his towel. 'You've got yourself so you just don't know where to turn.'

'You're laying yourself wide open,' Mr Wilkins's second told him encouragingly, as the burly publican spat heartily into the bowl. 'Now go in there and finish yourself off.'

The bell went for the second round.

The landlord soon knocked himself down. He got up after a count of eight, knocked himself down again, struggled up bravely after a count of nine, and knocked himself senseless.

They carried mine unconscious host out of the ring, and he soon revived.

The third and last round was a distinct anti-climax. Mr Dent continued to duck, weave, feint, side-step and hold. Occasionally he managed to hit one hand with the other, but he didn't succeed in getting in one decent blow during the whole three minutes.

The crowd gave him the bird.

As Mr Dent left the ring to renewed booing he waved once more to Mr Winstanley. He seemed unperturbed by his reception.

The second bout began sensationally. The businessman who answered to the name of Edwards rushed into the middle of the ring, hit himself violently in the balls, cried 'Below the belt, you swine', and collapsed in a groaning heap.

'A victory for that congenital bastard Levingham over the congenial loser Phipps-Partington, you see,' he told Reggie, when he had recovered sufficiently to speak.

Later that afternoon, Reggie saw Mr Winstanley again. Once more, the venue was the sun-room at Number Twenty-one.

'That boxing was ridiculous,' said the paunchy official.

'Thank you.'

'Absolutely ludicrous.'

'You're too kind.'

'Everybody reacted as though it was the most normal thing in the world.'

'We ask them to join in. They enjoy it. Children enjoy the ridiculous and what are adults but older children? Unfortunately, adults tend to feel it destroys their dignity to enjoy the ridiculous.'

'I think it's ridiculous to enjoy things as ridiculous as that.'

'Thank you again. As you're so enthusiastic, why not stay and have a look at us? We have wonderful food.'

'So Mr Dent says.'

'I don't really expect you to stay, Mr Winstanley. You have all your work to do. With Mr Dent away you must be snowed under. Irregularities with air vents are rife in Botchley, I hear, and sun-room extensions are the rule rather than the exception. You don't want to have to sit with a lot of strangers over our lovely food when you could be indulging in merry banter with your fellow officials over the meat pies in the town hall canteen.'

'How can I stay?' said Mr Winstanley. 'What could I tell people?'

'Tell your office you've got 'flu, and tell your wife you've got to go to a town planning conference in Harrogate.'

'That's not a bad idea.'

*

January gave way to February. Snow gave way to rain and rain gave way again to snow, as the winter continued to tease.

Jimmy and Lettuce got the photos of their honeymoon back, and everyone admired them.

'There seems to be a bus in every picture,' Reggie commented.

'Damned hard to get a picture in Malta without a bus in it. Nature of the terrain,' said Jimmy. 'Nice old buses, aren't they? Lovely shade of green.'

The granite of Lettuce's face was touched by sunlight as love and amused exasperation played upon her features.

'Interesting ticket system. Tell you about it some time,' said Jimmy.

'I can't wait,' said Reggie.

'Tell you now, then,' said Jimmy.

'No. Anticipation is such sweet pleasure,' said Reggie.

'No equivalent of our Red Rover, as such, though,' said Jimmy.

Lettuce spent her time helping Jimmy with his expeditionary activities, but it was understood that she could be used as reinforcements to plug any holes that might develop in the community.

'Stout girl,' was Jimmy's comment. 'Trouble-shooter. Feather in your cap.'

For the moment, however, there was no trouble to shoot.

There were no holes to plug.

Guests continued to pour in. Some had strange tales and quirks to relate.

There was the hotelier who owned a chain of small hotels and restaurants which bore famous names, but with the first letter missing. He owned the Avoy, Orchester and Itz in London, Affles in Singapore, Axim's in Paris, the Lgonquin in New York. The idea was that people would mistake them for their renowned equivalents. What actually happened was that some people said, 'Look. The first letter's dropped off the

Dorchester. It must be going downhill,' while the others said, 'Oh, look, some silly berk's trying to pretend that's the Ritz'. The final straw to his collapsing empire came when he stayed at the Avoy and found that its first letter had dropped off, so that the neon sign outside the grubby frontage read: 'VOY HOTEL'.

There was the research chemist whose sexual proclivity was for women who had glandular fever. Since all the women to whom he was attracted refused to go out with him because they were ill with glandular fever, his problem was one of loneliness and frustration.

Then there was the young homosexual who made supermarket trolleys and wire baskets at a small firm near the Potteries. Reggie excitedly informed him that his boss was also present, but the meeting between them was not a success. As the boss explained to Reggie, 'It wouldn't do for me to have an intimate relationship with a lad on the shop floor. We may both be one of them, but there's a worker-boss situation to be taken into account as well. A them and us situation. I'm one of them who's one of us, and he's one of them who's one of them.'

Reggie decided to convert the five garages into double bedrooms, to provide more accommodation.

The work was supervised by Mr Dent, with Mr Winstanley as his assistant. Both men enjoyed the reversal of their roles, but they got even greater pleasure out of the unauthorized change of use which they were helping to perpetrate. When Mr Pennell called round on the trail of his colleagues, he joined in the alterations with relish.

Another man to arrive at this time was Paul Pewsey, the photographer. He sat in the sun-room, confident, pale, superficially effeminate.

'I can only relate to, you know, things,' he said. 'I just can't relate to, you know, people. I'm in a not relating to people situation.'

Suddenly, to his own surprise, Reggie began to speak.

'This is because you see people as things,' he said, smiling hastily to take the sting out of his involuntary words. 'You see people as things which ought to relate to you. I think you've taken up photography not because you want to look at the world through your camera but because you want the world to look at you looking at it. Every photograph you take is really a photograph of yourself taking a photograph. You look like a homosexual but like to be seen in the company of attractive women. That way, you are an object of speculation and mystery. In fact, you are almost asexual, since you are more interested in being admired than in admiring. You want to be both the butterfly and the album. You're from a working class background and have joined the classless society, which as you know forms a very small and rather conspicuous class. I think that that is all I think and that you will be sorry that I've stopped talking about you.'

Paul Pewsey stared at Reggie in astonishment.

So did Reggie.

'Go on,' said Paul Pewsey. 'I love it.'

The arrival of Paul Pewsey was quickly followed by that of Clarissa Spindle, the designer, Loopy Jones-Rigswell, the playboy, Venetia Devenport, the model, and Byron 'Two breakdowns a year' Broadsworth, the *avant-garde* impresario.

In the wake of the newspaper articles and the television appearance, Perrins was becoming fashionable.

Hastily, Reggie widened the scope of his adverts. He inserted an advertisement in the programmes of twenty football league clubs. It concluded with the words, 'Yobbos accepted. Party rates for mindless louts.'

In the *Daily Gleaner* he proudly announced, 'Nig-nogs welcome'.

In the *Daily Gunge* he declared, 'Illiterate pigs warmly invited. Get someone who can write to apply to 21, Oslo Avenue, Botchley'.

*

Confidence was high at this time.

Even C.J. was throwing himself into the spirit of things. In the evenings, it was true, he preferred to remain in his room but by day he had become a fount of strength.

One day Reggie accompanied him on his commuting trip to London with a small band of guests.

'I have an idea,' Reggie said, as they assembled in the surprisingly spacious Genuine Hall of Number Twenty-one. 'You will never know, and need never see again, the other people in the compartment. So it's ridiculous to worry what they're thinking of you. Self-consciousness is the truly British disease, not bronchitis, homosexuality or tea breaks. Today we will overcome this self-consciousness. The conversation on the train will be utterly ridiculous. But I won't say any more. This is your show, C.J.'

'Thank you, Reggie,' said C.J. 'Our bodies are enclosed in conventional clothes. We carry conventional briefcases and umbrellas. But our minds are as free as air. They can swoop on ideas like swallows on flies. They can soar to flights of invention like a buzzard over the mountains.'

'Well put, C.J.,' said Reggie.

They set off down Oslo Avenue, six conventional commuters. The wind was razor sharp. They turned left into Bonn Close. They turned right into Ankara Grove. They walked down the snicket to Botchley Station. They waited for the eight fifty-two.

'May I suggest a simple device today, to get it off the ground?' said C.J.

'Please do,' said Reggie.

'We put urgle on the ends of words,' said C.J.

'Good thinking,' said Reggie.

'Thank yurgle,' said C.J.

Reggie couldn't hide his look of astonishment. C.J. smiled in return, acknowledging how extraordinary his transformation had become. Was this transformation genuine, or was

194

C.J. playing a game, or simply earning his salary? Or all of these things? There was no clue on his face.

At three minutes past nine, the long dirty blue snake that was the eight fifty-two slid noisily into Platform One. The train was crowded, and they all had to stand.

The conversation began.

'Eleven minutes lurgle.'

'Typicurgle.'

'Blurgle Southern regurgle.'

'Derailed rolling sturgle at Wimbledurgle, I belurgle.'

'Not a bad mornurgle.'

'Nurgle.'

'Not at all burgle.'

'Bit curgle.'

'Yurgle.'

'Looks like rurgle.'

'Or even snurgle.'

'I didn't gurgle where I am todurgle withurgle recognurgle a mornurgle that lurgle like snurgle.'

'Did it make you feel better?' Reggie asked at Waterloo.

'Definurgle,' came the chorus.

'You can stop now, for God's sake,' said Reggie.

Every morning after that, C.J. led his clients down Oslo Avenue.

Every morning, they turned left into Bonn Close.

Every morning, they turned right into Ankara Grove.

Every morning, they went down the snicket to Botchley Station.

Every morning, they caught the eight fifty-two.

Every morning, it was eleven minutes late.

Every morning, C.J. and the clients were dressed exactly like all the other commuters.

Every morning, they held absolutely ridiculous conversations, and proved that in spirit they had freed themselves from convention and conformity.

Every morning they all got seats.

\*

195

Towards the end of February the coquettish snow storms gave way to the real thing. A fierce depression in the North Sea pulled the cold winds from the steppes. The winds roared far to the North of Britain, and were sucked back by the deepening cyclone. On the biting north-westerlies came the snow.

A faint sun was still shining over Botchley when the first reports of blocked roads came through on McBlane's radio, blaring away in the steaming kitchen as he scraped Belgian salsify with fierce disdain.

Soon the first flakes were falling in Oslo Avenue. By now there were so many road works reports that there was hardly time for any records at all, but in other ways the snow was harmful. By morning there were sixteen inches of level snow, and drifts up to seven feet at the exposed end of Lisbon Crescent. No trains ran from Botchley Station. No further council officials came to inquire into the strange goings-on at Perrins. The guests' cars were hidden beneath the drifts.

Jimmy speedily arranged snow-clearing sorties. Systematic checks were made in the poorer parts of Botchley for old people freezing slowly to death in badly heated houses. Doctors were informed and proved not to be interested.

A survey printed in newspapers that were never delivered because of the drifts showed that Britain came seventeenth in the world snow-clearing league, behind Yugoslavia and Peru. There was ice in Ramsgate Harbour. Trains were stranded in the Highlands of Scotland and in Devon. All down the stern backbone of England, early lambs froze to death, and vets both shy and extrovert were stranded. Charms of goldfinches starved within sight of the oast houses of Kent.

But in Numbers Seventeen to Twenty-five, Oslo Avenue, everything was cosy. People poured out their problems to Doc Morrissey. They tried to tell David Harris-Jones about their sex lives. They formed barber shop quartets with Joan, boxed against themselves with Tom, enacted the great love scenes of literature with Tony, weaved baskets with Prue, and made snowmen with Linda.

'Pure art!' said Byron 'Two breakdowns a year' Broadsword, shaping his snowman excitedly, 'because totally ephemeral.'

In the evenings they helped McBlane prepare his superb food, they ate McBlane's superb food, they helped to wash up McBlane's superb food. And then they sat and talked as the smokeless fuel crackled. They shared cigarettes and bowls of Tom's loganberry brandy and prune rum. Every now and then, as if moved by some spontaneous force, they would all touch and embrace each other. Occasionally someone would strum a guitar, and a middle management shanty, or an import/export protest song would shake the rafters. From time to time a couple would drift off, make love and drift back in again. Yarns were exchanged, beautiful experiences related.

Slowly, the thaw came. A few guests left, to return to the outside world stronger and better than when they had come. Sincere were the thanks and generous the cheques. Typical of the tributes was one paid by a leading light in the Confederation of British Industry.

'When I came here, Perrin, I was dying,' he said. 'I was dying of a serious social disease. Complacency, Perrin. Terminal complacency.'

He puffed long and gently on his pipe as he made out his generous cheque.

'I'm not complacent any more,' he said. 'I'm a wiser, better, kinder, happier man. I'm honest with myself at last.'

These were the good times.

The centre of the little town was pulsating with life.

The light was fading, and the street lamps were on.

Shop windows were ablaze with light.

Reggie walked slowly down the long main street, lined with cheery buildings from many centuries.

A butcher handed an old age pensioner a lamb chop and refused payment.

A kindly young property developer trudged happily from house to house, seeking the views of the residents on what they would like to see done to the pretty little town of which they were so proud.

Six youths in the colours of Chelsea Football Club ran down the main street, chanting, 'Be fair to the Somalis. Bring peace to the Ogaden.'

The dignified man sitting outside the Bull and Flag smiled at them. They smiled back.

Strapped to the dignified man's chest was a board, on which was written, in a strong, elegant hand, 'Successful merchant banker. Please take generously.'

In front of the merchant banker was a bowler hat. It was half full of coins.

Every now and then a poorer member of the community bent down and took a coin. The merchant banker smiled.

Down the street in the opposite direction from the Chelsea fans came a swarm of Tottenham supporters. They were cleaning the windows of all the shops as they passed.

'What's the score, young man?' called out the merchant banker to the leading youngster.

'We lost six-five, didn't we, old timer,' said the Tottenham supporter, and a cheer rose from the whole ragged assembly.

Reggie opened his eyes and found Elizabeth watching him with interest.

'You had a smile like a Cheshire cat,' she said.

'I was dreaming,' he said.

He stretched and yawned.

'Monday morning,' he said. 'Another week's work.'

He leapt out of bed and pulled back the curtains.

It was not yet quite sunrise, and the garden looked bare in the cold light of dawn.

Yet Reggie didn't feel cold.

The last of the snow had gone, and the first snowdrops

were out. Soon the crocuses would come, then the daffodils. Spring was on the way.

Reality looked as beautiful as Reggie's dream.

Five guests began that Monday morning. They included the first yobbo, the first nig-nog, and a man who had crossed the path of Reginald Iolanthe Perrin before.

The first guest had a wet mouth and spoke very fast.

'I'm a philosopher,' he told Reggie, sitting on his chair so lightly that he gave the impression of balancing just above it. 'I believe that the art of philosophy is vital for mankind's survival. Politicians are finished,' he said. 'Such battles as they were ever equipped to fight have been won, even if the victories have been Pyrrhic.'

He laughed, and crossed his legs so violently that he almost fell off the chair.

'The relationship of politicians to the nation has become as that of top management to an industrial concern,' he said. 'They deal largely with economic management, not political principle. It's as inappropriate to elect politicians as to elect the top management of ICI.'

He flung his arms in the air with such force that his chair almost toppled backwards.

'The questions asked in the political arena today are "how" questions – "How do we manage our society?", not "what" questions – "What kind of society do we want?",' he continued. ' "How do we achieve continued growth?" rather than "Is continued growth desirable?" I believe, incidentally, that it is not, since the world's resources are finite, but it can't be abandoned without a fundamental change in our philosophy. So, I believe we must ask "what" questions instead of "how" questions. But how? Aha! Yes?'

'Yes.'

'One suggestion. Have philosophical elections instead of political elections.'

Reggie smiled.

'There now follows a party philosophical broadcast on behalf of the logical positivist party,' he said. 'This programme is also being broadcast on BBC2 and ITV.'

'Precisely. Totally unrealistic, of course, like everything worth striving for, because once you have something, by definition you can't strive for it. "I plan an expedition to Samarkand." "This is Samarkand." "Blast, that's scuppered that, then."'

'It's better to travel hopefully than to arrive,' said Reggie.

The philosopher looked at Reggie as if seeing him for the first time.

'Yes! Awfully well put, if I may say so,' he said.

'Thank you.'

Suddenly the philosopher slumped dejectedly. All the energy went out of him.

'I've arrived,' he said.

'What at?' said Reggie, concerned at the abrupt change in his guest's manner.

'Everything,' said the philosopher mournfully. 'I've solved all the problems of ethics, mathematics, logic and linguistics, all of them.'

'The whole lot?'

'The whole bang shoot. It's no use pretending I haven't. It'd be like crying, "Eureka, but mum's the word".'

'Or "I won't climb Everest, because it isn't there",' said Reggie.

'No, that's different,' said the philosopher.

'Just testing,' said Reggie. 'What are your solutions?'

'I can't reveal a word of it,' said the philosopher. He lowered his voice. 'I've had threats.'

'Threats?'

'The existentialist mob. The linguistic boys. The logical positivist mafia. I've been getting anonymous letters, heavy arguing on the phone, pseudo-jocular messages.'

He handed a sheet of writing paper to Reggie. A message

had been glued on to it in letters of assorted sizes. 'I think, therefore I am going to duff you up,' it said.

The philosopher nodded.

'I wouldn't have told anyone,' he said. 'I couldn't. It would have put every other philosopher out of work. It would have taken away the purpose of life. In finding the purpose of life, one destroys it. They didn't need to threaten me.'

Was this man genuine? Was he a phoney? Was he mad? Could his tale possibly be true?

There was no way of telling.

He wanted to say something brilliant.

'Well, well!' he said.

'Help me, Mr Perrin,' said the philosopher.

The yobbo entered the room awkwardly, shyly, nervously, arrogantly, defiantly, and plonked his eloquent body on the chair.

'Bleeding sub-human cunt, aren't I?' he said.

'Are you?' said Reggie. 'Well . . . er . . . hello.'

'Glenn Higgins. I'm a yobbo.'

'Are you?'

'Course I am. I'm a bleeding mindless lout. That bloke you've just had in here. Naffing philosopher, right?'

'Yes.'

'Philosophers don't stab the bleeding opposition with knives and break all the windows in their coaches, do they?'

'No.'

'Know why? Because they aren't sub-humans cunts. Listen. The way I look at it is this. Right? When his naffing lordship bleeding philosopher and I were kids, we were both in prams wetting our bleeding nappies and crapping all over the bloody place, right?'

'Right.'

'Now he's a philosopher and I'm a football hooligan, right?'

'Right.'

'They have philosophy conferences and that, all expenses paid, white-haired geezers giving these talks and that, right?'

'Right.'

'They don't have conferences of elderly football hooligans, all expenses paid, right?'

'Right.'

'When we're fighting, we reckon we're proving a point, know what I mean?'

'You're showing society that you don't give a damn for the established order of things, right?'

'Right. But it isn't society that's the bleeding loser, right?'

'Right.'

'I reckon it's a mug's game, being a sub-human cunt. Help me, Mr Perrin.'

The third guest to face Reggie across the sun-room desk shook hands briskly, flashed his white teeth, and said, 'I'm the nignog'.

'I'm sorry about that advert,' said Reggie. 'But I wanted it to stand out. I really do want to get some coloured people in. It's in danger of becoming a kind of therapeutic Cotswolds. Your name?'

'Clyde Everton Frank Johnson.'

'Ah!' said Reggie. 'Named after the three Ws, eh? Walcott, Weekes and Worrell. What a team that was. Stollmeyer, Rae . . .'

'I hate cricket,' said Clyde Everton Frank Johnson. 'I hate the way you talk to us about it all the time, as if that's the only contact we make. As if we're children. Black people are lovable when they're children. Cricketers and jazz singers remain so. Shit.'

'I couldn't agree more,' said Reggie.

Snodgrass scrabbled at the window with her paws, uttering plaintive supplementary miaows.

'What a lovely non-white cat,' said Clyde Everton Frank Johnson.

Reggie let Snodgrass in. She leapt on to Reggie's chair and he had to tip her off before he could sit down. She gave an injured squawk and settled down on the floor by the filing cabinets.

'You know why you all think we're lovable as cricketers, don't you?' said Clyde Everton Frank Johnson.

'Tell me,' said Reggie.

'Because cricketers wear white flannels,' said Clyde Everton Frank Johnson. 'Garbage. Do you know what I do for a living, Mr Perrin?'

'How could I?'

'Guess.'

'Well . . . bus conductor?'

'Schoolmaster.'

'Oh, I'm sorry,' said Reggie. 'It's just that . . .'

'Many of us have to do jobs which are below the level of our intellectual attainments?'

'Well, yes.'

'The joke is this, Mr Perrin. I'm doing a job which is above my level of intellectual attainment. I ought to be sacked. But I'm not. You know why?'

'I imagine it's difficult to sack a teacher,' said Reggie.

'It's because I'm black. They'd have asked me to leave long ago if I was white. Man, I'm really bugged with all this prejudice. Hasn't a black man even got the right to be sacked in this damned country?'

Reggie drummed on his desk with his fingers.

'What do you want me to do?' he said.

'Teach me not to hate,' said Clyde Everton Frank Johnson. 'Help me, Mr Perrin.'

'Have you heard of the Fraternity of Universal Love?' asked Mrs Enid Patton, from Trowbridge.

'No,' admitted Reggie.

Her lips worked even when no words emerged. Her hair sagged listlessly under the crushing burden of life.

203

'Two months ago I was expelled,' she said, 'For inviting into my kitchen a woman who wasn't a member of the Fraternity of Universal Love.'

A roar shattered the silence of that blustery morning in early March. A pneumatic drill was probing the surface of Oslo Avenue.

'You were expelled for that?' said Reggie.

'My family aren't allowed to speak to me. They're still members, you see,' said Enid Patton.

'After what happened to you?'

'The community's their life, Mr Perrin. My husband's a Regional Reaper. The elder boy's a Group Leader and the younger boy's an Elder.'

Reggie walked over to her, and put an arm on her shoulder. She had begun to sob.

'I understand,' he said. 'You've lost your family and your faith. I can't help you with the family, but I will say this about the faith. I believe that every virtue praised by religion, with the single exception of worship itself, is just as valid in the name of humanity if there's no God and no purpose in life.'

Mrs Patton turned a tear-stained face towards him.

'You shouldn't say such wicked things,' she said. 'May God have mercy upon you.'

'You mean you . . . you still . . . er . . .' said Reggie.

'God's road has many turnings,' sobbed Mrs Patton. 'Help me, Mr Perrin.'

Last of the five came the man who had crossed his path before.

It was none other than Clive 'Lofty' Anstruther, best man at the wedding that never was, Jimmy's partner in staccato speech and his secret army, who had vamoosed with all the weapons and money.

Reggie greeted him neutrally. He felt that it would be a betrayal of Jimmy to show friendliness and a betrayal of Perrins to show hostility.

Clive 'Lofty' Anstruther was tall and sinewy. No irony attended his nickname. He lit a cigar which, like him, was long, thin, brown and showing signs of age.

'Permission to smoke?' he said, after taking a luxurious puff.

'Certainly,' said Reggie.

'Well done,' said Clive 'Lofty' Anstruther.

'Why are you here?' said Reggie.

'Remorse. Fear of death. Conscience. All that palaver,' said Clive 'Lofty' Anstruther.

He sighed.

'Like to pay poor old Jimmy back,' he said. 'Hoping I might run into him some time.'

'That shouldn't be too difficult,' said Reggie. 'He's here.'

Clive 'Lofty' Anstruther seemed as near to turning pale as he would ever be.

'Here?'

'Yes.'

'Working here, for you?'

'Yes.'

'Splendid. Well done.'

'Yes, isn't it?'

'Help me, Mr Perrin.'

Jimmy was out all that day, on an expedition that involved the use of no less than six bus routes, so it wasn't until evening that the touching reunion took place.

Reggie invited both men to the Botchley Arms for a preprandial snifter.

The saloon bar was awash with furniture. Chairs and tables abounded. The walls had erupted with swords, plates and horse brasses. Shelves were covered with Toby jugs. The carpet was fiercely patterned. The only thing that could be said in its favour was that it was the best bar in Botchley.

Reggie sat in a corner, underneath a mauve wall lamp, a tank full of mouldy goldfish, and a warming pan of no distinction. He sipped his Guinness nervously. This was the ultimate test of his community. If Jimmy could make his peace with the man who had so grievously wronged him, there was no limit to what Perrins could achieve.

He had asked Jimmy to arrive fifteen minutes before Clive 'Lofty' Anstruther, in order to prepare him.

At last he arrived.

'Sorry I'm late,' he said. 'Cock-up on the back collar stud front.'

Reggie bought him a large whisky and reflected on the old-fashioned nature of the old soldier's attire. Where other men simply slipped on a shirt and tie, Jimmy had two collar studs, two cuff-links and a tie-pin to contend with each evening. He changed for dinner every night, out of one shirt with frayed cuffs into another shirt with frayed cuffs. Reggie suspected that he also had a shoe-horn, shoe-trees and his personal pumice stone, but this wasn't the time to ask. There were bigger fish to fry.

'I've got you here to meet someone,' said Reggie, when they were both seated. 'I hope you're in no hurry.'

'No. Lettuce is making herself beautiful. Be an hour at least.'

'Yes.'

'No slur intended, Reggie.'

'Jimmy, would you describe yourself as a charitable and forgiving man?' said Reggie.

'Other cheek, mote and beam, that sort of crack?'

'Yes.'

'Goodwill to all mankind, that kind of caper?'

'Yes.'

'Yes, I would, Reggie. Every time.'

'Would that include Tim "Curly" Beamish?'

Jimmy's mouth dropped open. His left eye twitched.

'Ah! That bastard. Ah well, that's different,' he said.

'It's goodwill to all mankind except Tim "Curly" Beamish?'

'Could put it that way. Johnny did me down, Reggie.'

A thought struck Jimmy, an event so unusual that it caused his hand to lurch and his whisky to spill.

'Not here to meet Tim "Curly" Beamish, am I?' he asked.

Reggie shook his head, and Jimmy relaxed.

'No,' said Reggie. 'Clive "Lofty" Anstruther.'

More whisky sloshed on to the table. In the tank, a fish abandoned life's uphill struggle. The other fish ate it. Jimmy gazed at the scene as if it was tenderness itself, compared to the emotions that he was feeling.

'He arrived this morning, to join our community,' said Reggie. 'He's had a change of heart. He wants to pay you back.'

'Think so, too,' said Jimmy.

Reggie put his hand on Jimmy's arm.

'I expect the highest standards,' he said. 'This is your supreme test. This is Australia at Lord's. This is Everest. This is your Rubicon.'

Jimmy breathed deeply, and forced a ghastly parody of a smile.

'Message received and understood,' he whispered faintly.

He downed the remainder of his whisky in one gulp, before he had a chance to spill any more.

Clive 'Lofty' Anstruther stepped anxiously into the bar. His face was tense. He approached them. He too tried to force a smile.

'Hello, Jimmy,' he said, holding out his hand.

There was a perceptible hesitation before Jimmy clasped the proffered extremity.

'Anstruther,' he said hoarsely.

'What are you having?' said Clive 'Lofty' Anstruther.

'Large whisky, please, Anstruther,' said Jimmy.

'Well done,' said Clive 'Lofty' Anstruther.

The former con man towered over the other customers at the bar. Reggie smiled at Jimmy.

'Well done,' he said.

'Just don't expect me to call him Lofty, that's all,' said Jimmy.

'Cheers,' he said.

'Cheers,' said Reggie.

'Cheers,' said Jimmy, after another slight hesitation.

'Long time, no see,' said Clive 'Lofty' Anstruther.

'Not surprising,' said Jimmy.

Clive 'Lofty' Anstruther cleared his throat.

'Jimmy?' he began.

'Yes?'

'Bastard business, that thing. Rotten show. Rifles and so forth.'

Jimmy swallowed hard and looked at Reggie.

Reggie nodded encouragingly. 'Everest,' he mouthed.

'Oh well,' said Jimmy. 'Water under bridge, Anstruther.'

'Never in army,' said Clive 'Lofty' Anstruther.

'Can't all be,' said Jimmy. 'Funny old world if everyone in army.'

'Pack of lies from start to finish.'

'Oh well.'

'What heppened to all the . . . er . . .?' asked Reggie.

'Weapons? Sold them. Dribs and drabs. Not a fighter. Yellow streak,' said Clive 'Lofty' Anstruther.

'Bad luck,' said Jimmy.

'Rotten through and through,' said Clive 'Lofty' Anstruther.

'Drew a lousy hand, that's all,' said Jimmy. 'All the other babies, two hearts, three no trumps, that sort of crack. You, no bid. Rotten luck.'

'Thanks.'

'Drink?'

'Thanks.'

Jimmy bought three large whiskies.

'Cheers.'

'Cheers.'

'Cheers.'

'Pay you back,' said Clive 'Lofty' Anstruther. 'Weekly instalments.'

He hunted in his pockets, found two grubby notes, and handed them to Jimmy. Jimmy stared at them.

'Harbour?' he said. 'Castle? What are these?'

'Guernsey notes,' said Clive 'Lofty' Anstruther. 'Legal tender.'

Jimmy put them in his wallet very carefully, as if he didn't trust them not to disintegrate.

'Remember the wedding you didn't turn up at?' said Clive 'Lofty' Anstruther.

'Yes,' said Jimmy. 'Bad business, that.'

'Don't blame you,' said Clive 'Lofty' Anstruther. 'She looked like the back end of a bus.'

'Married her just before Christmas,' said Jimmy.

'My God, is that the time?' said Reggie.

'Oh my God. Awfully sorry,' said Clive 'Lofty' Anstruther.

'Don't worry, Lofty,' said Jimmy. 'I like buses.'

They walked back up Bonn Close, and turned left into Oslo Avenue. Reggie felt a warm glow in his heart. The world was wending its way to his door, and saying, 'Help me, Mr Perrin.'

Many of their problems were difficult, but if he could reconcile Jimmy and Clive 'Lofty' Anstruther, he could solve them all.

Yes, there were the good times.

There would never be such good times again.

# 7   The Difficult Days

The crocuses appeared. So did a petty thief.

His existence came to light at a sex symposium presided over by David Harris-Jones in the sex clinic, alias his bedroom.

The double bed had been folded against the wall, and ten people sat round in a circle. Apart from David Harris-Jones, there were eight guests and Reggie, who was holding a watching brief.

The eight guests were Mr Winstanley; a depressed police Superintendent; the extremely shy vet, who appeared to be too shy to leave the community; a scientist who believed that scientific progress would eventually destroy mankind; an automation consultant, who believed that mankind would have succeeded in rendering itself surplus to requirements long before it was destroyed; a football hooligan from Sheffield who felt that, with United and Wednesday both down the plughole, being a football hooligan in Sheffield was a declining industry; a Highways Officer from Botchley Borough Council; and a British Rail traffic manager, who arrived seventeen minutes late, due to alarm clock failure.

The symposium began with a game of 'Sexual Just A Minute'. The guests had to talk for one minute on any subject connected with sex. They must not hesitate or repeat themselves or deviate from the subject. The aim of the exercise was to break down inhibitions.

The scientist described his favourite sexual activity. After eleven seconds he was buzzed for deviation.

The football hooligan spoke for one minute about a knee trembler in a back alley in Tinsley.

'Super,' said David Harris-Jones, when he had finished.

The automation consultant described a night he had spent with a lady electronics expert in Geneva. After fourteen seconds he was buzzed for repetition.

The Superintendent spoke for a minute about the prostitutes of Trudworth New Town.

'Super, Super,' said David Harris-Jones, when he had finished.

The extremely shy vet was buzzed after one second for hesitation.

Mr Winstanley spoke of Mrs Winstanley's uncanny resemblance to Kim Novak. He illustrated this with a snapshot and was very upset when he was buzzed for inaccuracy. He grabbed the photo and shoved it back in his wallet.

Suddenly he began to examine the contents of the wallet very carefully.

'I've been robbed,' he said. 'I can't believe anybody here would take money.'

The extremely shy vet spoke, so softly that only dogs could have heard him.

'What was that?' said Reggie.

'I lost ten pounds last Friday,' he said.

'Why didn't you say?' said Reggie.

'I did, but nobody heard me.'

'You ought to send for the police,' said the Superintendent.

'Two cases isn't much,' said Reggie. 'Leave it for a bit, eh?'

The Highways Officer talked about his obsession for Andrea Bovington of Accounts. Reggie didn't listen. He knew that, if the thefts continued, they could destroy the delicate balance of faith and trust that had been created in the community.

He tossed and turned long into the silent Botchley night.

'What's wrong?' Elizabeth murmured sleepily, shortly after three o'clock.

'It's those thefts,' said Reggie. 'It's like a rape in a nunnery.'

'Stop exaggerating, Reggie,' said Elizabeth.

'This is supposed to be a place of trust and faith, darling,' said Reggie.

Elizabeth switched on the light.

'Men!' she said. 'Everything goes well for several months, then you get two puny little thefts, and you start panicking.'

'You're right, darling,' said Reggie. 'I'm sorry.'

'This is a test of *your* trust and faith,' said Elizabeth. 'You've got to have faith in the thief's conscience. Trust him to see the error of his ways.'

'You're right, darling.'

'You expect everything to go well all the time. It's impossible. It's through set-backs that you prove your strength.'

'You're absolutely right, darling.'

'Don't just agree with everything I say, Reggie. It's extremely irritating.'

'You're abso . . . lu . . . go to sleep, darling. It's gone three.'

He kissed her and turned over to go to sleep. She was right. Faith and trust. Everything would be all right. Quite soon he was asleep.

He woke to find that she was no longer in the bed. She was over at the dressing table, hunting through her handbag.

'What are you doing?' he asked her sleepily.

'You made me wide awake with all your not sleeping, and then you went straight to sleep.'

'I'm sorry, darling.'

'I came for one of my pills. I've got cramp.'

'I'm sorry, darling.'

She put her handbag down on the dressing table.

'My purse has been stolen,' she said.

'Are you sure?' said Reggie, wide awake now.

'Of course I'm sure. You're going to have to take some firm action over that thief, Reggie.'

'You're absolutely right, darling.'

He tossed and turned until dawn.

*

That morning Reggie called everyone together in the living-room of Number Twenty-one.

The room was packed. There were seventy people present, including al the staff, all the guests, and McBlane.

'Ladies and gentlemen,' said Reggie, standing on a chair so that he could be seen by everyone. 'I'll be blunt. We have a petty thief in our midst. Three cases have been reported.'

'Four,' said the Deputy Borough Engineer of Botchley Council. 'I lost ten pounds last night.'

'All right,' said Reggie. 'Four cases of . . .'

'Five,' said Clive 'Lofty' Anstruther. 'I've lost twenty pounds and my watch.'

'Are we to put at risk everything we've built up so painstakingly,' said Reggie, 'because we've lost seventy-five pounds and a watch?'

'Digital,' said Clive 'Lofty' Anstruther.

'We mustn't let ourselves be eaten away by suspicion,' said Reggie. 'I regard these lapses as relics of a past, mis-spent life, committed by somebody who hasn't been here long enough to come fully under the spell of our community. I say to this person: Cease your crimes, and free your conscience, by handing back the seventy-five pounds.'

'And the digital watch,' said Clive 'Lofty' Anstruther.

In the morning there were two more cases of theft, and none of the money had been handed back. Reggie called another emergency meeting. Once again he stood on a chair and addressed the crowd packed into the living-room.

'We have not yet been successful in reclaiming the soul of our erring brother,' he said. 'I don't believe that this thief is evil or greedy. I believe that he's bored. The conventional channels have failed to provide the challenge that he craves. It's the risk, not the money that is the motivation here. I ask you therefore to eliminate the element of risk, and at the same time put this criminal to private shame, by a supreme act of faith. Leave your valuables lying around the house tonight.'

'Asking for trouble,' said Clive 'Lofty' Anstruther. 'I know the criminal mind.'

'Sometimes we have to ask for trouble,' said Reggie, 'in order to overcome it.'

That night three hundred and eighty-two pounds, four watches, two rings and a bracelet were stolen.

Reggie held his third emergency meeting in the crowded living-room.

'Help me nail the sod,' he said.

The Superintendent was about to depart on one of Jimmy's expeditions when Reggie asked him to lead the inquiries into the thefts.

'It's what I've come here to avoid,' he groaned, following Reggie into the sun-room.

The March sun was streaming in through the wide windows. In a gap between the houses in Lisbon Crescent a street lamp glowed a faint orange. There was a fault in the timing device.

'Please!' said Reggie.

The Superintendent sighed.

'How can I refuse you when you ask me so nicely?' he said.

There was a knock on the door. It was the automation consultant. He wanted to leave. He was disturbed by the petty thefts.

'Do you mind if the Superintendent asks you a few questions? Purely routine, of course,' said Reggie.

'Not at all,' said the automation consultant.

The Superintendent cleared his throat.

'Did you commit those thefts?' he asked.

'No,' said the automation consultant.

'Thank you,' said the Superintendent.

214

When the automation consultant had gone, Reggie remonstrated with the burly policeman.

'Why didn't you ask him any more?' he said. 'It wasn't exactly a searching inquiry, was it?'

'No point,' said the Superintendent. 'He isn't the type.'

'You shouldn't look at people that way,' said Reggie. 'That's stereotyped thinking.'

The Superintendent set off to pursue his inquiries, but not before Reggie had emphasized the importance of being discreet.

There was a faint knock on the door of the sun-room. Reggie had to call 'Come in' three times before the extremely shy vet entered.

'I'm leaving,' he mumbled.

'It's the thefts, isn't it?' said Reggie.

'It's burst the bubble,' mumbled the vet, 'but I would have had to have gone sooner or later.'

'You aren't conquering your shyness as quickly as you'd hoped.'

The extremely shy vet nodded.

Could he be the thief? Anybody could be. Even the Superintendent.

'Do you mind if I ask you a few questions?' said Reggie.

'No,' said the extremely shy vet.

'Did you commit those thefts?' he asked.

'No,' said the extremely shy vet.

'Thank you,' said Reggie. 'No further questions.'

Reggie knew that he hadn't made a conspicuous success of his first police inquiry, but he consoled himself with the thought that the extremely shy vet wasn't the type.

That afternoon both the football hooligans departed in high dudgeon, after their rooms had been searched. Before they left they punctured the tyres of every car in Oslo Avenue. Reggie was angry with the Superintendent.

'I suppose you searched their rooms first of anybody,' he

215

said, as they reviewed the day's events in the sun-room that evening.

'They're the types,' said the Superintendent.

'I wish you hadn't done that,' said Reggie. 'You didn't find anything, I suppose?'

'No, but it was one of them. You run a nice, middle-class place. No crime. You bring yobbos in. Crimes begin. What they did to those tyres proves what they are.'

'They did that because you searched their rooms,' said Reggie. 'You force people into the roles you want them to play.'

'God save me from idealists,' said the Superintendent. 'That's the one good thing about Trudworth New Town. No idealists.'

The Superintendent handed Reggie fifty pounds.

'What's that for?' said Reggie.

'I'm leaving,' said the Superintendent. 'This place has failed me.'

At the door he turned.

'You won't get any more thefts,' he said.

There were no thefts that night, nor the next night.

The exodus continued. The trendies decided that Perrins was no longer fashionable and proved mean with their money.

Mr Linklater, from the Town Clerk's Department of Botchley Borough Council, was ushered into the sun-room on the following day. He was a neat, concise man, who looked as if he was trying to cram his body tight into an invisible box. He sat very upright, holding his hands firmly into his sides.

'You have eleven of my staff here, Mr Perrin,' he said.

'Twelve, including you,' said Reggie.

'I won't be staying, though,' said Mr Linklater.

'They all said that,' said Reggie. 'A cup of my coffee, a couple of my ginger nuts, a quick gander at my community, and they're hooked. Would you like coffee and biscuits?'

'No, thank you,' said Mr Linklater firmly. 'The decimation of our staff cannot continue.'

'I didn't force them to stay,' said Reggie. 'It isn't my fault if working for the council is boring, the offices are dreary, the corridors are dusty, and the food in the canteen is vile.'

'May I see my staff?' said Mr Linklater.

'Certainly,' said Reggie. 'Let me show you around.'

They set off along Oslo Avenue. The bright sun was deceptive, for the air was still quite sharp.

'What a strange walk you have, Mr Linklater,' said Reggie. 'The way you bounce up and down, and hold your backside in so tightly, as if you're walking through Portsmouth on a dark night.'

That afternoon Mr Dent called on Reggie and told him that the Botchley Council contingent were all leaving.

'I'll be sorry to see you all go,' said Reggie.

'We'll all be sorry to see us all go,' said Mr Dent.

'Is it the thefts?' said Reggie.

'I suppose they've brought it on,' said Mr Dent. 'That and Mr Linklater explaining about our benefits and back pay and how we wouldn't lose any if we came back now.'

Mr Dent remained standing, by the door.

'Sit down,' Reggie urged him.

'No thank you,' he said. 'You'd be offering me your ginger nuts next and then where would we be? Back at square one. We couldn't stay for ever, Mr Perrin.'

'I hope we've had an effect,' said Reggie. 'I hope you won't forget that real you that you spoke of. That friendly, genial, delightful man.'

'Don't you worry,' said Mr Dent, smiling. 'He's here to stay.'

He looked embarrassed.

'We ... er ... I'm collecting a sum of money from everyone. We've agreed how much we'll all pay, according to how long we've stayed. I've ... er ... I've done a cheque for us all.'

217

Mr Dent removed the cheque from his wallet and looked it over carefully.

'It's not a lot,' he said. 'You aren't millionaires if you work for the BBC.'

He handed Reggie the cheque. It came out at more per head than the amount donated by all the trendies.

'Thank you very much,' said Reggie.

'May I ask you a question?' said Mr Dent.

'Of course.'

'What did you say to Mr Linklater this morning?'

Reggie told him.

'Out of my own pocket,' said Mr Dent, handing him two five pound notes.

That evening Clive 'Lofty' Anstruther's room-mate handed Reggie an envelope.

It contained two hundred pounds and a note.

The note read: 'Dear Mr Perrin. Couldn't face you. Sorry. Yellow streak. Had to leave. Place destroyed for me by thefts. Peace of mind gone. Mankind rotten through and through. Please find £100 for you, £100 for Jimmy. More follows. Lofty.'

Five days later, Reggie received a letter, second-class, post-marked London.

'A thousand pounds gone from your safe,' it read. 'Sorry. Rotten through and through. Fact of life. Don't want anyone else to be suspected. Not vicious. Don't try and find me. Waste of time. Love to Jimmy. Lofty.'

Reggie hadn't even known that there were a thousand pounds gone from his safe. He had failed the two yobbos. He had lost nineteen of his fifty-two guests. He called a meeting of his staff, in the living-room of Number Seventeen.

They sat around the walls in the wildly assorted chairs, and drank coffee out of the brown mugs, each of which bore its owner's name.

In a gesture of solidarity, they never drank out of their own

218

mug. The names were on the mugs merely to remind them of other, less fortunate organizations, where a less happy spirit prevailed.

Reggie was smoking an opulent cigar.

'The petty thefts have knocked Perrins, but they haven't destroyed it,' he said. 'Things were too easy. We'll be all the stronger for the experience. It may even be a blessing in disguise as new guests will soon take up the slack, and will probably prove better payers than the trendies or the council officials. We've all got to work a little harder, but don't worry. We shall succeed. Any questions?'

'Yes,' said Tom. 'Why are you smoking a large cigar?'

'It's a psychological ploy,' said Reggie. 'It'll give me an air of authority and opulence which will help to re-establish an aura of confidence and well-being.'

He drew on the cigar luxuriantly, and sighed contentedly.

'I hate the bloody things,' he said. 'But it's a sacrifice I'm prepared to make, for the sake of the community.'


Buds began to appear on the trees, daffodils bloomed in the gardens, and all over Botchley men oiled their lawn mowers.

The clock went forward, providing an extra hour of daylight in the evenings.

The March winds grew angry at mankind's presumptuousness. We'll show them whether winter's over, they howled. They hurled themselves against roofs, rattled upon double-glazing, sported with carrier bags and old newspapers, and sent daffodils reeling.

A container ship carrying thousands of tons of Worcester sauce from Immingham to Nagasaki crashed on to the jagged rocks off the west coast of Guernsey and was severely holed. Spicy brown tides roared up the holiday beaches. The rocks from Pleinmont to L'Ancresse were awash with vinegar, molasses, sugar, shallots, anchovies, tamarinds, garlic, salt, spices and natural flavouring. It was the worst Worcester sauce slick in modern mercantile history.

Six novelists began books about the incident. Five of the books were called *Worcester Sauce Galore* and the sixth was called *The Fall and Rise of Lea and Perrins*.

Deborah Swaffham arrived at the community.

Jimmy continued the endless task of clearing Botchley of litter all over again. It was an ecological Forth Bridge. He removed a sodden copy of the *Botchley and Spraundon Press* (*Incorporating the Coxwell Gazette*) from the bars of a gate in Reykjavik View, where it had been flapping in impotent anger. He began to read it, for other people's newspapers are always more interesting than one's own. His eye alighted on an article by 'The Gourmet'. 'In the gastronomic treasure house that is War Memorial Parade,' the article began, 'no jewel shines more brightly than the wittily named Oven D'Or.'

Jimmy had just reached: 'My companion plumped for the prawn cocktail and pronounced it as delicious as it was ample,' when a bloodcurdling yell came from round the corner.

He abandoned his reading, and led his expeditionary force into action for the first time.

Three youths were attacking a smaller youth in Lima Crescent.

Jimmy's six-man force rushed in, with the exception of the philosopher, who hung back as much as he dared.

Jimmy tore into the midst of the fray, grabbed two of the youths, and banged their heads together before they knew what was happening.

'Take that, you bastards,' he shouted, bringing his knee up into the larger one's groin.

Four members of the expeditionary force were not far behind him, while the philosopher faffed around ineffectually on the edge of the fight.

The three youths were soon overcome.

'Love and peace, you bloody louts,' Jimmy shouted at them, as they limped sullenly off along Lima Crescent. 'Love and peace, do you hear? Reckoned without Major James Anderson, didn't you?'

One of the youths turned, and intimated, though not in those exact words, that retribution might be expected.

Jimmy turned to the rescued youth.

'On your way, lad,' he said.

The rescued youth set off equally sullenly in the opposite direction, without a word of thanks.

'Ungrateful sod,' said Jimmy.

The middle-aged expeditionary force stood panting in the road, regaining its corporate wind.

'Right,' said Jimmy, the flint dying reluctantly from his eyes. 'Back to clearing litter.'

'Leloipe,' cried the philosopher. 'My God! My God!'

'Know what you're thinking,' said Jimmy.

'I very much doubt that,' said the philosopher.

'Can't all be men of action,' said Jimmy, putting a consoling arm round the philosopher. 'Rum bag of tricks if we were.'

'No, no, no,' said the philosopher irritably. 'When you fought, I was thinking that here we have war and history in microcosm.'

'Microcosm, eh?' said Jimmy blankly.

'Violence to stop violence. A peace-keeping force is a contradiction in terms. Fighting for peace is as absurd as making love for virginity. And suddenly that led me on and I saw a fatal flaw in my solution. I'm wrong. All my life's work – wrong!'

'Bad luck,' said Jimmy.

'It's wonderful, you fool,' said the philosopher. 'I've lost everything.'

'Leloipe,' he cried again, and the wind hurled his triumphant cry of failure along Lima Crescent towards the Arctic.

Later that afternoon, as the winds spent themselves slowly, the philosopher saw Reggie in the sun-room.

His face was exultant.

'I haven't solved all the problems of ethics, mathematics,

logic and linguistics after all,' he said. 'In fact I haven't solved any of them. Isn't it wonderful news? Aren't you happy for me?'

'Delirious,' said Reggie.

'My quest can begin again,' said the philosopher. 'The long search resumes. Please accept a cheque for four hundred pounds. I wish it could be more, but philosophers aren't millionaires.'

'I haven't earned it,' protested Reggie.

'You've flung me back into the exquisite cauldrons of doubt and speculation,' said the philosopher gratefully.

On her first day, Deborah Swaffham had been upstaged by Jimmy's little fracas.

On the Tuesday, she was upstaged by the petition. It was delivered at three thirty in the afternoon by Mrs E. Blythe-Erpingham, of Windyways, Number Eighteen, Bonn Close. It had been signed by one thousand two hundred and seventy-six residents.

The purport of the petition was that the presence of Perrins in the midst of Mrs E. Blythe-Erpingham and her friends was 'inconsistent with the character of this predominantly residential area'.

Reggie greeted Mrs Blythe-Erpingham courteously, and studied the petition carefully.

'Photostats have been sent to the leader of the council, our MP, and to the *Botchley and Spraundon Press*,' she said.

'*Incorporating the Coxwell Gazette*,' said Reggie. 'I do apologize for interrupting, but I think we should remember our friends in Coxwell. We're all brothers and sisters under the skin, are we not, Lady Blythe-Erpingham?'

'*Mrs* Blythe-Erpingham,' said Mrs Blythe-Erpingham.

'Lady Blythe-Erpingham to me,' said Reggie.

Mrs Blythe-Erpingham simpered.

'I thought it would be courteous to bring you a photostat,' she said. 'And I would like to assure you, Mr Perrin, that this is only because of the parking, the punctures, the publicity, and the undesirable types that your excellent project attracts. There is nothing personal in this whatsoever.'

'I'm glad to hear it,' said Reggie. 'There's nothing personal in *this* either.'

He tore the petition into little pieces and dropped them over Mrs Blythe-Erpingham's head like snow.

In the early evening, in the late sunshine, Reggie strolled around the streets of Botchley, marshalling his thoughts.

Why did I tear the petition up?

Why was I rude to Mr Linklater?

I can't afford these gestures. They can destroy my work.

I shouldn't want these petty triumphs.

He entered the Botchley Arms and ordered a pint of bitter. The landlord had a long, gaunt face and a long, pointed nose beneath which a brown moustache bristled acidly.

'These fine evenings are bad for trade,' he said. 'People pop out to the country when they see a bit of sun.'

Reggie felt an impulse to make a thoroughly rude reply.

No, no, no.

'I daresay it's as long as it's broad,' he said.

'That's exactly the way I look at it,' said the landlord. 'You've got to in this trade.'

On the Wednesday, it was the financial problems of Perrins that occupied Reggie, and enabled those posed by Deborah Swaffham to remain undetected. Elizabeth asked him to come and see her in the secretary's office. She was wearing a pair of severe horn-rimmed glasses which she affected when she wished to look businesslike rather than wifely. Her eyebrows rose at his large cigar, but she made no comment. Instead she gave a concise summary of their financial position.

'Our expenses have been enormous and have used up almost all our capital,' she said. 'During January and February we were full, and still only just exceeded our costs. We are now not full. We can't guarantee to be full all the time. We must therefore make economies.'

'I think those are long-tailed tits at the bottom of the garden,' said Reggie.'

'Reggie!'

'Sorry, darling, I missed some of what you said. I missed that bit about the finances.'

'Reality won't go away because you don't look at it, you know.'

'You're absolutely right, darling, but those tits are lovely.'

Concentrate, Reggie.

Elizabeth repeated her pithy summary of their financial position.

Reggie puffed his cigar thoughtfully.

'We'll have to make economies,' he said.

'Those cigars can go for a start,' said Elizabeth.

'But not short-sighted economies,' he said. 'I mustn't lose my authority, darling, much as I might wish to. What are our major expenses?'

'Salaries and food. Salaries you can't cut down on. McBlane is extravagant.'

'You're suggesting that I go and see McBlane and tell him that we must make economies?'

'Frankly, yes.'

'Man to man, straight from the shoulder?'

'Frankly, yes.'

'Are you absolutely certain we need to economize?'

'Frankly, yes. Are you frightened of McBlane, darling?'

'Frankly, yes.'

Reggie walked slowly through the living-room, bracing himself for his confrontation with McBlane.

The kitchen was filled with the pleasant aroma of prawns provençale. The pustular wizard of the pots was seated at the kitchen table pouring white powder over his left foot.

224

'Morning, McBlane,' said Reggie. 'Prawns provençale. Yum yum.'

McBlane grunted.

'Keeping the old feet in good condition, eh?' said Reggie. 'Splendid.'

McBlane replied. For all Reggie knew, he might have said anything from, 'Yes, I'm a bit of a stickler for pedicure', to 'Mind your own business, you Sassenach snob'.

'Splendid,' said Reggie, taking a calculated risk, for if McBlane had said, 'I have an incurable dose of McAllister's Pedal Gunge and will be bed-ridden ere Michaelmas', Reggie's reply of 'Splendid' would have been distinctly inflammatory.

'Splendid food all week,' said Reggie, as McBlane drew a thick woollen sock over his powdered foot. 'So good, McBlane, that a thought occurs to me. A chef of your calibre doesn't need expensive ingredients all the time. Any chef can make a delicious meal of parma ham with melon, crayfish thermidor, and syllabub. Only a genius like you could make a delicious meal of, shall we say, leek and potato soup and scrag end of lamb. In others words, McBlane, were I to say to you that a degree of economy was needed, just a degree, you understand, then a chef of your brilliance and subtlety might see that as a challenge. Point taken, McBlane?'

'Guidy and airseblekkt ooter her whee himsel obstrofulate pocking blae ruitsmon.'

'Jolly good. We'll say no more about it, then, McBlane.'

On the Thursday afternoon, in the Culture Room, alias the Websters' bedroom, Tony was instructing Deborah Swaffham in the dramatic arts. More precisely, they were studying *Antony and Cleopatra*, with particular reference to the relationship between the eponymous duo. Tony was taking the part of Antony while it was Miss Swaffham's task to portray the sultry temptress of the Nile.

Tony was feeling a certain lassitude, possibly as a result of

225

his superb lunch of Parma ham with melon, crayfish thermidor, and syllabub.

Deborah Swaffham had long blonde hair, full lips with a suspicion of a pout, a good figure and long legs covered in a golden down. All Tony's lassitude disappeared when she said, 'How do you think Cleopatra would have kissed?'

'I really don't know,' said Tony. 'I've never given it much thought.'

'I think she probably used lots of tongue and things, rather slowly and thoughtfully,' said Deborah Swaffham.

'Perhaps you'd better show me,' said Tony.

And so, Deborah Swaffham and Tony sat in an armchair in the Culture Room on that quiet afternoon at the end of March in Oslo Avenue, Botchley, and were transported back through two thousand years of history.

After Deborah Swaffham had shown Tony how Cleopatra would have kissed, Tony showed her what he thought Antony's attitude to breast fondling would have been.

When Tony put his tongue in Deborah Swaffham's mouth, she gave it a little bite, like the remnants of natural aggression in a sleepy domestic cat.

'I couldn't do this as myself. It's only because I'm Cleopatra,' she said.

'I find that hard to believe,' said Tony.

'Honestly, Tony. I'm very inhibited as me. If you came to my room and things, when I was me, I wouldn't be like this. But then you wouldn't want to come.'

'How do you know?'

'I'm unattractive to men. I have this frigid element which turns them off.'

'Rubbish.'

Deborah Swaffham looked into Tony's eyes.

He held her gaze.

'If you came to my bedroom in Number Seventeen, I'm lucky, I've got a proper bedroom and no room-mate, if you came there during dinner, because food is pretty draggy, isn't it?'

'Food is Dullsville, Arizona.'

'If you came this evening, would you still be able to feel attracted enough to me to try and help me get over my inhibitions and things?'

'I could try,' said Tony.

That evening Tony complained of indigestion – 'probably the crayfish, I've never really been into crayfish' – and told Joan that he'd miss dinner. As soon as she'd gone to eat, he sped along the road to Number Seventeen. He was awash with greedy waves of desire.

Outside Deborah Swaffham's bedroom, he paused to tidy his hair. Then he knocked and strode in, masterfully, without waiting for a reply.

The room was empty.

'Those meals were very expensive today,' said Elizabeth in bed that night. 'McBlane can't have understood what you said.'

'He understood all right. He's mocking us,' Reggie said. 'Tomorrow I'm going to sort McBlane out. Don't worry.'

Elizabeth took her reading glasses off and placed them on her bedside table. Then she turned towards Reggie.

'I'm worried,' she said.

'Everything's going to be all right,' he said. You'll see.'

Friday dawned cold and stormy. Patches of steely blue sky appeared only briefly between the angry clouds. Reggie walked slowly towards the kitchen and what might well be his final showdown with McBlane.

Adam and Jocasta burst from the kitchen, full of energy and high spirits on the first day of the school holidays.

'Been to see Uncle McBlane?' said Reggie, glad of an excuse for delay.

'He's been telling us a story,' said Jocasta.

'That's very kind of him, isn't it?' said Reggie.

'Yes,' said Jocasta doubtfully.

'Tell me' said Reggie, 'can you understand what Uncle McBlane is saying?'

'Of course,' said Adam. 'We're big.'

'You can understand every word?'

'Of course,' said Adam.

'Just checking,' said Reggie.

'Except words we don't know,' said Adam. 'Like syphilitic.'

'Yes, quite.'

Adam lowered his voice, confiding in Reggie, man to man.

'Uncle McBlane's stories aren't as nice as Uncle C.J.'s stories about ants,' he said. 'Uncle McBlane's stories are boring.'

'Fucking boring,' said Jocasta.

'Yes, you can understand every word Uncle McBlane's saying,' said Reggie.

He entered the kitchen purposefully. If the pimply genius of the herbs hadn't had a meat cleaver in his hand, Reggie's task might have been easier.

'Hello again,' he said. 'Superb meals yesterday, McBlane. Superb. Not perhaps quite as economical as I'd have wished . . .'

McBlane raised the cleaver.

'. . . but, as I say, superb.'

McBlane grunted, and brought the meat cleaver down savagely upon the hare that he was preparing.

'But,' said Reggie, 'and this implies no criticism, McBlane, but, and it is a big but . . .'

McBlane raised the cleaver once more.

'. . . well not that big a but. A medium-sized, almost a small but. But still a but. Well, almost a but.'

McBlane hacked another portion off the splendid creature so cruelly denied the opportunity to display its seasonal mania.

Hailstones rattled against the window panes. The sky was a

bruised magenta. A breeze swept through the kitchen, stirring the loose ends of McBlane's boil plasters.

'I gather you're still telling stories to Adam and Jocasta,' said Reggie. 'Splendid. I wonder if for their age some of the stories are a little spicy, like your wonderful seafood pilaff.'

McBlane held the cleaver poised in his right hand. His poisoned thumb was encased in a sling, stained red with the blood of hares.

'Not too spicy, I hasten to add,' said Reggie. 'Far from it.'

The cleaver thudded into the hare.

'But perhaps spice, so brilliant in your seafood pilaff, is a little less appropriate in your stories.'

'Baskard brock wee reeling brawly doon awa' wouldna cleng a flortwingle.'

'Come off it, McBlane,' said Reggie. 'Stop playing games with me, you mobile bandage emporium. You can make yourself understood when you want to, you pock-marked Caledonian loon. You're all right when you tell your dirty stories, corrupting the children's minds, you diseased thistle from Partick. You stand there, like a demonstration model for a lecture on skin diseases, a walking ABC of ailments from acne to yellow-fever, ruining us with your extravagances, laughing at us, mocking us. Well, rather like you, McBlane, it just won't wash.'

Reggie stopped.

So did the hailstones.

The silence was deafening.

McBlane walked slowly towards him, the meat cleaver clasped in his right hand.

The hairs on the back of Reggie's neck stood on end.

McBlane walked straight past him and picked another hare from a huge plate which was lying on the Scandinavian-style traditional English fully integrated natural pine and chrome work surface.

He was poker-faced, and spoke quietly.

He might have said, 'I applaud the spirit if not the justice of your rebukes', or, 'I'll endeavour to mend my ways in future', or even, 'You'll pay for this, you long streak of Sassenach piss'.

Reggie would never know.

Later that afternoon, a longer, fiercer hailstorm clattered down on Botchley. Some of the hailstones were the size of exceptionally large hailstones. They caused the abandonment of Tom's latest football experiment. Having failed with no opponents, trying to score for the opposition, and goals being illegal, Tom hoped that at last he'd solved the problem of removing the aggression from football. There were now two teams of equal numbers, each trying to score in the opponent's goal. There were rules, and breaches of the rules were marked by free kicks and penalties. Players who committed serious or repeated fouls were sent off.

When he was told that this was exactly how football was played, and that the system was not notably successful, he replied, 'Oh well, I always told you I wasn't a sports person'.

On the way home it seemed natural that Tom should find himself walking beside Deborah Swaffham. She looked extremely attractive in her Botchley strip, her cheeks and legs reddened by the stinging hail, and Tom felt acutely conscious of the flabby whiteness of his nether limbs.

The storm abated as they crossed into Addis Ababa Avenue. Deborah Swaffham swayed towards Tom. She clutched him for support.

'Sorry,' she said. 'I thought I was going to fall.'

She kept her arm round his waist. When they turned into Washington Road, he grew visibly nervous. He lifted her arm and removed it from his waist.

'Sorry,' she said. 'I know I'm not the sort of person who turns men on and things.'

'You are,' protested Tom.

'It wouldn't worry me so much if I was ugly,' said Deborah Swaffham as they turned into Oslo Avenue. 'It's knowing that I've got full, firm breasts and a flat, taut stomach and rounded hips, and long shapely legs, and things, and still I have this distancing effect which shrivels the male libido.'

Tom's voice came out in a ghastly, strangulated croak.

'I assure you my libido isn't shrivelled,' he said.

'You could come to my bedroom during dinner,' said Deborah Swaffham throatily. 'Unless of course I'm not exciting enough for you to miss your food.'

Tom looked round furtively, to see if any of the other footballers had heard. Nobody was near them.

'I'll be there,' he croaked. 'I'm not a food person.'

'I'm not hungry,' Tom told Linda that evening.

'Not hungry?' she said. 'Are you ill?'

'Yes. Ill. That's it. Ill,' said Tom. 'I need to go to bed.'

As soon as Linda had gone to dinner, Tom dressed rapidly and hurried to Number Seventeen.

He paused briefly outside the door to tidy his hair. Then he knocked, and plunged in, masterfully, without waiting for a reply.

The room was empty.

Tom went back to bed and lay there, deflated, angry and ravenous.

'I thought of bringing you some cheese and biscuits,' said Linda on her return. 'But I thought I'd better not, if you're ill.'

'Quite right,' said Tom. 'Well, what masterpiece did I miss?'

'Cold meats,' said Linda. 'McBlane has disappeared.'

The policeman arrived at midnight. Reggie went downstairs in his dressing gown, and talked to him by the remnants of the living-room fire.

Elizabeth waited anxiously. At last she heard the front door go, and Reggie came upstairs.

'It's McBlane,' he told her. 'He's broken an arm.'

'Oh my God,' said Elizabeth. 'Well, I'll have to do the cooking, that's all.'

'McBlane can cook,' said Reggie.

'You can't cook with a broken arm.'

'I'll go bail for him.'

'Bail?'

Reggie climbed into bed and kissed her.

'It wasn't his arm he broke,' he said. 'Apparently he went into that big pub by the roundabout on the by-pass.'

'The Tolbooth.'

'Yes. And he attacked a Salvation Army lady with his meat cleaver when she tried to sell him the *War Cry*.'

'Oh my God.'

'I imagine that's what she cried. Unavailingly.'

Reggie switched off the light at his side of the bed.

'I think I may have gone a bit far in what I said to him this morning,' he said.

'What did you say?'

Reggie told her. She looked at him in considerable alarm.

'Why did you say all that?' she asked.

He shrugged.

'People are saying you tore up a petition over Mrs Blythe-Erpingham's head.'

'Yes.'

'Did you?'

'Yes.'

'Apparently you were insulting to Mr Linklater from the Town Clerk's Department.'

'Yes.'

'Oh Reggie.'

'Yes.'

'You destroyed yourself at Sunshine Desserts, Reggie.'

'Yes.'

'You destroyed yourself at Grot.'

'Yes.'

'You're not trying to destroy yourself again, are you?'

232

'Of course not. I couldn't stand Sunshine Desserts and I didn't mean Grot seriously. This is my life's work. Why should I destroy it?'

Elizabeth hugged him tightly.

'I couldn't bear it if everything was destroyed all over again,' she said.

Reggie squeezed her hand tightly and pressed his body against hers.

They made love.

Afterwards, just before he drifted off to sleep, Reggie said, 'Everything'll be all right, darling. You'll see.'

Elizabeth kissed him on the forehead.

'You'll see,' he said.

By a stroke of ill-luck, the Tolbooth was the local of a reporter from Reuters and the arrest of the chef of Perrins, the community of faith and trust and love and peace, on a charge of assaulting a Salvation Army lady with a meat cleaver made good reading in several papers.

'McBlane's just an employee,' complained Elizabeth. 'But they make it sound as if all our ideals are in ruins.'

McBlane returned to work, but an atmosphere of gloom hung over Perrins.

Reggie took to drinking champagne. Rarely was a glass absent from his hand.

'It's a gesture,' he told Elizabeth. 'A touch of style. I have to re-establish confidence all over again. You know I don't like the stuff. It's far too gassy. It's like the cigars. But what are my lungs and my digestion, compared to the future of Perrins?'

He topped up his glass.

On Sunday evening, Reggie called an emergency staff meeting. The demoralized group sat around, in the varied old armchairs, drinking coffee listlessly out of each other's mugs. A small baize-topped card table had been set up for Reggie, opposite the fireplace. On the table was a pad of writing paper, a supply of pencils, and an auctioneer's gavel which Elizabeth had picked up cheap at an auction of the belongings of a deceased Spraundon auctioneer. It would come in handy for keeping fractious meetings in order. So far there had been no fractious meetings, but the gavel's brief hour of glory was at hand.

Reggie entered two minutes late. He had a fat cigar in his mouth and a glass of champagne in his hand. He sat at the table and waited for the conversation, such as it was, to cease.

'Ladies and gentlemen,' he said. 'Morale has declined and these things must be nipped in the bud. This meeting is to discuss which buds, and how they should be nipped, and in what. I'd like one firm suggestion for improving morale from each of you. Who'll be first?'

He met in turn the eyes of Elizabeth, Tom, Linda, David, Prue, C.J., Jimmy, Lettuce, Tony, Joan and Doc Morrissey. Did any man ever have such a staff?

'Get rid of Deborah Swaffham,' said C.J.

All eyes turned towards C.J., seated in a relatively smart sofa, facing the window.

'Is she the one with the . . .' said Reggie.

'Yes,' said C.J.

'Expelling people looks to me like an admission of defeat,' said Reggie. 'However, if you insist on that suggestion, I'll make a note of it.'

'I do,' said C.J.

'Perhaps you could give us your reasons,' said Reggie.

'Certainly,' said C.J. 'When I do a job, I do it properly. I have never in my life spoilt a ship for a ha'porth of spilt milk, and I don't propose to start now. So, when Miss Swaffham, during our role-playing session earlier this week, proposed a further extra-mural session one evening, I heard the trumpet call of duty. I abandoned the story I was writing for Adam and Jocasta, and she came to my room. We . . . er . . . we had a role-playing session.'

234

'What roles did you play?'

'It was her idea.'

'What roles did you play?'

'Doctor and patient.'

C.J. looked at Elizabeth, appealing for moral support as his reward for having left her alone throughout the community's life. She tried to smile encouragingly.

'I felt out of my element,' he said. 'I didn't get where I am today by playing doctors and patients with Deborah Swaffham.'

Reggie took his cigar from his mouth and gazed steadily at C.J.

'Did the role playing involve . . .?' he began.

'An examination? Yes,' said C.J. 'She was the patient, by the way.'

'Ah!'

'It was her idea. She took off her clothes . . .'

He shuddered at the memory.

'I didn't know whether I was coming or going,' he continued. 'I . . . I forgot myself, Reggie.'

'Forgot yourself C.J.?'

'It's been a long time. I think everyone knows how much I miss Mrs C.J.'

'It's a *sine qua non*, C.J.'

'Is it really? Well, there you are. Anyway, I forgot myself. She hit me. She hit me, Reggie.'

C.J. flinched as he remembered the experience.

'We got dressed in angry silence,' said C.J.

'Oh, I see,' said Reggie. 'You'd got undressed as well.'

'She was shy of undressing. Said she had an unsexy body. I said, "You haven't seen mine". She said it might help her if she did. Oh God.'

'Thank you, C.J.,' said Reggie. 'It was brave of you to tell us that. It only goes to show that we should leave medical matters to the Doc.'

'No,' said Doc Morrissey.

All eyes turned to Doc Morrissey. He was sitting on a hard chair pushed back slightly out of the circle to Reggie's right.

'She got up on the couch,' he said. 'She seemed very tense and vulnerable I just put my arm round her.'

'Where were you?'

'Oh. I was on the couch as well. I didn't want to be in an analyst-patient situation, with the inequality that that entails. I thought she would feel better, professionally, in an analyst-analyst situation, or patient-patient situation, whichever you like. Let's call it a person-person situation, if you prefer.'

It seemed that Jimmy didn't prefer, for he let out a thunderous snore from the depths of his shabby armchair. Lettuce kicked him gently from the adjoining chair, whose springs hung down like a prolapsed uterus. He jerked to life with a moan.

'Sorry,' he said. 'Must have nodded off.'

'He's not been sleeping since that business with Clive "Lofty" Anstruther,' said Lettuce.

'Sorry,' said Jimmy. 'Morale shot to ribbons. Bad show. What's meeting all about? Rather missed that bit.'

'It's about low morale,' said Reggie.

'Ah! Treacherous chap, low morale. Depressing sort of cove.'

Reggie banged on the card table with his gavel.

'Order,' he said. 'Finish your story, Doc, and then maybe we can move on from this woman.'

'She told me she had sexual problems,' said Doc Morrissey. 'I'm afraid I . . . I forgot myself as well. She flung me off the couch. I practically broke my . . . er . . . well anyway it's still pretty painful.'

'Were you able to make an assessment of her character?' said Reggie.

'Yes,' said Doc Morrissey. 'She's a cow.'

'My community psychologist, and that is your considered opinion. She's a cow. I despair,' said Reggie. 'Anyway, Doc, enough of all this nonsense. Do you have any suggestion for improving morale?'

'Yes, I do,' said Doc Morrissey. 'Get rid of Deborah Swaffham.'

Reggie groaned.

'Right,' he said. 'I want a woman's view next. Maybe then we'll begin to get some sense. Any ideas, Joan?'

'Get rid of Deborah Swaffham,' said Joan.

'Oh my God,' said Reggie. 'Joan! You haven't been taking your clothes off with Deborah Swaffham as well have you?'

'No, but Tony has.'

'Is this true, Tony?'

'No.'

'He's doing *Antony and Cleopatra* with her,' said Joan. 'She suggests going back to her room. What does my faithful husband say? "O'oh! Knock-out!" He's really into Deborah Swaffham. She's where it's at.'

'But she isn't,' said Tony. 'That's the whole point.'

'Children!' said Reggie. 'Why can't you be like David and Prue?'

'Please. Leave us out of it,' said David and Prue Harris-Jones.

They were sitting in identical armchairs, holding hands. They were wearing brown trousers and navy-blue sweaters.

'Self-satisfied prigs,' said Joan.

'Please,' said Reggie, banging his gavel. 'Can't we do anything except squabble and talk about Deborah Swaffham and fall asleep?'

'Jimmy can't help it,' said Lettuce. 'He's worked his heart out for you, and he's taken this Clive "Lofty" Anstruther business very hard. Haven't you, darling?'

Jimmy launched himself into a fierce snore. Lettuce kicked him with gentle affection.

Jimmy looked round the room in puzzled surprise.

'Some sort of meeting, is it?' he said.

'We're discussing the fact that you keep falling asleep,' said Reggie.

'Sorry. Missed that bit. Must have dropped off,' said Jimmy.

Reggie buried his head in his hands and groaned.

'Please. Let's move on, away from Deborah Swaffham,' he said.

'Hear hear,' said Tony. 'It's Prick Tease City, Arizona, that one. OK, so I did go back to its room. The cow wasn't even there.'

'No, I'm not . . . er . . . I'm not . . . er . . . not sure what I was going to say,' said Tom. 'Sorry. Carry on.'

'Tony would have,' said Joan. 'Pretending he was ill and not wanting any dinner. As if that would fool anyone.'

A vivid flush spread over the few bits of Tom's face that weren't covered by his beard.

'Tom!' said Linda. 'Oh my God. So that's why you said you were ill.'

'Oh my God,' said Reggie. 'Not you too! Perrins? Sodom and Gomorrah, more like.'

'She . . . er . . . she played football the other day,' said Tom. 'She's not a bad little striker actually. Pretty good distribution. She put through some fairly shrewd . . .'

'Balls!' said Linda.

'Exactly,' said Tom. 'I went to her bedroom to discuss tactics before the hailstorm. That's all. No, Poggle chops, nothing happened.'

'No, she wasn't there, you poor sap.'

Reggie banged the gavel down on the table. It broke.

'Wonderful,' he said. 'Even the bloody gavel doesn't work.'

He hurled it across the room. It struck the mug marked 'Reggie', breaking it.

'A symbolic moment,' he said. 'Perrins is finished.'

Elizabeth stood up.

'I'm disgusted with you all,' she said. 'Haven't we better things to do than insult each other?'

'Exactly,' said C.J. 'Out of the mouths of babes and little children.'

'What the hell does that mean?' said Elizabeth.

'It's obvious,' said C.J.

'It's meaningless, you stupid fool,' said Elizabeth.

'Darling!' said Reggie.

Elizabeth stood in the middle of the room, and glared at them all in turn.

'You're behaving like fools,' she said. 'We've had a run of bad luck, that's all. A few petty thefts. One act of violence from our chef. And a cow who makes a fool of you. So are we to expel her because she's awkward? This nation is full of doctors who refuse to have patients on their lists because they're sick or old. It's full of homes for difficult children which refuse to take children because they might be difficult. Is it asking too much to hope that here we have somewhere which can actually cope with the people for whom it's intended? I suggest that tomorrow Deborah Swaffham goes to the sex clinic. It's what it's there for. I suggest that we fight all the harder for the success of this project we believe in, and reveal these set-backs for what they are. Pin-pricks. And now, could we at last have some sensible suggestions?'

She sat down. Reggie smiled proudly at her.

There was a moment's silence. It was broken at last by Jimmy.

'Well, why don't you have Red Rovers, you stupid Maltese bugger?' he said. 'Oh. Sorry. Dreaming.'

In the morning, Mr Cosgrove of the Highways Department called round.

'You're using a residential street to park cars for business purposes,' he said. 'The police could get you on obstruction. This is a bus route, Mr Perrin, and the magistrates are very protective towards bus routes. A purge on bald tyres also suggests itself. We only have to give the word.'

Reggie spread his arms in a gesture of helplessness.

239

'I know very little about these things,' he said. 'We're very unworldly here.'

'People have been laying off you,' said Mr Gosgrove. 'You've friends in the Town Hall. But your friends may not be able to help you much longer. The vultures are gathering over Oslo Avenue.'

The bed had been folded away. David Harris-Jones sat on a hard chair, behind a desk, and Deborah Swaffham curled foetus-like on the settee with her long legs tucked under her.

'I'm off-putting to men,' she said.

'Maybe it's because when they visit you, your room is empty,' said David Harris-Jones.

'That's awful of me, isn't it?' she said. 'But when I was inviting those men back to my room and things, I didn't intend to get all frightened and leave the room empty. It's just they give off this aura of sexual aggression. I bet people like Tony had hundreds of pre-marital conquests before they were married. And there's something a bit sinister in the way those older men go about it, Doc and D.J. and things.'

'C.J.'

'I'm hopeless with names. Oh God, what a mess.'

Deborah Swaffham began to cry. Real salty tears trickled from her grey-green eyes.

David Harris-Jones didn't intend to walk across to the settee and sit beside her. He didn't intend to put his arm around her. And he certainly didn't intend that the limb in question should fondle her consolingly.

Yet all these things happened.

Deborah Swaffham tried to smile. David Harris-Jones handed her a tissue and she blew her nose.

'I don't think I'd be frightened with you,' she said.

David Harris-Jones closed his eyes and felt himself sinking.

'You don't give off an aura of sexual aggression.'

'Oh, thank you. Thank you very much.'

'I bet you had hardly any pre-marital conquests before you were married.'

'Hardly any,' he agreed. 'It wasn't easy to be a Casanova in Haverfordwest.'

'I bet you get premature ejaculation and dementia praecox and things.'

'Well, I . . . er . . . thank you very much. Super.'

'Come to my room at lunchtime, David, and teach me not to be frightened.'

'Well, I . . . er . . . thank you very much. Super.'

David Harris-Jones went round to her room at lunchtime.

It was empty.

He stalked out angrily and found Prue standing grimly by the garden gate.

'Good-bye,' she said.

'Well, I . . . er . . . oh God. Oh God.'


At lunch Reggie noticed the absence of David and Prue Harris-Jones. He knew that Deborah Swaffham, at that moment chatting animatedly to a newly arrived yobbo, had seen David that morning.

He hurried round to Number Twenty-three.

He met them coming down the stairs. Prue was carrying a suitcase and little Reggie.

'We're splitting up,' said David and Prue Harris-Jones.

Reggie felt as if he'd been hit by a sandbag filled with lumps of old iron.

A taxi drew up, and Prue stepped into it, taking young Reggie with her. Nothing Reggie or David Harris-Jones said could persuade her to change her mind. David stared after the disappearing taxi with vacant eyes.

'She's gone,' he said.

He began to whimper.

'Prue!' he said. 'Prue!'

He stared at the forsythia bush.

'Prue!' he said. 'Oh Prue!'

No miracle happened. The bush did not turn into his wife.

Reggie put his arm on David's shoulder, felt David's knees begin to buckle, and hastily removed his arm.

'How can I live without Reggie, Reggie?' said David Harris-Jones.

Reggie stalked the litter-free streets of Botchley angrily. Along Oslo Avenue he went, and down Bonn Close to the High Street. The purpose of his walk was to control his anger and direct it towards its natural target. Deborah Swaffham.

It began to rain, a sharp shower on a merciless wind. Large spears of rain.

There was just time for a drink at the Botchley Arms before closing time. Reggie ordered a pint of bitter and a whisky chaser. There weren't many people in the bar, just a few businessmen angling for some after-hours drinks, and two housewives chatting animatedly over their toasted sandwiches. They looked at Reggie as at some monster from outer space. This was the fiend who'd torn up Mrs Blythe-Erpingham's petition.

Anger welled up in Reggie.

Anger at Deborah Swaffham.

Anger at his staff.

Anger at himself.

Anger at Botchley.

Anger at the nation.

Anger at the Northern Hemisphere.

Anger at the whole damned, stupid world.

But anger above all at Thomas Percival Crankshaft, licensed to sell beers, wines and spirits.

Because at that very moment the landlord pushed his long, gaunt face towards Reggie and said, 'These cold wet days are bad for trade. People have sandwiches in their offices, in the dry.'

'What a miserable, mean, boring, petty-minded prick you are,' said Reggie.

\*

He hastened home to beard Deborah Swaffham in her den.

He must treat her as a human being and try to help her.

It wouldn't be easy.

At that time she ought to be taking part in one of the manifold activities which were still continuing, despite the traumas. Whenever she ought to be in her room, she wasn't. Perhaps now, when she oughtn't to be, she would be.

She was.

Reggie sat in an old wicker chair that Elizabeth had picked up in one of the leading antique shops in Botchley.

'Anyone can be frightened of men, Deborah,' he said.

Deborah Swaffham walked casually round the room. She glanced at the print of bygone Botchley. Suddenly she pounced on the door, and locked it. She removed the key.

'I'm not frightened of men,' she said. 'All that was a blind to get to see you. You're the man with the power and things round here, and power fascinates me.'

'Give me that key, Debbie,' said Reggie.

Deborah Swaffham dropped the key between her breasts.

'Come and get it,' she said.

'I will not come and I am not going to get it,' said Reggie.

Deborah Swaffham sat on the bed and began to unzip her dress.

'Please, Deborah!' implored Reggie.

'Call me Debbiekins, Reggie.'

Reggie closed his eyes and counted ten.

'I'm not going to call you Debbiekins, and you will please call me Mr Perrin, Miss Swaffham,' he said.

He opened his eyes.

She had removed her dress. Her legs were long and shapely.

'You can't help being what you are,' said Reggie. 'But you can help me to help you to become different from . . .'

'You don't find me attractive,' said Deborah Swaffham. 'Nobody does.'

She began to take off her tights. Reggie hurried over to the window.

'You are attractive,' he said. 'You're gorgeous.'

He undid the sash and tried to lift the lower half of the window. It had stuck. He pushed desperately and at last it opened.

He breathed in the bracing spring air, and looked down at the flower bed in the front garden below.

Deborah Swaffham advanced towards him.

'I put you off, don't I?' she said.

'You're lovely,' he said, shoving her backwards on to her bed as gently as he could.

He ran to the window and began to climb out.

'You just don't fancy me,' he heard her sob. 'You hate me.'

'I find you irresistible,' he cried as he jumped out of the window.

Jimmy and his expeditionary force, trudging home from an afternoon of carrying shopping bags for old ladies, were suprised to see the leader of their community leap out of a bedroom window yelling, 'I find you irresistible'.

Reggie would have crashed into the flower bed, if his fall had not been broken by several small rose bushes.

Jimmy sent the guests rushing off to look for Doc Morrissey.

'I can't move,' Reggie groaned.

Doc Morrissey arived with a makeshift stretcher.

'I need a doctor,' said Reggie.

'I am a doctor,' said Doc Morrissey.

There was a film of sweat on Reggie's brow.

'I mean . . .' he began feebly.

'Faith and trust, Reggie,' said Doc Morrissey.

Reggie nodded resignedly.

They put him on the stretcher, and carried him to Doc Morrissey's room. Doc Morrissey examined him carefully.

'Is anything broken?' said Reggie.

Doc Morrissey stood up with difficulty. His back creaked like rowlocks.

'You need a doctor,' he said.

Miraculously, nothing was broken. A sprained ankle, a twisted knee, a strained back, severe bruising and widespread abrasions – these things can be lived with.

Three guests left, declaring the place to be a shambles.

Reggie decided that he had no alternative but to ask Deborah Swaffham to leave. It was either the community or her.

He hobbled along the street to Number Seventeen. His face was covered with pieces of elastoplast. Painfully, a step at a time, he hobbled up the stairs. He limped along the corridor, knocked on her bedroom door, and hobbled in without waiting for a reply.

The room was empty.

None of them ever saw Deborah Swaffham again.

The April weather remained changeable, but the fortunes of Perrins were not. People crossed the road to avoid speaking to anyone connected with the community. They were banned from every pub in Botchley. Youths jeered at Jimmy's expeditionary force. Among them Jimmy noticed the three who had attacked the smaller youth in Lima Crescent. And the smaller youth.

Mr Dent paid them a visit.

'I've come to check your air vents,' he said awkwardly.

Reggie nodded slowly.

'Rats don't desert sinking ships any more,' he said. 'They condemn them for having irregularly spaced portholes and the wrong kind of hinges on the companionways.'

'I can't blame you for casting me as Judas,' said Mr Dent.

Reggie accompanied him on his inspection. He was still hobbling, but the little municipal official didn't seem to mind their slow progress.

'You still have friends in the Town Hall,' he said, peering at the bricks of Number Twenty-five. 'We're being as slow as we can, but the wolves are closing in on Oslo Avenue.'

'Thank you for warning me, anyway,' said Reggie.

When the inspection was over, they shook hands.

'That other Mr Dent you spoke of?' said Reggie. 'What happened to him?'

'He can't really cope with life. He's keeping a low profile, but he's there. A faint flicker of your work lives on in me. All is not lost, Mr Perrin.'

All is not lost.

Reggie took the farewell words of the likeable little official as his text for those difficult days.

He continued to keep up appearances, enduring his cigars and his regular doses of champagne. As soon as he was sufficiently recovered, he went to London and bought himself a whole new wardrobe of clothes including a velvet jacket which suited him to perfection.

'You know how I'm never happier than when I'm pottering around in old trousers and pullovers,' he told his staff. 'Well, that's one more thing I've had to give up for the cause.'

All the activities continued. Paintings were painted, baskets were woven, roofs were thatched, songs were sung, sexual problems were mulled over, and good deeds were done, ridiculous conversations were held on trains, and in the evenings they relished their bowls of apple gin and pear vodka, their protest songs and their acts of physical solidarity all the more for the fact that they were banned from every pub in Botchley.

It began to seem as if the community could gain new strength from its vicissitudes and new solidarity from its isolation.

All was not lost.

Not yet.

# 8  The Final Days

One day in the middle of April, Reggie's bank manager sent for him. He had good news and bad news. The good news was that Reggie wasn't in the red. The bad news was that the level of his reserves was ninepence.

Reggie spoke eloquently about the ideals behind Perrins. He reminded the anxious financier about the amazing success of Grot, and opined that a similar success could shortly attend Perrins.

The bank manager lent him ten thousand pounds.

'It's a lifeline,' said Reggie in bed that night, as Elizabeth struggled to find her place in her book. 'It's a reprieve. Nothing more.'

'We mustn't waste a penny of it, Reggie,' said Elizabeth.

'I agree. Not a penny. Tomorrow we'll get a lawyer for McBlane.'

Elizabeth lost her place in her book just as she had at last found it.

'Don't be silly, Reggie,' she said. 'McBlane is blatantly guilty.'

'I agree,' said Reggie. 'He's obviously blatantly guilty. But the press are going to be gunning for us. Peace Community Chef in Sally Ally *War Cry* Drunken Meat Cleaver Assault Scandal. We simply must put up some good mitigating circumstances, so that we don't look ridiculous in the eyes of future guests.'

Reggie slid his arm under Elizabeth's back and kissed her nose.

'I have a plan,' he said.

She groaned.

The little public gallery at Botchley Magistrates' Court was crowded. So were the press seats.

The court had been built four years ago. It was panelled in light woods which had been stained to give an appearance of age and tradition. In the centre of the ceiling there was a skylight, with a dome of frosted glass. There were three lay magistrates, two men and a woman. They looked decent enough to realize how absurd it was that they would hold the scales of justice in their unqualified hands.

At ten past eleven McBlane entered the court room. He looked gaunt and long-suffering. He was wearing a suit, and had left his boil plasters off in the interests of respectability, yet he still looked like a threat to a civilized community.

He took the book in his right hand, and repeated certain words after the clerk of the court. It is to be presumed that they were the oath, but they could equally well have been extracts from the timetable of the Trans-Siberian Railway.

He was asked if he was Kenny McBlane, chef, thirty-four, of Twenty-one, Oslo Avenue, Botchley.

His nods led the court to understand that he was.

Mr Hulme, a confident young man in a striped blue shirt with separate white collar, announced that his client was pleading guilty to the charge of committing grievous bodily harm upon Ethel Henrietta Lowndes, spinster, in the Tolbooth Hotel, Botchley, between nine and ten p.m. on the evening of Friday, March the thirty-first.

He also pleaded guilty to the charge of possessing an offensive weapon, to wit a meat cleaver.

He pleased not guilty to the charge of using abusive language.

The case for the prosecution was brief and clear. Mr Hulme questioned PC Harris only about the abusive language.

'You say he used abusive language?' he said. 'What did he say?'

PC Harris consulted his notebook.

'This is a note I made at the time,' he said. 'I said to him, "What exactly has been going on here?" He replied, "Ye steckle hoo flecking clumpthree twinkoff".'

'Would you repeat that, please, officer?' said Mr Hulme.

'He said, "Ye steckle hoo flecking clumpthree twinkoff".'

'The court will draw their own conclusions from that,' said Mr Hulme. 'Now, did any further conversation ensue?'

'Yes, sir. Further conversation ensued,' said PC Harris. 'I said, "Lor, luv a duck, you're going to have to repeat that". He said, "Ye steckle hoo flecking clumpthree twinkoff".' I said, "Never mind that, my good man. What are you doing with that offensive weapon, to wit a meat cleaver?" He replied, "Flecking sassen achenpunk schlit yer clunge". I said, "I don't advise you to employ language like that to me", and he said, "Schpluff".'

'And this is his abusive language?'

'Yes.'

'But you don't know what it means?'

'No.'

'Then how do you know it was abusive?'

'It sounded abusive.'

'It sounded abusive. It seems to me, officer, that he used elusive language.'

'Yes, sir.'

'Are you aware that using elusive language is not an offence in English law?'

'Yes, sir.'

'No further questions.'

Miss Ethel Henrietta Lowndes was small and lined like an old tea cosy. Her left arm was in plaster. She had an extremely unfortunate effect on the magistrates. The effect was of hostility towards McBlane.

Mr Hulme only asked two questions.

'Did the accused speak to you?'

'Yes.'

'What did he say?'

'I don't know.'

After the prosecution's case had been completed, Mr Hulme called upon McBlane to take the stand.

'Would you please give the court your version of what transpired in the Tolbooth Hotel on the evening of Friday, March the thirty-first?' said Mr Hulme.

The magistrates leant forward, and McBlane began to speak. He spoke fast and incomprehensibly.

'Would you speak more slowly?' said Mr Hulme.

McBlane spoke slowly and incomprehensibly. The magistrates leant further forward.

'What's he saying?' asked the chairman.

'I don't know,' confessed the young lawyer.

An impasse!

'It seems to me that we're up a cleft palate with no paddle,' said the chairman of the magistrates.

'Absolutely!' murmured C.J. in the public gallery.

'There is one possibility,' said Mr Hulme. 'There's a man in this court who does understand my client. It's his boss, Reginald Perrin.'

'That is correct, sir,' said Reggie, standing up. 'I'm familiar with his speech, and furthermore I was evacuated to Glasgow during the war, to avoid the bombing. Awa hoo frae broch acha blonstroom doon the crangle wi' muckle a flangebot awa the wee braw schlapdoodles.'

'I don't understand,' said the chairman.

'No, but I do,' said Reggie.

The magistrates decided that they had no alternative. Reggie was warned of the dangers of perjury, and sworn in as interpreter.

McBlane began his version of events anew.

'He says he'd been drinking quite heavily, and his speech was becoming slurred,' said Reggie.

McBlane continued.

'The lady from the Salvation Army approached him,' said Reggie.

McBlane resumed his narrative, at considerable length.

'She asked him to buy the *War Cry*,' said Reggie. 'He told her how much he admired the publication's splendid mixture of information and entertainment. He said he'd buy the lot and then she could go home and put her feet up. She didn't understand a word of what he was saying.'

McBlane spoke earnestly.

'When he reached to take the pile of *War Cry*, she thought he was trying to steal them,' continued Reggie. 'In the ensuing misunderstanding, they were scattered. He reached for his wallet, but drew out the meat cleaver instead. In his semi-alcoholic confusion he didn't realize this.'

'What were you doing with the meat cleaver?' interpolated Mr Hulme.

McBlane looked round the crowded room for a moment before launching into his reply.

'The meat cleaver was blunt,' said Reggie. 'He was taking it to a friend who sharpens meat cleavers. He was expecting to meet his friend in the Tolbooth, but he didn't turn up.'

McBlane continued his narrative.

'McBlane saw that the lady, whose cause he had been attempting to help, was terrified and regarded him as a violent criminal,' said Reggie. 'For one brief moment all the frustrations of his misunderstood life welled up. He made one angry blow which unfortunately broke the lady's arm. He bitterly regrets it.'

McBlane nodded vigorously.

He was fined fifty pounds on the charge of grievous bodily harm, and fifteen pounds for being in possession of an offensive weapon.

The charge of using abusive language was dismissed.

*

There was widespread press coverage of the case of the lady from the Salvation Army and the mad Scottish chef with the meat cleaver. In spite of, or possibly because of, Reggie's intervention, much controversy was stirred up.

It was suggested in some quarters that Reggie's interpretation had been a pack of lies. The Salvation Army were not pleased. The vexed question of the lay magistracy was fiercely argued. Reggie was besieged by reporters. Several guests left, and many forward bookings were cancelled.

Reggie plucked up his courage and sacked McBlane. He told him that the community couldn't be associated with violence in any shape or form. He gave him a week's notice and a golden handshake of fifteen hundred pounds.

McBlane promptly disappeared.

In the morning, the papers carried widespread coverage of his sacking.

'They preached faith and love,' he was reported as saying, 'yet they sacked me for one offence, after I'd promised never to do it again.'

The journalists appeared to have no difficulty in understanding McBlane.

Reggie made a handsome donation to the Salvation Army, and informed the newspapers that he was willing to reinstate McBlane.

McBlane returned and resumed his duties, striking superb gastronomic form immediately.

Reggie went into the kitchen and welcomed him back with a firm handshake.

'Talking of handshakes,' said Reggie, 'obviously now you will return your golden handshake.'

McBlane examined his poultry knife, to see if its sharpness still met his exacting standards.

'Or then again it might be simpler to regard it as an advance on your salary,' said Reggie.

McBlane raised the knife in his right hand.

'Another possibility occurs to me,' said Reggie. 'Perhaps we could regard it as a bonus for your truly splendid cooking.'

McBlane, apparently satisfied with the sharpness of the knife, replaced it in its drawer.

'McBlane?' said Reggie.

McBlane turned and faced him.

'You can make yourself understood when you want to,' said Reggie. 'I know you don't like us and you feel that society has given you a raw deal, but I didn't choose to be born English and middle-class. And I did support you in court, whatever my motives. Please, McBlane. Talk to me so that I can understand.'

'Ye flickle mucken slampnach nae blichtig fleckwingle,' said McBlane.

Reggie wagged his finger sternly.

'A bit more of your jugged hare wouldn't come amiss,' he said.

Four clients departed. Seven forward bookings were cancelled. Four thousand pounds of Reggie's loan had gone.

Every hour of need throws up a hero, and this one was no exception.

The hero was Doc Morrissey.

The ageing medico called on Reggie in his sun-room, on the afternoon following McBlane's return, and plonked a milk bottle full of colourless liquid on his desk with an air of suppressed triumph.

'Taste it,' he said.

Reggie poured a minute measure, sipped it cautiously, then spat it out.

'It doesn't taste of anything,' he said.

Doc Morrissey sat back in his chair and stretched his legs like a somnolent dog.

'Precisely,' he said.

'Well, thank you very much,' said Reggie. 'It's just what I wanted.'

'Your sarcasm isn't lost on me, Reggie,' said Doc Morrissey.

He leapt slowly to his feet, and began to give an impression of a brilliant scientist, pacing around the sun-room like a tethered greyhound on heat.

'It can control entirely our supplies of insulin and adrenalin, our sugar level, and blood pressure,' he said. 'It can cure us of all our suggestions and neuroses. It can keep our bodies in a state of perfect chemical equilibrium. It can do everything you're trying to do here.'

Reggie lifted the bottle to the light and examined the liquid. It was absolutely clear and totally lifeless.

'Why have I never heard of this?' he said.

'It's a new invention,' said Doc Morrissey.

Reggie turned the bottle round and round slowly.

'British invention?' he asked.

'I invented it,' said Doc Morrissey.

Reggie handed the bottle back to its creator.

'You invented it?' he said at last.

'My antennae have become pretty sensitive to nuances since I started looking into this psychology lark,' said Doc Morrissey. 'I detect a lack of confidence in your attitude, Reggie, and it pains me.'

Reggie went to the window and looked out, drinking in the white blossom on the apple trees and the delicate pink of the almond.

Four clients jogged by on the gravel path, followed by a breathless Tom.

Faith and trust.

'Are you prepared to stake your reputation on this working?' said Reggie.

'Without hesitation,' said Doc Morrissey. 'I bring it to you, Reggie, in your hour of need.'

*

254

Before dinner that evening, Reggie called a staff meeting. They drank coffee out of each other's mugs. It was six fifteen on a cool spring evening, and one section of the calor gas fire was on.

Reggie sat gavel-less at his card table and explained about Doc Morrissey's wonder drug. A milk bottle full of the stuff stood on the card table in front of him.

Doc Morrissey addressed them, his face touched with a becoming modesty. He said that the drug was made up of many ingredients with long names which would be meaningless to laymen. He proposed that the staff and guests should take regular doses of his cure-all.

'I'm sorry,' began Tom.

'So am I,' said Linda.

'I haven't said what I'm sorry about yet.'

'I'm sorry you're about to pontificate.'

'Well I'm sorry that you're sorry, Linda,' said Tom, 'but pompous Patterson is about to pontificate. Is it ethically desirable that we should expose people to this drug? Surely the real benefit that people get out of the place is the feeling that they have been involved in helping to create the improvements that have taken place in their mental adjustment to the environment as a consequence of the manifold activities that we provide?'

'We don't need to let them know they're taking it,' said Tom.

'We can't afford to look a gift horse in the mouth, or we may go down with a sinking ship,' said C.J. 'I didn't get where I am today by looking gift horses in the mouth and going down with sinking ships.'

Jimmy patted Lettuce's hand. The gesture was an admission that he also thought the ship was sinking, to join the flotilla of his past disasters. More ships had sunk under Jimmy than were afloat under the Royal Navy.

'Army put bromide in men's tea, subdue sexual feelings,' he said. 'Heat of battle, erotic fantasies dangerous. Chaps

255

falling in love with their bayonet frogs, that sort of crack. Ends justify means. I'm for old thingummy's wonder whatsit.'

'Me too,' said Lettuce.

'Good girl,' said Jimmy.

Reggie smiled.

'What are you smiling at?' said Elizabeth.

'Do you remember the English versions on Cretan menus?' said Reggie. 'Some of them had lamp chops, some had lamb shops, but we never actually found one that said lamp shops. Well, I was just thinking the same thing about Jimmy. He refers to Lettuce as "good scout", "stout girl", and "good girl", but he never, well so far as I know he doesn't, and I can only go by what I've heard, never uses the fourth possible combination "stout scout".'

There was a stunned silence.

'Reggie!' said Elizabeth.

'Sorry,' said Reggie. 'It's a bit of a red herring at this important time, but you did ask me.'

He began to sweat.

Concentrate, Reggie. This is no good.

Elizabeth gave him a worried look and he smiled reassuringly.

'Yes, well,' said Doc Morrissey, somewhat needled by the red herring. 'Are there any further views on my wonder drug?'

'Is it really going to work?' said Tony. 'Because I've had the pineapple whisky syndrome up to here and I don't feel like scoring any more revolting drinks unless it's going to be Results City, Arizona.'

'We've never had pineapple whisky,' said Tom.

'Children,' said Reggie. 'Please! Tony does have a right to ask if it's going to work, though. I mean, has it been tested at all?'

'A bit,' said Doc Morrissey.

'Ah! Good!' said Reggie. 'What on?'

Doc Morrissey glanced round the company uneasily.

'Pencils,' he said.

'Pencils?' said Jimmy incredulously.

'Pencils,' affirmed Doc Morrissey.

'What sort of pencils?' said C.J.

'HB, C.J.,' said Doc Morrissey.

'I didn't get where I am today by drinking liquids that have only been tested on pencils,' said C.J.

'Did the pencils show a marked lack of aggression?' said Tony.

'Come come,' said Reggie. 'It's all to easy to be sarcastic. It's a failing that I've slipped into myself once or twice, but it really is terribly negative. I'm sure Doc Morrissey had his reasons. Tell us, Doc, what's the point in testing the liquid on pencils?'

'Not much,' said Doc Morrissey. 'I didn't have any animals, though.'

'I'm glad,' said Tom. 'I'm against testing animals on principle.'

'Pencils are all right, though, are they?' said Linda. 'What about the poor old Royal Society for the Prevention of Cruelty to Pencils?'

'I think vivisection of Paper-mates is shocking,' said Joan.

'I was outraged to read about the propelling pencil that was trained to turn round and propel itself up its own sharpener,' said Tony.

'Please!' said Lettuce.

She rose from her armchair and stared fiercely at the assembly. She had a kind of beauty at that moment, as the Grampian Mountains sometimes do, when touched by the evening sun.

'I think it's pathetic to listen to you all being sarcastic about pencils when Doc Morrissey has stuck his head on the block for the sake of the community,' she said. 'I'm happy to take a dose of the medicine now.'

She sat down, and there was an abashed silence, broken

only by the twanging of a spring deep in the tattered bowels of her chair.

'Stout scout,' said Jimmy, patting her hand with proprietary pride. 'Count me in too.'

Reggie banged on the table with his fist.

'Hands up all those prepared to test Doc Morrissey's magic potion.'

The hands of Doc Morrissey, Jimmy, Lettuce, Linda and Elizabeth shot up.

'I may as well,' said David Harris-Jones. 'What does it matter if it kills me?'

'Oh get off your self-pitying backside and go and drag Prue back,' said Reggie.

'I happen to believe that she was justified,' said David Harris-Jones. 'I succumbed to craven weakness. It's Dolly Lewellyn from Pembroke Dock all over again.'

'Dolly Lewellyn from Pembroke Dock?' said Reggie. 'Who's she?'

'I don't really want to go into her, if you don't mind,' said David Harris-Jones. 'I didn't much want to at the time. One isolated lapse in a lay-by on the A1076 and I had to make thirteen visits to the outpatients department at Haverfordwest General. I knew then that I wasn't destined to be a Casanova. I didn't have another woman from that day till I met Prue, and now I do this. Men are such fools. I . . .'

David Harris-Jones suddenly seemed to realize that he was talking to the collected staff of Perrins.

He blushed.

'Sorry,' he said. 'I . . . I didn't . . . er . . . realize. Sorry. Tragedy must have loosened my . . . er . . .'

'Go and find her, wherever she is,' said Reggie.

'. . . tongue,' said David Harris-Jones. 'I will. I'll go to her mother's and find her, wherever she is. Tomorrow. But first, I'll take Doc Morrissey's potion.'

'Thank you,' said Doc Morrissey, whose lone hand was still

raised in a gesture of long-suffering patience. 'I wondered when we were going to get back to that.'

David Harris-Jones raised his hand. So did Elizabeth, Jimmy, Lettuce and Linda.

Linda looked at Tom.

'I still have moral qualms,' said Tom.

'If Doc Morrissey's drug had been given to Jack the Ripper, his victims wouldn't have died,' said Reggie. 'Do you think they'd have had qualms?'

Tom raised his arm slowly.

'It was probably just the qualm before the storm,' he said. 'Joke. Joke over.'

Joan looked at Tony. Tony looked at Joan.

'Oh come on,' said Joan. 'It's May As Well Be Hung For A Sheep As Lambsville, Arizona.'

Joan and Tony raised their arms.

'Oh well' said C.J. 'Never let it be said that I was the one ugly duckling that prevented the goose from laying the golden egg.'

'I promise you I'll never let that be said,' said Reggie.

C.J. raised his arm.

'And you?' said Elizabeth.

'Oh no,' said Reggie. 'Somebody has to remain totally unaffected in order to observe the results scientifically.'

Slowly, one at a time, all the hands were lowered.

'And what more natural than that that somebody should be McBlane?' said Reggie.

'Perhaps you'd like to be the first to drink,' said Doc Morrissey.

'Splendid,' said Reggie. 'Absolutely splendid.'

Trust and faith. He poured himself an inch of the potion.

'The dose is half a glass,' said Doc Morrissey.

'I want to leave enough for the others,' said Reggie.

'My resources are to all intents and purposes infinite,' said Doc Morrissey.

'Oh good,' said Reggie. 'Splendid.'

He drank his dose swiftly, and to his surprise he didn't fall down dead.

All the staff took their doses.

Reggie called a special meeting of the staff and eighteen remaining guests. Doc Morrissey spoke about the drug. The staff took their second dose, and Reggie asked the guests for volunteers.

All eighteen volunteered.

Afterwards, they shared cigarettes and swapped yarns. A squash player with a drink problem sang Cherokee love songs. A time and motion man who'd investigated his own firm and been declared redundant as a result sang his own compositions, bitter-sweet laments for a less ruthless age. An overworked builder, known throughout his home town as Mañana Constructions, told an interminable story about the amazing prescience of his cat Tiddles. The manager of a dry-cleaner's in Northamptonshire went into the garden and made love to a lady computer programmer from Essex. Snodgrass was quite shocked when she came upon them, shivering from cold and ecstasy, naked and dewy under the suburban stars.

In the morning David Harris-Jones set off for Prue's mother's place in Exeter.

McBlane prepared twenty-nine portions of chicken paprika, and C.J. felt slightly queasy at breakfast.

Shortly after breakfast, both Tony and Joan felt slightly ill.

By half past ten, all three of them, plus Linda, had retired to bed with stomach trouble.

By twenty to eleven, stomach trouble was already a euphemism.

News of the outbreak spread rapidly. So did the outbreak. Was Doc Morrissey's potion to blame?

At five past eleven, Reggie confronted the inventive ex-medico in his upstairs room at Number Nineteen.

'Five members of my staff are ill,' he said. 'Three guests are feeling queasy.'

'Four,' said Doc Morrissey. 'One just left me in a hurry.'

'Your potion's responsible,' said Reggie.

'It can't be,' said Doc Morrissey adamantly.

'How can you be so certain?' said Reggie. 'Tell me just what *was* in that liquid.'

A strange smile played on Doc Morrissey's lips.

'It was water,' he said.

'Water?'

'Plain simple water. You don't really think I'm skilful enough to create a drug that does all I claimed for it?'

'Well, I did wonder,' said Reggie.

'Oh you did, did you? I shall take that as a personal insult,' said Doc Morrissey.

Reggie sat on the couch.

'May I ask you why you presented us with a wonder drug which was in reality water?' he asked grimly.

'Faith and trust. It was a psychological, not a medical experiment, Reggie, but I didn't want you to know it was psychological.'

'You concealed it for psychological reasons?'

'Exactly. But I didn't want you to know that the reasons were psychological. Psychology, Reggie. I wanted you to think that I was concealing the ingredients because I couldn't remember their medical names. When in fact I was concealing them because there weren't any. Pretty good, eh?'

'Excellent.'

'It was all lies, Reggie. Even the bit about the pencils. I just tossed that in to add authenticity.'

'It wasn't a conspicuous success.'

'I felt that. I wanted you to gain confidence because you believed you'd taken a wonder drug.'

'I see. Then why is everybody ill?'

'I've no idea.'

Reggie looked Doc Morrissey straight in the eyes.

'I don't know how to put this without being mildly rude,' he began.

'Be mildly rude, Reggie. I can take it,' said Doc Morrissey, smiling the cheerily mournful smile of a man reconciled to his pessimism.

'Your medical reputation at Sunshine Desserts wasn't high. You weren't known as the Pasteur of the Puddings. This reputation wasn't enhanced when you were sacked from the British Medical Association for gross professional incompetence. It is possible that, far from inspiring us to confidence, your mystery panacea has provoked us to fear, that my staff are persuading themselves into illness. The obverse of the mind over matter syndrome, Doc. The dark side of the psychological moon.'

Doc Morrissey looked stricken.

'Mass auto-indigestion!' he said. 'It's possible.'

He clutched his stomach and groaned.

'Excuse me,' he said, and hurried from the room.

The epidemic continued to spread.

An accident prevention officer swooned on his way to the toilet, fell downstairs and broke his leg.

Reggie sent for a doctor. He arrived at twelve twenty-three. Eight members of the staff and nine guests were by this time ill.

'It's mass hysteria,' he told Reggie at the conclusion of his visit. 'I've known similar things in girls' schools, and what is this place but a girls' school where the pupils happen to be adult and predominantly male?'

'I see no similarity,' said Reggie.

'I only mean,' said the doctor, 'that the emotional soil is favourable to hysteria. Hysterical dysentery. Fascinating,'

'And what do you propose to do about it?' said Reggie.

'Ah, that,' said the doctor, as if treatment was an afterthought of little consequence.

He prescribed medicine for people on the National Health and a better medicine for the private patients.

'Thank you,' he said, as he set off down the garden path in a burst of tactless sunshine.

'Thank you,' he repeated, for all the world as if the epidemic was a charade laid on for his delectation.

The symptoms of dysentery are widely known and it is best to draw a veil over them. Suffice it to say that at one o'clock fifteen people were sitting down, and in only seven cases was it for lunch.

The seven lunchers tackled McBlane's hare terrine in circumstances that were far from propitious.

'Tidworth all over again,' muttered Jimmy cryptically.

All five attempted to make cheerful conversation over the chicken paprika.

'Worse than Ridworth,' declared Jimmy, still in gnomic vein.

It was a deflated trio that struggled with McBlane's superb lemon meringue pie.

Both men accepted coffee.

'Far worse than Tidworth,' asserted the gallant old soldier, rushing out to meet his Waterloo.

And so, when McBlane entered to collect the pudding plates, he found Reggie in solitary state, defiant to the last, alone on the bridge of continence as his ship was scuppered about him.

'Thank you, McBlane,' said Reggie bravely to the pock-marked Pict. 'A superb luncheon.'

The bad luck that had assailed Perrins seemed determined to continue to the last.

It was bad luck that the doctor should have a drinking acquaintance who was a stringer for several national newspapers, so that Reggie spent much of the afternoon fending off the queries from the gentlemen of the press.

It was bad luck that it should be on this of all days that the environmental health officer came to review the sanitation arrangements. At first, all went well. He began with an examination of the kitchen. As luck would have it, McBlane was preparing a marinade for boeuf bourguignon, and not powdering one of his extremities or recycling his boil plasters.

McBlane appeared to be, albeit unconsciously, an advocate of Cartesian dualism. I, McBlane, can be monumentally filthy, inventively scabrous and permanently itching. You, the kitchen, must be clean and gleaming at all times. In truth, however, it was emotion and not logic which created this spectacular dichotomy. McBlane loved his kitchen. Nay, more. He was in love with it. Romeo and Juliet, Antony and Cleopatra, McBlane and his kitchen, three great love stories, passionate, vibrant, ultimately tragic.

Violent death parted Romeo and Juliet. Violent death parted Antony and Cleopatra. The tragedy of McBlane's great love was different.

His passion was unrequited.

Why did the tough scion of Caledonia love his kitchen? Because he didn't dare give his love to a woman. Women would spurn him. He had too many skin diseases.

While the kitchen didn't love him, it didn't spurn him. It didn't know that he was covered in spots. McBlane, ever a realist, had settled for the kitchen.

The Environmental Health Officer didn't know any of this.

'Only one health hazard there,' he told Reggie. 'The chef.'

Their examination of the toilets was hampered by the fact that they were constantly occupied. The presence of people standing in agonized poses waiting to enter the toilets was explained away by Reggie as art therapy.

'They're representing the agony of the human struggle in modern dance,' he said.

'They look as if they're waiting to go to the toilet,' said the philistine official.

'You see what you're capable of seeing,' said Reggie.

The Environmental Health Officer told Reggie that he'd be turning in a very unfavourable report.

'What do you have to say to that?' he said.

'Excuse me,' said Reggie.

He spent three days in bed with hysterical dysentery.

The newspaper headlines included 'Hysteria Bug Hits Jinx Community', 'The Squatters of Botchley' and 'Perrin Tummy KO's Commune'.

Undoubtedly, the hysterical dysentery would have caused many of the guests to leave, if they hadn't been too ill with hysterical dysentery.

Gradually., the staff and guests recovered. Four guests did leave.

A post-dysentery evening was planned, in which they would drink from communal bowls of Andrews Liver Salts and Bisodol.

Reggie let himself out of the side door and then remembered that he was banned from every pub in Botchley.

He walked down Oslo Avenue, and turned left into Bonn Close, a sinister figure with the collar of his raincoat turned up against the penetrating drizzle of early May.

He turned right into Ankara Grove, went down the snicket to the station, and took the narrow pedestrian tunnel under the tracks. It dripped with moisture and smelt of urine.

He plunged into the streets of the council estate, on the wrong side of the tracks. Here the houses were poor and badly maintained. Every possible corner had been cut, in the interests of persuading the inhabitants that they were inferior, so that they would accept their role in society and commit the vandalism that was expected of them, thus confirming the people on the right side of the tracks in their belief that they were right to stick these people in council estates on the wrong side of the tracks. Thus mused Reggie bitterly as he slipped through the dark, inhospitable streets.

Beyond the housing estates came the damp backside of Botchley, a rump as pitted and pocked as McBlane's. The street lamps were widely spaced and feeble, dim as a Toc H cabaret, their faint yellow glow deepening the darkness of the night around them. Here the streets were like teeth – old, stained, badly maintained, and full of gaps. It was the sort of area that film companies use for their blitz sequences. Even the potatoes on the tumble-down, refuse-ridden allotments were suffering from planning blight.

At the far end of these streets lay the Dun Cow.

Reggie entered the public bar, a tiny, ill-lit, raucous place, where the beer tasted as if several elderly dogs had moulted in it.

But it had one great advantage. He wasn't known here, and so the ban would not be imposed. He ordered a pint and prepared to assault it.

'Holy God, it's Mr Perrin himself,' said a familiar Irish voice.

Reggie turned to find himself gazing into the agreeable features of Seamus Finnegan, the former navvy whom he had plucked from obscurity to become Admin Officer at Grot.

'Seamus Finnegan!' said Reggie.

'If it isn't, some bastard's standing in my body,' replied that worthy.

'Terrible beer,' said Reggie.

'It is that,' said Seamus Finnegan. 'Undrinkable.'

'Have another?'

'Thank you, sir.'

They sat in a corner, watching two youths in filthy jeans throwing inaccurate darts at a puffy travesty of a board.

'It's good to see you, Seamus,' said Reggie.

'Thank you, sir,' said Seamus.

'Come on, Seamus. We're friends. Less of the "sir".'

'Thank you, sir, but your insistence that I don't call you sir is based on a false premise.'

'What premise is that?' said Reggie.

He closed his eyes, shut his nose, and forced a sizeable draught of beer down his throat.

'You're thinking "Poor Seamus. I brought him out from the obscurity of the Climthorpe Slip Relief Feeder Road, a simple tongue-tied Irishman from the land of the bogs and the little people, I rescued him from the swollen underbelly of that fat old sow that is urban deprivation, I made him Admin Officer in the hope that his simple Irish idiocy would send the whole Grot empire tumbling about our ears, but with the true contrariness of Erin he proved to be a genius, and then I disbanded Grot, leaving poor old Seamus to return to the drunken monosyllabic slime of the road works, his only companions simple oafs, and the occasional inarticulate driver of an articulated lorry, back in the gloomy underbelly of the aforementioned sow of urban deprivation from which I had so irresponsibly rescued him",' said Seamus Finnegan.

Reggie gave a sickly grin.

'Well, yes, I suppose I was thinking something along those lines, if not in so many words,' he said. 'I'm terribly sorry, Seamus. It was a dreadful thing to do.'

'I own eight companies,' said Seamus Finnegan.

'I . . . Well, that's marvellous, Seamus. That's marvellous. So . . . er . . .'

'What am I doing drinking in this dismal hell-hole?'

'Well . . . yes.'

'It would be facile to suggest that success has not changed Seamus Finnegan. Success, sir, he's a feller that changes everything. But it doesn't mean that I don't have time to slip away from my spiritual Athenaeum and while away an idle hour with the mates of my erstwhile existence. To me, sir, class distinction is a horse of dubious character, a non-runner, a late withdrawal, as the actress said to the Catholic bishop.'

'Quite.'

'Same again, sir?'

'I'd rather a whisky, Seamus.'

'Yes indeed. A noxious brew.'

Seamus went to the bar, passed a few brief words with the mates of his erstwhile existence, and returned with two large whiskies.

'Seeing you here, Mr Perrin,' said Seamus Finnegan, as they clinked glasses, 'did not lead me to believe that you had fallen upon evil days. I don't judge a man from his surroundings. His innate character, he's the feller I look for. The old essential nature of the unique and individual homo sapiens, he's the man for me.'

'I am justly rebuked,' said Reggie with a wry grin.

One of the darts players farted. There was loud laughter. Life went on. So did Seamus Finnegan.

'However,' he said, 'curiosity is a frisky nag. She's liable to sweat up in the paddock, that one. And, sir, curiosity rather than social stereotype compels me, in my turn, to ask of you, "What are *you* doing drinking in this dismal hell-hole?".'

Reggie described Perrins and its situation as best he could. Seamus Finnegan's amiable ruddy face expressed shock and alarm, but when asked why, his garrulity vanished, and he displayed all the characteristics of an unusually introverted clam.

Next morning, at ten past nine, Seamus Finnegan called at Number Twenty-one, Oslo Avenue.

'Hello!' said Reggie. 'To what do I owe this pleasure?'

'Dark deeds,' said Seamus Finnegan.

Reggie led him into the sun-room. Seamus produced a briar pipe of great age, filled it with foul tobacco at his leisure, lit it, took a puff, seemed pleased and spoke.

'You remember my colleagues of last night?' he said.

'The mates of your erstwhile existence?'

'Them's the fellers. They're right villains, them lot. Well, they've been having inquiries from some yobbos and ruffians with a view to duffing up a certain community that has aroused resentment.'

Reggie's eyes met Seamus's, and a cold fear stabbed him.

'Perrins?'

'Yes.'

'When?'

'Saturday night. It's only rumour, but that's one horse you can never write off.'

'Thank you for warning me, Seamus.'

*

Reggie called a staff meeting for six thirty that evening.

At half past three, David Harris-Jones arrived back, without Prue. He was starving, and Reggie led him into the kitchen.

McBlane was upstairs, taking a rare opportunity to put his athlete's feet up, but Reggie managed to rustle up some leftovers.

'I got as far as Paddington, and nemesis overtook me,' said David Harris-Jones, between mouthfuls. 'I spent twenty-nine hours in one of the toilet cubicles. Can you imagine spending twenty-nine hours in the cubicle of a Western Region toilet?'

'The plight is horrific, the region immaterial,' said Reggie.

'Every graffitus is etched on my memory,' said David Harris-Jones, shuddering at the enormity of the obscenities.

'It was hysterical dysentery,' said Reggie. 'It's odd that you should get it in isolation like that.'

'The seeds of hysteria were sown before I left.'

When David had almost seen off another mouthful, Reggie asked him how things stood with Prue.

'She didn't believe me,' he said. 'She said I'd been visiting . . . that woman. I quoted the graffiti as proof. They seemed to make matters worse.'

Reggie nodded understandingly.

'Would you . . . er . . . would it be asking too much, Reggie? Yes, of course it would,' said David Harris-Jones.

'What?'

'Would you . . . no, it's stupid to even . . . but what can I do?'

'David!'

'Would you ring Prue and tell her it's all true, and I'm feeling absolutely . . . er . . .'

'All right,' said Reggie.

'. . . suicidal. Oh, thank you, Reggie,' said David Harris-Jones.

Reggie told Prue the full story of the hysterical dysentery.

'Well?' said David Harris-Jones, who had been hovering near the phone like an injured peewit. 'What did she say?'

'Very encouraging,' said Reggie. 'She said I must think she's a complete fool and rang off.'

David Harris-Jones groaned.

'What's encouraging about that?' he said.

'It wasn't what she said,' explained Reggie. 'It was the way she said it! She was icily cold.'

David Harris-Jones looked at Reggie in dismay.

'Let's go back in the kitchen and have a beer,' said Reggie.

David followed him less out of enthusiasm than out of an inability to formulate an alternative plan. Reggie got two beers out of the fridge.

'Don't you recognize Prue's anger for what it is?' he said. 'Cheers.'

'No. Cheers. What it is?'

'Love.'

'Love?'

'Fool that she is, she loves you.'

'I never want to set eyes on her again.'

'You see. You love her too.'

David Harris-Jones sipped his lager angrily. His concept of his own uniqueness was insulted by this revelation of how true the most dismal clichés of love are.

'A lesson in love from old Uncle Perrin,' said Reggie. 'You make too much of your quarrels because you quarrel too little. Tony and Joan make too little of theirs because they quarrel too much. There are six marriages in this place. Four will survive. Two may not. Gaze at Uncle Reggie's crystal ball.'

David Harris-Jones managed a faint smile. Reggie's lecture across the kitchen table continued.

'Your marriage will survive because you love each other,' he said. 'Tony and Joan's will survive because they don't. Elizabeth and I will survive because we've survived so much already. Jimmy and Lettuce will survive because there's no alternative. McBlane and his kitchen may not survive . . .'

'McBlane and his kitchen?'

'A great if one-sided love. There's a strain of desperation in McBlane, David, and one day he'll seek a response from his kitchen – it may be this kitchen, it may be another – which it's unable to give. All that talent, and no chance of happiness, David.'

'And the sixth marriage?'

'Tom and Linda. I fear that won't survive, because Linda will expect more than Tom can give, and Tom will expect less than Linda can give. Bear one thing in mind about my predictions, David.'

'What?'

'Nobody can safely predict anything about anyone. Now, to more serious matters.'

'More serious matters! It wouldn't be more serious to me if this place was going to be razed to the ground by hordes of Vandals and Visigoths.'

'It is.'

Once again, the staff gathered and drank out of each other's mugs.

Reggie explained the threat.

It was decided that they had three alternatives.

They could fight.

They could give in.

They could go to the police.

They soon decided – possibly against the wishes of David Harris-Jones and Tom – that they couldn't give in.

There was widespread reluctance to get involved with the police even if it would have been of any use on the hearsay of one eccentric Irishman.

Resistance was declared to be the order of the day.

Adam and Jocasta would be sent to the Perrymans' for the night, and McBlane wouldn't be included in the action, as it was doubtful whether killing eight yobbos with a meat cleaver would come into the category of justified self-defence.

Jimmy appeared to regret this decision.

The next question to be decided was the selection of a leader of the defence.

'You, of course,' said Tom.

'No,' said Reggie. 'This is a specific task. It calls for a natural leader. A man who seeps authority from every pore. Need I say more?'

'I don't think so,' said C.J.

'I refer, of course, to Jimmy,' said Reggie.

'Me?' said Jimmy. 'Good God.'

'Hear hear,' said Doc Morrissey.

'Was that "hear hear" to the appointment of Jimmy, or "hear hear" to "Good God"?' asked Reggie.

'I don't honestly know,' said Doc Morrissey. 'I just thought it was about time I spoke.'

Jimmy was elected defence supremo by ten votes to one.

'Elected unanimously,' declared Reggie.

'Hardly unanimously,' said C.J.

'Jimmy voted against himself,' said Reggie. 'A mere formality.'

'Didn't actually,' admitted Jimmy. 'Couldn't. Frankly, between you, me, gatepost, goodwill expeditions, fish out of water. Defence of HQ, repulsion of loutish elements, bingo, message received, can do, wilco, roger and out.'

'Splendid,' said Reggie. 'So one person voted against Jimmy. I wonder who that was, don't you, C.J.?'

'I certainly do,' said C.J.

'Now,' said Reggie. 'If anyone wants to leave, we must let them. Does anyone?'

Linda gave Tom a meaningful glance. He looked straight ahead, resolutely.

'I don't want to leave,' said David Harris-Jones. 'Heaven forbid. Leave you in the . . . er . . .'

'Lurch.'

'Exactly. My word, no. But . . .'

'Ah!' said Reggie.

'No,' said David Harris-Jones. 'Wait. It's . . . well . . . Prue. I think I . . . er ought to . . . er . . .'

'Go and bring her back in time to join the defences, because we need everyone we can get. Good thinking, David. Like your style,' said Reggie.

'Yes, well . . . er . . . yes,' said David Harris-Jones.

'Right,' said Reggie. 'It's now Wednesday. We have just three days. We'll have another meeting tomorrow night. I trust that by then Jimmy will have come up with a plan.'

'What about the guests?' asked Elizabeth.

There was a lengthy silence. Everyone had forgotten all about the guests.

Later that evening, Reggie told the fourteen remaining guests of the theat to the community. They had three alternatives. They could stay, they could leave, or they could leave for the weekend and return when the threat was over.

Three voted to leave, three to stay and eight to go away for the weekend.

When they discovered that the other guests would be leaving, the last three decided to go away as well.

At half past six the following evening, the staff met in the living-room of Number Seventeen for the last time.

They didn't know it was the last time.

They drank out of each other's mugs for the last time.

Some of them may have suspected that it was the last time.

For the first time, it was warm enough not to light the calor gas fire.

Perrins had survived one autumn, one winter and one spring. It would die just as its first summer began.

This time there were only ten members of staff present, as David Harris-Jones had gone to Exeter.

This time it was Jimmy who conducted the meeting. Reggie sat at his right hand.

At Jimmy's request, the chairs of the other eight had been

rearranged in three rows, like an armchair rugby scrum, facing Jimmy, who stood behind the card table with a baton in his hand, even though there was no plan at which he could point it.

If Jimmy felt any dismay as he looked down at his puny forces, he didn't show it.

'Good evening,' he began. 'Purpose of exercise, repulsion of yobbo invaders. Tell you my thought processes.'

'That should be good for fifteen seconds,' whispered Tony, from the second row of the armchair scrum.

Lettuce, who was in the hooker's position, turned round furiously, and hissed, 'Ssssssh!'

'Element of surprise essential,' said Jimmy. 'Must assume Finnegan has kept mouth shut. Enemy doesn't know we know they're attacking. Where will enemy expect us to be?'

'Inside,' said Elizabeth from the loose head position.

'Exactly,' said Jimmy. 'So where will we be?'

'Outside,' said Doc Morrissey from the middle of the back row.

'Precisely. In garden.'

'They'll see us if we're in the garden,' said Tony.

'Disguised,' said Jimmy.

'Ah!' said C.J.

'Precisely,' said Jimmy.

'What as?' said Joan.

'Exactly,' said Jimmy.

They looked at him expectantly. He didn't fail them.

'First thought, molehills,' he said.

'Disguised as molehills?' said Reggie.

'Yes.'

'Molehills aren't big enough.'

'Precisely,' said Jimmy triumphantly, as if their agreement over the unsuitability of molehills would clinch his military reputation for posterity. 'Exactly what I thought. Next thought. Compost heaps. Ten of us. Heap in each garden. Two bods in each heap.'

274

Jimmy's ragged army stared up at him in astonishment.

'I'm told that I keep saying, "I didn't get where I am today by whatever it might be",' said C.J. 'Well, I'm sorry. I'll endeavour not to use the phrase, in future. However, if I didn't get where I am today by any one thing above all other things that I didn't get where I am today by, it must be by being disguised as half a compost heap.'

'Compost heap, pros and cons,' said Jimmy, as if he hadn't heard a word that C.J. had said. 'Credit side, big enough, nice and warm, element of surprise when attacked by compost heap considerable. Debit side. Smelly, bad for morale, normally in back gardens, field of vision limited, delay in getting out of compost heap considerable. Careful consideration, but, on balance, thumbs down.'

Nobody demurred.

'Better idea, trees,' said Jimmy. 'Let them approach house, take them in rear, terrify them, nail the sods.'

If the staff had looked towards Reggie to nip the idea of being disguised as trees in the bud, they were disappointed. His attitude seemed to be that, having appointed his master supremo, he would stand by any plan that he might make.

On reflection, Jimmy's mention of compost heaps had been a master stroke, for it made being disguised as trees seem almost sensible by comparison.

Friday morning was spent preparing themselves as trees. Lettuce was i/c tree making.

Shortly after lunch Reggie answered the door to find Mrs C.J. with two suitcases.

'I want to be with him,' she said. 'You can't understand that, can you?'

'With difficulty,' said Reggie. 'I wouldn't want to, but I'm not his wife.'

He put the cases down in the hall, and escorted Mrs C.J. into the living-room.

'I simply don't care about the monastic restrictions,' said Mrs C.J.

'Monastic restrictions.' said Reggie.

'The celibacy. The dormitories. The sexual segregation.'

Mrs C.J. sat on the settee, with a sigh.

'I'm pooped,' she said.

Reggie stood facing her, in some perplexity.

'C.J. told me at Christmas,' said Mrs C.J.

'Ah!' said Reggie. 'Good for him. Very wise. What exactly did he tell you at Christmas?'

'About the monastic restrictions.'

'Ah! Let me get this right. C.J. told you at Christmas that we live in segregated dormitories and lead a life of celibacy?'

'Yes. You do, don't you?'

'What? Oh yes. Yes. Of course we do. Or rather did. Yes. We gave it up on Wednesday. Because of the attack. No doubt C.J. was going to write to you, after the attack.'

Reggie slumped into a chair.

'What attack?' said Mrs C.J.

Jimmy entered, disguised as an aspen.

'This is Mrs C.J.,' said Reggie. 'Mrs C.J., Jimmy.'

'Hello,' said Jimmy. 'Can't shake hands. I'm an aspen. Not bad, eh Reggie?'

'Excellent,' said Reggie. 'You're a dead ringer for a slightly mangy aspen.'

It was Mrs C.J.'s turn to look perplexed.

'Could you ask C.J. to come in?' said Reggie. 'Don't tell him why. Let it be a lovely surprise.'

'Will do,' said Jimmy.

Jimmy shuffled out of the room, shedding twigs on the carpet as he went. Reggie explained to Mrs C.J. about the attack, and Jimmy's master plan.

Soon C.J. entered. He went white when he saw Mrs C.J., and stood rooted to the spot, as if he was already an aspen.

'Good God,' he said. 'I mean, "Wonderful to see you, darling".'

He embraced his wife.

'You look horrified, C.J.,' she said.

'I am slightly,' said C.J. 'There's a nasty business happening on Saturday.'

'I've told her,' said Reggie.

C.J. sat beside Mrs C.J. on the settee.

'That was the only reason I looked horrified,' he said.

'C.J. doesn't want you mixed up in our arboreal deception,' said Reggie.

'Precisely, Reggie,' said C.J.

Mrs C.J. melted sufficiently to let C.J. put an arm round her.

'I presume you were going to write after the attack to tell me that the monastic restrictions had been lifted.'

'Monastic restrictions?' said C.J. 'What monastic restrictions?'

'The monastic restrictions of our community, that you told Mrs C.J. about at Christmas,' said Reggie. 'How until Wednesday we lived a strictly celibate life in segregated dormitories.'

'Oh, *those* monastic restrictions,' said C.J.

Jimmy re-entered, minus his costume, plus Lettuce.

'Top-hole aspen my clever Lettuce rustled up, what?' said Jimmy.

'A1,' said Reggie.

'You're being fitted for your box hedge at five, C.J.,' said Lettuce.

'I know,' said C.J. glumly.

Lettuce was introduced to Mrs C.J.

'How did you cope with the monastic restrictions.' said Mrs C.J.

'Monastic restrictions?' said Lettuce.

Mrs C.J. burst into tears.

Reggie ushered Jimmy and Lettuce out of the room.

When they were alone, Mrs C.J. hit C.J. across the cheek.

He stood up, holding his nose in his hands.

There was no blood.

'You lied to me,' said Mrs C.J. 'You hate me.'

'I love you,' said C.J., standing at the french windows,

looking over the bursting verdure of the garden. 'I lied to you because I didn't want you to come here till I'd finished my masterpiece.'

'Masterpiece?' said Mrs C.J. scornfully. 'What pack of lies is this?'

'Every evening, when the day's work is done, I retire to my room and write,' said C.J. 'My book will do for ants what *Watership Down* did for rabbits.'

He returned to the settee, and turned to face his wife.

'It's the only reason I didn't send for you,' he said. 'I could never have done my masterpiece and been with you. It would have been the last straw that broke the camel's hump.'

'What's this masterpiece of yours called?' said Mrs C.J.

'I've tried everything,' said C.J. '*Watership Ant*, *Watership Hill*, *Charley's Ant*, *Lord of the Ants*, *Ant of the Lords*, *Ant of the Flies*, *Ant of the Rings*, *No Sex Please we're Ants*, *No Ants Please we're British*.'

'Show me your masterpiece,' said Mrs C.J.

'You still don't believe me, do you?' said C.J.

He took Mrs C.J. to his room and showed her his masterpiece.

The fateful day dawned warm and sunny, innocent and smiling. They all felt foolish, as they prepared their disguises under Lettuce's supervision. It wasn't the sort of day on which it was easy to believe in attacks by bands of marauding yobbos. Mrs C.J. was determined to stay at her husband's side, and it was decided that they should both be part of the same box hedge.

Shortly after lunch, David Harris-Jones arrived with Prue.

'We're reconciled,' they said. 'We've come back to help in the defence of our community. Little Reggie's safe in Exeter.'

Prue looked radiant. David's radiance was tempered by fear.

'Unfortunately you haven't time to disguise yourselves as trees,' Reggie told them.

'Trees?' said David and Prue Harris-Jones.

Reggie explained the plan, and it was decided that they should stay in the house and act as reserves, in case any invaders broke through the leafy cordon.

By the time Linda drove Adam and Jocasta to the Perrymans', the sunshine had gone and there were menacing clouds.

It became much easier to believe in the threatened attack.

Jimmy gambled on the invaders not attacking before dusk. For, while Lettuce had done extremely well in the short time available, it has to be admitted that the deception would not have been effective in daylight.

As dusk gathered, and the rain began, Jimmy armed his band with clubs disguised as branches.

'I hope we don't intend to be violent,' said Tom.

'Of course not,' said Jimmy. 'But these people are louts. They're the dregs. It's the only language they understand.'

'We're supposed to be a community of peace and love,' said Tom.

'That's why we've got to nail the bastards,' said Jimmy.

He led his band of trees, shrubs and hedges to their stations.

Afforestation took place. The night began. The rain grew heavier.

Every twenty minutes a W288 slid past, a pool of golden light in the murk.

Ten o'clock, and not a yobbo in sight. A flock of starlings tried to roost in Joan. Somewhere, a larch sneezed.

The evening grew colder. The rain grew harder. They weren't coming.

They might come after the pubs closed.

They didn't.

At twenty to twelve the ridiculous, freezing, sodden, pointless vigil was rudely interrupted. Splitting the silence of the night came a screeching of brakes. A crashing of metal. A scream.

Reggie began to run.

'Phone for an ambulance, David,' he yelled into the house.

'Stay in your places,' called Jimmy. 'It's a diversion.'

'It's an accident,' said Reggie.

People converged on the junction of Oslo Avenue and Bonn Close.

So did trees, shrubs and a box hedge.

Both cars had horribly mangled bodies.

Reggie bent down to talk to the driver of one of the cars.

'It's all right,' he said. 'The ambulance is on its way.'

The driver opened his eyes, saw a length of box hedge scurrying down the road, overtaken by a hawthorn yelling, 'Let me through. Let me through. I'm a doctor', and fainted.

Later that night, they all sat in the living-room and shared a communal bowl of prune whisky. The smokeless fuel roared brightly in the hearth.

Miraculously, nobody had been seriously hurt. They had returned home, feeling foolish. Defoliation had occurred.

Now the feeling of foolishness had given way to a sense of relief. They were warm and dry and united by strong bonds of shared experience. Many of their relationships were informed with true affection, and the others with a very adequate facsimile.

Joan sang excerpts from Gilbert and Sullivan, and everybody joined in the choruses.

To everyone's astonishment, Tony blushed. Nobody could recall his blushing before.

'Would you like me to hit *Richard the Second*, Act Two, Scene One, and score the old John of Groat speech?' he asked.

'Please,' came the chorus.

'It's John of Gaunt actually,' said Tom.

'Same difference,' said Tony, and he launched himself into it.

He declaimed with rare fervour, and only made one small verbal slip, when he said:

'This blessed plot, this earth, this realm, this England,
This knock-out, teeming womb of royal kings.'

Everyone agreed that his rendition was splendid. 'Top-hole' was Jimmy's chosen epithet, and a man would have had to have been a veritable churl to have quarrelled with the old warrior's assessment.

'To try and follow that would be a case of the morning after the Lord Mayor's show before,' said C.J., 'but ... er ... well ...'

He glanced at Mrs C.J. She nodded eagerly.

'I wondered if you'd like to hear a short extract from my books on ants,' he said.

'Book!' exclaimed Elizabeth.

'On ants!' cried her equally surprised partner.

C.J. smiled at them all benevolently.

'I know what you're going to say,' he said.

'You didn't get where you are today by writing books about ants,' they thundered in unison.

'True,' said C.J. 'But on the other hand it's never too late for a leopard to change horses in mid-stream.'

He went to fetch his manuscript. Soon he returned, clutching a large sheaf of papers.

He sat down. His audience adopted the cautious pose of self-conscious embarrassment that people have when listening to the literary efforts of their friends – a determination not be patronizing mixed with a conviction that it's going to be dreadful.

He coughed.

'Every evening, throughout the time of the year that is called Nith,' he read, 'which comes after Glugnith but before the festival of Prengegloth, the ants of the Hill of Considerale Fortitude sit around and tell stories. And listen to them too, because if nobody was listening it would be pretty silly to bother.'

C.J. paused to chuckle, then resumed his narrative.

'"Tell us a tale, Great Ant Ogbold," squeaked little Squilblench. "Tell us the one about the journey of Thrugwash Blunk."

'"Okey dokey, then," said Great Ant Ogbold, smiling like a Cheshire cheese. "After all, it is Nith, and if we can't let our hair down during Nith, then things have come to a pretty pass.

'"In the dark years before anybody believed in the Great Sludd," he began, "a little ant named Thrugwash Blunk went on a journey.

'"His daddy didn't want him to go.

'"'Rolling stones butter no parsnips,' he warned him.

'"But Thrugwash Blunk went away, and got lost in the land of Threadnoddy, where there was a big fog, and he went round and round in eccentric circles.

'"Then he met a conceited owl, who thought he was the cat's whiskers and the bee's knees."'

C.J. chuckled again.

'"'Help me, owl, for I don't know where I am,' said Thrugwash Blunk, 'and I didn't get where I am today by not knowing where I am.'

'"'I'll tell you where you're at,' said the conceited owl. 'No sweat, baby.'

'"'Oh, thank you, owl,' cried Thrugwash Blunk, and suddenly, without any warning . . ."'

The yobbos came.

There was the almost musical sound of breaking glass from several directions. Everybody leapt to their feet and stood irresolute, not knowing in which direction to turn.

Everywhere there was crashing and shouting.

The first yobbo burst in through the curtains, yelling fiercely like a demented apache.

Everyone looked to Jimmy for leadership. This was his greatest moment.

At first he looked lost, still in the world of ants. Then he

282

pulled himself together and issued his orders. They were a model of succinctness, if not of precision.

'Get the bastards,' he roared.

All was confusion. Youths appeared from all directions. The staff scattered in all directions.

C.J. hurried towards the front door, clutching his masterpiece. He was too late. Two youths rushed in from the hall. One of them grabbed him and the other pulled the pages from his grasp. They had no idea what they were destroying. It was enough that he wanted it not to be destroyed.

The air was full of sheets of paper. Epic set pieces of ant life were ripped asunder, as C.J. and his assailants lurched around the living-room.

David Harris-Jones ran from the dining-room and up the stairs, chased by a youth with a knife. An older man followed, grappling with Reggie.

Elizabeth crept out of the kitchen, McBlane's pestle raised above her head, but just as she was about to bring it down on the head of the man who was grappling with Reggie, another man pulled her off, twisted her arm, grabbed the pestle, and knocked her senseless.

Tony, Joan and Doc Morrissey were conducting a running battle upstairs, in and out of the bedrooms.

In the kitchen, Prue, Linda and Mrs C.J. were fighting off the invaders like cats.

On the settee, three men were trying to hold Lettuce down. She was screaming and yelling, thrashing around like a dying whale.

A huge man with a twisted nose walked casually into the living-room and felled C.J. with one casual blow. He lay prone among the ruins of his book.

David Harris-Jones ran downstairs and collided with Tom, who was running upstairs. They crashed down the stairs together and landed in a heap at the bottom, with Tom on top of David.

'Get off me,' hissed David Harris-Jones, but Tom was unconscious.

David Harris-Jones pretended to be unconscious as well.

A very tall young man kicked Tom casually, as he passed him on his way upstairs. Tom didn't stir.

He kicked David Harris-Jones, and David groaned. The young man kicked him until he passed out.

Reggie and the older man were wrestling ferociously on the floor of the living-room.

Jimmy crawled over the carpet behind the heaving settee, a vase in his hands. He stood up, raised the vase, and aimed it at the biggest of Lettuce's assailants. Lettuce made one last titanic heave which propelled her to the top of the writhing heap. Jimmy brought the vase down on the back of her head. The vase shattered and she passed out. Jimmy looked down aghast at what he had done.

Upstairs, Joan locked herself in a cupboard. Doc Morrissey lay gasping for breath. Tony was the last to succumb.

The three wild women in the kitchen were finally tamed by the superior strength of their aggressors.

In the living-room, the three men who had been freed from the attentions of Lettuce turned on Reggie and Jimmy. The guiding spirit of the community and his defence supremo fought bravely, but age and numbers were against them. Reggie heard Jimmy murmur one single word in his ear. It was 'Dunkirk'. Then Jimmy passed out.

Reggie was on his own now. Further resistance was useless. He continued to resist, wildly, flailing arms and legs, yelling, screaming, a last berserk defiance amid the ruins of his dream.

And then he was falling. He couldn't see. Darkness was all around him.

He felt a sharp blow in the small of his back, then a stabbing pain in the ribs. A fierce buzzing filled his head, and he could hardly breathe.

He was falling again. He had thought that he was lying on the floor, and yet he was still falling.

He tumbled far beyond the floor.

He tumbled far beyond Botchley.

He toppled over the edge of the universe into the blackness between our universe and all other universes.

At last he fell no more.


He grew dimly aware that somebody was becoming conscious.

But who?

It must be he, if he was conscious of it.

He remembered dying.

Was this Hell?

He tried to move. The display team of the Chinese Acupuncture Service, the famous Red Needles, were practising massed acupuncture upon his body.

He tried to swallow, but his mouth seemed to be full of sour carpet.

He became aware of voices, groans, low conversation.

The yobbos! They'd come back.

A hand grabbed his wrist. He froze, waiting for further blows.

'He's dead,' said a voice, and with joyous relief he recognized it as Doc Morrissey's.

He opened his eyes.

'Buggered if I am,' he said. 'You won't get rid of me that easily.'

He managed to struggle agonizedly to his feet.

He looked round the room. Nobody had died. The whole staff were there, battered, bruised, but alive. Their faces were hideously distorted by contusions and black eyes.

A strange overwhelming pungency filled the air, and the carpet was covered in a fine multi-coloured dust. Pictures lay slashed on the floor, cushions and chairs had belched forth their innards, and there were torn sheets of paper everywhere. The curtains were billowing into the room as the wind tore through the gaping holes in the french windows. Reggie passed out.

\*

There followed a sombre week.

Every chair in all five houses had been smashed, every window broken, every drawer pulled out and upturned.

On his arrival home at five fifteen a.m. McBlane discovered that his herb and spice racks had been destroyed. He wept. Luckily for him there were no witnesses.

The spicy pungency was explained. So was the fine dust on the living-room floor. The whole house was covered in rosemary, thyme, sweet basil, tarragon, mace, dill, oregano, cayenne pepper, allspice, crushed chillies, paprika, coriander, nutmeg, turmeric, ground bay leaves, meat tenderizer, sage, ginger, cinnamon, cardamom, saffron, fennel and parmesan cheese. So were the remnants of C.J.'s manuscript.

Reggie put a consolatory arm on C.J.'s shoulder. C.J. winced, and Reggie speedily removed the consolatory arm.

'It was no good,' said C.J.

'It was a damned good first effort,' said Reggie.

Other comments included 'super', 'knock-out', 'top-hole yarn', 'I liked it, and I'm not an ant person' and 'the most interesting story about ants I've ever heard'.

'I realized that it was no good as I was reading it,' said C.J. 'I console myself with the thought that it's a long lane that has no turning.'

The police arrived at nine fifteen in the morning. They didn't believe Reggie's story of a private fight that had got out of hand, and departed in bad humour.

The doctor did believe Reggie's story. After the hysterical dysentery, he was prepared to believe anything.

Several people needed bandaging, splinting and strapping at Botchley General Hospital. Slowly, with agonizing delays, this was done.

As they tried to get comfortable in bed that Sunday night, Elizabeth asked Reggie why he had lied to the police.

'I don't want to be bothered with it any more,' he said. 'It's all over.'

And so it proved. The guests who returned after the weekend took one look at the devastation and fled.

The newspaper reports of yet another chaotic event at the jinxed community caused the cancellation of all remaining future bookings.

Reggie arranged with an estate agent to put all five houses up for sale, as soon as essential repairs had been effected. He borrowed money from his bank manager, against the sale of the houses. He hired an overwhelmed glazier who almost cried with joy when he saw the extent of the damage. The glazier had a glass eye.

Reggie offered his staff three months' wages in compensation. C.J., Tony and McBlane accepted. Tom and Doc Morrissey accepted one month's salary. The rest refused to take anything.

It was time for farewells.

'Bye bye,' said Reggie. 'Back to Godalming, eh?'

'Yes, the old house is still there,' said Mrs C.J.

They were standing at the front gate of Number Twenty-one on a lovely May morning.

'What'll you do?' said Elizabeth.

'I may see my brother about a job,' said C.J. 'There comes a moment in everybody's life when he has to swallow his pride.'

C.J.'s brother ran a pub called the Dissipated Kipper on the Hog's Back in Surrey. Reggie couldn't imagine C.J. working in a pub, but he supposed beggars couldn't be choosers.

C.J. extended his hand.

'Well, this is it,' he said.

'Yes,' said Reggie. 'This is it.'

Mrs C.J.'s handshake was limp.

'Never outstay your doodah,' said C.J.

'Absolutely,' said Reggie.

*

'Well, this is it,' said Jimmy.

'Yes.'

'Never forget Perrins,' said Jimmy. 'OK, final analysis, flop, crying shame. Brought me something, though. Biggest thing in my life. Lettuce.'

He kissed Lettuce on the mouth and clasped her hand affectionately.

'What'll you do?' asked Elizabeth.

'This and that,' said Jimmy.

'Especially that,' said Lettuce.

'Saucy girl,' said Jimmy. 'No, start small business, private bus company, foreign parts, that sort of crack. No cock-up this time. Buses on up and up. Buses are coming back everywhere, Reggie. Chap I know, offer of backing. Nigel "Ginger" Carstairs. Top drawer. All right, eh, Lettuce?'

'Absolutely.'

'Stout scout. Suppose you haven't any food, big sister? Odd egg, crust, that sort of caper. Bit of a cock-up on the . . . no, suppose you wouldn't have. Hard times, eh? Well well, chin chin.'

Jimmy and Lettuce clambered into the remains of Jimmy's old car. Reggie and Elizabeth pushed, and at the corner of Oslo Avenue and Bonn Close it burst into a parody of life.

Our last sight of them is of two beefy hairy arms, waving frantically.

One of the arms was Jimmy's. The other was Lettuce's.

Our last sound of them is of the car back-firing noisily, as if it shared its owner's military nostalgia.

'It failed in the end,' said Doc Morrissey, 'but nobody can say you didn't have a go.'

'Not a bad epitaph,' said Reggie. 'Here lies Reginald Iolanthe Perrin. Nobody can say he didn't have a go. Doc, we'll miss you.'

'Me too, Reggie. And Perrins didn't fail me. The discovery

288

of my unsuspected talent for psychology has done wonders for my self-esteem.'

'Where will you go?' said Elizabeth.

'There is a corner of Southall that will be for ever English. And there, one day in the not too distant future, Professor Morrissey, that old fraud, will teach his last English lesson, and die not desperately discontent.'

'Ciaou City, Arizona.'

'Absolutely. Keep him in order, Joan.'

'I will. No sweat.'

'No need. I'm a reformed character. And I owe it to you, Reggie. OK, it was a shambles, ultimately, but you've shown me where it's at. It's at maturity, Reggie. I'm into responsibility. I don't have unrealistic dreams any more. I'm going to buckle down to the hard grind of hard work. I'll be a millionaire in ten years.'

'Good-bye, Reggie. Good-bye, Elizabeth,' said David and Prue Harris-Jones.

'Sorry you called him Reggie?' said Reggie.

'No fear,' said David and Prue Harris-Jones.

'What'll you do?' said Reggie and Elizabeth.

'There are jobs for both of us in the old family firm in Haverfordwest,' said David and Prue Harris-Jones. 'Our wandering days are over.'

'We'll see you one day, though,' said Reggie and Elizabeth.

'Oh yes, we must,' said David and Prue Harris-Jones.

'Super,' said Reggie and Elizabeth and David and Prue Harris-Jones.

'Well, we've got a nice day for it,' said Tom.

'Bye bye, dad,' said Linda. 'Bye bye, mum. See you soon.'

'Bye bye,' said Adam and Jocasta.

'It's had such a good effect on them,' said Linda, getting into the car. 'It hasn't all been in vain.'

'Nothing is,' said Reggie.

'I shall take up the reins of estate agency once again,' said Tom. 'But I regret not one minute of the events that have transpired. Frankly, I was becoming a bit of a bore. Without you, Reggie, and not forgetting you, mother-in-law, I would have gone on and on, slowly but steadily ossifying, and I would have ended as pomposity personified.'

Tom held out his hand.

'A dream is over, Reggie, but because of that dream, reality will never be quite the same again,' he said.

'I'm so glad you won't end up as pomposity personified,' said Reggie.

'Come on, Tom,' said Linda.

'Coming, Squigglycrutch. I won't say good-bye properly, Reggie, mother-in-law, because we'll be seeing each other, we're family, and I don't like good-byes. I'm not a good-bye person.'

'Oh good. Well, good-bye,' said Reggie.

'Good-bye,' said Elizabeth.

'I fail to see the point of protracted good-byes,' said Tom. 'I'd like to say good-bye and get it over with. It may be a fault, but that's the way I am. Well, good-bye.'

'Good-bye.'

'Good-bye.'

'Good-bye.'

'Good-bye.'

'Good-bye.'

Reggie and Elizabeth dined alone that night. They sat at either end of the long table that had so recently been vibrant with gossip and pregnant with metaphysical speculation. Savage cuts disfigured the table top.

It was McBlane's last night. He served them with deep disdain four courses of superb foreign muck – borscht, sole dieppoise, osso buco milanese, and sachertorte. Large and rich though the meal was, it was also light and subtle, and they did full justice to it.

Afterwards they sat in silence, savouring this wonderful experience that had come to them in the midst of ruin. McBlane entered with the last of the sunflower brandy.

'Thank you for a superb dinner, McBlane,' said Elizabeth.

'Thank you,' said Reggie.

McBlane's lips parted. His teeth appeared. His cheeks creased.

He was smiling.

'Will you join us in a glass of sunflower brandy?' said Reggie.

'Eeflecking gaud loupin puir dibollolicking aud frangschlibble doon the brizzing gullet, ye skelk,' said McBlane.

The summer blazed. The refrigeration broke down in a cold store in Wapping, and twenty thousand pork pies were condemned. A survey showed that Britain had dropped to nineteenth in the world survey league, behind Malawi and Spain. Vandals smashed three osprey's eggs on Loch Garten. A Liberian tanker collided with an Albanian freighter off Northumberland, pouring oil on untroubled waters. Thirteen hundred guillemots died.

Numbers Seventeen to Twenty-five, Oslo Avenue, Botchley were sold.

There was just enough left, when all the debts had been paid, to enable Reggie to buy a modest house outright, which was lucky, as no self-respecting building society would have touched him now, and all building societies are self-respecting.

They could go anywhere. The Cotswolds, the Lake District, Spain, the Dordogne, Tierra Del Fuego.

They bought a three-bedroomed semi-detached villa in Goffley.

The address was Number Thirty-eight, Leibnitz Drive.

# 9  *The Aftermath*

On their first evening in their new home, they had a bottle of wine. They sat in the living-room, on hard chairs, for all the armchairs had been ruined beyond repair. The only other furniture in the surprisingly unspacious room was the old card table from Number Seventeen. It was laid for the evening meal. The dining table from Number Twenty-one, though not quite ruined beyond repair, was too big for Number Thirty-eight, Leibnitz Drive.

The floorboards were bare. The main windows afforded a view over a garden that was at once neglected and tame. The lawn was mottled with bare patches and studded with tufts of rank grass. In the middle was a small area of concrete, and on it stood a swing, swaying rustily in the midsummer zephyrs, in squeaking memory of the children who lived there no longer.

Around the lawn there were flower beds which appeared to have been planted with earth. Nothing green disturbed their virgin slumber. The evening sun was slowly sinking towards the roofs of the houses in Kierkegaard Crescent.

They drank their wine slowly, savouring every drop. It might be a long while before they could afford wine again.

'Supper ready?' inquired Reggie.

'It isn't much to write home about,' said Elizabeth.

'That's lucky,' said Reggie, 'because I don't intend to write home about it, since this is home. What is it?'

'Shin of beef casserole.'

'Shin of beef casserole. Yum yum.'

They ate with hearty relish, washing it down gently with the wine. All too soon the last of the food and wine was gone. Reggie sighed.

'Never mind, darling,' said Elizabeth. 'Something will turn up.'

Nothing turned up the next day.

Reggie went to the public library and scoured the newspapers for jobs. Elizabeth explored Goffley High Street, combing the shops for bargains. They met in the Bald Faced Stag, and allowed themselves one half of bitter each.

The pub was suffused with the aura of impending sausages.

'You managed to get something for supper, did you?' said Reggie.

'We're having goujons de coley.'

'Goujons de coley. Yum yum.'

Next day Reggie went to the public library and scoured the newspapers for jobs. Elizabeth explored Goffley High Street, combing the shops for bargains. They met in the Bald Faced Stag, and allowed themselves one half of bitter each. The pub throbbed with the threat of packet curry.

'How did you get on?' said Elizabeth.

'Absolutely splendidly,' said Reggie.

'Oh good.'

'Yes,' continued Reggie. 'The papers were full of adverts for people like me. "Amazing opening for washed-up executive. Geriatric Electronics requires unemployed post-menopausal loonie. Previous sackings an advantage. Bonuses for mock suicides. The successful candidate will have frayed trouser bottoms, anxious eyes and at least three major career cock-ups."'

Elizabeth patted his hand.

'Never mind,' she said. 'Something will turn up.'

That evening, black pudding ragout turned up.

'Black pudding ragout. Yum yum,' said Reggie, as Elizabeth dolloped lashings of the steaming dark mess on to his plate. Halfway through the meal, Reggie let out a tremendous sigh.

'Is it that bad?' said Elizabeth.

'It isn't the food,' said Reggie. 'It's me.'

'Darling!'

'I've brought you such trouble.'

'Don't be silly.'

Elizabeth clasped his hand firmly across the card table.

'I regret nothing,' she said.

Reggie smiled faintly.

'The Edith Piaf of Goffley,' he said.

'Please don't be depressed, darling,' said Elizabeth. 'I've said it before . . .'

'I'll say it as well this time,' said Reggie. 'Maybe it'll help.'

'Something will turn up,' they said in unison.

Next day it did.

A letter.

'Listen to this, darling,' said Reggie. 'It's from the Personnel Manager of Amalgamated Aerosols. "Dear Mr Perrin. No doubt you have heard of us." No. "As you probably know, we are one of the fastest growing companies in the highly profitable growth industry of aerosols. We produce both the can and the contents." Wow! "We are known equally for industrial chemicals, insecticides, furniture polishes and hair lacquers, while our air fresheners and deodorants are experiencing the sweet smell of success." Ha ha! "As you can see, we are also not without a sense of humour." No! "We feel that the inspiration behind Grot and Perrins must have ideas to offer the world of aerosols." They must be mad. "Perhaps you would care to telephone my secretary to fix an appointment. Yours sincerely, James A. Fennel, Personnel Manager." I wonder how they heard of me.'

'They did. That's what matters,' said Elizabeth.

'Yes, but . . . aerosols! I'll phone them at eleven. I mustn't sound too eager.'

Father Time, the bearded tease, moved slowly towards that hour.

'My name's Perrin,' he told Mr Fennel's secretary.

'Ah. Yes. When would it be convenient for you to come and see Mr Fennel, Mr Perrin?' she asked, in a brisk but sexy voice.

'Let me see . . . just having a look through my diary . . . yes. Tuesday or Wednesday afternoons would suit me best, as late in the afternoon as possible, especially if it's the Wednesday.'

'Thursday week at nine thirty.'

'Splendid.'

At last the fateful Thursday dawned.

Elizabeth brushed Reggie's suit with the brush which she had bought for that very purpose the previous day at Timothy White's.

'Thank you, darling,' he said.

She handed him his umbrella.

'Thank you, darling,' he said.

He kissed her good-bye.

'Good luck, darling,' she said.

The hazy blue sky was teeming with insect life, and swallows and swifts darted joyously over Reggie's head as he walked down Leibnitz Drive. He turned right into Bertrand Russell Rise, then left into Schopenhauer Grove. This led him on to the main road which wound uphill past Goffley Station. He struggled up the hill, feeling his age. The day was warm, still, sticky. The haze was thickening, and Reggie felt that it might rain.

He followed the crowds along the subway to platform three. A fast train roared above their heads, frighteningly close. Nobody turned a receding hair.

Would he soon be doing this day after day, he wondered.

Did he want to do this day after day, he wondered.

What could he do, day after day, if he didn't do this, day after day, he wondered.

Would he wonder the same thing, day after day, he wondered.

Opposite him, on platform four, there was a poster advertising the French railways. The gleaming train was gliding past the blue sea of the Cote D'Azur like a sleek snake. An observation car bulged on the snake's back like an undigested rat.

The eight eleven wasn't like a sleek snake. It was like a grubby blue worm with a yellow clown's face. It was also fourteen minutes late.

Do you, Reginald Iolanthe Perrin, take British Rail, Southern Region, to be your awful dreaded life, for better for worse, for fuller for dirtier, in lateness and in cancellation, till retirement or phased redundancy do you part?

I do.

I have to.

Place the ring of dirt around your collar. It will be there every day.

The train arrived at Victoria twenty-two minutes late. The loudspeaker announcement blamed passengers joining the train and alighting.

Reggie arrived at Amalgamated Aerosols at twenty-eight minutes past nine. It was a gleaming affair of glass and Portland stone. Two window cleaners were busy on cradles above the main entrance.

Reggie entered the foyer. It was all rubber plants and soft music. The receptionist had a soft, musical, rubbery voice. She told Reggie to go to the third floor, where Mr Fennel's secretary would meet the lift. Mr Fennel's secretary was twenty years older than her telephone voice, and no slouch where meeting lifts was concerned. She led Reggie along a central corridor. The walls were of glass from four foot upwards, affording a view of an open-plan rabbit warren where people worked and idled in full view of each other and everyone else.

Mr Fennel's office was right at the end of the corridor. He stood up and smiled broadly at Reggie, extending a welcoming hand. He was almost tall, with receding fair hair and an anxious air. He was fifteen years older than his secretary's voice.

'Bonjour,' he said. 'Bienvenu à Londres.'

'Bonjour,' said Reggie, surprised.

'Asseyez-vous,' said Mr Fennel.

'Merci beaucoup,'said Reggie, feeling capable of playing this kind of executive game until the vaches came home.

Outside, beyond the wall-to-wall glass, a splendid, delicately elegant Wren church was dwarfed by massively inelegant prestige office developments.

'Est-ce que que vous fumez?' said Mr Fennel in execrable rather than executive French, holding out a silver cigarette case initialled J.A.F., and filled with Marlboros.

'Non, merci,' said Reggie.

'Seulement les gauloises, n'est-ce pas?' asked Mr Fennel.

'Non. Je ne fume pas,' said Reggie.

Mr Fennel lit a cigarette.

'Bon,' he said 'Maintentant. A les affaires. Le temps et les courants de la mer attendent pour personne.'

'I don't understand. Je ne comprends pas,' said Reggie.

'Time and tide wait for . . . you're English?'

'Yes.'

'Are you sure?'

'There's no possible doubt about it.'

'You aren't Monsieur Duvavier?'

'No.'

'Oh hell. Well who are you?'

'Reginald Perrin.'

'Oh hell.'

'Sorry.'

'Not your fault. Is it Friday?'

'No. Thursday.'

'Damn! I've got tomorrow's files. Why the hell did you answer in French?'

'I thought it was some kind of executive game.'

Mr Fennel laughed.

As soon as Reggie joined in, Mr Fennel's laughter died abruptly.

'Now, what exactly did you want to see me about?' said Mr Fennel.

'You wanted to see me.'

'What? Oh. Yes. Ah. Bit stymied without my files. Millie'll be back in a moment. I'm a bit lost here. We were on the second floor. Now, what do I want to see you about?'

'I don't know. I presumed from your letter you were planning to offer me a job.'

Mr Fennel looked out of the window, as if he expected a passing sky-writer to remind him. London shimmered in darkening haze.

'You must be the bod F.J. wants to see,' said Mr Fennel at last.

'F.J.?'

'Our managing director.'

'Your managing director's called F.J.?'

'Yes. Why?'

'Nothing.'

'Perrin! Grot?'

'Yes.'

'You *are* the bod F.J. wants to see. Why didn't you tell me?'

'I didn't know I was the bod F.J. wanted to see.'

Reggie tried to keep the irritation out of his voice. Mr Fennel had three pens in his breast pocket. Reggie didn't like men who had three pens in their breast pocket and he didn't much care for being called a bod.

'F.J. seems to think you're the kind of bod we want,' said Mr Fennel.

'Oh good,' said Reggie. 'I'd certainly like to work in a high-growth, rapid-yield, multi-facet industry like aerosols.'

'Save that guff for F.J.,' said Mr Fennel.

*

'Come!' called F.J.

Reggie entered F.J.'s office. It was huge, and had large picture windows. The glass was tinted brown.

F.J. advanced to meet him.

'Perrin!' he said. 'Welcome!'

F.J. pumped his hand vigorously.

'I believe you know my brother C.,' he said.

Reggie felt his head swimming.

'So you *are* C.J.'s brother,' he said. 'I did wonder. I . . . er . . . didn't know there was a third brother.'

F.J. sat down behind his vast desk. Its tinted glass top matched the windows.

He looked rather like C.J., but a bit slighter. More tidy and self-contained.

'Oh yes,' he said. 'I didn't get where I am today without being C.J.'s brother.'

'Oh my God,' said Reggie. 'I mean . . . you say that too.'

F.J. laughed heartily.

'No,' he said. 'That was my little joke.'

'Oh. Thank God,' said Reggie.

'I'm very different from C.,' said F.J.

'Oh. Thank God,' said Reggie.

'Do sit down,' said F.J., indicating a low white leather chair shaped like a coracle.

Reggie sat down. The chair blew a raspberry.

F.J. roared.

'Good gimmick, eh?' he said. 'C. copied it. Didn't carry it through, though. My brother's too soft.'

'Soft?'

'All mouth and no trousers. You never let his manner fool you, I hope?'

'No! What? I should say not.'

'You weren't frightened of him?'

'Frightened of C.J.? Huh. Pull the other one.'

'Good. Now I am hard. Cigar?'

'Thank you.'

Reggie reached forward, but the chair was too far from the desk. He had to stand. He took a huge cigar from the large box on F.J.'s desk, and sat down.

The chair blew a raspberry.

F.J. laughed.

'Light?'

Reggie thrust himself out of the chair again, held his cigar to the flame offered by F.J., and sat down again.

The chair blew a raspberry.

F.J. laughed.

'Thoroughly discomfited, the hopeful employee quakes,' he said.

'Absolutely,' said Reggie.

'Do you fancy working here?' said F.J.

'I certainly do,' said Reggie. 'I'd like to work in a high-growth, rapid-yield, multi-facet industry like aerosols.'

'Save that guff for Fennel,' said F.J. 'He's the one who does the hiring and firing.'

'I've seen Fennel,' said Regie.

'You've seen Fennel?'

'Yes.'

'Ah!'

F.J. leant forward and glared at Reggie through slitted eyes.

'Nozzles?' he said.

'Pardon?'

'Nozzles. Views on. Think on your feet.'

'Well, I . . . er . . . they're those things you press on aerosol cans, but you can't see the arrow properly, so you point it the wrong way and cover yourself with freshener.'

'I like a man who can think on his feet,' said F.J.

He swivelled slowly round in his chair.

'Our laboratories in Boreham Wood are on the verge of a nozzle breakthrough that'll do for the aerosol canister what the apple did for gravity,' he said. 'Whichever way you point the canister, the spray will always emerge pointing away from you.'

300

'That's fantastic.'

'Is it not?'

Large drops of rain began to splatter against the windows.

'You and your good lady must come to Leatherhead and have dinner one day, Perrin,' said F.J.

'Thank you, F.J.'

'My good lady cooks an amazing lobster thermostat.'

'Oh. Really? That sounds . . . amazing.'

'You have to be very careful at what temperature you serve it. Hence the name.'

'Really?'

'No.'

'What?'

'There's no such thing as lobster thermostat. It's lobster thermidor.'

Reggie began to sweat.

'I know,' he said.

'Then why the hell didn't you say so?'

'Well, I . . .'

'You thought I was a pretentious *nouveau riche* ignoramus who'd got it wrong.'

'Well, F.J., I . . . er . . .'

'And fell headlong into my executive trap.'

'I certainly did, F.J.'

'Huh huh huh.'

'Absolutely.'

'You're not just another yes man, are you?'

'No, F.J.'

The rain began in earnest. It was quite dark outside and the lights in all the tower blocks shone brightly.

'May I ask you a question, F.J.?' asked Reggie.

F.J. regarded him sadly.

'Why have I got these flaps at either side of my face?' he asked. 'To help me fly?'

'No, F.J.'

'Those are my ears, Perrin.'

'They certainly are, F.J.'

'They're for listening. So, if you have a question, ask it. Don't waste time asking if you can ask it.'

'Sorry, F.J. The question is, F.J., did C.J. recommend me to you?'

'Yes.'

'Good gr . . . oh good.'

F.J. lifted one of his phones.

'Get Fennel please, Ingeborg,' he said.

He put the phone down. Almost immediately it barked. He lifted it.

'Fennel?' he said. 'I have your chap Perrin here . . . You thought he was *my* chap? No, no. He's your chap, I assure you. What do you think of him? . . . Well, it's not up to me . . . Well, I happen to believe he has a flair for unusual invention and is just the man for us, but that's irrelevant . . . You agree? Well, I hope for your sake you're right. It's your decision, Fennel.'

F.J. replaced his telephone on its cradle lovingly.

'You start on Monday fortnight,' he said. 'You'll be working in our air freshener and deodorant division.'

The fine weather returned, and the days passed slowly.

Elizabeth took a secretarial job with a firm of solicitors in Goffley, to start the week after Reggie.

Every morning they called for a drink at the Bald Faced Stag. Often they'd accompany it with a ham sandwich or a portion of gala pie with pickle.

They visited the Goffley Carpet Centre and stared in bewilderment at rolls of hideously patterned material. Eventually they settled on a carpet for the living-room. The price was astronomical.

They went for walks among the quiet yet subtly varied streets around their home. Often they walked down Sartre Rise and Wittgenstein View to the golf course. Between Wittgenstein View and Nietzsche Grove an old windmill survived from the days when all this had been open farmland. It had no sails. It was called John Stuart Mill, in memory of John Stuart, a Goffley landowner of bygone days. It was sad to look at the windmill and dream of the days when these gentle hills had been open fields.

One afternoon, as they crossed the golf course on footpath number seventy-eight, which followed the Piffley Brook to East Franton, the wife of a quantity surveyor hooked her seventh at the short twelfth, and the ball struck Reggie on the backside before she had remembered what you were supposed to shout to warn people.

But for the most part they were quiet times.

The first day of employment began.

Elizabeth brushed Reggie's suit, removing a minuscule crumb of toast from the lumbar region in the process.

She handed him his new briefcase, engraved with his initials 'R.I.P.'.

'Thank you, darling,' he said.

She handed him his umbrella.

'Thank you, darling,' he said.

She kissed him good-bye.

'Thank you, darling,' he said.

'Have a good day at the office,' she said.

'I won't,' he said.

Was this pessimism premature? Only time would tell.

Reggie walked down Leibnitz Drive, turned right into Bertrand Russell Rise, then left into Schopenhauer Grove. High in the summer sky a commuting heron flapped lazily towards the Surrey ponds. Reggie walked up the punishing slope to Goffley Station, showed his new season ticket, and stood on platform three, opposite the poster for the French railways.

This is the life for you, he told himself. This is the life that you are destined to lead. Your dreams have been out of place. They have caused great suffering and chaos.

303

Now you have a job, a new challenge, a new adventure. You must be thankful.

He told himself.

But not too thankful. You mustn't be craven or afraid. You're an old hand, and you mustn't allow yourself to be used as a doormat by anybody. Life is too short.

He told himself.

The train reached Victoria twenty-three minutes late. The loudspeaker announcement blamed chain reaction to the effects of the landslip at Angmering. He reached the office fourteen minutes late, and willed himself not to hurry as he approached the gleaming edifice of glass and Portland stone.

It was called Aerosol House. You will be impressed, it said.

Will I hell, replied Reggie's nonchalant walk.

He entered the foyer. You will feel dwarfed by our air of impersonal affluence, it said.

Cobblers, said Reggie's demeanour as he walked across the slippery marble floor from the sliding doors to the reception desk.

He took it at a steady pace, moving with determined though not over-stated authority.

'Perrin (air fresheners and deodorants),' he announced, employing oral brackets with a dexterity born of long practice.

'I'm not sure if he's in,' said the receptionist.

'No, I am he,' said Reggie. 'I am Perrin (air fresheners and deodorants). I start work here today, and I wondered where my office was.'

The receptionist checked her list. He wasn't on it.

'What exactly is your job?' said the receptionist.

Oh my God.

'I don't know.'

'You don't know?'

'No.'

'You're working here and you don't know what your job is?'

'Yes.'

304

'Oh.'

She checked her special instructions. He wasn't on them. She telephoned Mr Fennel. He was on holiday. It took the combined efforts of Mr Cannon of Admin and Mr Stork of Communications to locate his office.

Reggie sat on a black leather settee, surrounded by rubber plants, fighting against feelings of guilt and insignificance. It's not our fault, he told himself. You've done your bit, in that you've arrived successfully. It's Amalgamated Aerosols that should feel guilty.

And so he adopted a defiant, long-suffering look, until he realized that it might be interpreted as over-compensation for insecurity. And it was he who had talked of the dangers of excessive self-consciousness. Had he learned nothing?

At last his office was located. It was two one seven, on the second floor. Mr Cannon escorted him there.

'I'm sorry about this,' he said. 'There's been a big shift around, and Cakebread hasn't put the P139 through.'

They went up in the lift, and walked along the corridor lined with offices. They weren't open plan, and their doors bore names and titles. Perhaps he was about to find out what his job was.

No such luck. The legend on his door said simply 'Reginald I. Perrin.'

The windows overlooked the Wren church. The desk was of moderate size. There were green filing cabinets, and two phones, one red and one green. On top of a cupboard stood a mug and a bent wire coathanger. There was a communicating door to the offices on either side. The paint on the radiator was peeling, and the brown carpet was laid in strips that didn't quite meet.

'All right?' said Mr Cannon.

'Fine.'

'Jolly good,' said Mr Cannon. 'I'll leave you to your own devices, then.'

He was as good as his word.

But what are my own devices, thought Reggie.

He opened and shut three empty drawers.

There was a knock on the westerly connecting door.

'Come in,' he said.

A pert, self-confident young red-head entered.

'Mr Perrin?' she said.

'Yes.'

'I'm your secretary. I'm Iris Hoddle.'

They shook hands. Her smile was friendly.

'Coffee?' she said.

'Please.'

She returned shortly with a beverage that approximated vaguely to that description. Reggie explained the difficulty that he had experienced in finding his office.

'Mr Cakebread didn't put through the P139,' she said. 'This was Mr Main-Thompson's office, but he's gone to Canisters. There's been a big shift around. He's taken the in and out trays. He shouldn't have, they're like gold, but that's Mr Main-Thompson for you. Anyway, I've put through an F1765, so fingers crossed.'

'Thanks.'

He smiled at Iris Hoddle. She smiled back.

'They haven't exactly told me what you do,' she said.

'They haven't exactly told me what I do either.'

Iris Hoddle laughed.

'That figures,' she said. 'It's Fred Karno's Army, this place. Anyway, C.J.'d like to see you at ten thirty.'

Reggie spilt his coffee down his crutch, and stood up hurriedly. The hot liquid was burning his private parts.

'Damn!' he exclaimed.

He pulled his trousers and pants away from his skin. It was not an elegant way to stand before one's secretary on one's first morning.

'C.J.?' he said.

'Do you know him?' said Iris Hoddle.

'I have run into him,' said Reggie.

306

'He's just started here too,' said Iris Hoddle. 'He's Head of the Department.'

'He's my boss?'

'Yes.'

C.J. entered Reggie's office through the easterly connecting door. He didn't knock.

'Morning, Reggie,' he said. His eyes flickered briefly over Iris. 'Morning Iris.'

He held out his hand to Reggie. Reggie shook it.

'I'm next door,' he said. 'We can use the connecting door.'

'Ah! Splendid,' said Reggie.

He led Reggie into his office. It was twice the size of Reggie's and three times as plush. Reggie sat down gingerly. The chair didn't blow a raspberry. C.J. laughed.

'I leave all that to F.,' he said. 'These childish tricks seem to amuse him. Well, Reggie, we meet again.'

'We certainly do, C.J.'

'Adjoining offices, eh, Reggie?'

'Absolutely C.J.'

'We can be in and out like lambs' tails.'

'Yes, C.J.'

'*But*, Reggie, not in each other's pockets.'

'Definitely not, C.J.'

'Neither Mrs C.J. nor I has ever believed in being in anybody's pockets.'

'A wise attitude, C.J.'

'We're settled again in Godalming.'

'Splendid, C.J.'

'It's not splendid, Reggie.'

'Sorry, C.J. One small question about my work, C.J.'

'I'm all ears, Reggie.'

'What is it?'

C.J. laughed.

'They didn't tell you?'

'No.'

'That figures. This is Fred Karno's Army. You're my right hand, Reggie.'

'I am?'

'You're my think tank. Cigar?'

'Thank you, C.J.'

Reggie took a large cigar. C.J. proffered his lighter and Reggie held his cigar to the tiny flame.

'I've stuck my neck out over you, Reggie. "F.," I said, "you've always said that if things go wrong there's a place for me at Aerosol House." "There certainly is, C.," he said. "I've preferred to make my own way," I said, "but I'd like a job now, F., on one condition." "What condition's that, C.?" he inquired. "I want Reggie Perrin as my number two," I replied.'

'Thank you, C.J.'

C.J. smiled.

'I'm your boss again, Reggie.'

'Yes, C.J.'

'Not that that's why I've asked for you.'

'No, C.J.'

'It's not in my nature to gloat.'

'I should think not, C.J.'

'I've asked for you because you're an ideas man.'

'Thank you, C.J.'

C.J. leant forward and glared at Reggie.

'Do you remember that exotic ices project at Sunshine Dessert, Reggie,' he said.

'How could I ever forget it?'

'I like your attitude, Reggie.'

C.J. lifted his phone.

'Jenny?' he said. 'C.J. on red. Send Muscroft and Rosewell in.'

C.J. put his phone down.

'You . . . er . . . want me to do the same for aerosols?' said Reggie.

'You're a shrewd one,' said C.J. 'The world of air fresheners is in the doldrums, Reggie. The horizons of the small men here are limited. Pine, lavender, heather. Slavish imitation of the big boys.'

'You want new smells, C.J. Raspberry, strawberry and lychee.'

'Exactly, Reggie. I like your thinking.'

There was a knock.

'Come!' said C.J.

Two tall men wearing keen suits and enthusiastic shoes hurled themselves dynamically into the plush executive womb. They were introduced as Muscroft and Rosewall.

'You take your instructions from Perrin,' said C.J.

'Marvellous,' said Muscroft.

'Terrific,' said Rosewall.

'We're going for exotic air fresheners,' said C.J. 'The world is our oyster. The spices of the orient, and the wild flowers of the Andes are your playthings. Between us we shall transform a mundane visit to the toilet into a sensual wonderland. This is a biggie.'

'Marvellous,' said Muscroft.

'Terrific,' said Rosewall.

'Every dog has its day,' said C.J.

'It certainly does,' said Muscroft, Rosewall and Reggie.

When Reggie's two assistants had left the room, C.J. looked at Reggie earnestly. He lowered his voice.

'I don't want any funny business, Reggie,' he said.

'Absolutely not, C.J.'

'You've been on a switchback of fate, Reggie. You were discontented. You believed that there is a greener hill far away with grass on the other side. You set off in search of it. You discovered that there is no greener hill far away with grass on the other side.'

'There certainly isn't, C.J.'

'I'm glad to hear you say it. You've returned, Reggie, a better and a wiser man, and that's an order.'

'Yes, C.J.'

'I want you to familiarize yourself with the current state of play, odour-wise. There's a smelling in Boreham Wood tomorrow.'

'A smelling in Boreham Wood!'

'I like your attitude, Reggie. Edrich from Nozzles can take you in his car.'

C.J. stood up, and Reggie was not tardy in following his example.

C.J. held out his hand. Reggie clasped it.

'I hope we've learnt something about human relations amidst all the twists and turns of our entangled fates Reggie,' he said.

'I hope so, C.J.' said Reggie.

Reggie walked to the connecting door, and opened it.

'Reggie?' said C.J.

'Yes, C.J.?'

'We aren't one of those dreadful firms that would sack a man just because he always turns up fourteen minutes late. Good-bye, Reggie.'

He caught the six twelve home. It was nineteen minutes late, but he didn't let it upset him, because he was an older and wiser man.

He walked down Schopenhauer Grove, turned right into Bertrand Russell Rise, then left into Leibnitz Drive. He felt exhausted, but he didn't let it depress him. He told Elizabeth that he had had a good day at the office. He relished his lamb cutlets and apple charlotte. He slept the troubled sleep of the exhausted. He ate a hearty breakfast. He walked down Leibnitz Drive, turned right into Bertrand Russell Rise, then left into Schopenhauer Grove.

He told himself that he was enjoying this routine, because he was an older and wiser man. As he laboured up the punishing final straight to Goffley Station he consoled himself with the thought that, like life, it would be downhill in the evening.

Mind over matter, he told himself. All you have to do is

convince yourself that your hobbies are tedium and exhaustion, and that decay and decline are the most exciting processes in the world.

On the spine-crushing, vein-throbbing, armpit-smelling journey to Victoria, he tried to inject a sense of mission into his work.

'Roll on deodorants,' he said.

'I beg your pardon?' said the man opposite him.

'Sorry,' said Reggie. 'I didn't mean it to come out loud. That's what people must have said in the bad old pre-aerosol days. "Roll on deodorants." Sorry.'

He began to sweat.

Careful. Mustn't arrive at the smelling smelling.

Oh God.


Edrich from Nozzles drove him to the smelling at Boreham Wood. The laboratory was an undistinguished two-storey building at the back end of a large industrial estate. Edrich led him to a room which was like a doctor's waiting-room, bare with rows of hard chairs round the walls.

There were five doors in one wall. Each door had a small window, barred with a thick grille. Beyond the doors were the smell-proof booths. Reggie felt tired and crumpled. He had a thundery headache coming on.

Also present were Muscroft and Rosewall from Air Fresheners and Deodorants, Lee from Furniture Polishes and Hair Lacquers, Gryce from Communications, Price-Hetherington from Industrial Chemicals, Coggin from Admin, Taylor from Transport, Holmes and Wensley from the lab, Miss Allardyce from the typing pool, Miss Hanwell from Packing, and representatives for the National Smell Research Council and the Campaign for Real Aerosols.

Ten smells were to be tested, two in each booth. They were each handed ten cards numbered one to ten. They had to mark each smell, out of ten, for strength, pleasantness, originality and commercial appeal. They also had to say what the smell reminded them of, and suggest a brand name for it.

Everyone filled in their cards most assiduously.

'Marvellous, isn't it?' said Muscroft.

'Terrific,' said Rosewall.

'Fascinating,' said Reggie. 'A pretty stodgy range of smells, though. I'm looking for something that packs far more wow for our exotic range.'

'Marvellous,' said Muscroft.

'Terrific,' said Rosewall.

C.J. popped in just before lunch.

'Well, Reggie, which way's the wind blowing?' he asked.

'I came, I smelt, I conquered,' said Reggie.

'I like your attitude,' said C.J.

On his way home Reggie began to regret his actions.

Why had he done it? What was the use?

Out here in the open air, walking down Schopenhauer Grove, what had seemed an amazingly apt gesture in the claustrophobic booth in Boreham Wood seemed utterly stupid. I'm a lucky man, he told himself as he turned right into Bertrand Russell Rise. I have a lovely wife and two lovely children, even if one of them has married a bearded prig and the other has disappeared into the huge vagina of the pornographic film industry. There are worse things in life than bearded prigs and pornographic film industries, he told himself as he turned left into Leibnitz Drive.

'Did you have a good day at the office?' Elizabeth asked.

'Very good,' he said.

He enjoyed his lemon sole meuniere and rhubarb crumble. He slept the troubled sleep of a condemned man. He ate a hearty breakfast.

Elizabeth handed him his brand new briefcase, engraved with his initials 'R.I.P.'.

'Thank you, darling,' he said.

She handed him his umbrella.

'Thank you, darling,' he said.

She kissed him good-bye.

'Thank you, darling,' he said.

'Have a good day at the office,' she said.

'I will,' he said.

Why did you do it, he asked himself as he walked down Leibnitz Drive.

You're a lucky man, he told himself as he turned right into Bertrand Russell Rise. You live in a peaceful country.

You're free to walk through pleasant residential streets, he told himself, as he turned left into Schopenhauer Grove.

You're walking up the hill to Goffley Station. Trains have been invented. You're not ill. You have a roof over your head, clothes on your back and food in your belly. It isn't raining. Your credit rating will improve with time. Here comes the train. It's only twenty minutes late. You have a seat. Your newspaper is not a lackey of the government. You earn a good salary. You're reasonably personable and can make friends without extreme difficulty. Iris Hoddle is pleasant and helpful. Muscroft and Rosewall are marvellous, terrific people. You're happy.

Why did you do it?

The wheels were saying, 'You can still get away with it. All is not lost.'

He believed the wheels, because he was an older and wiser man.


'Something rather extraordinary seems to have happened at the smelling,' said C.J.

'Really? How extraordinary,' said Reggie.

'Normally nothing extraordinary happens at them,' said C.J. 'But yesterday it did. Cigar?'

Reggie took a cigar.

C.J. handed him the lighter.

Reggie knew that C.J. was looking to see if his hand was shaking.

He fought hard to keep it steady. At last the cigar was lit.

'What sort of extraordinary thing, C.J.?' he asked.

'The computer has processed the results of the smelling,' said C.J.

'Ah!'

'Exactly. "Ah!", as you so rightly say. This is what smell number one reminded its smellers of, Reggie. Mountains, five people. Snow, three people. Fresh water, two people. Larch forests, two people. Scotland, one person. Camping, one person. Bolivian unicyclist's jockstrap, one person.'

'Good lord, C.J. That is extraordinary,' said Reggie.

'Smell number two,' said C.J. 'Herbs, eight people. One person each for rockery, lavender, thyme, marjoram, spice factory, heather and Bolivian unicyclist's jockstrap.'

'This is astonishing, C.J.,' said Reggie.

C.J. picked up the sheet of paper from which he had been reading, and waved it violently at Reggie.

'Smell number three,' he said. 'Roses, fourteen people. Bolivian unicyclist's jockstrap, one person.'

'I can hardly credit it,' said Reggie.

'The same sorry story occurs with regard to all ten smells, Reggie.'

'Oh dear, oh dear.'

'I didn't get where I am today by having everything smelling of Bolivian unicyclists' jockstraps, Reggie.'

'I can believe it, C.J.'

C.J. gave Reggie a long hard look.

'Can you suggest any explanation, Reggie,' he said.

'I certainly can, C.J.'

'Ah!'

'A fault in the computer.'

'It seems a strange fault for a computer, Reggie. It doesn't have an electronic ring about it.'

'I grant you that, C.J.'

'Do you have any other suggestions, Reggie?'

Reggie returned C.J.'s gaze levelly.

314

'It looks as if somebody's playing silly buggers,' he said.

'It looks that way to me too,' said C.J. 'Who could it be, do you think?'

'I've no idea, C.J.'

A shaft of sunlight broke through the morning cloud and lit up the narrow steeple of the Wren church.

'I don't like it,' said C.J. 'Neither Mrs C.J. nor I has ever played silly buggers.'

'Perish the thought, C.J.'

'I intend to find out, Reggie. There will be an investigation.'

'An excellent idea, C.J.'

'Who do you think will head that investigation?'

'I don't know, C.J.'

'I do, Reggie.'

'Who, C.J.?'

'You, Reggie.'

'Me, C.J.?'

'You, Reggie. Good-bye.'

Reggie walked slowly towards his connecting door.

'Be thorough, Reggie,' said C.J. 'Leave no worm unturned.'

'I'll get to the bottom of it, C.J.,' said Reggie.

'I like your attitude,' said C.J.

Reggie entered his mean little office and sank into his chair.

Why did you do it, Reggie?

C.J. knows. C.J. knows that I know that he knows. I'm trapped.

I can still get away with it.

I don't want to get away with it.

He lifted the red phone.

'Perrin on red,' he said. 'Come in, Miss Hoddle, please.'

His heart began to thump.

His pulse began to race.

His ears began to buzz.

Damn it, he would not lie and evade the issue any more.

Miss Hoddle entered. He smiled at her.

'Sit down, Miss Kettle,' he said.

'Hoddle,' she said.

'I thought I'd call you Kettle for a change.'

Reggie!

'Take a saucepan, Miss Hoddle.'

Letter!

'Saucepan, Mr Perrin?'

'I meant letter, Miss Kettle.'

'Hoddle.'

I seem to be calling things by the names of household utensils. It's out of the frying pan into the colander.

Not colander. Fire.

Oh what the hell. May as well be hung for a sheep as a baking tin.

Miss Hoddle's looking at you, wondering. She's worried. She's a nice girl, and you're upsetting her.

Get it over with.

'To all present at the smelling yesterday,' he began. 'At the smelling yesterday somebody played silly buggers, and wrote that every single air freshener smelt of Bolivian unicyclists' jockstraps.'

Miss Hoddle stared at him in astonishment.

'That somebody was me,' he continued. 'I did it, and I'm not ashamed. I want you all to know why I did it. I did it because I believe that the whole thing is absolutely fish slice. Not only that. It is totally and utterly egg whisk.'

Silence filled the little office. Reggie smiled reassuringly at Iris Hoddle.

'Find out the times of trains to the Dorset coast, would you, please?' he said.

# A Selected List of Humour Available from Mandarin

While every effort is made to keep prices low, it is sometimes necessary to increase prices at short notice. Mandarin Paperbacks reserves the right to show new retail prices on covers which may differ from those previously advertised in the text or elsewhere.

The prices shown below were correct at the time of going to press.

# Love in the
# Time of Dragons

A novel of the Light Dragons

Katie MacAlister

# Love in the Time of Time of Dragons

A Novel of the  Light Dragons

HODDER

First published in Great Britain in 2010 by Hodder & Stoughton
An Hachette UK company

1

Copyright © Marthe Arends

The right of Marthe Arends to be identified as the Author of the Work
has been asserted by her in accordance with the Copyright, Designs and
Patents Act 1988.

A CIP catalogue record for this title is available from the British Library.

ISBN 978 0 340 99303 3

Printed and bound by Clays Ltd, St Ives plc

Hodder & Stoughton policy is to use papers that are natural, renewable
and recyclable products and made from wood grown in sustainable forests.
The logging and manufacturing processes are expected to conform to the
environmental regulations of the country of origin.

Hodder & Stoughton Ltd
338 Euston Road
London NW1 3BH

www.hodder.co.uk

*Shortly after I finished writing this book, my beloved furry girl Jazi died. She was my constant companion for twelve years, and literally at my side for the writing of every book, curled up on a bed next to my desk while I tapped away on the keyboard. She was spoiled, demanding, and obstinate in her desire to have her own way. She also gave me more happiness and love than I could ever have hoped for. This book is dedicated to her memory, which will forever remain bright.*

# Chapter One

"You're going to be on your knees saying prayers for hours if Lady Alice finds you here."

I jumped at the low, gravelly voice, but my heart stopped beating quite so rapidly when I saw who had discovered me. "By the rood, Ulric! You almost scared the humors right out of my belly!"

"Aye, I've no doubt I did," the old man replied, leaning on a battered hoe. "Due to your guilty conscience, I'm thinking. Aren't you supposed to be in the solar with the other women?"

I patted the earth around the early-blooming rose that I had cleared of weeds, and snorted in a delicate, ladylike way. "I was excused."

"Oh, you were, were you? And for what? Not to leave off your sewing and leeching and all those other things Lady Alice tries to teach you."

I got to my feet, dusting the dirt off my knees and hands, looking down my nose at the smaller man, doing my best to intimidate him even though I knew it wouldn't do any good—Ulric had known me since I was a wee babe puling in her swaddling clothes. "And what business is it of yours, good sir?"

He grinned, his teeth black and broken. "You can come over the lady right enough, when you like. Now, what I'm wanting to know is whether you have your mother's leave to be here in the garden, or if you're supposed to be up learning the proper way to be a lady."

I kicked at a molehill. "I *was* excused . . . to use the privy. You know how bad they are—I needed fresh air to recover from the experience."

"You've had enough, judging by the weeding you've done. Get yourself back to the solar with the other women before your mother has my hide for letting you stay out here."

"I . . . er . . . can't."

"And why can't you?" he asked, obviously suspicious.

I cleared my throat and tried to adopt an expression that did not contain one morsel of guilt. "There was an . . . incident."

"Oh, aye?" The expression of suspicion deepened. "What sort of an incident?"

"Nothing serious. Nothing of importance." I plucked a dead leaf from a rosebush. "Nothing of my doing, which you quite obviously believe, a fact that I find most insulting."

"What sort of an incident?" he repeated, ignoring my protests of innocence and outrage.

I threw away the dried leaf and sighed. "It's Lady Susan."

"What have you done to your mother's cousin now?"

"Nothing! I just happened to make up some spider-wort tea, and mayhap I did leave it in the solar next to her chair, along with a mug and a small pot of honey, but how was I to know she'd drink all of it? Besides, I thought everyone knew that spiderwort root tea un-plugs your bowels something fierce."

Ulric stared at me as if it were my bowels that had run free and wild before him.

"Her screams from the privy were so loud, Mother said I might be excused for a bit while she sought one of Papa's guards to break down the privy door, because her ladies were worried that Lady Susan had fallen in and was stuck in the chute."

The look turned to one of unadulterated horror.

"I just hope she looks on the positive side of the whole experience," I added, tamping down the molehill with the toe of my shoe.

"God's blood, you're an unnatural child. What posi-tive side is there to spewing out your guts while stuck in the privy?"

I gave him a lofty look. "Lady Susan always had hor-rible wind. It was worse than the smell from the jakes! The spiderwort tea should clear her out. By rights, she should thank me."

Ulric cast his gaze skyward and muttered something under his breath.

"Besides, I can't go inside now. Mother said for me to stay out of her way because she is too busy getting ready for whoever it is who's visiting Father."

That wasn't entirely true—my mother had actually snapped at me to get out from underfoot and do some-thing helpful other than offer suggestions on how to break down the privy door, and what could be more helpful than tending the garden? The whole keep was gearing up for a visit from some important guest, and I would not want the garden to shame her.

"Get ye gone," Ulric said, shooing me out of the garden. "Else I'll tell your mother how you've spent the last few hours rather than tending to your proper chores. If you're a good lass, perhaps I'll help you with those roses later."

I smiled, feeling as artless as a girl of seventeen could feel, and dashed out of the haven that was the garden and along the dark overhang that led into the upper bailey. It was a glorious almost-summer morning, and my father's serfs were going about their daily tasks with less complaint than was normal. I stopped by the stable to check on the latest batch of kittens, picking out a pretty black-and-white one that I would beg my mother to let me keep, and was just on the way to the kitchen to see if I couldn't wheedle some bread and cheese from the cooks when the dull thud of several horses' hooves caught my attention.

I stood in the kitchen door and watched as a group of four men rode into the bailey, all armed for battle.

"Ysolde! What are you doing here? Why aren't you up in the solar tending to Lady Susan? Mother was looking for you." Margaret, my older sister, emerged from the depths of the kitchen to scold me.

"Did they get her out of the privy, then?" I asked in all innocence. Or what I hoped passed for it.

"Aye." Her eyes narrowed on me. "It was odd, the door being stuck shut that way. Almost as if someone had done something to it."

I made my eyes as round as they would go, and threw in a few blinks for good measure. "Poor, poor Lady

Susan. Trapped in the privy with her bowels running amok. Think you she's been cursed?"

"Aye, and I know by what. Or rather, who." She was clearly about to shift into a lecture when movement in the bailey caught her eye. She glanced outside the doorway and quickly pulled me backwards, into the dimness of the kitchen. "You know better than to stand about when Father has visitors."

"Who is it?" I asked, looking around her as she peered out at the men.

"An important mage." She held a plucked goose to her chest as she watched the men. "That must be him, in the black."

All of the men were armed, their swords and mail glinting brightly in the sun, but only one did not wear a helm. He dismounted, lifting his hand in greeting as my father hurried down the steps of the keep.

"He doesn't look like any mage I've ever seen," I told her, taking in the man's easy movements under what must be at least fifty pounds of armor. "He looks more like a warlord. Look, he's got braids in his hair, just like that Scot who came to see Father a few years ago. What do you think he wants?"

"Who knows? Father is renowned for his powers; no doubt this mage wants to consult him on arcane matters."

"Hrmph. Arcane matters," I said, aware I sounded grumpy.

Her mouth quirked on one side. "I thought you weren't going to let it bother you anymore."

"I'm not. It doesn't," I said defensively, watching as my father and the warlord greeted each other. "I don't care in the least that I didn't inherit any of Father's abilities. You can have them all."

"Whereas you, little changeling, would rather muck about in the garden than learn how to summon a ball of blue fire." Margaret laughed, pulling a bit of grass from where it had been caught in the laces on my sleeve.

"I'm not a changeling. Mother says I was a gift from God, and that's why my hair is blond when you and she and Papa are redheads. Why would a mage ride with three guards?"

Margaret pulled back from the door, nudging me aside. "Why shouldn't he have guards?"

"If he's as powerful a mage as Father, he shouldn't need anyone to protect him." I watched as my mother curtseyed to the stranger. "He just looks . . . wrong. For a mage."

"It doesn't matter what he looks like—you are to stay out of the way. If you're not going to tend to your duties, you can help me. I've got a million things to do, what with two of the cooks down with some sort of a pox, and Mother busy with the guest. Ysolde? Ysolde!"

I slipped out of the kitchen, wanting a better look at the warlord as he strode after my parents into the tower that held our living quarters. There was something about the way the man moved, a sense of coiled power, like a boar before it charges. He walked with grace despite the heavy mail, and although I couldn't see his face, long ebony hair shone glossy and bright as a raven's wing.

The other men followed after him, and although they, too, moved with the ease that bespoke power, they didn't have the same air of leadership.

I trailed behind them, careful to stay well back lest my father see me, curious to know what this strange warrior-mage wanted. I had just reached the bottom step as all but the last of the mage's party entered the tower, when that guard suddenly spun around.

His nostrils flared, as if he'd smelled something, but it wasn't that which sent a ripple of goose bumps down my arms. His eyes were dark, and as I watched them, the pupils narrowed, like a cat's when brought from the dark stable out into the sun. I gasped and spun around, running in the other direction, the sound of the strange man's laughter following me, mocking me, echoing in my head until I thought I would scream.

"Ah, you're awake."

My eyelids, leaden weights that they were, finally managed to hoist themselves open. I stared directly into the dark brown eyes of a woman whose face was located less than an inch from mine, and screamed in surprise. "Aaagh!"

She leaped backwards as I sat up, my heart beating madly, a faint, lingering pain leaving me with the sensation that my brain itself was bruised.

"Who are you? Are you part of the dream? You are, aren't you? You're just a dream," I said, my voice a croak. I touched my lips. They were dry and cracked. "Except those people were in some sort of medieval clothing, and you're wearing pants. Still, it's incredibly vivid, this dream. It's not as interesting as the last one, but still interesting and vivid. Very vivid. Enough that I'm lying here babbling to myself during it."

"I'm not a dream, actually," the in-my-face dream woman said. "And you're not alone, so if you're babbling, it's to me."

I knew better than to leap off the bed, not with the

sort of headache I had. Slowly, I slid my legs off the edge of the bed, and wondered if I stood up, if I'd stop dreaming and wake up to real life.

As I tried to stand, the dream lady seized my arm, holding on to me as I wobbled on my unsteady feet.

Her grip was anything but dreamlike. "You're real," I said with surprise.

"Yes."

"You're a real person, not part of the dream?"

"I think we've established that fact."

I felt an irritated expression crawl across my face— crawl because my brain hadn't yet woken up with the rest of me. "If you're real, would you mind me asking why you were bent over me, nose-to-nose, in the worst sort of Japanese-horror-movie way, one that guaranteed I'd just about wet myself the minute I woke up?"

"I was checking your breathing. You were moaning and making noises like you were going to wake up."

"I was dreaming," I said, as if that explained everything.

"So you've said. Repeatedly." The woman, her skin the color of oiled mahogany, nodded. "It's good. You are beginning to remember. I wondered if the dragon within would not speak to you in such a manner."

Dim little warning bells went off in my mind, the sort that are set off when you're trapped in a small room with someone who is obviously a few weenies short of a cookout. "Well, isn't this just lovely. I feel like something a cat crapped, and I'm trapped in a room with a crazy lady." I clapped a hand over my mouth, appalled that I spoke the words rather than just thought them. "Did you hear that?" I asked around my fingers.

She nodded.

I let my hand fall. "Sorry. I meant no offense. It's just that . . . well . . . you know. Dragons? That's kind of out there."

A slight frown settled between her brows. "You look a bit confused."

"You get the understatement-of-the-year tiara. Would it be rude to ask who you are?" I gently rubbed my forehead, letting my gaze wander around the room.

"My name is Kaawa. My son is Gabriel Tauhou, the silver wyvern."

"A silver what?"

She was silent, her eyes shrewd as they assessed me. "Do you really think that's necessary?"

"That I ask questions or rub my head? It doesn't matter—both are, yes. I always ask questions because I'm a naturally curious person. Ask anyone; they'll tell you. And I rub my head when it feels like it's been stomped on, which it does."

Another silence followed that statement. "You are not what I expected."

My eyebrows were working well enough to rise at that statement. "You scared the crap out of me by staring at me from an inch away, and I'm not what *you* expected? I don't know what to say to that since I don't have the slightest idea who you are, other than your name is Kaawa and you sound like you're Australian, or where I am, or what I'm doing here beyond napping. How long have I been sleeping?"

She glanced at the clock. "Five weeks."

I gave her a look that told her she should know better than to try to fool me. "Do I look like I just rolled off the gullible wagon? Wait—Gareth put you up to this, didn't he? He's trying to pull my leg."

"I don't know a Gareth," she said, moving toward the end of the bed.

"No . . ." I frowned as my mind, still groggy from the aftereffects of a long sleep, slowly chugged to life. "You're right. Gareth wouldn't do that—he has absolutely no sense of humor."

"You fell into a stupor five weeks and two days ago. You have been asleep ever since."

A chill rolled down my spine as I read the truth in her eyes. "That can't be."

"But it is."

"No." Carefully, very carefully, I shook my head. "It's not time for one; I shouldn't have one for another six months. Oh god, you're not a deranged madwoman from Australia who lies to innocent people, are you? You're telling me the truth! Brom! Where's Brom?"

"Who is Brom?"

Panic had me leaping to my feet when my body knew better. Immediately, I collapsed onto the floor with a loud thud. My legs felt like they were made of rubber, the muscles trembling with strain. I ignored the pain of the fall and clawed at the bed to get back to my feet. "A phone. Is there a phone? I must have a phone."

The door opened as I stood up, still wobbling, the floor tilting and heaving under my feet.

"I heard a—oh. I see she's up. Hello, Ysolde."

"Hello." My stomach lurched along with the floor. I clung to the frame of the bed for a few seconds until the world settled down the way it should be. "Who are you?"

She shot a puzzled look to the other woman. "I'm May. We met before, don't you remember?"

"Not at all. Do you have a phone, May?"

If she was surprised by that question, she didn't let on. She simply pulled a cell phone out of the pocket of her jeans and handed it to me. I took it, staring at her for a moment. There was something about her, something that seemed familiar . . . and yet, I was sure I'd never seen her before.

Mentally, I shook away the fancies and began to punch in a phone number, but paused when I realized I had no idea where I was. "What country is this?"

May and Kaawa exchanged glances. May answered. "England. We're in London. We thought it was better not to move you very far, although we did take you out of Drake's house since he was a bit crazy, what with the twins being born and all."

"London," I said, struggling to peer into the black abyss that was my memory. There was nothing there, but that wasn't uncommon after an episode. Luckily, a few wits remained to me, including the ability to remember my phone number.

The phone buzzed gently against my ear. I held my breath, counting the rings before it was answered.

"Yeah?"

"Brom," I said, wanting to weep with relief at the sound of his placid, unruffled voice. "Are you all right?"

"Yeah. Where are you?"

"London." I slid a glance toward the small, dark-haired woman who looked like she could have stepped straight out of some silent movie. "With . . . uh . . . some people." Crazy people, or sane . . . that was yet to be determined.

"You're still in London? I thought you were only going to be there for three days. You said three days, Sullivan. It's been over a month."

I heard the note of hurt in his voice. I hated that. "I know. I'm sorry. I . . . something happened. Something big."

"What kind of big?" he asked, curious now.

"I don't know. I can't think," I said, being quite literal. My brain felt like it was soaking in molasses. "The people I'm with took care of me while I was sleeping."

"Oh, *that* kind of big. I figured it was something like that. Gareth was pissed when you didn't come back. He called your boss and chewed him out for keeping you so long."

"Oh, no," I said, my shoulders slumping as I thought of the powerful archimage to whom I was an apprentice.

"It was really cool! You should have heard it. Dr. Kostich yelled at Gareth, and told him to stop calling, and that you were all right, but he wouldn't say where you were because Gareth was always using you. And then Gareth said he'd better watch out because he wasn't the only one who could make things happen, and then Kostich said oh yeah, and Gareth said yeah, his sister-in-law was a necromancer, and then Ruth punched him in the arm and bit his ear so hard it bled, and after that, I found a dead fox. Can I have fifty dollars to buy some natron?"

I blinked at the stream of information pouring into my ear, sorting out what must have been a horrible scene with Dr. Kostich, finally ending up on the odd request. "Why do you need natron?"

Brom sighed. " 'Cause I found the dead fox. It's going to need a lot of natron to mummify."

"I really don't think we need the mummy of a fox, Brom."

"It's my hobby," he said, his tone weary. "You said I needed a hobby. I got one."

"When you said you were interested in mummies, I thought you meant the Egyptian ones. I didn't realize you meant you wanted to make your own."

"You didn't ask," he pointed out, and with that, I could not dispute.

"We'll talk about it when I get back. I suppose I should talk to Gareth," I said, not wanting to do any such thing.

"Can't. He's in Barcelona."

"Oh. Is Ruth there?"

"No, she went with him."

Panic gripped me. "You're not alone, are you?"

"Sullivan, I'm not a child," he answered, sounding indignant that I would question the wisdom gained during his lifetime, all nine years of it. "I can stay by myself."

"Not for five weeks you can't—"

"It's OK. When Ruth and Gareth left, and you didn't come back, Penny said I could stay with her until you came home."

I sagged against the bed, unmindful of the two women watching me so closely. "Thank the stars for Penny. I'll be home just as soon as I can get on a plane. Do you have a pen?"

"Sec."

I covered the phone and looked at the woman named May. "Is there a phone number I can give my son in case of an emergency?"

"Your son?" she asked, her eyes widening. "Yes. Here."

I took the card she pulled from her pocket, reading

the number off it to Brom. "You stay with Penny until I can get you, all right?"

"Geez, Sullivan, I'm not a 'tard."

"A what?" I asked.

"A 'tard. You know, a retard."

"I've asked you not to use those sorts of . . . oh, never mind. We'll discuss words that are hurtful and should not be used another time. Just stay with Penny, and if you need me, call me at the number I gave you. Oh, and Brom?"

"What?" he asked in that put-upon voice that nine-year-old boys the world over can assume with such ease.

I turned my back on the two women. "I love you bunches. You remember that, OK?"

" 'K." I could almost hear his eyes rolling. "Hey, Sullivan, how come you had your thing now? I thought it wasn't supposed to happen until around Halloween."

"It isn't, and I don't know why it happened now."

"Gareth's going to be pissed he missed it. Did you . . . you know . . . manifest the good stuff?"

My gaze moved slowly around the room. It seemed like a pretty normal bedroom, containing a large bureau, a bed, a couple of chairs and a small table with a ruffly cloth on it, and a white stone fireplace. "I don't know. I'll call you later when I have some information about when I'll be landing in Madrid, all right?"

"Later, French mustachioed waiter," he said, using his favorite childhood rhyme.

I smiled at the sound of it, missing him, wishing there was a way to magically transport myself to the small, overcrowded, noisy apartment where we lived so I could hug him and ruffle his hair, and marvel yet again that such an intelligent, wonderful child was mine.

"Thank you," I said, handing the cell phone back to May. "My son is only nine. I knew he would be worried about what happened to me."

"Nine." May and Kaawa exchanged another glance. "Nine . . . years?"

"Yes, of course." I sidled away, just in case one or both of the women turned out to be crazy after all. "This is very awkward, but I'm afraid I have no memory of either of you. Have we met?"

"Yes," Kaawa said. She wore a pair of loose-fitting black palazzo pants and a beautiful black top embroidered in silver with all sorts of Aboriginal animal designs. Her hair was twisted into several braids, pulled back into a short ponytail. "I met you once before, in Cairo."

"Cairo?" I prodded the solid black mass that was my memory. Nothing moved. "I don't believe I've ever been in Cairo. I live in Spain, not Egypt."

"This was some time ago," the woman said carefully.

Perhaps she was someone I had met while travelling with Dr. Kostich. "Oh? How long ago?"

She looked at me silently for a moment, then said, "About three hundred years."

# Chapter Two

"Ysolde is awake again," May said as the door to the study was opened.

I looked up from where I had been staring down into the cup of coffee cradled in my hands. Two men entered the room, both tall and well-built, and curiously enough, both with grey eyes. The first one who entered paused at May's chair, his hand smoothing over her short hair as he looked me over. I returned the look, noting skin the color of milky coffee, a close-cut goatee, and shoulder-length dreadlocks.

"Again?" the man asked.

"She fainted after she woke up the first time."

I eyed him. After the last hour, I'd given up the idea that May and Kaawa were potentially dangerous—they let me have a shower, had promised to feed me, and had given me coffee, and crazy people seldom did any of that.

"Ah. No ill effects from it, I hope?" he asked.

"Not unless you call fifty-two elephants tap-dancing in combat boots while bouncing anvils on my brain an ill effect," I said, gazing longingly at the bottle of ibuprofen.

"No more," May said, moving it out of my reach. "You'll poison yourself if you take any more."

I sipped my coffee with obnoxious noisiness as punishment for her hard-heartedness.

"I'm afraid there is little I can do for a headache." He nodded toward the man with him. "Tipene, when we are done here, e-mail Dr. Kostich and let him know his apprentice has recovered."

The second man was also black, but with much shorter dreadlocks. He nodded. Beneath the light-colored T-shirt he wore, I could see thick black curved lines that indicated he bore rather detailed tribal tattoos across his chest.

"We were just having some coffee while waiting for lunch," May continued, smiling up at the first man. "Ysolde says her brain is a bit fuzzy still."

"Not so fuzzy that I can't correct something that's seriously wrong," I said, setting my cup down. I addressed the man who stood next to May. "I assume you're Gabriel Tao . . . Tow . . ."

"Tauhou," he said, his eyes narrowed as he searched my face.

"Sorry, I have the memory of maple syrup when it comes to people's names. I was trying to tell your . . . er . . ." I waved vaguely toward May.

"Mate," he said.

"Quite." I didn't even blink over the odd word to use for a partner. What people called their significant others in the privacy of their own homes was not one iota my business. "I was just trying to tell her that I think you have me mistaken for someone else. My name isn't Ysolde. It's Tully, Tully Sullivan."

"Indeed," he said politely, taking the seat that May had been using. She perched on the arm of the chair instead, not touching him, but I could sense the electricity between them.

"I'm an apprentice mage," I explained. "You mentioned contacting Dr. Kostich—I'm sure he'd be happy to tell you that you've got me confused with someone else."

"Whether or not you are a mage remains to be seen. That you are Kostich's apprentice, we know. You were introduced to us by him almost two months ago, when you came to the home of the green wyvern to prevent an attack."

"Wyvern?" The word was mentioned earlier, but it took until now to sink in through the fog wrapped around my brain. If it meant what I thought it did, it would go a long way to explaining their odd behavior. "The kind that are . . . oh! That's why you mentioned dragons. You're them, right? Dragons?"

"My father is a dragon, and May is my mate," Gabriel said, taking May's hand. "Tipene is also a silver dragon, as is Maata, whom you will meet shortly. As, I need not say, are you."

I would have laughed, but my brain was still slogging along at a snail's pace. I gave him what I hoped was a jaunty little smile, instead. No wonder they seemed to be so very odd—they were dragons! "You know, in a way this is very exciting. I've never met a dragon before. I've heard about you, of course. Who hasn't? But I can assure you that I am *not* one of you. Not that there's anything wrong with, you know, being an animal. There's nothing wrong with that at all. I'm sure some very nice people are dragons. I just don't happen to know any other than you guys, and I just met you. Oh, hell. I'm babbling again, aren't I?"

"Yes," Kaawa said. "But that is all right. We understand."

"Do you?" I asked hopefully. "Good, because I don't understand anything since I woke up, not the least of which is why you'd think I was the same as you."

"You are Ysolde de Bouchier, silver dragon, and mate to Baltic, who used to be wyvern of the black dragons," Kaawa said, her gaze seeming to strip away all my defenses and leave my soul bare. I squirmed in my chair, uncomfortable with her intense regard.

"I think I would know if I was a fire-breathing shape-shifter with a love of gold," I said gently, not wanting to upset her because she seemed rather nice, if a bit odd. I racked my sluggish brain to remember everything I knew about dragons. "I'm afraid I don't even know much about you folk, although there's been some talk of you lately at the mages' commune, since Dr. Kostich has been forced into dealing with an uncontrollable, irresponsible wyvern's mate who evidently is also a demon lord. But other than that—sorry. I'm afraid you have me mixed up with someone else."

Doubt was evident on May's face as she glanced down at Gabriel. "Could you be wrong?" she asked.

He looked thoughtful as his mother shook her head. "I am not wrong," Kaawa said with determination. "Although I have seen Ysolde de Bouchier only once before, the image of her is burned into my memory for all time. You *are* Ysolde."

I rubbed my forehead, suddenly tired despite my five-week sleep. "I don't know what I can say to prove I am who I am. You can ask Dr. Kostich. You can ask the other apprentices. I'm human. My name is Tully. I live in Spain with my son, husband, and sister-in-law."

"Husband?" Surprise showed in Gabriel's eyes for a few minutes before turning to amusement. "You're married and you have a child?"

"Yes, I do, and I have to say that I don't at all see what's so funny about having a family," I said, frowning a little at the man named Tipene as he chuckled to himself.

"Nothing is funny about it," May said, but even she looked like she was struggling to keep from laughing. "It's just that Baltic is kind of volatile, and when he finds out that his precious Ysolde is alive with a husband and child . . . well, to be honest, he's going to go ballistic."

"That's tough toenails for him, but since I'm not his precious Ysolde, I don't particularly care."

"I think the time will come when you will care very much," Gabriel said, still amused.

"Doubtful. I have this policy about not wasting time on people who are big pains in the ass, and he sounds like a major one. Oh!" I grimaced. "He's not . . . er . . . a friend of yours, is he? If that major pain in the ass comment was out of line, I apologize."

May choked on the sip of coffee she was taking. Gabriel helpfully pounded her on her back while saying, "No, he is no friend to silver dragons."

"Gotcha," I said lightly as I got to my feet. "This has been a really . . . special . . . experience, but I should be on my way. Thank you for the coffee, and for taking care of me while I was out of things. I appreciate it, but my son has been left alone far too long, and I really need to get him from the neighbor who's been taking care of him."

"I don't think it's a very good idea for you to leave just yet," May said slowly as she and Gabriel exchanged yet another of those knowing glances.

"Look, you seem nice and all, but I'm getting tired of saying that I'm not this person you think I am—" I started to say.

"No, I meant that given your physical state, it would be best for you to stay here for a few days," she interrupted.

"My physical state? You mean the fugue?" I asked.

"Is that what you call it?"

"That's how the psychiatrist I saw referred to it. I assure you that although the fugues are inconvenient for everyone, once they are over, I'm fine. A little headachy, but nothing serious."

"You saw a psychiatrist about these … fugues?" Kaawa asked, her dark eyes watching me carefully.

"Well . . . yes. Once. I didn't know what happened to me, and thought …" I sat down again, biting my lip, hesitant to tell them I had thought I was going crazy. "Let's just say I was concerned about what was causing me to have them."

"What was the judgment of the psychiatrist?" Gabriel asked, also making me uncomfortable with his unwavering gaze.

I shrugged. "I only saw him once. Gareth didn't like me going to him."

"Gareth is your husband?" May asked.

"Yes." I tried to make a light little laugh, growing more and more uncomfortable in the situation. "Why do I feel like I'm playing twenty questions?"

"I'm sorry if it appears we're grilling you," May said with a tight little smile of her own. "It's just that you took us all by surprise, and now even more so."

"If you can tolerate another question . . . ," Kaawa said, moving over to sit next to me. I shifted on the couch to give her room, the hairs on my arms pricking at her nearness. There was something about her, some aura that led me to believe she was not a woman who tolerated either fools or lies. "When did you see the psychiatrist?"

I stared at her in surprise. "Er . . . when?"

She nodded, watching me with that same intent gaze.

"Well, let me think . . . it was . . . um . . ." I stared at my fingers, trying to sort through my memories to find the one I wanted, but it wasn't there. "I don't seem to recall."

"A month ago? Two months ago? A year? Five years?" she asked.

"I don't . . . I'm not sure," I said, feeling as lame as I sounded.

"Let me ask you this, then—what is your earliest memory?"

I really stared at her now. "Huh? Why would you want to know something unimportant like that?"

She smiled, and I felt suddenly bathed in a warm, golden glow of caring. "Do my questions disturb you, child?"

"No, not disturb, I just don't see what this has to do with anything. I really have to go. My son—"

"—will be all right for another few minutes." She

waited, and I glanced around the room. The other three dragons sat watching me silently, evidently quite happy to let Kaawa conduct this strange interview. I gave a mental sigh. "Let's see ... earliest memory. I assume you mean as a child."

"Yes. What is the first thing you remember? Your mother's voice, perhaps? A favorite toy? Something that frightened you?"

Supposing it wouldn't hurt to humor her, I poked again at the black mass that was my memory. Nothing was forthcoming. "I'm afraid I have a really crappy memory. I can't remember anything as a child."

She nodded again, just as if she expected that. "Your son is only nine, you said. You must remember the day you gave birth to him."

"Of course I do—" I stopped when, to my horror, I realized I didn't. I could see his face in my mind's eye, but it was his face now, not his face as an infant. Panic swamped me. "By the rood! I don't remember it!"

"By the rood?" May asked.

I stared at her in confusion, my skin crawling with the realization that something was seriously wrong with me. "What?"

"You said 'by the rood.' That's an archaic term, isn't it?"

"How the hell do I know?" I said, my voice rising. "I'm having a mental breakdown, and you're worried about some silly phrase? Don't you understand?" I leaped to my feet, grabbing the collar of May's shirt and shaking it. "I don't remember Brom's first word. I don't remember the first time he walked, or even what he looked like as a baby. I don't remember any of it!"

"Do you remember marrying your husband?" Kaawa asked as May gently pried my hands from her shirt.

Goose bumps prickled up my arms. I prodded, I poked, I mentally grabbed my memory with both hands and shook it like it was a brainy piñata, but nothing came out. "No," I said, the word a whisper as fear replaced the panic. "What's wrong with me? Why can't I remember anything?"

"It is as I thought," Kaawa said, taking my chin between the tips of her fingers so she could search my eyes. "Your memory has been expunged."

"Why would someone do that?" I asked, the words a near wail as I fought the desire to race out of the house and onto the first plane to Spain. "Did you do this to me?"

"No, child," she said solemnly, releasing my chin. "I suspect you have been conditioned to forget."

"Conditioned to forget my own son? That doesn't make any sense! Who would want me to forget him?"

"It's all right, Ysolde. Er . . . Tully," May said in a soothing voice, gently guiding me back to the couch. "I know you're scared by all this, but you talked to your son earlier, remember? You said he was all right."

I clung to that, fighting the rising fear that threatened to overwhelm me. "Yes, he was all right, although I really need to go home. I'm sorry, but I can't stay here any longer."

I made it all the way to the door before Kaawa's voice reached me.

"And what will you do if you have another fugue while your son is with you?"

I froze at that, turning slowly to face the room of people. "I only have them once a year. I believe I mentioned that."

"You told your son that you didn't know why you had it now. That was what you were referring to, wasn't it?"

I nodded, my shoulders slumping. "I shouldn't have had it until the end of October."

"And yet you had it now."

"But, Kaawa, that was—" May started to say.

The older woman raised her hand, and May stopped.

"I've only ever had them once a year," I told them all. "This was an anomaly. I don't know why it came early, but I'm sure it won't happen again."

"How can you be sure? You can't, not really. There is nothing to stop you from having another one right now, or an hour from now, or a week from now, is there?" Kaawa insisted.

I gritted my teeth in acknowledgment.

"What if you were driving a car with your son and you were suddenly sent into a fugue?"

"That would be very unlikely—"

"But it could happen," she pressed. "Would you risk his life?"

"It's never happened like this before," I said, but the horrible ideas she was presenting couldn't be denied. The fugue shouldn't have happened now, but it did. What if it came again, while I was with Brom? My gut tightened at all the terrifying possibilities of disaster.

"I think what Kaawa is trying to say is that until you know why you're having these . . . er . . . events, you should probably stay with us," May suggested.

"No," I said, shaking my head. "I've left Brom alone long enough. I must go home."

"What if—" She slid a glance toward Gabriel, who nodded. "What if your son joined you here?"

"I don't know," I said slowly. "I think it would probably be better to be with my family. Gareth may not be any great shakes as a husband, but he has looked after me this long."

"How long would that be?" Kaawa said, pouncing on my words.

"A long time," I said finally, not finding any answers in my brain.

"Would he have any reason for wanting you to be without your memory?" Gabriel asked.

I opened my mouth to deny such a thing, but remembered the manifestations. "He might. There is . . . when I have a normal fugue, I manifest . . . that's not the right word, really, but it's how I think of it . . . I make . . ." They all watched me with an avidity that made my skin itch. I took a deep breath and said the word. "Gold."

The two male dragons sat up straighter.

"You *make* gold?" May asked, her expression puzzled.

"Ahh," Kaawa said, sitting back, as if that explained everything.

"Yes. Gareth—my husband—says that I'm a natural alchemist. That's someone who can transmute base metals without a need for apparatus or any special elixirs or potions. Every year, when I have the fugues, he brings me lead. Lots and lots of lead, great huge wads of it, and leaves it in the room with me. When the fugue has passed, the lead has been changed into gold. I don't know how it's done, but he assures me that it's some process that happens when I'm asleep."

"That must be very handy," May said, somewhat skeptically, I felt.

I made a face. Whether or not she believed me wasn't the problem at hand. I was more concerned about this sudden loss of memory. Maybe it was me who was going insane, not them, as I'd first thought. "To be honest, I'd much rather do without the fugues. Especially if they're doing something to my brain."

"I imagine you would."

"I admit that's a curious talent to be given, and one that leaves me wishing I had some lead to place in your room," Gabriel said with a rueful smile, "but I don't follow the reasoning between that and why your memory would be wiped."

I made a noncommittal gesture, and for a second, a scene flashed in my mind's eye—Ruth, lying on a cot in a dimly lit hut, covered in boils, sweating and trembling with an illness while Gareth shook her, telling her I was awake, and demanding that she rise and take care of me. I tried to push the fragment of a memory, tried to see more, but there was nothing there, just a black abyss.

"I don't know," I said finally, sadly aware that I couldn't trust the images my brain suggested. There was no way to know if it was an actual memory, or a fabrication of a mind that more and more I was beginning to fear was not normal.

"I can think of any number of reasons why her husband might prefer her without memories," Kaawa said calmly. "For one, he might not wish for her to know what sept he's from."

"Sept?" I shook my head. "Gareth isn't a dragon. I would know if he was."

"Just as you would know if you were one?" Gabriel asked lightly.

"Yes, exactly." He raised his eyebrow and I hurried on. "Besides, Gareth is an oracle, and I've never heard of a dragon being an oracle."

"Just because no dragon has ever sought the position of oracle does not preclude the possibility of doing so," he pointed out.

"He's not a dragon," I insisted. "I would know. I've been married to him for . . ." I slid a quick glance at Kaawa. "However long it's been, I would know."

"I agree," she said, taking me by surprise again.

"You do?" I asked.

"Yes, child. You would know if your Gareth was a dragon." She laid her hand on mine, the gesture one that would normally leave me recoiling—as a rule, I do not like to be touched other than by Brom—but the gesture was a kind one, and offered an odd sort of comfort. "But there are other reasons he might like you to be without memories of what you do during these fugues of yours."

"What do you mean, what I do? I sleep," I told her.

She raised her eyebrows just as Gabriel did, giving her the same disbelieving expression. "How do you know?"

"I know. I mean, I must sleep. Otherwise, I would not have dreamed—" I stopped, not wanting to go into the oddly vivid dream I was having when I woke up.

The look she gave me was shrewd, but she said nothing about the dream, merely commented, "You wake without a memory. You may think you sleep, but what if you don't? What if your husband has you performing acts that he knows would be repugnant to you? Would he not want your memory wiped of them to protect himself? What if your son knows what he does—"

I bolted for the door, alarmed by the pictures she painted in my mind. "I have to go. *Now*!"

"Calm yourself, Ysolde," Kaawa said soothingly. Tipene had somehow gotten in front of the door before me and stood blocking the exit, his arms crossed over his chest.

"My *name* is Tully," I said through clenched teeth.

"I do not say that your husband is doing anything heinous," she continued. "I merely offered that as a possible reason why he might want you in a perpetual state of unawareness."

"Please let me leave," I said, turning to May. Of all the people in the room, she seemed the most sympathetic, the most familiar. "I must go back to my family."

She looked uncomfortable as Gabriel said, "We are your family, Ysolde. You were born a silver dragon. You need our help. You will stay here while we give you that help."

"I don't want your damned help!" I said, losing my temper, while at the same time I wanted to sob in frustration.

"You need assistance recovering your memory," Kaawa pointed out. "Even if you are not who we believe you to be, you cannot wish to live your life without any memories."

That stopped me, as did a thought that struck me as important. "Why didn't I notice before this that I can't remember things like Brom's birth?"

She was silent for a moment, searching my face before answering. "I suspect that whoever expunged your memory applied a compulsion that would keep you from being troubled by the lack. It is only a guess, of course, but you did not become distraught about it until I drove home just how peculiar your circumstances are."

I slumped down on the chair nearest the door, exhausted, mentally bruised and battered. "I just want my son."

"And you will have him. He will come here as soon as possible," Gabriel said.

Hope flared within the dullness of pain inside. "He's only nine," I said.

"May and I will fetch him ourselves," he answered smoothly. May smiled and twined her fingers through his. "We will let no harm come to him, of that I swear."

I watched him for a minute, not sure whether I should trust him or not. A worried little voice warned that I knew little about these people, but they had taken very good care of me for the last five weeks, and I felt an odd bond with May, almost as if I had known her for a very long time. She seemed comfortable to me, trustworthy, and after giving it some thought, reluctantly I agreed. "All right. If you bring Brom to me today, I will stay. For a little bit. Just until you help me discover my memories, so I can prove to you that I'm not a dragon."

Two dimples showed deep on either cheek as he smiled at me. I was unmoved by them. I didn't actually distrust Gabriel, but he didn't seem as familiar and comfortable to me as May, and the sense of power around him made me wary and left me feeling vaguely unsettled.

Brom, unfortunately, could not be whisked to me at a moment's notice. After a lengthy conversation with Penny, the American friend who had taken Brom and me to her heart, she promised to hand him over to Gabriel and May when they arrived in Spain later that afternoon.

"I've never been to England," Brom said when I told him he was to join me. "Not that I remember. Have I, Sullivan?"

I panicked. "Brom, you remember last Christmas, don't you?"

"Last Christmas? When you got upset because I asked for a dissection kit and you wanted to give me a Game Boy, you mean?"

I relaxed, the sudden fear that my memory issues were hereditary—or that someone had been abusing his mind—fading into nothing. "Er . . . yes. That's right."

"What about it?"

"Just remember that sometimes, you may not understand why things are happening, but they turn out for the best," I said in my "vague but wise" mom manner. "I want you to behave yourself with May and Gabriel when they get there, but if anything happens to them, you call me, all right?"

"Yeah, OK. Penny says I have to go pack now. Bye."

I hung up the phone feeling relieved, but at the same time I was worried. Could I trust Gabriel and May? Where was Gareth, and why had he left Brom for so long? And what was going on with my brain? Was I insane, or just the victim of some horrible plot?

"I need some serious therapy," I said aloud, thinking of the small garden plot that I shared with the other residents of our apartment house. It was my haven against daily trials and tribulations, providing me with boundless peace.

"All silver dragons like plants," Kaawa said from behind me. "May hasn't had time yet to take the garden in hand, but I'm sure she'd be happy if you wanted to tidy things up out there."

I whirled around to pin her back with a look. "How did you know I was talking about a garden?"

She just smiled and gestured toward the French windows. Gabriel's house, although in the middle of London, had a minuscule garden guarded by a tall redbrick wall. My heart lightened at the sight of tangled and overrun flower beds, and before I knew it, I was on my knees, my eyes shut as I sank my hands into the sun-warmed earth.

"I'll leave you here. It will be four hours before Gabriel will reach your son," she said, watching with amusement as I flexed my fingers in the soil, plucking out the weeds that choked a chrysanthemum.

"I know. The garden is as good a place as any to wait," I said, looking about to see how bad it was. There were only three beds. One appeared to have suffered some calamity, since the wild lilac bush in it was crumpled to the ground, and wild grass filled the rest of the bed. The second contained miniature rhododendrons run amok, tangled up with irises and what looked to be phlox. The bed I knelt before contained autumn plants, all of which were threatened by the rampant weeds and wild grass.

Kaawa left, and I spent a pleasant hour clearing out the chrysanthemum, amaryllis, and saffron sprouts, worrying all the while about what had become of my life.

# Chapter Three

"Where is she?"

The roar reached me, even hidden from view as I was in the farthest corner of the stable, behind the broken wagon that Dew, the smith, was supposed to have mended months ago.

The doors to the stable slammed shut with a force that I felt in the timbers behind my back. The horses inside with me protested with startled snorts and whinnies. Hastily, I set down the two kittens I had been nuzzling for comfort, returning them to their anxious mother before dusting off my knees and picking my way through the gloom of the stable. The man's voice was deep, and he spoke in French, not the English of the serfs, but there was an accent to his voice that I had never heard.

"Where are you hiding her?"

Anger was rich in that voice, anger and something else, something I couldn't define. I patted Abelard, my mother's gelding, and slipped beside him to peek out through a rotten bit of wood next to his manger, watching as the warrior-mage stomped across the bailey, my father and mother trailing behind him.

"We are not hiding anyone, my lord," Papa said, his tone apologetic.

My mouth dropped open in surprise. Papa never apologized to anyone! He was a famous mage, one of so much renown that other mages travelled for months just to consult with him. And yet here he was, following the warrior around, bleating like a sheep that had lost its dam.

"Kostya saw her," the warrior snarled, spinning around to glare at Papa, the tall guards moving in a semicircle behind him. "Do you call us liars?"

"No, my lord, never that!" Papa wrung his hands, my mother next him looking pale and frightened. "If you will just come back inside the hall, I will explain to you—"

"Explain what? That you are holding a dragon prisoner, a female dragon of tender years?"

"She is not a prisoner—" Papa started to say, but I stopped listening for a moment. A dragon? Here? I had heard tales of such beings, but had never seen one. Margaret told me they did not really exist, that it was just a bit of foolishness spoken by men who had too much wine, but once I had overheard my mother talking to her maid about a female dragon she had befriended in her youth. Perhaps Mama had hidden her here all these years. Who could it be? Leah, the nurse who tended both Margaret and me? One of my mother's serving women? The flatulent Lady Susan?

"I just wager you it's her," I told Abelard. "She is very dragonlike."

"Bring her forth!" the warrior demanded, and I pushed Abelard's head aside in order to get a better view of the bailey, watching with bated breath to see the dragon.

"My lord, there are circumstances that you are not aware of. Ysolde has no knowledge of her ancestry. We have sheltered her as best we could, indeed, raised her as our own daughter—"

My skin crawled. My blood curdled. My brain exploded inside my head. I stared at Papa, my papa, the papa I had known for my entire life, unable to believe my ears.

"—she has been protected from those who would ill use her, as sworn by my lady wife to the dragon who bore her here."

"Me?" I said, touching my throat when my voice came out no more than a feeble squeak. "I'm a dragon?"

"That is none of my concern," the warrior said now, his voice thick with menace. "She is a dragon, and evidently of age. She belongs with her own kind, not with humans."

My own kind? Scaly, long-tailed, fire-breathing monsters? A sob of denial caught in my throat, the noise almost inaudible, and yet as I stood there reeling from the verbal blows my father—the man I thought of as my father—dealt me, the warrior spun around, the gaze of his black eyes so piercing, I could swear he could see straight through the wood of the stable.

*Run*, my mind told me as the man started forward toward the stable doors, and I knew at that moment that he was one of them. He was a monster the like of which I'd never seen. My brain didn't wait for me to absorb that knowledge. *Flee*, it urged. *Flee!*

I didn't stop to question the wisdom of that command. I spun on my heels, racing down the narrow aisle
of the stable to the far corner, where a small window had
been cut in order to pass hay through from the fields. I
wasn't fast enough, however, not if the roar of fury that
followed me was anything to go by.

"Stop!" the warrior bellowed as I leaped through the
window, not even pausing as I hit the ground hard before
I was off again, racing around the pens holding the animals to be slaughtered, dashing between the small huts
housing craftsmen and their families, dodging chickens,
dogs, and occasionally serfs as I raced for the postern
gate along the west curtain.

"Lady Ysolde," John, the man on guard at the gate,
called in surprise as I rounded a cart loaded with wool
destined for the market, not even slowing down as I
flung myself past him and through the postern gate. "Are
you off to the village—hey, now! Who are you, and what
right do you have to be chasing Lady Ysol—oof!"

I didn't stop to see how John fared, although I sent up a
small prayer that he hadn't been hurt by the warrior. I ran
along the rocky outcropping that led down into the village, the moat not coming around to this face of the castle
since it would be impossible for anyone to scale the cliffs
that hugged the west and south sides. Behind me I heard
the noise of pursuit, but I had always been fast on my feet,
and I dug deep for speed as I leaped down the last of the
rocks and headed for the trees beyond the village. They
marked the edge of the thick forest where I had spent
many an hour, wandering pathways known to only a few.
If I could just make it there, then I could hide from the
warrior . . . and then what?

I didn't stop to answer that question. I just knew that

I needed to be by myself, to absorb the strangeness that had suddenly gripped me. And I couldn't do that with the intense, black-haired dragon storming around me.

He was still behind me as I skirted a newly plowed field, ignoring the calls of greeting from the serfs as I raced by, intent on my goal, greeting the dappled shade of the outer fringes of the forest with relief. I'd made it, no doubt due to the extra weight the warrior wore in the form of his armor. I risked a quick look behind me as I sped around an ancient birch tree. The warrior was about thirty feet behind me, but just beyond him, his guards approached on horseback, leading his horse.

"By the rood!" I swore to myself as I leaped over a downed tree trunk, heading for the densest part of the forest.

The sounds of pursuit were muted in the calm of the forest. Birdsong rose high above me as the swallows dipped and spun in the sunlight, making elegant arcs in the air. Patches of sunlight shone here, and I slowed down, trying to control my breathing, picking through the muffled noises of the animals of the forest as they went about their business. Somewhere near, a badger was snuffling along the ground, disturbing earth and fallen leaves. A woodpecker drilled a few yards away, while farther afield, foliage rustled and snapped as a large animal, probably a stag or hind, grazed. In the distance, the jangling of horses' harnesses was audible. I smiled to myself at that, pleased that the growth was too thick for the warrior's men to ride through.

I was just looking around for a suitable tree that I could climb and hide myself in when a man's voice sounded, uncomfortably near. "Where are you, *ché-*

*rie*? You do not need to be afraid of me. I will not hurt you."

I snorted to myself, trying to pinpoint the origin of the voice. Usually I had very good hearing, but the denseness of the trees and sounds of the forest combined to muffle the warrior's voice, making it hard to judge where he was.

"We want only to help you," he continued. I moved around the tree, clutching the rough trunk as I peered into the depths in the direction I thought the voice came from. A branch moved, but before I had time to react, a wren popped out and gave me a curious look.

"Are you frightened, *chérie*?"

I strained my ears, but it was impossible to pinpoint a direction. Which is the only reason I called out, "No."

Laughter edged his voice. "Then why do you run from me?"

"Why are you chasing me?" I asked boldly, moving to the cover of another tree, peering intently around it for any signs of the man.

"We only just learned of your existence from the mortals."

The scorn he put in the last words irritated me. "Those mortals are my family!" I yelled.

"No, *chérie*. We are your family. We want to bring you home, where you will be taken care of and taught."

I didn't think much of that statement.

"I know you have no knowledge of us," the man continued. Was his voice fainter? Had he been misled into moving away from me? "But we will correct that. We will teach you what it is to be a dragon."

His voice *was* softer. I smiled to myself as I hugged

the tree. "I don't wish to be a dragon, warrior. I wish simply to be myself."

Another man's voice called in the distance. I smiled again and turned around, intent on making my way out of the forest while the intense dragon and his guard stumbled around it searching for me.

The warrior was leaning on the tree behind me, watching me with a half smile that made my blood freeze. "That is all we wish for you, too—that you be yourself."

"How did you do that?" I asked, momentarily too intrigued to be incensed by his trick.

He shrugged and strolled toward me, all long-legged grace and power. "There are many things you will learn." He stopped before me, reaching out to touch my face. I slapped his hand. He laughed. "You have fire. You will learn well."

"And you are impertinent. What makes you think I'm who you think I am?"

"You need proof?" he asked, his eyebrows raised, but there was still amusement in his onyx eyes.

"That I'm a gigantic scaly beast who breathes fire? Yes, I think I'm going to need proof," I said.

"There is a way," he said, taking my arm, and with a quick jerk, he ripped the laces from the wrists of my tunic. He bent over my wrist as if he were going to bite it, paused, and looked up at me, an odd expression on his face. "How old are you, *chérie*?"

"My name is Ysolde," I said, trying to pull my arm free. His fingers tightened around it. "Ysolde de Bouchier, and I am *not* your *chérie*."

"How old are you?" he repeated, a stubborn glint in his eyes.

"I have seen seventeen summers, not that it is any concern of yours," I said primly.

He grimaced, then shrugged, and instead of biting my hand, he pulled me up against his chest, his arms around me in an unbreakable vise. "This is the test, *chérie*."

His mouth was on mine before I could do more than slap my hands on his chest. I was no stranger to being kissed—Mark, the brewer's son, was always happy to hide behind the ale barrels with me and kiss me as long as I liked—but this was not a kiss as I knew it. Where Mark's kisses had been interesting and vaguely pleasurable, this was a kiss of an entirely different variety. The warrior's mouth was hot on mine, hotter than I had ever experienced, hot and sweet and spicy all at the same time, as if he'd been eating spiced plums. His hands moved down my back, holding my hips, pulling me closer to his body, his tongue teasing the seam of my lips even as his fingers dug into my hips.

With a frustrated snarl, he suddenly pushed me away. I stood shocked to my toes by the kiss, watching with astonishment as he doubled over, sliding his mail hauberk off over his head. He stood back up, pulling off the padding armor, then the leather jerkin beneath it, his eyes glittering like sunlight sparkling off rocks in a stream.

"Now," he said.

"Now?" I asked, not understanding, taking a step back.

He made a noise in his chest that sounded like a growl, his arms around me again as he pressed me up against the tree trunk.

"Now I will prove to you what you are," he said just before his mouth descended again, his body holding me against the tree. Gone was the mail that stood between us; now I was smashed up against his body, aware of the difference between his hard lines and my softer curves. But it was his mouth that captured and held my attention as his tongue swept along my lips again, urging me to open them. I did so, goose bumps prickling down my arms as his tongue swept inside, touching my own, tasting me even as his hands pulled my hips tighter against his, his fingers cupping my bottom in a way that was shockingly intimate and wildly thrilling at the same time.

His tongue twined around mine, and I gave up all thoughts of fighting, tasting him as he tasted me, reveling in the groan of pleasure he gave when I mimicked his action and let my tongue dance into his mouth.

Heat blasted me then, heat of such intensity I swore I was going to go up in flames, the fire of it pouring into me and setting my soul alight. Impossibly, the kiss deepened, the warrior pulling me upward along the tree trunk until my feet dangled a good foot off the ground, my mouth at the same height as his. I wrapped my arms around his back and gave myself up to the heat, to the pleasure he was stirring with just the touch of his mouth. The heat was in me and around me and through me, and with every second it filled me, my heart sang. I was consumed by it, burning just as bright as the biggest bonfire, my soul soaring with the sensation. I didn't want it to stop, never wanted to stop kissing this strange, handsome man.

"That, *chérie*, is the test," he said, his face tight with some emotion as he let me slide down his body.

I blinked at him a couple of times, trying to regain my wits. "Test?" I asked stupidly, my mind clearly too dazzled by that kiss to do anything but parrot what was said to me.

"Only a dragon or a mate can take dragon fire and live," he said, his lips almost touching mine. His eyes were as deep and shiny as the bit of onyx hung in a pearl necklace that my mother sometimes wore.

"Who are you?" I asked, searching his face, memorizing it in order to tuck away the memory of that kiss.

A slow smile curled his lips. "I am the wyvern of the black dragons, Ysolde de Bouchier. I am Baltic."

Baltic. The name resonated within my head like a bell, repeating and echoing until I thought it would deafen me.

Baltic. The word spun around in my brain as I was swept up in a hurricane of thoughts, confused and tangled beyond hope.

Baltic ...

"Sullivan?"

My eyes shot open at the voice. I was disoriented, my brain feeling muzzy again, but as my eyes focused on the worried face peering down at me, joy leaped within me.

"How come you're out here in the dark by yourself? Are you OK?" Brom asked as I pushed myself up from the ground, where I'd evidently fallen asleep. Immediately I wrapped him in my arms in a bear hug to beat all bear hugs. "Geez, Sullivan, there are people watching."

I finished kissing his adorable face, giving him another hug just to reassure myself that he was really there. "I'm fine. Did you have any trouble at the airport?"

"Nope. Gabriel said there might be some problems, but he bribed a few people, and it ended up being OK after all."

I looked over Brom's head to where Gabriel and May stood, leaning against each other with that ease of longtime lovers. "Trouble with his passport?"

"Not that," Brom said before Gabriel could answer, squirming out of my hold. "With my mummies!"

"Your . . . you didn't bring those horrible things, did you?"

He shot me a look that was oddly adult in its scorn. "It's my work, Sullivan. You didn't think I was going to leave it behind so Gareth or Ruth could take it when I wasn't there? The customs dudes didn't want to let me bring them, but Gabriel gave them some money to look the other way. He says I can use a room in the basement as my lab. It's got a table and sink already, and he said he'll get me a big tub to soak the bodies in."

"How very generous of Gabriel," I said, trying not to grimace at the thought of Brom's current scholarly pursuits.

May laughed. "It actually sounds very interesting, if a little gruesome. Brom says he only works on animals that have died naturally, because he feels too much empathy to kill one for research purposes."

"For which I am truly grateful," I said, ruffling his mousey brown hair.

"That's not all. Gabriel says you get to give me some sort of a tattoo of the silver-dragon sept. He says most members of the sept have them on their backs, but I thought it would be cool to have it on my arm, so I can show it off."

"No tattoo!" I said firmly. "You're far too young for that. And I wouldn't know how to give you one even if you weren't."

"It's not really a tattoo," May said quickly. "It's more of a brand. It's done with dragon fire."

I stared at her for a few seconds. "Is that supposed to make it better?"

Gabriel laughed and pulled his shirt off, turning around. "All members of the silver sept bear the emblem marking them as such on their backs."

High on his shoulder blade was a mark that looked like a hand with a crescent moon on the palm.

"May has one too, although she wouldn't show me hers," Brom said, giving her a disgusted look.

"I don't take my shirt off in public quite as easily as Gabriel does," she told him.

"I don't care what it is," I said. "You're not having it. You're not a member of the silver dragons."

"Gabriel says I am because you're one of them."

"Well, I'm not." A thought occurred to me. "And I can prove it. You said all the silver dragons have that mark—well, I don't."

They all looked at me as if they wanted me to take my shirt off.

"She's right," Brom said after a moment of silence. "I've never seen anything like that on her back."

"You see?" I tried to keep the triumph in my voice to a minimum. "I wish you'd mentioned this emblem or tattoo or whatever it is before—it could have cleared things up instantly. I don't have any such marks on me."

"Well . . . except for that one on your hip," Brom said.

"That is a scar, not a tribal marking," I told him.

"Scar?" Gabriel asked, his gaze dropping to my midsection. "What sort of a scar?"

"Just the remnants of an old injury, nothing more," I said quickly.

"It's shaped kind of like this," my son said, holding his hands up, fingers spread, thumbs touching.

"Oh, it is not. It's just a simple scar!"

"Is it a figure resembling a bird?" Gabriel asked him.

"Of course it's not! And no, before you ask, I'm not going to—Brom!"

The child I had labored to bring into the world—even if I couldn't remember the event—grabbed the bottom of my broomstick skirt and lifted it, squinting at my exposed hip. "I suppose it looks kind of like a bird."

"You are in serious trouble, buster," I told him, trying to wrestle my skirt out of his grasp.

Gabriel started around the back of me, but stopped at a pointed look from May, who gave me a little smile, and said, "I'm sorry, Yso— Tully," as she bent her head to look at the mark that rode high on my hip. I'd never thought much of it, assuming that I must have had a painful fall sometime in my past.

I realized now that Kaawa had been right—something had made me not worry about the fact that I couldn't remember my past.

"I have to say, the part that I can see looks like a . . . well, like a phoenix," May said, examining the scar. "It disappears into your underwear, but it looks like those are outstretched wings."

"I think everyone has seen enough," I said, giving Brom one of my scariest mom looks.

He didn't even flinch, the rat.

"We could see this better if you took your underwear off," he pointed out.

"You did not just say that," I said through clenched teeth.

Confusion flashed across his face. "Yeah, I did. See, that part of it is underneath your underwear—"

I slapped his hand where he was about to yank down the side of my undies. "That is quite enough!"

"I'm sorry, Tully," May said, straightening up. "This isn't a scar. It's not a brand, though, either. I don't quite know what it is—it's like it's an anti-tattoo."

"Mayling," Gabriel said, clearly asking her permission to look at the silly scar.

She narrowed her eyes at him. "You do not need to be looking at strange women's hips."

"I'm a healer! I've seen women's bodies," he protested.

"Ysolde isn't injured!"

"You wouldn't recognize a sept emblem as I would."

"I think I would. I've seen enough of them now."

"You are far from an expert—" he started to say, but I had finally had enough.

"Oh, this is ridiculous." I jerked the material of my skirt out of Brom's hand and spun around, pulling the top side of my underwear down a few inches. "You want to see? Fine, you can see. Why don't we get Kaawa and your big friend in to see as well? Perhaps announce it on the street and bring in a few strangers!"

Gabriel ignored my little hissy fit as he stared at my hip for a few moments before his gaze rose to mine. His grey eyes were somber and considering. "I believe I have been mistaken."

"A voice of sanity at last!" I said, readjusting my underwear and letting the skirt fall back into place. "Thank you! It's nice to know there's someone who recognizes a scar when he sees one."

He shook his head. "That is no scar, Ysolde."

"Tully. My name is Tully."

"Your name is Ysolde," he said firmly, his eyes glittering strangely in the night. I opened my mouth to protest, but he continued. "I was wrong about you being a silver dragon. You do not bear our emblem. You do, however, bear that of the black dragons."

I closed my mouth and, taking Brom's hand, turned on my heel, walking back into the house and up the stairs to the room where I'd woken up.

Brom watched me for a few minutes before saying, "May says I can sleep in the room next to this one 'cause she figures you'll want me close by. I told her you didn't think I was such a baby."

"That was very thoughtful of May. I do indeed want you close by. I've missed you terribly."

He grimaced. "I hope you're not going to go all mom on me in front of everyone. I like them. I like Gabriel and May. They're nice, huh? Did you know May can go invisible?"

I shook my head, my brain numbed by the events of the day. What was happening to me? Was I losing my grip on reality, or was something more profound, infinitely more frightening, controlling my life?

"She said she's made up of shadows, but I think she was just teasing me, because she feels just like a normal person. But she showed me in the car coming here how she can disappear. She said you have to be born that way to do it, that she's something with a long name, and that's why she can become invisible."

A word nudged its way to the front of my mind. "Doppelganger."

"Yeah, that's it." He plopped himself down on the bed next to me. "Gabriel says if Gareth had been a mortal human, I could have been a wyvern, and one day challenged him for the job."

"Gareth *is* human," I said, feeling as if a thousand ants were marching up and down my body.

"Sullivan," he said with an exaggerated eye roll. "Have you seen those pictures of him and Ruth and you in old-time clothes? He's got to be at least a hundred years old. Maybe more."

"Pictures? What pictures?" I roused from my stupor in order to look at him.

"The ones in Ruth's room."

I dug through what remained of my memory. "I don't remember seeing any pictures in her room."

"In a box in the locked drawer in her bureau," he said, looking around the room with casual curiosity.

"How do you know what's in a locked drawer?" I asked, then realized just how stupid a question that was. "I don't care if your father gave you a lock-picking kit for Christmas—you are not going to be a cat burglar when you grow up, and you are not to hone your skills on your aunt's locked bureau."

"She has pictures of you, too," he said with blithe disregard to my chastisement.

"I highly doubt that. Ruth and I aren't the very best of friends."

"Yeah, I know, but she has pictures of you and Gareth and her, and you're all wearing clothes like out of that movie you made me watch."

I racked my brain, or what was left of it. "What movie?"

"The one you like to watch so much. You know, the one with the girls in long dresses and they walk around and talk a lot."

*"Pride and Prejudice?"*

He nodded. "Yeah, you were wearing stuff like that."

"They didn't have cameras during the Regency period," I told him, distracted by the thought of pictures.

Brom wouldn't lie, but he might have misinterpreted what he had seen.

"Whatever. I think I'll go move my stuff down to the room in the basement Gabriel said I could have."

I eyed him, his round face as dear to me as life itself. Thank god whatever was happening to me hadn't stripped me of memory of him altogether. "You will go to bed. It's well past your bedtime."

"I'm nine, Sullivan, not a baby," he said with exaggerated forbearance.

"Go to bed," I repeated.

He sighed and got to his feet, pausing at the door to send me a martyred look before saying, "Gabriel says he won't kick us out because we're not silver dragons anymore. He said you were born into the silver sept, and that they'd honor that, even though you were married to a black dragon. Did you know Gareth when you were married to the dragon?"

I closed my eyes and bowed my head, wanting to cry, wanting to scream, wanting to tell Brom that I had only been married once in my life, to his father. "Time for bed," was all I said, however, before escorting him to his room. I made sure that he was settled before disgusting him with not one, but three hugs, and two smooches to the head, which he tolerated, but only just barely. Clearly Brom was moving into that stage of life where motherly affection was a thing to be borne with much martyrdom.

"Sleep well. If you need anything, come and get me," I told him as I left the room.

"I'm glad you're OK," he said before the door closed. "Penny said you would be, but I was kind of worried. I didn't know you had May and Gabriel to look after you.

You know what I think? I think you're lucky they found you."

My heart swelled at the fact that he had been concerned. "Lucky?"

"Yeah. What if it had been one of the other dragons who found you? Someone not from your own group? What would have happened then?"

What indeed. "Go to sleep," I said, blowing him a kiss.

Silence filled my little room when I returned to it, but all it did was heighten the desperate confusion of my mind.

# Chapter Four

"I don't want to go."

The lid of my traveling basket closed with solid finality, punctuated by the muted sounds of weeping.

"I don't like him. He's arrogant," I added, watching as my mother's tirewoman tightened the straps on the basket so it wouldn't come open during travel. "Although he's a much better kisser than Mark, the brewer's son."

"He kissed you?" My mother moved into view, her face pinched and white as she glanced around my bedchamber. Margaret sat on the bed, weeping into her sleeve.

Sorrow at leaving her filled me, but anger at the sudden upheaval in my life was the emotion that rode me. "Yes. I don't see why I have to go with him."

"Mama, can't she stay?" Margaret begged, looking up with red-rimmed eyes.

I sat next to her on the bed and hugged her. Margaret and I had sometimes had a turbulent relationship, but she was the only sister I had, and I would miss her. Especially since I was being taken from my home against my will.

"I promised your mother—" Mama choked on the word before continuing. "I promised the one who was your mother that I would raise you as my own to ensure your safety. I have done so, but I know she would not have wanted me to keep you from your true family. I would not let you go, but indeed, I have no choice in the matter. And Lord Baltic said that no ill would come to you, not that I told him anything about your past. Still, he swore that you would not be harmed, and that is what we must hold to."

"I don't care what that Baltic says," I murmured, holding tight to Margaret. "I'm not an animal."

"I've explained to you, dear—dragons do not take their bestial form very often. They prefer to be in human form, and live amongst us as a mortal would." She gestured to the maids to carry down my traveling baskets. "Come, Ysolde. It is time. Lord Baltic is waiting, and I do not wish for his anger at a delay to fall upon your father."

"Lord Baltic can go stick his head in the pig's wallow for all I care," I said, stalking out the door after the maids.

Mama made noises of distress, but followed after me, speaking to herself as she ran over the things I was taking with me. "I asked him if he wanted the bed, but he said no, he wanted to travel fast. I have done my best by her, I hope he knows that."

Margaret hurried after me, wiping her face. "Ysolde will be able to visit us, won't she, Mama?"

"Of course I will," I said as our little procession

marched down the stairs to the great hall below. "No one can stop me from seeing you whenever I want."

"Is that so?" a deep male voice asked.

I turned my head as I stepped off the last step, meeting Baltic's ebony gaze with a level look. "Yes, that's so."

He watched me for a moment, then gave a jerky nod of his head. "We will do our best to make you happy, *chérie.*"

"Stop calling me that," I hissed through my teeth as I passed him.

His laughter rolled out across the hall in response.

The leave-taking that followed was not something I ever wish to live through again. I clung first to my mother, then my father, unable to keep tears from spreading tracks down my cheeks, their wetness blending with that of Margaret's when she hugged me, her face pressed to mine as she whispered her desire that I not be long in returning.

By the time the imperious Baltic lifted me onto my horse, I wasn't in much better shape than Margaret, although I had enough presence of mind to glare at him when he gripped my leg as he adjusted the stirrups.

"I am not a strumpet to be handled such," I snapped, my emotions frayed and irritated, placing my boot in the middle of his chest and pushing him backwards.

One of his guards, the one he called Kostya, a black-eyed devil if ever there was one, laughed and said something in a language I did not know.

Baltic shot me a look filled with ire, but said nothing. Before I knew it, we were riding across the bridge over the moat, the only home I'd ever known slowly slipping away behind me.

I didn't speak to any of the dragon men for three days.

On the fourth, I was sick of my own thoughts, tired of grieving for my lost family, and bored almost to the point of insensibility.

"Where are we going?" I asked that evening, when we passed through the gates of a small town.

Baltic, who was riding next to me, shot me an amused glance. "You're speaking to us?"

"Since I have no other alternative," I said in my most haughty manner. "I would like to know where these other parents of mine are."

We stopped in front of a small inn. The three guards dismounted; one of the men, a short, stocky man named Pavel, disappeared into the low opening of the inn. Baltic tossed the reins of his horse to a stableboy before helping me off my mount. "I am not taking you to your parents."

I stared at him in surprise. "Why not?"

He put his hand on my back and gave me a little shove toward the inn. Since it looked like it was about to rain, I went inside, ducking at the low beam at the doorway. The inn was of modest size, smoky and dark inside, but there were no foul odors as you will sometimes find in such places. To the right was a rough staircase leading to a floor above, while to the left was a common room filled with benches and rough-hewn plank tables.

"We do not yet know who your parents are. The mortal woman would not tell us the name of the dragons who left you with her, and although it would have been possible to get that information from her, such methods can take time, and I wished to be on my way. We will go to my home in Riga, and from there begin the search for your true parents."

I felt like a dog hackling up at his arrogant tone. "I suppose you expect me to be grateful you decided not to torture my mother!"

"No." He looked nonplussed. "She was not your mother. She was merely a mortal who had sworn her fealty to a dragon."

"Did you even talk to her?" I demanded, grabbing his arm when he was about to walk away from me. "Did you even ask her why I was left with her? You didn't, did you? You couldn't be bothered to find out what really happened!"

His eyes glittered dangerously, but I was never one to take heed when I should, and I saw no reason to start now. He leaned close, his fingers biting hard into my arm, his breath fanning my face as he growled, "You will not address me in such an insolent tone. I am a wyvern. You will show me respect at all times."

"I will respect you when you prove worthy of such an honor!" I snapped back.

His jaw worked as if he wanted to shout at me, but all he did was release me with a muttered oath. He started off toward the innkeeper, but I wasn't through with him. "Finding out the truth may have been beneath your concern, but it wasn't beneath mine! My mother told about the woman she knew from her youth, a woman who was gravely injured, and whom she healed. She told me about how they had remained friends until one day, the woman arrived covered in blood, bearing a baby—me—and begged her to hide the child away lest it be discovered by her enemies. She told my mother the name of that enemy."

Baltic froze and turned slowly around to face me, his expression blank.

I squared my shoulders and met his gaze without flinching. "Baltic. The woman said the one who would destroy her and the child was named Baltic."

With a snarl, he lunged at me, moving so fast I could barely follow him. I didn't even have time to scream before he spun me around, ripping off my cloak and shredding my surcoat. I ran forward, sobbing, intent on escaping the suddenly mad warrior, but he caught me, pressing me into the wall as he tore the cotte until only my chemise hid my skin from his view.

Even that wasn't enough. As I clutched the wall, terrified that in his animal frenzy he would tear the flesh from my bones, he jerked down my chemise until my back was exposed.

"Silver!" he snarled, releasing me suddenly. I half collapsed on the stairs, clutching my clothing to my chest, trying to understand what brought on this brainstorm.

"What is silver?" I asked, flinching when he kicked tables and chairs out of his way as he stormed across the room.

"The mark you bear."

"On my back?" I snatched up the cloak that lay on the ground, wrapping it around myself.

At the sound of wood being smashed, Kostya burst into the room, his sword in hand. "What is it?"

Pavel stood at the top of the stairs, silently watching as his master literally destroyed the meager furnishings in the common room.

Kostya frowned, looking from Pavel, to me, and finally to Baltic. "What's wrong?"

Baltic swore, profanely and with a fluency that I

couldn't help but admire. He slammed a chair into the wall. It exploded in a thousand little splinters. "Ask her!" he snarled, kicking debris out of the way. The innkeeper had run into the back room the second Baltic had become enraged. He peeked out of the door, quickly hiding when Baltic pulled out his sword and started hacking away at a barrel of ale.

"What have you done?" Kostya asked me, sheathing his sword.

"Nothing. Baltic is upset over a birthmark on my back."

"That is no birthmark!" Baltic yelled, his face red with fury as he started toward me, his sword still in hand. I backed up, stumbling over a broken chair, wanting nothing more than to get out of the way of the madman. He stalked forward, menace rolling off him, his eyes narrowed and focused on me.

I thought briefly of running, but knew I wouldn't make it more than two steps before he would be on me.

"I've done nothing to anger you," I said, putting on a brave front.

His lips curled. "You bear the mark of a silver dragon."

Behind him, Kostya looked shocked.

"Silver, not black! You are the spawn of a traitor, one who has betrayed us! I should kill you where you stand!" He raised the sword until the tip of it was pressed into my throat.

I stood still, confused why he should be so angry with me, but aware that if I showed the least sign of weakness, he would kill me.

"Baltic—" Kostya approached, stopping just short of us. His expression was wary, but I did not see in him the unwholesome fury that was in his master. "She is innocent of wrongdoing."

"No silver dragon is innocent," Baltic said in a low growl. Pain pricked my neck as the sword tip pierced my skin. I lifted my chin, keeping my gaze steady on his. "They will either rejoin us, or they will die."

"But this one knows nothing of our ways. She has not even accepted that she is a dragon," Kostya argued, gesturing toward me. "What purpose is there in killing her?"

Baltic opened his mouth to answer, but I was through being tolerant.

"His purpose is to bully and frighten," I said loudly. "He is a coward, nothing more."

His breath hissed in as he leaned forward. "No man has ever spoken those words to me and lived."

"I am not a man," I said, gritting my teeth against the burn of the sword as it slid deeper into my flesh.

"You would be dead if you were," he snarled, lowering the sword and stepping back.

"You wish to challenge me?" I asked, shoving him hard in the chest.

He looked so surprised by the action, I had to bite back the urge to laugh. Kostya's mouth dropped open into an O as I took two steps forward until I stood toe-to-toe with Baltic. "I will meet your challenge, warrior, but on my terms."

An odd look crossed his face. "What terms?"

"No weapons," I said, lifting my chin. "If you wish to challenge me, I will meet you body to body, but with no weapons, no armor. Just your fists against mine."

Pavel gave a short bark of laughter. Kostya's frown relaxed into a smug smile. Baltic's face remained expressionless, nothing but his eyes giving away any indication of what he was thinking.

"Very well," he said after a minute's silence. "But you must make it worth the ridicule I will suffer for such an indignity."

"Indignity!" He actually had the nerve to smile when I hit him on the chest. "Because I am a woman, you mean?"

"Because I am the wyvern, and you are merely a young female who has not yet learned her place." He handed Kostya his sword. "I will be happy to teach it to you, but I must have payment."

I eyed him as Pavel came down the stairs to help divest him of his mail and armor. Both guards were smiling. "What form of payment do you seek?"

"When I win the challenge, you will disavow your fealty to the traitorous bastard who rules your sept."

"I don't know any bastards other than Jack, the carter's brother, and he is simpleminded and hardly could be called traitorous."

"I refer to Constantine of Norka," Baltic said, all but spitting the words out.

"Well, I don't know him either, and I certainly haven't sworn fealty to him."

"Your parents must have, else you would not bear the brand of the silver dragons on your back." Baltic peeled off his leather armor and stood before me wearing nothing but boots, braies, and jerkin.

It struck me for the first time that he was quite comely for a man. The high, sharp cheekbones gave his face a measure of strength. His nose was thin and sharp, sitting below a broad forehead from which dark hair swept back. Twin slashes of straight black eyebrows drew attention to his deep, dark eyes beneath. His jaw was angular, but blunted at the chin, as if God had decided that he had too many angles in his face and wanted to soften the sharpness a little. But it was his mouth that seemed to hold an unholy attraction for me. His lips were full, the lower creating a down-turned crescent, while the upper had a gentle curve that belied the anger held within him.

"Do you agree to the terms?" he asked, and I realized I'd been staring at his mouth.

I cleared my throat. "You have neglected to state the full terms. I must have a boon if I defeat you."

All three men laughed loud enough that the remaining guard came in from where he had been tending to the horses.

"Lady Ysolde has accepted Baltic's challenge," Kostya told him when he entered casting curious glances around the now-destroyed common room.

"What challenge?" the guard asked. His name was Matheo, I remembered from the brief introduction Baltic had made when he took me from my home. Kostya leaned over and whispered to him. Matheo smiled broadly.

"You will not defeat me," Baltic said, and once again, I was possessed with the desire to slap him. "But let us live in the world of the impossible, and say that you do. What boon would you like of me?"

"I wish to go home," I said, my gaze steadfast.

He was silent for a moment, then made me a bow. "I accept the terms of the challenge. When would you like to begin?"

I looked around the room. It was only four warrior dragons and myself, the innkeeper wisely keeping himself out of sight.

"Is there anything wrong with now?" I asked, pinning my cloak so my hands were free.

"No." He waved a hand around the room. "Would you like to fight here, or would you prefer we go out—"

I moved swiftly. He dropped like a sack full of bulls, his body curling into a circle as he clutched at his privates, unable to speak except to gasp for air.

"You should never have taken off your codpiece," I said, gesturing toward that piece of armor that lay half hidden by the leather cuirass that had been discarded a few minutes before. "And I believe this qualifies as a win."

His guards, all three of them, stared with open-mouthed surprise as Baltic stopped writhing on the ground, his eyes open and glaring at me with promised retribution. He uncurled himself, his face beautiful and deadly.

"You . . . will . . . pay . . ." he finally managed to get out.

"No, I think you will pay—you will take me home." I kept my ground as he got painfully to his feet, his body hunched as if . . . well, as if he'd just taken a very hard kick to the privates. "Do you deny that I won the challenge?"

His face worked again, and I was certain that he was going to either spit at me or strike me, but he did neither; he simply turned and slowly made his way up the stairs to where the bedchamber was located.

The guard Matheo, after a long look at me, followed him. Pavel shook his head and gathered up Baltic's armor before doing the same.

Only Kostya was left with me, and he watched me with an expression that I found difficult to read.

"You do not approve of my method of winning?" I asked him.

He was silent for the count of six, then shook his head. "You are a woman. He is a wyvern. I would expect you to use whatever method you could to disable him. It is not how you struck the blow that you will regret."

"Then what?" I asked, feeling more than a little ashamed at the way I'd taken Baltic off guard.

Slowly, Kostya smiled. "There may come a day when you wish to enjoy those parts you have this day so grievously injured."

Heat flooded into my cheeks as he, too, made a bow, then went outside.

Had he seen me staring at Baltic's mouth, and assumed I was a woman of no virtue? I couldn't blame him if he did. I didn't feel particularly virtuous around Baltic, not with my mind reliving over and over again that kiss in the forest.

"By the rood," I swore to myself. "Kostya's right. But the saints help me, Baltic is driving me insane."

Guilt ate at me later, as I sat alone in a cramped bedchamber, nothing more than a closet, really, with a pallet crammed up against the eaves, a three-legged stool, and a cracked chamber pot.

The inn boasted two rooms—this one, and the larger room that took up the remainder of the upper floor—but as it was a communal room, one containing several pallets upon which Baltic and his guards would sleep, I had been given the closet. I walked the two paces that was the available free space, turned, and paced back, listening with half an ear to the sounds coming up through the floorboards.

Kostya had evidently made things right with the innkeeper, because earlier, when I had come in from using the privy, two lads and a frightened-looking woman were clearing away the debris left by Baltic's fit, and shortly after that, three new benches appeared. Two hours later the locals slowly arrived, no doubt reassured that the mad lord was safely asleep upstairs. The soft murmur of conversation drifted upward, livened now and again by a hearty laugh that was stifled quickly, as if the patrons feared causing too much noise.

"This is silly. He challenged me. He held a sword to my neck. I shouldn't feel the least bit sorry for what I did," I told myself, touching the spot on my neck where the sword had pierced my flesh.

The wound wasn't there. It had healed almost immediately, and if a thin trickle of blood hadn't seeped into my chemise, I might have thought I imagined it. I had changed my torn clothing once Pavel brought my traveling basket, but my chemise lay on top of it, the rusty stain a glaring accusation. I rubbed at the dried blood and tried to ignore the feeling of guilt and shame.

"It's no good," I said finally, and straightening my shoulders, opened the door and entered the main chamber.

There was no light but the moonlight that came in through the shutters. I held high the candle from my closet, scanning the pallets to locate the one Baltic had chosen. To my surprise, they were all empty, all but one.

I approached the dark shape cautiously. I couldn't tell which man it was—a fur was thrown over him, leaving only the tip of his head showing, and all the guards had varying shades of dark hair.

Setting the candle down on the ground next to the pallet, I reached out to pull back the fur just far enough to see who lay there, but before I could touch it, a hand shot out and grabbed my wrist in a grip that came close to grinding my bones. I cried out, and the man sat up, releasing my wrist when he saw it was me.

"What are you doing?" he snarled.

It was Baltic, and he didn't look any too pleased to see me.

"I came to see if you were hurt," I said, suddenly feeling very awkward. I gestured toward his legs. "In your . . . place."

He stared at me a moment just as if two carrots suddenly sprouted from my ears. "You came to see if I was hurt?"

"Yes. I know men are sensitive there. Well, you would have to be, wouldn't you? I mean, it's all just hanging there, right out in the open, not tucked away nicely like women. And I knew it would disable you, but I was thinking about it, and I realize that perhaps I took you by surprise, and that even though I said we'd start right then, you weren't ready for my attack. So I thought I would see if you were hurt. Seriously hurt, that is, because I know you were hurt, or else you wouldn't have rolled around on the ground as you did."

He sat through that entire speech without saying anything, but when I was finished he shook his head, and said in a quite reasonable tone of voice, "Yes, you hurt me. You damn near kicked my stones up into my belly. But you didn't permanently damage me, if that's what you're having this attack of conscience about."

"Are you sure?" I asked, kneeling down next to him. I wanted to check his parts, but couldn't think how to suggest that without sounding like I just wanted to ogle him. Which, sadly, I had to admit I wouldn't mind. "Perhaps I should make sure. My mother—Lady Alice—taught me much about tending ailments. I'm known throughout the keep for my healing skills."

He muttered something that sounded like a blasphemy against healers, then suddenly sat up straight. "You want to look at my cock?"

"I think it would be best if I examined your man parts for signs of injury, yes," I said, trying my best to look knowledgeable in the area of genitals. "After all, I caused the injury. If anyone should look at your ... er ... area, then I should."

He scooted back until he was leaning against the wall. "Go ahead," he said, crossing his arms.

I licked my lips nervously, biting my lower lip as I pushed the fur down his legs. He was dressed in a thin tunic and braies, and unless he had donned his armor, he would have no codpiece on under the tunic. Carefully I lifted the edge of his tunic. "Oh. My. Um. I was expecting ... hmm."

"What were you expecting?" he asked, pulling up his tunic in order to stare down at himself. "What are you hmming about?"

"Oh, it's nothing, really," I said, frowning just a little at his man parts.

"Like hell it is!" he said, sounding quite incensed.

I looked at him in confusion.

He sighed, closed his eyes for a minute, then opened them back up, and with a tight jaw, asked, "Are you going to examine my cock or not?"

I eyed the part in question. "I don't want to touch it if it's bruised."

"It's not bruised," he snapped.

"It looks ... angry."

"For god's sake, woman, it doesn't have emotions of its own!"

"Of course not. All right then. I will just check to make sure everything is as it should be." I put one hand on his shaft. He didn't move, the expression on his face suspicious.

"Well?" he demanded.

There was nothing for it. I put my other hand on his parts, lifting them to look for signs of damage.

A noise at the door had Baltic jerking up the fur, my hands trapped beneath it.

Kostya stood at the top of the stairs, giving us a puzzled look. "I heard loud voices. Is everything all right?" he asked.

"Yes!" Baltic answered through gritted teeth.

Kostya looked pointedly at me.

"Baltic's man parts are angry, and I was seeing if there was something I could do to ease the pain," I explained, not wanting him to think me wanton.

Kostya's expression went absolutely blank. Baltic ran a hand over his face, clearly trying to maintain a grip on his formidable temper. "It's not like that. She wanted to see if she had seriously hurt me. I told her she could look for herself to see that I wasn't."

"I see," Kostya said in a voice that sounded as if he were choking. "I'll just leave you to that, then."

He disappeared. A roar of laughter came up from below that had Baltic swearing under his breath as he shoved the fur down again. "For the love of the saints—get on with it, woman!"

"Very well." I lifted his shaft, looking for signs of injury, but saw nothing. Despite the knowledge that I was renowned in the village and by folk of the keep as a healer, I couldn't help but feel wicked as I touched him. I was no stranger to the sight of man parts—the male villagers frequently wore short tunics that left little to the imagination when the wind was high, but my mother had kept Margaret and me from bathing visitors, as was the common custom. Baltic's parts were . . . interesting. "You don't appear to have any injury," I added, suddenly feeling a bit breathless. I let his stones slide slowly from my fingers, and was surprised by both the sudden hitch in his breath and the fact that his shaft began to harden.

"You are becoming aroused," I said, looking at it.

"I'd have to be dead not to. Are you stopping?"

I trailed my fingers down the length of his shaft. It was gaining in stature, the skin of it sliding like the softest silk over a piece of polished ivory my mother kept in her sewing box. "Do you want me to stop?"

"Hell, no."

I continued to lightly run my fingers down it. "How much bigger will it grow?"

A short, pained-sounding bark of laughter escaped him. "I've never measured it. Why do you ask?"

"Idle curiosity. That part is pushing back. Is it supposed to do that, or did I damage it?"

"It's supposed to do that."

I slid one hand underneath the shaft, stroking it like I would a cat. Baltic groaned and closed his eyes, his hips rocking forward. "I'm enjoying this," I told him, feeling a sense of pride in the fact that I could arouse him with my hands.

Eyes of purest black regarded me, shimmering with something I couldn't put a name to. His lips quirked. "So am I."

"It seems rather monotonous, however," I said after a few minutes of repeated stroking. His shaft was fully aroused now, and I marveled to myself that he ever fit it into his codpiece.

"There are ... variations ... you can do," he said in a choked voice.

"Oh?" I looked down at the shaft. "Changes in pressure and speed?"

"No. Instead of your hands, you could use your mouth."

"You're jesting," I said, staring at him in disbelief.

His lips quirked even more. "I thought that would shock you."

I eyed his shaft again. "I'm not shocked. I'm just a little taken aback. If I were to use my mouth, that would give you pleasure, too?"

"*Chérie*, if you were to use your mouth, I would probably spill my seed within two seconds of your tongue wrapping around me."

"It's a sin to spill your seed outside of a woman," I said, parroting Father David, the priest at our keep.

"That is a human belief. Dragons do not hold with such foolish dogma. If you weren't a silver dragon, I would be happy to do as you suggest."

I touched the very tip of him with one finger. A bead of moisture had formed there, a tear that glistened as I spread it about the head of his shaft. "I don't wish for you to bed me, if that's what you are implying."

"Why not? You seem to enjoy touching me."

I met his black-eyed gaze with calm assurance. "One day I will marry, and I must save my maidenhead for my husband."

"Marriage is also a human tradition, one dragons seldom follow. Ysolde?"

"Hmm?" I spread the moisture around a little more, enjoying the sensation of it, wondering what he tasted like, and whether it would be a sin to find out.

His jaw tightened. "Nothing. Go back to your bed. I'm not injured, as you can—"

I bent over him and took the tip of his shaft into my mouth. He stopped speaking. In fact, for a few seconds, he stopped breathing. He just sat there stiff as a plank, staring with wide eyes as I tasted him.

It was . . . different. Different, but pleasant. He tasted hot, somewhat salty, but it was the feeling of his silken flesh against my tongue that gave me boldness. I slid my tongue around the head of it, and Baltic groaned loudly, clutching with both hands the linen covering the pallet.

"Stop!" he cried, his voice sounding as if he had a mouthful of stones.

I released him from my mouth, worried I had done something to harm him. "Did I hurt you?"

"No. You just have to stop, or else I'm going to—"

I took his shaft in my hand again, sliding my fingers around the flesh now made slick by my mouth. He groaned again, his hips thrusting forward as he growled, "Too late."

"I don't see how that's not going to count as a sin," I said, my hand full of his seed. "You'll have to do penance for that."

"I already am," he muttered, jerking up one edge of the pallet linen to clean my hand. He rose when he had done so, pulling me up and swinging me into his arms.

"What are you doing?" I asked, panicking slightly as he marched tense-jawed toward my closet.

"Taking you to bed."

"I told you that I don't wish for you to bed me."

"I heard you the first time," he said, his voice sounding rough and harsh.

He shoved open the flimsy door and dropped me onto the pallet.

"I'm serious. I don't want to hurt you again, but I will defend myself if you make me."

He dropped down onto his knees. "I don't bed silver dragons."

"Then what—"

"I'm just going to reciprocate."

I frowned as he pushed my feet apart in order to move between them. "Reciprocate what?"

His face lost its tense look as he suddenly grinned at me. "Bliss."

# Chapter Five

Bliss. What a lovely word it was. I lay on the bed and stared up at the shimmers from a streetlight dappling the ceiling of my room, listening to the faint sounds of London traffic, sounds that were muted by the fact that the house had exceptionally good windows, and by the time of night. It was two in the morning—deep night, someone had once called it.

I frowned. "Now where did I hear that?"

A sliver of light pierced the darkness of the room as the door opened a tiny bit. "Are you awake?"

"Unfortunately, yes."

Kaawa opened the door wider and gave me an inquisitive look. "I was passing your room a short while ago and heard you call out. I thought perhaps you were having a nightmare. Would you like some company?"

"So long as you don't mind being shut up with a nutcase, sure," I answered, pulling myself up to a sitting position. I clicked on the bedside lamp and watched as she hauled an armchair a little closer to the bed.

"That's a lovely caftan," I said, admiring the black and silver African batik animals on it.

"Thank you. My daughter sent it to me. She lives in Kenya, on an animal preserve. Why do you think you are a nutcase?"

I looked back up at the ceiling for a minute, debating whether or not I wanted to talk about the fear that was eating away at me. Kaawa seemed nice and motherly, but I didn't really know her.

Then again, there weren't too many people I *did* remember knowing.

"I think I might be mentally unstable," I said at last, watching her to see if she looked at all frightened of me.

She didn't look anything but mildly interested. "Because of the memory loss?"

"No. I think I might be schizophrenic. Or suffering from multiple personalities. Or some other mental disorder like that."

"You are having dreams," she said, nodding just as if she understood. "Dreams of your past."

"I'm having dreams, yes, but it can't be my past. I'm not a dragon. I'm human. Evidently mentally unstable, but human."

She was silent for a moment. "Struggling against yourself is not making the situation any easier, you know."

"I'm not struggling against myself. I'm trying to hold on to my sanity. Look, I know what you think, what everyone thinks. But if you were in my place, wouldn't you know if you weren't human?"

"Do you think humans have dreams of their past life as a dragon?" she asked with maddening calm.

"The only reason I'm having those dreams is because you people put it in my mind!" I said, my voice tinged with desperation.

She shook her head slowly. "It was a dream that brought you out of the month-long sleep, was it not?"

I looked at my hands lying clenched tight on the bed cover. "Yes."

"Child." She laid her hand on my arm. "The dragon inside of you wishes to be woken, whether you desire that or not. I will admit that you appear human to me, and I do not know how it can be that you have changed thusly, but deny it though you may, you are Ysolde de Bouchier, and you will not be calm in your mind until you accept that."

"Calm in my mind? At this point, I can't even conceive of what that's like." I took a deep breath, trying to keep from going stark raving mad. "I'm sorry. I don't mean to be the biggest drama queen there ever was, but you have to admit that this whole situation is enough to drive a girl bonkers."

"It is a test, yes," she agreed in that same soothing voice.

I just wanted to shriek. Instead, I took another deep breath. "OK, let's go into the land of totally bizarre, and say you're right. I'm a dragon magically reincarnated—"

"Not reincarnated—resurrected," she corrected me.

"What's the difference?"

"I am reincarnated—when my physical form has run its appointed time, I retreat into the dreaming and await a new form. I am born again, remembering all that has passed before, but with a new body. That is reincarnated. Resurrection is the bringing back to life of that which was dead."

I took a third deep breath. It's a wonder there was any air left in the room. "That's cool. You're reincarnated. I'm resurrected. We'll just move past that and get to the meat of my argument—if I'm a dragon, why don't I like gold? Why can't I breathe fire? Why can't I turn into great big scary animal shapes?"

"Because the dragon in you has not woken yet. I think . . ." She paused, her gaze turned inward. "I think it is waiting."

"Waiting for what?"

"I don't know. That is something you will find out when the time is appropriate. Until then, you must stop fighting the dragon inside you. The dreams you have, they are about your past, are they not?"

I looked away, feeling my cheeks grow hot as I remembered the highly erotic dream I'd just had. "They concern someone named Ysolde, and a man named Baltic."

"As I expected. The dragon part of you wants you to remember," she said, patting my hand as she rose. "It wants you to accept your past in order to deal with the present."

"Well, the dragon part can just go take a flying leap off the side of a mountain, because I want my life to go back to what it was."

"I don't think that's possible. It has stirred. It wishes for you to remember. It is time, Ysolde."

"Cow cookies!" I snapped. "No one tells me what to do. Well, Dr. Kostich does, but that's fully within the bounds of my apprenticeship. And he doesn't give me erotic dreams!"

"Erotic dreams?" Kaawa asked, a little smile on her lips.

I blushed again, damning my mouth for speaking inappropriately again. "I don't really think the type of dream matters as much as the fact that my mind is cracking."

"Your mind is doing nothing of the sort. Allow the dragon side to speak to you, and I think you will find your way through this trying time," she said from the door. She hesitated a few seconds, then added, "This is truly none of my business, but I have prided myself on my knowledge of history of dragonkin, and I admit to being very curious about this. . . . When you and Baltic met—did he offer to make you his mate right away, or did that come after Constantine Norka claimed you?"

I blinked in surprise, then gave a rueful chuckle. "Assuming the dreams are not a figment of my warped mind, then no, Baltic did not ask me to be his mate when we met. Quite the contrary. He came very close to killing me, and later told me he would never bed a silver dragon."

"Fascinating," she said, looking thoughtful. "Absolutely fascinating. I had no idea. Sleep well, Ysolde."

"Tully," I said sadly, but it was said to the door as she closed it.

"You look horrible," the fruit of my loins told me six hours later as I found the dining room. Brom was seated behind a bowl of oatmeal, a plate heaped high with eggs, potatoes, and three pieces of jam-covered toast waiting next to him.

"Thank you," I said, dropping a kiss on his head before taking a cup off the sideboard. "And I hope you're planning on eating all of that. You know how I feel about wasting food."

"That's just 'cause Gareth makes such a big fuss over money," Brom said, turning to May, who sat at the end of the table with a cup of coffee in front of her. "He's a tightwad."

"Quite possibly the fact that you eat like a horse has influenced his lectures regarding economy," I said, giving him a meaningful look. I lifted the lid to a silver carafe and peered in. It held coffee.

"If you prefer tea, we can get you some," May said, watching me.

"Actually, I'm really big on chocolate," I said with an apologetic smile. "I'm afraid the term 'chocoholic' applies to me far too well."

"I'm sure we can rustle up some hot chocolate," she said, rising.

"Don't go to any bother for me—"

"It's no bother. I'll just go tell Renata."

May disappeared, leaving me with Brom. I sat across from him, trying to make a decision.

"Gabriel says there's a museum here that has human mummies. Can we go see them?" Brom asked.

"Possibly. I have to see Dr. Kostich today, though. I was told he's in town, and I will need to see what work he has for me."

Brom's expression was made strangely horrible by the mouthful of toast and eggs he stuffed in. "Gabriel said Tipene or Maata would take me 'cause you're going to be busy with dragon stuff."

"Dragon stuff?" I frowned, idly rubbing my finger

along the beaded edge of the table. "What sort of dragon stuff?"

Brom thought for a few seconds, his cheeks bulging as he chewed. "It had some foreign word, like sarcophagus."

"*Sárkány*," May said, entering the room with a tall, athletic woman who towered over her. Like Tipene, she appeared to be of Aboriginal descent, with lovely dark skin that gave emphasis to her grey eyes. "This is Maata, by the way. She's the second of Gabriel's elite guards."

We exchanged greetings. Maata moved to the sideboard, loading up a plate almost as full as Brom's.

"Before you ask," May continued, retaking her seat, "a *sárkány* is basically a meeting where the wyverns discuss weyr business. Kostya called one for today."

"Kostya?" I sat frozen for a second as a face rose in my mind's eye.

"Yes." Both May and Maata watched me. "Do you know him?"

I blinked away the image, saying slowly, "He was in a dream I had."

"Kaawa mentioned you were dreaming of your past. It must be very confusing to you to see yourself but not be able to relate to it."

"Yes," I answered, falling silent as a young woman bustled into the room with a pot of hot chocolate for me. I thanked her, breathing deeply of the lovely chocolatey smell.

"The *sárkány* is called for three this afternoon," May continued, sipping her coffee.

"I'm sure we can stay out of your way while you have your meeting."

"That's actually not what I meant," May said with a

little smile. "The *sárkány* has been called so the wyverns can be introduced to you."

I sighed. "I'm getting very tired of telling people I'm not a dragon."

"I know. But I do think it would be good for you to meet them. If nothing else, they will be able to see for themselves that you're human."

"There is that. . . ." I chewed my lip for a moment. "All right. I will come to your meeting."

"Excellent!" May said, looking pleased. "Brom would probably find it pretty dull stuff, so Maata volunteered to take him to the British Museum to see the mummies."

I assessed Maata. She looked sturdy enough to take on a semitruck, and since she was one of Gabriel's elite guard, I assumed she was beyond trustworthy. "That's very kind of you, but I wouldn't want to impose," I told her.

She waved away the objection with a fork loaded with herbed eggs. "It's no imposition at all. I happen to like mummies, and am very interested in Brom's experiments with mummifying animals. Before I knew I was to be part of Gabriel's guard, I thought I might be a veterinarian."

"That's what Sullivan wants me to do," Brom said around another mouthful of food.

I frowned at him, and he made a huge effort to swallow.

"You are not a python," I told him. "Chew before you swallow."

"This is none of my business, but why do you call your mother Sullivan?" May asked.

Brom shrugged. "It's what Gareth calls her."

May's gaze transferred to me. "Your husband calls you by your last name?"

"Gareth is a little bit ... *special*," I said, pouring out more hot chocolate. It was excellent, very hot, just as I liked it, and made with Belgian cocoa.

She murmured something noncommittal.

"I've decided after talking with your ... er ... what do you call Kaawa?" I asked May.

"Call her?"

"Yes. I mean, you're not married to Gabriel, are you? Not that I'm judging! Lots of people shack up without getting married. I just wondered what you call his mother."

She blinked at me twice. "I call her Kaawa."

"I see."

She smiled, and I realized again that there was something about her that struck a familiar chord. "Marriage is a human convention. I've never been human, so I don't feel the need to formalize the relationship I have with Gabriel in that way. The bond between a wyvern and a mate is much more binding than a mortal marriage ceremony, Ysolde. There is no such thing as divorce in the dragon world."

Brom's eyes grew round as he watched her.

"Dragons never make bad choices so far as their significant others go, then?" I couldn't help but ask, trying hard to keep the acid tone from my voice.

"I'm sure some do," she said, glancing at Maata. "I've never met any, though. Have you?"

"Yes, although it is rare," Maata told me. "It is not common, but it can happen that two people are mated who should not be."

"So what do they do? Live out their lives in quiet misery, trying to make the best of what they have despite the fact that they have no hope, no hope whatsoever of any sort of a satisfying or happy connubial and romantic life?" I couldn't help but ask.

"What's connubial?" Brom asked around another mouthful of eggs.

"Married."

May hid her smile, but Maata openly laughed. "I would like to see the dragon that is content to live in quiet misery. No, if a mated pair is not compatible, they take the only solution."

I waited for her to continue, but she didn't. I had to know, though. My curiosity would not be satisfied until I asked. "And what's that?"

"One of them kills the other," she said, shrugging slightly. "Death is the only way to break the bond. Of course, usually the one who remains does not survive long, but that is the way of dragons. They mate for life, and when one mate is gone, the other often chooses to end his or her suffering."

"Cool," Brom said, looking far too fascinated for my ease of mind. "Do you know of a dragon who's died? I wonder if I could mummify something that big. Do they die in dragon form or people form? What happens to them when they're dead? Do you bury them like mortals, or do you burn them up or something else?"

"Enough of the 'like mortals' comment, young man," I told him. "You are a mortal. I don't care what anyone tells you—you are a perfectly normal little boy, albeit one with a bizarre mummy fascination."

"Sullivan is all over denial," he told Maata, who nodded her head in agreement.

"We are going to move on, because if we don't, some-one will find himself confined to his room rather than going to a museum," I said with a dark look at my child.

"Are you going to kill Gareth?" he asked me, com-pletely ignoring the look.

"What?" I gawked at him.

"Gabriel said you're married to a dragon named Bal-tic, but you're also married to Gareth. That means you have to get rid of one of them, and you don't like Gareth, so you should get rid of him." He frowned. "Although I don't want you to if you'll do what Maata said, and end your suffering."

"I assure you that I have no intentions to kill either myself or your father. Shall we move on? Excellent. I really need to see Dr. Kostich today. What time were you thinking of going to the museum?" I asked Maata.

"We can leave right after breakfast, if you like. There's enough to see there to keep us busy all day."

"I'd better take my field notebook and camera," Brom said, starting to rise from his chair.

"Sit," I ordered. "Finish that food or you won't go anywhere today."

He slumped back into his chair, grumbling under his breath about not wanting to waste valuable time.

"Tipene called Dr. Kostich yesterday to tell him you were awake, in case you were worried he didn't know," May told me.

"It's not that. I'm his apprentice. I have no doubt there's a huge mountain of work that's been waiting for me."

"What sort of work does an apprentice do?" May asked.

"Lots and lots of transcribing," I said, sighing. "We're

expected to copy out vast compendiums of arcanery, most of which are bizarre things that no one in their right mind cares about anymore. There are some useful things to be learned, like how to wield arcane destructive spells, but those come to more advanced apprentices. Ones at my level spend their days perfecting their wart removal spells, and ways to make a person's ears unstop. Last week—or rather, the last week I remember—I ran across the mention of a really rocking spell to make a person's eyebrows spontaneously combust."

"Wow," May said, an odd expression on her face.

"I know. Underwhelming, right?" I sighed and glanced at my watch. "Someday I'll get to the good stuff, but until then . . . I should be going now. Brom, I expect you to behave yourself with Maata, and not give her any trouble."

He made a face as I grabbed my purse, but his eyes lit up when I tucked a few bills into his shirt pocket.

"Don't forget, the *sárkány* is at three," May said as I ruffled his hair.

There was a slight undertone of warning to that, a fact I acknowledged with a nod as I left the dining room.

I'm not quite sure what sort of a reception I was expecting from Dr. Kostich, but I assumed he would express some sort of pleasure that I was once again amongst the cognizant.

"Oh. It's you," was the greeting I received, however. He looked over a pair of reading glasses at me, a frown pulling his eyebrows together, his pale blue eyes as cold as an iceberg.

"Good morning, sir. Good morning, Jack."

"Hi, Tully. Glad to see you're up and about again. You scared the crap out of us when you just keeled over a month ago." My fellow apprentice Jack, a young man in his mid-twenties, with a freckled, open face, wild red hair, and a friendly nature that reminded me of a puppy, grinned for a few seconds before some of the chill seeped off of our boss.

As Dr. Kostich's gimlet eye turned upon him, Jack lowered his gaze back to a medieval grimoire from which he was making notes.

"Thanks. I have no idea why the fugue struck me just then and not in October, as it should have, but I am very sorry for any inconvenience it's caused you," I told Kostich.

He tapped a few keys on the laptop before him and pushed his chair back, giving me a thorough once-over. I had to restrain myself from fidgeting under the examination, avoiding his eye, glancing around the living room of the suite he always booked when he was in London. Everything looked the same as when I had left it some five weeks before, everything appeared normal, but something was clearly wrong.

"I have been in contact with the silver wyvern, whom I believe you are currently staying with," he said finally, gesturing abruptly toward a cream and rose Louis XIV chair. I sat on the edge of it, feeling as if I had been sent to the principal's office. "He informed me of a number of facts that I have found infinitely distressing."

"I'm sorry to hear that. I hope that perhaps I can explain some of the circumstances and relieve you of that distress," I said, wishing I didn't sound so stilted.

"I have little hope that will happen," Kostich said, steepling his fingers. "The wyvern informed me that you are not, in fact, a simple apprentice as you represented yourself."

I glanced over at Jack. His head was bent over the grimoire, but he watched me, his gaze serious. "You know, Gabriel is a nice guy and everything, but he and May have some really wild ideas. I don't hold with them at all," I said quickly, just in case he thought to wonder about my mental status. Lord knows I was doing enough of that for both of us.

"In fact, the wyvern tells me that you are a dragon, and were once a member of his sept," Kostich continued just like I hadn't said a word.

I flinched inwardly at the grim look on his face. I knew from the rants he'd made over the past year that Kostich did not like dragons very much. "Like I said, wild ideas. He's wrong, of course. Everyone can see I'm human!"

"No," he said, taking me by surprise. "That you are not. You appear human, yes, but you are not one. I knew that when you applied for apprenticeship."

"You did?" I had a feeling my eyes were bugging out in surprise. I blinked a few times to try to get the stupefied expression off my face. "Why didn't you say something to me?"

He shrugged. "It is not uncommon to find those of mixed heritage in the L'au-dela."

"I'm not . . . mixed heritage."

"I assumed that you had one human parent, and one immortal, as does your husband."

I gawked at him. "You're kidding, right? Gareth? My Gareth? He has an immortal parent?"

"Your husband is of little concern, except when he interrupts me with demands and foolish threats," he answered, shooting me a look that had me frozen in my chair. "You are aware, are you not, of the Magister's Code by which we live our lives?"

"Yes, sir," I said miserably, sure of where he was going.

"You will then be in no surprise to find that due to the violation of statute number one hundred and eighty-seven, you have been removed from the rolls as an apprentice."

A little zap of electricity ran through me as his words sank in. "You're kicking me out?" I asked, unable to believe it. "I know you're pissed about my unexpected absence, but to kick me out because of it? That hardly seems fair!"

"I do not get 'pissed,' as you say." His pale blue eyes looked bored. "That is a useless emotion. You have been stripped of your apprenticeship. Furthermore, as of this moment you are under an interdict prohibiting you from using any of the knowledge you have gained during your time as my aide."

He sketched a couple of symbols in the air. They glowed white-blue for a moment before dissolving into me. "But, sir—"

"Strictly speaking, an interdict is not necessary, since you have limited powers." He peered at me in a way that left me shivering with unease. "You haven't been using your powers lately, have you?"

"No. You know I'm not comfortable doing so without a good deal of preparation." I squirmed in the chair.

His lips tightened. "I am well aware of that fact. That you wasted my time and resources trying to teach you, a dragon, one who has no ability to handle arcane power, is something I shall not forget for a long time."

"But I have power," I protested. "It may not be a lot, and I may not be terribly comfortable with it, but I've learned tons of things from my time as your apprentice! I can take off even the most stubborn of warts. Eyebrows live in fear of me! My neighbor had a case of prickly heat, and I had that sucker gone and her toes back to normal in nothing flat!"

His lips thinned even more until they all but disappeared into each other. "You have been my apprentice for seven years, and yet you still struggle with the most elemental of skills. Jack has been with me for six months, and already he has surpassed your skill tenfold!"

I glanced at Jack, wanting to protest that it wasn't my fault, that magic didn't come easy to me. But the words rang in my head that dragons could not wield arcane power.

"Now that I know the truth about you, there is little wonder that you failed to progress in your studies as you should have. I don't know how I could have been so blind, so foolish as to believe your stories that you simply needed more time to learn the ways of the magi, but I assure you that I will not make the same mistake a second time. You are released from your duties, Tully Sullivan."

Pain lashed me at the invocation of my name. I stood up, not knowing what I could say or do to make him change his mind. "I was making progress," I said sadly. "I almost have that spell down to clear out a plugged ear."

"A child of four could deal with the earwax spell better than you after four months' study at it," he snapped.

"I've tried," I said simply, my spirits leaden.

"Foolishly, yes. I have not doubted your devotion; it is your ability for which I've made allowances, and now that I know the reason for your lack, my path is clear."

"I'm sorry," I said, ridiculously wanting to cry. "I never intended any deception or insult to you, and if there was some way I could make it up to you, if there was some epic sort of task I could undertake, or some hugely intricate bit of magic I could perform to show you how serious I am about my career as a mage, I would do so."

He was silent for a moment, and I was convinced he was going to turn me into a toad, or worse. But to my surprise, he said slowly, "There is, perhaps, a way you could serve me. It will in no way influence my decision to remove you as apprentice, but if you truly wished to be of service to the L'au-dela, then perhaps we can come to an understanding."

I bit the inside of my lip, wanting to tell him that if I was going to do him a favor, I expected to be reinstated to my position, but I had been acquainted with him long enough to know that he couldn't be pressured into any act. But perhaps I could sway him with my devotion and dedication.

"What would that be?" I asked.

"There is a dragon that you have no doubt heard of," he said, his voice deep and persuasive. "He is known as Baltic, and he possesses most alarming skills and abilities, one of which is to enter and leave the beyond at his whim."

I sat somewhat numb, wondering if the whole world revolved around the ebony-eyed Baltic.

"I wish to know how he has come by the arcane skills he has shown on numerous occasions. His companion, whom we captured the day you collapsed, refuses to talk despite being threatened with banishment to the

Akasha. I also wish to know how he obtained Antonia von Endres' light sword, and remove it from him."

"Baltic has a light sword?" I asked, confused. "But that's made up of arcane magic. No one but an archimage could wield it."

"And yet he does, and quite proficiently, I will say," he answered, rubbing his arm as if it hurt.

"You want me, an apprentice of little power and skill—"

"You are no longer an apprentice," he interrupted quickly, his eyebrows making elegant arches above his long nose. "Nor can you wield any power with the interdict upon you."

"You want me, with no power and skills, completely unable to work any sort of magic, to take a priceless sword away from a dragon mage-warrior?" I shook my head. Even to me it sounded like the sheerest folly. "I wouldn't have the slightest clue how to do something like that, even assuming I could."

"Your inability to see all the possibilities is your failing, not mine," he answered, his attention returning to his laptop.

"But I don't even know how to find this Baltic—"

"When you have something to report to me, you may contact me. Until then, good day."

"Perhaps if we were able to talk this over—"

He looked up, power crackling off him. I was at the door before I realized he had compelled me to move. "Good *day.*"

A few minutes later, I stood outside the hotel, buffeted by happy tourists and visitors, numbly aware of people and traffic passing by me, but unable to sort through my thoughts. They all seemed to whirl around in a horrible jumble that I doubted I could ever unravel.

The silver dragons thought I was mated to Baltic. The dreams I had focused on Baltic. Dr. Kostich wanted me to retrieve something from Baltic. "I'm beginning to hate that name," I muttered to myself.

The doorman shot me a curious glance. I moved a few feet away, not sure where I was going to go. "Can I help you?" the doorman asked.

"I . . . I have some time to kill. Is there a park nearby?" I asked, falling back on an old standby that never failed to leave me comforted.

"Six blocks to the north, ma'am. Straight up the street."

I thanked him and walked quickly, needing the calming influence of green, growing things to restore order to my tortured mind. I felt better almost the instant my feet hit the grass, the scent of sun-warmed earth and grass and leaves from the trees that ringed the park fence filling me with a sense of well-being.

There were a great many people out in the park that day, no doubt enjoying the late summer day before the fall gloom set in. Groups of children raced after Frisbees and remote-controlled helicopters, couples lay in languid embraces, harried mothers and fathers herded their respective broods, and great giggling groups of schoolgirls clustered together to fawn over a musical group that was setting up on an entertainment stage in the corner of the park.

I headed in the opposite direction, breathing deeply to fill my soul with the smell and sensations of green life, eventually settling on one of two benches that sat back-to-back next to a boarded-up refreshment stand. No sooner had I slumped onto my claimed bench than two young women who appeared to be in their late teens hurried over and grabbed the one behind me, shooting me brief, curious glances.

I smiled and closed my eyes, turning my face up to the sun, hoping they wouldn't stay long in such an out-of-the-way place, not when a band was going to be playing elsewhere.

The girls evidently decided I was harmless, because they started chatting in voices that I couldn't help but overhear.

"I can't believe that he had the balls, the steel balls, to tell me he'd rather go visit his parents in Malta than go with me to Rome, but he did, and that was it, that was just it as far as I'm concerned. I mean, Rome versus Malta? Rome absolutely wins."

"Absolutely," the second girl said. "You are so right to dump him. Besides, that leaves you free for doing a little shopping in Italy, if you know what I mean. Italian men are so lickable, don't you think?"

"Some of them," the first girl allowed. "Not the really hairy ones. They are just . . . ugh." She shuddered and I started glancing around to find another spot. "I mean, my god, the things they stuff into their Speedos! It's positively obscene!"

My phone burbled at me just at that moment, causing me to send up a prayer of thanks as I flipped it open, expecting to hear Brom asking if he could have another advance on his allowance for some horrible instrument of mummification. "Hello?"

It wasn't his voice that greeted me, however. "Sullivan? What the hell are you doing still in England?

Brom said you were staying there! Is this some sort of a joke?"

"Gareth." The two girls glanced over their shoulders at me. I half turned away and lowered my voice. "I wondered when you would think to call me."

"Think to call you? Are you daft? I've been trying to get hold of you for weeks. What is Kostich making you do?"

"It's a bit complicated," I said, mindful of the girls, although they seemed to have moved on to judging the qualities of every male who wandered past. "I'm still here because I had an episode."

"What?" His shriek almost deafened me. "When? How? What the hell are you thinking?"

"I wasn't—I was asleep. And I don't know how or why, it just happened. I've been staying at the house of some people Kostich was working with. They took me and Brom in."

"Did you manifest?" he asked quietly, but I could hear the eagerness in his voice.

"No. But that brings up a very good question—how long have I been doing that?"

"What?" His voice was wary.

"How long have I been making gold for you? Dr. Kostich says you're immortal. How long have we been married?"

"You know how long we've been married—ten years. You've seen the license."

I had? "I don't remember any of that. Have you been doing something to my memory?"

"What the hell are you talking about?" He sounded furious now, speaking in a low, ugly voice that sent goose bumps up my arms. "If you're trying to distract me because you manifested for some bastard who took you in—"

"I just told you I didn't. Fortunately, no one had large chunks of lead lying around."

"Fortunately? You stupid bitch. Do you have any idea how much that's going to cost us by missing it? How the hell am I going to tell Ruth?"

"I don't know, and I don't appreciate being called names. Look, Gareth, things are a bit confused right now. Dr. Kostich kicked me out of the magister's guild, and I—"

"He *what*?" Profound swearing followed, for a good two minutes. "What did you do?"

"Nothing, I swear."

"Then why did he kick you out?"

"It's because of these"—I cast a glance over my shoulder, but the girls had their heads together, watching as three young men in soccer outfits strolled past— "because of some dragons."

"Dragons?" he repeated, his voice suddenly very small.

"Yes. The people I'm staying with are dragons. They've asked Brom and me to stay with them for a bit while I try to figure things out."

Silence filled my ear for a good minute. "Get out," he finally said.

"What?"

"You heard me—get out. Get away from the dragons."

"Don't you think that would be rude? They've given me a lot, Gareth. The wyvern's mother herself tended me while I was in the fugue—"

"Get out, you stupid woman! Do I make myself clear? Get out before they kill you!"

"You are watching way too much TV, Gareth, you really are." I kept my voice low, but allowed anger to sound in it. "If these people wanted to kill me, all they would have had to do was to dump me in the Thames while I was asleep."

"Listen carefully to me, Sullivan," he said, breathing heavily. "You may think they're your friends, but they aren't. You have to get away from them, today, right now."

"That's not going to be quite so easy," I said, hesitating. I really didn't want to talk to Gareth about Gabriel and May. Somehow, it seemed that it would taint the relationship if I were to try to explain them to him. "I told them I'd stay for a while. I'm having . . . well, they're kind of dreams, and they're—"

"I don't want to hear about your goddamned dreams!" he thundered, breathing like a bulldog for a few minutes before continuing. "I can't leave just yet. Ruth and I are . . . we're following up a potential client. But I'll send someone to help you."

"Will you please stop doing the Darth Vader impression and listen to me?" I lost all remnants of patience with him. "Brom and I are fine. The dragons aren't going to hurt us. We don't need anyone to help us, because we're fine, just fine!"

"Be prepared to leave tonight," Gareth said. I clenched my teeth against screaming in frustration. "Don't tell anyone. Stay in your room."

"By the rood, Gareth! If I wasn't already going insane, you'd be enough to push me right over the edge, do you know that?"

"Wait a minute—did you say Brom was there?"

"Yes! Yes, I did! Hallelujah and let fly the doves! You actually listened to something I said!"

He cursed again, but under his breath this time. "Well, it's of no matter. They can't want him. You'll just have to tell him to stay there until Ruth or someone can get him."

"You're nuts," I said flatly, so flabbergasted that he actually expected I would leave my own child, my brain couldn't come up with anything more than that.

"They won't harm him," he said testily. "Just make sure you're ready to leave."

The very idea that Gareth was willing to abandon Brom, his own child, to people he considered dangerous was so obscene, I sat staring at the grass in utter disbelief. At that moment, I knew the marriage was over. I could not remain married to a man who cared absolutely nothing for his son.

Gareth, obviously taking my silence for compliance, warned me again to have nothing to do with the dragons until I could be rescued.

"What do you expect me to do even if I were to leave the dragons?" my curiosity forced me to ask. "I'm not an apprentice anymore, and I've had an interdict placed on me. I can't practice arcane magic at all."

"You'll get your job back," he said grimly.

"How?"

"That's your problem," he said, echoing Dr. Kostich. With one last word of warning he hung up, leaving me to shake my head. It was all so much to take in—first the dragons, then the dreams, and now the scales falling from my eyes where Gareth was concerned. How had I lived with such a monster for all those years?

"Holy Mary, mother of god," one of the girls behind me said as I tucked my phone away in my purse. "Get a look at those two. Mmrowr! I call the back one."

"Oh! I was going to call him. I suppose I'll have to take the tall one in front, then. What do you think—seven? Seven and a half?"

"Are you kidding? He's too intense. He probably has OCD or something. Five at the most. Now, the one behind him, he's a definite eight point nine."

I glanced between them to see who they were talking about. Two men were walking parallel to the bench, some thirty feet away. I couldn't see much of the far man, although glimpses indicated he was in his late thirties, with short dark hair and a slight goatee. An intricate Celtic tattoo wrapped around his biceps was made visible by a black sleeveless shirt. His companion, nearest me, was taller, and of a similar coloring. He also wore black, unremarkable except for the way the wind rippled the man's shirt against his chest. He moved swiftly, his long legs making nothing of the expanse of the park, his body moving with an almost feline grace.

Something about him struck me as familiar. I turned a little more to get a better look as they continued past. The nearest man, the one with the graceful walk, had shoulder-length dark chocolate brown hair that was pulled back from a pronounced widow's peak into a short ponytail. He was clean-shaven, although a faint hint of darkness around his jaw hinted at stubble.

"Maybe I should go for the tall one. I love me some manly stubble," one of the girls said, as if she'd read my mind. "He's just one hundred percent delicious. Hey! Why don't we see where they're going, and if they'd, you know, like us to go with them?"

The second girl looked hesitant as she watched the ponytailed man. "I don't know. Mine looks kind of intimidating, doesn't he?"

I agreed. He did look intimidating. He also looked sexy as hell. I wished I could indulge in a little illicit daydreaming about him, but I had enough on my plate without dwelling on the lamentable state of my personal life.

My gaze slid to him again, and once more I was struck with a sense of the familiar. It was as if something inside of me recognized something inside of him—a foolish notion if ever I'd had one, and of late, I'd had nothing *but* foolish notions.

To my surprise, the first man stumbled and came to a stop, turning full circle as he scanned the area. He hesitated when he faced us, and the first girl squealed and nudged her friend as she rose to her feet, blocking my view.

"Look! They've seen us! Let's go over to them. Come on, Dee!"

Her friend was slower in getting up. "I don't know that they're looking at us, Sybil."

"Don't be stupid," the first girl said, grabbing her purse. "It's as clear as day! Let's go say hello."

The two women headed toward the men. I tried to watch them but my vision started to fog, as if I were suddenly enveloped in a cocoon of cotton wool. I clutched the back of the bench to keep from pitching forward, but it was no use. I fell.

Pain burst to life in my head in waves of red that pounded and pulsed stronger and stronger until I thought it would explode from me.

"Stop!" I yelled, and miraculously, it did.

I opened my eyes and glared at the two men who faced each other over the altar of the cathedral, the echoes of their shouting disturbing the dust motes that danced in the thin sunlight streaming through the lovely stained-glass rose window. I turned to the man on my right. Slightly taller than me, of a thick, muscular stature, with golden brown hair and almost identically colored eyes, he reminded me of one of my father's prized bulls. "Baltic has done nothing to harm me, *nothing*."

"He has sworn to destroy all silver dragons who do not submit to his obscene demands," Constantine Norka said, glaring at Baltic. "Why would he bring you to me unless you were damaged?"

I held up a hand to stop Baltic's retort, which I knew would be loud and vicious. "He didn't harm me because he is a man of honor. He swore to take me home, and he did, although"—I shifted my gaze to give him a reproachful look—"I meant my father's keep, not to be delivered into the hands of dragons."

"You belong to my sept," Constantine said, his hands fisted.

"Your *sept* belongs to me!" Baltic snarled.

"For the love of the saints, please don't go through that again!" I said, rubbing my forehead. The remnants of a headache, caused by listening to the two wyverns circle each other snapping and snarling for the last hour, still lingered. "The fact is that he did as he said."

"Including spending the nights in your bed?" Constantine asked, his gaze tight on Baltic.

I raised my eyebrows and considered whether I should respond with maidenly indignation, or a more worldly approach. I decided for indignation. "My maidenhead is intact, if that is what you are desirous of knowing. Baltic did not bed me."

"No? Then why do his men say he was in your cabin every night?"

I thought of the weeklong journey from England to the southern coast of France. It was true Baltic had visited me each night—I had been unable to refuse him, and had, in fact, learned much about what pleased him, and what drove him to the point of losing control.

"I was afraid of the journey," I said truthfully. The sea was a foreign thing, and I did not trust or like it.

The corners of Baltic's mouth curved upward.

"It's true that when we were on the ship he came into my cabin at night, but it was to comfort me."

That also was true, although more of a half-truth. I would have to seek a confessor in my new home.

Constantine made a noise of disbelief, but I raised my chin and said calmly, "I say again that my maidenhead is intact. If you insist on an examination, I will submit to one."

"No," he said, never taking his eyes off Baltic, who was still smiling faintly, an amused look in his obsidian eyes, as glossy and shiny as polished stone. "I will accept what you say."

"Thank the heavens. And now, I would greatly appreciate it if someone would tell me where my family is. My dragon family. So long as I have been ripped from the only parents I have known, I would like to meet the ones who gave me up."

Constantine's hands flexed, but at last he stepped away from the altar, finally turning his gaze to me. In the distance, the song of the monks could be heard as they prayed in a smaller chapel. "It grieves me to tell you this, but your parents are dead, Ysolde."

"No," I said, stopping when he tried to take my arm and lead me out of the cathedral. "They can't be. I came all this way to find them."

"I'm sorry. Your father died in battle with your *savior*." His words and expression were bitter as he nodded toward Baltic. "Your mother did not long survive him. They were a very devoted pair. I did not know you survived—your mother told us you had drowned. I don't know why she placed you with mortals rather than her own kin, but we rejoice that you have been returned to us."

A deep sense of sadness leached into my heart, filling me with a black despair. I lifted my gaze to meet that of Baltic. He was waiting for me, his eyes guarded, his face devoid of emotion. "You killed my father?"

"We are at war," he said. "Lives are lost during wars, Ysolde."

I nodded, tears filling my eyes, my heart so heavy I couldn't speak.

"Come. I will take you to your mother's family. They will welcome you," Constantine said, one hand on my back as he escorted me down the aisle of the cathedral, his guard falling in behind him.

I paused at the great double doors and looked back. Kostya and Pavel had joined Baltic at the altar. All three watched me. I wanted to thank Baltic for honoring his word to me, even when it meant he had to meet with his most hated enemy. I wanted to tell him how much pleasure he had given me in our nights together. I wanted to tell him that I was no longer angry that he took me away from the only family I'd known.

I said nothing. I simply looked at him, then turned and accompanied Constantine out of the cathedral and into my new life.

"You will be cherished now, Ysolde," Constantine reassured me. "We have much to teach you, but you will learn that by-and-by."

# Chapter Six

*By-and-by*, I thought, my heart filled with so much sadness I knew it must shatter into a hundred little pieces. *By-and-by*.

By-and-by? No, that wasn't right.

"I said hi. Hello? Howdy? Hidy ho? Hi hi hi?"

I blinked, the fog evaporating into nothing, the back of the bench once more solid under my hand. In front of me sat a large shaggy black dog, panting in the sunlight, long streamers of drool dribbling from his slobbery lips. I looked around for the dog's owner, but no one was there.

"There you are. Ysolde, right?"

My eyebrows raised, I looked down at the dog. The voice was coming from him.

He tipped his head to the side and I swear he winked at me. "Wow, you look like hell. How ya doing after that header you took into Ash's marble coffee table?"

"Er . . ." My jaw sagged slightly. "Do I know you?"

"Yeah. We met at Aisling and Drake's house during the big birthing hullabaloo. I'm Jim. Effrijim, really, but that's way too girly for a butch guy like me. You look kind of funny. You didn't see me when May ordered me into human form, did you? Because that would explain why you look like you're seeing a three-headed alien dance *A Chorus Line*."

"Human form," I repeated stupidly. "No, I was . . ."

I was dreaming. In the middle of the day? Panic gripped my stomach with clammy fingers. Now the dreams were coming to me while I was wide awake? "Dear god, the shock treatments are going to be just around the corner if my brain keeps going at this rate!"

"Ya think?"

I stared at the dog; my thoughts panicked.

"Ouch. You look like you're gonna pass out or hurl. If you're going to do the latter, can you aim away from me? This magnificent coat takes forever to dry after a bath."

"I'm all right," I said, managing to get a grip on my errant emotions. "You're a dog, but you can use human form?"

"I'm a demon. Sixth class, so it's OK. I'm not going to rip your entrails out and drape them over a tree or anything like that. Besides, Aisling would lop off my package if I did that. She's always threatening to lop off my package. I think she's got a secret genitalia fetish, if you want to know the truth, but she's a nice enough demon lord otherwise, so I don't make a big deal about it. You sure you're OK? Hey, put your head between your knees or something—you're as white as Cecile's underbelly fur."

I did as the dog—demon—suggested, wondering where I knew him from. Before I could even complete that mental sentence, I corrected myself. Demons, I remembered hearing one of my mage instructors say, were always referrcd to by means of gender-neutral pronouns. Why, I had no idea; it just was. "You said I know you?" I asked after a couple of minutes of trying to get a little blood back into my brain.

"Now you're all red," it said, giving its shoulder a lick. "You don't remember me?"

"I don't remember anything," I said with more honesty than I liked.

"Yeah?" Its eyes narrowed on me. "That looks like an interdiction on you. Kostich kick you out of mage's camp?"

I looked down to my chest where a faint blue swirly pattern glowed. "I'm not even going to ask how you know that, because frankly, if I have to listen to one more bizarre thing today, I'm just going to curl up in a little ball and pretend I'm a hedgehog, and then where would Brom be?"

"Who's Brom?"

"My son."

"Oh, man! You have a son? Does Baltic know about it? If he doesn't, promise me I can be there when you tell him, because he's going to go totally psycho dragon. Well, more psycho dragon than he already is, which I gotta tell you is pretty wacked out."

I took a deep, cleansing breath of the grass-scented air. "For the sake of my sanity and my son, I shall now pretend you aren't saying anything. In fact, you're not even here. I'm all alone. And now I'm going home."

"Where's home?" the demon asked, getting up as I gathered up my purse and started off toward what I hoped was the street. It didn't seem to take the slightest offense to my comments, but on the other hand, it also didn't seem inclined to leave me alone.

"Barcelona."

"That's gonna be a hell of a walk."

"I'm staying with some people in town."

"May and Gabriel, yeah, I heard Ash dumped you off on them because you're Baltic's long-lost love. What's it like doing the humpy-jump with a crazy dragon?"

I glanced down at it as I walked. "You are the single most strangest demon I have ever met."

"Face it, babe—I'm the best, aren't I?" it asked, cocking a furry eyebrow at me. Catching sight of someone, it yelled, "Hey, Suzanne! Look who I found!"

A small blond woman hurried over, a leash and a plastic bag in her hand. "Jim! There you are! I thought I'd lost you. Oh, you're Ysolde, aren't you? Hello."

"My name is Tully," I said. "Although to be honest, I'm about ready to give up and change my name because no one listens to me."

"Ysolde's feeling crappy," Jim told her. "I think we should take her home. Wouldn't want her to turn into road pizza because no one was here to watch her."

Suzanne glanced at her watch, but agreed.

"That's not necessary. I'm quite fine on my own. I'm just a little insane, not bad enough I would do something crazy like take off all my clothes and dance on Nelson's Column."

"Damn," Jim said, looking disappointed.

"I think perhaps we should accompany you," Suzanne said, giving me an astute look. "You seem somewhat distraught."

"Distraught . . . insane . . . it's really a moot point by now."

They came with me as I strolled toward Gabriel's house, my thoughts a jumbled mess that I didn't want to examine. Jim chatted nonstop all the way, insisting on accompanying me inside.

"If you want to pay back my chivalry with belly scratches, go right ahead," it said, rolling over onto its back at my feet when I collapsed bonelessly onto a leather couch in a green-and-brown-toned study.

I complied silently, my thoughts still tangled around the vision, Gareth's cruelty, and my newly granted membership in the Club of the Mentally Bewildered.

"Suzanne says you're not feeling well?" May said, coming into the library with Gabriel on her heels. "Jim, really! Do we need to see that?"

"Can't have belly scritches without barin' Jupiter, Mars, and the really Big Dipper," Jim answered, its back leg kicking slightly in the air as my fingers found a particularly itchy spot on its stomach. "Oh, yeah, baby. I really dig chicks with long nails."

"Time to go," May said, prodding the demon with the toe of her shoe. "Thanks for bringing Ysolde back, Suzanne. We'll take it from here."

"But I want to stay!" Jim complained as it followed Suzanne out of the room. "I never get any excitement anymore, what with Drake not letting anyone in the house unless he has five references and a comprehensive background check...."

The door closed on the demon's voice. Gabriel knelt next to me, tipping my chin up to look into my eyes. I let him look, feeling mentally battered. "What has happened to you?"

I hesitated for a moment, remembering Gareth's words. "They will kill you," he had warned, but that didn't make sense, not on an intellectual or an emotional level. The only vibe I was getting from May and Gabriel was one of sympathy and concern.

"Baltic," I said, licking my lips, my thoughts finally stopping their endless spinning to coalesce into one solid thought. My voice was rough, my lips dry, as if I'd been exposed to the elements for a very long time.

May murmured something and moved over to pour me a drink. It was spicy, very spicy, redolent of cloves and ginger and cinnamon, and it burned as it went down my throat, but it was a good burn. It filled me with energy as it pooled in my belly, allowing me to focus my thoughts.

"What about him?" Gabriel asked.

I took another sip, enjoying the burn. "Is Baltic here? In London?"

Gabriel and May exchanged glances. He said, "He was here the day you collapsed. After that, we believe he returned to Russia."

"To lick his wounds, most likely," May added. "He was soundly defeated by Gabriel, Kostya, and Drake. Three of his guards died, and we captured his lieutenant, a woman named Thala."

"Well, unless I really am going insane, I think he's returned. I believe I saw him in Green Park." I explained about seeing the two men, and the vision that followed, although I left out specific details. "There's just one thing that confuses me—the man I saw in the park does not look like the man I've seen in my dreams. If it's Baltic I've really been dreaming about, then he couldn't be the man in the park."

"Yes, he could," Gabriel said slowly, getting to his feet. "I think something happened when Baltic was reborn. I think it changed his appearance, both dragon and human."

"He was reborn?" I asked.

"Of course—you don't know. Or rather, you don't remember," Gabriel said. "Baltic was killed three hundred years ago."

Well, that was a bit of a kicker. "Who killed him?"

"His right-hand man. Kostya Fekete."

"Kostya?" I gaped at him, truly gaped. "Tall, black hair and eyes, little cleft in his chin, square jaw—that Kostya?"

"Yes. You've seen him?"

"In my dreams, yes, but he is Baltic's friend."

"Was. He *was* Baltic's friend," Gabriel said. "The day came when Kostya realized that Baltic's mad plan to rule the septs was destroying the black dragons, and he put an end to it by killing Baltic, but not before the damage was done. The black dragons were all but exterminated."

"By who?" I asked, my voice a whisper.

"Constantine Norka, the wyvern of the silver dragons."

I slumped back, my brain reeling. It was just too much to take in, especially since I realized with a shock that, cling as I might to the idea that I was insane, I was beginning to believe that they could all be right, and I really was a freak of nature, a dragon trapped in a human body.

How sad is it that insanity was preferable to that?

Three hours later I sat surrounded by dragons. Evidently a *sárkány* was a big deal, being held in a large conference room of a very chic hotel, and attended by a number of people who looked perfectly ordinary. A long center table that would seat about twenty dominated the room, while chairs lined the walls. A podium stood at one end of the room, and at the other end a huge white screen was lowered, indicating there was going to be some sort of visual display.

I let my gaze wander around the clumps of approximately thirty people standing and chatting. Without exception, the expressions turned toward me were hostile. Tired of that, I looked at my neighbor to the right. "How long do these things usually last?"

"Depends," Jim said.

"On what?"

"Whether or not your boyfriend starts mowing everyone down like he did in Paris."

I shook my head, not sure if I should goggle at him, blink my eyes in surprise, or do the "water on a duck's back" thing and let it all roll off me. "I think I'll go with 'roll off me,'" I told Jim.

"Really? Like roll in the hay? With someone else, or with Baltic?"

"Baltic tried to kill people at a *sárkány*?" I asked, taking a firm grip on myself. I had decided that I would not go insane. Brom needed me, especially now that I knew what a bastard his father really was, and I couldn't take care of him if I was locked away, drawing pictures on the padded walls using only my own drool.

"Yeah, a while back. I wasn't there because Aisling was about to pop with the spawns, but I heard it was a real Wild West shoot-out. Until May exploded the dragon shard and blew up the top floor of the hotel."

I let that, too, roll off. In fact, I would have just sat back and closed my eyes in an attempt to let everything and everyone roll off my back, but a woman was approaching us with a glint in her eye.

"Jim, so help me, if you're bothering poor Ysolde—"

the woman said as she stopped in front of us, her hands on her hips.

"Hey, I'm just sittin' here partaking in polite chitchat, being my usual Mr. Helpful self. Right, Soldy?"

"The name is Ysolde," I said stiffly, then realized what I'd said. "No, it's Tully! Tully! My name is Tully, not Ysolde. Oh dear god, now you people have me doing it!"

"This is Aisling, my demon lord. She had twin spawns the day you keeled over in her house," Jim told me as Aisling clucked her tongue sympathetically at my outburst.

"You're a demon lord?" I asked, finding it hard to reconcile the image of the pretty woman with curly brown hair and hazel eyes, and a being who commanded demons.

"Yup. May says you don't remember anything, not that we met, but still, that has to be a serious pain in the butt. I'm married to Drake. He's the wyvern of the green dragons. That's him, over there, the good-looking one."

I looked to where she was pointing. Several men were clustered together at the far end of the room. I hated to say anything because they all looked pretty darn good to me, but a vague sense of recognition twinged in the back of my head when my gaze reached a tall man with dark hair. "And are you a dragon, too?" I asked Aisling.

May entered the room just as she laughed. "Oh, lord no. I was as human as they come before I met Drake. I was a courier, and we met when he stole the aquamanile I was taking to Paris. It was very romantic."

Jim choked, coughing and hacking as if he'd swallowed a hairball. "Romantic!" it finally said. "Man, if you knew what sort of hell she put us through while she was deciding to hook up with Drake—"

"Silence, furry demon." She smiled at May as she joined us. "It was almost as romantic as May and Gabriel's courtship."

May rolled her eyes. "What courtship? One minute I was myself, the next Gabriel was there demanding I be his mate. Not that I minded, but still. Oh, there's Cy. That means Kostya won't be very far away. Excuse me a minute."

"I forgot for a minute she was a doppelganger," I said as May crossed the room to join the woman who'd just entered. Although they were dressed differently, and the other woman's hair was longer, it was clear they were identical twins.

"Cyrene is more or less the mate to Kostya," Aisling said. "It's kind of confusing, really, but basically, he's accepted her as his mate, but she isn't technically a wyvern's mate, if you get my drift."

"I don't think I do, no."

"Well, as I understand it, it means that she is his mate in the eyes of the weyr, but can't be taken by another wyvern."

"Kidnapped, you mean?" I asked, confused how that could have bearing on anything.

"No, taken as in challenged for. Say if Bastian—he's the handsome blond on the right—if he wanted Cy as his mate, he couldn't challenge Kostya for her, because she's not technically a wyvern's mate. Whereas he could challenge Drake for me, or Gabriel for May, because we are mates. Does that make sense?"

"Only if it means that there is some bizarre rule to

this world that says one man can steal someone else's wife. Er . . . mate."

"Archaic, huh?" Aisling asked with a little shrug. "That's the dragons for you—they look hip and modern and may have lusts for all things technological, like Drake, but deep down, they're still in the fourteenth century."

"You mates should unionize," Jim suggested, wiping a tendril of drool on the empty chair next to it. "Mates Local 51. Make a new rule prohibiting mate swapping, and go on a sex strike if they refuse to negotiate."

Aisling looked at her demon with a startled expression. "That's not a bad idea," she said.

"Really?" Jim sat up a little straighter. "Can I watch when you tell Drake that you're not going to let him chase you naked through the house anymore?"

"You were supposed to be asleep!" Aisling said, leaning across me to pinch the demon on its shoulder. "You did not see us! You couldn't have!"

"Let me tell you, the sight of nursing boobies flopping all around while you tear through the house isn't something I'm going to forget anytime soon," Jim added, leaning away from me so Aisling couldn't reach it again.

"That's it! From now on, I'm locking you into the bathroom at night!"

"You're just lucky Drake didn't put an eye out with his gigantic—"

"Silence!" Aisling roared, and all of the occupants of the room turned to look.

She smiled at everyone before turning a look on Jim that would have scared a couple of years off my life. "Ignore Jim, please," she added. "It has moments of derangement. Oh, look, there's Chuan Ren and Jian. Chuan Ren is the red wyvern. Those are her bodyguards with her, although I don't see her mate, Li. Jian is her adopted son. I'll take you over and introduce you. She hates me, so it's always fun to say hi."

Aisling spoke cheerfully enough as we strolled over to the newest arrivals, a group of four people, all Asian, three men and one woman. The woman had long, straight black hair, and a figure that belonged on a runway. Two of the men were rather short but powerfully built; the third was tall and also would have been perfectly at home as a model.

"Hello, Chuan Ren. Hi, Jian, nice to see you again. Hi, Sying and Shing. This is—"

"Ysolde de Bouchier," the woman named Chuan Ren said, her gaze locked onto mine. "So, you are not dead as they said you were. Too bad."

She turned on her heel and marched off, her two guards in tow.

"She's in a good mood today, I see," Aisling said to the remaining red dragon.

He made a face. "Chuan Ren has had a trying time the last few weeks. Her mate, Li, has disappeared."

"Oh no! I'm sorry to hear that, although he obviously can't be dead or we'd know it," Aisling said, glancing at Chuan Ren.

"How would you know?" I asked.

"Wyverns can't survive the loss of their mates," she said simply before waving at the blond she'd called Bastian. "I'd better see what the latest gossip is about Fiat before things start. Ysolde, it was a pleasure to meet you at last. If you need any help with things, let me know. I know how hard it is trying to come to grips with some of the dragon lore."

She left us, and after another moment of polite chat with Jian, I was about to return to my chair when I turned and saw a man standing in the doorway staring at me, his eyes burning with black heat.

"Kostya," I said, the word a whisper on my lips.

He nodded slowly, stalking toward me. "It's true. They said it was, but I didn't see how it could be possible. I saw your body. I saw your severed head."

I touched my neck, horror crawling up my skin at his words.

"I . . . I really don't know what to say to someone who tells me he saw my severed head," I admitted. "'Hi' seems a little bit of an anticlimax."

I swore he was going to bare his teeth at me, but he managed to stop. "A miracle has happened, Ysolde de Bouchier."

"Tully Sullivan. I'm thinking of having it tattooed on my forehead."

"A miracle has happened, and now the time has come for you to pay in like coin for all the deaths, for all the suffering."

"Punky! There you are!" May's twin appeared at Kostya's side, alternating glances between me and him. "Hi, I'm Cyrene. You must be Ysolde. May's told me all about you. I don't blame you one bit for losing your memory. I would have, too, if I'd had to be mated to Baltic."

"Pleasure to meet you," I said, unable to break Kostya's gaze.

He leaned forward, his voice low. "If there is any

justice in the world, you will suffer as long as the black dragons have suffered."

"Kostya, I thought Drake said you weren't supposed to scare Ysolde," Cyrene scolded, taking his arm and tugging him toward the big table. "Ignore him. He's a bit grumpy because we ran out of his favorite cereal for breakfast."

He stopped glaring at me and transferred his glare to her. "You did not just tell her that! For the love of the saints, woman, I am a wyvern! You do not tell people I'm grumpy over breakfast foods!"

"If someone makes a fuss about not having Cap'n Crunch, then that someone is just going to have to take his lumps," she said, blithely unaware of his furious gaze. "Come on, I think they're waiting for us."

Kostya turned without another word and stomped over to the table, Cyrene at his side. I returned to my chair and watched with interest as the wyverns gathered around the table. There were only five chairs there, and before they sat, Gabriel, Drake, and Kostya all made a point of retrieving a chair and placing it next to theirs. The guards and the other dragons in attendance all took up spots on the chairs lining the wall.

Jim gave me a poignant look, but bound to silence as it was, it said nothing. I was grateful for that, since it meant I could try to sort through my mental turmoil while the dragons went through the formalities of their meeting.

"Kostya Fekete," the blue wyvern named Bastian said. "You have called this *sárkány* on behalf of the black dragons. State your business."

I looked up from where I'd been sightlessly staring at my hands.

Kostya stood at the foot of the table and looked at all the wyverns present. "I am here to seek reparation. The mate of Baltic has revealed herself, and the black dragons demand that she be held liable for the crimes he committed against the weyr."

"What?" I asked, standing up, so stunned by Kostya's demand I forgot that May warned me not to speak before I was called upon. "That's ridiculous!"

Bastian frowned at me. "You have not yet been recognized by the weyr. Please remain—"

"I will not remain silent!" I stormed over to the table, suddenly furious. "Certainly not while you people accuse me of something I didn't do."

"You are the mate of Baltic," Kostya snarled. "By the laws that govern the weyr, you are just as responsible for his actions as he is."

"I am not his mate. I am not even a dragon! I'm human! You all must be able to tell that!"

The wyverns exchanged glances.

"You see? No one is denying it, because it's true. I'm human."

"You appear human, yes," Drake said in a voice that held an Eastern European accent. "But Gabriel's mother assures us that your dragon self resides within you, simply waiting for you to waken it."

"Even if that's true, that doesn't give you people the right to try me for a crime I didn't commit! Don't you watch *CSI*? That's totally illegal!"

Kostya's scowl darkened. "You are a mate, *his* mate. And unless you'd like to bring him before us, then it is you who will pay the price for his crimes."

"What crimes, exactly? The war with the silver dragons that Gabriel said wiped out your sept?" I made a disgusted sound. "If the dreams I had were actually echoes of the past, then you were a part of that sept, too, which means you were a part of the war. How many silver dragons did *you* kill, Kostya?"

He snarled something extremely rude under his breath. "We are not discussing my actions. I have made my peace with the weyr."

"Oh, did you really?" Furious, I did something I never do—I made a scene. I leaped onto the conference table and stomped down its length to stand in front of Kostya. "You supported Baltic in everything he did! Everything! He couldn't pass gas without you telling him how fabulous he was!"

Kostya growled, positively growled as he leaped to his feet, his chair flying backwards several feet. "That is not true!"

"Do your friends here know just how much of a yes-man you really were? Do they know how you followed him around like a puppy, doing anything he demanded?"

"My past has nothing to do—"

"Do they know how you let Baltic hold a sword to my throat and threaten to kill me just because I was born a silver dragon?" My voice rang out loudly.

The entire room was silent.

"Er . . ." I cleared my throat as I realized what I'd just declared. "That's assuming that I am what everyone says I am, which I still maintain is very unlikely."

Kostya, goaded into a fury, yelled at me. "I am not to blame for Baltic's actions! I kept him in check until he rescued you. He was unbalanced then, but he became uncontrollable after you sided with Constantine Norka against him."

"I what?" I asked, feeling at a loss.

"I might have been able to reason with him if it wasn't for you!" Kostya accused me. "He wanted you. He was willing to take you despite the fact that you were a silver dragon."

"Should we be offended by Kostya's implication?" May asked Gabriel. "I have my dagger. I could poke him with it a few times."

Cyrene shot her twin an outraged look.

"Perhaps later," Gabriel told May.

"But you spurned him, and bound yourself to Constantine Norka instead!" Kostya's face was dark with anger. "Baltic was furious! His madness knew no bounds after that."

"I really don't know what you're talking about," I said, my anger starting to cool. I looked around at the dragons gathered at the table, embarrassed by my show of temper. "Sorry, can I just . . . thank you," I said as Bastian stood and held out a hand to assist me off the table.

"You cannot deny what happened in the past," Kostya said, his voice and face sullen.

"I wouldn't dream of trying. But I don't think I've gotten to this betrayal in my visions. I assume it will come at some point, but I have to say that I find it difficult to believe."

"Kostya, this is old history," Drake said, one eyebrow raised at the black dragon. "The blame for the Endless War has long since been settled. You cannot try Ysolde for that crime."

"There wouldn't have been an Endless War but for her!" Kostya declared.

"I thought Chuan Ren started that war?" Aisling leaned close and asked her husband.

Chuan Ren narrowed her eyes at Aisling, her mouth moving silently as if she was speaking a curse.

Aisling quickly drew protection wards over herself and Drake.

"Kaawa said Ysolde tried to stop the war by bringing the dragon shards together to re-form the dragon heart," May said. "She would hardly do that if she was responsible for the whole thing."

"That was later, after she realized what she had started," Kostya said stubbornly.

"You know, not even I think that makes any sense," Cyrene said, looking at him. "Seriously, punky, I think we're going to have to go to some anger management classes. You need to learn how to let go and move on."

"The black dragons—" he started to say.

"Are not the reason Ysolde has been called before the *sárkány*," Drake interrupted in a forceful voice.

"Exactly what crime did Baltic commit that you're all so intent on punishing me for?" I asked, suddenly tired and emotionally drained.

Drake looked at me with eyes that held infinite sadness. "The deaths of sixty-eight blue dragons, killed by Baltic almost two months ago."

# Chapter Seven

Silence filled the conference room as every person—every dragon—looked at me. I shivered, rubbing my arms against a sudden chill.

"Lucky me. I'm out of it for five weeks, lose my job, learn my husband is a rat to beat all rats, and now I find out that evidently I'm the girlfriend of a homicidal maniac. Is that it? Is that all you guys have to hit me with? Because I'm not quite over the edge yet."

"There is the matter of who held Kostya prisoner in his aerie for seven years," Cyrene said thoughtfully. "No one seems to know for sure who captured him there, but I think it was your mate, so by rights, you should be charged with that, too."

"Thank you," I told her. "That did the job."

Before anyone could react, I spun around and started for the nearest exit. I didn't make it, naturally, but I knew I wouldn't.

Kostya was there at the door. "You will not escape justice again, Ysolde de Bouchier."

I slapped him. It felt so good, I slapped him again, then stepped back, my hand over my mouth because I'd never struck another person in my life.

That I could remember.

Well, there was nailing Baltic in the groin, but that was just a dream.

"I'm sorry," I stammered, horrified. "I don't know what came over me. Not that you didn't deserve it, because if anyone deserved to be slapped, you did, but still, I'm shocked that I actually struck you. Did I hurt you?"

Cyrene screamed and ran toward us, clearly about to launch herself at me, but Kostya caught her before she could attack.

I just stared at them as she struggled to get free, cursing me roundly as she fought him, my eyes filling with tears. I'd never felt so alien, so alone, so completely out of my depth. I just wanted to sink into oblivion.

"Sit down," Kostya told Cyrene when she had worked out the worst of her swearing.

"She struck you! Twice! No one hits my dragon and lives to tell about it!"

"Go sit down," he commanded.

"No!"

"Cy, it was an open-handed slap," May said as she took her twin's arm and forcibly steered her toward the table. "I'm sure Kostya will survive it."

"I'm very sorry," I told him again.

To my surprise, rather than look angrier with me, he rubbed his abused cheek and looked thoughtful.

"Ysolde?" Gabriel indicated the table. "I believe since the subject of the blue dragons' deaths has been broached, you would be welcome at the *sárkány* table. Perhaps we can discuss the issue more calmly."

"I'm not at all a violent person," I told him, allowing him to escort me to a chair he placed on his other side. "I can't even spank my son."

He said nothing, just held out a chair for me.

"You must understand that the weyr does not seek to punish an innocent person," Bastian said, taking charge of the meeting again. "But there are laws that govern us, and as Kostya said, one of those laws holds that wyverns' mates are held accountable for the actions of their wyverns."

"What about other dragons?" I asked, too weary to be incensed.

Bastian looked confused. "What other dragons?"

"What about a normal dragon's mate, a non-wyvern. Are they held accountable, too?"

"No," he said, frowning.

"Why not?"

Silence fell on the table. Drake cleared his throat and answered, "Wyverns' mates are unique in dragonkin. They have power of their own, and are accorded a place of honor in the sept second only to the wyvern himself. Mates always support the wyverns' decisions, and thus the law was set into place recognizing that position and power."

"Let me make sure I have this straight. You all think that because I was alive two months ago, unaware of any of you, unaware of Baltic, unaware of anything but doing my job as an apprentice for Dr. Kostich, and being a wife and mother, you seriously expect me to believe that I am guilty of the deaths of sixty—"

"Sixty-eight," Bastian interrupted.

"My apologies. I didn't mean to make light of that tragedy. Where was I? Oh, you want to hold me responsible for the deaths of dragons I didn't even know existed in the first place? Is that what you're saying?"

Drake's gaze dropped. Gabriel and May exchanged uncomfortable glances. Kostya coughed softly and scowled at the table. Bastian looked into the distance. Chuan Ren smiled at me, showing far more teeth than was called for.

"Do I want to know what the punishment is for killing sixty-eight blue dragons?" I asked.

No one looked at me. "The punishment for a crime of such a heinous nature outside of a declared war is death," Bastian said at last.

"Lovely. You want to kill me for someone else's crime. That certainly sounds like justice to me."

No one said anything to that bit of sarcasm, either.

I thought of fighting, thought of running away, thought of damning them all and just letting them make me a scapegoat, but something inside me finally reached a breaking point.

"There is something going on with me," I said slowly, looking again at my fingers spread on the table. "Much as I want to deny it, I am willing to admit that I have some sort of a connection to this person named Baltic. Despite that, no one can deny that I *am* human, and it is for that reason that I do not, cannot, *will not* admit that I am the dragon named Ysolde. However, if any of you can prove to me that I am, if you can show me that what I'm experiencing is due to a dragon hiding inside of me, then I will acknowledge the laws of this weyr, and will accept the punishment for the deaths of those dragons."

That got their attention. They didn't look happy, though.

"That seems reasonable to me," Aisling said, nudging her husband with her elbow. "Of course you want proof that you're really Ysolde. We'll just have to show you that it's so. I'm not sure how we'll go about doing that other than giving you time to find yourself, so to speak. That's only right and fair, especially since the weyr is asking you to give up your life. Doesn't it seem fair to you, Drake?"

His frown cleared. "It would seem that such a demand is not unreasonable given the circumstances. What say the other wyverns?"

"I agree wholeheartedly," Gabriel said quickly. "Ysolde must have proof. She must be easy in her mind that she is who we know her to be. It would be a gross misinterpretation of the weyr laws to condemn her without her acknowledging her dragon self."

"I agree," Bastian said, a bit to my surprise since it was his sept members who had been killed. I thought if anyone would have wanted to see me condemned, it would be him. But he actually looked relieved, and turned to Kostya. "What do the black dragons say?"

Kostya pursed his lips as he looked at me.

"I think she needs to be smacked upside the head," Cyrene muttered. Kostya shot her a glare, then said, "I am influenced by the memories of what Baltic did to the black dragons because of Ysolde. Long have I sought to see her pay for the pain and suffering she caused us for her treachery with Constantine Norka—"

"She was a silver dragon," Gabriel said abruptly. "She agreed to be his mate. That can hardly be said to be treachery!"

Kostya leaped to his feet, his face red with anger. "Baltic wanted her for *his* mate!"

"Then he should never have handed her over to Constantine, saying he didn't want her!" Gabriel shot back, jumping up as well.

"Oh, *that* makes me feel good," I said softly.

"That discussion is not pertinent at this time," Bastian said, pounding on the table with his fist until the two dragons retook their seats. "Kostya, how say you?"

He sat down with a huff, his arms crossed, his expression black. "I will agree to a temporary stay so long as it's for a reasonable amount of time."

I was taken aback by his agreement. That left one wyvern.

"Chuan Ren?" Bastian asked her.

"The red dragons don't care what happens to the woman," she answered. "Kill her, or do not kill her, it is of no concern to us. We are only interested in the whereabouts of Baltic."

"Why do you care where he is?" May asked.

Chuan Ren just smiled again. It wasn't a pleasant smile.

"We are agreed, then, that Ysolde should have time to . . . what?" Bastian asked, looking puzzled. "How does one find oneself?"

"My mother says the dragon inside her is waiting to be woken," Gabriel said. "That is what must be done."

"But how do you go about doing that?" Bastian shook his head. "I've never before met a dragon who didn't know he was a dragon, who wasn't able to *be* a dragon."

"I think I may know of a way to do that," May said thoughtfully. She sat up a little straighter when she realized all eyes were on her. "There is a house in the country that belongs to Baltic."

"It is mine now," Kostya interrupted. "I have claimed it on behalf of the black dragons."

"That's right, we have," Cyrene said. "It's a bit too big as houses go, and needs a lot of redecorating, but it has a nice pond. Kostie says we can dig up the garden to enlarge the pond into a small lake."

Kostya gave his mate a thin-lipped look that she ignored.

"When I bore the dragon shard, it caused me to react quite strongly to the house." May's gaze turned to me. "It actually had me feeling things that I believe you felt while you bore the shard."

"I bore a shard?" I asked, refusing to cope with one more bizarre thing. "A shard of what?"

"A dragon shard, one of the five pieces of the dragon heart."

I closed my eyes for a minute. "Is the dragon heart something that's going to make me completely lose the tiny shred of sanity I'm holding on to? Because I have to tell you, if it is, I think I'd rather just not know about it."

May laughed. "It's not that bad, honest."

"The dragon heart is made up of five shards. Each of the wyverns here possesses a shard," Gabriel told me. "For a while, May bore the same shard that you bore.

Just as she did, you successfully re-formed the dragon heart—imbued with the power of the First Dragon—and allowed it to reshatter into five pieces."

"That sounds very clever of May and me, and I'm thrilled to bits to hear it despite the fact that I don't have the slightest idea of the significance of any of that, but so long as it has no bearing on whether or not there is a dragon curled up inside me, I'm willing to move on."

"Brava," Aisling said, applauding until her husband scowled at her.

"I take it you think that if I were to go to Baltic's home—"

"My home! It belongs to me now!" Kostya said.

"Pardon me, Baltic's former home, that it would somehow prove I'm a dragon? Will I start setting things on fire? Burst into scaly lizard form? Suddenly become fascinated with gold?" I asked, too tired to mind my manners as I should.

"Judging by what I felt when I was there, yes, I think you'll have some sort of a definitive experience," May said.

"But Ysolde doesn't bear the Avignon Phylactery anymore," Kostya said.

May slid an unreadable smile toward her wyvern. "No, but I can attest to the fact that once you've borne a shard, it changes you. I'm sure it changed Ysolde, too."

"It sounds like a good idea to me," Aisling said.

"With Kostya's permission, we will take you to the house in question tomorrow," Gabriel said. "You will not, I hope, mind if May and I accompany you?"

"I will be there as well," Kostya said.

"Oooh. That sounds interesting. Can we go?" Aisling asked Drake.

He raised his eyebrows and looked at Gabriel. "We have no reason to, but if Gabriel—and Ysolde—have no objection, I admit that I am curious to see if the house does have some effect on her."

Gabriel stated a time, and everyone agreed to meet at the house. I sat back in my chair, drained by the emotions I'd been through in the last few days, wanting nothing more than . . . I sighed to myself. I didn't even know what I wanted anymore, other than peace of mind.

I expected to dream that night, and I did. I closed the door to Brom's room after seeing him settled for the night, wished May a pleasant evening, and stepped into my room, and straight into a maelstrom of testosterone.

"You are too late, Baltic," the man who stood in front of me taunted. "Ysolde has spoken the words. She has sworn fealty to me. She is now my mate."

I stepped to the side to look around Constantine. Baltic and about ten men emerged from the trees that formed a gentle curve around the cliff top where we stood, Kostya and Pavel immediately to his rear.

Instantly the silver dragons pulled their swords, surrounding Constantine and me.

"Is that true?" Baltic asked me, his expression as stormy as the sea that raged behind us.

I took a step forward, but Constantine put his hand out to stop me. "You will address me, and not my mate. Ysolde is mine. You will never have her."

"Why are you here?" I asked Baltic, shrugging off Constantine's hand and pushing past his guards. They made a move to stop me, but fell back when I glared at them.

"Why do you think I'm here? I came to claim my mate," Baltic answered, his eyes glittering darkly.

"Your mate? You said you didn't want me. You said you would never have anything to do with a silver dragon," I cried.

"I said I would never bed a silver dragon," he corrected. "I have since changed my mind. You are my mate. I sent a messenger telling you I would come to claim you as such."

"I know of no messenger!" I said, shocked and horrified.

His expression darkened. "I should have known that Constantine would claim you for himself rather than let you be mine."

"Ysolde, my dove, let me deal with this," Constantine said, his voice warm and rumbly and comfortable just as it had been for the three months while I had been with him in the south of France.

I spun around to face him, suddenly filled with knowledge that left me furious. "You knew he was coming for me, didn't you? You knew my heart was breaking, and still you kept his message from reaching me. By the rood! That's why you pressed me to make the oath to you! You deceived me!"

"You are my responsibility," Constantine said, taking my hands in his.

Baltic positively growled. Kostya, his eyes on the silver guards, held him back.

"I promised to care for you that first day when you were given to me," Constantine continued. "I could not help but love you, my precious dove. Can you blame me for wanting you as my mate?"

How stupid I'd been. How stupid and naïve, falling for the honeyed words and the promise of a lifetime of being loved, when in reality, I was being used as an instrument in a war that had raged for two hundred years. I pulled my hands from his and backed up, sickened by the way he'd fooled me. The guards looked to Constantine, but he lifted his hand to stop them. "You told me I was the one meant to be your mate, but all the while you knew Baltic was coming for me. You watched as I pined for him, pined for the love I would give my soul to have, and yet you bound me to you? Why?"

"I love you," he said, his eyes glowing with a strange golden light. "How could I let the one thing I love more than life itself go to a madman, a monster who would destroy our sept rather than let us live in peace?"

I couldn't look at him any longer. "You say you love me, and yet you ensured that I would spend the remainder of my days a shadow of what I could have been."

Constantine reached out for me, but let his hand drop before he could touch me. "You are merely confused, Ysolde, not truly in love."

"How do you know?" I lifted my head to glare at him. "How do you presume to know what's in my heart? You won't even listen to me! I told you that I loved him, Constantine, and you just told me he would rather see me dead than alive."

"You—" he started to say.

"No," I said, cutting him off with a sharp gesture. "I know my own mind and heart. I love Baltic. If he had asked me to be his mate, I would have accepted."

Baltic smiled, a slow, smug smile.

"That doesn't mean I'm not furious with your high-handed dealings," I told him over my shoulder.

His smile slipped a notch.

"Even knowing what he is, knowing what he's done

to our people, to your own family, you would bind yourself to him?" Constantine asked, his voice reflecting the anger now in his eyes. "You would let him use your body, taint your soul?"

I met his gaze, my own steady. "I would do what I could to bring calm to this troubled time."

"You swore fealty to me," he answered.

"What choice did I have?" I countered. "You deceived me!"

He was silent for a moment, pain flickering across his face.

"If only you had told me the truth," I said softly, putting my hand on his arm. "I have great respect and affection for you, Constantine. You are a wonderful wyvern, and a generous, loving man. But much as I honor you as such, I would never have pledged myself to you if I had known the truth. You tricked me into becoming your mate simply to spite the man who holds my heart. How can I find happiness with you knowing that?"

Baltic stepped forward. "Constantine Norka, by the laws governing the weyr, I challenge you by *lusus naturalae* for your mate, Ysolde de Bouchier."

Constantine and I both stared at him.

"*Lusus* what?" I asked.

"*Naturalae*. It has many meanings, but to dragonkin, it applies only to one thing—the ability to steal a mate," Constantine answered, eyeing Baltic with palpable hostility.

"It is not stealing if I win the challenge," Baltic said, striding forward. At a gesture, all of his men but Kostya remained standing where they were. Likewise, Constantine nodded at his guard, who gestured the others back.

The dragons spread out until they formed a loose circle, in the center of which the five of us stood. "Do you accept the challenge?"

"I do," Constantine said, his stance aggressive. "Ysolde is young and confused. She has not yet had time to adjust to our ways. I am convinced that with time, she will realize what a tragedy her life would have been if she spent it with you."

"I dislike being spoken of as if I weren't standing an arm's length from you," I told him somewhat acidly. "I am not invisible, nor am I witless. This is *my* life you're talking about, and I demand the right to have a say in it."

"You are female," Constantine said abruptly. "You are young and inexperienced with the ways of dragons. You will allow me to decide what is best for you."

"I am the one who found her," Baltic said arrogantly, swaggering forward until he stood a foot away from us. "I will decide what is best for her, and that is to become my mate."

"Does no one think it is a good idea for me to decide what's best for me?" I asked.

"No!" both wyverns said.

I crossed my arms and looked daggers at both of them. "I think you're both obnoxious. I've changed my mind. I don't want either of you. I'll take Kostya instead."

Kostya's eyes widened in surprise and something that looked very much like dismay. "Er . . ."

"Are you trying to make me jealous?" Baltic asked, irritation pulling at his lips.

"No. If I were, I would do this." I walked toward Kostya, but he evidently read the intention in my eyes because he backed away from me. I stopped, stomped my foot in irritation, and demanded, "Stop running away from me and let me kiss you!"

"I'd really rather you didn't," he said with a wary glance at his wyvern.

"Ysolde," Baltic said in an even, almost disinterested tone of voice.

I marched over to him, narrowing my glare until it could have sharpened the edge of his sword. "What?"

"You don't have to attack Kostya to make me jealous, *chérie*," he said, the irritation in his face replaced with wry amusement. He gestured toward Constantine. "I'm ready to fight him to the death for his audacity in claiming you. I don't think I could get much more jealous than that."

"Oh." I thought about that for a moment, then took a step closer to him, not quite touching, but close enough I could feel the heat of his body. I looked deep into his eyes, searching there for the answers I so desperately sought. "You really want me for your mate even though I'm a silver dragon?"

"Yes." A muscle in his neck twitched.

"Why?"

His eyes took on the same wary look Kostya's had just borne. "Why?"

I prodded his arm. "Yes, why? Why do you want me for your mate?"

"Eh . . ." He looked from me to Constantine, who was standing watching us with a black scowl. Baltic squared his shoulders and leveled a haughty look at me. "That is unimportant. Only the fact that I have claimed you should matter."

"It matters to me," I said, and put my hand on his chest, over his heart.

Behind me, Constantine took a step toward us.

"You are female. You do not know what you're saying."

"By the rood, I don't. Tell me, Baltic. Why me?"

"Because," he said, his eyes glittering darkly. "Just . . . because."

"Do you love me?" I asked.

His jaw tightened. "That is none of your business."

I laughed; I couldn't help but laugh at him. Love in marriage was only a dream, my mother had once told me, and yet I knew she loved my father. She had also said that some men have difficulty admitting to such tender emotions, and clearly Baltic was one of them.

"I think it is my business. It's important to me, Baltic. I would like to know—do you love me?"

He stepped closer until his chest was pressed against my arms. "This is hardly the place to discuss such a thing."

"I think it's the perfect place," I said, gesturing at all the dragons, hesitating a moment when I noticed that every single one of them wore expressions of pain identical to the one on Baltic's face. "I must know. I will not bind myself to a man if he doesn't love me."

"That's foolishness," Baltic scoffed, and the dragons scoffed with him, murmurs of agreement rippling around us.

"Nevertheless, I must know. So I ask you a third time—do you love me?"

He looked around wildly before leaning in. "There are others here, woman!"

"I know."

"You expect me to say it right out in front of them?"

"Constantine did," I said, nodding toward him. Constantine straightened up and looked noble. "He didn't have any problem saying it."

Baltic growled deep in his chest, rolling his eyes heavenward for a moment before he said in a low and ugly voice, "Fine! I love you. Now get the hell out of my way so I can kill your mate."

I don't know what I would have done had Constantine not attacked Baltic at that moment—probably tried to reason with them, although hindsight tells me they wouldn't have listened. It is moot speculation, regardless, because the second the words left Baltic's lips, Constantine's body shifted, stretching and growing and elongating into the form of a silver-scaled dragon with scarlet claws. He flung himself at Baltic with a snarl that left my blood cold.

Baltic shifted as well, but his form, slightly smaller and less bulky, was ebony colored, with curving translucent white claws that flashed in the air as he lunged at Constantine.

Teodore, one of Constantine's guards, tried to restrain me, but I shook him off and stalked forward to where the two dragons were rolling around on the ground, blood arcing in the air as one of them struck true.

"Stop it!" I yelled, my hands fisted in impotence. I wanted to strike both of them back into their senses. "I will not have th—"

Constantine's tail lashed out as he threw himself forward onto Baltic, who just barely rolled out of the way in time. I screamed as I was knocked backwards several yards. Instantly Constantine was there, in human form, leaning over me and cradling my head. "Ysolde! My dove, my cherished one—have I harmed you?"

Baltic shifted back into human form as well, jerking

Constantine off me and onto his back, the glittering silver point of a sword digging into his neck.

"You have lost your mate, your sept," Baltic said, panting, "and now your life."

"No!" I yelled, leaping up as he raised his sword overhead, clearly about to cleave Constantine's head from his body. I threw myself forward over him, looking up at Baltic. "Do not kill him."

Baltic's eyes narrowed on me. "You have a change of heart?"

"No. I will be your mate. My life is bound to yours from this moment forward. But only if you spare Constantine."

His jaw worked, and for a moment, I thought he would refuse. But slowly he lowered his sword, grabbing my arm and pulling me to my feet. "By the grace of my mate, I will let you live," he told Constantine. "But only because she desires it."

The sight of Constantine's face haunted me as Baltic led me away.

# Chapter Eight

"After it's dehydrated, I take out the natron that is in the inside, and put cloth soaked in resin and more natron inside the body. Then I get to paint the whole thing with resin. That takes, like, three weeks to dry, so I want to get started right away. I think I have enough resin to do the whole fox."

"Whether or not you do is moot. I think you've spent enough time with your unnatural hobby. I'd like you to make yourself sociable today so May and Gabriel don't think you're a ghoulish little boy who is obsessed with dead things."

"Dead things are interesting," he protested.

"Regardless, I think you can leave your experiments alone for one day and socialize instead. How much?"

I paid off the taxi driver when he stopped in front of Gabriel's house. A strange man was at the front door, about to ring the buzzer as Brom and I got out.

"Hullo," the man said.

"Hello." I gathered up the bags of shopping from the floor of the taxi, eyeing the man as I did so. He had a long face that I thought of as typically English—not too long, but sort of ruggedly handsome—with dark blond hair and bluish grey eyes.

He examined me just as obviously. "You wouldn't happen to be Ysolde de Bouchier, would you?"

I took a deep breath. "My name is Tully Sullivan."

"That was going to be my other guess," he said, laughing. It was a nice laugh. He looked like a nice man, with a bit of a roguish twinkle to his eye, but still, nice.

"Your husband sent me," he said, taking me completely by surprise. "Name's Savian Bartholomew."

Nice? He was the devil incarnate!

"Gareth sent you?" Brom asked. "How come?"

"You must be Brom. It seems he wants you and your mother kept safe from some very bad dragons until he can come and get you," Savian said.

"Eek! Go away!" I said, shoving him toward the taxi.

"Eh?" he asked, looking confused as he clutched the side of the taxi in order to keep from being pushed inside.

"The gent want to go somewhere?" the taxi driver asked.

"Yes! He wants to go far, far away," I said.

"I do not! Stop shoving me, or I will be forced to subdue you!" Savian said, struggling when I tried to force his head down so I could push him into the cab.

"Sullivan, I don't think that man wants to go anywhere," Brom commented from his location on the sidewalk.

"Yes, yes, what the lad said!" Savian squawked as

I grabbed his ear and managed to get his head inside. "Help! I'm being kidnapped!"

"Just the opposite, actually," I grumbled, grunting as I gave a mighty heave that forced his shoulders in. "Just go already!"

"Never! Why are you doing this?" he yelled, somewhat muffled since I blocked most of the door with my body in an attempt to get rid of him.

"Can't you take a hint, you annoying man? Shoo! I don't want you!"

"But your husband—"

"Is a complete idiot! Now go away before I lose my temper and turn your eyebrows into warts!"

"The lady is crazy," I heard him tell the cabdriver in response to his inquiry about what was going on. "I think she fancies me."

"I'm a great and . . . urgh . . . powerful mage . . . unph! . . . and I will . . . dammit, let go of the door! . . . I will smite you with all sorts of unpleasant spells."

"Help!" Savian said to the taxi driver.

The man watched him impassively. "I would, mate, but I don't like the sound of that smiting."

"She's not a mage!" Savian said, yelping when, desperate to release his hold on the car door, I bit his arm. "Where's your male empathy? Go pull her off me! I'd do it for you!"

"Stop inciting innocent people to help you, or I'll turn your testicles into turnips!" I yelled, head butting Savian's back. "Now get the hell into the cab!"

"I will die before I submit to your brutal ways!"

"Argh!" I bellowed, and was just mentally thumbing through the list of spells I knew that might possibly help me, when the front door opened.

"I thought I heard voices—Ysolde! Who is that you're trying to bend in half . . . *agathos daimon*! Savian? What are you doing here? Don't tell me you've come to work for Gabriel again. I thought that, after the last time, you swore you'd never take another job from a dragon."

"Er . . ." I paused, suddenly wary as May rushed out onto the sidewalk.

"Save me, May! This madwoman is trying to bend me into all sorts of unnatural positions! I think she's already broken my liver and quite possibly one or both intestines," Savian called from the cab.

"You big baby," I said, releasing him as I gave May a feeble smile. "I barely laid a finger on him, honest."

"She didn't even turn his testicles to turnips, like she said she might," Brom offered helpfully. "I would have liked to have seen that."

I narrowed my eyes at him. He grinned back.

"Turnips?" May asked, looking from me to Savian as he unfolded himself from the car, clutching his sides.

"It was all just a little bit of fun," I said, putting my arm around Savian. "Wasn't it, old friend?"

He whimpered and clutched his sides. "My liver! Don't hurt my liver again!"

"You know Savian, too?" May asked.

"Ow! My neck!"

"Too? You . . . uh . . . know him?" I countered, releasing the pincer hold I had on the back of his neck.

"May and I are old friends. She's never tried to hurt me," he said, shooting me a belligerent glare as he shuffled away from me and over to her.

"Oh. Uh . . ." I coughed and tried to think of an excuse to get the man alone for a few minutes. "Isn't that a coincidence. We've known each other for . . . oh, forever."

"I've never seen her before in my life," Savian told May. "Don't leave me alone with her. She's vicious. I think she was trying the Vulcan neck pinch on me."

"Hmm," May said. "Why don't we all go into the house?"

I trailed behind them as they entered the house, thinking furiously.

"So what are you doing here?" May asked Savian as I closed the door behind me.

"Savian!" I said, interrupting the man as he was about to answer. I smiled brightly and took his arm, dragging him toward the room I knew to be a small, unused study. "We have so much to talk about! Why don't we go in here and have a cozy little chat, just the two of us, all nice and private-like."

"Help! She's going to smite my testicles!" Savian shrieked.

"You can bet I will if you keep up all that whining," I said through gritted teeth as he fought me. "Stop struggling and you won't get hurt."

"Famous last words!" he said, trying to pry my fingers off his arm. "Damn, lady, you have a grip like a . . . like a . . ."

"Dragon?" May asked.

"Yeah, like a . . ." He stopped struggling and gave me a long look, squinting at me slightly. "Hey. She doesn't look like a dragon."

"That's because I'm not one," I said, flinging open the door. "Now let's have a little chat about this business."

"What business? Have you hired Savian to do something?" May asked, standing in the doorway.

"Not Sullivan, Gareth," Brom piped up from the hall, unloading the books he had purchased from the bookshop where we'd spent the last hour. "He's trying to save us from some bad dragons."

"Go and play with your mummies!" I ordered, pointing toward the back of the house.

"You said I couldn't!"

"Don't do as I said—do as I say!"

He rolled his eyes and mumbled something about people not making any sense, but he duly trotted away toward the depths of the basement.

"Maybe we'd all better have a little chat," May said, giving me a long look as she entered the room. "I'd like to hear about the bad dragons."

"Who is bad?" Gabriel asked, following her in. "Savian! What brings you to our humble abode?"

I sighed and slumped into a heavy leather chair. "Well, I tried."

"Yes, you did. Despite your best attempts at mutilation, my liver will live another day," Savian said, groaning pitifully as he eased himself onto a long, low leather couch.

Gabriel looked at May. "What's wrong with him?"

"Evidently Ysolde was trying to turn his testicles into warts."

"Eyebrows to warts, testicles to turnips," I corrected wearily. I lifted a languid hand toward Savian. "Go ahead. Tell them. Ruin what remains of my life."

He ignored me, speaking to Gabriel. "I was sent to rescue a fair maiden and her small bundle of boyish joy from the clutches of a gang of murderous dragons. No one told me that the maiden had the strength of a dragon, and an unnatural interest in my balls."

"I have no interest in your balls. I never had an interest in your balls, other than wanting them to go away, preferably with you attached."

"Our clutches?" May said, looking appalled.

"It's not like it sounds," I said hurriedly, before she and Gabriel were insulted.

"Who hired you?" May asked Savian.

"Man by the name of Gareth Hunt."

I glared at him, and his hand moved protectively over his crotch.

"Why would your husband feel you needed rescuing?" Gabriel asked in a soft, completely misleading voice. The air positively crackled with anger.

"You see what you've done? Are you happy now? Everyone is mad at me," I told Savian.

"When you go around threatening to smite people's balls, I don't blame them!"

"Ysolde?" Gabriel asked, clearly expecting some sort of an explanation.

"I'm going to remember you," I told Savian before I turned to Gabriel. "Gareth called me a few days ago, and warned me that I was in danger if I continued to stay with you. I told him that you had been nothing but generous and attentive in your care of me while I was asleep, and even brought Brom to me, but he . . . well, Gareth is very single-minded. Once he gets an idea, he clings to it with the tenacity of a terrier with lockjaw. I assure you that I have absolutely no complaints about your hospitality, and I do not intend to be stolen away. That's what I was doing when May found us. I was trying to get rid of this annoying man."

"I am roguishly charming, and not at all annoying!" Savian protested.

May and Gabriel exchanged a loaded glance.

"Fine, you're the most charming man I've ever met. Now please consider yourself unemployed. You can keep whatever my husband paid you—he deserves to lose the money for doing something like this against my wishes."

"Since you are at a loose end," Gabriel said to him, opening the door and gesturing, "perhaps I could speak to you about doing a little job for us. Ysolde believes she's seen Baltic in town, and I'd like for you to find him."

"I'm not going to get my head bashed in again, am I?" Savian asked, grunting as he rolled off the couch and onto his feet. He slid me a glance as he followed Gabriel out of the room. "Or my liver ruptured?"

The door closed quietly behind him.

I looked at May. "You think he can find Baltic?"

"He works as a thief taker for the L'au-dela," she answered with a wry little twist to her lips. "That's how I met him. But sometimes he freelances, and he's a very good tracker. If anyone can find Baltic, Savian can. Are you going to be ready to go in an hour?"

I nodded.

"Good. We'll all go down together. It should prove to be interesting, eh?"

She left me with a little smile that made me wonder what she knew.

"Oh," I said three hours later as the car rounded one last gentle curve and cleared the willow and lime trees that formed a half circle in front of a magnificent house. "Oh, my. It's . . ." Words simply failed me.

"I know," May said, sighing as she gazed upon the redbricked front of the Tudor mansion. "Isn't it just? I would try to get it away from Kostya, but I suppose if anyone has a right to it, you do."

"It's perfect," I said, my face pressed to the window as I tried to take it all in. The house itself was perched on a gentle hill, a typical example of Tudor architecture, with a center square tower that rose with stately grace over the rest of the house, mullioned windows, stone quoins, and parapets that seemed to sweep upward to the sky. "Just . . ."

"Perfect," May finished the sentence, nodding her head. "The very words I said when I first saw it. But Ysolde, there's more. There's a maze. And gardens."

"Gardens?" I craned my neck to look around Gabriel, who was sitting in the seat opposite May and me. "Where?"

"Over there. You can just see a little splash of color."

"Ooh," I breathed in a heady sigh.

"Sullivan likes plants," Brom told May with a tolerant look at me.

"She was born a silver dragon. All silver dragons like plants," Gabriel said, opening the door as the car stopped. He held out his hand first for May, then for me. I stepped out and my heart was suddenly lightened.

"I feel like I should be singing," I said, turning slowly in a circle to take in the lovely soft velvety lawns that spread out endlessly before us.

"I know just how you feel. I was the same way," May said.

A yew maze was at the right, casting coolly intriguing shadows in its pathway. To the left of the house was a formal garden, and I took three steps toward it before I remembered I wasn't here to see it.

"Sorry," I said, turning back to the others.

May laughed and said, "Don't worry. We understand."

A second car pulled up behind ours, a sleek antique Rolls-Royce that disgorged Aisling, Drake, and Jim, along with Drake's two redheaded guards.

"Wow!" Aisling said, leaning back to look to the top of the tower. "This is a heck of a house! No wonder you like it so much, May. It's absolutely gorgeous! Is that a maze? Jim! Don't do that right there!"

"When you gotta go, you gotta go," the demon complained, but lowered its leg and wandered off to a less central shrub, saying as it went, "Don't let Ysolde turn into a dragon and go all psycho, or blow up the house, or whatever it is she's going to do, until I'm back."

"You're going to blow up this house?" Brom asked, looking around him with curiosity, but nothing else. "With what?"

"Nothing. Ignore Jim—it's deranged. Your mom isn't going to blow up anything, least of all this house," Aisling said as she started up the low front stairs. The double doors opened and Kostya and Cyrene came out, very much the lord and lady of the manor.

I wanted to shove them both in the pond I'd seen a hint of as we stopped in front of the house.

"You made it, I see," Kostya said somewhat sourly, his gaze flickering between Drake—who I had learned that morning was his brother—and me.

"Shall we go inside?" Gabriel asked, taking May's hand and leading her up the stairs.

I sent one last poignant glance toward the flower garden, my heart crying at the thought of it in the hands of Cyrene. "It wants someone who understands it, someone who will love it and nurture it," I murmured as I slowly climbed the five stairs to the door.

"You OK, Sullivan?" Brom asked, waiting for me at the top. "You look kind of funny."

I smiled and gave his shoulder a squeeze as we entered the door. "I just really like this pl—"

The world went black the second my foot crossed the threshold. I heard voices exclaiming, and someone calling my name, but it seemed to come from a long distance away. I turned away from the blackness, moving back out into the sunshine.

*Another vision*, I thought to myself as I went to the garden without consciously making the decision to do so. *I hope this one doesn't last too long. I'd like to see the garden for real before we have to leave.*

As I reached the area where the garden had been, I realized that something was different this time. For one, the flowers and shrubs seemed to shimmer in and out of focus, and nothing like that had happened in the previous visions or dreams. For another, two people stood in the center of a tangle of greenery. As I moved past a young willow tree, I caught sight of a third person standing to my left, a dark shadow unmoving against a tree. A gardener or workman of some sort, I thought, and dismissed him as I turned back to the couple.

It was me . . . or rather, it looked like me, and I realized with a shock that it was the me of the visions, the person whose experiences I had felt and lived. She was smiling up at a man whose back was to me, but I could tell by the love shining in her eyes that it was Baltic.

I moved around to the other side of the willow, wanting to hear what they said, but not wishing to disturb the vision.

"That's too many," Baltic said, frowning at the me-Ysolde. She poked him in the arm, and his frown melted into a smile. "You'll leave me no room for the house. We'll have nothing but garden."

I looked behind me. The house was there, but like the flowers and shrubs of the garden, it seemed to shimmer and fade in and out of view.

I was seeing a memory of the land as it was before the house and gardens had been built.

"And here, Madonna lilies and pinks, heartsease and leopard's-bane. Campion over there, against the wall, and daffodils and violets down by the pond. On that side, we'll have beds of wallflowers and lavender, marjoram and roses, great long beds of roses of every hue. And we'll have an orchard, Baltic, with apple trees, pears, plums, and cherries, and on the long summer days, we will sit beneath one and I will love you until you fall asleep in my arms. We will be happy here. At least . . ."

A shadow fell over her face. She looked into the distance for a few seconds.

"*Chérie*, do not do this to yourself."

"I can't help it. What if it was true, Baltic? What if I was his mate?"

"Constantine wanted you as all males want you," Baltic said, taking her loosely in his arms. "But you were not meant to be his mate."

"How do you know?" She looked troubled, and I understood the worry and guilt she felt at causing pain in another.

"I just know. If you were to die, I would cease living. That tells me you are my true mate, and no one else's."

"But you don't *know*—"

"I know," he said, catching up her hands and kissing her fingers.

She hesitated, and Baltic smiled and brushed a strand of hair off her face before pulling her past me, toward the place where the house now stood. "Enough of these dismal thoughts. I have something that will please you. I have designed the house. If you approve of it, it will be done by Michaelmas."

"I will get started on the gardens right away," she answered, smiling up at him again. My throat ached at the joy in her face, at the love that shone so brightly in her eyes. "And there I will pledge my fealty to you, surrounded by the sweet-smelling flowers."

He growled something in her ear I couldn't hear, and she ran off ahead of him, laughing, her long hair fluttering in the wind as he chased her out of my sight.

I held on to the tree for a moment, my fingers clutching painfully at the bark, possessed with a sorrow so great it seemed to leach up out of the ground.

A noise caused me to look up, and I noticed the third figure as he took a step away from the tree against which he'd been leaning. He dropped suddenly to his knees, his head bowed, his shoulders shaking as if he'd given in to the most devastating anguish, the grief that racked his body so profound, waves of suffering rolled off him, choking me with his despair and hopelessness. Mindlessly I stepped forward, driven to comfort him by the bond of one living being to another, even knowing as I did that this shadow figure was beyond my reach.

Gravel crunched beneath my foot and the figure looked up, getting clumsily to his feet. He stepped out of the shadows of the trees and my breath caught in my throat, my heart pounding so loudly I thought it would burst out of my chest.

"Ysolde?" His voice was ragged and raw, as if he'd swallowed acid. He stared at me in stark, utter disbelief.

"You're . . . Baltic?" I asked.

My voice seemed to bring him from his stupor. He took a step toward me, stumbling, his head shaking all the while his eyes were searching me, searching my face, trying to tell if I was real or not. "It cannot be."

"I saw you in the park. You *are* Baltic, aren't you?"

"You . . . live?"

"Yes," I said, chills running down my arms. He looked nothing like the man in the visions—except for his eyes. Those were the same onyx, glittering like sunlight on a still pond. "My name is Tully now."

He stopped a few feet from me, reaching out tentatively, as if he wanted to touch me, but was afraid to do so.

"Ysolde?"

A woman's voice called my name. Baltic froze, then whirled about.

"That sounds like May," I said, frowning as I gazed back at the house. "I wonder how she got here?"

"Silver mate!" Baltic spat, running a few yards away from me as if he sought something.

May emerged from behind the tree, smiling as she saw me. "There you are. We've been looking all over for you. We thought something might have happened to— *agathos daimon*! It's Baltic."

"Yes, he is sharing the vision with me," I said. "How is it that you're seeing it, too?"

"Run!" May said, grabbing my arm and pulling me after her as she took to her heels.

"You don't understand. I need to talk to him—"

"Not here in the shadow world," she yelled, her grip like steel on my wrist.

"Ysolde!" Baltic's roar was filled with fury like nothing I'd ever heard.

"This way!" May jerked me brutally as I tried to stop, pulling me so hard I slammed into the side of the car, seeing stars for a few seconds.

"Whoa!" Brom said, hurrying over to me, concern written all over his face. "You just appeared, like, right out of the air! Sullivan?"

"I'm all right. Just a little dazed."

"Baltic is here," May gasped, throwing herself on Gabriel. "In the shadow world. He almost had her. We barely escaped."

"Then he will be"—as Gabriel spoke, the air gathered and twisted upon itself, stretching to form the figure of a man who leaped forward out of nothing—"soon upon us."

"Don't hurt him!" I cried as Gabriel and Kostya both jumped on Baltic. "Let me talk to him—"

"Hold him!" Drake ordered, coming around the far side of the car.

"Oh, man, I can't believe I almost missed this," Jim said, running down the stairs with Aisling right behind it.

"I'll put a binding ward on him," she called as she started to sketch a shape in the air.

"No!" I yelled, catching her hand to stop her. "Why are you people doing this? Stop, all of you! This has to stop!"

Baltic screamed an oath in a Slavic language, shaking off both Kostya and Gabriel. For a moment, for the time it took to pass from one second to another, his gaze met mine. Anger and hope and pain were in it, but before I could blink, he was gone.

"Holy cow," Brom said, his eyes huge as he waved his hands around the spot where Baltic had stood. "I need to learn how to do that!"

"He's gone," I said, inexplicably feeling as if a part of me had just died.

"He's run back into the beyond," Kostya snarled as he wiped blood from his nose. "He is nothing but a base coward. He has escaped us by that means before because he knows only May can follow him."

"Aargh!" I screamed, suddenly filled with the same fury that I knew must have possessed Baltic. I grabbed Kostya by the shirt and shoved him backwards, slamming him up against the car.

"Sullivan?" Brom asked, his voice full of wonder.

"Why did you do it?" I yelled at Kostya, grabbing his hair and banging his head into the car. "You were his friend! He trusted you! And you betrayed him just as all the others did!"

A wildcat landed on my back, biting and clawing and pulling at my own hair.

"Make her stop, make her stop!" Brom yelled, dancing around us as all three of us—Kostya and Cyrene and I—fell to the ground.

It took a moment for them to separate us—Cyrene refused to let go of me until May pried her hands out of my hair—but by the time they did, the strange sense of anger had passed, leaving me shaking and panting with the aftereffects.

Aisling handed me a tissue to mop up the blood from the scratches that Cyrene had left on my face. Brom leaned into me, wordlessly needing reassurance. I hugged him, resting my cheek on the top of his head, fighting the sobs that threatened to shake me apart.

"Well, we wanted some proof that she was Ysolde," Aisling said as Cyrene cooed over Kostya while he gently felt the back of his head. "I guess you could say that was pretty definitive, huh?"

# Chapter Nine

"Do I have to call you de Bouchier now?" Brom asked as I tucked the journal in which he kept his science experiment notes into his backpack.

"No, of course not." I stood up, wanting to hug him again, but I'd already done that, and he had placed a firm "one hug per leave-taking" moratorium on me twenty minutes earlier.

"But that's your name now, right? That guy who appeared used to be your husband before you married Gareth?"

I sighed. There wasn't any way I could deny what life insisted on beating me over the head with. "Yes, I think he was."

Brom leaned in close, his eyes on May and Gabriel as they held a brief confab with Maata and Tipene. "So why is everyone trying to hurt him?"

"It's kind of a complicated story," I whispered back.

"But I'm going to do my best to stop them so that we can talk to Baltic."

"Is he my stepdad now?"

"I . . . we'll talk about that later."

"What's Gareth going to say when he finds out your first husband is still alive?"

I sighed again. "We'll talk about that later, too." I looked up to where Maata and Tipene approached. "I'm not really happy about this."

"We won't let anything happen to him," Maata said, giving Brom a little punch in the arm. He grinned and punched her back. She pretended to flinch, which made him grin all that much harder.

"We were just reunited. I don't like being separated again."

"It is just a precaution, and will not be but for a day or two. Aisling and Drake will take very good care of Brom," Gabriel said in a soothing voice that did nothing but make my jangled nerves more jumpy. "Drake takes his security very seriously now that his children have been born, and I would not be honest if I didn't admit that your son will be safer with them than he would be here should Baltic attack."

I waited until Brom and the two silver bodyguards left, waving with as cheerful a smile on my face as I could put there, but the second the car drove off, I turned on Gabriel. "Why do you persist in the belief that Baltic is going to attack your house?"

He took my arm and escorted me back inside, making sure the elaborate security system that monitored the doors was set. "He's done it before. He blew up our previous house, and destroyed much of the entryway of Drake's. You were there that day—that is how your head was injured."

I touched a little scar in my hairline. I'd wondered how I'd come to get that.

"Now that he knows you are alive, he will put two and two together and arrive at the conclusion that we have taken you in for protection, and he will do everything in his power to steal you from us."

"But that's just the point," I said tiredly, rubbing the headache that throbbed in my temples. "There's no need for him to steal me, as you put it. I want to speak with him. No, I need to—I need to talk to him in order to clear up all the things I don't understand."

"I don't think that would be terribly smart right now," May said softly. "Baltic is . . . I hate the use the word 'insane,' but he's not mentally balanced, Ysolde. You don't remember the things he's done to the silver dragons, to his own people, but Gabriel was there two months ago when they discovered the corpses that Baltic had left when he cut a deadly swath through the blue dragon population."

"No sane being, dragon or otherwise, could have done the things that were done to them," Gabriel said grimly.

His normally bright gaze was dark with remembered pain.

I looked down at my fingers, unable to justify that I was bound to a man who was homicidal.

"You said he looked surprised to see you," May said. "That means he didn't know you were alive, so he's probably frantic to find you now. And you can take it from us that an emotionally upset Baltic does not make for a pleasant companion."

"All I know is that I must have some time to talk to

him. I realize you want to capture him so he can face the charges that are now hanging over my head, but isn't there some neutral ground where we can meet him and talk to him, find out if he really is deranged?"

They were silent for a minute before Gabriel finally said, "I will present that suggestion to the weyr."

What he didn't say was that it would do no good.

I nodded, still rubbing my temples.

"You are fatigued," Gabriel said. "You should rest now. You may have a disturbed night if Baltic chooses to attack tonight."

"Would you like me to send some supper up to you?" May asked.

"Actually, I'm famished. I'd love some food."

"You go upstairs and get into bed, and I'll have Renata whip something up for you."

An hour later I was full of ginger chicken, fresh snow peas, and an intention that I prayed Gabriel and May would never find out. Dressed in jeans and a sweatshirt, I slung my bag over my back, pressed a red button that blinked slowly in a tiny little panel set into the corner of the windowsill, and cautiously opened the window, bracing myself for a siren.

Silence greeted me. I sighed in relief that the switch deactivated the alarm on the window, and peered out. I was three stories up, with no convenient drainpipe, balcony, ivy stuck to the building, or ladder casually leaning against the side of the house. There was literally no way out but to jump to the ground.

"Talk about your leap of faith," I muttered as I sat on the windowsill and swung both legs over the edge. "I just hope to heaven that this works or I'm immortal, because if I'm not, I'm going to be in very bad shape."

I took a deep breath, closed my eyes, and held out my hands as I whispered the light invocation, a spell used to temporarily guard mages from harm. A faint golden glow rippled up my body, skimming the surfaces, leaving me with a familiar tingly feeling that told me I was surrounded by arcane power. "So much for an interdiction, Dr. Kostich," I said somewhat smugly, and jumped off the windowsill.

"Ow." I spat out the bit of dried lawn and dirt and a very startled beetle. "Ow. Dear god in heaven, ow."

The light spell didn't work. That became apparent to me about half a second after I left the windowsill, and just before I hit the ground of the tiny garden spread-eagled and facedown.

I touched my nose, wondering if I'd broken it. "Ow." It wobbled back and forth just fine, so I gathered that it wasn't shattered, as it felt. I sat up slowly, gingerly moving my arms and legs. Everything on me hurt, but nothing seemed to be more than bruised. Either the spell did work after all, or I was immortal.

"Wish I . . . ow . . . knew which it was," I muttered to myself as I got painfully to my feet and limped off around the side of the house. By the time I took a few steps, I was moving a bit easier.

"Now to find Savian," I said as I glanced up and down the street. There was little traffic at this time of night, just a few cars passing. As I started off toward a busy intersection where I hoped to find a taxi stand, a car passing me suddenly slammed on its brakes with a squeal of tires on wet pavement that was painful to the ears.

To my amazement, the car backed up, and a door to the backseat was flung open.

"Get in!" the man who emerged said.

I stared at him in amazement. "How did you—"

*"Get in!"* Baltic didn't wait for me to comply; he simply picked me up and tossed me into the car, following me with a growl to the driver. Before I could pick myself off the floor, I was flung backwards when the car shot off like a rocket.

"Hey!" I struggled to sit upright, allowing the man next to me to pull me upward onto the seat. "That was totally uncalled-for! I am not a sack of potatoes you can just toss around!"

"Under no circumstances do I regard you as a sack of potatoes."

"Good." I gave him the meanest look I had. "If you intend on blowing up Gabriel's house, you can just think again!"

To my surprise, a little smile flickered over his lips. "I see that the centuries have not diminished your desire to tell me what to do, mate."

"I'm not your mate," I said primly, untwisting the sweatshirt that had been whipped around my torso when he'd thrown me into the car. "I may have been in the past, but now my name is Tully, and I would appreciate it if you would call me that."

"Your name is Ysolde de Bouchier, and you are my mate. Why have you sought refuge with the silver dragons?"

I glanced at the driver.

Baltic followed the path of my gaze, and said something in a language I didn't understand.

"I'm sorry. I don't speak Russian."

"That was Zilant, not Russian," he said.

"Well, I don't speak that, either."

"Yes, you do."

"No, I don't."

"You do. I taught it to you myself."

"I'm happy to argue with you about this all night, but honestly, there are approximately a thousand questions I have for you, and we aren't going to get to any of them if we spend all our time on whether or not I know a language."

"I have a solution to that—don't argue with me."

"You are just as bossy as you used to be, do you know that?" I told him, poking him in the chest.

He grabbed both my arms and pulled me over until his nose was a fraction of an inch from mine. "And you are just as argumentative and lacking in respect as you used to be."

We stared at each other for a minute. He narrowed his eyes. He sniffed the air. "Why do you not smell as you should?"

I pushed myself out of his grip, straightening my sweat-shirt a second time. "Well, I am sorry I offend you, but you have no one but yourself to blame for that, Mr. Disappear into the Beyond. Rather than take a bath, I opted to go find Savian in order to force him to find you so I could talk to you, which, I would like to point out, I wouldn't have had to do if you hadn't disappeared like you did."

"You might think it's an afternoon's frolic to face three wyverns bent on your destruction, but I have other ways I'd prefer to spend my time," he said dryly.

I smiled to myself. I didn't remember the Baltic from my dreams having a sense of humor. "All right, I will grant you the right to make a timely escape—they were unfairly ganging up on you. But that doesn't give you the right to make insulting personal comments by telling me I stink."

"I didn't—for the love of the saints, mate! I did not say you stink!"

"You did, too! You said—"

"I said you do not smell as you should, and you do not." He held up a hand when I was about to protest. "You do not smell like a dragon."

"Oh. Well. That's probably because I'm not—hey!"

Baltic lunged at me, burying his face in the crook of my neck. "You smell . . . human."

"I *am* human," I said, my body suddenly coming to life in a way that almost stripped the breath from me. It was as if his touch electrified me, sending little zaps of pleasure down my skin. His hair brushed my cheek, and it was all I could do to keep from grabbing his head and kissing him until he was insensible.

"You are not. You are a dragon."

"No, I'm human. My name is Tully, and I'm human now. I've only just decided to accept the fact that in the past I was a dragon named Ysolde, but now I'm human, and are you *licking* me?"

I couldn't stand it. The feel of him against me, the scent of him, something almost indefinable, like the smell of a rain-washed sky, pushed me close to the edge of my control. When his tongue licked a flaming path along my collarbone, I knew I had to stop him. I heaved him away from me with all my strength.

He licked his lips, an indescribable look on his face. "You taste the same. How is it that you smell differently but you taste the same?"

"How do I know?" I said, shakily trying to regain my wits and keep from flinging myself on him. "I'm still trying to get over the fact that you were dead and now you're not. Where are we going, by the way?"

"I am stealing you from the silver wyvern," he said with great satisfaction.

"You can hardly be said to be stealing me if I come with you of my own accord, not to mention escaping the house to go find you."

"I would expect nothing less from my mate," he said with that same satisfaction.

I sighed, probably for the fifteenth time that day. "I seem to be sighing a lot lately," I commented.

"That is because you were pining for me. Why did you not tell me you were alive?" he demanded.

"Have you always been this arrogant and egotistical?" I asked, then continued quickly before he could answer. "No, don't bother to tell me. The few visions I've had answer that question. I will tell you what I know, but I warn you that it's just going to raise more questions than answers."

It took the whole of the ride to a large house about an hour outside of London for me to tell Baltic what had happened since I woke up in Gabriel's house.

"You knew I was alive but you did not seek me out immediately?" he asked as we stopped outside a gate, the driver punching in a security code.

"People mentioned you, yes, but most of the time, I figured I was nuts and made you up," I answered, watching the driver in order to memorize the code, just in case I ever needed to make a fast escape.

"You are not insane."

"No, I gather that, but if you woke up remembering hardly anything, and having the most vivid dreams of your life about a bossy man who threatened to kill you at one point, what would you think?"

I turned to him, a stab of pain piercing my heart at

the pain visible in his eyes. "Oh, Baltic!" Without thinking I took his hand in mine, pressing it against my cheek. "I wasn't avoiding you. I truly didn't believe you were real until I saw you in the park, and then I knew I had to find you, to talk to you. You have to understand that it's been very difficult to accept that what I was reliving weren't just imaginings, but shadows of the past."

His fingers curled around mine, and he leaned forward to kiss my fingers as we drove up a paved driveway to a rather squat, blocky white Regency-era house covered with ivy on the front. "When I saw you this afternoon—I thought for a moment that I, too, had gone mad."

I smiled and rubbed his knuckles against my cheek. "I had no idea you were real. You were watching the past?"

"Yes. I do sometimes. Usually, it's too painful."

Anguish appeared to rise within him at the memory, and once again, I was helpless against it. I wrapped my arms around him, holding him against the pain, wanting to bring only light to his darkness. "It saddened me, too, seeing them—us—so happy, knowing how things ended."

"Nothing has ended," he said, his mouth moving across my temple with gentle little kisses that almost left me weeping. "You are here now. Life has begun again."

I turned my face into his neck, kissing his pulse point, but saying nothing.

The car stopped in front of the house, and I took a minute to gaze around before allowing Baltic to escort me inside. The grounds were pleasant, if a bit bare of anything but a tennis court and a hint of a swimming pool in the back.

Baltic led me inside, turning back for a moment to speak with the driver. I looked around, curious as to whether this home would be as soul-satisfying as the other. The entry hall was done in shades of white and egg cream, with white tile on the floor, an elegant staircase in white to the right, and a magnificent crystal chandelier. It was very pretty . . . and completely barren of warmth or soul or heart.

"Come," Baltic said holding out his hand, having finished with the driver. I noticed that he, too, set the security alarms before escorting me to a room that opened onto the entryway.

I ignored his hand, needing a little distance to keep my mind—not to mention libido—under control. "So, this is—ack!"

He leaped on me, positively leaped on me, pulling me down onto the couch, his mouth hot on my skin.

"Baltic!" I shrieked, trying to push him off me.

"We will now mate," he announced, just like that was the end of the story.

"Like hell we will!"

He kissed me then, kissed me with enough fire that my feet were burning by the time he was done.

"Whoa," I said, gathering my wits together enough to push him back. "I can't do this. You have to give me some time. Besides, there's something I haven't told you about—"

"There is no time," he interrupted, sliding his hands beneath my sweatshirt. "I must claim you as my mate now, before another can do so."

"Now hold on here a minute!" I seized his wrists and stopped his hands from moving farther. "I agree that we have a lot to talk about, and I'm ashamed to say that I enjoyed that kiss more than I should have."

"There is no shame in what we do," he interrupted again. "We are mated."

"We are not mated. We may have been mated in the past, but that was before you died. I don't know for sure what happened to me, but—"

"You died, as well."

I stopped and stared at him. "You knew that?"

"You died right before me." Pain filled his eyes and he closed them for a moment, his face twisted with re-membered agony. Without thinking, I moved closer, putting my hand on his chest. "I was in the tunnel be-neath Dauva. Kostya had turned traitor and was trying to kill me. I was just about to disembowel him when my heart stopped, and I knew you had been killed, knew that bastard Constantine had finally made good his threat and destroyed you rather than let me have you."

"Constantine killed me?" I asked, goose bumps rip-pling up my arms and legs. "But . . . he said he loved me."

"He swore that if he could not have you, I should not. And without you, I would have no life." His eyes opened and tears filled mine at the depths of pain so visible on his face. I pressed myself against his body, wanting to comfort him, wanting to ease the agony that time did not lessen. "My heart died with you at that moment, and I knew I would not survive. So I let Kostya kill me. It was easier than surviving the few remaining hours I had."

"I'm sorry," I said, blinking back tears.

His mouth brushed mine in a gentle acknowledgment of what I offered. "It wasn't your fault. I know now that you were only trying to stop the war. But you were once my mate, and you will be so again, now, this minute. I must claim you, Ysolde. We must mate as dragons mate, so that all will know you are truly mine once again."

I slipped out of his arms, my stomach sick and cold. "If things were different, if my life had not turned out as it had, I would accept your offer. But there is something you don't know, and aren't going to like."

"What?" he asked, gripping my arms tightly.

"I have a husband. He is an oracle."

Anger flared in his ebony eyes. "You have taken a lover?"

"No, I have taken a husband. Had taken. I don't remember marrying him, and for that matter, don't particularly like him. In fact, I'm planning on divorcing him, because he's a bastard. But I must have had nicer feelings for him at some point, because why else would I marry him?"

A muscle in his neck twitched. "You said your memory has been destroyed. You are not to blame for taking a husband."

"I'm glad you think so, but he is my husband, regardless, and I'm sorry, Baltic. It may not be much of a marriage, but I would be less of a person if I were to be unfaithful. I can't sleep with you until I am separated from him."

"You are my mate," he repeated stubbornly.

"Yes, I think I would be, but I have some moral values, and one of those is to not commit adultery."

The muscle twitched again. "This is not an issue. I will kill this husband who dares claim what is mine, and then you will be able to give yourself to me freely."

I laughed; I just couldn't help myself. He was so earnest, and it tickled my funny bone. "I appreciate the fact that you have absolutely no qualms about killing an innocent man, but that would be even less tolerable to me than straying. No. You will not kill my husband."

"Stop saying that word," he snapped, releasing me to pace the width of the room.

"I'm sorry. I will endeavor not to talk about him." It was an effort, but I managed to keep from smiling.

"I realize that you feel some mortal emotions toward this . . . person . . . but you are a dragon. You are my mate. You must be claimed. It would be dangerous for you to remain as you are."

"Dangerous," I said, skeptical to my toes. I managed to keep from throwing myself on him, knowing if I did, I wouldn't be able to resist him a second time.

"You are a wyvern's mate. If other wyverns were to see you and know you for what you are, they could steal you from me," he said, and I realized that he was deadly serious.

"I hate to break this to you, but unless there are some septs that I don't know about, I've seen all the wyverns. I met them all at the *sárkány*. No one even looked twice at me, at least not in the way you're implying."

"Nonetheless, you could be claimed by another." He paced past me, his hands behind his back. "I can't tolerate that. Once, I let you slip away from me—I have learned from that mistake, and will not do so again."

My heart warmed. I couldn't help it. Oh, he was being arrogant and pushy and domineering, but none of that really mattered, not when I could see the insecurity and fear that he tried so hard to keep from me. "I appreciate the fact that you want to protect me, but it's not necessary."

"Even now they are plotting to take you!" he said stubbornly.

"Who?" I asked, confused.

"The unattached wyverns, Bastian and Kostya. They have seen you, and they want you."

"Oh, for the love of all that's good and glorious! It's flattering that you think every wyvern out there is panting after me, but you're way off the scale here, Baltic. No one gives a damn about me, at least not in that sense. You really do take the cake, do you know that?"

"I have no cake!" he said, deliberately misinterpreting me.

I slapped my hand down on the table, frustrated, amused, and wildly aroused, all at the same time. "Well, that's a shame, because I could sure go for a piece right now."

"If you are hungry, I will feed you," he said somewhat grumpily

"Maybe later," I said with a smile. I looked around the room, examining the few objets d'art scattered around. "This is a very pretty house."

The sitting room was also done in white and egg cream, with beige and white striped overstuffed armchairs, less substantial black and gold Regency chairs, and a honey oak parquet floor.

"It's abominable, but it has an excellent view of the surrounding area, so I will be able to see attackers before they can strike."

I stopped in front of the long fireplace, tipping my head as I examined him. He looked the same as he had earlier—chocolate hair pulled back in a short ponytail, the widow's peak drawing attention to his high brow, his eyes just as piercing as they had been in my dreams. I sensed power about him that I realized with a shock was his dragon fire, carefully leashed, but present nonetheless. "Is that how you think? In terms of people attacking you?"

"Dragons, not people."

"Well, perhaps if you didn't run around slaughtering other dragons, you wouldn't have to protect yourself from them when they seek revenge."

A frown pulled his eyebrows close. "If you are referring to the wars—"

"Actually, I'm not," I said, heedlessly interrupting him. "I'm talking about the sixty-eight blue dragons you killed a couple of months ago."

He said nothing for a moment, pulling a long cream and gold curtain across a floor-to-ceiling window before turning to consider me. "What would you think if I told you that I was not responsible for those deaths?"

"I'd say . . ." I thought for a moment, my lips pursing. "I'd say that everyone believes you are."

He shook his head. "That is not what I wanted to know."

"It's what you asked," I pointed out.

"But it is not what I wanted to know, a fact of which you are well aware." To my surprise, he smiled. "If you had any doubt that you are a dragon, Ysolde, the fact that you avoid answering a direct question should be proof positive."

"You should do that more often."

"Point out reasons why you should recognize the fact that you're a dragon?"

"No, smile."

His smile faded. "I have had no reason to do so."

"Maybe not, but a sense of humor is right at the top of traits I find sexy in a man."

"You already think I'm sexy," he said with arrogant ease, strolling toward me with the same sense of a panther gliding silently down a jungle path that I remembered from the other Ysolde's life.

"In the past? No doubt. But there are a whole lot of sexy men around today." I kept my voice light, striving not to let him hear the smile in it.

He paused, a moment of uncertainty in his face. "You find this other man, this husband, sexy?"

"Gareth? Lord, no." I frowned, wondering about that.

"Then why did you mate with him?"

"Physically, you mean?"

He nodded, watching me with the intensity of a panther, too.

"I don't really know. I must have slept with him at some time. That's what married people do. But . . ." I sat and tried to examine the still impenetrable mass that was my memories. "No. There's nothing there. I can see his face, and I know he's a bastard, and I don't wish to be married to him anymore, but beyond that, it's pretty much a void."

"That is a small comfort," Baltic said with a wry twist to his lips. "What man is it you find sexy, then? Is it Gabriel? You find him arousing?"

I couldn't help but smile at the sudden look of sheer outrage that passed over his face. "Why on earth would you think that?"

"You are a wyvern's mate," he snorted. "He is a wyvern, and you were staying in his house. Did he touch you?"

"Even if he wanted to—and I assure you, he views me as nothing more than a big pain in the ass—May would kill him. And quite probably me, although perhaps she'd let me live because if she killed me, she'd feel obligated to take in Brom."

"Who is Brom?" he asked, his frown back. "Is he yet another man who arouses you?"

"I think lots of men are sexy, but that doesn't mean squat," I said, trying not to laugh again.

"It does to me."

"Pfft. Like you haven't ever seen a woman and thought she was attractive?"

"No," he said in complete seriousness.

I gawked at him, just a little gawk. "Oh, come on, Baltic."

"You doubt my word?" he said, bristling at the implication that I thought he was lying.

"I think you're trying to make me feel bad, yes."

He sighed a very exaggerated sigh, pulling me to my feet. I stepped away immediately, knowing that just being close to him would leave me indulging my carnal desires. "Ysolde, you are my mate. I desire no other woman than you. I would not try to make you feel bad. I would not lie to you, a fact you should know."

"All right, I apologize for doubting your word," I said humbly, moving over to the window. Although my body screamed to be near him, my mind knew it was wiser to put a little distance between us.

"Good. Now tell me where this Brom is so that I might geld him."

I laughed again, amused by the flash of ire in his eyes.

"You laugh at me, woman?" he said, stalking toward me.

I laughed even harder, holding him back with a hand on his chest. "Please do not geld my son."

He blinked at me. "Your son?"

"Yes. Brom is my son. He's nine. I think you will like him. He's a little odd, but very clever, and has an amazing range of interests, including a love of history. I'm sure he'd love to talk to you about the things you've lived through."

A muscle in his neck twitched. "You had my son with another man?"

"No, I had *my* son with another man."

His hands fisted, his face a veritable storm cloud of anger. "By rights he should be mine! You are *my* mate! Any child you bear should be mine!"

"Oh, grow up," I said, tired and suddenly annoyed.

I thought he might explode at that.

"I had Brom nine years ago. Nine years ago! So you can just deal with it, or not, but I warn you, I love Brom with all my heart, and I will not tolerate you treating him as if there is something inferior about him."

"You love *me* with all your heart," he yelled.

"Do you always yell?" I shouted back.

"Yes!" he snarled.

"Fine!" I bellowed.

He was so angry I swear his eyebrows were bristling, and before I could finish my sentence, he was on me again, his arms as hard as the oak floor beneath us, his mouth hot and demanding and just as exciting as it had been in my dreams. His tongue was everywhere, twirling around my tongue, tasting me, firing my blood with little touches that seemed both gentle and demanding at the same time. He filled my senses, overwhelming me with the scent and taste and feel of him pressed up against me.

And then the fire came. Actual fire, the kind that burns things down. One minute I was kissing him, feeling as if I were on fire, and the next I really was. For a second I panicked, sure I was going to be horribly burned, but just as I was about to fling myself away from Baltic's fire, an amazing thing happened—something inside me shifted. It was as if the entire world seemed to go slightly out of focus for a moment, then snapped back to its normal clarity.

The fire that threatened to char my skin suddenly danced along it instead, leaving me with a sensation of warmth, but nothing more. Well, nothing more that was harmful—it also fired up the burn inside me to new levels, until I wiggled against Baltic, doing a seductive little dance that I'd never done before. He groaned into my mouth as his fingers dug into my behind, pulling me tighter against him as his lips and mouth and dragon fire consumed my every thought.

"You love *me* with all your heart," he growled, his control very close to snapping.

As I told myself that I really needed to stop before things went too far, the words he had spoken sank in through the miasma of lust and love that raged in my brain, settling into a righteous annoyance.

"You know, I really hate people telling me what I do," I answered, biting his lower lip, and not gently, either. I didn't break the skin, because I didn't wish to cause pain, but it was the sort of a nip that would make him take notice.

And take notice he did. "You dare bite me?" He

reared back, shock evident on his face as he touched his lower lip.

"Yes—yes, I do." With my hands on my hips, I took a menacing step forward. "I don't like being told what to do! So you can just stop this Mr. Demanding bit and kiss me properly, or not kiss me at all!"

"Now you are telling *me* what to do!" he stormed, taking a step forward until his chest rubbed against mine. "I don't like it, either. And as for the kiss, Madame Bossy, I will kiss you any way I see fit. I am the wyvern here, not you!"

"Madame Bossy!" I gasped.

Nose-to-nose, we glared at each other until I couldn't help it, and laughed. To my surprise, Baltic's lips twitched; then a rusty chuckled emerged, which cascaded into an outright guffaw.

My heart sang as I watched him laugh until tears wetted the corners of his eyes.

"Ah, *chérie*," he said, putting his arms around me again. "Thus it has always been between us, eh?"

I brushed the hair out of his eyes, my fingers tracing the satiny length of his eyebrow. "I don't remember."

"You are the only one who has ever made me laugh," he said, kissing the corner of my mouth. "You used to say outrageous things, things I would not tolerate from any other dragon. Then when I was ready to throttle you, you'd tickle me, or perform some other silly act to lighten my mood, and make me think that life could not be any better."

His confession touched me, making my eyes burn as I dabbed away the remnants of laughing tears on his lashes. "Many things have changed about me, Baltic, but

I'm afraid I'm still prone to saying outrageous things. Did I hurt you when I bit you?"

"No." His hands slid down to pinch my behind. "But do not do it again."

I giggled.

"You *do* love me with all your heart."

That was a statement, but there was a shadow in his eyes that had me answering quickly, "Yes, I do. I've just met you, and yet I've loved you for centuries. I love both you and Brom."

"Equally?" he asked, pinching me again.

"Yes," I said, keeping my smile to myself.

"You should love me more." His voice had a faintly disgruntled hint to it.

"That, my little periwinkle, is about a toe and a half over the line." I slid out of his arms. It took more than a little effort to do that, since my body badly wanted to stay smooshed up to his, but the way my insides were humming, it was that or give in to him.

"Why do you push me away?" he asked, his eyes hot with desire.

"I . . . you overwhelm me."

"Good."

"No, it's not good. At least, not until things are straightened out with my husband. Now . . . what were we talking about? I've lost track."

"We were discussing your refusal to mate with me," he said, his eyes still smoldering with heat.

I held my tongue, not wanting to make another pass on that particular verbal merry-go-round. "You said you wanted to claim me in order to protect me. That claiming business is just an oath of fealty, isn't it?"

"That is part of it, yes."

"Can we do the swearing without the sex?"

"It is possible, but unheard of."

"Well, you'd better start hearing it, because I will agree to accept you as a wyvern, but I won't have sex with you. Not until I can resolve the issue of my husband. I fully intend to get a divorce from him, but until I have a chance to tell him I want one, to tell him that we are officially separated, there will be no sleeping together."

He dismissed the entire issue with a little wave of his hand. "I will take care of any concerns you have about the mortal."

"I'm not so sure he is mortal," I murmured, thinking back to what Dr. Kostich had said.

"It matters not. He will cease to be a problem." Baltic stood in front of me, a handsome, vital man who had suffered untold centuries of anguish. I touched his cheek, touched the hard planes of his face, tracing my finger along his high cheekbones and around his eyes, those beautiful black eyes that had a slight upward tilt, giving him a faintly Slavic look.

I brushed a strand of hair off his cheek. "How did we both come to be alive again?"

He captured my hand, kissing the tips of my fingers, his eyes never leaving mine. "I don't know how you came to be resurrected. But I will find out, *chérie*. I will find out."

"What do I need to say to swear fealty to you?"

"Whatever is in your heart."

I laughed. "My heart is confused at this point, so I wouldn't look to it for any help. But I ought to be able to come up with something. Let's see . . . I am Tully Sullivan, and I—"

"You are Ysolde de Bouchier. This other name, this mortal name, has no bearing on us," he insisted.

"I happen to like the name Tully—*fine*. I am Ysolde de Bouchier, also known as Tully Sullivan, and I hereby pledge my fealty to you, Baltic . . . um . . . is Baltic your first name or last name?"

"It is my only name. I have no other."

"Oh. All right. That's very movie star, but that's fine. I hereby pledge my fealty to you, Baltic, wyvern of the black dragons. No, wait, that can't be right. Kostya is the wyvern of the black dragons. He was at the *sárkány*."

Baltic swore. "His traitorous hide deserves only to be split on the end of my sword."

"Please tell me you're not going to fight him for control of the black dragons," I said, unable to handle the thought of what I knew would be a huge battle between Baltic and everyone in the weyr.

"By rights I should, but I will not. I am no longer a black dragon."

"You're not?" I looked him over as if that would tell me anything. "What sept do you belong to? Not the silver dragons?"

He shifted into dragon form, his body covered with glittering white scales.

"You're a white dragon?"

"Not white—light," he said as he shifted back, holding out his hand. Light formed there, stretching out to form a white and blue sword. "When I was reborn, I became something new, something not seen before—we are light dragons, you and I, Ysolde. Our dragon form reflects the fact that we encompass all colors, just as light does. We wield arcane magic, which other dragons cannot do. Ours is a new sept, with only the two of us as members."

I digested that. "That sword belonged to Antonia von Endres, didn't it?"

"Yes." He glanced at it. "She gave it to me long ago."

"Why would she give you something like that?" I asked. "That sword is famous in magedom, and although you're not a slacker at arcane abilities, you're not a mage."

He tossed the blade up, catching it on the tip of one finger. It balanced perfectly. "Antonia gave it to me because she said I gave her great pleasure."

"What sort of great pleasure?" I asked, a sudden roar of anger whipping through me so great that it drove off my intention to tell him that Dr. Kostich had asked me to take the sword from him. "Great pleasure as in, oh, I don't know, sex?"

"She was my lover, yes." He frowned, shaking his hand so that the sword dissolved into nothing.

"You screwed her for a sword?" I asked, my fingernails digging into my palms with the effort to keep from shaking him. I knew my anger was unreasonable, but I was powerless to stop it.

"Why are you so angry?" he asked, looking thoughtful all of a sudden. "Are you jealous?"

"Of course I'm not jealous! What do I have to be jealous of? I mean, it's not like the man I just told I loved beyond all reason informed me he's been out bonking anyone who has mage toys, is it? It's not like he just admitted infidelity, oh no! It's not like you're standing right there with your penis all bulgy and poking me"—I gestured at the fly of his pants, which was looking rather strained after our steamy kiss—"and telling me that it's been visiting other women, not because you are seeking another lover, but so you can have a fancy mage sword! It's not like that at all, is it, Baltic?"

He looked delighted, the bastard. "You *are* jealous!"

"You are the most obnoxious, reprehensible, despicable man I've ever met."

"I am a dragon, not a man."

"Gah!" I yelled, and slapped both hands on his chest.

He covered them with his own, doing that lovely rusty chuckle that made my knees go all weak despite the fact that I wanted to knock his block off. "*Chérie*, I remember many times you threatened to emasculate or decapitate me when you believed I was looking at other females, but I had thought the centuries we spent together had eased your suspicions."

"Just tell me this," I said, grabbing a fistful of his shirt. "How many times did you betray me?"

Anger followed surprise in his eyes. "What cause have I ever given you to believe I would do such a thing?"

A horrible silence followed, one that was filled with my brain suddenly pointing out that time actually existed before I met Baltic. "Er . . . you knew her before you met me?"

He sighed, unclenching my fingers from his shirt. "Yes."

"But you never told me she'd given you a mage sword."

"I had no cause to use it," he said, shrugging. "I did not have the skills at that time to wield it. It was only after I was reborn that I was able to do so."

"So you didn't sleep with her after you met me," I said, wanting to make absolutely certain of that point.

"I took no females after I met you." He started to smile, but suddenly looked away.

I pounced on that. "Oh, really?"

He made a vague gesture, a flicker of embarrassment in his eyes. "There was a barmaid in Bordeaux, but I did not rut with her. I tried, but I could not."

"What a goddamned shame," I growled, wanting to punch him all over again.

"She was not my mate. I thought I would ease my lust on her, but I could not. I knew then that I must have you and no one else." He took my clenched fists in his hands, stroking his thumb across the top. "That is when I sent to Constantine to let him know I was claiming you."

The fury inside me melted away into a dull throb. "It's very hard to be angry at someone when he's just told you he can't have sex with another woman because he wants you instead."

"You have no need to be angry. I have not given my-self to another, as you have." His voice was etched with acid.

"I can't help it if I lost my memory and got married. And wait a minute, are you saying that you haven't had sex in"—I did some quick calculations—"over three hundred years?"

"I have not had a female since I met you, no."

I blinked, unable to keep from asking, "Have you had a male?"

He looked outraged. "No! I do not lust after males, as Pavel does. I have been mated, and to a dragon, that bond exists for all time."

"Pavel your guard? He was gay?" I asked.

"That is the mortal term for it, yes. He enjoys both males and females equally."

I picked up on the present tense of that sentence. "Whoa! He's still alive?"

"Yes. He has been in London, but I expect him back shortly. Are you going to accept me as your mate, or not?"

"Er . . . yes. I'm sorry, I was just distracted by the thought of . . . never mind."

He gave me the oddest look. "You were distracted by the thought of Pavel with another male? Do you lust after him?"

"No, of course not! I don't even know the guy. It's just that, sometimes . . . well, you know, sometimes guys with other guys . . . it's just kind of . . . er . . . hot."

I thought his eyeballs might pop right out of his head.

"Hot? You are aroused by males making love to each other?"

"No! Not normally! Just once in a very rare while. It's kind of . . . titillating."

"I see." He didn't look like he saw at all, what with his lips pursed and his arms crossed over his chest.

"You don't ever think that once in a blue moon, it can be sexy?" I asked.

"No." He thought for a moment. "Two females together, yes. That is always arousing. Especially if they are oiled. But males? No."

"Well, see, I don't get the two girls together thing. It just doesn't ring my chimes at all. Does Pavel bring his dates here often?"

He stared at me for a minute. I cleared my throat. "Sorry. None of my business. What were we talking about?"

"You were saying the words of fealty." He paused. "You really are aroused by the thought of two males?"

"Only very rarely! Sheesh! I'm sorry I mentioned it! Let's move on."

He nodded, then asked suspiciously, "You do not wish for me to engage in sexual acts with another man—"

"No! God almighty, Baltic! That's the last time I'm ever going to share a sexual fantasy with you!"

"It's a fantasy of yours, seeing two men together?" he asked.

I walked over to the wall and banged my head against it a couple of times.

"I do not understand you," he said, a thread of puzzlement in his voice. "You have changed since you were resurrected. My Ysolde would never have wanted to see—"

"Enough!" I yelled, storming over to him and punching him in the chest. Hard. "Move past it or I'm walking out of here right now!"

His lips thinned, but he said nothing.

"Thank you. Now, I suppose I should start over, shouldn't I?" I stopped, pursing my lips as I looked at him. "You're still thinking about it, aren't you?"

"No." Five seconds passed. "Is it the thought of the men engaged in the sexual act itself, or some other facet—"

"Argh!" I yelled, and ran out of the room, out of the hall, and out of the house.

# Chapter Ten

Eventually I made the oath, outside under the stars, with the light breeze wafting around us.

"Are you sure you do not wish to mate?" Baltic asked politely as soon as he confirmed the oath, swearing to honor and protect me above all others. "I know how you like to be outside. We could do it out here, if you like."

I chuckled to myself. "Thank you, but until I have a chance to talk to my husband, sex will be out."

A sly look came into his eyes as he slowly pulled me over to his body. "There was another time when you refused to let me bed you, and yet we still managed to bring exquisite pleasure to each other."

"Yes," I said, unable to keep my mouth from moving toward his. My lips brushed his with a wanton display of need. "I very much enjoyed that dream."

"It was not a dream, *chérie*," he murmured against my mouth, his hips moving with persuasive sweeps against mine. "It happened. It can happen again."

"Except this time, I'm not a naïve seventeen-year-old who doesn't know what she's doing," I said, moaning softly when his mouth moved over to my neck, his lips burning my flesh, but it was a good burn, a heat that set my entire body alight.

He pulled back for a moment, his lips curling at the edges. "You knew what you were doing by the time we reached France."

I shared the smile until I felt his hands on the waistband of my jeans. I covered them with mine. "Baltic . . . I'm sorry. I can't. It's . . . there's too much up in the air. I'm not comfortable doing this with you until I talk to—"

He covered my mouth with his, stopping the words. "I won't do anything you do not desire, *chérie*. But you have spoken the words of fealty, and you are now my mate. You must bear the mark of my sept."

I held on to his shoulders as he unzipped my jeans, sliding his hands over to my hips, pushing the material down. "Just where exactly do you intend to put this mark?"

He grinned as he cupped me intimately, his thumb rubbing on my pubic bone. "I thought here."

"Well, you can bloody well think again!" I said, squirming against him nonetheless.

"Here?" He touched the crease of my thigh.

"That would hurt like hell. No."

"How about here?" He pulled me to him, his hands on my butt, giving my cheeks a little squeeze.

"I'm thinking that's fairly disrespectful, don't you?"

He gave a mock sigh, then whipped off my sweatshirt before I could protest, nuzzling my breasts. "Then it will have to be here."

"Over my heart?" I thought about that for a moment. It pleased me. "All right. Wait—don't you have one?"

"I was the only member of the sept until you accepted me. You will have to give me the mark."

I was about to tell him I hadn't the slightest clue how to go about doing that when he opened his mouth and breathed fire on me. It hurt like the dickens for about two seconds; then the heat soaked into me, swirling around until it settled in my groin, pooling in places that hadn't been pooled in for centuries. I looked down to see my bra gone, and Baltic licking my left breast, a strange swirly symbol burned into the flesh. As I watched, the redness of it faded until it was the same color as the mark on my hip—a sort of dark tan.

"Now you have been marked as my mate, although I would appreciate it if you didn't show people," he said, kissing my breast. "Your form, although apparently human, pleases me, and I do not wish for others to ogle you."

I thought seriously of throwing everything to the wind—Gareth, my moral values, decency—and just letting Baltic make love to me until the sun rose high above us. "I wish I could make love to you," I said, gasping when he took my nipple in his mouth. My fingers dug into his shoulders.

"I will if you desire it," he murmured, rubbing his cheek against my breast.

"I can't," I said, pulling his face up to mine. "I shouldn't even be kissing you. That's wrong, too."

"Nothing is wrong between us. But if you do not wish for me to do that, then I will not," he said, sucking my bottom lip.

"I think that would be best," I said, my fingers caressing the long sweeps of muscles in his shoulders. "Until things are worked out."

"Then I will not pay homage to your magnificent breasts, either," he mumbled, his mouth kissing a wet, steamy trail down to my chest.

"That would definitely be over the line," I said, my back arching of its own accord as he swirled his tongue around my nipple, the latter so tight and hard it positively ached with the need for his touch. I groaned again, gripping his shoulders as he tormented first one breast, then the other with long, hot strokes of his tongue.

"Were you to give yourself to me, I would bathe your sublime belly with fire," he said, pulling me down to the ground.

"But I haven't, so you won't," I said, threading my fingers through the cool silk of his hair.

"Of course not." Baltic lifted his head from where he was kissing the curve of my hip, and breathed fire on my stomach. It shimmered along my skin until it was absorbed back into his mouth as he laved a path to the other hip.

"The memory of your scent and taste has driven me almost mad with desire," he murmured into my pelvic bone, his hands gently pushing my underwear down over my hips. "The idea of experiencing it again fills my thoughts."

"That would be far too wrong to do now," I said, my eyes almost rolling back into my head when his tongue flicked across secret, intimate parts of me, parts that tingled with awareness and a need that I couldn't allow.

"I will not taste you, then," he said just before his mouth possessed me in a way that had me clutching the grass, my hips thrusting up against him.

"Thank you for not doing that," I gasped, almost coming off the ground when he sank a finger into me.

"You are so hot, *chérie*. Tell me you burn only for me."

"Only for you," I repeated, mindless with passion and desire now, wanting him like I'd never wanted anything, tears leaking from the corners of my eyes as I struggled with my conscience.

He moved over me, his clothing gone, the hard lines of his body pressing me down, into the earth. I felt him rub against my inner thigh, a hot brand that my body wept for. He framed my face in his hands, kissing me with a long, slow stroke of his tongue against mine.

"Let me love you, Ysolde. Let this happen. Since I was reborn, I have lived every moment in despair because I lost you. Let me worship you now as I've longed to do all those years."

I held on to him, sobbing now. "It's wrong, Baltic. I'm married to another man."

"You don't even remember marrying him. Perhaps you were forced. Will you remain faithful to a man who would so abuse your trust?"

"I don't know," I sobbed, wanting to shift my hips and allow him entrance into my body. I wanted him with a fever that threatened to consume me. "I don't know."

He rolled off me, and I curled up into a ball on the grass, crying for my lost memory, crying for the years that Baltic spent alone. Warmth covered me as he curled himself around me, keeping the cool night air from my naked flesh, comforting me despite his own pain.

"Thank you," I said when I had managed to bring my emotions back under control. I turned to face him and gently pushed the hair from his cheek. "Thank you for protecting my honor, even when I was willing to forgo it."

"You are my mate. I could never force you to do anything you did not want."

I stroked my hand on his chest, the sensation of the soft black hairs making my fingertips tingle. "When I give myself to you, Baltic, I want it to be all of me. I don't want my ties to another man to be there between us, tainting it, tainting the beauty of what we will have."

He looked down at me, the light of an almost full moon bathing the planes of his face in harsh shadows, but his eyes glowed with an obsidian inner light. Slowly he nodded, and touched my lower lip with his thumb. "You were always thus. You never did anything halfway—it was with your whole heart, or not at all."

"I sound like I was very annoying," I said with a little self-conscious grimace as I sat up to retrieve my clothing.

"Not annoying—honorable." He watched me dress, arrogantly naked, still aroused. "It irritated me at the time, but I learned to live with it."

I couldn't help but laugh at that as I finished dressing. I eyed him, guilt pricking away at my scruples. "I feel guilty about that," I said, waving at his penis, which was in no way returning to a more quiescent state.

He pursed his lips as he looked at it. "Why?"

"I more or less led you on. There's a term for that, and I'm appalled that it is applicable to me. Would you . . . I feel ridiculous even saying this after the big scene I just made, but would you like me to take care of it?"

"Yes," he said so fast I laughed again. I sank to my knees next to him, laying a hand on his thigh. "You would do this for me? It would not violate your sense of duty and honor?"

"It does, but not as much as the guilt of what I allowed to happen."

He shook his head, rising up on one elbow and catching my hand as I reached for him. "You did not *allow* me to touch you, Ysolde; I wished to seduce you. I did everything I could to sway you to that goal."

"And I enjoyed every minute of it," I said, slipping my hand from his. "Deep down, I knew if I told you to stop and really meant it, you would. And you did. So we are both to blame for how far things got carried, and although I would never do this for another man, although I feel I am still bound to my husband until I can tell him otherwise, you are the man I would choose to be with. For that reason, I wish to repay your kindness to me with a little kindness of my own."

"It is not kindness," he said as I bent over him, swirling my tongue around the very tip of him. He fell back, his eyes crossing as his hips thrust upward. "It is ecstasy."

"I have to get back to Gabriel's house."

"No."

My shirt went flying.

"They're going to be wondering what happened to me. I don't want them to worry. I have to go back."

"No."

My pants joined my shirt. I stood with hands on hips as I glared at Baltic, who was still naked, and quickly returning me to that state. "I can see where this is going, and it's not going to happen. I will sleep alone tonight."

"No."

My bra arced through the air, landing with a whisper on my shoes.

"Why on earth did I ever think you were a reasonable man?" I cried, slapping my hands on my legs.

He looked up from where he was about to remove my panties, honestly surprised. "I don't know. I'm not reasonable."

"I'm glad you admit that. Baltic, I'm not going to sleep with you."

"You are my mate," he said, yanking the last of my clothing off, and scooping me up in his arms at the same time. He carried me over to a large bed, covered in a quilt of white and gold. "I will not make love to you, but you will sleep with me from this night forward."

"That's going to be a little bit difficult to explain to Brom," I said, sliding beneath the cool linen sheets. For tonight, I saw no purpose in demanding he return me to Gabriel's house. Everything would come out in the morning, since I couldn't hide from either Gabriel or May the fact that I'd found Baltic. Besides, the reconciliation between Baltic and the weyr had to start at some point, and I'd much rather that it began sooner than later.

"Where is this child who should be mine, but who is not?"

"He's with Aisling and Drake because Gabriel insisted that you were going to attack his house. And just so you know—love me, love my son."

He snorted. "I was going to rescue you from Gabriel until I saw you outside."

"Nice change of subject," I said, amused. "But it's not going to change anything. Besides, Brom is a good kid. You'll like him."

"I will not," Baltic said grumpily, and lay down with his arms crossed.

I leaned over him and raised an eyebrow.

"I will tolerate him because he is of your blood, but no more," he conceded.

I slapped a hand down on his chest, and tapped my fingers. "I would hope that once we are free, you will take an active role in his life as a loving, supportive stepfather."

His expression was mutinous. "You ask me to raise this child of another man as if he were my own?"

"Yes. I expect you to love and cherish him. Brom deserves that. His own father doesn't give a damn about him."

He gritted his teeth. I narrowed my eyes. We made quite a pair.

"Very well," he finally snapped, rolling over onto his side so all I saw was his back. "I will do so, but that is the last concession I will make to you! I am the wyvern. You are the mate. It is you who must yield to me from this moment on."

I smiled and snuggled into his back, feeling a weight lift from me that I hadn't been aware of. Things were going to work out all right despite the overwhelming odds. I could just feel that they were.

Fire raged in and around and through me.

"This has got to end!"

"There is only one way it will end—my way!" A shadow flickered through the flames, a black shadow of the man I loved so dearly, and who was destroying not just his beloved sept, but my heart as well.

"Baltic, you will not win! You have decimated your own ranks trying to beat Constantine into submission, but it is for naught! And now that the green dragons have sworn to aid them against you, it is doubly foolish to pursue what is nothing more than a stupid rivalry!"

"Rivalry!" Baltic snarled and stalked across the room of our bedchamber, grabbing my arms in a painful grip. "He has tried to steal you from me. Three times he has tried! He is out there now, rallying yet another force to try to bring down Dauva so that he might take you. Is your love for me so fleeting that you would wish to see both Dauva and me destroyed?"

"You are being overly dramatic once again."

He spun away from me as I spoke, staring out of the narrow window to watch the countryside as if he expected to see a wave of silver dragons at the foot of the castle.

I looked at him, this man I loved, and knew that something would have to be done to stop him. The course he was taking was one of madness, one that could have no good end.

"My love, you know I have chosen you above all others," I said, sliding my arms around his waist and leaning into his back, pressing my cheek against it to hear his heart beating so strong and true. "You are my life, Baltic. I do not want to be Constantine's mate any more than I want this endless war to continue. You must find a way to end it, to make peace amongst the weyr. You are the only wyvern strong enough to do it."

"There can be no peace for me so long as Constantine lives."

"The war between you and Constantine is private, but the results of it are going to tear apart the entire weyr. This war did not begin with me, and I will not have it end with me!"

He turned, the muscles in his jaw tight, his eyes blazing with black fury. "What would you have me do? Go to Constantine with my tail between my legs and beg him to spare the black dragons? Would you have him absorb our sept into his without so much as a whimper? Would you have him strip everything from me?"

"The silver dragons have been autonomous for over a century now," I argued. "You never sought to force them to rejoin this sept until Munich!"

Baltic snarled an invective. "That was the day I knew the true depths of his treachery. To steal you two days after you had been brought to bed—"

Pain laced through my insides at the reminder. I looked down, tears welling in my eyes at the memory of that time. My poor little babe who did not live through the birth. Baltic grieved the loss as much as I did, but he did not see the truth behind the tragedy. I knew it was a sign that I should not bring life into a world that was filled with so much hate, while he went almost mad with rage and an intense need for revenge.

He stopped speaking, taking me in his arms and holding me so I could weep silently into his chest. "There will be other children, *chérie*. I swear to you there will."

"There won't be if there is nothing left for them," I said, looking into his eyes "You are using the war as an excuse to hurt Constantine. It has to stop, Baltic, or there will be nothing left for us."

"Do you have so little faith in your own sept?" he asked, his arms tightening around me.

"I have only faith in the black dragons, but you are not being honest with them."

He pulled back, strapping a leather scabbard around his waist. "We are at war. They know that."

"But you are allowing them and everyone else to believe you have some grandiose plan for domination over all the septs. You should ask yourself why you are so hesitant to tell them what your true purpose is."

Fire flashed in his eyes, manifesting itself in tangible form as it twisted up my body. "I will do anything to keep you safe. Anything!"

"Including sacrifice innocent lives? It isn't right, Baltic! If I didn't know better, I'd say you were mad!"

A slight noise heralded the arrival of Pavel, who stood in the open doorway, his eyes watchful. "My pardon for interrupting. All is ready. Do we ride?"

"Yes." Baltic bent down to kiss me, his lips sweet, but my heart broke nonetheless. "You will be safe here, *chérie*. No one has ever breached Dauva, and no one ever will. I will send word to you as soon as I can."

"Don't go," I said, knowing it would do no good.

"Constantine approaches Warsaw. I can't let him cross the Vistula."

I bowed my head for a moment while he slid his sword into its scabbard. "If you will not stop this war, then I will," I warned as he strode across the room to the door.

He paused and looked back at me, a question in his eyes.

"I will bring together the five shards of the dragon heart, and I will use them to end this battle between you and Constantine."

"The rumors about the dragon heart are grossly exaggerated," he said simply, and left. Pavel gave me a thoughtful look before turning to follow him.

"Stay safe, my heart," I whispered even as my own was shattering.

It took me two weeks to travel to Paris from Riga. The city was still in a shambles; the plague that had been triggered by the dragon war a century before continued killing mortals without prejudice. Rotting corpses of nobility and serfs alike festered in the streets, the stench almost unbearable. Outside of the city proper, the air was a bit cleaner, although carts laden with the dead rumbled by with a frequency that was unnerving.

From the safety of a clump of birch trees in Montfaucon, I watched the small group of people gathered, three men and a woman. One man I recognized. The other two—one blond, one dark-haired—were strangers, as was the woman, who was clinging to the dark-haired man in a manner that bespoke of intimacy. The dragons spoke together for a moment. I stepped out, wary lest the plea Kostya had made was some sort of a trap.

"We were not sure you would come," he called to me as I made my way through the boggy ground to where they stood on a small hillock. The woman squawked when one of the men disengaged her from his person and tried to shoo her away.

I accepted the hand Kostya held out to help me over the remains of an uprooted tree. "You knew I was in Paris. Why wouldn't I meet with you?"

"Come back to the inn with me," the woman cooed to the tall, dark-haired man. She was all but falling out of her bodice, and the look she gave him would be clear to a blind man.

"Go away, woman. I told you that I have business to attend to," the man answered, trying once again to shoo her away.

"With her?" the woman asked, glaring at me.

"Yes, but not the sort you understand. Leave me now or you will make me angry."

"What will you do if I don't?" she asked coyly, trailing her fingers up his arm. "Will you paddle my bottom?"

"No."

"Then what?" Her hand moved around to the front of his breeches.

He turned and breathed fire on her.

She ran screaming from the field, the hem of her skirts smoking.

"Mortals," the dark-haired man said in a disgusted tone, and proceeded to turn his attention to me. Both he and the second man eyed me with frank curiosity. I returned the compliment.

"This is Allesander de Crovani," Kostya said. "He is the younger brother of Mercadante Blu, the wyvern of the blue dragons."

Allesander made a bow, his light blue eyes watching me with amusement. He was slightly taller than me, had hair almost as pale as my own, and was slight of figure, but I sensed strength in him that I would not underestimate.

I murmured the polite responses and was introduced to the third man, the fire-breather. "This is *my* brother, Drake Fekete. He is heir to Fodor Vireo."

I looked at the man in surprise. "You are not a black dragon?"

"No." He had a different sort of accent, one that reminded me of Eastern Europe. He shared Kostya's height and general coloring, but his eyes were a pure, brilliant green. "Our grandmother was a reeve. She mated twice."

"I see. And Kostya is Baltic's heir . . . how unique it

will be to someday have wyverns of two different septs in the same family. Does it cause competition between you and Kostya?"

"Only with women," Kostya said, shooting his brother an irritated look.

"There is no competition," the latter said with blithe indifference.

"True words." Allesander laughed, giving Kostya a little nudge. "The women all go for Drake and give your scowls a wide berth, eh?"

I had no doubt of that. Drake seemed like the ultimate lady's man, if the tavern wench was anything to go by. "Do your wyverns know you are here?"

Both men nodded. "Merca wishes for an end to this battle between septs," Allesander said stiffly. "If you can bring it about, you will have the gratitude of the blue dragons."

"And green," Drake said quickly. "We, too, are tired of fighting our brother septs. We wish for peace in the weyr once again."

"I'm surprised the war continues if everyone is so desirous of its end. Certainly the mortals must be praying peace will return to the dragons," I said softly.

"It would end but for your mate and Constantine," Allesander said with an edge to his voice. "If they would settle their differences, we could band together and force Chuan Ren into an accord. But divided as we are . . ." He shrugged and looked away.

"Then we shall have to pray that the dragon heart can do what the dragons themselves cannot," I said, glancing at Kostya. "Baltic does not know I am here, but he is suspicious of your absence. I fear that he may discover I have come to Paris."

His eyes held mine with a fervor that made me uncomfortable. "We will have to risk that. Do you have the Modana Phylactery?"

"Yes." I touched a spot on my cloak. Beneath it, the phylactery hung between my breasts. "I have it with me. Were you successful with Chuan Ren?"

"I was." He reached into his doublet and removed a small box. "This is the Song Phylactery."

"I shudder to ask what it cost you to borrow it."

He grimaced. "It's better if you don't know."

I turned my attention to the other two men. "I take it that you have your respective septs' shards, as well?"

Both men nodded.

I raised my eyebrows as I glanced at Kostya. "Then all we are missing is the shard belonging to the First Dragon. Do you know where the Choate Phylactery is?"

"Yes. I have it, as well."

"How did you get that?" I asked, amazed. From what Baltic had mentioned over the last two centuries, the Choate Phylactery's whereabouts had been unknown since the weyr had formed.

He looked away. "That is another thing you don't want to know."

On the contrary, I very much wanted to know, but now was not the time to pursue such an intriguing subject. "Then nothing is stopping us from doing it now," I said, my palms suddenly damp at the thought.

"No." Kostya turned to a small satchel on the ground. He pulled out a wool cloth and spread it out, gesturing toward it. I knelt on one corner and removed my cloak, shivering a little in the cool morning air as I pulled the gold-chased vial housing the dragon shard from beneath my chemise.

One by one, the other dragons knelt at the remaining three corners of the blanket, each removing from their safekeeping the phylacteries that bore the precious shards.

"Baltic never told me much about the shards," I said nervously, rubbing my palms on my skirt before placing the shards in a line before me. "All he said is that there are five of them, and that together, they make up the dragon heart, the most powerful relic known to dragonkin. What exactly is the dragon heart? And why does it have so much power? It can't really be the actual heart of the First Dragon, can it?"

Kostya shrugged.

"I know less than you do about it," Allesander said. "All I have been told is that it is too powerful to remain whole, and thus it was broken into shards and placed with each sept for safekeeping. Except the silver dragons, but that is only because your sept was not formed when the heart was first sharded."

"So I gathered. Drake, do you know anything about it?"

Drake glared over my head to a point in the distance. I turned to look. Three women were clustered together at the edge of the bog. All three waved and giggled when they noticed he looked their way.

"I take it you're not mated," I said, unable to keep from smiling despite my nerves.

He snorted. "Nor will I be, if I have a choice. Women are good for one thing only, and I don't need a mate to get that."

"Evidently not." The women clutched each other and giggled more, waving and calling to him, trying to tempt him over to them. I looked again at the shards, touching each one of them, hoping against hope that I would be able to do what needed to be done. "Well. Shall we get started? Do you have the words, Kostya?"

"I have them," Allesander said, pulling out a piece of battered parchment. He handed it to me, grimacing at the large blots on it. "I'm not very good at writing, but I took it down just as I heard it from Merca."

"It's in Zilant," I said, deciphering with some difficulty the handwriting on the parchment.

"Yes. You speak that, don't you?"

"I've picked up a little over the last century." I read silently for a moment. "All right, shall we try?"

"I would prefer that you succeed rather than merely try," Kostya said, his face grim. "There will be no black dragons left if we do not stop your mate."

Guilt weighed heavily on me. "I've tried to stop him, I truly have."

"This war is not your doing," Drake said, his arms crossed over his chest as he knelt across from me. His eyes were almost like a cat's, so brilliant were they.

"I did not start it, no, but it continues because . . ." I hesitated, wanting them to know the truth, but wary lest they use that information against Baltic somehow. Drake and Allesander said their respective septs desired peace, but could I trust that? The dragons had been warring for over a hundred years, and I was no longer sure whom I could trust.

"It continues because Constantine, Baltic, and Chuan Ren will not be happy until there are no dragons left but their own," Kostya said bitterly, making a sharp gesture.

"That's not true. Baltic does not desire the elimination of other septs. . . ." Their expressions told me it was useless to continue. I sighed and placed the shards before me. "The sooner we do this, the sooner we can have peace. Let us begin."

The Zilant words were unfamiliar on my tongue as I spoke them, awkward and jarring to the ear as I made an invocation to the dragon heart. The air grew thick and heavy over the shards as they started to vibrate, a hum coming from them that grew louder as I spoke. I watched them with some wariness, not sure what would happen when the heart re-formed, and wanting to be ready to wield it.

As the last word fell heavily from my lips, the hum from the shards ceased, and all was silent for two beats of my heart. We held our respective breaths as the shards seemed to emit a light that twirled and spun around itself, taking the phylacteries with it. It grew brighter and brighter until it blinded me. I turned my head to avoid looking at it, but was compelled to turn back when a face began to form in it, the face of a dragon, one who was as brilliant as the light itself. The dragon's eyes were filled with the knowledge of all times, as old as the earth itself, the past, present, and future all mingling together in their depths. I knew without a doubt in my mind that I was looking at the First Dragon, he who formed the septs and weyr, the creator, the father of every dragon who lived, and who would ever live.

The First Dragon looked at me, searing a path straight down to my soul, his eyes closing slowly, but not before I saw a profound sadness in them that made me want to fling myself forward and weep until I had no more tears.

The spinning mass of shards exploded in a nova of blue-white light that seemed to pierce us, passing through our bodies and minds and souls until it was the only thing that existed, and we were no more.

Two hours later I stood at the inn and watched as the small band of five black dragons I had brought as guards saddled our horses. Kostya stood next to me, watching silently.

Female squeals of delight came from the inn. I glanced over my shoulder. Drake had his arms around the three women who had waited so patiently for him at the bog, escorting them upstairs to a room where he would no doubt partake of their wares. I had already bid him farewell, as I had Allesander.

"What would you like me to tell Baltic?" I asked Kostya, returning my gaze to the yard.

"About the shard?" He glanced at my chest.

I touched the spot about two inches below my breastbone where a small diamond mark now resided. Inside me, the shard that had once belonged to the First Dragon thrummed with a life of its own, the shard mourning with me for the future that I feared would come to pass. "No, although I don't understand how you can be so sure that the shard's rightful owner will not be distressed that I am now the phylactery for it. I would be happy to explain to whoever it is, if you give me the name—"

"I told you the responsibility was mine," he said, a flicker of something in his eyes causing me to wonder. "I will deal with the owner. You have no need to fear that she—"

"She?" I asked as he bit off the word and looked suddenly furious. "By the rood! This shard belongs to Chuan Ren?"

"Belonged," he said, shooting me an annoyed glance before turning his glare onto the courtyard.

"Why would she give you both shards?" I asked, shaking my head.

His jaw worked for a few seconds; then he said, "She didn't."

"The green dragons are renowned thieves," I said, as a few facts slid into place. "Your brother is a green dragon. You had Drake steal the shards from Chuan Ren, didn't you?"

His shoulder twitched. "The Song Phylactery will be returned to her."

"But not the Choate Phylactery," I pointed out, amused despite the situation. Chuan Ren would be livid when she found out. I would have to warn Baltic that she would likely wish to reclaim the shard.

"That can't be helped." Kostya took a deep breath and turned to me, his face hard and unyielding. "I wish things were different, Ysolde, but you must realize that I cannot stand alongside Baltic any longer. You must see that."

Sadness gripped me at his words. "You of all people know why he is continuing the war. You are his oldest friend, his most trusted guard. If we could reason with him together, if we could make him see that Constantine is not really a threat—"

"But he is," Kostya interrupted. "In that I wholeheartedly agree with Baltic. The silver dragons are a threat to every black dragon. They must return to us, or we will face an eternity of destruction."

"You said earlier today that Baltic was unduly perpetuating the war, and now you insist that he continue to do so? You don't make any sense, Kostya."

"There is a difference between trying to retake what is ours, and attempting to control the entire weyr."

"You know full well that Baltic has no desire to take over all the septs," I said, disgusted with his stubborn refusal to admit the truth.

"No?" He gave me a long look. "Ask yourself why he does not simply kill Constantine and bring the silver dragons back into the weyr."

"I will not argue about this anymore; we've both said everything there is to say." I sighed. "My concern is for the immediate future. Are you sure you don't wish to return with me? Surely peace would be worth trying to reason with Baltic again."

"He is past the point of listening to reason, and I will not have the last few black dragons slaughtered for no purpose. Ysolde—" He bit off what he was going to say, hesitating before finally saying, "You must be aware of what is in my heart. I loved Baltic as a brother, but I cannot let him destroy our world. Either he will stop, or I must stop him, by whatever means possible."

Fear gripped my stomach at the deadness in his eyes.

"You would destroy us," I said simply.

"If that's what it takes to stop him, yes." Kostya took my hand and bowed over it. "You will be well enough to travel?"

"Yes," I said, the world suddenly bleak and lifeless.

"What will you tell Baltic?"

"The truth." I met his gaze and carefully pulled my fingers from his. "I will tell him the truth."

# Chapter Eleven

"Good morning. Suzanne, isn't it? I don't know if you remember me, but I'm Tully Sullivan. I've come to fetch my son, Brom."

"I could not easily forget you, Ysolde," the green dragon said as she smiled and stood aside so I could enter Drake's house.

I glanced down the street to where a sleek black BMW sat. It had been all I could do to keep Baltic in the car, having to swear to him that I wouldn't go into the house by myself.

"My car is double-parked, so I think I'll just stay out here in case the police come," I said, waving a vague hand toward Baltic's car. "If you could just tell Brom to get his things together, I'll take him out of your hair."

"He's been no problem," she said. "I'm sorry, but I must shut the door. Drake would have my hide if I were to leave the door open. He's a bit crazy over security just now. Are you sure you don't want to come inside?"

"No, it's no problem. I'll just wait out here for Brom," I said, leaning against the white stone railing.

She gave me an odd look, but closed the door. Two minutes later, when I was trying to think how to broach a difficult subject with Baltic, the door opened. I straightened up, expecting to see my son, but instead a furry black demon in dog form marched out. "Heya, Solders! Oooh, sexy top, babe, very sexy top. I like how your boobies are kind of smooshed up over the neckline."

I looked down at the black stretch corset-style lace-up top I'd bought an hour earlier. My boobs did seem to be a bit more pronounced than was normal, but Baltic had expressed nothing but approval for my choice, going so far as snake his tongue down into the valley between my breasts. I put a stop to that, naturally . . . after an appropriate amount of time. "I just bought it at a small boutique this morning. It was on sale. Do you think it's too risqué?"

"No," Jim said, eyeing my boobs with glee. "If you bend over, will you pop out?"

I gave it a dirty look. "You are a demon. You aren't supposed to even notice things like uplifted breasts."

It rolled its eyes. "I may be a demon, but I'm a boy demon, and I'd have to be stuck in the deepest, darkest, most heinous of all of Bael's dungeon cells, suffering the worst torture imaginable, not to notice a fine pair of ta-tas when they passed by, and even then, I'd be thinking about them the whole time."

I mumbled something rude, turned to face the door, and did an experimental bow to make sure nothing untoward happened. "It's fine; you can suck your tongue back in," I told the demon when I turned around to face it.

"You take all the fun out of ogling. Hey, what's that on your left boob?"

I glanced down and edged the neckline over to better cover the sept mark. "None of your business. Where's Brom?"

"Packing his things. You're taking him away? Aisling said he was going to stay a couple of days because your crazy boyfriend was going to blow up Gabriel again."

"My crazy boyfriend will do nothing of the—" I stopped myself, getting a grip on my temper. "I don't have a crazy boyfriend, and no one that I know of is going to blow up Gabriel's house. Thus, yes, I am here to get my son. I hope to heaven you haven't been filling Brom's head with all sorts of inappropriate breast and Baltic talk. He is only nine."

"Naw, he's a good kid, and besides, Aisling told me if I showed him my collection of *Breasticles Monthly*, she'd have my noogies nailed to the wall. We've been good. Well, we did sit up until two in the morning watching old Hammer horror films because Ash and Drake took the spawns out to the country for a couple of days, but I promised to help watch Brom. And what's sitting up until two in the morning if not watching, eh?"

"I shall be sure to speak to him about staying up so late," I said with a mom frown.

The demon grinned. "You gotta let him have some fun. That's why I let him see pictures of my girlfriend, Cecile."

My jaw sagged just a smidgen. "You have a girlfriend?"

"Yeah. Black Welsh corgi with a fluffy white belly, and ears that beg to be sucked on. She's the cutest thing on four legs. She's getting up there in years, but that's OK;

I'm over three thousand years old, myself. Who's that in the car?" it asked, peering around me toward Baltic.

"Just a friend giving me a ride." I moved to block its view. I was about to distract the demon with something, anything, when the door opened again, this time disgorging Brom and his backpack.

"Sullivan, can we go to the British Museum again?"

"Good morning to you, too," I said, hugging him.

"Morning. Can we? Maata said she'd take me again if Gabriel and you said it was OK."

"Er . . ." I glanced back toward the car. Baltic's silhouette could be seen in it, moving in an impatient manner. I'd agreed to stay with him in his house, but I didn't want to break that bit of news to Brom with Jim standing right there, ready to carry the information straight back to Drake.

Momentarily distracted, I gave a little mental chuckle, realizing why Drake had seemed vaguely familiar to me when I saw him at the *sárkány*. The memory of Drake with the three women draped around him at the tavern in Paris left me wondering if he'd really changed from the womanizing tomcat he had once been.

"Sullivan?" Brom nudged me.

"We'll talk about it later, OK? Right now I want to get going. Nice to see you again, Jim."

"Kid's got mummies on the brain," Jim said to me, suddenly lunging to the side, hurrying past me toward the car. "Hey, is that who I think it is?"

"By the rood!" I swore, dashing after him, Brom on my heels. "Jim! Come back here! Heel!"

"That only works if you're my demon lord or duly appointed representative thereof, neither of which you are," it said as it came to a stop by the car. "Holy cheese and tiny little crackers! That's—"

I clamped my hand around its muzzle with one hand, glancing back to the house. The door opened, and Suzanne stepped out, obviously looking for Jim.

"Of all the . . ." I jerked open the car's back door, telling Brom, "Get in the front!"

"What are you doing to Jim?" he asked, standing there frowning at me as I heaved the demon halfway into the car.

"Why is it all I seem to do lately is shove people into cars? Just get in, Brom! Jim, so help me god, if you bite me, I'll bite you back!"

The demon's eyes widened as I grasped it firmly around the rib cage and shoved the last bit of it into the car, more or less tumbling in after it. We fell in a tangle of arms and furry legs onto the floor of the car.

"Get going!" I yelled to Baltic, struggling to get free of dog legs.

"What is this?" Baltic said, glaring over the seat at us. "Why are you bringing a demon with you? We have no need of a demon, mate. Release it."

"Heeel!" Jim wailed, its teeth clenched shut due to my grip around its muzzle.

"Wow, you're the guy who came after Sullivan," Brom said, getting into the front seat. He and Baltic regarded each other for a moment.

"Som-un heeell ee!"

"You should have been my son," Baltic told Brom.

Jim kicked with both its back legs, loosening my hold on its mouth.

"I'm being demon-napped!"

"OK," Brom said to Baltic after a moment's thought. The two nodded, just as if that settled the matter.

"Aisliiiing!"

"Be quiet, you pestilent little furball!" I yelled, wrestling it to the floor of the car as Baltic, finally noticing Suzanne, who now stood with her hands on her hips calling for Jim, put his foot on the gas and shot out into traffic, pulling a U-turn that narrowly missed sideswiping a Harrods van. "You brought this on yourself! If you hadn't been so nosy, I wouldn't have had to do this!"

"Aisling is going to go nutso-cuckoo on your butt when she finds out what you're doing!" Jim said, deliberately wiping its slobbery lips on me as I got onto the seat, leaving long, slimy tendrils of drool on my arm.

"You think so? Well, maybe your precious Aisling just needs to watch out, because I'm not some pushover, you know. I'm a mage, and mated to the baddest ass in the dragon world," I said as I looked around for something to wipe off the slobber.

Brom looked speculatively at Baltic. "That's you?"

"Yes. If you were my son, as you should have been, you, too, would have a badass."

"Hmm," Brom said, still thoughtful.

There was nothing in the back of the car, no tissue, no towel, no napkin. Nothing. I eyed the demon's fur.

"You wouldn't!" it gasped.

"If you give me any more grief, I'll do a whole lot more than smear you with your own saliva!" I threatened, bending down to wipe my hand on the floor mat.

It sucked in its breath. "Geez, and I thought Ash was mean! You ever want a job as a demon lord, you'd fit right in. Hey, is that your nipple?"

I eeped and jerked upright, tucking my breast back

into my shirt. Evidently it did not pass the bending-over test after all.

"Keep your eyes to yourself, and—Baltic!" I screamed and pointed at the side of a building we were about to hit because he had turned to look back at Jim's comment about my nipple. "Eyes on the road, mister!"

"I specifically asked you not to bare your breasts to others," he said gruffly, casting angry little glances at me in the rearview mirror.

"Jim isn't a person, and I didn't exactly bare myself— oh, it doesn't matter. Just keep your eyes on the road."

"It is difficult. These people do not drive properly," he said, transferring his glare to a young man on a scooter who flipped him off as he zoomed past us.

"City traffic is always bad . . . wait a minute. What do you mean they don't know how to drive properly? You *do* know how to drive, don't you?"

"Of course I know how to drive. I am doing it now, am I not?"

"Oh, man," Jim said, covering its eyes with its paw. "We're all gonna die."

"Yes, you are driving," I said, "but since I'm the one who drove us into town this mor—red light!"

Baltic slammed on the brakes, sending us fishtailing into the middle of the intersection. Luckily, the light had just changed, so the cross traffic had time to avoid hitting us.

"Will you stop distracting me with irrelevant things?" Baltic said, irritation dripping off each syllable.

"A red light is not irrelevant. Do you have a driver's license?" I demanded.

"I am eleven hundred years old," he snarled, jerking hard on the steering wheel as he sent us spinning out of the intersection. "I don't need a mundane license to drive!"

"We're doomed, I tell you, doomed!" Jim wailed.

"That is a pedestrian crossing!" I yelped as Baltic came close to mowing down two elderly ladies and their little wheely baskets of shopping.

"I did not strike them," Baltic said, his tone injured. "You make too much of a few near misses, Ysolde."

I looked back. One of the little old ladies was staggering to the zebra crossing barrier, her hand to her chest, while the other was making an extremely rude hand gesture at us. "Right, that's it. Pull over."

"Why?"

"When my fabulous form is crushed and burned into an unrecognizable blob of goo, would you please tell Aisling so she can summon me back?" Jim asked.

"Oh, be quiet. We're not going to d—*Baltic!*"

"What now?" he snarled, his teeth gritted and his knuckles white on the steering wheel as he drove in a serpentine fashion down the road, ignoring the blaring horns, anatomically impossible suggestions, and shrieks of horror.

"This is a one-way street!" I bellowed, leaning forward over the seat to try and wrap my arms around Brom in a desperate attempt to protect him from imminent death.

"I'm only going one way!"

"Yes, the wrong waiiiiiiiiieee!"

"Wow." Brom's voice came from the depths of where I had him smashed against my chest. "That really is your nipple. What's that mark near it?"

"Stop looking at my boobs!" I roared as Baltic, in blatant disregard of the fact that he was driving against traffic, and indeed was now up on the sidewalk scattering pedestrians hither and yon, turned to see just how badly I was popping out of the corset top.

"You will not be purchasing garments from that shop again," he said sternly. "I do not approve of this belief you cherish that exhibition games will arouse me. They do not."

*"Pull over!"* I screamed, pointing to a parking lot.

He pulled over, the sounds of horns, crumpling metal as cars avoided him but ran into parked vehicles, and breaking glass following us to the car park.

The second we stopped I was out of the car, marching around to the driver's side. I yanked open the door and pointed at the backseat. "I will drive!" I said, daring Baltic to defy me.

He glared, his eyes narrow slits of obsidian. "You are impugning my ability to drive a vehicle, mate. You will cease doing so, and get back into the machine."

"Please," Jim whimpered from the back. "Let her drive. I don't know how many more magnificent forms I can find."

My glare turned into a thing of fulminating beauty.

"Very well," Baltic said with haughty graciousness as he got out of the car. He stared pointedly at my chest. "But you must stop showing everyone your breasts. I realize that your rebirth has caused you to develop odd sexual preferences, but I will not tolerate my mate exposing herself to all and sundry. If you wish to display them, I and I alone will be your audience. You must resign yourself to this, mate."

"Oooh," Jim said, sitting up straight. "What sorts of odd sexual kinks other than flashing nip do you have, Soldie?"

"I am not exposing myself to anyone!" I said, then looked down and saw I was doing just that. I tucked my right breast back into the shirt, saying, "Well, dammit! I don't normally do that! And I don't have odd sexual preferences, so you can just stop whatever suggestive comment you were about to make, Jim."

"I was just going to ask if it involved sticks of butter or cloven-hooved animals," it answered.

"You cannot deny the overriding desire you harbor to watch Pavel with—"

"Gah!" I yelled, wanting to tear out my hair. I slapped my hand over Baltic's mouth, instead.

"Who's Pavel? And what does she want to watch him do?" Jim asked, leaning forward over the front seat.

I glared at it for a second as I slid behind the steering wheel. "Get in," I told Baltic.

He crossed his arms. "I will not share a seat with a demon."

"Hey! I can hear you!"

"I'll sit with Jim," Brom said, giving me a considering look as he scrambled into the backseat.

"There, you see? My son is kindly allowing you to ride shotgun."

"*My* son," Baltic said, giving me another of his patented annoyed looks.

"What?"

"He is *my* son. By rights he should be, and you said you wanted me to treat him as such, so I am doing that. I claim him as my son. You, Bram—"

"Brom," my child corrected him.

"You will cease being the offspring of the usurper who stole Ysolde from me. You are now my son."

"OK," Brom said, not the least bit ruffled by that idea.

"There, you see? I have fixed things," Baltic told me.

"Lovely. Great. Wonderful. I'll get you a Dad of the Year T-shirt later. Can we get going now? I hear police sirens, and if we don't get out of here now, we're going to have a whole lot of explaining to do."

"Yeah. Demon-napping is a federal offense now, I hear," Jim said as Baltic got into the passenger seat.

It was a *very* long ride back to Baltic's house.

"What are we doing here?" Brom asked as I stopped an hour later. He peered out the window at the white house.

"We're going to be staying here with Baltic."

"For how long?"

"Until I can rebuild Dauva," Baltic replied as he got out of the car. The door to the house opened, and a man emerged. "Ah. Pavel is back. Good."

I looked over the roof of the car to the man I recognized from my dreams. He started down the steps toward us, stumbled when he saw me, and stared with huge eyes. "Is that . . . it cannot be . . . is it?"

"Yes," Baltic said, marching over to me in order to wrap his arm around my waist and pull me into his side. "My mate lives."

"So do I, no thanks to Baltic's driving," Jim said as it peed on the back tire. "Nice place. Can I go home now?"

"No," I said, digging my elbow into Baltic's ribs. Brom was watching us with fascinated eyes.

"Aisling's going to open a serious can of whoop-ass on you when she finds out what you did, you know," Jim told me. "And bodacious boobies or not, I'm not going to stop her. I was supposed to go to Paris today to see my beauteous Cecile, and now I won't be able to suck her ears or snuffle her butt or lick her belly or any of the things I wanted to do."

Brom transferred his gaze to Jim, equally fascinated.

"You bared your breasts to the demon, too?" Baltic asked with outraged eyebrows.

"No, of course I didn't! I've told you several times now that I have no desire, fantasy, or other urge to bare anything to anyone, least of all my breasts. I have never, *ever* deliberately showed my breasts. So please stop insisting that's all I can think of. It just doesn't happen, OK?"

Pavel, Jim, and Baltic all eyed my cleavage.

I looked down, swore, and hiked up the neckline yet again. "Gah!"

"We are going to have a long discussion regarding these sexual fantasies of yours," Baltic told me, tugging me toward the house.

"I do not have an exhibitionist fantasy!" I yelled.

"What's an exhibitionist?" I heard Brom ask Jim.

I spun around and sent the demon a look that had it grinning. "It means someone who likes shopping at small boutiques," it said.

"One step out of line, demon, and I'll . . . I'll . . ."

"Or you'll what?" it asked, tipping its head to the side.

Before I could answer, Baltic paused and shot laser beams from his eyeballs. Well, all right, not really, but the effect was the same. Fire blossomed in a circle around the demon, causing it to dance and yelp.

"Cool," Brom said, looking with speculation at Baltic.

"All right, all right! Call off your wacko boyfriend! I'll behave!" Jim tried to blow out flames that licked up its tail. "Not the package! Anything but the package!"

"See that you do behave," Baltic said, extinguishing the fire with a flick of his eyes. He turned to Pavel and spoke in a low tone of voice, the latter casting periodic glances my way.

I sighed to myself and pulled out my cell phone as we all entered the hall. "I suppose I should tell Aisling that you're with me, Jim, and all right. It wouldn't be fair to make her worry you'd been kidnapped by someone who meant to destroy you."

Jim made a face. "Yeah, well, about that . . ."

"What?" I asked when its voice trailed to a stop.

"Normally I wouldn't worry, because as soon as Ash realized I'd been demon-napped, she could summon me back to her, but she's not going to realize I'm gone. Well, she is, but not. If you get my drift."

"Not in the least. What are you babbling about?"

Jim sighed. "My ride to the airport was due when you showed up. Suzanne probably thought that's where I went. I told you I was supposed to go to Paris."

"Ah, well," I said, not too worried about Jim's missed trip. "I'm sure you can go another time."

"I don't want to stay here," Brom suddenly said, giving the hall a good long look.

"Why not?" I asked, worried that he had gotten the wrong impression from Baltic's possessive hold on me. Or rather, the right impression, but without an explanation that would help him understand the complex relationship that even I wasn't sure I completely grasped.

"I want to go back to Gabriel's house, where I have my lab set up."

Baltic whirled around. "What is this? My son does *not* prefer the house of the silver wyvern over mine."

"Gabriel told Brom he could use a room in the basement to perform his experiments. He likes to mummify things."

"I'm a mummologist," Brom told Baltic.

"The silver wyvern gave you a room?" Baltic's eyes narrowed. "You are *my* son. I will give you . . ." He thought for a moment. "I will give you an entire building. There is a barn to the north—you may use that."

"Cool," Brom repeated; then his face fell. "But all my stuff is at Gabriel's house. My natron, and my dehydrator, and my dead fox, and everything else."

"I will give you new things. Better foxes, better natron."

I raised my eyebrows. "Do you even know what natron is?" I asked him.

"No," he said, blithely waving away the question. "But the natron I give to my son will be the best quality."

"If you want to dump Gareth for Baltic, I wouldn't mind," Brom whispered to me, clearly enjoying Baltic's determination to outdo what he thought of as a rival.

"Thanks. I'll keep that in mind," I told him with a little flick of my fingers to his ear.

Pavel made a little bow to me. "I am pleased to see you again, Ysolde. It has been a very long time. You have not changed at all."

Baltic said something in that language I didn't understand.

Pavel looked a bit startled, shooting me a look that I had a hard time deciphering as I answered, "It certainly has. And thank you."

Pavel gave Baltic a little nod and took off into the depths of the house.

"Brom, why don't you and Jim go outside and look around," I said.

"OK. We can look at the barn. I wonder if there's anything dead in it. . . ."

"Weird kid you got yourself there," Jim said over its shoulder as it followed Brom out the front door.

"Just see that you mind your manners," I warned it. "And don't try to escape, because you won't like how Baltic deals with pests."

"There is some business I must attend to," Baltic said, pulling out his phone.

"What sort of business?" I asked somewhat suspiciously. "Dragon business? Because if so, I want to talk to you about that."

"No, mundane business."

"You mean human-type business? I had no idea dragons did that sort of thing."

He shrugged. "Most of my fortune was claimed by others when I died. It takes some time to rebuild that, and since I will need a good deal of funds to restore Dauva, I must deal with business affairs."

"Oh. I wish I could give you some money, but I don't make very much as an apprentice, and Gareth funds us from the yearly manifestations. So I'm pretty much broke."

"I do not seek fortune from you, mate. Only your love."

I glanced down the hallway as Pavel crossed from one room to another. "Er . . . does Pavel live here with you?"

"Of course. He is my oldest and most trusted friend. He survived when the others did not." Baltic paused in checking his phone messages and slid me a glance. "Are you sure you do not lust after him?"

"Dammit! How do you know what I'm thinking? Are you a mind reader, too?"

He sucked in a huge breath, approximately a quarter of all the air in the house. "You *do* lust after him!"

"No, I do not! For heaven's sake, Baltic! I don't give a hoot about him, not in that way. I was just a bit curious about whether or not . . . oh my god! You didn't! Oh! You *did*! I can see by that expression, you did! You told him about me and my fantasy about guy-on-guy action, didn't you!"

Mollified, Baltic ceased seething at me and punched in a number on his phone. "Yes. He said you could watch the next time he has a male lover over."

"Oh! I can't believe"—I whomped him on the arm—"I *can't believe* you told him that! I am going to die of embarrassment! I will never be able to look him in the eye again! I'm never going to forgive you! How could you do that to me!"

Baltic just looked at me, waiting.

"Do you think he's going to have a guy over soon?" I couldn't help but ask.

He frowned. "I don't know. You shall have to satisfy your lustful ways upon me until he does, and even then, you may watch only, not participate. And you will not bare your breasts to Pavel or anyone else."

I gave him a look that should have shriveled his testicles. "I have no desire to have an orgy! All I said was that sometimes it was a bit interesting!"

"So you say," he muttered darkly, heading for a room I assumed was his study.

I swore under my breath at the obstinate, jealous, infuriating man, and wondered which of my male acquaintances I could hook up with Pavel.

# Chapter Twelve

The day was as dark and damp as my mood, the smell of snow heavy in the air. Bright Star, my mare, moved restlessly beneath me as we waited at the foot of the hill, watching as a line of men and horses wound its way in and out of the woods, moving toward us like a massive centipede.

Baltic rode at the lead, as he always did, without a helm, his hair lank from the misty rain, straggling over his mail like inky fingers.

"What are you doing out of the keep?" he yelled when he emerged from the last of the forest that surrounded Dauva.

"I came to greet you." My gaze passed from him to count the number of dragons who followed. It was a much smaller number than had set off, no more than a quarter returning. Sorrow, these days a constant companion in my belly, gripped me painfully. "You did not stop Constantine?"

"No." It was just one word, but in it was the full measure of despair that bound Baltic so tightly. His eyes were as bleak as his expression, flat, and without any hope. His shoulders were bowed, as if he were yoked to a great weight. "He comes for you, *chérie*. He is only a day behind me, less if he did not rest at night."

I shook my head, unable to believe it. "Why is he doing this? He knows I love you. He knows I want only you. I would never remain with him even should he take me from you."

He reached me, his stallion's head hanging as low as my spirits. The horses and men looked exhausted, clearly at their limit of strength. I knew Baltic would have pushed both hard.

"Why?" Baltic gave a hoarse bark of laughter. "He believes he can sway you, turn you against me."

"He's wrong," I said, urging my mare around so that we rode into the bailey together.

"He has sworn that if he cannot have you, I shall not."

I glanced at him, startled by the pain lacing his voice.

"Yes, my love," he said, taking my hand in his. His gauntlets and bracers were stained brown with blood. "He has threatened to kill you if he cannot steal you from me, this one who professes his great love for you."

"He is a fool," I said grimly, the dull thud of hooves on the dirt the only sound.

Baltic noticed the silence. He lifted his head, glancing around. "Where is everyone?"

"I sent them away."

He looked at me for a moment, his eyes so stricken I wanted to crush him to my bosom and comfort him.

Slowly, he nodded. "Why let others suffer for my folly?"

I said nothing until I had him inside, arranging for the two remaining maids to bring water for a bath. Pavel, silent and filthy with blood and dirt, helped me remove Baltic's armor.

"I'll send one of the maids to help you," I told Pavel as he gathered up the discarded mail.

His lips twisted in a wry half smile as he bowed and closed the door quietly behind him.

"It's over, *chérie*," Baltic said, slumping into the chair before the fire. "Constantine will win. He will take Dauva, take you, and I will die."

I knelt before him, my hands on his knees, sliding up his legs to take his hands in mine. "Then I will die, too. For I will belong to no one but you."

"I would rather you lived," he said, a faint smile coming to his lips, but there was no humor in it. "I would rather we both lived."

"There has to be a way we can stop this, stop Constantine. He has all but destroyed this sept."

"There are only eighteen of us left," Baltic said in a voice stripped of emotion.

"Dauva is strong. We will survive," I said, refusing to give in to the despair that tainted the air around us.

"It is strong, but with time, Constantine will find a way in. We can hold it only so long with only a handful of men." Suddenly, he lifted his head and looked about the chamber. "Where is Kostya?"

"Er . . . about that." I rose and opened the door for the maids, who lugged in four leathers of water. I waited until they were gone before continuing. "I realize that now is not the best moment to break this news to you, but ... well ... I'm carrying ... that is to say—"

"You're with child again?" Hope flared to life for a moment in his eyes. "*Chérie*, how can you think I would not be pleased with that news?"

"No, I'm not going to have a child. It's something else I'm carrying," I said, sick with the knowledge of what I had to say. I took a deep breath and said quickly, "While you were fighting Constantine, I went to Paris. There I met with Kostya and a green and a blue dragon. I told you that I was going to use the phylacteries to re-form the dragon heart, and so I did, only ... I failed. It wouldn't allow me to re-form it, and when it broke into the shards again, instead of going into the Choate Phylactery, it ... it went into me. Into my body."

Baltic stared at me as if he'd never seen me. "You would use the dragon heart against me?"

I marched over to him and slapped him, not hard, but shocking him enough that he leaped to his feet. "That is for even thinking that I would do such a thing."

Fury roared through him in the form of his dragon fire, a fury that spilled out onto me, twining around my legs, climbing higher and higher until I was alight with a spiral blaze. I welcomed the heat from it, merging it with my own, taking it into me and burying it deep into my soul.

For a moment, I thought Baltic was going to explode with anger, but amazingly, his fire banked and his lips quirked. "Ah, my love, what would I do without you?"

"Be wholly and utterly miserable," I said, pleased to see the life come back into his eyes. "And probably rut with every woman with two legs."

His hands slid around my waist. "You are the only woman I know who would dare greet her wyvern with the news that she now bears a piece of the dragon heart. We shall have to give you a name, now."

"I have a name," I protested.

"Phylacteries are always given names. If you are now the phylactery for the Choate shard, then it shall have to take a different name."

"We'll worry about that another time. What I need to know is how to get it out of me."

He shrugged, watching as the maids made another trip in with more water. "That I do not know. No dragon has ever been a phylactery before."

"Wonderful." I wondered if there was some learned person I could speak with, someone familiar with the dragon shards and heart.

"You did not say where Kostya is. He came back with you, did he not?" Baltic asked as he pulled off his thin linen shirt.

I knelt again and helped him with the crossties on his leggings. "Actually, he didn't."

"He left you to travel from Paris to Dauva alone?" he asked, frowning down at me.

I gestured toward the bath and went to a chest for the soap. "I wasn't alone. My personal guard went with me."

"So I should hope." Water splashed as he got into the tub. "Where is he if he is not here?"

I took a deep breath, watching as the maids poured in the last of the hot water. When they were done and we were alone again, I dampened a sea sponge and swirled it around on the soap I made especially for Baltic. It was scented with frankincense and myrrh, his favorite. He watched me closely as I knelt next to the tub and began washing him.

"My mother would never let me wash anyone," I said, wishing to avoid the pain I knew was coming. "I see now why she did so. It's very sensual, this spreading of soap on a man's body."

Baltic, distracted by the feeling of my fingers stroking across his skin, slippery little trails following each of my fingers as I lathered up the soft hair of his chest, glanced downward. "I am filthy, and riddled with fleas and lice, *chérie*. If you continue to stroke me that way, you will end up sharing the bath, and will not thank me for allowing my vermin to visit you."

I smiled, enjoying the hard muscles that lay in smooth ropes beneath his satiny flesh. Reluctantly, admitting the truth to his statement, I soaped up the sponge again and handed it to him, rising to fetch clean clothing as he briskly washed himself.

"Now you will tell me what you have wished to avoid," he said, washing the long ebony lengths of his hair, leaning forward so I could rinse the soap off with one of the remaining leathers of water.

"Kostya has forsaken you," I said simply, grabbing a linen cloth when he leaped to his feet, wincing as soapy water streamed down into his eyes. I mopped off his face, toweling his hair, and saying quickly, "He believes what all black dragons believe—that you seek to control the weyr. He refuses to be a part of it any longer. It was he who summoned me to Paris. I told him of my plan to use the dragon heart to stop the war, and he arranged for the other septs to loan me the shards so that it could be done."

"I wondered how you had arranged that," he said in

a deceptively mild voice. I wasn't fooled—he was beyond angry, beyond furious, his fire barely contained.

"Sit back down and finish bathing. I do not wish to share my bed with your friends any more than I would a bath," I said wearily, pouring him a cup of wine.

"So he has acted at last," Baltic said, slowly sitting down, absently washing his body as I retrieved a fine comb and a paste made from white bryony and honey that would kill the head lice. "I suspected he would, although I had not thought he would involve you."

I said nothing for a few minutes, rubbing the paste into his hair, then combing it over and over again until I was satisfied.

"You do not leap to his defense?" Baltic asked as I washed the paste out of his hair.

"What is there to say that I haven't already said?" I asked, pouring the last leather of water over his head. "He believes you to be a madman, willing to throw away the lives of everyone in the sept in order that you might rule supreme over the weyr. I don't blame him for leaving you—if I were he, I would do the same."

He shot me a look that sought reassurance. I leaned forward and gently kissed him, taking his breath into my mouth as my lips caressed his. "I am not Kostya, my love. I will never leave you."

"If I can't stop Constantine, you will not be left with the choice."

"There is always a choice," I said, holding up a cloth for him. "We just need to find it."

The heat of the fire melted away, easing into a different sort of warmth. Sunlight poured over me as I sat on the stone front steps of Baltic's house. I blinked as my mind was once again returned to the present, no longer disconcerted by the ease with which I slipped in and out of the visions.

"Whatcha doing?"

I looked up from where I had been hugging my legs, my chin resting on my knees, and moved the pad of paper upon which I'd been making a list before I'd slipped into the vision.

Jim plopped its big butt down next to me.

"Making a to-do list. I thought you were out with Brom."

The demon made a face. "He found a dead mouse and is looking it over to see if it's too far gone to mummify or not. Kid's a little weird, Soldy—you have to admit it."

"'Eccentric' is, I believe, the term you meant to use," I said with a gimlet glance. "He is very intelligent. He has interests beyond those of lesser children."

"Whatever. What's on your list?" It peered at the tablet. "'Call Aisling.' You better put on a pair of asbestos earplugs, 'cause she's going to be Miss Pottymouth of 2010 when she hears what you did to me."

"She seems like a reasonable person," I said with complacence I did not feel. "I'm sure I will be able to explain."

Jim snorted. "That's not a word that's often applied to her, but you're just going to have to find that out for yourself. What's next on the list? 'Call May and apologize for disappearance.' I like May. She feeds me."

"That is an excellent pointed look, but it is wasted on me. I'm sure you already had breakfast, and it's not lunchtime yet."

"You think this fabulous form stays looking this way without any help? Nuh-uh! I gotta give it all sorts of vitamins and minerals and fresh, lightly grilled cuts of beef."

"I'm sure you'll survive until lunch."

"I wouldn't count on it. Number three ... oooh. That's going to be a doozy."

"Yes, it is."

Jim's face screwed up as it thought. "If I was you, I'd try and find a neutral place to meet the wyverns. Because if you just march into a *sárkány* with Baltic, they'll grab you both."

I gave the demon a long look. "Why are you being helpful?"

Its eyes opened wide. "Me? Helpful? Not on your shiny pink ass. I'm a demon, remember?"

"Yes, but you're being helpful. That is totally against the norm so far as demons go."

"Yeah, well." It paused to suck a tooth. "I'm more than just a normal demon. I'm like Demon Plus with super whitening power. How're you going to get Baltic to agree to meet with the other wyverns?"

"What makes you think he wouldn't?" I asked, quelling a feeling of worry about that very subject.

It rolled its eyes at me. "He's the dread wyvern Baltic! The big kahuna during the Endless War. He's probably killed more dragons than everyone else put together."

"Oh, he has not!" I said, shifting uneasily.

"You kidding? Mr. 'We use his name to scare little dragons into being good' Baltic? He's like Genghis Khan and Vlad the Impaler and Stalin all rolled into one scaly package."

"Baltic is not scaly! Almost never!"

It cocked a furry eyebrow at me. "Face it, Soldums—you don't get the kind of reputation Baltic has by work-

ing well with others, and that's what number three on
your list is asking him to do."

I looked down at my list, sighing to myself as I admitted the truth. "He used to be scary. Now he's different."

"A kinder, gentler maniac is still a maniac, chicky. Tell
you what—you send me back to Ash, and I'll tell her
and Drake that Baltic isn't the hyperderanged, mass-
murdering psycho bastard they think he is, OK?"

"No," I said firmly, putting a little tick mark next to
item number three. "We're not going to tell them that.
We're going to prove it, and the only way we can do that
is to get everyone together, the wyverns and Baltic and
me, so we can work things out in a civilized manner."

The demon eyed me curiously as I stood up, filled
with determination. "You think you got a way to make
all that happen?"

"I think I have a way to make Baltic understand that
he will have to speak with the wyverns, yes. You forget
there's a death sentence hanging over my head. He may
be adorably arrogant, but I doubt very much if he will
allow the weyr to kill me. I'll simply point out that if he
wants that sentence lifted, he's going to have to go with
me to speak to the wyverns."

"Uh-huh. That's just part of it, though, the Baltic side.
How are you going to get the wyverns to talk to him?"

"That's the easiest part of all," I said, patting it on its
head.

"Yeah? What do you have up your sleeve? A magic
mongoose or something?"

"Nope." I paused at the door and tossed the demon a
smile. "I have you."

I closed the door gently on the sound of its sputter-
ing.

The phone calls, as I suspected, weren't the most pleasant ones of my life.

"Ysolde!" Aisling gasped when I got through to her. "Are you all right? We just got home. May's here, and she said you've been kidnapped. Did you get away from Baltic? Has he hurt you? If he has, you just let me know. I'm a professional—I'll take care of him. I'll just summon Jim from Paris, and we'll—"

"Er . . . I appreciate that offer, but it's not necessary," I interrupted. "About Jim . . . Aisling, Jim is with me."

"It's what? Why is it with you? Oh my god! Baltic kidnapped Jim when he grabbed you, didn't he? That bastard! That fire-breathing bastard! He had just better watch out the next time I see him, because I will do all sorts of evil things to him. He won't ever have children, for a start. And I think I know of someone who can curse him—"

"I would really appreciate if you didn't do any of that," I said, laughing. I could feel her surprise at the laughter, which, I admit, died quickly as I confessed, "Baltic didn't kidnap Jim—I did."

The silence that followed the statement was broken only by the noise of another receiver being picked up. "Ysolde? It's May. You're all right? Are you hurt in any way?"

"She said she took Jim," Aisling said, breathing somewhat heavily into the phone.

"She did? I thought it went to Paris."

"It was supposed to."

"Then why did Ysolde kidnap it?"

I sighed. "Because it saw that Baltic was with me. Look, this is going to be impossible to explain over the phone. I just didn't want you thinking that Jim was in any danger. It's here with us—"

"With you and Baltic? What the hell?" Aisling said, her voice rising.

"Oh, knock it off," I said irritably. Although I knew I had committed the wrong, I had expected that they would understand why I had done it.

"Did she just tell you to knock it off?" May asked Aisling.

"Yes, she did," Aisling answered, sounding rather bewildered.

"I'm sorry for my rudeness, but honestly! I thought if anyone would understand what's been happening, two wyverns' mates would," I said firmly. "Surely you two understand the strength of the bonds that tie you to your particular dragon. The same applies to me, no matter if I am in human form or not."

"But—" Aisling started to protest.

"No, there are no buts. You're the ones who were so bent on insisting that I'm Baltic's mate! For the love of all that's holy, you were ready to condemn me to death because of that!" My own voice was rising now. I made an effort to stem my growing anger.

"I never wanted you to die," May said quietly.

"Well, me either! I may be a demon lord, but I'm not a *bad* demon lord," Aisling said quickly.

"You accepted Baltic as your mate?" May asked.

I rubbed my forehead. Another headache was blossoming. "Yes, I did. And because of that, I want to call a *sárkány*."

"Um . . . all right," Aisling said. "I guess since you're a member of the silver sept, you can do that."

I didn't correct the incorrect assumption. "I want to discuss with the weyr these deaths of the blue dragons. Baltic and I will attend the *sárkány* together."

An intake of breath greeted that statement, but it was impossible to tell which woman made it.

"Since I know the weyr believes Baltic to be guilty of those deaths, and I believe he's innocent, we must have the opportunity to discuss the situation with everyone. For that reason, Jim will remain in my custody until it's over."

"You do realize that all I have to do is summon it, right?" Aisling asked.

"Oh, yes, I know you could summon it in a heartbeat." I crossed my fingers. "But you won't."

"I won't? Why not?"

"Because you are a woman of honor," I said firmly, praying my assessment of her character was sound. "In addition, you realize that Baltic needs to meet with the wyverns, and you know that they won't mind their manners unless they have a compelling reason to do so, and you, as a fellow wyvern's mate, understand the importance of making them act reasonably. For that reason, you'll allow Jim to be a hostage for the wyverns' good behavior."

"I'll do all that?" she asked, but I heard amusement in her voice, and I knew I had her support.

"You will. Jim will stay in my protection until Baltic has met with the weyr and been given safe passage out. I will not allow anyone to railroad him."

"Railroad him?" Aisling's voice lost the amusement.

May spoke softly, with no real inflection to her voice. "You have to understand that we have experience with Baltic, and although I realize you are his mate, and thus you want to protect him, he is not innocent of the blue dragons' deaths. Gabriel was there. He saw the bodies. He questioned the two survivors."

"I have always heard that dragons valued their honor, which is why I will ask the wyverns to agree to allow us safe passage to and from the *sárkány*. Jim will be returned to you safe and sound once we are away."

Aisling was silent for a minute. "All right. I will trust you. But so help me, if Jim is harmed in any way—"

"It won't be. I just want the same guarantee for Baltic."

Aisling snorted.

I gave her my cell phone number and told her to call me when a time for the *sárkány* had been set.

"Ysolde . . ." May's voice stopped me as I was about to hang up.

"Yes?" I asked, somewhat wearily. I didn't like having to be the bad guy, but someone had to end the conflict between Baltic and the weyr, and instinctively I knew he would not take any steps to do so on his own.

"Baltic . . . forgive me for asking, but you don't think he's using some sort of a thrall on you? We haven't known you long, but you don't seem like the sort of person who would tolerate, much less protect, a man who murders in cold blood."

I smiled sadly at my feet. "No, he hasn't enthralled me. That would involve sex, and . . . well . . . we haven't."

"Baltic didn't jump you the second he could?" Aisling asked, clearly agog at the notion.

"No. He might have wanted to—all right, he *did* want to—but I'm married. He understands that until I can talk with my husband and inform him that I wish to have a divorce, I don't feel it's morally right to do all the things we'd like to do."

Silence greeted that pronouncement. I was about to hang up again when May said, "That's very interesting."

"I'm glad my lack of a sex life is fascinating to you," I said dryly.

"I'm sorry, that sounded rude, didn't it? It wasn't intended that way. Ysolde . . . you said you had memories of the past. You must remember that dragons are very dominant when it comes to claiming their mates physically. That goes double for wyverns," May said.

"Oh, yes," Aisling added with a little chuckle.

"Yes, but this is different. That was in the past. This is now, today, in the present," I explained.

"Just the fact that you accepted him as a mate and he hasn't . . . well! I think that says something," Aisling added. "I think that says a lot of something."

"Yes, it says he has restraint. Call me when you have the time and day for the *sárkány*," I said, and hung up the phone, relieved it was over. "I just hope the rest of my plans go so well."

# Chapter Thirteen

Idly, I rubbed my cell phone and wondered if I'd put the cart before the horse. Baltic hadn't denied that he had killed those blue dragons, and yet I had seen a moment of hurt in his eyes before he answered with a typical dragon nonanswer. "I couldn't love someone who was a murderer," I said aloud to the empty room. "I couldn't."

"What couldn't you do?" Baltic asked from the doorway, causing me to jump.

"I'll tell you if you answer two questions for me."

His eyebrows rose as he strolled across the room to me, all coiled power and sexy hips. "Just two?"

"Yes. The first is whether you had any involvement with the deaths of the blue dragons."

He paused for a second, giving me an unreadable look. "You have already asked me that question, and I have answered it."

"No, you gave me a nonanswer."

"What purpose would I have to kill blue dragons?"

I ground my teeth. "You know, this dragon thing of not answering a question outright is driving me nuts."

"It shouldn't. You are prone to the same trait."

"I am not! I'm human! I don't do that! Now please, just answer the question—did you have anything to do with those deaths?"

"Yes."

My stomach dropped like a lead weight. I was so sure he would deny it. "You did? You killed those dragons?"

"No."

He stood near to me, not touching, but close enough that I could feel his dragon fire come to life. "You just said you did!" I all but wailed.

"No, I said I had something to do with it. I did not kill them, but I knew that their deaths were possible."

"I don't understand." I wanted to run screaming from the room and at the same time I wanted to wrap myself around him, reassuring myself that he wasn't the monster everyone thought he was. "Who killed them?"

He said nothing.

I put my hand on his chest, over his heart. "Baltic, this is important. The weyr thinks you are responsible for the deaths of all those blue dragons. In fact . . . well, we'll talk about that later. But right now, I really need to know—who did kill them?"

"I had forgotten how persistent you can be when you desire something," he said with a sigh, placing his hand over mine. "I will tell you, but only because you are my mate and I trust you. Fiat Blu killed the dragons."

"Fiat Blu? He's part of that sept?"

"Yes. His sept was taken from him by his uncle."

"Why would Fiat kill his own people? And why would you know about it?"

His arms snaked around my waist, pulling me into a gentle embrace. I let my fingers wander up the thick muscles of his arms, enjoying the solid feel of him, the tingle that seemed to come to life in the air around us whenever we touched. It was a sense of anticipation that left my body extremely aware of the differences between us.

"I have no quarrel with the blue dragons or Fiat. A few decades back, when I returned to life, he gave me shelter. Later, when he lost his sept to his uncle Bastian, he sought my aid in recovering control, but he disappeared a month ago. I do not know where he has gone to ground."

"You didn't try to stop him from killing innocent dragons?"

A flicker of pain crossed his face. "I did not think he would carry out his threat. He is unbalanced, mate, but I did not believe he would massacre members of his own sept. I was mistaken."

"Those poor dragons." I spent a moment sending up a silent prayer that they found a better life before something Baltic had said finally nudged my awareness. "Wait a second—a few *decades* back?"

"Why are you making that horrified face?" He frowned, puzzled.

"You said a few decades ago, when you were reborn."

He made an annoyed gesture. "I died after you were killed, Ysolde. I've told you that."

"But you were reborn right away, weren't you?"

"No. Life was not returned to me until almost forty years ago."

I stared at him in confusion. "But when was I reborn?"

"I don't know."

"Dr. Kostich said my husband wasn't mortal. If he's not, and I was reborn right after I died . . . oh my god!"

"What?" Baltic asked as I reeled back from him.

I pointed a finger at him. "You're younger than me!"

The look he gave me was almost comical. "What does age matter?"

"Oh, it matters if you're three hundred years old and the man you're dating is . . . what? Thirty-five? Thirty-six?"

"Thirty-nine."

"Great! On top of everything else, I'm a cradle robber."

"We are immortal. In our past lives, I was six hundred years older than you. Therefore, I'm still three hundred years older."

"It doesn't work that way," I said, disgruntled.

"You are making something of nothing," he said, trying to pull me back into his embrace.

I held him at arm's length. "Tell me this, then; why were we brought back?"

He said again, "I don't know."

"How were we resurrected?"

"Do I look like an encyclopedia of the resurrected? I tell you I do not know!"

"Who is responsible for bringing me back?"

He glared at me. "You are beginning to annoy me, woman."

"They're important questions! I would like some answers!"

"I do not know the answers!" After a moment's silence, he slid me an odd look. "This man who married you—does he know about your past?"

"I thought so," I said slowly. "He certainly has always known about the fugues. . . ."

"Then we will gain that information from him before we sever him from you," Baltic said with decisiveness.

"How is it *you* were reborn?" I asked, still wondering how long I'd been alive.

"Thala arranged it." He glanced away, something about his expression immediately catching my interest and setting my Baltic radar pinging.

"Who is Thala?"

His lips pursed slightly as he gazed out of the window. "A necromancer, of course."

Necromancers, I remembered from some long distant store of knowledge, had the power to raise the dead as liches. "Glory of god! You're a lich?"

"No, of course not. I am a dragon. You've seen that for yourself," he said, still not meeting my eye.

The radar cranked up a notch. "Necromancers only raise liches."

"When they raise humans, yes. But a dragon is different."

"Oh." That seemed to make a tiny bit of sense, and as I had little knowledge of the art of raising the dead, I didn't dispute the statement. "Why would she raise you? Did you know her before you died?"

He tried to keep his head turned, ostensibly scanning the fields outside the house, but I moved around to block his view. His face was filled with something that looked like chagrin. "Yes, I knew her. Her mother was Antonia von Endres."

"Ah, the daughter of your mage friend? I see." A horrible thought struck me. "She's not *your* daughter, is she? This Thala person?"

He looked appalled. "Christos, I hope not. Not after we ... er ..."

My jaw sagged a little. "You slept with her, too?"

"No. Perhaps. Just five or six times," he said, every word making me see red. He waved the thought away. "No, I could not be her father. Thala once mentioned that her father was a red dragon."

"Where is this girlfriend of yours? Does she live here, too? Are you hiding her from me? If you think I'm going to share you, you're madder than everyone says you are! I—"

"Your jealousy pleases me, *chérie*," he said, smiling one of those arrogant, smug male smiles that men are prone to when they think women are gaga over them.

"Yeah? Then you're going to love this," I answered, making a fist and aiming it for his gut.

He caught my hand with a laugh. "You are making yourself angry over nothing. Thala lives here, yes, but she is not my lover. She was briefly, but as with her mother, that was before you were born."

"Where is she now?" I asked, mollified enough to allow him to uncurl my fingers and kiss the tip of each one.

"Your silver dragon friends have her."

My eyebrows shot up as he gently bit the pad on one of my fingers, heat flaring to life deep in hidden parts of me. "They do?"

"They captured her two months ago. I assume she is still alive, although I have not been able to locate where she is being held." His gaze turned thoughtful as he released my hand. "You are in an ideal situation to do that."

I tamped down on the spike of jealousy that rose at the suggestion. "Possibly. But—"

He stopped me with a raised hand as he turned toward the window. "Who is that? Who has made it past my security?"

The crunch of gravel being crushed beneath a car's tires reached my ear.

"I have not authorized anyone to visit us," he announced, and bolted for the front door.

I ran after him, worried that Jim had somehow summoned the police or some other form of help.

It wasn't the police who emerged from the small rental car.

"Who the hell are you?" Baltic roared as he stormed down the stairs. A woman had emerged from the car, a slight woman with brown hair and pale green eyes. She flinched as Baltic leaped down the last three stairs and pinned her against the car. "You? How did you get in here?"

"Eek!" she cried, trying to squirm away. "Tully, help me!"

"Tully?" Baltic spun around and glared at me. "You know this woman?"

"Yes. She's my sister-in-law, Ruth. Which means that must be my husband."

"Husband!" he said, his eyes lighting with unholy pleasure.

Gareth slowly emerged from the car, his mouth hanging open as he stared at Baltic. Gareth in his best moments wasn't a terribly attractive man—he stood about my height, had no hair on the top of his head, and possessed a somewhat weak chin and narrow eyes that made me think of a particularly obstinate ferret.

"Holy Mary, mother of god," Gareth said now as Baltic rounded the car, clearly about to grab him. "You said

silver dragons! You said you were with the silver dragons! You didn't say it was Baltic!"

Baltic paused at his name on Gareth's lips, squinting
at him in the bright sunlight. A flicker of recognition
glinted momentarily in Baltic's eyes, causing me to stare
at him in stunned surprise. "How do you know who he
is?" I asked, gesturing toward Gareth.

Gareth backed up, his hands in the air as if to surren-
der or protect himself as he stared at Baltic. "Good god,
she really did it. You're alive again! Holy Mary!"

"You know my husband?" I asked Baltic, running
past Ruth. She grabbed at my arm as I passed her, but I
shook her off.

"Husband? He is not your husband!" Baltic snorted.

"Yes, he is. He's Brom's father."

"I am Brom's father! You yourself witnessed the oath
between us!"

"I don't understand any of this," I said, rubbing my
forehead again. "How do you know Gareth and Ruth?
And how did you two know where to find us?"

"Attack him!" Ruth shrieked to Gareth, almost hopping with excitement. "Kill him, you fool! He'll ruin everything we've worked so hard for!"

"I can't kill a dragon," Gareth said, bolting as Baltic started toward him again. Gareth grabbed my arms
and held me like a shield before him. "I didn't know
she could do it! She's tried for all those centuries, and I
didn't think she would ever do it! Holy Mary!"

"Will you stop saying that and tell me what's going
on?" I snapped, trying to get free of his grip.

"Release my mate," Baltic said in a low growl that
made the hairs on the back of my neck stand on end.
His eyes were burning with black fire, and I could sense,

even from the few yards that separated us, that he was about to pounce.

"You can have her!" Gareth shrieked, and flung me at Baltic, making a dash for the car.

"Hey—oof. Ow!" I rubbed my nose where it connected with Baltic's chin. "What on earth is going on?"

"He will tell you," Baltic snarled, lunging for Gareth.

"No! There's nothing to tell! I swear to you! Gark!"

Before I could so much as blink, Baltic was on the other side of the car, one hand clamped around Gareth's throat as he held him a good two feet off the ground. "How did you find us?"

"Man . . . hired . . . save Tully . . ."

"Savian Bartholomew," I growled, my fingers curling into fists. At a look from Baltic I explained, "He's a thief taker and some sort of übertracker. Gareth sent him to rescue me from the silver dragons. No doubt Gareth hired him again to find me."

Baltic snarled something obscene as his fingers tightened around Gareth's throat. "You took my mate!"

"Stop that! You're hurting him!" Ruth shoved me aside with a force that sent me reeling into Brom and Jim, who had raced outside at the sound of raised voices.

"Hoo. Maybe I'm not sorry you demon-napped me," Jim said, watching with wide eyes as Ruth leaped on Baltic's back.

"Hey!" I shouted. "Get off of him!"

"You got a video camera?" Jim asked Brom.

"No. Sullivan won't let me get one."

"Shame. I bet we could make enough money to choke a mummy with a video of your mom and that lady going at it."

"No one is going at anything—" I started to say, but

then Ruth started beating Baltic about the head, and fury rose within me. I threw myself over the hood of the car, grabbing Ruth around her waist and yanking her off Baltic.

She snarled something that had Brom looking shocked before lashing out at me with her legs, taking me down in a sort of scissor move.

"Tell her!" Baltic growled, shaking Gareth like he was a rag doll. "Tell her the truth!"

"There's nothing to tell," Gareth gasped, his face bright red as he struggled to get air into his windpipe.

Ruth punched me in the eye, snapping my head backwards, causing me to see little white stars for a moment. "Let go of him!" she yelled again, and abandoning me, threw herself onto Baltic's arm.

"Oh man," Jim said, strolling over to peer down at where I lay dazed. "That's going to leave a shiner. Hey, I can see down your top. That's a sun symbol on your boob, huh?"

Brom joined him. "Looks like it. Is that a tattoo?"

The twinkly white stars started to fade and I became aware of the fact that Jim had its nose about half an inch away from my left breast.

"Naw, it's a dragon mark. Pretty. Kind of Celtic looking with all those swirly bits on the sun's rays."

"Ack!" I yelled, shoving the demon back.

"Hello! I am not a piece of furniture," it said as I used it to get to my feet. "You grab my coat like that, you're going to rumple my fur! Aw, man! You did rumple it! Now I'm going to need brushing."

"Get off him, get off him!" Ruth was chanting as she threw all her weight into Baltic's arm in an attempt to break his grip on Gareth.

Baltic shot a look at her and set her hair on fire.

"Eeek!" She ran screaming away, slapping at her head.

"Fires of Abaddon! What I wouldn't give for a camcorder! That scene alone would have made us the hit of YouTube!" Jim said, watching Ruth run in a circle, beating her head.

"Baltic, stop it!" I said, limping over to him, my left eye starting to swell. "I know you don't like Gareth—at this point, I don't like him, either—but that's no reason to kill him. He's got to stay alive so I can divorce him. A widowhood just wouldn't be nearly as satisfying."

"You can't divorce him because you're not married to him," Baltic snarled, giving Gareth another shake before releasing the hold on his neck.

Gareth crumpled to the ground, one hand clutching his neck, gasping for air.

"Why do you keep saying that?" I asked, gingerly touching my eye. I could barely see out of it.

Baltic strode over to Ruth, grabbing her by the back of her collar and frog-marching her over to me. "Tell her," he demanded, giving Ruth a shove forward.

Ruth and I had never been the best of friends; indeed, she barely tolerated Brom's and my presence, but the look she shot me now was pure loathing. "He's not your husband. He's mine."

My mouth dropped open.

"Hoochiwawa," Jim said, whistling. "I didn't see that coming."

"Gareth's married to Ruth?" Brom asked.

"You're married to him? You're not his sister?" I touched my head, wondering if I'd hit it harder than I imagined when Ruth knocked me to the ground. "Are you sure? Gareth just told me a few days ago we'd been married for ten years."

She gave a choked little laugh as she squatted next to Gareth, who lay still struggling to breathe. "After five hundred years, I think I would know my own husband."

"Five hundred . . . oh my god. Dr. Kostich was right. He is immortal. But . . . why did he marry me, too?"

"He had to, you stupid twit! He had no other choice but to marry you when you suddenly decided you wanted to marry a mortal."

Beyond me, Baltic growled.

I kept my eyes fixed on Ruth. "I wanted to marry someone so Gareth married me instead? It was the gold, wasn't it? That's why he did it."

"Of course it was," she snarled. "We couldn't let anyone else have it, could we? And then you wouldn't stop talking about having a child, and my poor darling had to play stud to your mare. But he hated every minute of it! He told me so repeatedly!"

I digested this, my emotions tangled with anger and fury and hurt and quite a bit of confusion. "But . . . how did you know that Gareth was married to Ruth?" I asked Baltic.

"Ruth is the sister to the one who resurrected me," he answered, glaring at her as he moved over to stand next to me.

"If you're really married to him, then—" I glanced at Brom, and for the second time in a few minutes, rage whipped through me.

"Ouch. You know, even immortals can suffer from brain damage," Jim said, leaning over my shoulder as I whomped Gareth's head repeatedly into the side of the car.

"How dare you use my body! How dare you pretend you were my husband! How dare you do whatever it is you did to me just so I would make gold for you! It really was you who wiped my memory, wasn't it? Just so I didn't know what you and Ruth were doing to me! By the rood, I'll hang your guts from the highest tower!"

Gareth struggled feebly, but he was no match for me. Ruth would have attacked, but Baltic grabbed her by the arm and kept her back while I took out a little of what was evidently centuries of abuse on the man who had deceived me so cruelly.

"How dare you treat Brom the way you did!"

"Uh, Sullivan? I think he's passed out," Brom pointed out.

I released my hold on Gareth, suddenly horrified at what I'd done. "Oh my god! I tried to kill my husband in front of my own child!"

"Ex-husband, I think," Jim said.

"Non-husband," Baltic corrected, releasing Ruth as I leaped to my feet and clutched Brom to my chest. "'Usurper' is a better term."

Ruth cradled Gareth's head as I hugged Brom tightly. "Honey, I know you must be frightened and confused by what I just did to your father—"

"Actually, I was wondering if I could kick him."

"—and I have no excuse for it, none at all, but you know I'm not a violent person, and you must understand that I just had a very bad shock, and I lost my temper. Please, tell me you understand!"

"I understand," Jim said, lifting its leg. "You wanted to beat the crap out of him. I think pretty much anyone would after he played nook-nook with you all that time when he was really married to Scrunchy Face, here."

"Grah!" Ruth snarled, lunging at Jim as it peed on Gareth's foot.

The demon bared its teeth, and Ruth collapsed back onto Gareth, patting his cheeks and sniffling to herself.

"Brom?" I asked, releasing his head. He reeled backwards for a moment, his eyes huge. "Are you all right?"

"I couldn't breathe," he said, giving my boobs a wary glance.

"I'm sorry. It's just that I'm so very, very worried that you misinterpreted the little argument your father and I had."

"Little argument?" Jim snickered. "If you call beating someone to a pulp on the side of a car a little argument, then I don't want to see you when you really get pissed."

"It's OK, Sullivan," Brom said, patting my arm in a supportive manner. "I don't blame you for trying to kill Gareth. If you get mad at him again, and really do bash his brains in, can I mummify him?"

"Just tell me this, Gareth," I said, glaring down at where the man I had thought of as my husband was trying to pull himself up. "Did you ever really want Brom and me?"

He touched his swollen bottom lip, grimacing at the sight of blood on his fingers. "I wasn't going to let you get away from me, not the goose who laid the golden eggs every year."

My anger turned cold and settled in the pit of my gut. "So rather than let me have a life of my own, you bound me to you to ensure you could use me each year." I glanced at Brom, wanting to yell at Gareth for bringing into the world a child he didn't want and didn't care about, but Brom had had enough shocks for the day. "As of this moment, you are no longer a part of our lives. I don't want to see you again, and I will take legal action if you attempt to see Brom."

Gareth sneered as best he could with a battered face. "I don't give a damn about—"

Baltic moved faster than I could follow, grabbing both Ruth and Gareth and flinging them into the car. "He will not bother either of you again. You are both mine now."

"And thank the stars for that," I said, giving Baltic a grateful look that had him doing a double take.

"Whoa. I know what that's going to mean," Jim said, nudging Brom on the hip. "I think you're going to want to look away. You're too young to see what Baltic's about to do."

"You haven't heard the last of us!" Ruth swore as she started up the car. "We will not be treated this way! You may think you can hide behind the dragon, Tully, but you are beholden to us! You are ours, not his!"

"Right, that's it!" I yelled, suddenly furious again. I started toward the car, pushing up my sleeves. "You want a piece of me? You can have a piece of me!"

"Didn't your mom say she wasn't violent?" Jim asked Brom.

"Yeah."

"You can have a piece of me *right now*!" I yelled, jumping toward the car door. Just as I grabbed it, Ruth, evidently thinking twice about taunting me, jammed her foot on the gas. Baltic wrapped an arm around me and lifted me off the ground, leaving me waving my fists at the car as it spun down the drive, spewing bits of gravel behind it.

"You know," Jim said, looking thoughtfully at me as

Baltic set me down, "I used to think Ash was perfect for the role of demon lord—you should see the way she pinches me, and there's no excuse for her starving my fabulous form on those diets she keeps letting the vet talk her into—but I'm starting to think that you've got her on the 'beat the bejesus out of immortals' scale."

"One more crack out of you, demon, and you're going to need a whole lot more than a brushing," I told it, giving it one of my annoyed mother looks.

"That's exactly what I'm talking about," Jim said to Brom.

"Yeah," Brom said, agreeing.

"Well," I said, all wound up after the scene with Gareth and Ruth, "Gareth had it coming to him. Using me like he did . . . the rat!"

"I would have killed him for daring to touch what was mine, but for one thing," Baltic said.

"Brom?" I asked, figuring he would not want to kill Gareth in front of a child any more than I did.

"No." His gaze dropped to mine, and I flushed at the sight of the naked desire burning in its depths. "Now you are truly mine."

I didn't even have time to digest that before he bent down, slung me over his shoulder, and walked into the house.

"Baltic!" I shrieked, Jim and Brom trailing after us. "Put me down this instant! What did I say about treating me like I was a sack of potatoes?"

Baltic paused inside the hall, and I pinched his back, assuming he had come to his senses.

"Hey, Balters, just a little hint," Jim said, giving us a knowing look. "Aisling says she hates it when Drake gets all aggressive with her, but she sure grins like a fool afterward, so you might just want to take all that screeching with a grain of salt."

"I am not screeching!" I said, outraged, glaring at the demon. "You are going to be so sorry—Baltic! I said set me down!"

"There you are. Take care of my son and the demon," Baltic ordered Pavel, who emerged from the study.

"Dammit, I demand that you release me. I am not Aisling! I do not like arrogance!"

"What's Baltic doing with Sullivan?" I heard Brom ask as Baltic leaped up the stairs, apparently not feeling my weight slung over his shoulder at all. I spent a moment admiring that fact before I slid my hands down his back and only just refrained from pinching his butt.

"You don't wanna know. I mean, you will in about ten years, but for now, it's just going to mess with your head. You gotta trust me on this. Hey, who do I have to crotch-snuffle to get lunch around here? I'm starving, and my coat goes to Abaddon in a handbasket if I don't get five proper meals a day. You got any fresh horse-meat, Pavel?"

# Chapter Fourteen

"I want to give you something," Baltic said as he closed the door to his bedroom.

"I just bet you do. I want to give you something, too—a piece of my mind. What on earth do you think you're doing, carrying me off like you're some sort of a primitive caveman? What will Brom think?"

"My son will understand that I wish to spend time alone with you, where I may worship every inch of your soft, delicious body, and where you will pleasure me endlessly until I am a shattered wreck of a dragon."

I thought about that for a moment. Brom was fine with Pavel there. Jim would be watched, and Gareth, that bastard bigamist, was no longer a factor in my life. Was there any impediment to me flinging myself on Baltic and giving in to all those desires that had built up over centuries?

No, there was not! "All right," I squealed as I suited action to thought and flung myself on him.

He wasn't expecting that, because the weight of my body suddenly hitting him sent him staggering back-wards a few steps. "*Chérie*, you must wait. I have some-thing for you."

"Oh, yes, you certainly do," I said, nuzzling his neck as I slid my hand down his chest, and further below to stroke the length of him through his pants. He groaned, his eyes closed for a moment as I felt him growing in thickness and length.

Suddenly, he pried me off him. "Ysolde, you must wait."

"You are kidding me!" I said, glaring at him with irate intent as he turned his back on me and strode over to a tall bureau. "You were begging me to do this yesterday, and now you don't want me?"

"I never beg," he scoffed, searching through a drawer of the bureau. "I am a wyvern, and your mate. I do not need to beg."

"You want to bet?" I growled, my arms crossed and my eyes narrowed as I watched him. I knew he wasn't indifferent to me—a simple glance at his fly negated that idea. "You were all over me yesterday. Why are you spurning me now?"

"Wyverns don't spurn, either," he said, his voice somewhat muffled as he squatted, his head in a deep drawer at the bottom of the bureau.

"Well, you're sure doing something, and it is not cel-ebrating the fact that Gareth is a lying bigamist, as you should be doing. Instead, you're poking your head in some sort of a desk. What is it you're doing there, Bal-tic? Going to write a few letters? Pay some bills? Cut up pretty pictures and make a collage? What's that?"

He stood before me, a small wooden box in his hand.

Engraved on it, in gold, were two stylized medieval-ish dragons, their necks crossed. He put the box into my hands. "It is a gift for you."

I turned it over, examining it, my fingers sliding over the smooth, highly polished wood. "What is it?"

"Open it."

I traced the long lines of one of the dragons on the top, and looked up at Baltic. "If it contains a wedding ring, you can just take it back. I've had enough of marriage, thank you."

He made an impatient gesture. "Marriage is for mortals. You are my mate. That is for all time."

"Till death do us part," I said softly, then smiled. "And beyond."

"Open it," he repeated.

I glanced at the big bed behind me. The room was decorated in shades of cream and a cool blue—attractive, but completely not his style. "Why don't I open it later, after I've given you all that pleasure you think you're due?"

"I know I am due it," he said with maddening arrogance, then nudged my hands. "Open your present."

"I like to anticipate gifts. Once you open them, the anticipation is gone."

"Open it!" he said, a little line of frown starting to form between his brows.

"Let's have oral sex!" I said brightly, moving backwards toward the bed, patting it with a seductive glance toward him. "You like that! I remember that you do! You take off all your clothes and lie down here, and I'll give you a tongue bath that you won't ever forget."

"For the love of the saints, woman, open the damned box!"

"And you say you never spurn! You just spurned my offer of a blow job, something I thought no living man could do."

He started toward me, a look in his eye that said he'd reached the end of his pretty nonexistent patience.

"Fine!" I said quickly, crawling onto the middle of the bed while I clutched the box. "But I just want you to remember that you're the one who didn't want oral sex. Stop giving me that look! I'm opening it. See? The lid is . . . ahhh."

It wasn't really a word I spoke; it was more an exhalation of emotion. The box held a small object, somewhere between an oval and a circle, made of metal, but now dulled with age and time.

Recognition prickled along my skin as I gazed at it, waves of electricity seeming to ripple down my arms and legs. I knew this object. I knew it well, and yet it was both as familiar to me as the beat of my own heart, and foreign, something I had never seen before.

"Love token." I spoke the words without even being aware of it. "It's my love token. You made it for me. But how . . . ?"

"It was at Dauva, in my lair. You placed it there, along with all the valuables in the castle, before Constantine attacked. Kostya raided most of the lair, but he left that."

So faint I could barely make it out, a roughly drawn tree was engraved into the silver token, with three upper leafy branches, and two lower ones bearing hearts.

I smiled, a faint memory returning to me. "It's made of silver so it would not distract you when I wore it."

He watched me closely. "You remember it, then?"

"No. Yes. Both." I reached out to touch the token,

wanting to feel it, to weigh its age in my hand, but the second my finger touched the metal surface, the world began to spin.

I cried out, feeling as if I would fall, but strong arms caught me, warm and familiar, his touch stirring the embers of desire that were always within me. The room darkened, the colors shifting from light to dark, large amber pools lit by tall standing candelabras, the light of the candles flickering and shimmering along the shadows of the room.

Figures shimmered, too, the figure of a man and a woman.

"A love token?" the woman said, smiling at the man. "For me?"

"I made it for you when I sailed from Riga to France."

"It's a tree," she said, and her voice resonated within me, my lips parting to speak the next words with her. "A tree with hearts?"

"A tree because I knew it would please you. Three branches for you, me, and the sept," Baltic then and now said, one voice slightly echoing the other.

I was pulled toward the figure of my other self as if I were made of nothing but light and shadow, hesitating a moment as I glanced back at Baltic. He nodded and I let myself merge with the memory of my former self. Baltic's face changed as he, too, allowed himself to sink into his former being.

"And two hearts," Ysolde and I said at the same time as we smiled up at him.

"I give you this token as a pledge of my heart," he said, and tears pricked in my eyes at the love shining in his.

Ysolde and I kissed him, clutching the token to our chest. "It's the most wonderful thing I've ever received. I can't believe you made it for me."

"You have sworn to be my mate, and for me there is no greater bond, but you were raised with mortals. I thought you would like it."

I was so touched, both at the time, and again now, that he would go to such lengths to please me. "It couldn't have been easy to make it," I told my Baltic as the other Ysolde cooed happily at the token before offering him her mouth again.

The two Baltics shimmered, the image of one overlaying the other.

"It wasn't. I'm no artist. I almost severed my fingers a couple of times engraving the image in it."

"Make love to me," I pleaded as the other Baltic scooped up my former self and carried her to the gigantic canopied bed.

Baltic glanced at the memories of us when I moved against him, sliding my hands around to his back, stroking the muscles there, and wiggling my hips in brazen invitation. "Here? With them?"

"They're us. We're in your bedroom. Please, Baltic. I've waited so long for you, and now I can have you. You wanted to claim me yesterday—well, now I'm all yours."

"First you are aroused by the thought of males loving males; then you wished to bare your breasts to everyone with a pair of eyes in his head; and now you want to engage in mating with other people?" He bent and picked me up, carrying me to the bed with an expression that mingled irritation with desire. "We will have a long discussion about these fantasies of yours, *chérie.* I am willing to oblige you this once, but I warn you—you are my mate, and I have no intention of sharing you."

He laid me down on the bed next to the other Ysolde, who was now clad in what I recognized as a thin chemise, the black-haired Baltic kneeling between her legs, slowly pushing the chemise higher and higher.

"Whoa," I said, unable to take my eyes from them, my own emotions as conflicted as Baltic's. "This is . . . wow. On the one hand, it feels like we're watching two people about to make love. But it's us. So how can it feel so very . . . oooh. . . . kinky?"

Baltic, who had been removing his clothing, glanced over at the ghostly pair before returning his attention to me. He stood next to me, his hands on his hips, his penis fully aroused and saluting me. "As I said, we will have a discussion about this at a later time."

I looked at his groin, making a mental measurement before sliding a quick look over at the other version of him.

"What are you doing?" he asked, accusation heavy in his voice as he climbed onto the bed.

"Nothing!" I said, quickly looking back at him.

His black eyes narrowed on me as he, too, knelt between my legs. "You were comparing me to him, weren't you?"

"Of course I wasn't! What gave you that idea?"

"I saw you looking at my rod. You looked at it, and then looked at his. You were making comparisons!"

"He is you," I said, pointing at the other Baltic.

"The fact remains that you were judging my rod against his."

"I was not!" He stared at me. I stared back at him.

After about five seconds, I added, "Besides, it doesn't matter. You're bigger now."

"Aha! I knew it!"

"Look, you're making a big fuss over nothing," I said, gesturing toward the other couple. I glanced at them as I spoke, but the words dried up on my lips, and my eyes bugged out when Ysolde, lying next to me, groaned and clutched the sheets, her head thrashing from side to side as Baltic pleasured her with his mouth and hands. My mouth hung open as I blinked at the sight. It was so wrong to watch such an intimate moment between two people—but those two people were us. That was me having an orgasm that caused me to arch up off the bed, calling Baltic's name. "By the rood," I managed to get out as I watched.

Baltic smiled smugly. "You always were fast to please."

"By the rood!" I repeated as the other version of him crawled up her body, licking her with both his tongue and dragon fire. She growled, twining her legs around him as he eased himself into her warmth, her hands clutching his butt and pulling him tighter.

"Ysolde," Baltic said.

*"By the rood!"* I yelled as Ysolde arched again, her hips jerking upward. Her Baltic murmured something in her ear, pulling out just long enough to move his arms under her legs so that they rested on his shoulders, angling her pelvis for maximum penetration. "Can you do that to me, please? Like right now?"

He sat on his heels, frowning. "I do not like the fact that the sight of others making love excites you so much, *chérie*. You should be focused on me only."

"I am focused on you. Holy—is he doing what I think he's doing?"

"You wished to have a child," Baltic said, not paying the least bit of attention as his other self crammed a couple of pillows beneath Ysolde's behind, on his knees as he thrust into her with hard, fast movements. "I was simply trying to help you conceive."

I blinked, unable to look away until Baltic bit my ankle. "Mate, I am the one you should be staring at with that look of lust and desire and besotted fascination!"

"Jealous?" I asked him, trying to look at both Baltics at once. It wasn't easy.

"That would be foolish—" Even he stopped to look as the other version of us, with cries that were unmistakable for anything but those of completion, fell off the side of the bed.

"I knocked myself out for a few minutes by hitting my head on the floor," Baltic commented as I peered over at them.

Sure enough, Ysolde was on the floor, making soft little happy noises, stroking the sweaty back of the man who was still evidently embedded in her, her legs rubbing up and down on his. He didn't move.

"I hope you weren't hurt seriously."

"I wasn't. Now if your voyeuristic desires have been satisfied, will you please attend to me?"

"Sorry," I said, scooting back to my spot. Baltic looked peeved now. "But if you could do just what the other Baltic did, minus the falling on the floor and cracking your head, that would be really, *really* fine with me."

"It is right that you wish to give me a child since you gave one to the usurper," he said, approval softening his frown. "But first, I must claim you properly as my mate. Afterward, we will make a child."

I opened my mouth to tell him that one son was enough for me, but I remembered the pain in his face when he had spoken to my past self of the child we'd lost. "We'll talk later about adding to the family, all right? At this moment, I really would like you to do something other than frown at me."

He dipped his head and bathed me in fire.

I screamed and almost came off the bed, my breath caught in my throat as he started pulling off my clothing. As it did before, the fire seemed to dance on my skin, pulsating as it moved up my legs to my stomach.

Baltic pulled off my jeans, sandals, and underwear with a sweep of his hands. I writhed on the bed as the fire swept upward. The corset top seemed to melt off me as Baltic snapped the laces one by one until all that stood between me and his fire was my bra.

"You, too, are bigger," he said just as his head bent over the valley of my breasts, the bra coming off easily. His breath steamed my flesh, making me yearn for the inferno I knew he could build within me.

"I am not!" I looked down at my breasts. "You really think so?"

"I know it. You were plentiful before. Now you are"— he cupped one breast in his hand, his thumb gently rubbing across my nipple—"very abundant."

"Fire," I begged, squirming against him as his tongue flicked out over my now-aching breast.

"You must learn to use your own fire," he chastised, taking my breast into his mouth. I moaned and grabbed great handfuls of the sheets just as the past Ysolde had done, my breasts thrusting upward.

"Fire!" I ordered, and writhed happily when he chuckled and said, "So demanding. That, too, has not changed," before allowing his dragon fire to pour out of him and wrap itself around me. It burned, but it did not harm me. It warmed, but it was nothing compared to the inferno blazing within. It teased my flesh, but only Baltic's touches, soft caresses with his mouth and fingers, made me feel like I was one continuous erogenous zone.

"Embrace the fire, *chérie*," he mumbled into my breastbone as he slid lower, kissing and burning a path down to my stomach. "Claim it as your own. Use it. Shape it. Make it be what you want it to be."

I wanted to. Oh, how I wanted to, but I couldn't focus my thoughts on anything but the magic of him as he slid even lower, nipping at my hips with sharp teeth, soothed by long, slow strokes of his tongue.

"Accept the fire, my love."

"I . . . I can't," I said as he nudged my knees apart.

"You can. You are my mate. You are a light dragon. Accept it." Heat poured over me as he sent his dragon fire up my body again, the flames licking along my skin before sinking deep into me. His hands swept up my thighs, pushing them wider, his mouth hot on the sensitive inner flesh as he kissed a fiery path to my very core.

"I don't think it's possible," I said, a fever of need and want and desire all mingled together, causing a pressure within me to push higher and higher.

"It is. You must try, Ysolde. Give the fire back to me." I moaned again at the feeling of his mouth as he breathed fire on the most sensitive of flesh, gasping when he sank a finger into me. "Use it, mate. Use the fire."

A long, low cry tore from my throat as the pressure continued to build, fueled by both his fire and the passion he was triggering with every flick of his tongue.

"Now!" he demanded, and my body trembled on the brink of something so profound, I couldn't begin to understand it. The pressure inside me gave with a rush as the fire that I had absorbed roared to life, pouring out of me to consume him.

He made a noise deep in his chest, part growl, part mating sound that my heart recognized and answered. My body wasn't just alight—I *was* the flame. Baltic suddenly reached underneath me, flipping me over onto my stomach, the arm beneath my belly pulling me upward as he covered my back.

"Mate," he growled, his body hard and aggressive on mine. I arched again, unable to keep from moaning with sheer, utter ecstasy as he thrust into my body, his penis a brand that only drove the pressure inside me to the point where I knew I was going to explode.

The feeling of him within me, of my muscles trembling around him, was enough to push me over the edge. I spiraled into an orgasm unlike anything I thought possible, my soul merging with his as he joined me in a moment of absolute rapture.

My legs gave out and I collapsed onto the bed as he roared one word, his hands beside my hips as he continued to pound into me with short, fast thrusts until at last he, too, collapsed.

I tried to make sense of what had happened, but my brain gave a little whimper and told me I was on my own. I lay shaking with the sense of power that our joining had brought, Baltic's heavy body pressing me into the soft mattress.

"Did we die again?" I asked when I recovered enough ability to move my mouth.

A soft, rusty chuckle sounded in my ear. "No, but it was a close thing."

"Dear god," I said as, pulling me with him, he rolled onto his back. "Was it always like that? Because I'm serious, Baltic—I don't know if my heart can stand that every night. I'll have to take up an aerobics class, and I hate that sort of thing."

"It has always been and will always be thus between us," he said, moving my limp body so I lay draped over his chest, one of my legs caught between his. "You will learn to adjust to the more strenuous dragon matings, just as you learned to harness your fire."

"That wasn't my fire. It was yours. I just used it," I said, too drained to do more than smooth my hand over his still-heaving chest.

"It was both."

Next to us, a body hit the bed.

I glanced over, smiling as the past Ysolde dabbed tenderly at a spot of blood on her Baltic's forehead. He tolerated that for a moment, then pulled her over him, catching one of her breasts in his mouth. "Goodness. You appear to have had a lot of stamina then."

He didn't even look, just smiled, his eyelashes thick sable crescents as he lay with his eyes closed. "Give me five minutes, and I will show you that I have improved in that way, as well."

"You might have improved, but I think another round would be the end of me," I commented, unable to keep from watching when Ysolde impaled herself on the past Baltic. "You know, it's really too bad we can't interact with them."

He cracked open one eye and looked at me. "Why?"

I gestured to where his previous self bucked, Ysolde riding him as if he were an unbroken stallion, and pursed my lips a little. "Well, if we could, you and the other Baltic could . . . you know . . ."

The look he shot me was so outraged I giggled. He slapped my behind, then rubbed away the sting before closing his eyes. "Many people have told me to go fuck myself, but I never expected my mate to actually suggest that I do it."

I giggled even more, kissing the pulse in his neck, my body and heart and soul happier than they had ever been.

# Chapter Fifteen

My suggestion was, I thought, extremely acceptable. "How about Strand Palace Hotel? It has conference capabilities, and their big business suite is available tomorrow."

"Are you kidding? After what happened the last time Baltic came to a *sárkány* in a hotel?" Aisling's voice was filled with scorn. "I don't think so!"

"Why, what happened?"

"He tried to shoot everyone present!"

"Oh, that. One moment, please." I covered the mouthpiece of the phone and turned to where Baltic stood glaring at me. "Did you really go to a *sárkány* recently and shoot the participants?"

"Yes." The answer was given in a grumpy tone, which, given the look on his face, was no surprise.

I took a deep breath. "You do realize how difficult it is to get the wyverns to agree to meet you on neutral ground so we can talk about things, don't you?"

"What the weyr does or thinks is none of our concern. We are outside of them. They do not matter to us."

"They matter to me," I said.

He continued to glare. "Not as much as I matter to you."

"Of course not, and stop being so insecure. I've loved you for over four hundred years. I think you can relax."

"The other you loved me. This you . . ." He raked me up and down with a wary gaze. "This you is different. You have unnatural desires. My old Ysolde would never have left me to try to position herself between two lovers."

"I didn't try anything of the sort! I just moved off you and happened to roll exactly where the old version of us was going at it. Again. For a third time in the space of an hour." I narrowed my eyes at him. "You only managed once."

His eyes blazed black fire at me. "I told you to give me five minutes and I would recover enough to pleasure you again! You are the one who stopped me. You did not wish for me to start again!"

"Regardless, I did not deliberately roll under the other you and get my jollies from him pounding away. Although I really liked the looks of that little swirl thing he was doing. Do you think we could—" A faint voice in my ear reminded me that I was on the phone. Evidently, my hand had slipped off the mouthpiece.

"—arguing with him. No, not about meeting us, about sex, I think. Evidently he only did things once and she wanted three times. And it sounds like there may have been another couple involved."

"Um," I said, giving Baltic a glare of my own. "I'm

sorry you had to overhear that, Aisling. Baltic drives me a little batty sometimes."

"Only sometimes?" she asked; at the same time he snorted and said, "It is your bizarre fantasies that make me insane."

"My fantasies are not the least bit bizarre!" I said loudly.

"No, of course not," Aisling said, laughter in her voice. "Although I have to say, you're the last person I had pegged for a swinger."

I took another deep, deep breath, and managed to hold on to my temper. "All right, a hotel is out."

"Yes. Our house is big enough if we open up the downstairs to make one big room."

I glanced at where Baltic was now pacing beside me, his hands behind his back. He glared at the floor as if it personally offended him.

"I think we're going to have some objections to the neutrality of that location. How about Hyde Park? That's large."

"Too public," Aisling said. "And too many portals there. If the dragons start fighting, things can happen, and I'm not back to full Guardian duties yet. What we need is something private, yet roomy."

"How about Baltic's house, the one with the garden?" I asked, my spirits lifting just thinking about it.

He raised his eyebrows at the suggestion, looking strangely thoughtful.

"Let me check." Muffled voices followed that, too muffled for me to make out. "An objection has been raised for that location, as well. It's been pointed out that you could escape to the beyond there."

I sighed. "Tell May hello."

"She says hello," Aisling duly repeated. "May wants to know if they should bring Brom's and your things, or if you'll be picking them up?"

"If it's not too much trouble, that would be lovely. I guess that leaves us with only one solution."

"What's that?"

I kept my eyes on Baltic as I spoke. "You'll just have to come here. Baltic's house isn't huge, but there are ample grounds, and I think everyone would feel better if we held the *sárkány* out in the open."

"No!" Baltic bellowed, whirling around to face me. "You would bring my enemies here?"

"They wouldn't be your enemies if you stopped shooting at them!" I pointed out.

"And blowing up their houses," Aisling said. "And trying to steal their mates."

"Yes, and blowing up their houses, and . . . what was that?"

"Stealing their mates. Didn't May tell you? May, didn't you tell her that Baltic was trying to steal you with the shard?"

"Gargh!" I yelled, and for the first time, I felt Baltic's fire raging within me of its own accord.

"Oops. I take that as a no," Aisling said softly. "Oh dear. I think I set Ysolde off—"

"You tried to take May?" I yelled, clutching the phone so tightly, my knuckles were white. The pressure built within me, and I spat out a fireball the size of a grapefruit that slammed against his chest, rocking him backwards. "You tried to claim another mate?"

Baltic looked stunned for a moment, then worried. He absorbed the fire, his hands spread in placation. "*Chérie*, it wasn't like that at all—"

"Don't you *chérie* me, you scaly-skinned monster! You wanted May! You never really wanted me, did you? I was dead, so you looked around for the first piece of dragon ass you could find, and you tried to take her!"

"I wanted the shard, yes. I wanted it so that the dragon heart could be re-formed. I never really wanted the silver mate—"

"Then why did you try to take her?" I spat out another fireball, this one a little larger. He caught it before it could slam into him, extinguishing it as he slowly came forward, hesitantly, as if I were a dangerous animal.

I narrowed my eyes and wished I could switch into dragon form.

"My intention was to remove her from the silver wyvern, not to claim her for my own mate. He should never have had a mate in the first place."

"Oh, really? Why not?"

He looked disconcerted and waved away the question. "That is a matter for another discussion."

"I don't think so!" I held the phone back up to my ear. "Aisling, are you still there?"

"Er . . . yes. Ysolde, I'm sorry, I had no idea that you didn't know about—"

"Why shouldn't Gabriel have a mate?" I asked, ruthlessly interrupting her.

"Ysolde, you will not question others when I am here to answer anything you wish to know," Baltic said arrogantly, but I shot a bigger fireball at him, one that knocked him back a couple of feet, onto the couch. He dropped the arrogance and went straight for seduction. "My love, you distress yourself unduly over a minor incident."

"He cursed them to never have a mate born to them," Aisling said succinctly.

"Please hold. A curse, Baltic?" I asked, wrapping my fingers across the mouthpiece again.

"You were dead! Constantine killed you! That damned Kostya was trying to hack off my head! I had to curse someone, and Constantine ripped my life from me by killing you. Of course I cursed them!"

A memory of the pain he suffered when I was killed shimmered in his eyes and effectively squashed my ire. "You're going to have to lift the curse, you know."

His expression darkened. "I do not *have* to do anything, mate."

"You cursed the silver dragons because their wyvern killed me. But I'm not dead any longer."

"You are also not the same Ysolde you were."

"I do not have strange sexual kinks!" I yelled, slamming the phone down on the table. I poked him in the chest because I knew it would irritate him. "Things just conspire to make it look that way! By the rood, Baltic! Just because a little guy-on-guy action isn't objectionable to me, you think every little peccadillo is some majorly perverted desire on my part! Oh, hell." I looked down at the phone, picking it up carefully. "You heard that, didn't you, Aisling?"

A muffled laugh followed. "I'm afraid we all did, thanks to the invention of the speakerphone."

"Oh, god." I closed my eyes for a moment, overcome with embarrassment. "I will give you directions to the house."

"You will not tell them where we live!" Baltic ranted behind me.

"I trust you will continue to honor the agreement regarding Jim. Once the *sárkány* is over, I will turn it over to you."

"Your turn to hold," Aisling said, but she had an actual hold on her phone. A slight humming noise filled the earpiece.

"Mate! I forbid you to do this!" Baltic said, grabbing my arm.

I set the phone down, turning to face him, sliding my hands into his hair, gently removing the leather thong. "I love you, Baltic."

"I will not allow—er . . ." His tense jaw relaxed as I nibbled along it, gently biting his lower lip. His hands, which had been gripping my arms, moved around to cup my behind, pulling me tight against him.

"I love you more than anything in the world, but I would like us to live in peace with the weyr. Please do this for me. For us." I sucked his lower lip into my mouth and tried to summon his fire, but it seemed to be banked. "Fire?"

It roared through me as he claimed my mouth properly, his tongue being every bit as demanding as he was. Just as I was seriously contemplating wrestling him to the floor and indulging in a few acts I'd seen my past self perform, the door opened.

"Fires of Abaddon, they're still at it? Brom, my man, you don't want to see this."

"Don't want to see what? Oh. Sullivan is kissing Baltic."

"Father," Baltic said, breaking off the kiss to inform Brom.

"Huh?" my son asked, eyeing me as if I were one of his experiments. "How come your hands are on her butt?"

"I like her butt," Baltic said, giving the object in question a little squeeze. I bit his chin. "You will refer to me as 'Father' henceforth."

"But your name is Baltic," Brom pointed out.

"Hey, is that Aisling I hear squawking on the phone?" Jim asked as it wandered over to where I'd set down the receiver. "Ash, babe, you there?"

"Oh, damn, I forgot her again." I turned in Baltic's arms, but he didn't release me.

"It is not fitting that you refer to your parents by their names. It does not show respect. You will therefore refer to me as 'Father.' I will leave it to your mother to decide if she wishes to tolerate you referring to her by her surname."

"No, it's cool," Jim said, plopping down next to the table, its head lying next to the phone so it could talk and hear. "Pavel made sage-roasted game hens for lunch, and I had a whole one to myself. He needs to give the recipe to Suzanne because it was seriously yummy. And Ysolde said she was going to brush me later. No, they stopped kissing, although Baltic's hands are almost on her boobs. Right in front of the kid, too."

Baltic's hands, which had indeed been moving up from my stomach, froze.

"I don't like 'Father,' " Brom said, his brown eyes serious as they considered Baltic.

"Papa?" I suggested, placing my hands over Baltic's and leaning back into his chest. Despite the worry of the upcoming *sárkány*, I felt aglow with happiness. That Baltic cared so much about how Brom referred to him was a good sign. Brom would have a real father at last, one who cared about him.

"Yeah, yeah, but you're overreacting, Aisling. I'm fine—no one's hurting me. Ysolde keeps giving me scary mom looks, but I don't think she can help it. Besides, it's wild seeing Baltic being all lovey-dovey with her. How the mighty can fall."

Brom wrinkled his nose. "I'm nine, Sullivan, not two. How about 'Dad'? The others at the mage school call their fathers Dad. Most of them. There's that weird kid who calls everyone Carrot, but no one pays much attention to him."

Baltic's fingers twined through mine. "You sent my son to a mage school?"

"Dr. Kostich thought he might have some talents in that direction, so I enrolled him in it. Unfortunately, he seems to have inherited my lack of abilities when it comes to things arcane."

"Ixnay on the ecretsay ummonsay," Jim said, casting a worried glance my way. "Oh, great, now she's giving me another of those looks, the kind that says I'm going to be sent to my room without supper."

"You will if you don't give me the phone," I told it.

"Gotta go. Pavel said he's doing goulash for dinner, and he promises it'll be almost orgasmic."

"What's—" Brom started to ask.

"Out!" I told the demon, taking the phone from it. "Brom, Baltic will be happy with 'Dad.' You go practice saying it somewhere else, please. And Jim, so help me god—"

"I know, you'll skin me alive or some other heinous act if I explain to Brom what 'orgasmic' means. I didn't actually mean to say that in front of him. Sometimes I forget he's only a kid."

"That's all right," Brom said, patting Jim on the head as the two of them exited the room. "Sometimes I forget you're a demon. You want to play catch?"

"Naw. Let's go play on Pavel's Xbox. He's got a road-racing game I love."

"Aisling?"

"Still here. And you have my permission to yell at Jim. I can't believe it'd say something so inappropriate in front of a child. Honest to Pete! It knows better than that! Drake, stop trying to take the phone away from me! I'm not done."

"I take it we're off speakerphone?"

"Yes, I thought after that last argument, it would be better. Drake wishes to speak with Baltic, but I did want to remind you that should anything happen to Jim, I will rain down destruction as you've never seen it. Not that I think you'd do anything to it, because you seem very maternal, and we moms have a sense about those things, but I feel obligated as its demon lord to say that. Fine! You can have the phone. Sheesh, pushy dragons . . ."

"Oh, Aisling?" I said, smiling to myself.

"Yes?"

"The next time you have Drake alone, ask him about a small inn in Paris called the Hangman's Balls. Mention the year 1699."

"All right," she said slowly. "I will. Here's Drake."

"A moment, please," I told Drake when he asked for Baltic. I held the phone to my chest. "You will be polite."

"I am a wyvern," he said airily.

"You will not say rude things to Drake no matter what he says to you."

"You may leave. I will speak with the green wyvern by myself."

"We are trying to establish a relationship with these people. Please remember that."

He tried to take the phone. I hung on to it. "You may leave now, Ysolde."

"Not until you promise to be good."

"I'm always good. Give me the phone."

"Just remember what I've said, that's all."

"I am not a child who needs to be schooled in matters of weyr etiquette," he answered, trying to pry my fingers off the receiver.

"You're also notoriously short-tempered, don't give a damn what anyone else thinks, and have a chip on your shoulder approximately the size of Rhode Island."

"Mate," he said, a warning light in his eyes.

"Yes?"

"Do your many and varied sexual kinks run to spankings?"

"I don't have sexual kinks, and no—you wouldn't!" I gasped as he tried to pull me over to the chair. "All right, I'll leave, but if you mess things up after I've worked so hard to straighten them out, I will make your life a living hell—just see if I don't!"

As I closed the door I heard him say, "What? Yes, it worked. I recommend using the threat of it as a method of controlling an unruly mate—"

# Chapter Sixteen

"By the rood, they can't be early, can they?" I paused on my way through the French doors in the sitting room to peer out of the glass next to the front door. A car was pulling to a stop. "I'm not ready! We don't have all the beverages out to the field yet, let alone the canapés!"

"I can help you with the canapés," Jim said, licking its lips as it emerged from the kitchen hauling a large basket. "Oooh, visitors?"

"If your demon lord came early just to catch us by surprise—oh, no!"

"Who is it?" Jim asked, peering around me. Its eyebrows rose. "Heh. This ought to be fun."

"What is Savian doing, telling everyone in the Otherworld where I am?" I muttered as I set down the tray of cut glass crystal goblets and opened the door. "Good afternoon, Dr. Kostich."

"Tully," he said, inclining his head toward me. "I trust

you will excuse my unannounced arrival. I have matters of great import to discuss with you."

"Actually, I'm a bit busy today. Could you come back another time? Say, next year?"

The look he gave me said much, and none of it was in my favor. He strolled past me into the house, casually tossing over his shoulder, "I assume you have the von Endres blade by now. I have come to collect it."

"Oh, lord," I swore, looking heavenward for a moment. "Why me?"

"What's going on . . . oh man. Greetings, your eminence," Jim said, almost groveling toward Dr. Kostich. I didn't wonder that the demon, normally the most flip of beings, had adopted a respectful air. Clearly it had come into contact with Dr. Kostich before.

I turned slowly back to the foyer, trying to think of a diplomatic way to explain to the head of the Otherworld that I would not be stealing Baltic's sword.

"What are you doing here?" Kostich asked, staring at Jim where it sat in the center of the narrow hall.

Jim dipped its head again in a doggy bow. "Ysolde's making me be a pack mule. I didn't know you were going to be here, though. Not that there's anything wrong with you being here," it added quickly as it backed up a few steps.

"I dislike demons," Dr. Kostich told it, his eyes narrowing and his fingers twitching as if he might cast a spell.

"Ysolde!" Jim almost yelped, hurrying over to press into my leg. "You promised Ash to keep me safe! Don't let him do anything to me."

"You're a demon," I told it, patting it on its head

nonetheless. "He can't harm a demon. No one can but a demon lord. Not permanently, anyway."

"Wanna bet?" Jim peeked out around my leg at my former employer.

My eyebrows rose. "You can harm a demon? Not just its form, but the demon itself?"

Dr. Kostich just smiled.

"Don't worry, I won't let anyone harm you," I said meaningfully. "Jim is my guest, Dr. Kostich."

The demon moved out a few steps. "Hostage is more like it. Ysolde demon-napped me. Not that I mind, because she's cool and all."

"I can't imagine why she would want to do that—" The words dried up on his lips as Baltic emerged from a back room. He paused at the sight of Kostich. The two men stared at each other.

"Uh-oh," Jim said, backing up again.

"You!" Kostich said, pointing dramatically at Baltic. "It is you!"

Baltic shot me an irritated glance.

"I didn't tell him where we were," I answered the look. "Savian did."

"Now you will pay for your crimes against the L'audela!" Dr. Kostich announced, and began to cast what I knew was a morphing spell.

"I really should have killed you when I had the chance," Baltic snarled, holding out his hand. The light blade materialized in a burst of blue-white light.

"No!" I yelled, running to stand between them. "I will not have this! Not now! Not today! Not when I haven't made the lemon sorbet yet!"

Baltic, in the act of raising the sword over his head,

presumably to strike down Dr. Kostich, paused and frowned at me. "Lemon sorbet?"

"For after the *sárkány*. I thought a little lemon sorbet and some ladyfingers would be refreshing."

He lowered the sword, his lips tight as he turned to face me. "This is not a party, Ysolde!"

"Lemon sorbet does not constitute a party," I pointed out.

"Regardless, I will not feed my enemies!"

"Might I interject a note of seriousness into this bizarre conversation—" Dr. Kostich started to say.

"Don't think it will do any good," Jim answered as I pushed my way past Dr. Kostich to face Baltic.

"They are our guests, and I will be damned if I have it said that people came to my house and I did not offer them common hospitality."

"Sorbet is not common hospitality," he argued. "It's dessert."

"I thought people would like something to cleanse their palates after the canapés!" I said, slapping my hands on my thighs. "Pardon me for being civilized."

"Canapés? Now you have canapés?" His face was beginning to flush, always a sign his temper was slipping. "What next, champagne?"

Pavel emerged from the door leading to the basement, a cardboard box in his hands bearing the name of a famous brand of champagne. Baltic looked at him in disbelief before turning a scowl on me. "That's my vintage Bollinger's!"

"It won't hurt you to share."

"With people who want me dead!" he yelled.

"I completely understand their feelings," Dr. Kostich said. "About the von Endres sword—"

"That's it," Baltic said, raising the sword again. "I'm killing him; then I will deal with you, mate."

Dr. Kostich took a step back, his hands going through the intricate twists and turns of a morphing spell.

"You will not hurt him! I will never forgive you if you hurt him!" I told Baltic.

He glared at me, his eyes sparking onyx, his jaw tight with tension. "You are pushing me too far, woman!"

"I just want everyone to get along!" I yelled, so frustrated I could . . . well, yell. "Why can't people stop trying to kill each other and steal things from each other and so help me god, Dr. Kostich, if you complete that morph spell, I'll slap you with one myself!"

My former employer lifted his nose, his fingers dancing in the air as they drew near to completing a particularly detailed morph spell that would turn Baltic into some other form. "You are under an interdict. Your magic does not work."

"Wanna bet?" I snarled, and pulled hard on the dragon fire within me, letting my own fingers do a little spell casting.

A banana materialized out of the air and fell to his feet.

He stopped his morph spell. Everyone stared at the banana.

"Um. That was supposed to be a slavering tiger," I said, prodding the fruit with the toe of my shoe. "I guess the interdict is making my magic wonky."

"Understatement time," Jim said, sniffing it. "You want me to pretend I'm a tiger and stab the archimage with it?"

We all ignored Jim.

"You should not be able to even cast a spell," Kostich said, giving me a long look. "It is not possible that you can do so with the interdict placed upon you."

"My mate is not a normal woman," Baltic said, hauling me into his side with his free arm. With the other, he waved the sword at Kostich. "She is a light dragon. She is beyond your understanding."

"You!" Kostich snapped again, glaring at Baltic as he gathered up arcane energy into a bluish white ball.

"Here we go again," Jim said, taking the banana to the bottom step of the staircase. "At least I have snacks for this show."

"Don't you dare!" I told Kostich just as he released the arcane ball. Baltic parried it with a flash of his light blade.

"Very Wonder Woman," Jim said, its mouth full. "How are you with bullets?"

"Oh!" I yelled, glaring at the mage, rolling up my sleeves. Baltic hauled me back as I was about to pounce on my former employer. "Let go of me, Baltic! No one throws arcane magic at my man!"

"Dragon," Jim corrected.

"Move out of the way," Kostich warned, pulling on his power to form another arcane ball. "I shall smite the dragon where he stands!"

I twisted in Baltic's grip, shoving him hard to the side. Kostich's ball of power shot past us and hit a vase standing on a pedestal, exploding both into a bazillion tiny pieces.

"Steeeerike!" Jim said, tossing the now empty banana peel onto the floor in front of Kostich.

"What the hell are you doing?" Baltic asked as I continued to shove him toward the drawing room. "Leave me be, mate! I must attend to that deranged mage once and for all."

"I am not deranged!" Dr. Kostich bellowed, turning as he pulled together yet more power, forming it between his hands into a sphere that glowed blue. "Now stand still, damn you, so I can smite you!"

"Oh, no, he's not deranged," Jim said, cocking an ironic eyebrow.

"Stop it!" I shouted as Baltic yanked me sideways, out of the path of the ball of power. It went through the window, shattering the glass along the way.

"You are so going to pay for that window!" I said, storming toward Kostich.

"Mate, will you get out of the way so I can kill the mage?" Baltic snarled, his blade flashing from side to side as Dr. Kostich, muttering imprecations under his breath, quickly threw tiny little sparks of light at him one right after another.

"No one is killing anyone—you bastard!" I gasped as Dr. Kostich, whirling around when the wind caused the door to close loudly, sent a blast of arcane power into the tray of leaded crystal goblets. "Those were for the après-*sárkány* lemon sorbet! Right! That's it! No more Miss Nice Whatever-the-hell-I-am!"

"Dragon," Dr. Kostich said at the same moment Baltic said, "Mate," and Jim added, in not nearly a quiet enough voice, "Crazy lady?"

I snatched up a small Chippendale chair with a cream and pale blue striped seat, and lunged toward the mage with it held out before me, as if I were a lion tamer and he were a particularly obstreperous lion. "Back! Back, I say! You can't have the sword! You can't have Baltic;

he's mine! Go away, and don't bother us again! Er . . . do I get paid for the last two weeks even though you put the interdiction on me? Because I haven't seen my paycheck deposited yet, and I promised Brom he could pick out a large dehydrator for his birthday, and that's only a couple of weeks away."

A burst of whitish blue light flared in front of me, the chair I held disintegrating as the arcane power blasted it to smithereens. I stared in surprise first at my hand, which held one surviving leg of the chair, then up to Dr. Kostich. "You aimed that at me!" I said, aghast.

A low growl of anger came from Baltic, and suddenly, the room was full of a white dragon, fire erupting around him as he slammed into Dr. Kostich, the two of them tumbling to the highly polished marble floor in a confusion of dragon limbs, tail, and flailing mage legs.

"No one touches my mate," Baltic snarled, pinning Kostich to the ground, puffing a few wisps of smoke a scant inch from Kostich's face.

"Oooh. He's drooling on him. That's just completely gross," Jim said, watching from the safety of the stairs.

"Those who live in glass houses," I told the demon before marching over to Kostich's head and poking at him with the chair leg. "And you owe us for this chair, too! It was an antique!"

Kostich squawked something, his face beet red, his body writhing as he desperately tried to get air into his squashed lungs.

No one heard the front door open until the voice spoke.

"Are we early? Oh. Er. Hello, Dr. Kostich."

"Heya, Ash," Jim said, hopping down the stairs to

greet its demon lord. "Lemon sorbet's not ready yet. Why don't you come back in an hour?"

"Uh . . ." I blinked at the people crowding the doorway. Aisling, Drake, and his two redheaded bodyguards were crammed into the door, all with the same identical expressions of surprise. "Hi."

"Hi," Aisling said, looking at where Baltic was flattening Dr. Kostich. "Hello, Baltic. I don't think we've formally met."

"Do you know who I am?" Dr. Kostich spat out, somewhat breathily, to be sure. "I lead the Committee!"

I straightened up and smiled at the dragons as Aisling stepped carefully over the broken crystal goblets, Drake right behind her. "You are a little bit early, but that's all right, although as Jim says, the sorbet isn't ready yet. Oh, hell! Jim!"

"I can have you all banished to the Akasha! I'm just that powerful!" Dr. Kostich wheezed.

I ignored him and turned to glare at the demon.

"What? Who? Me? I wasn't smelling his butt!" Jim said quickly, backing away from where Baltic lay crushing Dr. Kostich.

"You're all going to be charged for these grievous crimes against my august person!"

Baltic swung his neck around to send a little circle of fire at the demon. I caught the fire as it passed me and tossed it back to him with a frown.

"You're supposed to be elsewhere, so that Aisling has to make Drake do what she says!" I told the demon. "You can't be a hostage for their good behavior if you're right here!"

"That's not my fault," Jim said, sitting on Kostich's foot.

"Including the demon, who has just broken my foot! Get off, you soulless beast of Abaddon!"

"Aisling is the one who came early," Jim added.

I frowned at the woman as she stopped in front of Baltic and Dr. Kostich. "You did this deliberately, didn't you? You came here early just so you would catch me in the middle of my preparations, just so you could make me look bad. That's really not at all nice, and after I went to the trouble of making a cheesecake!"

"What sort of preparations?" Drake asked, pulling Aisling back a couple of paces when Dr. Kostich freed one hand and tried to grab her. "Were you setting traps for us? Arranging for an ambush? Another bomb?"

"Lemon sorbet and canapés," Jim said, drooling on the mage's leg. "Ysolde let me taste-test the smoked salmon rolls, too. Speaking of which, I'd better get back to the kitchen. Brom is in there with Pavel, helping him with the cucumber-crab munchies, and the kid has a hollow leg. I bet he's getting to lick out the dish."

"I insist that you free me!" Dr. Kostich demanded. "I will not be able to eat canapés if my ribs are crushed into my lungs!"

"You're *catering* the *sárkány*?" Aisling asked, looking almost as if she didn't believe it.

"There, you see? Even the green mate agrees it's ridiculous to serve food at such a time," Baltic told me with infuriating self-righteousness.

"I am not catering anything," I said with a frown at both of them. "I'm just making a few little nibblies to enjoy while we're discussing this issue of whether or not they're going to execute me."

"What?" Baltic asked, his head whipping around to me.

"I'll tell you about it later," I said, nodding toward the others.

"You'll tell me about it now!" he ordered, tapping his claws in an annoyed fashion.

"Argh!" Dr. Kostich yelled.

Baltic shifted his forefoot so his claws weren't directly on Kostich's face. "What do you mean, whether or not they will execute you? What reason does the weyr have for wishing you dead?"

"That's it! I have reached the end of my patience. I will destroy you myself if no one is going to save me from this fat dragon!"

"He is not fat," I snapped, and thought seriously about kicking the archimage. "All dragons look like that!"

"You wouldn't say that if you were lying here in my place," Kostich grumbled.

Jim opened its mouth to say something, but stopped when both Aisling and I glared at it.

"Er . . . why *is* Baltic lying on Dr. Kostich?" Aisling asked.

"Well, you know, I've heard a rumor that Ysolde kind of likes a little mano a mano action—" Jim started to say. I threw the chair leg at it, followed by a small ball of arcane magic. Midway to the demon, it turned into another banana. "Ooh, more snacks. Thanks."

"Mate, you will answer me!"

"I can't see. Everything is going black. If you kill me, I swear I will haunt you all!"

"Did you just conjure a banana at Jim?" Aisling asked, taking a step to the side to watch Jim eat the banana.

"Yes." I sighed, gesturing toward my former employer. "He put an interdict on me. None of my magic works right."

"You shouldn't have magic, period, and you won't by the time I'm through with you and this obese behemoth—"

"Oh, for heaven's sake," I said, tugging on Baltic's tail. "Let him up. If we're going to have explanations, we'd do better having them in a civilized manner."

"With lemon sorbet and bacon-wrapped mushroom caps," Jim agreed.

Baltic glared down at Kostich, who was moving feebly beneath him, but shifted back into human form, dusting himself off as he got to his feet.

The two green dragon bodyguards helped Dr. Kostich up, half carrying him over to a chair where he collapsed, breathing heavily and spreading fulminating glares amongst everyone present.

Silence fell. Baltic and Drake stared at each other for a few seconds.

"Baltic," Drake said at last when Aisling nudged him with her elbow.

"Drake Vireo," Baltic said, acknowledging the greeting.

They stared some more, not outright growling at each other, but I could tell their hackles were up.

"Drake," Aisling said, the word full of unspoken meaning as she nodded toward us.

He sighed. I tried not to giggle at the martyred look on his face. "You look well, Ysolde. As does your mate."

"Thank you," I said, glancing at Baltic. He stared moodily at Drake. I pinched his arm. He continued to stare. I dug my nails into his wrist until he snapped, "For god's sake, woman! I am the dread wyvern Baltic! I do not make polite conversation!"

"You do now. Go ahead. It won't hurt you."

He took Drake's martyred look to a whole new level of pain. "My mate has decreed that you are welcome in our home."

"You can do better than that," I said, pinning him back with one of my most effective mom looks.

"One day, mate, you will push me too far!" he informed me with narrowed eyes and flared nostrils.

I kissed the tip of his nose. He just looked even more outraged.

"Go on. You can do this."

A small wisp of smoke escaped one nostril. I smiled at it; his answering scowl promised retribution at the earliest opportunity. But in the end, he managed to say to Drake, "Your appearance is much as I remember it from the last time I saw you."

"Now that didn't hur—"

"The last time you tried to kill me, that is," Baltic interrupted. "When you ran me through with a long sword, and tried to decapitate me with a battle-ax. I believe you also shot a few crossbow bolts into my legs in an attempt to break the bones."

Silence filled the hall again. Drake studiously picked a piece of nonexistent lint off his sleeve.

"And if I'm not mistaken, you had a dagger or two that you used on my spleen."

Aisling stared at her husband, who was now blithely examining a painting on the wall.

"Not to mention the grappling hook that you creatively used by sinking it deep into my—"

"That's your idea of a welcome, is it?" I asked, stopping Baltic before he could make me sick to my stomach.

He shrugged. "I didn't mention the two morning stars he used to try to bash out my brains. I could have, but I knew you would prefer to keep things on a social level."

"I think that's one for our team," Jim said, nodding its approval.

Aisling transferred her gaze to it. "Hello! You're *my* demon! You're on our team, not theirs!"

"Soldie kidnapped me. That means I'm on her team until she lets me go. Right, guys?"

"Why do I suspect that the only reason you want to be on my team is because I have a kitchen full of canapés?" I asked it.

"A demon has to have priorities."

"Jim, heel," Aisling said wearily.

"Oh, fine!" I stopped the demon as it was about to obey. "Just go right ahead and ruin all of my plans! You aren't supposed to be here yet. Jim is supposed to be hidden away! I try to have a nice *sárkány*, but no, everyone has to ruin it."

"Hello," May said, popping up behind the two red-haired bodyguards who had taken up positions behind Drake. She slipped between them, looking around with interest. "Are we late?"

# Chapter Seventeen

"**W**hy does Dr. Kostich have his shirt off?"

"I'm checking for broken ribs," the mage answered May, looking up. "Is the healer here? I will need witnesses to the assault charges I will be laying against these dragons."

"Yes, he's here. Gabriel?"

The two guards moved aside to allow Gabriel's entrance.

"Good afternoon, Ysolde." His eyes flickered to Baltic, narrowing on him.

The air positively bristled with electricity. I scooted in front of Baltic, so my back was against his chest. "No fighting. I'm tired of fighting. People who fight will not get any lemon sorbet. If you insist on ignoring me, I will turn you into a banana. Got that?"

"Oh, man!" Jim complained behind us. "Way to ruin a good *sárkány*."

Gabriel looked startled. "A banana?"

"Her magic is off. Dr. Kostich did something to her," Aisling told him.

"Interdict," Dr. Kostich snapped, still feeling his ribs. "The fat dragon and she will pay for this."

"He is not fat!" I yelled. "He's just big-boned! Look!" I yanked the tail of Baltic's shirt out of his pants, pulling it up to expose his belly. "See? Classic six-pack!"

"Oooh, very nice," Aisling said, admiring Baltic's lovely ripple of muscles.

He rolled his eyes and tucked his shirt back into his pants.

Drake set fire to Aisling's feet.

"I was just looking," she told him. "I'm allowed to look."

Drake's eyes were shiny emeralds. Pissed-off shiny emeralds. "No, you're not."

"Look, you're in enough trouble already, Mr. Having Foursome Orgies in Medieval France."

"It's all that lemon sorbet you're feeding him, no doubt," Dr. Kostich said to me, pulling up his pant leg to look at his shin. "Very fattening. Well, you won't have any of that while you're suffering for eternity in the Akasha, so you might as well enjoy it one last time."

"Lemon sorbet? I love lemon sorbet," a light, airy voice said, followed by the arrival of May's twin, Cyrene. "Where's the sorbet?"

Kostya was on her heels, a fact Baltic didn't realize until the black wyvern entered the house.

"Traitor!" Baltic suddenly roared, shoving me aside, shifting into dragon form again. I tripped over Jim and fell onto the bottom stair, my head hitting the chair leg where it lay.

"Baltic!" Kostya screamed in reply, and he too

changed. Everyone scooted to the sides of the hall as the black and white dragons tumbled around, their claws slashing, dragon fire blasting everything.

"I have had enough!" I yelled at the top of my voice, and snatching up the chair leg, started beating the two dragons with it. "You boys are not going to fight in my house!"

"Uh-oh. Someone's in trouble with Mom," Jim said. "You better watch out, Balters, or she'll bananate you."

"Mate!" Baltic protested as I whomped him on the butt with the chair leg.

Kostya snarled and lunged at Baltic, but I smacked him under the chops with the chair leg, causing him to stop and shake his head, a shocked look on his dragon face.

"You change back, both of you, or else it's banana time!" I said, shaking the chair leg at them.

"This is intolerable," Baltic said, shifting back as he stalked toward me, his hands on his hips. "You will not treat me in this manner! I am a wyvern!"

"Of what sept?" Kostya asked, wiping a thin trickle of blood from his nose as he, too, shifted into human form.

"We'll get to that at the *sárkány*," I said, absorbing the fire that Baltic snorted on me. "Calm down, please, Baltic. I know you feel that Kostya betrayed you, but . . . but . . . oh, no, not again . . ."

The world spun. I reached out blindly, desperate to find Baltic, his hand catching mine just as I swirled into nothing.

Nothing but white. It was all around me, biting cold and deep into my blood, roaring in my ears. The roaring resolved itself into the sound of the wind, an endless shriek that whirled around and through me.

The white ebbed and flowed in time with the wind, and I realized that I was standing in the middle of a blizzard.

"Snow," a voice said behind me.

I turned. Baltic still held my hand, looking around us with interest.

"What are you doing here? This is a vision. You're not supposed to be in my visions."

"I participated in the last one you had," he pointed out.

"That wasn't really a vision. It was just more a reliving of a moment in time, triggered by the love token." I touched the chain I wore around my neck, the token lying between my breasts, my fingers trailing down the front of the fur-lined cloak that was clasped about my neck. "This is different. This is the same sort of vision or dream that I've had before."

"Perhaps the shaman is right, and your dragon self is urging you to wake up," he suggested, turning around. "Dauva. We're on the hill outside of Dauva."

"I don't think it's quite that simple."

"Ysolde!"

I whirled when my name was carried on the wind.

"Constantine!" Baltic snarled, reaching for the sword that he no longer carried.

A dark shape emerged from the whirling snow, his hair white with it as he stretched his hands out to me. "My love, you should not be out here. If one of my men had seen you cross before I did—"

"You will die for that!" Baltic shouted, leaping forward to grab Constantine, but nothing met his grasping hands, his momentum sending him straight through Constantine to a deep snowdrift some feet behind.

"I had to come," I heard myself say, evidently locked into the past enough to repeat what I'd said so many centuries before.

"Mate!" Baltic gasped, getting to his feet. The pain in his face was almost more than I could bear. I reached out for him, but it was Constantine who took my hand.

"My love, I knew you would come to me one day."

"No!" Baltic snarled.

"No," I repeated, pulling my hand from Constantine's grip, and shaking my head, the hood of my cloak sliding back, leaving me exposed. "My heart belongs to Baltic, and it always will."

Baltic stood up to his knees in the snow, his dark eyes watchful and wary.

"I came here not to give myself to you, but to plead with you to leave. Leave now, before anyone else dies. This battle between you and Baltic is for nothing, a senseless slaughter, and I will not have the blood of any more innocent dragons staining my soul."

"You are my mate." Despite the roar of the wind, Constantine's voice was low and rough. "He took you from me. It is my right to reclaim you."

"She is mine!" Baltic growled.

"You know that Baltic holds my heart—I've told you that often enough. You must believe me when I say nothing will change that. Please respect my decision, and leave us in peace."

I started to turn back toward Dauva, but he stopped me, gripping my arm. "I can't let you go, my love."

"Do not!" I snarled, whirling around and slapping his hand off me, fury causing my dragon fire to spill over and form a ring around him. "Do not use that word! You do not love me, Constantine! You cannot love someone whom you systematically destroy!"

He reeled back a step. Baltic tried to shove him, but there was nothing there for him to touch. Instead he fought his way through the snow to where I stood. "I always knew he was mad. Look at his eyes, mate. Look at his face."

I had to admit, Constantine's eyes glinted with a strange light, even in the middle of a snowstorm.

"He has turned you from me," Constantine said sadly, bowing his head. "I must do what I must do, Ysolde. I have sworn to protect you, and I will do that the only way I know how."

"Protect her?" Baltic yelled at the figure of Constantine. "It's me you want to destroy—you always have, ever since I challenged you for the right to be heir."

"I am tired of protesting against your folly," I said, suddenly exhausted from the weight of all those dragons who had died, and would die, for no real purpose. Baltic's words sank in and I glanced at him. "You challenged Constantine?"

"That is the true reason this war has continued. He was named by Alexei as his heir, but I knew he held only his own interests close to his heart, not those of the sept. I challenged him for the right to be heir, and won. He never forgave me for that, and soon after I was named wyvern, he rallied a handful of dragons, lying to them, bribing them, convincing them that they could never be happy under my rule."

It made sense. It made all too much sense. Constantine was a man of great pride; all wyverns were. And for him to lose both the sept and me to Baltic . . . I wasn't surprised it would generate a deep, seething hatred that would spread to everything Constantine perceived as belonging to Baltic.

"There is no hope if you remain with him," Constantine told me, passing a hand over his face as if he, too, was weary.

"Only because you are too foolish to see it," I answered. "I must return before Baltic notices I am gone."

"At this moment I'm probably in the caves, fending off Kostya's attempt to sneak into the castle through the lower passages," Baltic said, then whirled around to face Constantine, swearing in Zilant as he did so. "This is when he killed you! Flee, mate! I will keep him from striking you down."

I turned on my heel and started down the steep incline toward the exit of the bolt-hole I'd used to escape the keep unnoticed. I wanted to stop, to grab Baltic and make him leave with me, but my body had to follow its actions of the past. "You can't," I called to him as I slid down a small slope toward a clutch of trees that loomed up grey in the whipping snow. "You can't touch him, remember?"

He swore long and profanely, starting after me.

A sudden blast of icy wind sent me sprawling forward. Behind me, Constantine called out my name. "Ysolde!"

I looked over my shoulder, but could see nothing, no sign of Constantine or Baltic.

"Mate! Where are you?" Baltic cried, his voice faint as most of it was whipped away on the wind. "I can't see you. Run from him! Don't let him find you!"

"I can't," I answered, getting to my feet. As I did so,

the wind lifted my cloak and swirled it around me, blinding me as a sudden blow struck my back.

I screamed, struggling both with the snow I'd fallen into and with the cloak, heavy and wet, effectively capturing my legs. I fell back into the snow and the whiteness consumed me, leaching into my being until I was as pure as it was, suddenly adrift.

The white swirled around with a beauty that brought tears to my eyes . . . until I noticed the red in it.

"What . . ." I gasped as I rose higher, and I realized I was looking at myself, at the past Ysolde lying facedown, a fan of crimson staining the snow and the cloak. "Baltic! Oh my god, Baltic!"

"I'm here." He stumbled into view, stopping when he saw the figure holding a long, curved sword.

"Noooo!" Baltic howled, falling to his knees, his head thrown back in agony.

Constantine stood at my feet, looking at my body with eyes that were flat and devoid of all expression.

A drop of blood sluggishly gathered at the tip of the sword he held, trembling with the force of the wind, finally releasing to fall with infinite slowness onto the field of white.

My eyes blurred. I turned my face out of the stinging wind and noticed a trail of crimson spots that led away from my dead form, away from Constantine, but before I could say anything, the sound of Baltic's cry echoed in my ears. The whiteness darkened, thickening and re-forming itself into a dark, dank, confined space.

Baltic was on his knees, his head thrown back, in the same position of anguish, but now it was he who held a sword in his hands.

The last few notes of the echo faded away, and I realized I was in one of the caves beneath Dauva.

Baltic slowly turned his head and looked beyond me. "It is over."

"It should have been over a century ago," a voice said, the shadow behind me resolving into Kostya. "But you would not listen to me. No more black dragons will die for you, Baltic. You are the only one who will die, and with your death, the sept will be free." Kostya raised his sword high. "You need not fear for the fate of Ysolde. I will see that she is taken care of."

Baltic merely laughed, the sound of it horrible, filled with hopelessness and anguish that had no end and no beginning. He bowed his head, letting his sword fall to the stony ground with a dull clatter. "At least I will be with her again."

I screamed and leaped forward to stop Kostya, tears streaming down my face, but I was just as unsubstantial as Baltic had been at the scene of my death. I heard the sword cut through the air, but could not watch the sight of Kostya killing my love. I spun around, a spray of blood hitting my cheek, mingling with my tears as I collapsed, sobbing as if my heart had been destroyed.

"My love, do not do this. It is over. I am here. You must return to me now. Ysolde, heed me!"

I opened my eyes, finding myself on the floor, cradled against Baltic's chest, my face and his shirt wet.

"I'll kill him," I said, my throat aching and my voice hoarse.

"Is she all right?" May asked. "Did she hit her head when she fell? Gabriel, maybe you should look at her."

"Now you know how I feel," Baltic said, the faintest hint of a smile on his lips.

I pushed myself away from him, the memory stark in my mind as I got to my feet.

"You," I said, my voice low and ugly as I started toward Kostya. "He was unarmed when you killed him!"

Kostya's eyebrows rose, and he had the nerve to look shocked as I grabbed my chair leg and raised it over my head.

"No, mate." Baltic caught me as I ran toward Kostya, intent on destroying him.

"You dropped your sword! You weren't even holding it when he killed you!" I yelled, fighting Baltic to get to Kostya.

"Eh . . ." Kostya looked startled for a moment, then frowned. "What are you talking about?"

"I was dead by then," Baltic said, wrapping both his arms around me and pulling me tight against his body. "Ysolde, I was dead. Constantine had killed you. I could not exist without you. It didn't matter that Kostya struck the blow—I could not have survived without you."

"It seems I have arrived at a most interesting moment," a light Italian voice said.

I spat out a word I would never have said in front of Brom, dropped the chair leg, and turned in Baltic's arms to hold him tight.

"Apparently, Ysolde just had another . . . er . . . dream, for lack of a better word," Aisling said slowly. "And I think Baltic went with her."

"Ah," Bastian said, obviously confused.

"Constantine did not kill Ysolde," Gabriel said, looking angrier than I'd ever seen him.

"We saw him," Baltic said as I sniffled one last sniffle into his shirt, turning to face the others who stood in a semicircle around us.

"You've taken Jim?" I asked Aisling, noticing that the demon wasn't present, although my spirits were too dulled to care much.

"No." She gave me an odd look. "We had an agreement, and we're standing by it. Jim will remain with you until the *sárkány* is over. Right now it's in the kitchen, no doubt trying to mooch food away from your son."

"You saw him?" Drake asked us, frowning slightly. "You saw Constantine kill Ysolde?"

I hesitated for a moment, remembering the trail of blood that led away from my body.

"Yes," Baltic said, his arms tight around me. "We saw him standing over her lifeless body, a sword in his hand that dripped with blood. There was no one else there, just him."

I said nothing. The situation was too charged to discuss the trail of blood at that moment. The dragons were all on edge enough; I would have to speak later with Baltic, when we could discuss what it meant.

"No," Gabriel said, shaking his head as he looked at his mate. "I can't believe that. It doesn't make sense. Constantine wouldn't do that."

Baltic growled something very rude. "Did you know him?"

"No." Gabriel's fingers flexed. "But my father served as his guard. He would not have done so had Constantine been without honor."

"Well, I *did* know him. There was no one else with Ysolde's body. I myself witnessed him telling her that he would do what he had to do. Is that not so, mate?"

I nodded. "He was furious with Baltic, and wanted nothing more than to destroy him. He said he felt affection for me, but . . ."

I stopped speaking, unwilling to speculate in front of the other dragons.

"Do not distress yourself again, mate," Baltic murmured in my ear, his arms tightening around me.

"That doesn't make sense," Gabriel said, shaking his head, his hand seeking May's hand as if for comfort.

"Believe it, or don't believe it—I don't really care. In fact, at this moment, I'm inclined to go along with Baltic's assertion that we don't need anything to do with any of you, or with the weyr." I clutched the love token I'd hung on a silver chain, sick of the constant struggle that seemed to fill my life now.

"Well, I have no idea what to say to that," Aisling said, glancing at Drake. "I have to admit, though, that I'm starting to think that maybe talking with Baltic is a good thing."

Bastian strolled over to us, and before either Baltic or I could react, punched Baltic smack-dab in the nose. "They tell me you're Baltic even though you do not look like him. I am glad. You will suffer for a very long time before you die for the deaths of my dragons."

I held Baltic back when he would have jumped on Bastian. "Please, don't," I begged him. "He'll just hit you back, and then I'll end up turning him into a banana, which means I'll have to ask Dr. Kostich for help, and he'll just call you fat again, and that'll lead to me wanting to punch out his lights, and we'll all end up brawling until there's nothing left but you, me, and a bunch of bananas. And some melted lemon sorbet."

Baltic looked like he was going to go ahead and deck Bastian anyway, but when I touched his cheek and said, "Please?" he refrained.

"Febales!" he grumbled, his expression as black as his

eyes. "I hope you like the looks of be with a crooked dose, because he just broke it."

"Oh!" I said, examining his face. His nose was swelling rapidly and had a decided list to the right. "Oh, dear. I don't know how to set a nose. Gabriel, do you?"

Gabriel stood silent, his lips in a mutinous line.

"I'm sure he does," May said, prodding her mate in the side. "Go on."

"No," Gabriel said, staring daggers at Baltic.

Bastian and Kostya nodded their agreement with Gabriel's obstinate stand.

"Oh, for the love of all the saints!" I said, pushed almost past my point of patience. "It's just a nose!"

"I'b fide," Baltic said nasally.

"You're not fine. You need that set properly. Gabriel, please do this. If you insist on being stubborn, you can do it for my benefit, not for Baltic's."

"Do you have any idea how many times he's tried to kill me, kill my mate, or steal her in the last few months?" Gabriel said, pointing at Baltic. "I'm not going to set his damned nose."

"I nebber tried to kill your bate," Baltic said with as much dignity as one could have with a nose approaching the approximate size, shape, and color of a ripe apple. "Steal her, yes. But not kill her."

"I won't do it!" Gabriel said, but at a look from May, he marched forward, muttering things under his breath that I felt were better to pretend I didn't hear, grabbed Baltic's nose between his thumb and forefinger, and gave it a quick jerk. A horrible snapping sound made everyone present cringe. Everyone but Baltic, who swore profanely as he felt his poor, abused nose.

"There. It's set. Can we get on to the part of the day where we sentence Baltic to death?"

A banana clipped him alongside his head. He shot a startled look at me.

I, wearing an innocent expression, tended to the tiny bit of blood that seeped out of Baltic's nostril, and said, "Why don't all of you go out to the north pasture, where a tent and tables and chairs have been set up for the *sárkány*. Baltic and I will check on the canapés, although at this point, I don't really give a damn about them either, but my mother raised me to show guests common courtesy even if it killed me. Which it did, but that's neither here nor there."

# Chapter Eighteen

"Did I see artichoke hearts? I love those." Cyrene peered anxiously down the table. "With garlic and parmesan? Does anyone see them?"

We were in the north pasture, a large open field mottled with wild grass and bare earth. I would have preferred a more civilized setting, but the only way I could get Baltic to agree to have the *sárkány* at his house was allowing it to be held in an open field, where no one could hide in ambush. I didn't think the wyverns would do something like that, but agreed with him that it would be best not to take foolish chances.

The ladies were seated around a couple of tables pushed together. The wyverns were together in a small clutch, obviously discussing something about the *sárkány*. Baltic stood alone, watching everyone with a glower that would have leveled a T. rex.

Pavel and I had spent the day in the kitchen, making a few snacks that I intended on serving after the *sárkány* itself, but it appeared that all the discussion about the lemon sorbet had set appetites on edge.

"Here's a plate for you and Jim," I told Brom as I handed him a tray with two plates piled high with hors d'oeuvres and canapés. "You may eat it in the kitchen, and afterward, Pavel said you could play with his video game machine."

"I don't see why we can't stay out here and watch Kostya have a couple of hissy fits," Jim complained, nosing the tray to see what was on it. "Hey, we don't get any of the famous sorbet? My mouth is all set for it!"

"I left some for you in the freezer, and I prefer that you and Brom stay out from underfoot during the meeting. Speaking of which, don't pester the dragons, either. All the guards are remaining in the house, and none of them looked very happy."

"Yeah, yeah, I can handle a couple of bodyguards."

"Don't handle them—leave them alone. We had enough of an argument to get them to leave the wyverns out here alone."

"She just wants us out of the way in case Kostya comes unglued on Baltic again," Jim told Brom as they started toward the house. Brom stopped and turned back, a suddenly worried look on his face.

I muttered something rude under my breath about Jim's big mouth, hurrying over to Brom. "Sweetheart, nothing is going to happen. It's just a meeting."

"Oops," Jim said, looking contrite. "Uh . . . yeah, B-man. I didn't mean that Kostya was going to hurt Baltic or anything. Besides, if he tried, your mom would turn him into fruit."

"That's right," I said, giving Brom a quick hug. "No one is going to get hurt."

He continued to look worried. "Can I talk to Baltic for a minute? I mean Dad?"

"All right," I said slowly, wondering if Jim had been saying anything to him about the fact that the weyr wanted Baltic executed. I glanced over at the man in question, who was standing with his arms crossed, watching everyone with grim suspicion. At my nod toward Brom, he strode over. "Brom wishes to speak with you."

He raised his eyebrows and looked expectantly at Brom, who squirmed slightly and said apologetically, "Can I talk to him alone, Sullivan?"

"Er . . . certainly." I moved off to check that the sorbet was still packed tightly in ice and not melting under the warm summer sun, before standing behind my chair.

"Oooh! Is that pesto?" Cyrene made happy little noises. "This is so good, Ysolde. You have to cater all the *sárkánies*!"

"Thank you, but I think I'll pass on that offer."

After a few minutes, Baltic returned, his expression unchanged. I watched Jim and Brom return to the house before turning to him. "What was that all about?"

"He was worried about you."

"About me? Hell! Jim must have told him about the execution order."

"No. He was worried that if the weyr did something to me, you would be left helpless. I told him that he had nothing to worry about."

"Because I'm not weak or feeble or without the ability to take care of myself," I said, nodding my approval of the way he dealt with Brom's concern.

"Because the weyr has no control over me," he corrected.

A horrible feeling came to life in my gut. Before I could warn him of it, the wyverns marched over to the table, Kostya taking up a spot at the head. "The wyverns are all present. The *sárkány* can commence."

"Would you pass the crème fraiche cherry apricot scones?" Aisling asked May, who sat diagonally across the table from her.

I moved to stand next to Baltic, slipping my hand in his to both offer and receive comfort. His fingers curled around mine, making the fire in me stir just a little.

"This *sárkány* is called to order to address the issue of the deaths of the sixty-eight blue dragons in France."

"This olive tapenade is fabulous," May said, moaning with delight as she popped a tapenade pinwheel into her mouth. "Almost orgasmic with the touch of cognac."

"Present are the wyverns of all five septs, with the exception of Chuan Ren, who has sent her son Jian to act in her stead."

Jian acknowledged the comment, taking a bite of a pesto, basil, and tomato freschetta.

"Who has the arancini?" Aisling asked, looking around.

"Lemon thyme, or mozzarella and basil?" Cyrene asked, holding up two plates.

"Oooh. Lemon thyme, please. Sweetie, would you like more arancini?"

"This is like a bizarre love child of Martha Stewart and the Nuremburg trials," I whispered to Baltic, noting that a couple of glasses were empty. I slid my hand from his and fetched a covered pitcher.

"Baltic, former wyvern of the black dragons, you have been charged by the weyr with the deaths two months ago. How do you plead?"

"I do not plead anything," he said loudly, his voice once again normal due to the ice pack I'd made him hold on his nose. "I do not need to answer the charges. They are ridiculous, and without proof."

"More iced tea, anyone?" I asked, holding up the pitcher. No one said anything, although Kostya looked like he was about to explode. "No? Champagne, then?"

"Christos!" Kostya swore, slamming his hands down on the table as everyone held up their glasses for a refill. "This is a *sárkány*, not a brunch! Can we get on with the meeting?"

"There's no need to be quite so testy," I said as I poured champagne, making sure to splash his over the side. "I don't see why we can't do this in a civilized manner."

"Civilized coming from a dragon . . . that's certainly an oxymoron," a voice said behind me.

"I thought you were going to get rid of him?" Baltic asked as Dr. Kostich strolled up.

Kostya sank into his chair, banging his head gently on the table a couple of times.

I narrowed my eyes at my former employer. "I did. I called him a taxi and saw him get into it."

"I decided it would be wiser for me to remain here, where I can keep an eye on you and the hefty wyvern until the watch comes to detain you both," he said, looking over the buffet table. "Does that herbed goat cheese have garlic in it? I'm allergic to garlic."

"I give up," Kostya told Cyrene. "I can't fight herbed goat cheese and champagne."

"It's very good herbed goat cheese," she said, offering him a bite.

"Mate!" Baltic said, his hands on his hips, clearly expecting me to do something.

"What do you want me to do?" I asked. "He's an archimage!"

"A fact neither of you seems to give its due respect," Dr. Kostich said, somewhat garbled since he'd just stuffed a mini cherry scone into his mouth.

"He's placed an interdict on me. You've seen how it makes my magic go awry—I couldn't make him vanish, even if I had that sort of power."

"You never were much of an apprentice, although I will admit you tried," he said, taking a loaded plate to a free chair at the table.

"Not to mention the fact that he's the head of the L'au-dela," I finished.

"Is he supposed to sit with us? I thought this was just for wyverns and their mates," Cyrene asked Kostya, frowning at the archimage.

Dr. Kostich ignored her. "Hence the fact that the watch is, at this very moment, speeding its way here to arrest you."

"What does it matter?" Kostya answered, his features set in a pout. "No one is listening to me. No one cares about anything but their bellies. No one wants to see justice done. I'm the only one here who is actually concerned about making Baltic pay for his heinous crimes—are those crab and papaya rice rolls any good?"

"Your watch cannot touch us," Baltic told Kostich, who frowned at him, but was unable to speak due to another mini scone he was eating. "Dragons are not governed by the L'au-dela. He has no authority over us, mate, so you need not fear that his threats are anything more than idle."

"I assure you they're quite real," Kostich answered, bits of crumbs flying as he spoke around the mouthful of scone.

*"Voulez-vous cesser de ma cracher dessus pendant que vous parlez?"* Aisling murmured.

Dr. Kostich, sitting across from her, stared.

"Sorry. I've been dying to find a chance to say that," she said, brushing the crumbs from in front of her plate. "Rene will be so proud."

"That's right," I said slowly, thinking about what Baltic said. "Dragons aren't part of the L'au-dela."

"Dragons aren't, no," Dr. Kostich said, taking the glass I'd set down for Baltic, sipping the champagne with a thoughtful look. "Quite a decent vintage. My compliments. As I was saying, your chubby mate is right—I have no authority over dragons. However, I do over humans, and you, my ex-apprentice, are close enough to human to count as one. It is true that I would have a hard time punishing him, but you are a very different matter, and since I can't have the one who perpetrated the crimes against me, I will take the next best thing: you."

"Just once I'd like to be charged with something that I've done," I said. "What do you think you're going to do to me?"

"I've already told you—banishment to the Akasha."

A horrible feeling gripped me in cold, clammy hands. Banishment to the Akasha was no laughing matter—the place the mortal world thought of as limbo was not one which many beings ever escaped. "You can't do that," I protested.

"I can, and I will."

"Baltic?" I asked, turning to him, suddenly worried. "What will happen to Brom and you? I don't want to go to the Akasha."

"You won't, *chérie*. I would never allow it. This mage is blowing hot air, nothing more."

Dr. Kostich glanced at his wrist. "The question will become moot in less than an hour when the watch arrives to take Tully away."

"Touch her, and you will die," Baltic said simply.

Kostich pointed a fork at him. "It's that sort of attitude that has kept the dragons and the L'au-dela at loggerheads for centuries. Even your ambassador was arrogant and impossible to deal with."

"Ambassador?" Aisling asked Drake. "We have an ambassador with the L'au-dela?"

"Fiat," he answered, his eyes bright as he watched us.

"That was the former ambassador. We received notice he was excommunicated, or whatever it is you dragons do, and removed from the post. We are awaiting the appointment of a new ambassador, to whom I will certainly lodge detailed complaints about my treatment at the hands of that behemoth."

"Archimage or no archimage," I said through gritted teeth, "knock off the references to Baltic being large. It's only his dragon form that's big."

"You know," May said slowly, looking distracted, "something has just occurred to me. Ambassadors have diplomatic immunity, don't they?"

Lightbulbs seemed to go off in many heads at that moment. I looked thoughtfully at May.

"Yees," Aisling drawled. "What a good idea. The weyr

needs an ambassador, and Ysolde needs protection from Dr. Kostich."

The latter glared over the table at her as he helped himself to more champagne.

"If Ysolde was ambassador, he couldn't touch her, and voila! Two problems solved at once. What a perfect solution."

"No, it isn't," Kostya said, in the process of consuming a mound of food piled high on his plate.

"Oh, stop being so obstinate," Aisling told him. "We know you don't like Baltic, but Ysolde hasn't done anything wrong. There's no reason she couldn't be the ambassador for the weyr. She certainly will do a better job of it than Fiat."

"She's not a member of the weyr," Kostya pointed out.

"I'm not?" I asked, feeling somewhat adrift, both conversationally and emotionally. "I thought I was a silver dragon."

"You were silver, then black, but now you are neither, and as such, you are not a member of the weyr," Drake agreed with his brother.

"There's an easy solution to that," May said.

Everyone turned to look at her.

"Baltic's sept will have to join the weyr."

Kostya snorted. "That would never happen. The weyr would not tolerate the blight dragons."

"Light," Baltic snarled, starting toward him. "We are *light* dragons. You are the blight."

Kostya leaped up, his hands fisted.

"Oh, lord, there they go again," Aisling commented to the table. "And I thought it was bad with Kostya and Gabriel. You'd better get your bananas ready, Ysolde."

"No," I said.

"No?" May asked, watching as Baltic and Kostya both turned surprised gazes upon me.

"No. If they are so hell-bent on fighting, they can fight."

Kostya smiled. Baltic shifted into dragon form.

"Definitely overweight," Kostich said, eating a bacon-wrapped scallop.

"But in human form," I told the two dragons. "And with no weapons. Just fists."

A little puff of smoke escaped Baltic, but after a moment's thought, he shifted back to human form, eyeing Kostya. "Fisticuffs, eh? It's been several centuries since I've had that pleasure."

Kostya tossed off his jacket and rolled up his sleeves. "The pleasure is going to be all mine, Baltic."

"Over there, not here," I said, pointing to the other side of the pasture that was mostly dirt. "I don't want any more of this crystal broken. You can have five minutes to beat the living daylights out of each other, and after that, you have to behave in a polite, decent manner. Do you both agree to the terms?"

Kostya's gaze was shifty. "Define decent."

"No more leaping up at every little thing you perceive as an insult. I'm tired of you two being at each other's throats, and I imagine everyone else is tired of it, too."

The women nodded. The men avoided meeting my eyes.

"You wouldn't mind if their sept was in the weyr, would you?" Aisling asked Drake as Baltic and Kostya moved off about sixty feet, Bastian and Jian going with them, whether to referee or to cheer Kostya on, I had no idea.

"It's not quite that simple," Drake said. "There are rules to admitting a sept. I'm not even sure that Baltic actually has one."

"But if he did, they could join, and then Ysolde could be ambassador, and Dr. Kostich could—" Aisling bit off what she was going to say as the mage looked at her.

Baltic, with a yell, flung himself at Kostya, who answered by twisting to the side and landing a nasty kick on Baltic's thigh.

"Could what?" Kostich asked, his pale eyes intense.

"Leave us alone?" she asked sweetly.

Dust rose from the field where the two men were now circling each other, periodically lashing out with arms and legs.

Kostich made a derisive noise. "I have never sought anything from dragons other than the sword that rightfully belongs amongst mages, a fact you should well know, Guardian."

"There is no place in the weyr for a sept that slaughters members of another in times of peace," Gabriel said, watching interestedly as Kostya head butted Baltic, who roared in outrage. The two men went down in a cloud of dust.

"Baltic didn't kill those blue dragons."

"So you say." Gabriel's silver gaze switched to me. "But we have only your word to that effect. It is hardly enough for the weyr to dismiss the charges."

"If you are going to go through that argument again, I shall go watch the combatants. I believe a little spell increasing the black dragon's speed is in order. . . ." Dr. Kostich rose from the table, tossed down his napkin, and strolled off toward the fight.

My chin went up as I addressed Gabriel. "I see now why Baltic has been so resistant to meeting with you. Your mind is already made up."

Silence fell . . . silence tinged with the grunts and muffled cries from the two men who were once again on their feet, dirty, sweaty, and dabbed with blotches of crimson.

"He had to have done it. He was working with Fiat," Gabriel said, sounding as if he was trying to convince himself.

"So were you, from what Jim told me," I countered, my ire starting to rise.

Gabriel looked startled. "I am not conspiring with Fiat!"

"Not now, but you have. Or did Jim lie when it told me that you helped Fiat poison Aisling and take her as his mate?"

The silence fell again.

"You bloody bastard! I just had that set!" Baltic yelled in an outraged voice, grabbing Kostya by the throat and flinging him a few yards. "That's it! If I'm going to have a crooked nose, you're going to have one as well!"

Both men disappeared again into the gently swirling cloud of dust.

"Oh, dear, I hope not. I like Kostie's nose the way it is," Cyrene said, not even looking at the two combatants.

"Well?" I asked Gabriel, who appeared very uncomfortable.

"She's got a point, you know," Aisling said. "You were working with Fiat then."

"I was trying to stop him from doing worse than he did!"

"My point is merely that it's possible that Baltic could have helped Fiat obtain one goal, but wasn't wholly in accord with his plans. Which is what he did."

"It comes down to proof," Drake said slowly. "You have none that he is innocent of the crimes, and we have witnesses that say he was with Fiat in France during the time of the killings."

I looked at them all sitting around the table, so frustrated with everything that I could scream. How could they not see that Baltic was innocent? How could they believe he could ruthlessly kill so many dragons? "Let me ask you this, Drake: have you ever known Baltic to kill dragons in cold blood?"

"He has killed many dragons, of all septs," Drake said, avoiding the question.

"This is a waste of time," I said, disgusted. I knew then that we would never get the wyverns to understand that Baltic was innocent.

"I am afraid continued arguments would be fruitless, yes," Drake said.

I looked down at my hands for a few moments, my fingers clasped so tightly together that they were white. "Baltic will not allow himself to be martyred, nor will I."

"You leave us no options," Gabriel warned.

"You must understand that if Baltic refuses to answer for the charges laid against him, there will exist between us a state of war," Drake said.

"No," Aisling said, her face pinched. "Not another war?"

War. The word reverberated in my heart, tearing off little pieces of it. War again. With war came death and destruction, and suffering that would know no end.

"Not again," I whispered.

"What war?" Cyrene asked, looking confused.

I wanted to explode into a million pieces and drift away on the wind. I wanted to go to sleep and not wake up. I wanted to hide in Baltic's lovely house that made my soul sing, and never leave it.

I wanted Baltic.

"The war between Baltic's sept and the weyr," May said sadly.

"They've declared war?"

"You've declared it on us," I answered.

"You do not have to tread this path," Drake said, his eyes dark.

"You won't allow us to do otherwise."

"A war is not to be undertaken lightly," he said, taking Aisling's hand. "It affects everyone in the sept. Those who are at war are considered viable targets for attack."

A cold chill swept over me, piercing me with fear greater than any I had ever known. "Brom," I whispered, a horrible vision in my head of him being used as a hostage. Or worse.

"We do not attack children," Drake said stiffly, ire flashing in his eyes. "Mates, however, are a different matter."

"Nothing has changed," I said softly, despair filling me at the knowledge of what lay ahead. "There was a war then, just as there will be now. There was death and pride and the refusal to admit a lost cause then, and it's all being repeated. I know how it will end, and I will not allow that, not again."

"There has to be something we can do," Aisling said to Drake.

He shook his head.

I looked up, tears bright in my eyes as I stepped first on the chair, then onto the center of the table. "I won't have it!" I shouted, opening my arms up wide. "If you won't end this now, then I will!"

"What's she doing?" Cyrene asked as Drake leaped to his feet, grabbing Aisling and pulling her back away from the table.

I closed my eyes, allowing Baltic's fire to swell within me, growing in intensity, building the familiar sensation of pressure as I summoned the words that would send them all far away from me.

"Kostya?" Cyrene said worriedly as she started to back away from the table.

"Run, little bird," Gabriel told May as he hauled her to her feet, giving her a shove toward the house.

"What's going on?" Aisling asked as Drake, having difficulty in making her follow him, bent down and scooped her up. "Drake! What do you think you're doing?"

The air around me rippled, gathering in a circle with me at its center, the power swelling inside me as I shaped it, visualizing the only possibility left to me. "Taken with sorrow," I cried, allowing the fire to consume every iota of my being as I used it to cast my spell.

"I thought she was under an interdict?" May asked Gabriel as he told her again to run.

"Kostya?" Cyrene asked again, her voice more strident. *"Kostya!"*

"All I cast from me," I said, my voice ringing like the purest bell. It must have reached Baltic, because suddenly he stopped pummeling Kostya and turned to face me.

Kostya tackled him, but Baltic simply flung him to the side as he started toward me, Dr. Kostich on his heels.

"Is she casting a spell? It sounds like a spell," Aisling said.

"Devoured with rage," I bellowed, the fire beginning to flicker along my skin as I raised my face to the sky, my heart sick with knowledge that nothing would ever be right.

Dr. Kostich ran toward me, flinging away his glass. "Stop her! That's a banishing spell! You must stop her!"

"A banishing spell? Mages can't send people to the Akasha," Cyrene called to him. "Can they?"

"No, but she can remove us from this location. Just stop her!" he shouted.

"But her spells don't work," Cyrene said, turning back toward me.

Baltic sprinted past Dr. Kostich, reaching me just as I released his fire, channeled into the vision of what I wanted most. "Banished so you will be!"

For a moment, nothing happened. It was as if the world held its breath to see what effect the interdict would have on the spell. Baltic skidded to a stop next to me, his eyes shaded like dark pools of water glinting in the sunlight, and then suddenly, the air shimmered again, thickening, twisting, morphing itself into the shape of a dragon.

"The First Dragon," I heard May gasp.

Heat shimmered on my skin like electricity, crawling up and down my arms and back as the dragon looked first to May, then to me, his eyes filled with infinity. Like Baltic, he was white, but more than white—all colors seemed to dance in harmony, illuminating the dragon, a soft glow wrapped around him that shifted and moved.

Baltic leaped up to stand behind me, his body warm

and strong and so infinitely precious, tears burned behind my eyes. The First Dragon looked at him and
smiled, shifting into a human form, that of a man . . .
and yet, it wasn't a man. Not even his human form could
hide the fact that he was a dragon.

Around us, the other dragons stood frozen, staring at
him, their expressions ranging from stunned disbelief to
outright awe. I knew just how they felt.

"Why did you call me, Baltic?" the First Dragon
asked, his voice as strong as the wind, but softer than
the lightest down.

"It was my mate who summoned you, not me," he answered, his arms sliding around me protectively.

"I . . . I didn't know I was going to do that. I meant to
do something else." I was so shocked by what I had done
that it was almost impossible to speak.

The First Dragon's eyes, those uncanny, all-knowing
eyes, turned from Baltic to me. I felt the impact of his
gaze right down to the tips of my toes. He reached toward me, touching my forehead.

"Remember." The word seemed to echo in and around
me, a haze coming up over me that was like nothing I'd
experienced before in either a fugue or the visions that
I'd had of the past.

The haze turned white, whipping around me with an
icy bite. Once again I stood on a snowy hillside, a blizzard raging around me.

But this time, the others were present as well. It was
as if the First Dragon had simply lifted up everyone
standing in the field and placed us in a different time
and place. We stood in a circle around two forms, one
fallen, scarlet still staining the snow at the First Dragon's
feet.

"A life has been given for yours, daughter," the First Dragon said.

My dead form shifted, then slowly stood up, whole again, my eyes vacant and unseeing. "Who gave it?" the other Ysolde asked.

"It was given willingly."

"Baltic? Did he—"

"Much is expected of you." The First Dragon's words were whipped away on the wind as soon as he spoke them, and yet they resonated within me. "Do not fail me again."

As the last word faded on the howl of snow and ice and wind, the First Dragon touched the risen Ysolde's forehead in the same spot he'd touched mine, and she collapsed onto the ground—but she wasn't dead. She hunched over, sobbing, buffeted by the snow before finally getting back to her feet, staggering down the hill and into the white oblivion.

# Chapter Nineteen

"Fascinating. Absolutely fascinating. That almost makes up for the fat dragon sitting on me."

I shook my head, more to clear my vision than to disagree. The white mist in front of my eyes slowly evaporated, the vague figures resolving themselves into familiar people.

"That was an interesting experience," Aisling said somewhat bemusedly as she leaned into Drake. "Is that what all your visions are like, Ysolde?"

"No." I turned to Baltic, needing to feel his fire, needing his love. I clutched his silk shirt, shaking it in a demand for reassurance. "Do not fail me *again*? I failed the First Dragon before? When? What did I do? I don't even know him! How could I fail him, if I don't even know him? Is that why I was killed? Because I failed him somehow? Why didn't anyone tell me I was supposed to do something for him? Glory of god, man, why aren't you answering me?"

He gently pried my hands off his shirt, his thumbs stroking over my fingers, squinting at me with an odd look on his face as he did so. "I will answer you if you stop talking long enough to let me do so. What is on your forehead?"

"Who cares about my forehead!" I wailed, feeling as if the earth had suddenly dropped out from under me. "The First Dragon is pissed at me! I failed him! Dear god, Baltic, he expects much of me. What much? What am I going to do?"

"It's the sept emblem," he said, still staring at my forehead, suddenly looking very pleased. "It is a sun. The First Dragon has marked you."

"Is that good?" Aisling asked Drake.

"Yes," May said before he could answer, smiling a secretive sort of smile. "To hold his regard is an honor."

"Which is interesting, considering that he knew your name," Drake said to Baltic, looking extremely thoughtful.

I was still having problems with the idea that I'd somehow failed the First Dragon in the past. "What did he mean, much was expected of me? What sort of things are expected?"

"I don't know," Cyrene said, looking confused. "Should I know?"

"Yes, how is it the First Dragon knows your name?" Kostya asked Baltic, one eye swollen shut, his nose bleeding, and his lower lip cut.

Baltic evidently fared better than Kostya had—there was a red lump on his jaw, and a jagged-looking cut over one eye, but his nose didn't appear to be broken again despite his growls during the fight. He didn't respond to Kostya, instead watching me, looking very much like a cat who'd gotten into a bowl of cream.

"This changes things," May told Gabriel.

He frowned. "How so?"

"She can summon the First Dragon. Don't you see? She's tied to him. And so, assumedly since the First Dragon recognized him, is Baltic. You can't war with a sept that has ties to the First Dragon."

"Absolutely not," Aisling agreed. "I don't know as much about him as May does, since she dealt with him when she re-formed the dragon heart, but what I've heard makes me think that summoning him is almost an impossible act."

"We've just witnessed such an act, so it cannot be impossible," Dr. Kostich commented from where he was sitting, drinking Baltic's expensive champagne.

"No, but Aisling's right—I talked to Kaawa after I re-formed the heart, and she told me that the only way to summon the First Dragon was to re-form it—and that has only happened a couple of times. Ysolde did it three hundred years ago. I did it two months ago." May's gaze shifted to Baltic. "Kaawa didn't mention other times it has been re-formed."

"The dragon heart has only been re-formed four times," Baltic said, his gaze on my forehead again. I *tsk*ed to myself and rubbed it, not feeling anything different. "Attempts have been made several times, but it is not an act that is easily accomplished."

"There, you see?" Aisling said, prodding her husband. "You have to cancel the war now."

Slowly, he shook his head. "This changes nothing."

"Agreed. Baltic refuses to acknowledge the weyr's decision; therefore, he is at war with us," Kostya said, his eyes as black as deep night.

"Gabriel?" Drake asked.

Gabriel and May had been exchanging a glance filled with meaning. "Agreed," Gabriel said slowly, turning to me. "I'm sorry, Ysolde."

"Not as sorry as I am," I said, my throat tightening with tears.

"Bastian? Jian?" Drake asked the two silent wyverns.

"All I seek is retribution for the deaths of my sept members," Bastian said reluctantly. His gaze examined Baltic for a moment, the hostility which had been banked in his eyes slowly fading as he shook his head. "I don't know what to believe anymore. It seems inconceivable that the First Dragon would tolerate someone who would murder his descendants, and yet, the evidence is there—Baltic was with Fiat."

I slid a look up at Baltic. "You're tired of denying it, too, huh?"

"Extremely so."

"I will agree with the other wyverns," Bastian finally said, looking at Jian.

"Chuan Ren welcomes the opportunity to war," he said.

"And you?" I couldn't help but ask.

He inclined his head slightly, his expression unreadable. "I am my mother's son."

"Typical dragon answer," Aisling said, snorting to herself.

"Then we are in concurrence," Drake said.

Gabriel's face was somber as he said, "Ysolde de Bouchier, born into the silver dragons, it is with deep regret and no little amount of sorrow that I pronounce you ouroboros."

Something inside me gave at his words, some intangible little connection to him and May and the other silver dragons. It was as if tiny little silken cords were suddenly severed.

"Ysolde de Bouchier," Kostya's deep voice said. I looked at him, tears filling my eyes. "Once mated to a black dragon, I pronounce you ouroboros."

I reeled backwards into Baltic. He righted me, his face dark with anger as he glared at the wyverns.

"You are henceforth named ouroboros and outside of the weyr," Drake said, his face impassive, but his eyes glittering with emotion. "From this moment, a state of war exists between us. Should you seek mediation with regards to this, you may request a parlay with any wyvern recognized by the weyr. Safe conduct will be granted to and from the parlay."

I bit back a sob. Everything was going wrong again. "I don't want any more deaths," I told Baltic, clinging to him shamelessly.

"There won't be," he said, looking over my head at the other wyverns. "So long as they leave us alone."

Gabriel looked like he was going to say something, but just shook his head instead, and with his arm around May, walked away.

"Ysolde—" Aisling reached out to touch me, but Drake took her hand, pulling her after him as they, too, left. "Please send Jim back tonight. I imagine you're getting pretty tired of it by now."

Bastian and Jian, with an exchange of looks, murmured something and followed them.

"Ah. Looks like the watch has arrived at last," Dr. Kostich said, glancing toward the drive. A black van was parked behind the wyverns' cars. He slid a glance toward us, hesitating for a few moments. "I believe in light of the day's experience, I would be willing to drop the charges of assault against me on the condition that you give into my keeping the light sword of Antonia von Endres."

"You are mad," Baltic said.

"On the contrary, I'm quite sane. I am also very serious that Tully will pay for your abuse of me on the occasion of your attack on the silver wyvern's house, as well as today." He lifted his hand, and a couple of men emerged from the van, jogging across the field toward us.

I clutched Baltic's hand, panic swamping me. "You are not taking me to the Akasha!"

"No, he is not," Baltic said calmly.

"It's your decision," Kostich said, looking only mildly interested in the whole affair. "The sword or your mate. Or do you intend to be in a state of war with the L'audela, as well as the weyr?"

"So help me god, if I didn't have this interdict on me, I would turn you into a fruit salad," I told him.

His eyebrows rose. "I never knew you had such a temper. I would never have engaged you had I known. It will matter little to you in the Akasha, however. Bryce, Dermott, please take Tully Sullivan into custody. We will return to Suffrage House in Paris where a formal trial will be held tomorrow—"

Baltic snarled an invective, jerking his hand out to the side, the motes of air gathering around it until a long, shining blue-white sword formed. "The day will come, mage, when I will claim this sword again."

"Indeed?" Dr. Kostich caught the sword as Baltic hurled it at him. "You may try, dragon, you may try. I will accept this in lieu of punishment for your mate. Tully . . ." His mouth tightened as he looked at me.

I lifted my chin and gave him a look that let him see Baltic's dragon fire raging inside me.

"The sorbet was excellent. My compliments."

He strode off with two puzzled-looking members of the watch, his hand rising to deflect the arcane ball–turned-banana that I hurled after him.

"Damn him. Damn him!" I railed, turning to Baltic. "Why did you give that to him? I know you loved that sword."

"If I told you that you mattered more to me than anything, even something so unique as the light blade, would you do unnatural things to me?" he asked, his fire simmering in both of us.

"I've told you I don't do unnatural things! Why you insist on thinking my simple little common everyday sexual fantasies are bizarre and depraved is beyond me."

He just waited, his eyebrows raised in silent question.

"What sort of unnatural? You mean something like tying you down and coating your entire body with chocolate so I can lick—"

A noise behind me reminded me we weren't quite alone. I spun around, my cheeks heating as Kostya gave me a very odd look.

"Tying him down, hmm?" Cyrene said thoughtfully. "Milk or dark chocolate?"

"Milk. Belgian. Or Swiss," I answered.

"Melted, of course?"

"You can do so ahead of time, but I think it would be more fun to melt it right on him with dragon fire."

"Hmm," she repeated, looking at Kostya.

He cleared his throat, trying to scowl but seemingly

not able to with Cyrene's speculative gaze on him. "If I see you again, Baltic—"

"You will try to kill me," he answered wearily, sliding an arm around my waist. "Yes, I know—again."

Kostya was silent for a moment, some of the antagonism leaving his face. "I am glad you are not dead after all, Ysolde."

"Thank you. It's nice to be alive," I said with no little irony.

He bowed to me, then glanced at Baltic. "I would have taken care of her."

Baltic waited for the count of five before answering. "I know. I never distrusted you with regards to my mate."

"You never had cause to," I said, frowning a little at Kostya. "Not since that time when you showed up to claim me, and Kostya ran from me because he was afraid I would accept him, instead."

A little smile flickered at Kostya's lips at the memory, and for a moment, I was transported back to happier times.

"Oh, really? I'm going to want to hear about this," Cyrene said, tugging on his arm. "Come on, let's go home. I want to swim in the pond."

"The pond," I said, thinking of that beautiful home, with the even more beautiful grounds.

"That house was built for Ysolde," Baltic called after Kostya. "She will have it again."

"You can try, dragon," Kostya said in mimicry of Dr. Kostich. "You can try."

We stood together alone in the field, the afternoon sun beating down on us, the smell of the warm earth sinking deep into my soul, where Baltic's fire resided.

I let my gaze roam over his face, over the high, Slavic cheekbones, along his widow's peak, to the eyes that shone like polished ebony. "Everything is wrong, Baltic."

"Not everything."

"We're at war with the weyr."

He shrugged. "We don't need them."

"We do. They are our kind. More importantly, I want to be a part of the weyr. I want there to be peace between us."

He took my hands, his mouth hot on my fingers as he kissed them. "I don't know that I will be able to give you that."

"We'll work on it together, OK?"

He said nothing.

"Then there's the First Dragon. How do you know him?"

He dropped my hands and wrapped an arm around me, gently urging me toward the house. "If I tell you all my secrets now, what will you have to worm out of me with your inventive sexual persuasions?"

"Typical dragon answer. I can't tell you how annoying that is."

"I am not typical. I am the dread wyvern Baltic."

"You are the annoying wyvern Baltic, that's what you are. What are we going to do about this thing that the First Dragon expects of me? How can I do whatever it is when I haven't the slightest idea what he was talking about? And how did I fail him in the past?"

"Questions, questions, you were always full of questions," he sighed, pulling me tighter against his body until his heat became mine.

"What about your sword? That's not right that you should just hand it over to Dr. Kostich."

"There is a difference in surrendering something temporarily, and relinquishing the same," he said cryptically.

I glanced up at him, squinting against the low sun. "If you're going to steal it back from him, I want to help. I can't believe I slaved for that man for all those years. Talk about ungrateful. Do you think Kostya would let us buy that house? This one is nice enough and all, but that house is just so us. And while I'm thinking of it, who was it who gave his life for me? It wasn't you, was it? You were already dead. So who did that? I wonder also if I need to get a divorce from Gareth. Were we even really married, or did he just say we were?"

Baltic sighed again. "You wear me out with all these questions, mate. Can you not think, instead, of all the ways in which I will use chocolate upon your body?"

"Stop distracting me. I'm angsting, and I can't do it if—wait, on *my* body? Oooh. Now that is kind of kinky. . . ."

Have you read Katie's earlier novels?

The Silver  Dragon novels

featuring May and Gabriel

*Playing With Fire*
*Up in Smoke*
*Me and My Shadow*

are all available as Hodder paperbacks.

Read on for an exclusive extract from

# Playing With Fire

HODDER

# Chapter One

"Good twin calling evil twin. The weasel crows at midnight. How copy?"

"Oh, for mercy's sake . . . I'm busy! Stop sending me silly messages in code! If you have something to say, just say it; otherwise, radio silence, remember?"

"You're no fun anymore. You used to be fun, but lately, I've noticed a change in you. Is it menopause, May?"

Cyrene's question took me aback so strongly, I stopped creeping down the darkened hallway and blinked in dumbfounded surprise at the mirror that hung on the wall opposite.

No reflected figure blinked back at me.

"Are you still having your period? Do you experience hot flashes at night? Are you now growing, or have you at any time in the recent past grown, a mustache?"

"Goddess help me," I murmured to no one in particular, and tried my best to ignore the perky little voice that chirped so happily in my ear as I continued to make my way down to the dark and deserted room. I thought for a moment of just turning off the miniature radio that allowed Cyrene to contact me, but knowledge born of long experience with my twin reminded me of the folly of such an idea.

"Boy, you really are in a grumpy mood if you won't rise to the bait of menopause," she said in a mildly disgruntled voice.

I stopped briefly to admire a beautiful dull–sea green vase that sat in a glass-fronted display case before slipping silently across the room to the door opposite. "That's because it was completely ridiculous. You're older than me, which means you'll be menopausal before me."

"I'm barely older than you. Just a few years, really. A thousand at the most. What are you doing now?"

Trying to keep from going mad, I wanted to say, but I knew better than to do that, too. Cyrene being helpful was survivable. . . . Cyrene hurt, depressed, or unhappy could have dire repercussions that I truly didn't want to contemplate. "I'm in the library, approaching the office. Which could well have extra security, so radio silence from here on out, OK?"

"You said I could help you." The petulance in her voice was potent enough to make my lips tighten.

"You're helping me by guarding the front of the house." I sidled up to the door and gave it a good long look. There were no wards that I could see. I held up my hand, lightly placing my fingers on the wood. Nothing triggered my sensitive danger alarm.

"I'm on the *other* side of the street!"

The doorknob turned easily, the door opening with the slightest whisper, which bespoke attentive care by the house staff. "Gives you a better view."

"In a tree!"

"Height gives you an advantage. Hmm." Across the small room, another lovely antique display case stood, this one lit from within, the yellow light spilling out of the case and casting a pool on the thick carpet beneath it. There were a couple of pieces of object

d'art in the case, but it was the slender glass vial that
sat alone on the center shelf that held my attention.

"Hmm what? I think I'm getting bugs. There are
definitely bugs in this tree. What hmm? Did you find
the thingie?"

"The Liquor Hepatis? Yes. Now, hush. I have to
figure out how this case is protected."

"This is so exciting," Cyrene whispered. "I've never
been a part of one of your jobs before. Although this
watching business is a bit boring, and I don't see that
it's necessary if you said this mage is in England somewhere. I mean, after all, it's a mage!"

The disdain in her voice was evident even over the
tinny radio.

"I never did understand what you have against
mages. They're just people like everyone else," I murmured as I eyeballed the mundane electronic alarm.

"Oh, they think they're so high and mighty with
their arcane magic and deep, dark secrets of the universe. Bah. Give me a nice simple elemental spell any
day. Mages are very overrated. I don't see why you
don't just go in and get the thingie."

"Overrated or not, Magoth said this particular mage
was gone, but his staff is here, and not even a mage
would leave something as valuable as an arcanum of
the soul unguarded," I answered, disabling the alarm.
Mages, as a rule, dislike modern security measures,
usually preferring to rely on their own arcane resources, and the owner of the case before me was
no different.

I smiled at the spells woven into the wood itself,
intended to keep intruders out. They had no effect on
me, however, so once I tossed a small, aluminum-
coated piece of cloth over the minute security camera
bolted high in the corner of the room—it wouldn't do

to have images of me recorded for all posterity—I
simply opened up the case and reached for the vial.

Something glimmered for a fraction of a second to
the left of the Liquor Hepatis. I jerked my hand back,
narrowing my eyes at it.

"Did you remember to cover the camera?" Cyrene
asked suddenly. "You don't want them seeing you
when you decloak."

"I'm not a Klingon bird of prey, Cy," I said absently, scanning the shelf holding the glass vial. There
was nothing else visible. Had I seen just a reflection
from the vial, perhaps? A bit of light creating a prism
from the glass? Or perhaps the mage had done something to the vial that was beyond my experience?

"No, but you can be seen when you do anything
requiring concentration. Or so you say—I couldn't see
you when you juggled at the party we gave in Mar-
rakech."

"The discussion about you using me as a party trick
is going to have to wait for another time," I murmured, shaking my head at my foolish thoughts. The
owner of this house might be a mage, but he had a
misplaced confidence in his ability to keep his Liquor
Hepatis safe. I reached for it again, catching another
momentary glimpse of something tantalizingly just out
of the range of my vision. *"Agathos daimon!"*

"What?"

*"Agathos daimon.* It means—"

"Good spirit, yes, I know. I've heard you mutter it
often enough. Why you can't swear like any normal
person is beyond me. What are you *agathos*ing
about, anyway?"

I turned my head to the side, my peripheral vision
catching the sight of a small lavender stone box sitting
behind the vial. The second I tried to focus on the
object, it vanished.

"There's something else here. Something . . . important."

"Important how? Can I come down out of this tree yet? I'm getting eaten alive here."

"No. Stay there until I'm out of the house." I removed the vial, securing it in an inner pocket of my leather bodice as I gave the case another look, but nothing was there. I turned my head again, my fingers groping blindly along the slick glass of the shelf. They closed on a small, cold square just as the lights in the room burst on.

"Agamemnon's tears!" Cyrene squawked in my ear. "Someone's there! There's a car out front and lights just went on in three different rooms—"

"Thanks for the warning," I whispered through my teeth. Voices outside the room heralded someone's imminent approach. I glanced quickly around the room, desperately hunting for a dark corner where I might hide, but the room was far too bright for that.

"I'm sorry! I was picking bugs off my arm and didn't see the car pull up. What's going on? Why are all the lights in the house on? Oh, no—I think one of the men is a mage. He's . . . yes, he's a mage! He's probably the owner! Mayling, you have to get out of there!"

She wasn't telling me anything I didn't know. I leaped to my feet as the doorknob started to turn, jamming a chair underneath it to keep the door from opening.

"Mayling!" Cyrene yelled in my ear, in her excitement using her nickname for me once again.

I ran for the window, praying I could make it outside into the darkness before the door opened. The door burst into a thousand pieces, turned to ash, and drifted slowly to the ground as I jumped onto the table next to the glass.

"Mayling!" Cyrene's bellow was loud enough to

hurt. A man's shape appeared in the doorway, pausing for a moment as he evidently heard my twin.

"Mei Ling!" he cried, running forward, obviously hearing Cyrene but misinterpreting my nickname for a proper name. It wouldn't be the first time that had happened. "It's the thief Mei Ling!"

Instinctively, I shadowed when I heard the men's voices, but the room was too bright to remain hidden. Just as soon as he looked toward the window, the man would see me. I had no choice but to go through the window.

"*Agathos daimon,*" I repeated softly to myself as I put my hands over my head and flung myself through the glass.

"There!" the man cried as pain burst into being all over my body. "She's there! I heard someone say her name! It's the thief Mei Ling on the ledge outside!"

The blessed warm darkness of a late March Greek evening embraced me, making me all but invisible to watchful eyes as I raced down the narrow ledge, shinnying down a pipe to the ground.

"Where are you? Are you all right? *Mayling*!"

"I'm fine. I'm outside the house, but stop yelling or the mage's people will find you," I hissed into the microphone. "Can you get out of the tree without being seen?"

"Oh, thank the gods you're all right. I just about had a heart attack! Yes, I think I can get down. There's a handy branch right . . . oomph!"

Across the street from the elegant villa located in Nea Makri, a small resort town outside of Athens, a black, vaguely human shape fell to the ground. I hurried around the edges of the square, avoiding pools of light from the houses until I reached my twin.

Her face, lit dimly from the lights at the nearest

house, looked up at me as I stopped next to her. "I fell."

"I saw. You all right?"

She nodded, peering at the house as I quickly pulled her to her feet. "What are they yelling? I can't make out the words."

"It's probably nothing but a lot of swearing. Oh, and my nickname. Well, not my nickname—the other name."

"What other name?" she asked as I hurried her away from the house and down the dark side street where we'd left the rental car. "Oh, you mean that Asian thing that someone made up?"

"They made it up because they heard you yelling my nickname in Dresden when I helped the naiad sisterhood get back the icon that was stolen. Fortunately, they were looking for an Asian person and paid no attention to little old me."

A guilty look flitted across her face. "I didn't know that people would think that was your real name. Besides, that was at least ten years ago. Surely they've forgotten that by now?"

"Hardly. The fame of Mei Ling lives on. . . ."

We stopped in front of the car. I was about to pull out the car key but realized with some surprise that I was holding something.

"What's wrong?" she asked as I stared at my hand. "Goddess! You're bleeding! You went through the window?"

"Yes." I unfurled my fingers and stared at . . . nothing.

"We'd better go," she said, taking the key and unlocking the door. "I'll drive. You can slump down so you're less obvious. I know no one can see you when you do your cloaking thing, but they'll see the blood that you're dripping everywhere. It's a good thing you're my twin, or you'd have to go to the hospital."

"If I wasn't your twin, I wouldn't have been in a position to jump through the window in the first place," I answered automatically, tracing out the shape of a small stone box. "Whatever the mage used on this is pretty powerful. I still can't see it."

"See what?" she asked, pausing to peer into my hand. "The cuts? They'll heal in a few minutes."

"I'm not worried about that—I have been stabbed, shot, and nearly disemboweled, and I know full well I'll heal up quickly enough. It's this," I said, ducking as Cyrene shoved me into the car.

"What, exactly?" she asked, gunning the engine. "Hotel?"

"Yes, please. It's a box. Look at it from the corner of your eye."

"I can't see anything when I'm driving—oh! It's a box!" she exclaimed, her gaze flickering between my hand and the street.

"I think it's crystal. I think—" My fingers, which had been stroking the invisible box, must have pressed a small, hidden switch, for suddenly my soul sang. I felt rather than saw a luminous golden glow radiating from the box, a beautiful light of such wondrous beauty, it seemed to fill me with happiness.

Cyrene swore and slammed on the brakes, jerking the car onto a thankfully empty sidewalk, her eyes huge.

I stared down in astonishment at the source of the unseen but still tangible ethereal glow.

"What the—what is that? Gracious goddess, it's . . . it's . . . ."

"It's quintessence," I said, breathing heavily as I allowed the glittering brilliance to sink deep into my bones.

"The what now?"

"Quintessence. The fifth element."

Slowly, I closed the lid of the box, the light ending with an abruptness that left my soul weeping.

"Like the movie, you mean? With Bruce Willis?"

"What?" It took a moment for her words to penetrate the fog that seemed to settle over me with the loss of the light. "No, not that. That's just Hollywood. The fifth element is something alchemists strive to find. It's the essential presence."

"Essential presence of what?" she asked, carefully pulling back onto the road, but quickly pulling over again when police cars burst out of a cross street, sirens wailing and lights flashing.

"Everything. It's the above and below. The embodiment of that force we call life. It's the purest essence of . . . being."

"Is it valuable?" Cyrene asked, a calculating expression stealing across her face.

My fingers tightened around the box. "Priceless. Beyond priceless. Invaluable. Any alchemist would kill to have it."

"Hmm."

I knew what she was thinking. Cyrene had expensive tastes, and no practical ability to save money. I was sure she was going to suggest putting the quintessence up for bid, but that was something I couldn't allow. "No," I said.

Her lips, recently plumped and now shaded a delicate pink, pouted in a manner that I knew made grown men swoon. "Why not? I bet we could get a lot for it."

"For one, it's not mine." I stroked the bumpy crystal lid with worshipful fingers.

"Well, I know Magoth will want it, but that's not what he sent you there to get, right? So he doesn't need to know we have it."

I shook my head. "If Magoth thinks I was even *near* a quintessence . . . well, the phrase 'hell hath no fury like a demon lord denied' charges immediately to mind. I can't begin to describe the horrible things he'd do to me to get it. And to you, for that matter."

She shot me a quick glance as we drove through the city to the commercial center, where our hotel was located. "Me? A demon lord can't do anything to me. I'm immortal!"

"So am I, and he could snuff me out as easily as a candle flame."

"I can't believe you never learned this, but demon lords can't kill elemental beings, naiads included," she said with gentle chastisement. "Everyone knows that."

"So the lore goes, but do you seriously doubt you could escape Magoth's wrath?"

"Er . . ." She thought about it for a moment, her lips thinning. "No."

"I didn't think so. No, dear twin, this little box is not going to Magoth . . . and we're not going to sell it. There's nothing else for it—I'm just going to have to return it to the mage."

"It seems such a pity," she said, pulling into the underground parking lot that sat beneath our modest hotel. "Maybe he won't know it's gone. I think you should just hold on to it for a bit and see if he even notices that you have it."

"Did you give up morals along with your common sense?" I asked.

Cyrene parked the car, turning to me with an exaggerated roll of her eyes. "My morals are just fine, and you can stop making that face at me. I just think we should talk this over a bit. It's invisible, so maybe the mage has forgotten about it."

I leaned forward until I could peer directly into her blue eyes. "Priceless, Cyrene. Literally . . . priceless."

Avarice lit her face for a moment.

"Even if I was the sort of person to steal something for myself—and I'll reiterate the fact that I'm not, since you seem to conveniently forget that whenever temptation raises its head—there's no way I'd keep this. It's just too valuable. That mage is going to move heaven and earth to get it back, and frankly, I could do without having anyone else after my head."

She sighed and got out of the car. "You take life too seriously. We definitely need to work on getting you a sense of humor, not to mention a sense of fun!"

"There is little time for fun when you have my job. And speaking of that, I wonder what the mage will do since his people heard my name," I said, slowly getting out of the car. My skin was hot and tight at spots where dried blood pulled at it. The cuts I'd received going through the glass were mostly healed, but I still looked like hell.

She spun around, her hand at her mouth. "Oh, May! I'm sorry! I didn't think of that—do you think they'll connect Mei Ling with you?"

I let the corner of one side of my mouth curl into a rueful smile. "I don't see how they can. They didn't get a good look at me, and they think it was Mei Ling, infamous international cat burglar, and not a simple doppelganger from California."

She grimaced. "Me and my big mouth."

"Oh, it's not that bad—it means less attention on me if everyone is looking for an Asian woman. Ugh. I can't go into the hotel like this. I'll shadow walk to my room. Will you be OK?"

She'd had a century to practice the long-suffering look she bestowed upon me, but my lips twitched at it nonetheless. "I'm not inept, May! I am perfectly capable of entering a hotel and making my way to my room without encountering any assassins, thugs, anarchists, or muggers, thank you."

"Sorry," I said, contritely.

"Honestly! You treat me like I'm the child and you're the parent, when it's the other way round. I'm almost twelve hundred years old, you know! Just because I need a little help now and again doesn't mean I can't do *anything* without you. . . ."

She marched off to the elevator with an indignant twitch of her shoulders. I followed more slowly, avoiding the overhead lights and taking the less-used stairs as a question danced elusively in my mind.

How on earth was I going to get the quintessence back to the mage without being caught?